THE TOLTEC CUP

THE TOLTEC CUP

A NOVEL OF OLD NEW YORK

NYM CRINKLE
(A. C. WHEELER)

With a New Introduction by Erick Kelemen

EXCELSIOR
EDITIONS

Published by State University of New York Press, Albany

Excelsior Editions is an imprint of the State University of New York Press

For information, contact State University of New York Press, Albany, NY
www.sunypress.edu

Library of Congress Cataloging-in-Publication Data

Names: Wheeler, A. C. (Andrew Carpenter), 1835–1903, author. | Kelemen,
    Erick, writer of introduction.
Title: The Toltec cup: a novel of old New York / Nym Crinkle (Andrew C.
    Wheeler); with a new introduction by Erick Kelemen.
Description: Albany: State University of New York Press, [2022] | Series:
    Excelsior editions
Identifiers: LCCN 2021050874 | ISBN 9781438488899 (hardcover) | ISBN
    9781438488905 (ebook) | ISBN 9781438488899 (paperback)
Subjects: LCGFT: Thrillers (Fiction). | Romance fiction. | Novels.
Classification: LCC PS3165.W6 T65 2022 | DDC 813/.4--dc23/eng/20211015
LC record available at https://lccn.loc.gov/2021050874

10 9 8 7 6 5 4 3 2 1

CONTENTS

NEW INTRODUCTION

Erick Kelemen

Andrew Carpenter Wheeler's first novel, published in 1890, *The Toltec Cup*, is full of mysteries and misunderstandings that make it a great-great-grandfather of novels and movies like *The Da Vinci Code, National Treasure*, and *The Name of the Rose*. But perhaps most interesting to today's readers are the novel's remarkable depictions and connections with New York City and its people.

The Toltec Cup is a sprawling tale of conspiracy and love triangles. At the center is a mysterious silver cup covered in hieroglyphs that goes missing just days after its owner's death. John Wilder, a New York Metropolitan Police inspector, grows suspicious when someone offers a huge reward for the cup's return. Wilder discovers that the owner didn't unintentionally kill himself, as he had been told. Who, after all, accidentally stabs himself through the heart—twice? Wilder traces the reward to Colin Carteret, an artist engaged to the murdered man's daughter, but Carteret swears he'd never heard of the cup until he saw the reward posted in the paper. Together, the men follow the cup's trail to one of New York's slums, a beautiful young woman, Manuella Castleton, and a syndicate that believes that the cup will lead to an extraordinary buried treasure.

Andrew Carpenter Wheeler was already famous as the theater and music critic "Nym Crinkle" when he wrote *The Toltec Cup*. Born in New York City in the 1830s, Wheeler started as a journalist at the *New York Times*, who memorialized him in 1903 as "An aggressive and original writer."[1] Wheeler was for a time editor for the *Milwaukee Sentinel* and worked during the Civil War as a war correspondent, covering pivotal and bloody battles in Tennessee, including the battle of Pittsburgh Landing, also known as Shiloh. After the war, he adopted the Nym Crinkle pen name and became a contentious but thoughtful critic. In his second stint at the *New York World*, under Joseph Pulitzer, he became one of the highest paid journalists in the city. Wheeler may have enjoyed arguing more than having a consistent opinion, but, in the words of one theater historian, in an age when "Most critics were hacks[,] Wheeler took his work very seriously."[2] In addition to writing about theater, Wheeler also wrote *for* it. While most of his efforts appear to have been unsuccessful, he seems to have collaborated anonymously in two successful melodramas, *The Still Alarm* and *Blue Jeans*, both of which were eventually turned into silent films.

The Toltec Cup announces from its two subtitles that it sits between genres. The original subtitle on the book's title page reads *A Romance of Immediate Life in New York City*. And certainly a love triangle between Colin, Rose (his fiancée), and Manuella plays a significant role. But the idea of "romance" excludes the detective plot that holds the book together. This tension is compounded by the second subtitle, which appears on the novel's cover: *A Tale of the Here and Now in New York City*. But readers who expected the "here and now" to be New York City in 1890 would have been mistaken. Instead, Wheeler set his novel some thirty years earlier, from the summer of 1862 through the summer of 1863, culminating in the secessionist and racist violence popularly known as the New York City Draft Riots. Both the "*Here and Now*" and "*Immediate Life*," of the subtitles are best understood figuratively.

One of Wheeler's acquaintances reported that Wheeler was aiming for "old-fashioned plot, intrigue, and varied movement," such as one would find in *The Count of Monte Cristo*.[3] As Wheeler writes in the novel's dedication, he wanted to see whether "the elements of familiar life all around us" could hold something as interesting as "the far off golden afternoons of Boccaccio or the silver nights of Scheherazade." The novel indeed delivers an incident-filled, exotic adventure, but sets it in mundane New York with mundane New Yorkers. They are not princesses and knights in shining armor, even if the novel sometimes jokingly describes them that way.

New York City is so important to the novel that it is almost a character itself. Even when the story takes the train to the suburbs, Manhattan's gravitational pull is obvious. The setting in bucolic Westchester, for instance, is mainly along the Croton Aqueduct, Manhattan's essential fresh water source, and the plot turns in part on details of the aqueduct's basic maintenance. *The Toltec Cup*'s New York is a dynamic, changing landscape, and Wheeler takes pains to describe places such as the Gas House District, the Bowery, Union Square, Harlem, and the Meatpacking District as well as their diverse people. This is a New York that was already disappearing for Wheeler's contemporaries in 1890 and is largely gone for us. In fact, it was already disappearing in the novel itself. When Manuella's grandfather secretly buries the cup near Turtle Bay Cove (roughly where United Nations Headquarters now stands), there's nothing there but a brewery and some goats grazing around the rocky outcroppings. When he returns a few weeks later, the place is already transformed. Builders have excavated the spot and are putting up more tenements and brownstones for the city's floods of newcomers. The place the man knew has vanished with the cup.

Wheeler's vision of New York as a place means that even mundane details carry significance for its detective plot. The layout of apartments in a tenement house in the Gashouse District matter enough that the novel provides a floor plan. (This inclusion is especially interesting when one remembers that in 1890 Jacob Riis included a floor plan for Lower East Side tenements in his groundbreaking photo essay about Manhattan's slums *How the Other Half Lives.*) The floor plan makes clear that the details of New York living matter: it matters that guests must ascend the steps to go through the front door of Mrs. Hannige's boarding house but that unwanted guests can coax their way in through the servant's entrance below street level to interrogate unsophisticated but honest maidservants. It also matters that Mrs. Hannige's house is on 15th Street, across from the Century Club, whose building is still there today, though the club long ago moved. The facticity of the novel led some reviewers to identify it as a fourth genre: the roman à clef, satirizing prominent New Yorkers of the day. To read this novel is to be a little like a tourist, led on an adventure through an 1860s New York City by an 1890s New Yorker, a writer with a journalist's precise eye but also with a native's great fondness for his always-changing city.

Wheeler's celebrity as Nym Crinkle seems to have been enough that publisher Lew Vanderpoole paid him a $10,000 advance. The sum was outlandish even for Gilded Age New York—the equivalent of almost $300,000 in 2021—and may have been a sales gimmick. (The information in fact comes from an advertisement for the book.[4]) And it may also be a fabrication, as Vanderpoole was as much a con man as a bookman. Three years before, Vanderpoole had sold *Cosmopolitan* what he claimed was his translation of a supposedly unpublished novel by George Sand, *Princess Nourmahal. Cosmopolitan* paid Vanderpoole some of the fee but demanded to see Sand's manuscript before they began printing. Vanderpoole claimed she was a relative of his and that he had translated her work from memory. *Cosmopolitan* had him arrested, but the charges were dismissed on a technicality. His case was widely and gleefully reported. A newspaper in Kinderhook that used to employ Vanderpoole noted, "Unless [he] has acquired a knowledge of French since he left here, he knows nothing of the language."[5] Vanderpoole, undaunted, later published the novel under George Sand's name.

Vanderpoole had financial problems often. Four years after the publication of *The Toltec Cup,* in 1894, Vanderpoole attempted to borrow £1,000 from the son of the Lord Chief Justice of England and Wales. Vanderpoole claimed he had four million francs tied up in a French bank until the next year and needed money to bribe the bank into early access. When his lie was discovered and he was arrested, Vanderpoole objected, "I have received no money. He [the Lord Chief Justice's son] has not lost anything. Why should I be locked up?"[6] Vanderpoole then tried to shift blame, claiming he was working on behalf of someone else. New York City has a reputation for attracting and perhaps nurturing a type of bamboozler with big dreams, fast talk, and questionable morals. Vanderpoole seems to have been one of them.

As a journalist and dramatist with extensive connections, Wheeler must have known of Vanderpoole's character. Perhaps Vanderpoole, having convinced an investor that Nym Crinkle's name would create an immediate bestseller, really did offer a huge sum to publish *The Toltec Cup*. Perhaps Wheeler welcomed the risk of publishing with Vanderpoole, given that his best theatrical successes to date, such as *The Still Alarm*, had been lowbrow. Given Vanderpoole's own fortune hunting and his ability to create mysterious sources who disappear when needed, it might be there was no more perfect publisher for *The Toltec Cup*.

The Toltec Cup received some reviews as vicious as a theater critic with enemies ought to expect. One writes of Wheeler: "A failure as an author, he is, of course, an excellent critic, as he has written so many poor things himself that he recognizes one the moment he sees it."[7] But other reviewers praise *The Toltec Cup*'s depictions of New York, which "show a remarkable power of description. . . . The conditions of tenement house life, the party at Dr. Follen Sanger's in Gramercy Park, the anti-war meeting at Brannagan Hall, are well described. The local scenes, as the terrace in Nineteenth Street, are drawn with great skill."[8] Another reviewer compared Wheeler's sketch of the poor favorably to those by Dickens.

Nevertheless, *The Toltec Cup* was probably not the hit Vanderpoole and Wheeler hoped for. Two years later, Wheeler's second novel, *The Primrose Path of Daliance*, received almost no notice. Wheeler kept writing theater reviews as Nym Crinkle for a few more years (his legal name appears under the pen name on both novels), then retired it. When he returned to writing essays and novels, he adopted a new, more secret alias, J. P. M. or J. P. Mowbray, taken from his second wife, Jennie Pearl Mowbray, who claimed coauthorship many decades later. Doubleday brought out his final novel, *The Conquering of Kate*, in the month after he died.

Some sources claim that Wheeler is buried in Sleepy Hollow Cemetery. But while Wheeler's daughters from his first marriage, Grace and Minnie, are buried there, Wheeler is in fact buried next door, as it were, in an unmarked grave in a lot owned by Eliphalet Wheeler, his father, in the Old Dutch Burial Ground in Sleepy Hollow.[9] It is hard not to take this fact as emblematic. In his day, Wheeler was one of the most prolific and widely read writers, and his death attracted national notice. Today, few know of him and fewer read him. *The Toltec Cup* is now a rare book, nearly impossible to find. Now, thanks to SUNY Press, it is available to anyone with an interest in nineteenth-century New York, in Andrew Wheeler, in Nym Crinkle, or in Lew Vanderpoole.

A few warnings. As might be expected for a novel of this age, this book contains casual racism, antisemitism, bigotry, and sexism. In my view, it is much less than one might expect, and the narrative is rather soundly on the side of inclusiveness. It uses the word "nigger" once (chapter sixty), putting it on a placard carried by a mob who are decidedly *not* the good guys. The novel describes two murders in explicit but not extensive terms (chapters four, six, and fifty-eight), an abduction (chapter thirty), and rioting leading to violent deaths (chapter sixty).

The text of this edition has been silently and lightly emended to correct obvious typographical errors.

NOTES

1. "Death of Andrew C. Wheeler," *New York Times*, March 11, 1903, 9.
2. Thomas K. Wright, "Nym Crinkle: Gadfly Critic and Male Chauvinist," *Educational Theater Journal* 24, no. 4 (December 1972): 370–82. https://www.jstor.org/stable/3205931. Citation is to p. 382.
3. B. B., "Highways and By-Ways," *The Epoch* 7, no. 170 (May 8, 1890): 219–20. Citation is to p. 220.
4. In *The Critic*, July 19, 1890, i.
5. "Lew Vanderpoel's Case," *Philmont Sentinel* (Philmont, New York), October 19, 1887, 1, col. 2 (an unsigned article quoting an article from *Kinderhook's Rough Times* [Kinderhook, New York]).
6. "Events in the Old World," *The Sun* (New York), August 19, 1894, 1, col. 2.
7. H. B. S. "The Toltec Cup," *America: a Journal for Americans* (Chicago) 4, no. 20 (August 14, 1890): 556.
8. "The Toltec Cup," *Book News* 9, no. 98 (October 1890): 54. The article reprints a review that appeared in the Philadelphia Press.
9. Jim Logan, Superintendent, Sleepy Hollow Cemetery, email messages to Erick Kelemen, February 5, 2021, and January 13, 2022.

DEDICATION

To all the well-remembered friends, who, on the bleakest of winter nights, around the jolliest of wood fires, listened to the spinning of this yarn and cried for more, I now dedicate it, in its formal efficacy of cold type, which, I am sure, can never have half the charm that one poor voice had under the stimulus of wondering faces.

As the story now goes out into circles that are measureless to me and that cannot be lit by the same single glow that warmed us, it is only fair that, on your behalf, no less than on mine, I should tell new listeners what it was we set out to do.

You will bear me witness that we were to make a story of incident and not go to the heart of Africa or the Glaciers of the Moon for our material.

We were to find our adventure, our knights, our maidens and our ogres, our dusky coverts, our crouching panthers and our coiled serpents in the *here* and the *now* of a life that is spread out in the blessed sunshine, or is hiding in the congenial darkness under our very eyes. We were to bind this material together with the golden wire of romance and see if the current of a healthy sentiment would go over it. Our purpose was a homespun and perhaps a heterodox purpose to the doctrinaire criticism of today; at all events we did not want to convert or appal anybody. We only wanted to know if the elements of familiar life round about us still retained any of the plasticity and possibility of romance and could be made to cohere with something of the entrainment that shone in the far off golden afternoons of Boccaccio or the silver nights of Scheherazade.

That was our privilege. It was the privilege of sheer beguilement, but it will have grown into a modest duty if it should still prove to be interesting, without having been compelled to be prurient or morbid or to have sought in sexual passion what can only be found in human love.

Then perhaps, some readers that I shall never know or see, will in far off places glow with something of the warmth and sympathy of the circle where, in the watches of the night, we summoned these everyday faces to walk in our fire-lit fantasy.

A. C. WHEELER
(Nym Crinkle).

THE TOLTEC CUP.

CHAPTER I.

THE ADVERTISEMENT IN THE HERALD.

On the 15th of July, 1862, Mr. Oliver Enniston died. The occurrence was mentioned in the public prints at the time, for he was a well-known business-man, and the accident which caused his death was a remarkable one. He had gone out upon the veranda of his country home at Coe's Grove, the accounts said, late in the evening. While sitting there with some ladies, one of them expressed a desire to have a camelia. In endeavoring to cut the flowers in the garden with a poignard, he had fallen upon the weapon, which entered his left side and killed him.

On the second day of September of the same year, Mr. John Wilder, then employed in the central office of the Metropolitan police, cut with his penknife from the *New York Herald* the following odd advertisement:

L OST OR STOLEN.—A Toltec cup of solid silver, of unique design, eight inches in height, ten inches in circumference at the rim, elaborately engraved with hieroglyphics. Its intrinsic value is not quite twenty dollars, but its value as a memorial will insure a reward of $500 to any one who will cause it to be returned to the owner.

COLIN CARTERET,

Coe's Grove on the Hudson.

Mr. John Wilder thought there was something sufficiently novel in this announcement to think over. Five hundred dollars for a stolen cup was not offered every day.

In the course of the morning, he sauntered into old Syphon's on Broadway. It was an establishment for the sale of curios.

"Have you got such a thing as a Toltec cup?" he asked of the old man.

"A what?"

"A Toltec cup."

"Never heard of such a thing in the whole course of business. Toltec? Why, that must be Mexican or Aztec."

"Do you mean to say," asked Wilder, "that an old curiosity hunter doesn't know what a Toltec cup is?"

"Yes," replied Syphon, "that's what I mean to say. Where did you hear of it?"

"I'm looking for one—want to make a purchase. I should have thought you were just the man."

"See here," said Syphon, "you musn't take me for an archaeologist, I'm only an antiquary," and he lifted one eyebrow with self gratulation at the nice distinction. "I don't say there isn't such a thing in the books—only that it never came my way. Why don't you go up and see Colonel Perebeau at the Museum? He's up to all that kind of stuff."

The next day Wilder happened to be passing Simpson's pawn broking shop in the Bowery. Thinking of his advertisement, he stepped in.

There were three women with shawls over their heads, and one or two flash-ily dressed young men at the counter. Wilder stepped behind one of the narrow partitions meant to shelter timid applicants, and the clerk, who evidently knew him, came to him immediately.

"Want to see me?"

"Just a word," said Wilder, as the man leaned over so as to be confiden-tial,—"any Toltecs been offered lately?"

"Any what?" asked the man turning his ear to the officer.

"Toltecs."

The man scratched the back part of his head with his pen and made a gri-mace as if it hurt him.

"You've got hold of a patter that beats me," he said. "You'll have to put it into English."

Wilder then took the advertisement from his pocket and showed it to the man, who read it with some difficulty two or three times. Suddenly an idea seized him and he handed it back to the officer with a smile.

"Misprint," said he. "No such word in the language. The d____d newspa-pers got it wrong."

"What should it be?"

"I'm blessed if I know, but you can bet your salary it aint Toltec and there aint no such thing—cause if there was, we'd know of it. We take in all there is, from coffin plates to steam engines, and cups is a specialty of ours. There aint been a cup turned up for a week and the last one was washed."

John Wilder was not easily discouraged. It didn't take him long to ascertain the meaning of the word Toltec, and the assurances of the pawnbroker that there was no such thing, only convinced him that this piece of property was out of the range of vulgar experience.

The word nestled in his mouth strangely. He found himself repeating it the next morning when he got up. He studied the advertisement in leisure moments and the conviction grew that there was a mystery connected with it that would be worth unravelling.

John Wilder was in many respects an interesting character. It is true he had been in the employ of the Central Office for some time, and had come to be called inspector, but in mental equipment and personal appearance he was altogether unlike the usual special of the police force. That celebrated criminal lawyer John Braham, said to him one day: "John, I never could understand how with your head you got on the force, or how you escaped being a lawyer." To which John had said rather jocosely, "I suppose the reason why I escaped being a lawyer is that I know more about human nature than I do about crime."

This answer was more sagacious than either of them at the time suspected.

"The man I want," said the celebrated Vidocq, "must have a woman's faculties in a man's body." What he meant was that the officer must possess that power of intuitive and rapid induction which we see oftenest in women.

John Wilder possessed this faculty. His instinctive inductions were marvelously accurate. His deductions were often wide of the truth.

Some kind of conclusion arrived at by an unknown process, told him that the advertisement he had cut from the paper meant exactly what it did not say. All his experience, aided by his reason, gave him to understand that, at the best, somebody had lost an heirloom or a token, whose value was in its association, and that its recovery was extremely problematical.

The inclination of his mind was to ponder dreamily over the odd announcement.

That kind of judgment which was the result of vocation, told him that it would be a wild goose chase, and that other and more pressing and practical duties claimed his attention.

He was boarding at this time at his sister's, Mrs. Hannige's in Fifteenth street, and that personage found him in the morning sitting on a trunk, in his shirt sleeves, with his head between his hands, in a deep reverie.

"I do believe you're in a trance," she said. "I knocked hard enough to break my knuckles."

"Have you got some breakfast ready?" he asked, jumping up with sudden vigor.

"Ready? Yes, this hour; but you don't mean that you are in a hurry for it?"

"Yes, I am. I want to catch an early train. I'm going to Coe's Grove."

CHAPTER II.

O'REARDON'S TERRACE.

A September afternoon. The season had been unusually prolonged. Broadway had not yet got its autumn stir. The summer runaways hugged the country and the seaside. Save the familiar tramp of the New England regiments passing through to the front, to the rather worn song of "John Brown's Body Is a Marching On," there was little going on in the city to disturb the public lethargy of a very hot September.

A man of remarkable appearance stood on the corner of Astor place and Third avenue, looking down Eighth Street toward old St. Mark's in the Bowery, whose white, blistered spire reached up above the dust laden trees, and whose clock has insisted, ever since Peter Stuyvesant died that it is a quarter to one.

The bit of green looked very inviting through the golden-hued dust of the streets on this drowsy afternoon, and the man regarded it thoughtfully.

He had a foreign air. His face, dark, wrinkled, and almost cadaverous in its shrunken flesh, was nevertheless that of an alert, intelligent man. He was at least fifty years old, but his beard was yet dark, save for a gray and white tuft on one side, and his mustache which completely hid his mouth, was jet black. As he lifted his quaint silk cap to wipe, with a blue cotton handkerchief, the perspiration that was trickling down his temples, he showed a shining cranium from which the hair had long departed.

Asked to guess at this man's character and occupation as he stood there, you might have said he was an Austrian doctor who made a precarious living out of his poor and superstitious countrymen. If he turned his face toward you with his quick nervous action, and you saw his little brilliant black eyes under their shaggy brows, and noted the hollow temples and the prominence of his almost Semitic nose, it is also possible, you might have thought him a Pole and a political refugee.

There was something foreign in the green-hued cloth of which his old-fashioned and somewhat rusty surtout coat was made, and save for the ruby as big as a filbert that gleamed like a drop of hot blood in the cravat at his throat, you might have concluded that he was very poor.

He looked round as he wiped his bald head, very much as if he wanted to see who had noticed him, and then crossing the avenue, went down the street in the direction of the church.

A number of youngsters were playing on the walk under the trees. The grass looked cool and green through the iron fence, and the entrance way to the old church, which was some little distance from the street and much higher than the sidewalk, was quaintly quiet and rural. He did not notice any of these things but turned up the Second avenue, crossed one of the twin parks under the shadow of St. George's, and looking back once or twice, plunged into the populous region that lies toward the river. There were no more green shadows now. Once over the First avenue and he was in the dirtiest, densest, and aridest quarter of the city. Eighteenth, Nineteenth and Twentieth streets, are all built up with great uniform houses, six and seven stories high, that are known as "tenements" and that shut out the sun from the numerical ditches below.

Looking down any one of these streets, you will see two unvarying walls facing each other, with thousands of windows in them and in nearly every open window is a human being leaning upon the sill and watching the life in the streets below, and each street itself presents an unrivaled vista. It is peopled with thousands of children, who are dashing across the roadway, encumbering the walks in sportive association, shouting, singing, playing ball, organizing processions, dancing, with hands joined, round the organ grinders, fighting, flinging stones and giving a shimmer to the perspective. They all live here and the street is their only playground. A wild jargon assails you. You see that the neighborhood is tremulous and discordant with more life than it can contain: a great, barren, overcrowded region where the inhabitants seek the street to escape from homes that have been provided for them. Toward the river it gets even worse, for the houses are older and dirtier and more densely packed, and here in Nineteenth street, within the noxious breath of the great gas houses, with their tanks, stands, on the north side, the row of tenement houses, six-stories high, that has been known for years as "O'Reardon's Terrace." There is a tradition that long before the region became so thickly settled, the original owner had a row of little frame houses on a bank here. But with the growth of the city and the rise in property, he pushed them upon the rear of the lots and put this six-storied row up in front. The original name descended from the cottages to the barracks, without any other reason than local inability to make a better or more appropriate one.

O'Reardon's Terrace has now seven houses and they are all exactly alike. But it is at the middle house that our strange gentleman in dusky green surtout stops, and it is with that house that our story deals, for in it, is the most important personage in the strange events that are to be related.

This house is, in most respects, the exact counterpart of the six. Each story contains two families and their condition is inversely to their height. Thus, the first floor tenant, John Grinch, who is a butcher, and whose shop is nearly opposite, is, in the local scale of social values, of more importance than Philip Brainsby, the letter-carrier who has the first floor back.

Mr. Grinch has three daughters and a stalwart wife, and is himself a great, rubicund, goodnatured, carnivorous fellow who belongs to the first battalion of the Butchers' Independent Mounted Troop, and on gala days makes a sensation in front of his residence with his large-boned white horse and yellow trappings, and the clanking of his sabre when he mounts and cavorts round the neighborhood, to the infinite admiration of the crowd. It is worth a loitering five minutes to see him throw the bridle to a boy and go clanking into the first floor front on these occasions. His three daughters carry on a systematic vendetta with the two daughters of the architect on the floor above them, who work at envelope-folding somewhere and put on the airs of Nineteenth street belles, on Saturday nights when they get their money. These second floor girls are known as Dory and Cory, their fond father having had an early illusion that one would grow up Corinthian like her mother, and the other would expand into the Doric style like himself, which it is perhaps pertinent to observe they never did.

Just how the warfare originated between these families, it would be hard to tell, but there is reason to believe that it had its roots in the superior Saturday night attractiveness of the architectural Pitwilks and the Croton water. And here it is necessary to explain that in O'Reardon's Terrace it was difficult to get any water above the first floor when the first floor faucets were open, and Miss Fanny Grinch, burning with envy, one Saturday night conceived the diabolical idea of opening the faucets whenever she thought the Pitwilks were in need of water. As this ingenious scheme cut the Croton off from all the other floors above, the deprivation usually resulted in a rumbling protest and a consummating procession down the stairs of all manner of disgruntled people.

Then as the two Pitwilk girls, arrayed in their best garments, were very apt on Saturday nights to stand in front of the Grinch's windows and elicit disparaging remarks from their beaux, touching the Grinch's, it was not long before the Grinch's took to leaning their elbows on the sills and returning the compliments, and as the Grinch's had much the best of it in volubility and rhetoric, the Pitwilks were driven from the sidewalk to the fastnesses of the second floor. It was about this time that the flower pots in the Pitwilk's window-conservatory began to fall. Mary Grinch got a whack over her cerebellum from a geranium in a sardine box, and a few days later when the water was cut off for an hour, Fanny received a tremendous blow from a pot of dead gilliflowers. These horticultural amenities at times embroiled the whole family. When Fanny was combing the fertilizer out of her back hair and mingling tears with broken pottery, her mother was racing over to the meat shop to summon the butcher. Sometimes he came over in his white apron, looking very ponderous and peaceable, and he would call up the stairs with strenuous dignity:

"Now, sir, this' ere thing's got to be stopped, sir, I want you to distinctly understand."

And somebody with equal strenuousness would call down:

"Who are you, sir? What the devil are you talkin' about, sir, anyway?"

Then Mr. Grinch would go back to his meat saw much relieved and Fanny would open the faucets.

Immediately above the architects, lived Mr. and Mrs. Gridlegrean with seven children. Mr. Gridlegrean worked in a factory somewhere at the manufacture of cordage and marine tackling. He was a quiet, industrious Englishman, who could sing Dibden's songs with a funny little bass voice and had a mortal terror of being burnt out, which his wife had grown to share with him. Under the influence of this dread, he had organized his family into a domestic fire brigade or life saving corps. The eldest boy, about fifteen, had charge of the fire escape tackle which was kept under the bed, and his two brothers were his assistants. The four girls were organized into a subsidiary corps that gathered up the wardrobe and Mrs. Gridlegrean herself was a valuable auxiliary in holding the ropes. It was Mr. Gridlegrean's custom to rehearse his family by calling out "fire" at inopportune and unexpected moments, when his domestic establishment was locked in the deepest slumber. On such occasions there was a general rumpus over the sleeping architect's head. The stalwart young Gridlegrean sprang to the window, dragging his tackle after him; the various departments tumbled out of bed and fell to gathering the chattels and on one or two occasions the astounded Mr. Pitwilk had seen a stream of Gridlegreans shooting past his window late at night in all degrees of drapery, on some kind of flying trapeze.

In the remoter altitudes of this house there was known to be a woman called "the widder," whose husband was a sailor and came home at long intervals and thrashed her and went away again. From her apartments there issued at unseasonable hours, during her husband's absence, subdued sounds of revelry which sometimes rose to the shrill murderous tones of an affray. Then the other tenants in their disquiet waking, would hear the heavy tramp of the policemen on the stairs, the sound of something soft being pulled down, and after awhile all would be quiet again.

This widow had a rapscallion son of twelve who lived a vagabond life on the street and was known in the neighborhood as "Cokey Tim." The adjacent gashouses were forever turning out vast quantities of coke and the steaming carts were forever going through the streets delivering this fuel. The boys of the vicinity made a regular practice of robbing these carts, and their method of doing it was for one of their number to climb upon the tailboard of the vehicle and throw the lumps of coke from the load over his shoulder into the street, as the cart was going on its way. At this work Tim was an expert, and it was believed the drivers winked at him. At all events, he seldom got a cut of a whip and, save when a policeman shouted at him, had matters all his own way. It was this immunity that had got him the title of Cokey Tim. His chief boast when not robbing the coke carts, was that he could lick any of the Eighteenth street gang that wasn't twice his weight. He was a vicious, pugnacious, little brute and the terror of all the tradesmen in the neighborhood.

Back of this widow's, on the fifth floor, a girl known in low professional life as Clianthe Mignon, and in private life as Betsey Wood, lived with her mother, and over them was an unexplored region where cart loads of emigrants were occasionally tumbled in and had been seen sitting round on their green boxes, smoking their pipes and patiently waiting for something. Their existence in the place was accounted for by the fact that one of the emigrant runners at Castle Garden had hired the whole floor and used it to turn newly arrived groups of foreigners into, while he was making advantageous bargains with railroads to send them West. This gave a distinctive flavor to the house.

There was usually a crowd of jabbering steerage passengers, smelling of oakum and bilge water, choking the stairways and making an unnecessary noise with their boxes. They were always coming in and going out. They were never known to stay. They broke the stairs, dug the plaster out of the walls in getting up, only to sit round when they got up, and wait—then they split the balusters and scratched the hand rails in coming down again. Sometimes it happened that a departing group with their chattels, met an arriving troupe with theirs on the narrow stairway. Then there was a horrible confusion and inextricable muddle in mid-air, especially if one party happened to be Irish and the other French or Hungarian, and all the female tenants on these occasions leaned on the hand rail and looked down the well-hole with a sense of proprietorship in the diversion.

This strange but periodical gladitorial combat was very apt to be intensified by one other circumstance, if it happened on Saturday, and that other circumstance was this, Mr. Ned Skillet who lived back of the Pitwilks and was a conductor on the Second avenue horse railway, had two sons who turned the hallways on that particular day into a railway system of their own, assembling all the boys of the house and using the handrail for a tramway. As each human car started down the rail on its stomach, young Skillet who acted as starter, would make the air blue with his remarks about "headway" and "knocking down" and "clearing the track."

To drop in at O'Reardon's Terrace at a moment when the railway system was in full operation and the emigrant system had tied itself into a knot on the stairs, was to produce a lively sense of the incomprehensible intensity and jargon of the life that went on there.

The first thing that attracted the old gentleman's attention when he arrived at the Terrace was a little placard on the side of the door of this house. He put on a pair of horn spectacles and read it:

TO LET.

FOURTH FLOOR FRONT—

Enquire of Mc'Gloine on the corner.

He looked into the dirty hallway, where a score of children were playing, and then picking his way through a game of ball and a group of costermongers, he crossed the street to Gustav Lever's little "Dutch Grocery," and lingered about the doorway watching the entrance to the centre house in the Terrace.

He may have stood there fifteen minutes, then apparently satisfied, he went off down to the corner of Avenue A, entered the drinking saloon known as "McGloine's" and presently came out with a young Irishman who was in his shirt sleeves, smoking a large cigar and swinging a bunch of keys with careless official skill in a circle, occasionally throwing them up with one hand and catching them with the other. This personage was accosted familiarly as they went along by several people as "Patsey," and one old woman with a bucket of coke on her arm called him Patsey McGloine and wanted to know, as she struck an attitude and measured his companion from head to foot, what he "would be after givin'em." To which Patsey, with ready politeness, replied "something new and nice, Mrs. Dooley, and don't you forget it."

The two men then went up the stairway of the centre house, the elder betraying his age as he toiled after the stalwart young Irishman.

They found the interior of this house to be almost as noisy and characteristic as the street. The hallway is narrow and badly lit. There is a score of children playing at tag in it and bedraggled women are talking over the handrail of the staircase. There are mingled odors of tobacco smoke, cabbage and onions. The floors, walls and stairs are a dark greasy color that suggests dampness, but is only dirt. Long lines of chalk and charcoal mark the height of the artistic children in the house, and a recent cartoon on the wall of the first landing represents "Mike MacCarthy, the Sixteenth street beat," and has an inscription issuing from his mouth conveying this pleasing personal information. It has been suffered to remain some time, not so much on account of the genius of the artist, as on account of a war that sprung up between the second and third floors as to whose duty it was to scrub it off. Each story, as the visitor ascends, is worse than the preceding one. There are half clothed people on all of them looking down the wellhole, watching their children or husbands sitting on the steps, so that the visitor has to wait for them to rise and let him go by, which they do as if it were a gratuitous favor not stipulated in the lease. They stand in the dark corners "sparking," gossiping, scolding. With each ascent the children get dirtier, younger, and more unreasonable; the smells more pungent and the obstructions more numerous. Pails of ashes and garbage, tubs of soaking clothes, bundles of wood and boxes of coke, multiply as you go up.

Arrived on the fourth floor, the strange gentleman, a little short of breath, asked in a somewhat acrid voice, but in good English:

"Who lives on this floor?"

The question was evidently intended to appear incidental, but the slight eagerness with which he bent his head to catch the answer ruined the intention.

Then Mc'Gloine, who paid very little attention to his tenants, unlocked the door of the front apartment and throwing it open with a free and easy gesture, took the cigar from his mouth and said:

"On this floor? Why there's a genteel family in there; do you want me to get their reference?"

"What's the name?"

Then Mc'Gloine walked to the open window in the empty room, leaned out and began a shouting conversation with somebody in the opposite house, leaving his tenant to inspect the place at his leisure. There was nothing to see; the suite of five rooms were soon examined and save for an army of Croton bugs that swarmed audibly over the walls and floors, nothing that could attract attention. The man gave a quick glance into each apartment and came back to the front room. Then Mc'Gloine gave a parting shout and withdrew himself from the window without looking at his companion; he merely said interrogatively—"all right?" and going to the door, held it for the tenant to come out.

"Is that your style, old man?" he asked as he locked the door.

The old man, with a good deal of quiet dignity, turned about and said:

"Come to your office and I'll give you a check for the rent."

Mc'Gloine took his cigar out and whistled a note of surprise. Then the men went downstairs, repaired to the corner saloon and the agent received a check for fifteen dollars. It was drawn on the First National Bank and was signed in full: Zabdi Ben Plonski.

While this was going on, there was sitting at the window of one of the rooms in the rear suite on the same floor, an old man, who was known in the neighborhood as Gentleman Evans. There was a leathern-bound and somewhat dilapidated ledger on his knees, but he was staring vacantly out upon the roofs and gas tanks of the rear view, just now ruddily lit with the setting sun.

This old man is the father of Mrs. Jacob Sitwhite whose husband rents the rooms. He is at least seventy years old. There is an air of serious, almost pathetic contemplation on his face, which is a remarkably benign one and must have been handsome at sometime, for his watery eyes show their rich brown color yet and his mouth has not lost its generous curves. His short, thin, white, side whiskers soften a face that is already benignly effeminate. His garb betrays the struggle of poverty with gentility. The scrupulously white collar is a little frayed and the old-fashioned black stock about his neck is a little rusty. His black coat and vest have been brushed threadbare and his shoes which have been patched many times, are carefully blackened.

This is Mr. Eben Evans, or as the people in the house call him, "Mr. Gentleman Evans." He has seen better days, but is little more than a pensioner now on the Sitwhites.

He had been a moderately prosperous coal merchant, and as late as 1859 was living in his own house in Stanton street, adjacent to his coal yard. Here he had been surrounded by his family consisting of three daughters and their mother. These children, brought up in a comfortable home by an indulgent father, were chiefly unfortunate in their marriages. The eldest, Martha, died in childbirth one year after her marriage with a well-to-do silversmith. The second daughter, Manuella, married a civil engineer, who was killed two years after by the premature explosion of a blast somewhere in Pennsylvania. He left a little property and his widow came with her infant daughter to live with her father in Stanton street. This child became the pet of the old man. She was eight years old when in 1850 her mother died. About this time Mr. Evans' misfortunes set in. He was led into some kind of speculation in coal by a partner and ruined, and Cynthia, the remaining daughter (Cynthy they always called her) who inherited very few of her father's traits, except his weakness, made the acquaintance of one John Sitwhite, a handsome but shiftless fellow and, in spite of her father's mild protests, married him and went off West.

This reduced the Evans household to grandfather and granddaughter, and the misfortune in business and the disappearance of his last child, only served to intensify the affection that had grown up for Manuella.

All attempts to straighten out his business failed. He would not listen to any plan that was not obviously honest and in accordance with his simple method, for years. He got a notion into his head that the accounts had not been rightly balanced, and his friends began to understand that the sudden blow had in some way affected his judgment and they adopted toward him that conciliatory tone which was the result of pity and a general sense of the hopelessness of his case. He continued to live in the brick house in Stanton street until 1859, but he mortgaged the property and let the money slip through his hands. In fact by the time Manuella was seventeen, Mr. Evans was incompetent to manage his own affairs, and the girl saw, when she was brought home from boarding school, in her sixteenth year, that some kind of an inexplicable but gloomy change had taken place in the household. She was bright and beautiful and loved her grandfather with the double affection that was meant for father and mother, but she could give him no assistance and little counsel, because a hopeful hallucination possessed him that somehow things would presently right themselves, and because her ignorance of the practical world was beautifully prodigious.

Matters went steadily on from bad to worse. The mortgage was foreclosed on the Stanton street property; the old friends who had sat around his table in his days of prosperity fell away. John Sitwhite, after a profligate career in the West, in which he tried to do several things for which he was unfit, left a load of debts behind him, came back to New York with two children and was glad to go to work at any rough employment that would earn him ten or twelve dollars a week. In 1860 he drifted into one of the gas houses on Avenue A, where he got twelve dollars a week as foreman of a gang of coke shovellers, and his family went to live in O'Reardon's Terrace.

A little later the Evans establishment was closed out by a merciless execution. Manuella found out too late that her grandfather had put the papers in the suit against him carefully away in one of his ledgers and forgotten all about them. She saw the men carry out the piano and take down the pictures, and she found her grandfather in tears when she went to him for an explanation.

They had reached at last the condition of almost absolute poverty, having only a few hundred dollars in the savings bank, left her by her mother, which must now go to support her helpless grandfather and herself.

So, in their extremity, they went with the Sitwhites to board, in O'Reardon's Terrace, until something better turned up, Mr. Sitwhite agreeing to the invasion after some protestations, in consideration of the few dollars a week that was paid over out of the girl's little capital.

Once in the humble home of the tenement house, the former friends and acquaintances of Manuella were cut off by an impassable chasm. Only one had come over and bridged the yawning separation by a visit. This was a girl of French extraction, known in the family as Therese, who had been employed as a maid in the Evans household when the daughters were all at home. She was a wayward, superstitious, and rather handsome young woman, whose irregularities had been several times overlooked in consideration of her skill in dressing hair and her cleverness generally in toilet matters. She went utterly astray one day; disappeared entirely for awhile and had been well nigh forgotten, when she suddenly returned and told a penitent story to Mr. Evans, who with his usual weak generosity not only forgave her at once, but helped her materially with money and good advice. She stayed some time and looked after the young Manuella and then disappeared again.

This girl had visited the Evanses twice since their removal to the Terrace. She had come suddenly and as before, with a penitent story, and as before had been kindly received by Mr. Evans, but Manuella with instinctive dislike had avoided her and knew nothing of her troubles. Her first visit was made on the twenty-third of July; her last visit was on the fifth of August.

Existence in such a house, it can readily be seen, was anything but pleasant to Manuella, who had been surrounded all her life with the comforts and most of the advantages that affection could supply.

The coarseness and familiarity of the strangely various natures in the house shocked and surprised her; nor could she find much relief in the rooms of her aunt, for Mrs. Sitwhite, who was never regarded as of the sweetest disposition in her father's family, had long since fallen into a querulous and complaining habit under the wear and tear of poverty and the disappointments of matrimony. If she had ever had a reasonable hope of reaching the comfortable and quiet life of her earlier experience, she had given it up. Years of failure and incessant drudgery had worn her down to a careless, mechanical loyalty, and her protests and complaints were no longer guarded in language nor moderate in manner.

She had unquestionably been dragged down to this condition by her husband. It really seemed as if he had found his level in the gas house. At all events, he accepted the life of dull unpromising labor as if it was the best that could be done. He went about his work with the regularity of a machine. He came home hungry and tired; he smoked his pipe, plagued his children, had a quarrel with his wife, and went early to bed to snore loudly. Now and then McGloine caught him on a Saturday night, with his wages in his pocket, and if he came back tipsy or was brought back by Mrs. Sitwhite before he had spent all his money, as had been the case two or three times, he was apt to be maudlin and reproachful, rather than vicious. On such occasions his fancy was very apt to exaggerate the inoffensive Mr. Evans into all manner of terrible impositions.

To add to the domestic distress of the Sitwhites and their lodgers, it should be mentioned that within a year or two Mrs. Sitwhite had been troubled with a growing affliction that took the form of a chronic influenza, and it was her chief reproach to Sitwhite that she had caught it from him. This may have been true; at all events John, when he was married, suffered very severely with prolonged attacks of coryza, which entirely left him after he began to work in the gashouse.

The five rooms occupied by the Sitwhite's were narrow, ill-ventilated and badly arranged. At the rear end of the hall was a small apartment used as a kitchen; this opened into the largest room of the group, which was family parlor, dining room and nursery. There were three doors in it, two of which led to bedrooms in the centre of the building and the suite was completed by an additional dark room beyond, that could only be entered from the hallway.

It is necessary that this scheme should be clearly understood, and the [following] diagram, which represents the fourth floor, is also a plan of all the groups of rooms above and below it.

It will be seen by this drawing that the front and back groups on the floor do not correspond exactly, and it may be explained that the builder, Mr. O'Reardon,

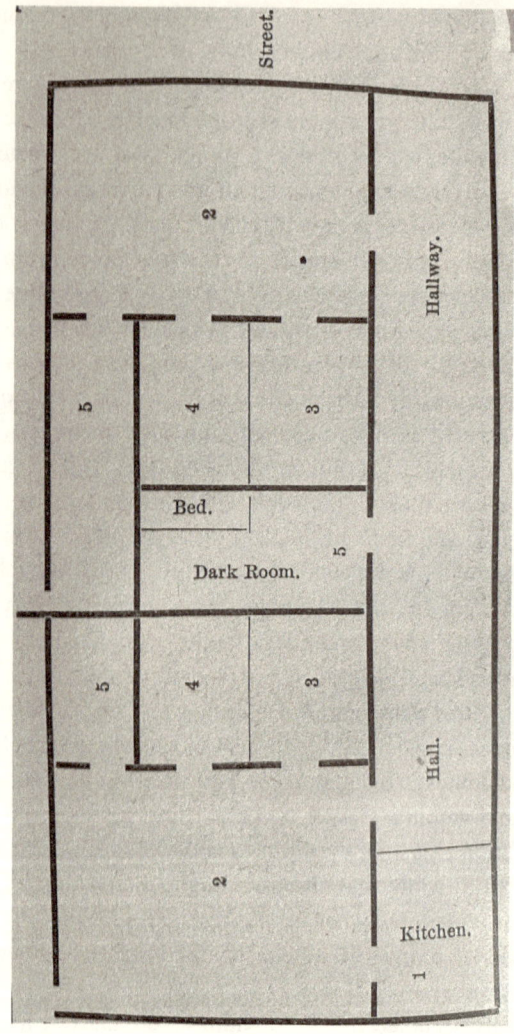

had originally constructed his tenements with the intention of letting each floor of eight rooms to one family. He soon found that his applicants did not want so many rooms and could not afford to pay so high a rent. He then promptly divided each floor into two groups as we now have them, and he added two rooms by putting up thin partitions across what was an interior passage-way or hall, from front to back, one of which (shown by the projecting line) is the dividing mark between each suite of apartments. The dark room (numbered 5) had been intended for a common store room for both families, but the impossibility of making families use anything in common, without providing each floor with a committee of arbitration and a guard of policemen, quickly led him to abandon this idea. He cut off two feet of the room, converted it into a pantry or closet and let the room go with the back groups—this being an offset against the superior advantages of the front suites in their outlook upon the panorama of the street.

The wooden partition which extended across the passage-way and shut each family into its own domicile, was made of thin tongue and groove pine boards, which had shrunk a good deal, but the seams had afterwards been covered with cheap wall-paper.

The disposition of the Evans household was simple and uncomfortable enough. The largest of the sleeping rooms (No. 8), was occupied by Mr. and Mrs. Sitwhite and their two children; the smaller chamber adjoining it, was given to Manuella, and Mr. Evans, who was not supposed to care particularly about the light, was consigned to the dark room (No. 5), where he slept upon a cot with his head against the closet, in which he kept and guarded with an absurd care, his old coal yard ledgers and other relics of the past, in which nobody but himself had the slightest interest.

It was in the large family room that Mr. Evans sat while Plonski was hiring the front suite. His chair was drawn up to the open window, through which came super-heated puffs of heavily loaded air from the tin roofs and brick walls. But the arid view was broken by one square gap of a few feet between chimneys and gashouses, and across the narrow perspective of that chasm, gleamed the dancing waters of the East River, with a tantalizing inch or two of the misty blue hills of Long Island.

This bit of outlook, so dismally framed, was the one perpetual picture hung there in the prosaic gallery of Manuella's home life. It had its regular and familiar visions and its little surprises. The big, white steamers that went up Long Island Sound, glided punctually across it at the same moment like stately phantoms, every afternoon, and the girl could see, with her clear young eye, the black masses of people on the upper deck, and her active fancy could almost hear the band playing. At other times the chasm seemed like a telescopic tube turned upon some other world—a little picture of far away showers falling upon the hillside; rifts of clouds in gold and dun way down on a distant horizon and the gleam of a white sail idly drifting on the river and reaching unbroken into purple depths.

It is doubtful if Mr. Evans vision or thoughts were quite equal to all the miniature details of this opening. He looked, indeed, along the line of break in the walls, but he was evidently in a reverie. His thin, wrinkled, but delicately formed hand lay upon the open page of the ledger on his knees, with one finger outstretched as if he had been guiding his eyes along the lines of faded figures.

There were two children boisterously playing upon the floor; one, a boy of three or four years, only half attired, was driving a coke cart extemporized out of a rattan chair, to which a younger sister was harnessed with strips of muslin and who was protesting in angry tones but to no effect, against the driver's use of Mr. Evans' cane as a whip. The experiment ended in a rousing thwack of the cane across the girl's head, and an immediate altercation in which she was pushed backward and received another thwack from the wall on the opposite side of the head. At the height of the fracas the door opened and Manuella came in from the hallway.

She wore a plain mantle thrown round her shoulders, over a light summer dress, and had a common brown chip hat upon her head as if she had been walking. She entered radiantly as if from some other condition of life than that seen in this place. In the momentary pause, as she took in the situation, there was the unconscious dignity of innocent youth and the marvelous grace of high health and perfect function. As to her beauty, there could be no argument. It asserted itself instantly and needed no explanation to the observer. It was of that general and baffling kind that cannot well be scheduled. She looked taller than she really was, owing to her erect carriage and the unconscious imperious-ness with which her head was thrown back. But her face dispelled any idea of haughtiness. Its breadth between the large, smoky gray eyes would have ban-ished that if the graciousness of expression and a certain dreamy wonderment in the eyes themselves had not been there. Her hair, which was like old gold seen through a glass of brown sherry, came out on her forehead under the chip hat in wanton convolutions and was swept back in a loose mass over her ears. Her eyebrows were several degrees darker than her hair and as cleanly arched as if Giotto had swept his umber pencil there. They were lifted in surprise a moment as she looked at the group in the room. Then, without saying a word, she took the boy by the arm, opened the kitchen door and thrust him quickly, but not violently, into the adjoining room and came and dropped down on her knees in front of her grandfather, picking up his still outstretched hand and holding it between her palms as she did so.

"O, Grandpa," she said with unmistakable tenderness in low rich tones; "how long have you been here? I must have stayed a deal longer than I intended. See, there goes the six o'clock boat."

"Yes, Ella," he replied, putting his other hand in a weak way upon her chip hat and then withdrawing it "Why don't you take your bonnet off?"

She withdrew the pins that held it and let it drop behind her on the floor. Then she lifted his hand and placed it on her head, where it rested limply on the wavy brown hair.

"You've been worrying your poor brain over that hateful old book again. Let me shut it up. I want to have a real good talk with you before they come in. Does your head hurt you to-day?"

"No, my dear," he replied; and his voice was thin but pleasant. "My head's clearer than it has been for weeks. That's why I've been trying to fix up some of my accounts."

"I've been thinking of a way," she said cautiously, "to give you more time and have you less disturbed, so that you will be better able to attend to them."

"What way, my dear?" he asked with just the least anxiety.

"Well," she continued, beginning to feel about for phrases, "I'm going to earn some money myself and then we can move up town into nicer rooms, and—"

Here she stopped. She knew by the movement of his hand on her head that she had alarmed him, and she lifted her eyes slowly to his as if guilty of a wrong.

"Ella, what are you thinking about?" he asked. "What will you do to earn money?"

"Something nice and respectable and easy," she said. "I can go into Maxwell's store on the Sixth avenue and get seven dollars a week."

He was trying to get up on his feet.

"My child," he said, with real concern in his tone, "you must not think of this. I cannot permit it; I really cannot. You are a Castleton, remember."

She pulled him back into the chair with strenuous affection.

"Listen to me, Grandpa," she said impulsively. "I am a woman now. Have you forgotten that? I must have clothes." She said this with a faint flush as if it were a slight to remind him of it. "I must earn a little money to keep myself respectable, and I am sure we both shall be a great deal more comfortable when I do it."

"Manuella," replied the old man with an almost painful air of authoritative tenderness. "You must not talk this way; I have brought you up too carefully. I will take care of you. I will see that you have all that you want."

"We are very poor, Grandpa, and you are not as strong as you were once."

My dear," he said, "you do not know the world as I do. You will commit some dreadful mistake. No, no, we can do better than that. You shall have clothes."

"How," she asked, with genuine wonder, "shall I get them?"

"You forget," he said, "that I have the means of getting them. You are young and impatient, but it is all right now."

"What is all right?"

"You shall hear; yes you shall hear. I have a surprise for you, my darling."

There was a new exaltation in his tone that arrested her attention.

"Do you mean, Grandpa, that you will go into business again?" she asked, fearing to hear that it was the same old fancy.

"Yes, yes," he replied, "in good time, but it's not that. I have something else. It will make you comfortable and happy. I will not permit you to go and associate with the people who are unworthy of you, my beautiful child, when I have the means of supplying you with the comforts you desire."

She was looking at him with a lovely wonderment, and in her unconscious eagerness she had caught hold of him as if to prevent him from lapsing into his usual imaginative helplessness.

"Yes," she said, attentively, "what have you got, Grandpa?"

"I have got," he answered, and he bent down to her and softened his voice, "I have got the cup, my child; don't forget."

Then she got up. A look of weariness came into her face. She merely said, "Yes, I had forgotten it," and began to busy herself with her duties.

CHAPTER III.

"WHAT IS THAT WOMAN AFRAID OF?".

It was an unusually bright September morning when John Wilder got off the train at Coe's Grove, and sauntered up to the country tavern not a thousand feet away from the station. It was an inviting old moss-grown hostelry, shaded by poplars and flanked by two country roads. All the gentry of the neighborhood must pass it to come to the station. Broad and decayed wooden steps led up to a spacious veranda, screened all over by Virginia creeper. A stable and hitching-shed for teams adjoined the house. A triangular bit of worn clover stretched out in front round one of the poplars, and in the shade stood Jared Sprinkler, the proprietor, in his shirt sleeves, discussing the points of a plowhorse with a farmer, while the animal gnawed at the bark of the poplar.

Mr. Wilder stared into the little barroom under the veranda, the door of which stood open. It was a basement room quaintly indicative in its appointments of the patrons, the proprietor and the place. On one side, a short, well-worn counter, behind which a few heavy decanters bore labels—Gin and Tansy, Applejack, Medford Rum, Rye Whiskey, etc. In the center of the room a large cast iron stove, grown permanently red with its winter fires, with the ashes still bulging from its unhinged door and the iron railing that surrounded its sand-box still polished by the feet of the worthies who gathered round it to drink applejack and discuss the vital affairs of the township when the weather drove them indoors. Against the wall—a rough settee, its arms carved into grotesque unsightliness by many jack-knives, and on the walls last year's circus bills, printed notices of sheriffs sales and the time tables of the Hudson River Railroad. At the one short window looking out under the veranda, asleep with last week's *Herald* in his hand, was a red-nosed, sun browned veteran, whose crutch balanced across his stomach was regularly undulating with his heavy abdominal breathing.

Mr. Wilder took in everything like a camera, at one flash. He then went back to the lawn and addressed himself to Mr. Jared Sprinkler.

"Can you tell me," he said, "if there is a person living in Coe's Grove by the name of Carteret, and how I can find him?"

Mr. Jared Sprinkler, thus interrupted in a horse-discussion, looked at the newcomer carelessly with his eyes, but his mind was not so easily diverted. His reply was:

"A man that will work a horse up to her time in a stone field would put his wife to churnin' on her wedding day. You can't tell me nothin' about horses."

Then he picked up the animal's off leg and looked at the hoof, remarking as he did so, "never heard of anybody o' that name."

"What's the name?" asked the other man, putting his hand to his ear as if he were deaf.

"Carteret—Colin Carteret," rather loudly.

Then a female voice from the veranda said:

"Why, Pop, that's the young man at Enniston's, don't you know?"

Mr. Sprinkler slapped the mare on the flank with his open palm. "She's been pulled down, Rube," said he, "and she wouldn't do for my work." Then a moment later, as he ran his hand critically down the animal's leg—"If there's a new young man in the village leave Nancy Ann alone for finding it out."

John Wilder looked around and saw a buxom and freckled young woman in highly starched calico smilingly leaning out of the veranda window on her elbows and inviting a conversation by her manner.

Mr. Wilder was not the man to disappoint her. He summarily left the men, walked up the wooden steps and accosted her.

"O, yes," she said with ready volubility, "Mr. Carteret's a painter. He's up at Enniston's."

"Who's Enniston?"

She looked at him with surprise.

"Enniston—don't you know, that got killed. It was in all the papers."

"Was it, indeed," said Wilder, taking a seat near the window. "Do you know now I've forgotten all about it. Was it a railroad accident?"

"No, indeed," with something like pride in the consciousness that it was no such ordinary affair. "He fell on a dirk one night two months ago and killed himself. Why, everybody heard of it. Did you come from the city?"

"Yes, I did," replied Wilder.

"Well I should 'a thought you'd heard of Ol Enniston then. He was a city man."

Wilder was in a brown study—a dim recollection of having heard or read something of the accident was awakened by the girl's words. It then occurred to him that the event had been reported as having taken place at Cosgrove, that being the abbreviation of Coe's Grove, and he had not associated it with this place.

The girl, finding that she had an entirely fresh subject to impart her story to, seated herself sidewise on the windowsill with an evident desire to be cross-questioned.

"I wish," said Wilder, "you'd tell me about it. I do have a slight recollection of reading about it in the papers. It was an accident, you say?"

"O yes. You see he went down in the garden to cut some flowers with a dirk, and his foot caught and he fell on the dirk. There was a party there; he was going to cut the flowers for a young lady. I've got a scrap book full of it; would you like to see it? I cut them all out of the papers."

With scarcely any interruption she produced her book and placed it in his hands with just the least bit of pride—not so much at her work as in her possession.

It proved to be a collection of newspaper clippings about Mr. Oliver Enniston and the accident; obituary notices, editorials from the county press, resolutions passed by the deacons of the First Reformed Church, a funeral sermon preached by Dr. Beresford Flocton and a poem written by a "sympathizing friend."

Mr. Wilder went through the book in his usual deliberate manner. Exclusive of the funeral sermon, there was not much of it and it did not take him long to possess himself of the contents.

The accounts agreed mainly as to the occurrence. It was regarded as a most shocking accident that had removed an estimable and influential townsman and bereaved a most devoted family. There was not the slightest suspicion attached to his character or name. He had died in his wife's arms two hours after the accident, attended by Dr. Wollendorf, the nearest physician, and had been profoundly mourned by the whole community.

Meagre as the details were in those particulars which would be most likely to interest a detective, still there was something about the affair, thus suddenly presented to Wilder's mind that awakened an inquisitive interest.

The very piece of information that would be first sought by any reader was not furnished by the book. So he said to Nancy Ann, as he closed it.

"Why should Mr. Enniston cut flowers with a dagger?"

"Why, you see," she replied with a patness that showed this to be an expected question, "Miss Hardynge came out on the balcony where Ol Enniston and Mr. Seymour were smoking and she saw the white flowers in the moonlights—they were camelias—and she wanted one; so Ol Enniston took the little dirk out of her hair and went down to cut it. That's how it was—it's simple enough. I know all about it, because Barney the gardener who used to come down here every morning for the papers when Mr. Enniston was home, has told me pretty much all there was."

"Does he come down any more for the papers?"

"No, I guess Mrs. Enniston don't read 'em—anyway she told Mrs. Plogget, who done her cleaning, that they annoyed her. It don't take much to annoy some folks. She said she didn't want him hanging round the tavern. Hanging round—I'd like to know. O, she's way up if there ever was one."

Wilder smiled good-naturedly. "So Carteret stops up there, does he?"

"I don't say he's there. He goes to the city sometimes and stays several days. Barney drove him down for the ten-forty day before yesterday and I haint seen him come back. You bet that affair made a fuss here. The first I heard of it was when Bill Newman came over in the morning from Wollendorf's and said Ol' Enniston was dead. I spose you want to see Carteret about pictures?"

"Yes," said Wilder reflectively. "He's a smart painter."

Half an hour later, the officer was walking up the river road in the direction of Enniston's. It was a very beautiful rural highway and especially lovely on this bright autumnal morning. Handsome residences and well-kept parks betokened a scattered community of well-to-do residents who had selected the river bank for their homes. The great lawns swept down in green vistas to the Hudson, and glimpses of the blue water were caught through the reddening maples and the bronze chestnuts.

The Enniston place, as it was called, was at least a mile from the station, northward. From the description Wilder had obtained from Nancy Ann, there was no difficulty in finding it. It stood on the river side of the road, a handsome cream colored brick residence, surrounded by broad lawns enriched with old trees and well-kept shrubbery. A blue gravel road swept in a great curve from the highway through the trees to the house.

Half way up the approach he met Barney, the gardener, who stepped out of a thicket with a pruning knife in his hand. He was a stout, red-whiskered Irishman in a blue shirt. He doffed his hat and wore a deferential manner.

"Morning, sir," he said. "We expected you yesterday. If you'd sent a telegram, I'd a had the trap down for you."

"This is a good-natured ass," Wilder said to himself, as he took the man in. "The walking was good and I preferred it," he replied. "Is your mistress at home?"

"She's always at home now, sir. She's not been out of the house for a fortnight, save the goin' to church."

"Yes, I suppose she's been pretty badly smashed up and don't even have any company."

"Divil a one, sir, savin' the docther."

"Wollendorf. I see."

"Wollendorf is it?" said Barney with sudden energy. "May the ground swaller Wollendorf. It's the praste I mean."

"Dr. Flocton?"

"Divil a man else has been on the place, barrin' the lad Carteret. What would she be sendin' to the lawyers fur, if it wasn't for Wollendorf? It's yoursel' could be doin' me a good turn, sir, while your hand's in," added the man, taking off his straw hat and suddenly assuming an air of appeal.

Wilder struck a match deftly on the sole of his shoe, lit a cigar very deliberately, gave one or two puffs with his head thrown back, and looked round at the landscape. By that time he had struck the safe mean of reply.

"Barney," said he, "you've got a magnificent place here. Can you see the river from that grove on the north of the house?"

"You can't see it no better anywheres," replied Barney. "I took out almost fifty trees on that slope so as Mr. Enniston could see it from his window."

"O, I thought it was Mrs. Enniston wanted to see the river."

"How the divil could she see it, when her room's on the other side of the house?"

"I'd like to walk over there," said Wilder, "and see the scenery before I go in. You can tell me what I can do for you while I smoke my cigar."

The two men sauntered leisurely along the winding paths toward the grove.

"How far does the property extend in that direction?" pointing southward.

"To the row of Junipers," replied Barney, "that's Wollendorf's place—the doctor. It's him that makes the fuss."

"Yes," said Wilder thoughtfully, "and I can't see what's got into the old man."

He looked sidewise at his companion, who trudged along. "Old man" was a risk, but it was evidently a safe guess.

The gardener struck his forehead with his knuckles.

"It's crazed he is, sure. The old rat ought to be in the asylum. Never a word was said agin Mr. Enniston till he set it goin'."

"Perhaps you're right. It's a crazy story to set going. If he'd told something that people might believe—"

"That's it. There's no more chance of a man like Mr. Enniston killing himself, than o' my being archbishop. Wasn't I with him the whole time? There weren't no saner nor sounder man on arth. No sir, Mr. Enniston wasn't such a gummach as to go down into his garden to kill himself on his own flower beds, before the young ladies with a hairpin, when he could a gone up in his own room and took the top of his head off dacintly, if he was minded."

Wilder found that it was judicious to let Barney run, so to speak, and the man once started, kept on, with an occasional steer from the officer.

"You see the place aint what it was when he was alive," he said. "You wouldn't see them stalks a comin' up like that. He knowed what a gentleman's place ought to be. But what does that painter know? Lord, the more dead limbs and rotten trunks, the better he likes it. What's this he calls it—picterest? Well, bless me, if I see any sense in it, but he's got hold of Rose and what's my opinion good for now?"

"You are speaking of Carteret?"

"I am. He's a nice enough young man and I spose he'll be in the family, but what's he know about grounds? You see they've sacked the stableman and the boy and expect me to do all the work and take care of the place as well. Look at it. That's what I wanted to speak to you about. If you could manage to put in a word about the grounds and necissity of kapin them up, don't you mind. It'ud be for the good o' the property."

"Is Mr. Carteret at home?" asked Wilder.

"He'll be up at noon; didn't Rose tell me to have the phaeton ready for the train?"

They had sauntered back to the house. Wilder hesitated a moment and then concluded to see Mrs. Enniston.

He allowed the gardener to go up the steps, open the door and usher him into the parlor, where he awaited the arrival of Mrs. Enniston.

This was the saloon room where the party had been held on the night of the accident. There were three long Windows that opened out on the broad front Veranda, and through the chinks of the closed blinds he saw the shrubbery and flowers where Enniston had met his death. On the north was a large bay. The green bank outside was so high that a person standing there when the window was open could easily look into the room.

The parlor was richly furnished and frescoed. A grand piano muffled in a thick cover, stood obliquely out from the corner. There were portraits on the walls and costly ornaments scattered about, but the room wore an air of deser-tion that long-closed rooms acquire. There was a handsome photograph album on the centre table, but it was too dark to read the inscriptions.

As he stood turning the leaves, Mrs. Enniston, with quick but noiseless step, came suddenly into the room from the hall, and as she stood in the ray of light from the window, Wilder saw a stately and somewhat austere woman of forty, whose face appeared even whiter than it really was against the prevailing gloom of the place.

"My servant has told me that you came from my lawyers," she said, with a firm and slightly sharp voice. "Please take a seat."

"Madame," said Wilder, "your servant has made a mistake. I do not come from your lawyers. I came here about the cup."

"Cup?" she repeated with astonishment. "I do not understand you, sir."

"The Toltec cup," Wilder explained. "It was this advertisement of Mr. Carteret's that brought me," and he felt in his waistcoat pocket for the news-paper clipping.

The lady was staring at him while she supported herself with a hand on the back of a heavy chair.

"What are you?" she asked with an authoritative iciness.

"I am an agent of the police department, employed only on special business, but in this case simply attracted here by this reward," and he held out the paper for her to look at it.

Without the slightest attention to it she repeated the words, "agent of the police." She had taken a step backwards.

"Let me explain," began Wilder.

"No explanations are necessary," she said, haughtily; "you could not have gained admission to my house had you not deceived my servant. I request you to leave it."

"Madame," said Wilder, a little nettled, "I had no intention of annoying you. An invitation in a newspaper signed by Colin Carteret is my only apology."

"Mr. Carteret is not here and is not master when he is here." Then she opened the door.

There was no room for parley, and a moment later Mr. Wilder found himself on the gravel walk.

For the first time in his life he was chagrined and puzzled. The question that he naturally asked himself was, "What is that woman afraid of?" Then a moment later he chuckled as he added mentally, "Woman-like, she has taken the very method to defeat herself. I'll have the secret now, if there is one, in spite of her."

He walked rapidly down the road. The beauties of the landscape were unnoticed. He was in a profound study. He waited at the station until he saw a phaeton driven up by a handsome black eyed girl, whose photograph he had seen in the album. She had come to meet Carteret. Barney did not accompany her. "These young people are lovers," said the officer. The moment the train was in he saw a good looking young man, jauntily dressed in blue flannel, making for the phaeton. He touched him on the shoulder.

"A word with you, Mr. Carteret." Thus addressed, the young man turned a frank, kindly face upon the officer.

Wilder could be summary when he chose, and he was not to be frozen out this time.

"I am an officer from the city," he said. "I came to see you about the advertisement of the lost cup. I want to catch the next train down and I will only detain you a few moments."

Mr. Carteret made an apology to the young lady and stepped aside with Wilder.

"You don't mean to say that you came up here expressly on that business?" he asked.

"Yes," replied the officer, "and I have been up to see Mrs. Enniston."

The young man looked amused. "You didn't get any information from her, I'll swear. The fact is, I know no more about that advertisement than you do, and I have been much annoyed by it. I did not insert it and cannot for the life of me see what motive any one else had in printing it."

This was said with an ingenuous sincerity that left no doubt of its truth.

"Was there a cup stolen from the house?" asked Wilder.

"Why, yes. A cup disappeared about the time of Mr. Enniston's death—but we only knew of it through the row that old Job Ackerman kicked up when it was missed."

"You say it disappeared about the time of Mr. Enniston's death?"

"Yes, I believe it was missed on the day of the funeral."

"And was nobody suspected?"

"Upon my word, I couldn't tell you. Mr. Ackerman was the only one who took any special interest in it and as he went away to South America shortly afterwards, there was nothing more thought of the affair. I hadn't heard it mentioned since, till this advertisement appeared."

"To whom did it belong?"

"To Mr. Enniston. I believe it was some kind of a relic. He kept it in his room."

"Was no other property missed at the time?"

"Nothing that I ever heard of."

"One word more, Mr. Carteret. Who are Mrs. Enniston's solicitors?" and Wilder took out a book and pencil to write down the answer.

"Burton & Dunn," replied Carteret. "Trinity Building."

Wilder put back the book and pencil without writing the names.

"Were they Mr. Enniston's lawyers?"

"Yes, sir."

Here the men separated. Just three hours later John Wilder was in Burton & Dunn's law offices.

CHAPTER IV.

JOHN WILDER STUMBLES ON THE FIRST FACT.

John Wilder found Mr. Albert Burton, the senior partner, in his chair, reading the first edition of the evening paper. As he was well known to that gentleman, having been employed on one or two occasions to gather special information, he had no hesitancy in explaining that he had been up to Coe's Grove on the matter of an advertisement, and had accidentally learned from Mrs. Enniston's friends of her annoyance and of her application to the attorneys for advice and assistance.

Mr. Burton, leaning back in his chair, ran his hand through his flowing white hair and lifted his white eyebrows, which looked not unlike tufts of cotton on his florid face.

"By all that's treacherous," said he, as he took musk pink from his lapel and began to sniff at it. "I forgot that matter and you're just the man to attend to it."

With that he got up and going to a secretary surmounted by vast ranges of pigeon holes that were filled with papers, he pulled therefrom a package of letters and began turning over the endorsed ends. When he had found what he wanted, he returned to his seat with two folded notes and adjusted his glasses.

"Mrs. Enniston," he said, "sent me this letter about two weeks ago. You may read it."

Wilder took the missive, which, with the exception of a few lines relating to the settlement of the personal debts of the late Mr. Enniston, read as follows:

Coe's Grove, August 15.

* * * * It was, however, business of quite another nature and far more serious, which led me to address you this time. I have been very much annoyed by vague reports concerning Mr. Enniston's death. Somebody, I felt sure, was circulating stories that were untrue. Of course, they only reached me in the vaguest shape and I could do no more at first than feel uncomfortable; but they have increased of late; and I am now satisfied that they have one author, a Dr. Wollendorf of this place.

For some reason—Heaven only knows what it is—he has set in motion the cruel and unfounded suspicion that my husband was not killed by accident, but committed suicide. Have I no protection from such a man? Shall he be permitted to slander the memory of the dead and wound the feelings of the living? Please advise me as speedily as your business will permit.

Respectfully,

Jane Enniston.

Wilder read this letter in his slow, careful manner and then handed it back to the attorney.

"In reply to that note," said Mr. Burton, "I wrote to Mrs. Enniston, promising to look after Dr. Wollendorf and advising her to give herself no uneasiness concerning the idle rumors of a gossiping village, took no further action in the matter until, three days ago, I received the following."

He then passed a second letter to Mr. Wilder, which read as follows:

COE'S GROVE, Sept. 1.

Messrs. Burton & DUNN:

I am compelled again to call your attention to the matter of which I wrote you on the fifteenth. As the attorneys and executors of the estate, I thought it proper to ask your aid in this delicate matter. Please inform me at once if you can assist me.

JANE ENNISTON.

"I intended," said Mr. Burton, "to send our man Coffin up, but he has been away for three days. This is one of those annoyances that need only diplomacy and tact, and I think you can manage it for us. In a stagnant town like Coe's Grove, they must have something to talk about. All you will have to do is to let this Dr. Wollendorf know that we intend to defend our client's interests and name and that he had better be prudent. Mrs. Enniston is probably nervous and irritable, for the accident was a terrible shock to her and she exaggerates the importance of the scandal. When do you go?"

"I shall run up in the morning," replied Wilder. "You had better give me a letter to Mrs. Enniston. She is very peculiar."

Mr. Burton wrote the following note:

"JANE ENNISTON—

Dear Madame: Officer John Wilder is a confidential agent of our firm and we have given him instructions to look into the matter of which you wrote. We have great confidence in his ability to manage the affair to your satisfaction.

Respectfully,

BURTON & DUNN."

Thus equipped, John Wilder found himself the next morning before the tavern of Mr. Sprinkler at Coe's Grove. Nancy Ann greeted him with a broad smile from the sill of the tavern window upon which she sat, attired in starched pink. He had changed his dress completely, and she noticed it with ill-concealed approval. In the place of the loose flannel suit and soft hat he had previously worn, he now had on a dark cutaway coat and a silk hat. This alteration lifted him in the girl's estimation from a drummer or commercial agent, to a patron of the fine arts, and she raised her style of addressing him a tone or two in the gamut of respect.

She noticed in the alert woman's way, the gold chain which peeped delicately and respectably from beneath his vest, and she saw that a diamond ring glittered on his finger. She wondered if he had worn that before and if it had escaped her.

As he came across the triangle of lawn beneath the poplar, she saw that he was a good-looking man of about thirty-five, tall, and straight and sinewy, with a firm but elastic step and a swing of his arms from the shoulder that betokened muscular vigor.

To a more discerning physiognomist than Nancy Ann, his face would have betokened something more interesting than his occupation, as he touched his hat and looking up, saluted her. It was one of those faces that have a deceptive mildness, almost vacuous at times, and at others, the rather thin lips and gray eyes wore a placid inflexibility that made one uncomfortable. The vague expression could only be interpreted to mean a relentless power of waiting.

His spare face was close shaven, save that a short yellowish moustache had been left on his lip.

Nancy jumped with alacrity from the window sill and leaning over the balustrade of the high veranda, said:

"O, sir, you'll catch him this morning. He came up yesterday. Won't you come in and sit down?"

"Just a moment," replied Wilder "I'd like to look at that scrapbook of yours once more," and he sat down on the wooden bench under the windows. "You don't object to my seeing it again do you?"

"Not a bit," she said, "I keep it to show; why, that's what I made it for."

It only took a second to reach through the winder and take it from the table. Wilder turned the leaves over and kept up a conversation of the common-place kind with the girl. He wanted to fix the dates of Mr. Enniston's death and funeral in his mind. It did not take him many minutes to do this, and then, seeing that the girl was watching him with interest, he said:

"O, here it is; I wanted to find this name. I knew a man once of the same name. Who is Job Ackerman?"

"He? Why, he was Mrs. Enniston's brother. He's a sea captain. He's sailin' round the world somewhere now, I suppose. Anyway, he hasn't been here since the funeral. He stopped with the Enniston's all that summer."

"He's a sailor, is he?" remarked Wilder reflectively.

"Yes, and a smart one I guess, for he used to come down and give Zebe McCutchen, who had a Haverstraw sloop, a lot of points; I've heard him tell it. Then he took the Enniston's all out in Commodore Bageley's yacht that summer and they were gone a week."

"I don't think that can be the man I knew," said Wilder, shutting up the book. "My man was an auctioneer and he didn't have a sister."

"Are you going back to the city to-day sir," asked Nancy Ann, tempering curiosity with an extra touch of respect.

"I don't know; I suppose Mr. Sprinkler can give me a bed somewhere if I don't?"

"Law! I kin; Pop don't run anything but the bar and the stable. You kin have half a dozen if you want 'em. Business haint been so dull in a year. Cosgrove always was a prim place but it's extra quiet this season. Deacon Fancher did talk o' havin' a camp meetin' here this fall, but the Sing Sing folks fit agin it. It would'a' made trade. Are you goin' up to Enniston's?"

"Yes, I shall walk up there this morning. I suppose I'll catch the whole family at home."

"That's Mrs. Enniston and her daughter Rose," replied the girl, as if she wished to intimate that it wasn't much of a family to catch.

"Then you don't include Mr. Carteret in the family?"

"O, no; he's company, I guess. He's Rose's beau, don't you know. Law, they're so sweet; it's town talk and it's been goin' on nigh a year."

Wilder either despaired of getting any more information immediately or concluded that it was not prudent to exhibit his curiosity, for he changed the subject, and after making a few commonplace remarks about Cosgrove and the railroad, he left Nancy Ann, promising to stop on his return if he concluded to stay over, and in half an hour he stood once more on Mrs. Enniston's front steps. He did not encounter the gardener, and to his surprise the door was opened before he had rung the bell, and a young woman who was going out, started a little and then recognizing him, smiled at her own trepidation.

John Wilder bowed and said without any waste of words that he came from Mrs. Enniston's lawyers and desired to see that lady.

"She is not at home at present," replied the girl, "but may come in at any moment. If you have business with her you had better wait. Will you come inside?"

Thus invited, Wilder once more walked into the parlor and Miss Enniston, who proved to have none of her mother's antipathy to the officer, threw open one of the blinds and let a flood of light into the room.

"Is Mr. Carteret at home?" asked the visitor.

"He is on the grounds somewhere. I was just going to look for him. You were here once before, were you not?"

"Yes," said Wilder. "On that occasion I came about the cup."

"Cup"; she repeated with a genuine look of ignorance. "What cup?" and then before he could reply she exclaimed: "O, you mean Mr. Ackerman's cup that was lost on the day of the funeral."

"Yes," he said, with a waning interest, seeing that she knew little if anything of the present mystery. "Did not Mr. Carteret mention it?"

"No," she answered bluntly. "Are you an officer?" looking him all over as if his dress was not in keeping with that idea.

"I am afraid that is what they call me sometimes," he said. "But I should not like to be regarded as one at present. My business with your mother is rather of a legal character."

"If you do not mind sitting alone for a few minutes," she replied, still regarding him with curiosity utterly devoid of apprehension, "you will be pretty sure to see her."

Then backing away she made a girlish half bow, and he heard her little boots go rapidly down the front steps.

He sat for several minutes with the picture of the girl on his retina, and he could not help contrasting her passionate face, black eyes and easy unconventionality with the white and frigid countenance and austere demeanor of her mother. "She must take after her father," he said to himself, "and in that case, her father was a handsome man."

He turned over the leaves of the album on the table and saw her photograph in varying poses and costumes. He noticed that the face lost a little of its womanly charm in profile owing to the pronounced curve of her forehead and the projection of her chin, but what it lost in charm it gained in individuality.

As he sat turning the heavy pages of the book, a step was heard in the hall and Barney appeared in the doorway. He stood there a moment with his hat in his hand somewhat irresolute, but wearing a most serious countenance that instantly indicated to Wilder that the man had a disagreeable duty to perform.

Wilder got up and going toward him, anticipated him. Laying his hand on his shoulder with a touch of familiarity and an air of easy authority, he said:

"Well, my man, I suppose Mrs. Enniston has warned you against me."

"Indeed she did," replied Barney. "She said I wasn't to let you into the house."

"That was right," remarked Wilder. "You see I came here without getting a letter from her lawyers and she didn't know me. This time they have sent me with a letter to her. Now the best thing we can do is to understand each other at once. Her friends are trying to help her, but they have to humor her a little because she's so queer in her notions. So you mustn't take her at her word too quickly—do you understand? I'll get her affairs straightened out for her, if she is not too hard to manage. Carteret and Rose understand this. The young lady was here a moment ago. She let me in. Where is Mrs. Enniston now?"

"She's gone over to the doctor's with the phaeton."

"Wollendorfs?"

"Divil a bit, no. The praste's—Flockton."

"I'll wait for her as I've got an important message. Did she tell you I was an officer?"

"She did and she warned me not to answer any questions." Wilder smiled and put his other hand on Barney's shoulder.

"You see how queer she is," he said. "You'd think now that I hadn't come here to serve her, wouldn't you? Women are the hardest creatures to handle when you want to do them a good turn; why, I know all about this Enniston affair, but a man has a little curiosity when he gets into the very house, don't you know, and stands in the very room, that's all. Miss Enniston told me all about it, but she was in such a hurry to get out with her young man, that I wouldn't keep her. This is the room where they had the party that night."

"The same, sir."

"It was a warm night, wasn't it?"

"It was indeed, sir."

"And I suppose this parlor was full?" looking about as if trying to recall the scene of a crowded room.

Barney shook his head. "Why, as to that, sir, it was only a little family affair. None o' your city blowouts."

"O," said Wilder, "that was it. I had an idea it was a big celebration. I was looking at the pictures in the book here. Enniston was a fine looking man."

"You never said a thruer word, and a gentlemen every pound of him."

"Another," continued Wilder, going to the table where the album was lying open, "Is Mr. Ackerman."

It was a photograph of a square built man of forty-five, sunbrowned and wearing a short, reddish beard and moustache.

Barney assented and Wilder turned over the pages, pausing for a moment as he came to the picture of a stout gentleman with short, white, side whiskers, a broad hard face with high cheekbones and a mild clerical expression that seemed to belie the contour of his face.

"Dr. Flockton?" he remarked, looking at Barney who nodded his head.

"But this I don't know," and he pointed to the face of a man of thirty, whose general appearance was of that wide awake order that we call smart. It was the jaunty, self satisfied, well kept and well dressed man of the world, with a business air, an oiled moustache and a white spot or two on his shirt front that told where the light had flashed from diamond studs.

Wilder waited a moment while Barney leaned over and inspected it.

"O, thrue. That's Mr. Seymour He was a friend of Mr. Enniston's. He was only up here once or twice, and the last time I saw him was the night of the party."

There were several pictures of Enniston, one of Carteret and one of Mrs. Enniston, very severe and erect, and finally, the likeness of a handsome brunette with jet black hair and eyes and elegantly attired in furs.

Wilder pointed his finger interrogatively at it, merely saying, "fine looking woman, that."

Barney took the book up and shifted it about as if he could not focus his recollection and then suddenly replacing it, said, "Miss Hardynge, of course. I brought her up myself that afternoon."

"What afternoon?"

"The day o' the throuble. She and Mr. Seymour came on the 3:50 express. She's an old schoolmate o' the young lady's."

"There must have been quite a party, Barney, after all."

"Divil a one else, barrin' Mr. Carteret and the help."

Wilder closed the book. As he did so, the sound of wheels on the blue gravel made the gardener start and he went to the window.

"It's the misthress," said he, with just the faintest show of trepidation. In another moment he opened the door and Mrs. Enniston and John Wilder stood face to face. Before they could say a word, Barney had slipped down the steps, with something more than his usual alacrity, to look after the horse.

Erect and as frigid as a statue, Mrs. Enniston advanced but a step beyond her parlor door and stood blankly staring at the officer.

Wilder was the first to speak, "Madame," he said, "I bring you a letter from your lawyers, who have sent me back here," and he held out the missive for her.

Without making the slightest motion to receive it, and without changing the stony stare with which she regarded him, she replied with a chilling deliberation:

"I did not ask them to send you back."

"Quite true," said Wilder, "but in response to your application, they selected me because they thought I was competent to serve you, and that I am anxious to do."

"I endeavored," said Mrs. Enniston, as she put her hand lightly on the knob of the door, so lightly that Wilder was unable to detect in it any intention to steady herself. "I endeavored when you entered my house before to make you understand that I did not desire your assistance, and there must be some way in which I can protect myself from it. Evidently you have gone to my lawyers and thurst yourself into this private affair. Is it plain to you now, when I tell you that I consider it an unpardonable piece of impertinence, and no man who had the instincts of a gentleman would come back here after being ordered out?"

Wilder winced a little, in spite of his training and coolness.

"You are certainly the mistress of your own affairs, madame, so long as they remain private affairs, and I regret that you choose to treat with rudeness the attempt of your legal advisers to assist you."

"I shall most assuredly remain mistress of my own house, if my lawyers will permit it," she said, "and will thank you to retire without conversing with my servants."

Then without waiting for an answer, she stepped to the hall door and calling to Barney, who was just turning the horse and phaeton into the road to the stable, she said:

"Come back here. I wish you to go to the station with a telegram."

Then a moment later as Wilder passed her in the doorway, and as if remembering that the two men would come together at the village, she added:

"I'll go myself when this gentleman has left the grounds."

Wilder was nettled and disappointed. His professional pride had been touched. He had been wantonly insulted, it appeared to him, and worst of all he had been completely outgeneraled by the inflexible and cutting frankness of a woman.

He walked slowly and reflectively down the road and Mrs. Enniston passed him in the phaeton about a stone's toss from her own gate without giving the slightest heed to him. He looked after her and said to himself: "A clever, strong woman that. I wonder what she is afraid of."

Then an idea seemed to strike him suddenly.

He was in front of Wollendorf's place, though the house was hidden by locusts and dogwood.

An Irish woman was driving a cow along the path by the fence. He asked her where Dr. Wollendorf lived.

"Beyant there," she replied, jerking out her elbow in the direction of the locusts. "It's not a good dhocter as has a rusty gate. Go on to the house without paint and ye'll find a man without luck."

He pulled open the rickety gate in the palings and went up the long grass-grown road to the locusts. When the house was discernible, it proved to be one of those low farm houses refitted in parts. A great roofed veranda ran nearly the whole length of it. It was weather beaten and mossy and on its ridge pole were collected, in a long line, innumerable pigeons. Nevertheless there was something inviting in its roomy homeliness, and there was an air of seclusion and content about it, curtained off by dogwood and lilac bushes from the world.

In the center of the great porch the steps lead up to an open door. He went up and rapped with his knuckles on the inside casing. No one answered. He heard nothing but the cooing of innumerable pigeons. The door opened into a large room that was like the building—all length; and on the opposite side was another door standing wide open. He looked in. No one was visible. Then he walked across the room to the other door to see if the occupants were all in the rear garden. One or two pigeons that had strayed into the apartment ran out before him. He found that another immense porch extended along the rear of the house, level with the room; and at one end of it, attired in what had been once a rather gaudy dressing gown and with a Turkey red smoking cap on his head, stood a portly man of fifty-five. His long iron gray hair flowed backward behind his ears and fell on his shoulders. His profile was Romanesque and his attitude one of contemplative reverie. He was feeding a flock of birds with sunflower seed which he took from the pocket of his dressing gown and threw across the balustrade upon the grass below.

Wilder went slowly up to him.

"Dr. Wollendorf, I believe."

"Yes. Who's sick?" without turning his head.

"I came to see you on a matter touching Mrs. Enniston," said Wilder. "I represent her attorneys."

The doctor turned a large, benevolent face upon him slowly, looked him over with a pair of great liquid chestnut eyes and then went on feeding his pigeons.

"In the matter of certain scandalous reports," continued Wilder, "touching the peace of mind of our client, Mrs. Enniston, I have been instructed to see you and take such steps as the interview suggested to protect the lady."

Doctor Wollendorf brought his hands together with a slap, to knock the dust off, picked up a long-stemmed porcelain pipe from a wooden bench and began filling the bowl with tobacco from another pocket in his dressing gown, still keeping his attention upon the feeding pigeons. This task occupied him at least a minute, during which time Wilder stood waiting for an answer. Finally the doctor having filled and lit his pipe and taken two or three preliminary puffs, turned round and said:

"Well, sir, what steps does the interview suggest?"

"Mrs. Enniston complains," rejoined Wilder, "that you are the author of certain malicious stories or gossip concerning the nature of the late Mr. Enniston's death, which are annoying and scandalous."

Dr. Wollendorf wore a calm and dignified demeanor as he puffed his pipe and looked rather indifferently at Wilder.

"My friend," said he, "I don' circulate stories of any kind and am not given to gossip. I have something else to do; but you had better go back and tell Mrs. Enniston's lawyers that the best thing they can do for Mrs. Enniston's peace is not to stir this matter."

"It is not proposed to stir matters, but to quiet them," suggested Wilder.

"Then you have gone the wrong way about it. I have no theories, no curiosity, no animosity to actuate me; but facts are facts and I do not propose to falsify them."

"But it seems that you have circulated the story that Mr. Enniston committed suicide."

"It's false," quietly replied the doctor. "I never intimated it, but if I had any reason to believe that he did, I should not hesitate to assert it."

"Then you do not think that he committed suicide?"

"I never said so."

Dr. Wollendorf stood impassively regarding Wilder a moment, then he motioned with his hand to the wooden bench and the officer in obedience to the mute invitation, sat down.

"Are you one of Mrs. Enniston's lawyers?" the doctor asked as he sat down himself a few feet away, and put the elbow of the arm that held the pipe into the supporting palm of his other hand.

"No," replied Wilder promptly.

"What are you?"

"I am a special agent employed to attend to such cases as this."

"Humph," grunted the doctor. "Special agent. Is that the latest euphony for meddling policemen?"

"No," said Wilder with a slight smile. "As I told you, my errand is rather a suppressive than a disturbing one. Mrs. Enniston's lawyers are sensible men and understand perfectly her morbid condition of mind and the folly of attempting to correct the idle gossip of a chattering village. The best they could do to pacify her was to send a discreet agent with good sense enough to learn what facts there were and to consult with her intelligent friends about them. I came to you thinking we might quietly put our heads together."

The doctor regarded Wilder out of the corner of his big brown eye with an expression of growing mildness that seemed to say: "This man is not the ordinary impertinent understrapper."

"You must understand," he said slowly, "that I have almost as much repugnance to being mixed up in public discussions and investigations as Mrs. Enniston herself. I've an invincible dread of the annoyance that is sure to follow if you begin to re-examine the cause of Mr. Enniston's death. That alone would have kept my mouth shut; but at the same time I want you to understand that when it comes to a statement of facts, I do not intend to disguise them or falsify them. It is for Mrs. Enniston's lawyers to decide how far they will press me for those facts."

"Perhaps," said Wilder, "the best course would be to place the facts in my possession and then we can together do what is best both for your comfort and Mrs. Enniston's."

"I haven't the slightest objection, sir," replied the doctor. "The absurd story has been published to the world that the late Mr. Enniston fell accidentally upon a poniard and received a mortal wound, and his friends and the public have accepted the story. I was called that night to attend him, being the nearest physician. I arrived at the house at twenty minutes past nine. I found him in his own room on the second floor upon a lounge, drenched in blood, and the house, which was full of visitors, in an uproar. I got the wrappages off him as quickly as possible to make an examination. Mrs. Enniston and her brother, Mr. Ackerman, were in the room. Most of the guests and servants were huddled panic stricken, in the hallways. He was in a dangerous state of excitement and the first thing he said was, 'Doctor, I've met with a terrible accident. I must speak to you alone—put them all out.' The tones of his voice betrayed how great had been the hemorrhage. Mrs. Enniston stood near him, pale and inflexible, and at this request gave him a look that said plainly she would not leave the room. 'Tell me as quickly as you can,' he said, 'how long can I live?' I got the things off him, managed to send Mrs. Enniston for cloths and asked Mr. Ackerman to step outside for a moment. The instant we were alone he said in an anxious whisper, 'Quick, tell me how long I've got. I have an important communication to make to Ackerman and Carteret.'

"'My dear sir,' I said, 'you are bleeding like an ox, and it is imperative that you remain as quiet as possible and do not try to converse.'

"I found upon examination that he had *two* almost vertical wounds in the fifth intercostal space. I had my finger in both of them, and from the nature of the hemorrhage, I suspected that the instrument, whatever it was, had grazed the aorta. I told him flatly that I didn't believe he could live half an hour, and he died in exactly twenty minutes from that time.

"Now, sir, it is not necessary for me to tell you that a man does not fall *twice* accidentally on a dagger, and even if he did, it would be physically impossible for him to drive it downward in the direction those wounds took."

"But it would not be impossible," remarked Wilder, "for him to have driven the instrument downward himself with his right hand?"

"Certainly not. But as there is not the faintest motive discernible in his life, or conduct, or actions before the event to explain why he should do so, and no possible reason for saying it was accidental afterwards, and not the slightest grounds to suppose that a man like Enniston would select his shrubbery on the night of a party for such an act, I have not thought of it."

"Then you think," said Wilder, "to put it plainly, that he was—"

"I don't care to think any further into the matter," replied the doctor. "There is a mystery here that I have not tried to solve. The family have withdrawn themselves almost completely from society and I do not know that a discreet prudence in their interest does not dictate silence."

Wilder meditated a moment, then he said: "I must say that that conclusion surprises me a little. It seems to me at first glance that the honor of the dead man and justice to his family demand some consideration."

"The conclusion—and I did not say it was a conclusion," replied the doctor, "is based upon the deep conviction in my mind that his family are as much in the dark as we are and quite as innocent. To re-open the matter would therefore subject them to public annoyance certainly and to public disgrace probably, without any reasonable prospect of either public or private good. You do not appear to me to be swayed entirely by professional considerations, and I put it to you this way because there is sometimes even in justice a golden reticence."

"Doctor," said Wilder, "you have been good enough to treat me with a frank confidence that deserves fair dealing on my part. Before I tell you how I came to be interested in this matter will you kindly describe to me the incidents that preceded the death of Mr. Enniston—I mean the story as told by the people in the parlor?"

"They are easily told. The party, which was a small one, consisted of Enniston, his wife and daughter; Mr. Anson Seymour; Grace Hardynge; Mr. Ackerman and Colin Carteret. Enniston and Seymour, about nine o'clock had gone out on the front balcony to smoke their cigars. There were some white flowers blooming in front. The papers said they were camelias, but I think they were chrysanthemums. Miss Hardynge came out on the balcony a moment after Seymour had left Enniston, and seeing the flowers in the moon-light, exclaimed "How beautiful. I'd like one for my hair." Her hair is very black. She says Enniston looked very white, and she thought he and Seymour had been quarreling, but he merely said, "Permit me to cut you one," he then took the poignard out of her hair and went down the steps. At that moment some one called to her from the room and she disappeared from the balcony. The next thing that was heard was an exclamation from Job Ackerman who had gone to the window and saw Mr. Enniston staggering, pale and bloody, to the steps where he fell. The wounded man declared that he had fallen on the dagger, and Mr. Seymour denied in the most emphatic manner, that he had quarreled with Enniston, declaring on the contrary, that their short conversa-tion had been of the most friendly and confidential character."

"Thank you," said Wilder, as the doctor finished his account. "Let me tell you now how it was I stumbled on all this."

The doctor got up, went to the balustrade and looked over at a pair of pigeons that had run fighting under the steps. He came back a moment later, after knocking the ashes of his pipe out on the balustrade.

"Proceed, sir," he said, with a very slight interest in the narrative.

"On the second," continued Wilder, "I happened by mere accident to see this advertisement in the *Herald*," and he once more pulled from his pocket the little slip, now pasted for preservation on a piece of cardboard.

The moment he read this, Dr. Wollendorf turned squarely about and for the first time evinced an unmistakable interest. He reached and took it, put his spectacles on and read it carefully.

"When did you say this was in the *Herald*?"

"On the second."

"Have you seen Carteret?"

"You had better let me tell you all that has occurred," replied Wilder. "In my own way, it will be more connected and take less time."

He then rehearsed all that the reader already knows, telling in a straightforward way how he came to visit Coe's Grove; how he had been mistaken for someone else by the gardener; how Mrs. Enniston had refused to listen to him and denied all knowledge of the cup; how Carteret had declared that the advertisement was as much a mystery to him as it was to the officer; and finally how he had stumbed upon the fact that Mr. Enniston had not died by an accident.

"Now you will see," he said, "that this chain of remarkable circumstances is not only sufficient to awaken the keenest interest in a man trained to investigate mysteries, but it would warrant my making a deposition, having a post mortem, and I had almost said making some arrests. If I were to allow myself to be influenced by Mrs. Enniston's insulting treatment, I think I could cause her a great deal of trouble."

"But of course," said the doctor, "you are not that kind of a man. I am curious to know how you connect the cup with Mr. Enniston's death."

"It connects itself. It disappeared from his room on the day of his funeral."

Doctor Wollendorf got up at this point, with rather more eagerness in his manner than he had yet evinced, and began refilling his pipe. He stood for a moment with his back to Wilder, as if in deep thought, for he spilled a good deal of tobacco on the floor of the porch. Finally he turned about and said, "What do you intend to do in this matter?"

"That's not a fair question, Doctor," Wilder replied. "It looks to me as if there was some kind of a conspiracy here. What I want to know is something more about this cup."

"And you think you can find it?"

"Well, as to that, I don't think that it is possible to hide anything permanently so long as conduct makes footprints, as do legs."

The doctor was pacing up and down the porch now in his slippers, and puffing vigorously at his pipe. "Most extraordinary," he muttered. Suddenly he came to a halt and asked, "What motive do you assign for the publication of that advertisement and the use of Carteret's name?"

"If you will tell me how a cup can be worth so much trouble, I will give you a motive."

"It may have been a memorial, an heirloom, or something of the sort."

Wilder smiled and shook his head. "It will not do," he said. "Your way of saying it, is the first thing against it."

He got up, looked at his watch. "I may have occasion to consult you again," he said.

"Yes, do," said the doctor. "Let me give you a glass of home-made wine."

"I suspect," said Wilder, as he held the wine in his hand and looked at the doctor with a smile, "that the advertisement is what we call a stall."

"A what?"

"A stall. It was put up by somebody who wished to find out who was interested in the cup, by watching who came to Carteret. Your wine is excellent. I hav'n't drunk any home-made wine since I was a boy. It reminds me of my grandmother's excellent vintage."

CHAPTER V.

WILDER STUMBLES ON THE FIRST CLUE.

John Wilder, on returning to Mr. Sprinkler's tavern from Dr. Wallendorf's, saw Nancy Ann and the red-headed girl who had charge of the telegraph office in the railway station, with their heads together. A suspicion immediately beset him, and it was confirmed half an hour later by Nancy Ann herself, who came smilingly into the little sitting room of the hotel and under the pretence of adjusting the old-fashioned chairs and white "tidies," betrayed a new order of interest in her guest when she asked him, with what was intended for a look of great significance, if he had found any pictures up at Enniston's. He instantly suspected that the telegraph operator had sent a dispatch for Mrs. Enniston which had divulged his vocation, and that the operator without betraying the nature of the message, had informed Nancy Ann that he was an officer. So he met the new difficulty very squarely by saying, "Miss Sprinkler, if I were you, I'd tell that girl over at the depot that if she wants to keep her place, she had better keep her mouth shut."

This gave Nancy Ann a little start in spite of herself. "Why," she exclaimed with more volubility than discretion, "she didn't tell me anything," which only made Wilder smile. He merely remarked to himself, that the telegraph girl was worth cultivating.

Mr. Wilder remained in Coe's Grove two days and in that time made a number of quiet observations. He then, when about to return to New York, received a note from the doctor asking him to stop in for a moment if he came up that way. So he once more called on Dr. Wollendorf.

"My dear sir," began that gentleman with considerably more affability than he had hitherto shown, "I wanted to say to you before you went away to-day that my lack of tact in telling you about Mr. Enniston's wounds has worried me a great deal; simply because I am sure you are now going to stir up a public scandal that will result in no good whatever and lead to immeasurable annoyance to both Mrs. Enniston and myself. I have thought the whole matter over. I am satisfied that there is no possible benefit to be derived from any form of investigation, and that Mrs. Enniston's conduct to you was the result simply of a reasonable repugnance to publicity and scandal. As you have been sent here to look after her interests and the interests of peace, don't you think it will be best to drop the whole matter?"

"No," replied Wilder, laconically. "Is that all you wanted to say to me?"

"Your business and your visits to me are already known in the village," continued the doctor, "and I suppose you have satisfied yourself by this time that your attempts to nose into this matter can have only one result, and that is, unnecessary and vain discomfort to everybody connected with it."

Wilder looked up from the negligent attitude he had assumed in one of the doctor's chairs. As the doctor waited for an answer, he merely said, "No, I don't think so. Have you any more questions to ask me?"

For a moment or two there was an embarrassing silence. One man walked heavily up and down the floor. The other sat indifferently making a mental inventory of the things in the room.

Finally, Wilder seeing that the doctor was really distressed, said to him:

"Doctor, you are too sensible a man to take this rural view of the matter. I have no present intention of going to the authorities or of making a public scandal. You can give me some valuable assistance. It will be the best possible way to save both yourself and Mrs. Enniston from annoyance, for if you do it, I will promise you to take no public step without consulting with you or notifying you."

"Ah," exclaimed the doctor, "you have found, as I suspected, that there is absolutely nothing upon which to hinge an excuse for a detective."

"On the contrary," said Wilder quietly, "I have found out a great deal. Some of it I do not mind telling you when you get calmed down."

The doctor stopped walking. Wilder saw what may be called a gleam of curiosity break through his phlegm.

"I'm not so good a talker as you are," he added a moment later, "so I'll tell you what I have to say in a short order. I have found out that you know something about that cup, and I want to find out what it is."

The doctor was evidently trying to appear unconcerned. The effort was discernible. "Nonsense," he said, and went for his pipe. When he came back, Wilder proceeded leisurely.

"I have been followed here and watched as I believed I would be. Somebody wants that cup and doesn't know where it is. Do you?"

"No, sir," replied the doctor with unnecessary energy. "I am not in the conspiracy."

"You were in the house when it was taken," said Wilder.

"My friend," said the doctor, giving two or three vehement puffs at his pipe and resuming his heavy tread of the carpet, "to save you from a great deal of round-about nonsense, and not to save myself from your suspicions, I will tell you frankly all that I know about the cup."

"Do," said Wilder. "It may save me a great deal of trouble and you a good deal of annoyance."

The doctor then sat down and after some reflective work at his pipe, began as follows:

"Last summer a year ago, the Ennistons went away for a fortnight. Enniston himself and a party went off on a yacht. Mrs. Enniston, I believe, went to Newport. The house was left in charge of two servants—the man Barney and an old woman. One night I was sitting on that back porch rather late and had my attention attracted to what I thought was a curious ignis fatuus, but it turned out to be Enniston's man Barney coming across the field and swinging a lantern. He tumbled through the gate and came up the steps white with fright and said there were ghosts in the house. I told him, of course, that he was a damned idiot and had abandoned the place to burglars; but I put on my coat, took my pistol and went back with him. I found the place in great confusion and then learned from him what had occurred.

"He had been sitting in the lower kitchen, just after locking up the house; he had put on a kettle of water to make himself a glass of hot toddy before going to bed, and had sat down by the kitchen table to look over an old illustrated paper while waiting for the water; when he thought he heard some one moving over head. As the old woman was snoring in her chair within sight, he was naturally startled, and picking up the candle, went to the dumb waiter to listen. He had not been there a minute when the water began to boil over and made so much noise that he put the candle on the shelf of the waiter and went to the stove to remove the kettle. While in the act of moving it he turned round, and to his horror saw the waiter slowly ascending with his candle on it. In a state of unreasonable fright he lit his lantern and came plunging across the lawn to me. I went over the entire house with him. Mr. Enniston's room on the second floor had been ransacked. There was an old-fashioned fireproof safe in the room, the door of which stood open, and the contents, consisting of family silver, papers, and some jewelry, were scattered on the floor. So far as could be ascertained nothing had been taken. On this account Barney insisted that the visitors were ghosts. I hardly adopted his theory and came to the conclusion that robbery was not the object of the visitors. The man insisted that every door and window had been fastened, and I naturally concluded that whoever had disturbed the place had been secreted in the house before it was closed. These conclusions were made more probable by the fact, which I learned afterward, that before Mr. Enniston went away he had taken something out of the safe and sent it to New York for better security.

"Now, sir, on the night that Mr. Enniston died, as I told you, I was alone with him for a few moments. In that time he asked me to unlock the safe and bring him a bundle of papers. I did so, and saw standing on a shelf in the safe a unique silver goblet. He died before he could make any disposition of the papers and they were taken from his hand and put back, the door of the safe pushed to, with the bunch of keys hanging in it, and may have stood so during the excitement. As you already know, the cup was missed when they came back from the funeral, and Mr. Ackerman made so much fuss over it that I learned most of the particulars. He declared that the corpse had not been left alone during the whole time intervening between the death and the funeral; that he himself locked the safe and removed the keys just before the under-taker took the body from the room, and that the door of the apartment was locked, and Barney, an old and trustworthy servant, had guarded the room when the household were at the cemetery. Yet, when he returned, he found the cup gone. When you showed me the advertisement these circumstances con-nected themselves in my mind, and you can easily understand my interest and curiosity. There; you have my whole experience and all that I know concerning the cup; but the fact that Mr. Enniston did not meet his death by accident only added to my perplexity, while Mrs. Enniston's conduct naturally increased my wonder."

Wilder listened to this recital and then asked:

"Whom did Mr. Ackerman suspect in the house?"

"No one in particular. The fact is, he was so excited and perplexed that he lost his head for awhile and made all sorts of accusations, searching the ser-vant's trunks and ransacking the whole house, until Mrs. Enniston put a stop to the proceedings by declaring that the cup was not worth so much annoyance. As an example of his condition, he accused the French maid, whose name I have forgotten, of having taken the property, when it was shown that she was the only person in the house who was not in the room at all, having been confined to her bed, from which she got up to go to the funeral, riding in the carriage with Mrs. Enniston, and was not out of her sight till they returned, when they found Mr. Ackerman already there. He searched all her trunks and made her so indignant that she left the employ of Mrs. Enniston two or three days afterward, walking to the depot empty handed."

"Mr. Ackerman appears to have had a level head," remarked Wilder.

There was the slightest possible contempt in the look with which the doctor regarded him. "Have you reached his conclusions?" he asked.

"I hardly know what Mr. Ackerman's conclusions were," replied Wilder, "beyond the fact that the cup had been taken out of the room between the time of Mr. Enniston's death and the return of the family from the funeral."

"You say that as if you thought it a very simple problem. It did not appear so to Mr. Ackerman. The room was never empty; the windows have wire gauze frames screwed into the sashes. It could not have been thrown from the win-dow; the safe was locked; the family did not leave the corpse alone."

"Pardon me," said Wilder. "You are asserting things that you are not certain of. The safe may not have been locked, and the room may have been deserted long enough to have the cup abstracted."

"But how could it be taken out of the house? No one left the place, and the girl that Mr. Ackerman suspected was absent at the time it was taken."

"My dear sir, you are asking me several questions. Let me ask you one. Don't you know how that cup went out of the house?"

"No, sir," said the doctor with emphasis and promptness. "I do not."

"Then I will tell you," replied Wilder. "It went out in that coffin."

Both men regarded each other in silence a moment. Then Wilder said: "You can save me a great deal of trouble, being a doctor. You can have the remains up, and I'll prove it to you."

"Why, you don't expect to find the cup there?"

"Certainly not," with a smile. "But I expect to find that the grave has been opened before and the cup removed." Dr. Wollendorf emitted a long column of smoke that was not unlike a ponderous note of exclamation.

"I am bound to admire your fertile imagination," he said. "It reminds me of Dumas."

"I believe," replied Wilder. "That you men of science make use occasionally of what you call a working hypothesis; when all the facts square into it, you use it. Suppose you try my hypothesis with these facts. I assume a conspiracy to get possession of the cup. It places its agent in the house. The cup is ingeniously taken out, but it miscarries, and the original conspirators are still looking for it. Is there any other hypothesis that will account for everything, including the advertisement?"

"But it doesn't account for Mr. Enniston's death."

"I'll account for that when the time comes. Murder is child's play beside the prodigious difficulty of finding out how a cup can be valuable enough to warrant such extraordinary proceedings."

After this conversation, the doctor and Wilder were on better terms. The doctor discovered that Wilder was a "man of faculty" as he termed it, and he began to feel that whatever the mystery of the cup might be it would be unravelled in time if this cool, shrewd worker kept at it.

Wilder, on the other hand, felt a little discouraged. He had spent a good deal of time, and up to this point had utterly failed to obtain a single clue to the possible cause of Mr. Enniston's death. The whole community was opposed to anything like a suspicion of that gentleman's integrity and spotless character, and Wilder already saw that he was regarded by the towns people with anything but encouraging looks. He hung about with keen eyes and alert ears for another day, but the mystery remained unbroken. Then he determined before he left Coe's Grove to make an effort to have the Enniston grave opened. He was well aware that this could not be done without Mrs. Enniston's permission, unless he got an order from the Coroner, and he didn't for a moment think of getting either. But one morning he walked over to the cemetery and found the superintendent, a round-shouldered giant who had been promoted from the grave-digger of the village churchyard to the Master of the "Hillside Home," as it was called.

To his agreeable astonishment he found this man to be anything but a strict disciplinarian in his own domain. He did pretty much as he pleased, and the fact that up to that time the "Hillside Home" had not been largely patronized and was in great part still wild, owing to a lack of funds to clear it, he was little interfered with. In a short familiar conversation with this man he made the covert proposal to pay him handsomely if he would quietly open the Enniston grave for him and Dr. Wollendorf; and the man to his astonishment said there wasn't any trouble about that, "If you don't steal the late respected and don't go round blabbing," said he, "I'll open it for you, and much good may it do you."

Wilder then got Dr. Wollendorf, and later two laborers set about the work of opening the grave for them. It was late in the afternoon when the task was begun. The one grave was in a twelve foot enclosure, surrounded by a stone coping and iron chain. The men were experts; the soil was light and it did not prove much of a task. Wilder sat down on the curb and watched the operation until the men's heads disappeared below the level of the plot. Then he went to the opening and said, "Understand, I don't want you to touch that coffin with your spades. When you are within reach brush the soil off with your hands." As he turned to retrace his steps he noticed something thrown out with a shovelful of dirt. He turned it over with his foot. It was a piece of cotton cloth. He picked it up daintily and spread it out on the grass. It proved to be a napkin stained with soil and rumpled. He pointed it out to Dr. Wollendorf. Just at that moment one of the men in the pit called to him. The fellow had reached a depth of nine feet and had run an iron rod down into the bottom of the grave.

"See here," he shouted, "there's no coffin here."

"Are you sure?"

"Dead sure," said the man.

Wilder walked thoughtfully away.

"Well," said Wollendorf, "they appear to have stolen the whole establishment this time."

"Nonsense," replied Wilder, who had fallen into a reticent mood. "Nothing of the sort."

The men were shoveling the earth back again. The doctor and Wilder watched them silently a moment. Then the former said:

"Is there anything more to be learned?"

"Not here," replied Wilder. "Let's go."

A few minutes later the doctor remarked guardedly, as if a little afraid of offending his companion in his present mood, "You appear to have made up your mind to something. Has your hypothesis tumbled to pieces?"

"I was thinking," said Wilder, "what could have induced Mrs. Enniston to take that body up, unless it was the fear of our intermeddling. Doctor, she's a much cleverer woman than we have given her credit for."

"How do you know she took it up."

"I know it because she is the only person who can have a motive for removing it. The persons who wanted the cup didn't want the body. To be hampered with that would imply insanity. But Mrs. Enniston was not going to let you get your fingers into those wounds again. I had a suspicion of something of that sort when that old ruffian consented so readily to have the grave opened and I remember now that he remarked in an aside, 'much good may it do you.' I rather like his stupid craft."

"But what has Mrs. Enniston done with the body?"

"Simply put it in a receiving vault, under lock and key, so that prying doctors and others cannot get at it without committing sacrilege and burglary at the same time," replied Wilder. "You see, you are not the only person that knows that Mr. Enniston did not die by accident."

Dr. Wollendorf was silent for some time and very thoughtful. The men walked along the grass-grown avenues of the cemetery in silence. Presently the doctor said:

"I'm sorry I had anything to do with this affair. There is no telling where it will end."

"Yes," added Wilder, "I'm sorry myself. If the State should get hold of it, you'd be a valuable witness, especially since you came privately to see the grave opened."

The doctor let a grim smile steal over his face. "Do you know, Wilder," he remarked, "that we appear to be slipping into the roles of Dr. Faust and Mephistopheles."

"But there isn't any Marguerite in this case, is there?" asked Wilder rather quickly.

"No, no," exclaimed the doctor even more quickly; and that answer and the manner of it, set Wilder off on a new train of thought.

He left the doctor on the highway and walked moodily back to the station.

In recapitulating his experience, he had to confess himself baffled. The more he learned of the Enniston affair, the more unaccountable appeared the actions of all parties concerned. He had assumed a confidential air to the doctor, but he acknowledged to himself that he was now about to leave Coe's Grove without a working clue—and once out of Coe's Grove, there was little possibility of pushing an investigation.

Instead of taking the train, he put up at Sprinkler's, avoided Nancy Ann and spent the day wandering off up the road alone and moody. Turn the thing in whichever way he might, it baffled him and at the same time stimulated every bit of pride that he had in his vocation and reputation. He tried to get some of the villagers into conversation, only to find one impenetrable and comfortable belief, that "Ol' Enniston had met with an accident and they "didn't want no impertinent folks from the city pryin' into a good family's affairs." The village blacksmith said, in his hearing, that "it wouldn't be comfortable for any man who set lies afloat about 'Ol' Enniston."

One or two things were now clear to Wilder's mind. Enniston had met with foul play and the cup had disappeared immediately afterwards. Mrs. Enniston knew or suspected something and was acting either from a fear of discovery that sprang from guilt of simply from a wife's desire to shield her family and the memory of her husband. He felt that he had stumbled on a mystery of unusual import, but no amount of thinking or imagining threw the least light upon the possible value or significance of the cup, or upon it's connection with a tragedy.

He remained at Coe's Grove upon one pretext or another three days, bending all his craft and address to discovering Enniston's antecedents, but finding nothing.

No one could have borne a better character than he. Nothing of the vaguest kind was whispered against him. He had no enemies; no quarrels; no misfortunes. His habits, associations, and tastes, removed him entirely from the atmosphere of suspicion. Everybody that knew him spoke of him with hearty approbation or a sincere respect, and no one had ever heard of his having disagreed with his excellent wife.

The result of Wilder's endeavors was, that at the end of three days he had discovered nothing and on the morning of the fourth day he got up determined to return to the city.

He was cross and taciturn. Nancy Ann met him and he gave her short answers and was almost rude. She brought him his satchel and held it out at arms length as if she were afraid he would snap at her. He walked over to the railway station. The red-headed telegraph operator was staring at him through her little wicket. He had half an hour to wait before the train arrived. He walked moodily out and lit a cigar. As he did so, Barney the coachman, drove up to the station with a team. He had come down to send a dispatch and to get one of the horses shod. The smith's forge was only a stone's throw from the station and in full view. Having sent the dispatch, Barney went over to the forge and a moment later he was idly walking up and down before the open door waiting for the horse. Wilder joined him, with no definite purpose in his mind. He had twenty-five minutes to wait. In spite of Barney's reluctance, he drew him into a conversation. A number of private conveyances were coming to the depot and as the two men went over to Sprinkler's to get a drink, Wilder asked to whom one of them belonged. Barney knew everyone. The conversation then fell into the following shape:

"You appear to know everybody in the village," said Wilder.

"I ought to. I was raised here, long before the Ennistons came."

"Yes, you have a good eye for faces—I noticed that when I first met you. You're one of those fellows who never make a mistake in a face. You'd make a good detective, Barney."

"As for that sir, I can tell a man when I see him, but I'm not so good with the women. I think it's the dress like. I've made mistakes when they had their backs to me."

Barney swallowed his apple jack with gusto. Wilder looked at his watch. They sauntered out to the little green triangle and stood under the poplar. By the merest accident Wilder reverted to the subject.

"Well, I suppose it isn't so hard to know everybody in a place where there are no strangers."

"That's just it," replied the man. "We've got'em by heart, loike. Sometimes a man like yourself pops in and we don't know much about'em."

"Do you remember?" asked Wilder, "how Mrs. Enniston was dressed on the night of the party?"

The applejack had loosened the man's tongue a little. "That's not much to remember," said he, "when she's dressed pretty much the same as long as I've known her—always in black. But I ought to remember that night, for that's the time when as I tell you, I found one woman was pretty much like another, when you can't see her face. I got fooled on the dress that time."

Wilder had fifteen minutes. "Tell me about it," he said. "You needn't make it long."

"O, there's nothing to it. You see she came up on a late train that day and I came down for her. This team was a fresh one then and a little anxious. I was afeard they wouldn't stand the train, so I drove'em round out o' sight and came back to wait for her. The train got in before I reached the ladies' room. I jest looked in the door and I saw Mrs. Enniston standing with her back to me and a satchel in her hand, waiting. I went right up and took hold of the satchel, sayin' somethin' about drivin' the team around, when the woman drew back and looked at me and I saw it wasn't Mrs. Enniston. You see the dress had fooled me."

"You had never seen the woman before?"

"Divil a sight. She didn't belong here."

"Did you ever see her again?"

"I never did. O, bedad, yes; I did. I passed her on the road when we went up. She was talkin' with Hi Tucker by the roadside. I think that's your train sir, a'comin'."

"Who's Hi Tucker?" asked Wilder.

"It's the widow Tucker's boy. They live on the aqueduct. He used to bring the berries down to the hotel. There's your train."

"Never mind the train," said Wilder. "Let's take another drink. I'm going to wait over."

From that moment John Wilder's manner changed. It was the vaguest hint, but something told him he had stumbled on a new source of information. He cracked a joke with Nancy Ann. He told Barney that he ought to make his fortune with his memory, and the moment the man was gone, he hunted up Mr. Sprinkler and got a horse and buggy. "I want," he said, "to find the widow Tucker's by the straightest road,"

"All you have to do sir." said Mr. Sprinkler, "is to strike the aqueduct and keep along the stream till you come to the hollow. The widow's moved down to Tarrytown. When you see the gatehouse, the old woman's cottage'll be about a quarter stretch this side. You'll know it by the sunflowers: hold her up on the off side—she's apt to sheer goin' through the woods."

It was a long ride southeastward through one of the most beautifully pictur-esque tracts on the Hudson. Once in the old shadowy road that ran along the banks of the Pocantico, the great green wall of the Croton aqueduct was guide enough. Half a mile east of the widow's house, he encountered a bare-footed lad of twelve on the roadside, throwing stones up a great beech tree and incit-ing a red terrier to vertical but futile leaps up the trunk after some treed animal.

"How far to Mrs. Tucker's?" halloed Wilder.

The boy pointed with his hand up the road and Wilder saw the yellow gleam of sunflowers.

"Are you Hi Tucker?" he asked.

The boy nodded his head and the dog broke out in a new order of demon-strative barks at what he considered an unwarrantable interruption.

It was a canopied spot, all lush with moss and vocal with the frogs in the neighboring stream. He saw that it would not do to frighten the boy into prevarication.

He sat there half way out of the buggy holding the reins loosely and his voice had a mellow echo as if the damp evening woods were repeating his words with eagerness.

"Look here, Hi," said he, "that's a nice dog. I'd like to buy him. What have you got in the tree?"

"Chipmunk," replied Hi carelessly, as if it were the regular thing. He held his head down and the loose peak of his cap hung over his eyes, as he struck his big toe into the moss and began digging little holes.

"I'll give you a dollar for him, and you can keep him till I come up in the winter and get him. But you must not sell him to anybody else—mind," and he took out one of the crisp green bills that were then in vogue and held it out.

The boy came over to the buggy in a wondering way with his hand outstretched for the money.

"I'd like him for a little cousin of mine," said Wilder. "What's his name?"

"Jiz," replied Hi, with his hand outstretched.

"Here, Jiz, come here Jiz," said Wilder coaxingly. But Jiz backed away, and mingled contempt and bitterness in his bark.

"Here's your dollar," and Wilder handed over the crisp bill. "But the fact is, I'm so busy I don't know whether I shall have time to come after him or not. He won't bite, will he? You see I'm looking for a sister of mine. She came up to Coe's Grove on the fifteenth of July. You remember, that was the day Mr. Enniston died. She was dressed in black and went up the road that evening. Don't you know, she stopped you and asked you something."

"Yes, sir," said Hi, promptly. "I know, but I didn't know she was your sister."

"Of course not, how could you know that? I'm afraid she's got sick somewhere and I want to bring her home."

"What made her run away?" asked Hi.

"She was foolish, poor girl."

"She didn't run away. She went to Mr. Enniston's," said the boy innocently as he turned the greenback over in his hand, "'cause she asked me where he lived."

"Yes, she was acquainted with Mrs. Enniston."

"No, she wasn't." said Hi, promptly. "She says to me, 'Boy, where's Mr. Ennis live?' I said I don't know Mr. Ennis. 'Don't lie,' says she, acatchin' hold o my arm. I aint alyin' says I. 'Don't he live in a big house up this road?' says she. Not as I knows, I said. Enniston lives up there, mabbe he's the one. 'What's his first name?' says she. Oliver, says I."

"That's right," remarked Wilder. "What'd she do then?"

"She didn't do nothin'. She looked at me a minute queer and went off up the road."

"Did you ever see her again?"

"Yes, sir. I seed her when I was goin' home, asettin' on a flat rock inside of Shorey's Grove with her head down. She must a' been sick."

"When you left her on the road, where did you go?"

"I went to Sprinkler's to get the old woman's pail."

"How long were you there?"

"I d'now, sir."

"Well, did you go right home?"

"No, sir. I went down to the sloop dock with Bill Yerkin to swim."

"How long did you swim?"

"I d'know, sir."

"Was it dark when you went home?"

"Yes, sir."

"Did you see her eyes?"

"No, sir. She had a veil on."

"Well, Hi, I guess that's all I want to know. I guess you can keep the dog and the dollar. I shan't have time to come for him. Can I turn my horse round up the road?"

"Yes, sir."

CHAPTER VI.

THE GHOST IN THE SHRUBBERY.

Events now began to press upon John Wilder. He went immediately from Hi Tucker to the ticket office of the railway station. His object was to find out, if possible, if the strange woman had bought a return ticket. The young man in charge was ignorant and supercilious. Did he look like a fellow who could remember every lady that bought tickets through that hole? Besides, he wasn't in charge of the office at that time. Nick Bixby had been there, and he was laid up with the rheumatism at Wood's Corners. There was nothing for it but to go to Wood's Corners. Wilder found Bixby in bed, and that young man remembered the woman answering to wilder's description. She had bought a ticket for Peekskill, and had gone up on a late freight.

There was but one thing to do now, and that was to find this woman. He met Carteret on the train going to New York. They went into the smoker and got into conversation. From him Wilder had a fresh account of the persons present on the night of the party at Enniston's, and it agreed strictly with what he had been told before. There was no such person there as this strange woman. Where was she during the time between Hi Tucker's meeting her in Shorey's Grove and the death of Mr. Enniston? Wilder did not tell Carteret of his discovery, but he learned from him some interesting facts. Mr. Enniston had been his guardian, his best friend and his patron; and the death of that gentleman had been an incalculable misfortune to the young man. He was engaged to Rose Enniston, but her mother did not know it, and opposed the intimacy so strenuously since her husband's death that it was only through Rose's stubborn insistence that he went there at all. Dr. Wollendorf had always been very fond of Rose, and she and Carteret often met at his house when Mrs. Enniston was not aware of it. The young man had a studio in what was known as the Tenth Street Building, near the Sixth Avenue, and he cordially invited Wilder to visit him.

The most important piece of information obtained in this interview related to the life and habits of Mr. Enniston in the city. Wilder learned that he often stayed away from home for a week at a time, and during the spring and summer had kept a furnished room in Bond street. Carteret was very guarded in speaking of his patron, but Wilder reached the conclusion from several things the young man unintentionally said that Mr. Enniston was much more a man of the world than Dr. Beresford Flocton and the rest of the community at Coe's Grove suspected.

A week of unremitting search ensued, and on the twenty-third of September he had run down the game.

The tedious and minute steps taken, the patience and persistency that could not be wearied or discouraged can be best imagined by a succinct account of the results. Wilder first saw Seymour, the gentleman who had sat on the veranda with Enniston the night of the fatal occurrence. That personage was the junior partner in a woolen house in Church Street. The moment he understood the nature of Wilder's visit he flatly refused to talk about the matter and told the officer that he considered it a piece of brutal impudence to mention the subject.

"I want that conversation on the balcony between you and Enniston," said Wilder.

"Well, by Heaven, you'll not get it," retorted Seymour; "and what's more, if you attempt to get it out of me I shall take it as a personal insult. Do you understand that?"

"I shall get it, nevertheless," replied Wilder, cooly.

"Will you? How will you get it?"

"I'll get it out of that shrubbery."

With that threat they parted.

Wilder went to work to find where Mr. Enniston had roomed in Bond street. It was three days before he discovered the woman who had then kept the house, for she had moved to Greenpoint. She was a garrulous, shabby-genteel type of lodging-house keeper and after a long and tedious cross-examination, Wilder learned that a Mr. Ennis had hired a suite of rooms of her on the second floor and often slept there with his male friends. He had never had any female friends there except his cousin, who was a poor girl that he was trying to assist. The woman only knew that her name was Kate, and that she was in a sewing machine establishment on Broadway. She was tall and beautiful and pale. She had come two or three times and inquired for Mr. Ennis when he was away.

He then found out from Carteret that Mr. Enniston had no female cousin, and it took him two days more to work all the sewing machine establishments on upper Broadway. After many discouragements and rebuffs, he at last found that one of them had employed for a few months, a young woman by the name of Kate Havilland, whose disappearance corresponded with the date of Enniston's death. The proprietors had no record of her life or knowledge of her home, but she had been intimate with a forewoman who probably knew, and the forewoman had got married and was living somewhere in Harlem. By questioning about fifty girls, he at last obtained the address of this woman and having found her, learned that Kate Haviland's home was in Deposit where her mother lived, and the forewoman had thought she had gone home, sick. "She acted like a girl who had been crossed in love." On the morning of the twenty-second, Wilder was in Deposit amid the smell of the tanneries and was hunting patiently for Kate Haviland's mother. At last he found her in a humble home some distance from the village, living with a negro servant—old, infirm, and pious. She knew nothing about Kate's later career, except that her mother's instinct told her the girl had not been going right, and now she had received a letter from her saying she was dying in Philadelphia. This letter was dated the twentieth and was written at the Samaritan Hospital, as the letter-head indicated. At twelve midnight, Wilder was in Philadelphia. As he stepped into the depot, he met a comrade from the Central Office, one Sergeant Odell, who had come on from New York to "work a case of the queer." His anxiety to reach if possible, before it was too late, what he understood to be a dying woman, made him a little impatient at the red tape of the hospital officials. But he got in on the morning of the next day. He was informed that Dr. Sanger, who appeared to have sole authority, had gone to New York. But the patient was still alive and had improved a little within twenty-four hours though her death was looked for at any moment. The hospital was in process of repair. The whole of the west wing had been torn down to be rebuilt and enlarged under Dr. Sanger's directions and plans, and, at the time of Wilder's visit, the new walls were up fifty feet and covered with scaffolding. He had said to Sergeant Odell in the morning, "If you do not hear from me before three o'clock, I wish you'd stop at the hospital—I may need you in a delicate matter as witness," and Odell had promised to call for him. After much delay, Wilder was permitted to see the patient alone on the plea of purely private business, and to his astonishment he found a very beautiful woman propped up in bed, who appeared to be expecting him. She looked him all over eagerly, with large, brown eyes that had an invalid shadow round them, and then motioned to a seat. There was an ominous silence for a moment. On the woman's part, there was an intuitive, almost clairvoyant perception of the nature of her visitor's errand.

"I have been looking for you, Miss Havilland, for a week," Wilder said at length.

"I know it," she replied with a strange, cold voice. "You needn't stare at me that way; I haven't got anything to be afraid of—I haven't had from the first. The doctor will tell you I'm out of your reach. I knew that before he did. I wanted to die and they couldn't save me. You want a mystery cleared up—that's what you want. Well, I can clear it; I can't carry it any longer. They'll tell you I mustn't talk, but it relieves me. If I could have talked and cried I wouldn't have died."

She spoke very rapidly and clearly, with just a little vehemence in her manner.

"I wish," said Wilder, "that you would tell me your story entirely—you have guessed that I am an officer. It cannot injure you now and it may save innocent people from suspicion."

"O, I'll tell it," she continued. "It begins away back in Deposit. Do you know why I left that place? It was because I had my father's hot Southern blood in me—his mother was a quadroon, because I was a reckless, headstrong girl. That's what they said up there. They lied. I left because I was hunted. You can't understand it—you're a man. My curse was good looks. They wouldn't let me alone. I was the best looking girl in that town; I couldn't help it, could I? I didn't make my looks. I was poor and I tried, God knows, to be honest. No, it aint the old story. You think I was ruined—I wasn't. I ran away because they wanted to marry me to a rich man that I hated. I said I'd work my fingers off first. I had a cousin in New York. He got me employment. It was in a photographer's on Sixth Avenue—his name was Brandon. I thought I was happy and independent then, but it was a mistake. Brandon took a great fancy to me and made pictures of me all the time. Then his wife got mad and jealous. She accused me of leading her husband astray, and he stood by and never said a word in my defense. Then I was ordered out of the house. When I found that this affair hurt me even with my cousin who thought there was something wrong, it made me desperate. I answered an advertisement for saleswomen in a large furnishing store and got six dollars a week to stand all day on my feet behind a counter. My feet ached so I could hardly walk home at night. Then one of the girls told me that I could get twenty dollars a week in one of the big theatres with my looks and have my days to myself. So I answered another advertisement and got a situation at Niblo's Garden. Then my cousin wrote home that I was going to the bad. I got a letter from my mother the first night I went on in the piece and it made me so ill, I could hardly keep my knees from sinking under me. I didn't have much to do. I was one of the ladies in a queen's train, and I had nothing to say and when it was over, I felt that I had won my way in spite of everything. I heard a good many people asking, 'who is she?' and the next night, I got three letters. One of them said the writer had fallen desperately in love with me and would throw me a bouquet in the second act from the left hand box. I took the letters to the stage manager and he laughed at me and said I'd get used to that. The bouquet was thrown on and the queen got it, but there was a note in it which she sent to me. It said the writer would come behind the scenes and see me at the end of the piece. The man did come on with the manager of the theatre, who introduced him to me as Mr. Stern. He treated me respectfully and asked me if he might see me home. I tried to make some excuse, but he insisted, and he did. It was a great comfort to have somebody for a protector and Mr. Stern seemed to think a great deal of me. I believe he was an honest man, but somehow I didn't care for him. He was at least forty-five years old and seemed to be a man of the world. He came every night after that and I got to expect him. He'd walk all the way to my door and leave me there as regularly as if he had to do it. This went on for three weeks. Then he called on me one day and asked me if I would take a ride with him. We went out of town some distance and he told me all about his affairs; said he was a widower with an income and was willing to marry me if I'd let him. He warned me of the dangers of the theatre, asked me all about my family and wanted to write to my mother. O, I don't know what he didn't say, but I told him I couldn't think of marrying just yet. I'd think about it for six months. He came to the theatre nearly every night and when I got better acquainted, I made inquiries about him and I found that he was a respectable gentleman; a great theatre man and very well off. One reason why I let him wait upon me was that it saved me a deal of annoyance. You can understand that. One night about six months after I had first seen him, he brought a friend on the stage with him and introduced him. It was a Mr. Elkins. They were very intimate. Two nights after, Mr. Elkins came without Mr. Stern, who he said had been called out of town, but with another friend, a Mr. Ennis, a very fine looking gentleman, who tried to make himself as pleasant as he could. Elkins said Stern had asked him to come up and put me in a coupé I did not object. I thought Mr. Stern was very thoughtful. When the play was over, they had some trouble in getting a carriage. Elkins ran off to find one, leaving me standing with Ennis. I don't know how long he was gone, I was so taken up. But when he came back, he made an apology—said that a friend of his had met with an accident and Ennis would have to see me to my home. I don't know how it was, but I did not object. I had got over objecting I suppose to such trifles. I don't remember anything but that it was the pleasantest ride I ever had. Somehow Ennis won my respect at once. He was as tender and gentle as a woman—faugh, no! Women are not gentle. He was handsome and had the air of a true gentleman. I wondered when I got in bed if I should ever see him again. There was something in his treatment of me different from anybody else. I wasn't afraid of him. You may laugh, but I would have trusted that man even with my honor. I know better now and here I am. I used to look all over the faces of the audiences night after night, to see if I could see him, and one night I did see him standing against the wall in the parquet, and before I knew it, I showed my pleasure in my face. At the end of the act, I ran down in the dressing-room and looked in the glass. I wondered if he would come and see me. I said to myself, O, what a fool you are to think of him—and I saw myself get red in the face. But I couldn't help it.

"I did not see him again that night, but a bunch of flowers was sent to me by a boy with Ennis's name on the card. I tried very hard not to be unpleasant to Mr. Stern, but he said I was cross—perhaps I was. I shouldn't have been, for he was a true friend. About a week after that, they commenced to rehearse a new piece at the theatre in the mornings and Elkins came there. He spoke to me during the intervals, complimented me on getting on so well, and said Ennis had asked after me several times. I don't remember what I said, but the next day Ennis came to the rehearsal and walked home with me. When we were alone, he said he wasn't sure but he had made himself believe that I recognized him in the audience on the night that he sent the flowers. I told him I had. 'And you seemed pleased to see me,' he said. I forget what answer I made, but I remember we came under a light as we walked, and he looked suddenly in my face, and I felt I was very red. He pulled me closer to him and whispered 'you really wanted to see me, didn't you?' and tried to hide my liking for him as well as I could, telling him that it wasn't exactly the thing for him to talk in that way, seeing that I knew him so slightly. But I was in a kind of whirl. I scarcely knew what I said or what I meant. I only knew that it was a new kind of happiness to be talked to as he talked to me. He asked me if I did not get tired and faint before the play was over and hungry and I said yes, and before I knew it scarcely, we were in a saloon. After that he came to the rehearsals several times, and I got to looking for him. He also told me that he walked out mornings on the Fifth Avenue, and I met him one morning and went all the way to the Central Park with him, and we lunched there together. It was then he told me that he loved me. Men had told me that before, but I never believed it before. Nobody ever seemed to think so much of me or to be half so much in earnest. He knew I liked him. I couldn't hide it. Well, I told him so. I lived in a kind of a dream after that. It was the happiest part of my life. He came to Mrs. Willis's, where I boarded, to see me. He advised me to leave the theatre. I told him that I was doing well there, but that if he wanted me to, I'd leave it. He said he'd get me a situation temporarily in a quieter place where I would not be so exposed to the attentions of men. That seemed to annoy him. After awhile I shouldn't have to work at all. I thought I knew what that meant and my heart gave a great leap. He brought me a ring. I took it as an engagement ring. Sometimes I did not see him for three or four days and then I got melancholy. He said he had to go out of town to see his mother. I asked him why he did not write to me when he could not come. I wanted to hear from him every day. He said I must control myself and promised to send me a letter, but he never wrote.

"After I got the ring, I let him buy me dresses as presents. I had them made to please him. He seemed to be so proud of me." Here Miss Havilland broke down and what with tears and sobs; it was some time before she could go on again. After awhile, she resumed rather fiercely:

"He was, too. He must have thought more of me than anybody else. What can a poor girl know till she's suffered? I couldn't tell. I sat in his lap and he told me all about his father, who was a dreadful severe old man, and how necessary it was for us to be discreet for a year. I never doubted him. If I did, he'd kiss me and I forgot everything. Then I went into the sewing machine rooms to get rid of Stern and the rest of 'em, and moved to a boarding house in Bleecker street and spent all my spare time in making up a stock of clothes for myself, working like a beaver night and morning, and singing over it as if there was never to be any more trouble. If Mr. Ennis had in all that time said or done anything that was improper for a virtuous girl to hear, I believe I should have loved him less. He must have known that. I loved him because he was good and different from anybody else. He asked me one day how I would like to live in a little cottage at Harlem and be mistress of it.

"I clapped my hands like a child at the idea and said—anywhere with him. 'Perhaps I'd like to go to Europe. How would I like to spend a season in Paris first?' I was fool enough to believe this meant a wedding trip. Well, I ought to be hung, sir. A woman, who is such a fool, isn't fit to live. I was infatuated. If he'd asked me to lay down my life for him, I believe I'd have done it and been happy. But all the world couldn't have made me believe he didn't love me better than anybody else on earth. I could see that he couldn't stay away from me long. I knew that I could make him do anything I pleased. I felt that his eyes hung on me every step I took, and that when he tore himself away from me, his tenderness wasn't put on. He said over and over again that the greatest happiness that could come to him would be when he would not have to go away from me at all—and when he held me in his arms, I would say—Well, have patience; by and by we'll be together forever—and he'd press me closer and sigh. We had a thousand little secrets in that time. We talked of what we would do when we lived only for each other, and where we'd go and he'd finish by saying, 'Well, well, you must be discreet.' All this was in June. He was away for a week and I was worried to death, watching out the window and listening for his ring at the door, and going to bed crying because I had not seen him. When he came back he said his father was suspicious and he had to stay with him to pacify him; that we would have to be more careful than ever, because he could not afford to sacrifice his father's influence and help just yet. I asked him a great many questions then and he evaded some of them, but I had no suspicions. He said he would take me to his father if I said so, but it would knock all his plans over. I said no, whatever he thought was right, I would consent to. I showed him most of the work I had completed. I was just like a school girl and I looked upon him as my husband. He was never out of my mind. If another man looked at me I felt a new indignation for his sake. I used to sit all day in the showrooms thinking of things I could say or do to please him when he came, and picturing the future home that should be ours. In July he told me he should be away for several weeks and that I must take it easy. You won't believe it, but I hung on him and begged him not to go. He said he must; that I could write to him just as often as I pleased if I sent my letters enclosed to Elkins. When he came back he said, 'he hoped that everything would be so fixed that he would have no more trouble.' I was to wait for that time and hope—and I promised.

"I saw him on the sixth of the month. He paid me a visit in the evening and we walked out together. He said everything was working smoothly and hopefully. In the fall we should be together, but he would not be in town again till the end of the month. I was to work along quietly, and write to him every day and keep our matters secret. Till then, he would be in misery without me.

"Somehow, from what he said I got the idea that he meant to surprise me when he came back. All along I had caught the notion from his talk, that my patience and fidelity and secrecy would be suddenly rewarded. I fancied that he meant to take me to the cottage in Harlem, and that idea grew on me so that I made all sorts of little plans in my mind how I'd fix it, and spent my pocket money buying little ornaments and pictures and saving them for a surprise on my part. My trunk was full of them. I used to sit down on the floor at night and take them out and talk to myself like a child about them, saying, that's to go on the sitting room mantel, and that's to hang over the dining table, and this we'll put in the hall."

Here she broke down again and gave way to a convulsive fit of weeping.

"Well, on the fourteenth, just as I came home in the evening who should call but Mr. Stern. When I went down in the parlor, he got up with pity and earnestness and came to meet me. 'My poor girl,' he said directly, 'you haven't treated me right, and I shouldn't have called on you if it hadn't been that I want to warn you against a villain.'

"I dropped his hand and drew myself up."

"'Don't get unreasonable,' he said, 'what I tell you is the truth.' Something shot through me like a hot wire, but it was gone in a minute. 'You're jealous, Mr. Stern,' said I.

"'No,' he answered, 'that isn't it; but whether it is or not, it don't make any difference. The truth is just the same—you've taken up with a villain.'

"The blood flew in my face. It was indignation. 'It's a lie,' I screamed. 'You'd ought to have known me better than to have come here with such a story. Mr. Ennis is a rival of yours.'

"'Ennis?' he answered; 'his name isn't Ennis.'

"I laughed in his face. I wouldn't have believed it if an archangel had proclaimed it. I felt sorry for Mr. Stern. 'You ought to be ashamed of such business,' I said. 'You're too old a man. I shall tell Mr. Ennis of it, rest assured.'

"'Kate,' said he, 'I am not lying, as you must find out sooner or later. Where is this man?'

"'Mr. Ennis's gone to his father's,' I replied.

"'His father's?' says Stern. 'Why, he's at his own place, up at Coe's Grove.

"I wouldn't hear any more. The man seemed such a wretch that I couldn't listen to him. I told him I was in constant communication with Mr. Ennis; knew all his affairs better than anybody else, and was already as good as his wife. He was true and honest and brave; that was more than I could say for other men. He looked at me with pity and astonishment, but my blood was up. Then he went away, asking me to remember that he had said nothing unkind and that I would always find a friend in him; and I said I had all the friends I wanted. I felt nothing but anger and pity for Stern that night. I got out my trunk and looked at the ornaments and little presents. There was a pair of slippers I had worked myself. There was a Bible with a place for a family record. There was a beautiful meerschaum pipe and a cigar holder, and lots of other things, and as I looked at them there wasn't a doubt in my mind, or anything but the most innocent, girlish happiness. But when I woke up the next morning it seemed as if something must have happened in the night. I had a feeling as if an accident had occurred somewhere, but I had forgotten what it was. The first words I said were—not Ennis. I couldn't help thinking over the whole affair. It seemed so cruel to Ennis, and he away. When I got to the warerooms it seemed to me that everybody looked at me reproachfully, as if they were saying, 'I wouldn't go on working quietly if that was said of my husband.'

"The one feeling that took possession of me was the awfulness of the lie that had been told about my darling. It seemed as if I must fly to him and tell him. I couldn't work. I broke all the needles, and when the machine wasn't running I could hear my heart beat. I got worse and worse, so I told the forewoman that I was ill, and went out and walked up Broadway very rapidly. Something seemed to drag me along quickly. I couldn't stop and look at anything. I said to myself, 'Must I suffer this way till the end of the month?' It was a beautiful day; why not get on the train and go to Coe's Grove? That would settle it, besides I'd see him if he was there and get a kiss. When this came to me I turned about, went straight to my room, put on a plain black dress and taking a light shawl and satchel started for the railroad depot. It was evening when I got there. The train left at six o'clock and I had to wait. It was 7:30 when I got to Coe's Grove.

"I stood in the depot among the people not quite sure what to do, when a man came up and spoke to me. Then I walked out into the village without knowing where I was going. I had been thinking in the cars what I would say to Ennis and it seemed to me now that if I found him he would direct me what to do. I was acting in a stealthy manner without knowing it. I had my veil down and was bent on finding him before I thought of anything else. I met a boy on the road and asked him where Mr. Ennis lived. He did not know such a man. He said: 'Mr. Enniston lives on the turnpike a mile up. That's Mrs. Enniston's carriage just gone by.'

"I made him give me a description of the house and then went on walking as fast as I dared without attracting attention. 'Don't know such a man,' I kept repeating to myself. There was a brook crossed the road. I was feverish and thirsty. It ran down into a grove of trees. I got through the fence and wandered into the thicket and sat down by the stream on a big flat stone. I had the strangest feeling. I couldn't tell what it was. It seems now as if my eyes must have been staring in expectation of something. I heard the familiar sounds of the frogs and it reminded me of my country home. I thought there was something unfeeling in the beautiful water that curled at my feet. I don't know how long I sat there. It was a long time for I did not know what to do. I heard a piano faintly playing in the distance and occasionally a woman's voice singing 'Home, Sweet Home.' I got up and staggered a little. It was dark under the trees and I caught my dress several times in the bushes and stepped into holes of water, but I did not think of it. When I got to Enniston's place it was dusk, and the house was lit as if there was a party there. I was tired and faint, but instead of going straight in as I had intended to do, I stopped at the stone wall and peeped though the trees at it. The devil put it into my head to go in and creep around the grounds first. God knows I had no idea of discovering anything. I only wanted to see my dear and put my arms around him and hear him tell me again that he loved me. The place was thick with trees. I put the light shawl around my shoulders and went stealthily up the graveled walk in the shadows. The lights from the open windows fell in the spaces about the house and I heard loud voices and laughter, so I went under the trees around to the side where there was a bay window. I must have stood within—no further than that table from it. I held on to a tree and looked in. There were ladies and gentlemen and some one was singing. I could hear what they said; a lady was standing near the window and some one came up to her and said 'Mrs. Enniston, has your husband run away?' She said, 'No, he prefers to smoke his cigar on the veranda.'

"I was clutching the tree with my finger nails as if I expected every minute to drop down. I know now that my mouth was open and I was gasping as if I wanted air. But I got calmer presently.

"I stared at that woman as if she had done me a dreadful injury. But I saw a beautiful girl come to her and call her mother and I remember that sad white face. It was easy to glide through the trees toward the veranda without being seen. There were two men smoking with their feet on the rail. I came within two yards of them and could hear every word they said. It was Ennis and Elkins. O, I was cool enough now. I happened to touch my hand to my face when I pulled my veil up, and it felt so cold it gave me a start. I heard Elkins say, 'Well, old boy, it's a ticklish piece of business and you'd better not go any further with it.'

"'Yes,' said Ennis, 'but how will I drop it? The girl loves me to distraction. I had no idea when I set out that she would go on in this way. I supposed, of course, that like all the rest of them, she liked one lover till she got another. It was begun as a mere bit of intrigue to kill time and, by Jove, it's going to end in a serious melodrama. I expect every minute Kate will hear I'm married and then the city won't contain her.'

"'Yes,' says Elkins, 'she'll make it pretty lively for you if she does, but you can buy her off, can't you? S'pose I go and see her; tell her you've been called to Europe suddenly; get her weaned, you know, gradually.'

"'I wish you could,' said Ennis. 'It's getting to be an awful weight on me. Once out of this scrape I'll keep out.'

"Somebody called Elkins and he went in, leaving Ennis alone. I was very close to him. I could have reached, over and touched him. I don't know why I did it, but I stepped out of the trees softly and stood, with my white shawl on, against the dark hemlocks, in full view, with the light from the bay window falling directly on me. I must have looked like a ghost. Suddenly he turned and saw me and gave a start, clutched the rail and jumped up. Just as he did so, somebody came to the window and I stepped back into the shrubbery. If I could have died then all would have been right. I looked up through the trees at the stars and said, O, God, let me die, and my voice sounded like another person's. I put out my hands and steadied myself. It seemed as if there was no God and I had just discovered it.

"Then I heard Ennis coming down the steps. I was leaning against a tree inside the shrubbery. He came to me with a dagger in his hand.

"'Kate,' said he, 'for God's sake go away. You'll ruin all our plans, why did you come here?' I looked at him with speechless misery. I was saying to myself, or the devil was saying in my ear, 'This is your darling, this infamous, lying hypocrite and wretch. This is your love.'

"He must have noticed my agony and felt sorry for me, for he put on a coaxing air and coming close to me, said, 'Now, Kate, listen to me.' That was all he said. He held the dagger in his hand with the hilt out. Before he could prevent it I seized it and struck it into him. I would have struck him again then, but he caught my arm. He looked down at the blood running out on his shirt bosom and said, 'Merciful Father, girl, you've killed me. I deserve it. Go, go, and let me die.' The moment he let go of my arm I struck him again. Then he seized the weapon and staggered out of the shrubbery with it in his hand. My first impulse was to follow him and kill myself on his doorsteps. But then I thought of the wife and daughter. The contempt and pity and disgust of his friends turned me. I would not give them that satisfaction. I'd throw myself into the river. I turned to go. My dress caught in a branch of the shrubbery. I tore it away and slunk like a cat through the trees, not knowing where I went. Before I knew it I was at the rear of the house and saw someone standing under the window. It was a man. The trees hid me and I stopped. I don't know why I did. I listened. He was talking in a low voice to someone in an open window. I heard every word that was said; it seemed to me in my condition so strange and unearthly, 'Have you got it?' the man said, and a woman's voice replied, 'No, but it's in the next room. Go away.'

"Then there was a scream in the house and the sash was let quietly down."

CHAPTER VII.

MR. SEYMOUR IS NONPLUSSED.

Scarcely had this extraordinary narrative come to a close, when there was a rap at the door and Wilder was informed that some one had called for him. He went out; saw Sergeant Odell at the portal; told him that he would not need him, but would meet him an hour later and go to New York with him; returned to the sick room where he remained probably half an hour longer in company with the matron, Mrs. Maxwell. But during that time occurred an unexpected event that influenced the lives of more than one person in the story, though it would have been impossible at the time to see in it any other than an entirely disconnected accident.

Sergeant Odell, who had been a contractor before he had joined the police force, seeing that a very large addition was being made to the hospital and that the men were using steam derricks to hoist the large stones, walked leisurely over to the wing, and, meeting with a former acquaintance at work there, stood directly under one of the derricks upon which hung a block of granite weighing at least a ton. While standing there a loud cracking report was heard, a shout went up from the men and the derrick parted and fell splintered within two feet of a group of laborers. One of the arms struck Sergeant Odell upon the head and he fell off the platform into the excavation below, a distance of ten feet. When they picked him up he was dead.

Wilder did not hear of this until he came out of the hospital. He had learned from the matron that the doctors had pronounced Miss Haviland's case hopeless; that she had lain for days in a swoon receiving no nourishment and had all along declared that she wanted to die. Dr. Sanger who had attended her personally for the last fortnight and was deeply interested in the case would be back at night.

The awful accident to his companion, delayed and pained Wilder exceedingly. He stayed over to look after the remains and started with them for New York a day later.

He saw now for the first time that two distinct motives of action governed the events at Enniston's house and that the murder of Mr. Enniston had nothing to do with the cup. The only connecting link was Kate Haviland's unexpected corroboration of his suspicion that the maid Therese was implicated in the conspiracy.

Never before had he employed his faculties on a case which had so many surprises and led by devious paths to such slow and unexpected results. He asked himself when he reached New York, if the game were any longer worth the candle, seeing that the tragic side of it had turned out to be an ordinary case of woman's revenge and the girl was dead. Now that the mystery of Enniston's death was cleared up, the matter of the cup would no doubt turn out to be a common burglary. Then the advertisement recurred to his mind, and he found that it was impossible to shake off the suspicion that there was something behind all this of graver importance than a mere cup.

All at once he received a letter from Dr. Wollendorf. It had been directed to the Central Office.

"I wish," it said, "that you would make me a visit at your earliest convenience. The result of your endeavors to fit this town to your hypothesis has led me into serious difficulties, and I should like to consult you. Having made me an object of rural suspicion and persecution, perhaps you can make me an object of sympathy long enough to lend me your professional aid."

Wilder smiled at this and merely asked himself—What has Mrs. Enniston been up to now? At his leisure he wrote to the doctor, promising to run up in a few days, and then he set about trying to find Therese. This was even a more difficult hunt than that for Miss Haviland, and necessitated another visit to Coe's Grove. He tried to get rid of this by using Carteret and went over to the Studio and asked that young man to find out, if he could, from Rose or Barney, how the girl's trunks were marked when they were sent away. In the course of a few days it was discovered that they had been sent to the French pier in New York. All attempts to track them failed. Similar attempts to find out from Mrs. Enniston how the girl had got into the Enniston family, were frustrated by Mrs. Enniston's incorrigible manner.

Then one day Wilder walked into the private office of Anson Seymour again and shut the door behind him.

The merchant turned on him gruffly. Wilder cut him short at once.

"Mr. Seymour," said he, "I am an officer. It is to your interest to behave yourself. I don't propose to be bullied this time."

Seymour looked at him with white and speechless amazement.

"I told you," continued Wilder, "that I would get that conversation on that balcony. Do you want to hear it?"

"By God, sir—" exclaimed Seymour.

Wilder interrupted him. "If you have an ounce of discretion about you, you'd better use it," he said. "I have seen and talked with Kate Haviland. It becomes you to try and act like a gentleman to me at least. I regard you as a sort of partner and adviser in that girl's ruin. I have no intention of laying this case before the authorities at present, but there is a great deal in your d——d insolence that tempts me to do it. Let me add that if that insolence goes beyond a certain point, I shall simply put the irons on you and take you to the nearest station. I hope you understand me now."

In this game of bluff, Wilder was more than a match for his man. Seymour was painfully nervous.

"What do you want of me?" he asked, with something of a modified manner, but unmistakable anxiety.

"I want you to go to Coe's Grove with me and see Mrs. Enniston."

"I'll see you——"

"Excuse me," said Wilder, "you'll go."

"Will I?" asked Seymour, with a look of mingled stubbornness, terror and curiosity, that was almost laughable.

"Yes, you will, because it is to your interest and Mrs. Enniston's. Your friend was murdered in his own shrubbery. I don't know that there is any possible good in making that public now, because I left the girl dying, and while justice is out of the question, publicity would injure a respectable family. But there is another case connected with a French woman who was in Mrs. Enniston's employ at the time. She's a thief and I want to find her. Mrs. Enniston will give you the information that I want and that will put me on her track. You'll do that Mr. Elkins, or Mr. Seymour, because I want you to."

Wilder's companion underwent a momentary struggle, then, with the elasticity of a commercial mind, he tried to adapt himself to the situation. His face softened a little. "You've got me in a hole haven't you?"

"No, sir; you've got yourself in a hole, but I've no desire to take advantage of it in the way you suspect. The whole of this unfortunate affair is now in the hands of two persons. You are one of them, I am the other. What Mrs. Enniston knows or suspects, I cannot even guess; but as I am not a blackmailer or a bully, it is not my desire to use my knowledge for personal revenge. Let me finish," he said, with the same deliberation as Seymour was about to ejaculate something. "In the pursuit of what you can readily understand was a public duty, I have been personally insulted by both you and Mrs. Enniston. You seemed to think that I was in some sense a criminal, bent on disturbing the good name of society. I want you to understand that I represent society in this matter and between the comfort of Mrs. Enniston and the public exposure of an Ennis and an Elkins who have circumvented the death of an innocent girl, I don't think society would hesitate long."

"Do you mean to say that the girl killed Enniston in his shrubbery?"

"Yes," replied Wilder. "Didn't you know it?"

"No. I had a horrible suspicion of something, but how could I know it? He swore he had fallen on the dagger. It's a d——d dreadful mess."

"You are thinking of the exposure."

"Not altogether. I'm thinking of the wrong." Then a moment later in a reflective way, "I'd do anything to fix it up."

"Now we understand each other," said Wilder. "It's curious how long it takes a business man to get a square view of some things. We might have fixed it up in five minutes if you had not insisted on being a bully."

" I s'pose a man is likely to do a good many rash things when he gets into this kind of a d—d scrape," replied Seymour in a helpless kind of a way. "What do you want me to do?"

"This woman Therese," said Wilder, "went into the Enniston house, I suspect, under peculiar circumstances. I want to trace her. She has nothing whatever to do with the Enniston murder. I want you and Mrs. Enniston to produce the girl. She's a common thief."

"Produce her," exclaimed Seymour; "a common thief—me?"

"Understand me. Produce the information I want and I'll get her. We needn't disturb the other matter. Mrs. Enniston never liked her. I want to know how she got in there; where she came from; and, if possible where she went. You see Mrs. Enniston's mouth is sealed to me for obvious reasons. But you can get all this."

"And you agree—?"

"I agree to let the Enniston affair alone, unless it comes before the public in some new way that I cannot prevent."

"But there is no necessity of your going with me."

"Perhaps not."

"Well, sir, I'll see what I can do. Poor Ol Enniston! I never thought the thing would come to this. Why, the girl looked as meek as a saint. Killed in his own shrubbery! My God, what a mess."

"When will you go?"

"To-morrow. Where shall I address you?"

Wilder wrote an address on a card.

This was on the twenty-seventh. On the twenty-ninth he received a line from Seymour asking him to call. The moment he went into the private office, Seymour took a letter from his pocket and handed it to him, saying, "There's your woman."

Wilder took the soiled sheet of paper. It was written over with a pale ink in a crabbed and exceedingly fine hand as follows:

452 E. 19, New York.

Mrs. Oliver Enniston,

Coe's Cove, New York.

Respected Madame: I write to inform you that your lost property has been placed in my hands by Therese Thibeaudeau to be returned. The poor girl is heartbroken and I believe is really penitent. She is overcome with remorse. At her request I write to you. I am a businessman and a man of honor. You may trust me, so may Mr. Carteret. If you think I am entitled to any part of the reward offered for the cup, I shall humbly receive it for my granddaughter's sake who is beautiful and good. If you could see her you would love her. I have taken great care of the cup. Therese has gone away and I hope you will forgive her. Hoping to hear from you, I remain, dear madame,

Your obedient servant,

EBEN EVANS.

NEW YORK, Sept. 24th."

Wilder held the note paper in his hand and repeated the name "Thibeaudeau," several times. It was not a common name. He dropped his eyelids half way in that introspective feat of overhauling every brain cell in search of an old impression. Seymour spoke to him once or twice, but he did not reply. Finally he looked up at his companion as if asking what he had been saying.

"I merely remarked," said Seymour, "that I have in substance Mrs. Enniston's reply as she remembered it. Here it is." And he read from penciled memoranda in his own hand the following:

COE'S COVE,. Sept. 25th.

EBEN EVANS:

In reply to your letter of the twenty-fourth, Mrs. Enniston can only say that she has offered no reward for a cup, and does not wish it returned. The miserable creature who stole it has made mischief enough in my house and I do not wish to hear of her or the cup again. You are welcome to it and can make it a present to your beautiful granddaughter."

The first impression that this made on Wilder showed that he was something of a philosopher as well as a detective. If his somewhat vague thought had been expressed in words, it would have been, "How near a fine imperious independence can come to sheer stupidity. It's much easier for a woman to stumble over her own pride than for a man to fall over a toy dagger."

But he came out of this mood. "Mr. Seymour," he said, "you have done me an unexpected service. I'll just take that address in Nineteenth Street. With regard to the Enniston affair, if anything should occur touching your interest, I'll communicate with you at once."

"Is there anything I can do for you?" asked Seymour, laying his hand on his check book.

"Yes," said Wilder, "do me the kindness to try and understand that a man can be a gentleman and have a sense of honor, who isn't in your line of business."

CHAPTER VIII.

THERESE THIBEAUDEAU'S STORY.

Wilder's intention was to go at once to Eben Evans. Other duties interfered, and talking one day with a ward detective in the Third Precinct, he got upon the track of Therese Thibeaudeau. The ward officer had said, "The girl you want must be one of McCune's gang. You know McCune, 'The Mink,' he was up for sneak thieving about a year ago, and was mixed up in the Anderson arson case at the Dry Dock. He had a woman in train, and hang me if I don't think that was one of her names. I shouldn't wonder if Capt. Spears could put his hand on her."

This surmise proved to be correct. Capt. Spears did approximately put his hand on her, and on the thirtieth Wilder found her in a low quarter near the river on the East side. She had two rooms, where she and a paramour were living. She proved to be a woman of thirty, of French extraction; tall and still good looking, with small dark eyes, a swarthy skin with a scar on the right temple, and a face prematurely wrinkled about the mouth and very shadowy under the eyes. The marks of dissipation were obvious enough and her eyelashes were heavy with the grease paint of recent decoration, some of which in a drunken sleep had rubbed off and stained her forehead. She was in a collapsed and nervous condition with terror and exhaustion, and was dressed in shabby finery that was soiled and crumpled. Wilder very soon found that she stood less in fear of him and the law than of some personal enemy who was looking for her, and that she was so beset with superstitious terror that it was difficult to reason with her. After a great deal of diplomacy and the exercise of consummate tact, seeing that she thought he knew most of the incidents of her eccentric career, Wilder succeeded in getting from her the story of her connection with the cup. This narrative, with the colloquial breaks closed up and the irrelevant matter omitted, was in substance as follows:

"I came to America from Toulon when I was an infant. My father died in New York when I was twelve years old. I was brought up by a woman named Seagrist, who kept a saloon in Division street. She abused me, and I ran away when I was fifteen and got to Philadelphia, where I was arrested as a vagrant and put in an asylum. I stayed there a year and was taken out by a French hair dresser, who taught me how to dress hair. I was with him two years and got to be very smart; but I fell in with a man in his place, who coaxed me to go to New York and set up with him in the same business. We were together about six months. Then I went to one of the theatres as hair dresser, and an actress afterwards hired me to go with her. I traveled for a year and saved up some money. When I came back to New York I got acquainted with a man named Saunders who had a stable, and married him. We lived a cat and dog life for three years; he gave me this mark on the temple. He left me and went to California and I went back to hair dressing. I had bad luck. I fell sick and got out of money, and after struggling along went into Mr. Evans' family. He had a partner by the name of Rankin, who was a villain and made love to me secretly. I did not suspect him though. He used to come to Evans' house and act disagreeable enough. He fooled me completely and got me to go away and live with him. I found then that he was a gambler and was fooling Mr. Evans too. They failed one day. I think it was Rankins' fault. I hated him. I went back to Mr. Evans and he treated me like a father, but I never told him.

"Rankin, when he found I was back there, began to injure me. I had an acquaintance by the name of Villers who came to see me sometimes. He was a kind of drummer. He had plenty of money and took me to balls and clubs. He was a Socialist. He introduced me one night to a man by the name of Plon, who took a great fancy to me. They wanted me to join one of their societies. About this time Saunders came back. He had always liked me, in spite of his brutal treatment. He claimed me as his wife. He was a desperate sort of man and I was afraid of him. He came to the Evans' house and kicked up a disturbance. He wanted me to go and live with him. I was afraid of him. He followed me nights, and finally I left Evans' and went to live with a woman in Norfolk street who kept a lodging house. I did this to get away from Saunders. Plon came there and got me employment. He sent me off several times to transact business for him and always paid me well. He used to go away for a week at a time, and I never knew what his business was. He was gone one time—it was in sixty or sixty- one—for six months. The Norfolk street house was a pretty bad place. In March, sixty-one, Plon came back suddenly and asked me if I wanted to make five hundred dollars. I was hard up. He said if I would go into Mr. Enniston's house, at Coe's Grove, and get a cup that was there, he would give me five hundred dollars. I didn't like the job and then he offered me a thousand. He said I could do it because they had advertised for a maid. He came to me four times about it. He coaxed and threatened. I asked him what he wanted to do with the cup. He said it had been stolen from a Spanish family and they were willing to pay a big price to get it back. He seemed to know all about the Enniston house. He showed me a drawing of the rooms, told me where Mr. Enniston slept and where the cup was kept. I asked him who would protect me from the law. He said he would; that there wouldn't be the slightest danger of the law, if I did what he told me. Finally he offered to give me two thousand dollars if I would undertake this, and then I thought if I got that money I could go away and set up business in some Western city, so I consented. I was pretty low down then, and I had some pretty rough acquaintances. Plon gave me a hundred dollars in advance and two letters to Mrs. Enniston, which I think were forged.

"I went to live in the Enniston house in April, eighteen hundred and sixty-two. It wasn't pleasant for me. The place was away off in the country. I didn't see anybody and had to live a quiet life; besides, Mrs. Enniston took a dislike to me before I had been there two weeks. I was there a month before I found out that the cup was kept in Mr. Enniston's room in a safe. He did business in the city and came home very irregularly. When he was away his room was locked. In the summer there was a good deal of company and it was livelier. I got the run of the house then and made myself useful to the women. But my room was in the attic and I began to despair of ever getting hold of the cup, because Mrs. Enniston watched me so closely. In June Mrs. Enniston's brother, Mr. Ackerman, came there from South America, and he and Enniston used to sit up late at night in Enniston's room talking. I could hear them distinctly in my chimney flue, after the family had gone to bed. Once I slipped down stairs in my stocking feet and listened at the door. I could make out enough to know that they were talking about the cup. I heard Ackerman say it was worth millions. This frightened me a little, for I thought it was only a common ornament that Plon wanted. I didn't see how I was to get into that safe and then get the cup out of the house. I tried to get Mrs. Enniston to let me do the chamberwork, but she always managed to keep me down stairs in the mornings and when I came up, Enniston's door was locked. I laid awake nights thinking of every plan I could, but I began to be discouraged. Then Plon made it worse by sending McCune. Do you know McCune?" asked the narrator.

Wilder put his hand in his breast pocket and pulled out a photograph. "Is that the man?" he asked.

"Yes," replied the woman in a helpless way, as if she meant to acknowledge that Wilder knew all her evil associates.

"Well," he sent McCune up there twice to hurry me up and that scared me. As I tell you, there was a good deal of company in the summer coming and going, and one day something occurred that gave me fresh hopes. There was a big thunder storm. The wind blew down part of one of the chimneys and it made the roof leak so that the water ran into my room and through the floor. Then I was put down in the hall bedroom next to Mr. Enniston's room temporarily, while they fixed the roofs and walls.

"There was to be a family party on the fifteenth of July and I think this storm was on the twelfth. Anyway, the house was torn up for two days and the workmen were going and coming past my door. Enniston was home overlooking the work and he left his door open pretty much all the time. He seemed to be a good natured man of the world and not at all like his wife.

"It struck me once or twice that I might get up a little harmless flirtation with him, as he treated me very kindly, but somehow it didn't come around that way. One morning when I came out of my room, his door was open and he called to me. I walked in promptly. He was shaving at a glass and his back was to me. All he said was, 'Oh, Therese, if you are going down stairs, tell one of' em to send me up some water that is hot.'

"As I stood there I saw the cup for the first time. The safe door was open. I hurried down, got the water myself and was coming back with it when Mrs. Enniston came out of the room they called the library and asked me where I was going with that pitcher. I said Mr. Enniston had asked me to bring him some hot water. She took the pitcher out of my hand and carried it up herself. I hated her then. There was something so superior in her quiet way that it maddened me. Then I began to think that I would never do what Plon wanted. I couldn't see any way to it, but I made up my mind to stay till after the party and then tell Plon it was no use. It was the next night that Mr. Enniston met with the accident. The whole house was thrown into an uproar. He was brought up stairs and laid on a lounge in his own room. I heard everything from my chamber. The doctor came and they were left alone. I held my ear close against the door that was in the wall and I heard the doctor open the safe and take something out. I did not hear him close it. Then it flashed into my head that perhaps my chance would come yet. If I could get in there during the excitement, no one would think of the cup. While I was thinking of this and getting nervous, I went to the window which was open, and saw McCune standing on the lawn against a tree, and hidden from the lighted parlors down stairs. He asked me if I had got it. I made some reply in a whisper and motioned him to go away, and shut the sash.[*]

"I waited in the room the whole night long without closing my eyes. Mr. Enniston died about an hour after the accident and the room was never left without somebody in it. Once Mrs. Enniston tried the knob of my door and then rapped to see if I was in it. It was a dreadful night to me. The next day I pretended to be sick and kept to the room, listening. The funeral was on the eighteenth in the afternoon at three o'clock. At two o'clock there was a con-sultation of friends below, before the ceremonies began. Mr. Ackerman was in the next room and I could tell by the sound that he was examining the papers in the safe which stood within three feet of my door. All at once he was sent for to confer about the arrangements down stairs. I heard Barney

---

[*]Therese's recollection of this is not quite accurate. She must have gone to the window before she put her ear to the door, and before the doctor arrived, if Kate Haviland's statement is correct.

ask him if he would step down a moment. My heart beat. I did not hear him close the safe. He said, 'Yes,' and the two men went down stairs. I peered out of my door. There was a murmur of voices below. Enniston's door was ajar. They were all taken up with the funeral. I stepped out into the hall and listened over the balusters. I put my hand on Mr. Enniston's door—it swung open. I must have been crazy. Before I knew what I doing, I was in the room. There stood the coffin on the trestles, with the hinged lid unscrewed. The safe door was partly open. In an instant I had the cup in my hands. It was small and light. As I clutched it, I heard the voices in the hallway below. I knew I could not take it to my room. The windows were covered with wire gauze. I was desperate. I don't know how the thought came into my miserable head. There was a napkin on the table. I wrapped it round the cup. Why, I don't know, and going to the coffin, I lifted the lid, and with all my strength, pushed the cup out of sight down by the side of the dead body, just in time to escape Mrs. Enniston and Mr. Ackerman who were coming up in deep consultation. When my door was shut I felt so weak in my knees that I sank down on the floor, but I crawled to the partition door. I heard Mrs. Enniston and Mr. Ackerman conversing in low tones, and it seemed to me that Mr. Ackerman went to the safe and pushed it to and took the key out. I shivered all over for fear Mr. Ackerman would look into the coffin. I heard the undertaker come up and ask Mrs. Enniston if he should close the coffin, and I had a new spell as I thought that he would be sure to look in and notice the disarrangement of the clothes. The next moment I heard the sound of his screw driver and then I knew that nothing had been seen, and that the cup would go out of the house. Mrs. Enniston had told me in the morning that she expected me to accompany her to the cemetery. I put on a dark dress and rode in the carriage behind her. It was all very dreadful to me. I could not get that white face out of my head as I had seen it lying there helpless, while I was stealing its property. It seemed to me that I had committed some horrible crime in a fit of insanity. When I came back to the house, I was really ill. Mr. Ackerman had got there first. I told Mrs. Enniston that I was so weak I must go to bed and she sent the doctor to me. I had had no sleep for two nights, and I went off into a doze with my head buried in the bedclothes. When I woke up it was dark. I went to the window and—heaven help me— the first thing I saw in the night was Mr. Enniston standing on the lawn beckoning to me. His hand was raised above his head as if to curse me, and I sank down on the floor with a moan. I must have fainted. In the morning there was a dreadful row. Mr. Ackerman had missed the cup. Everything was turned topsy turvy—my trunks were all pulled out. I was cross-questioned and insulted and Mrs. Enniston had to take my part. I never saw a man go on so as Capt. Ackerman did. If I had thought the loss of the cup was going to break him up in such a way, I don't think I'd have touched it. He got so violent that Mrs. Enniston had to request him to remember that he was in a mourning family. I made his accusations an excuse for going away, and I left there on the third day after the funeral. I came straight to New York and went back to Mrs. Maxwell's in Norfolk street. She saw something was the matter with me at once, but she slept with me that night. I was waked up about three o'clock in the morning. She had got out of bed, lit the gas and was standing in the middle of the room staring at me with fright. I begged her to tell me what had happened. She said: 'You had better tell me. What have you been doing?' I was confused—I didn't understand then that I must have been talking in my sleep. It seemed to me that she must have found out everything. I tried to pacify her, but she wanted me to go away. She said I'd bring bad luck on her. I begged her to let me stay, but she would not. I had to get up and go out of the house at four o'clock in the morning. I went up to the Bowery and every policeman stopped and looked into my face. I felt like a doomed woman. I wandered over to Mr. Evans' house in Stanton street and found he had moved away. I sat down on the steps and groaned. He was the only true friend I had. I thought if I didn't do something to remove the curse, I should go mad, and then as soon as it was sunlight I hunted up Villers. He was always willing to do anything I asked him. I told him I was in trouble. He asked me if I wanted money. I told him no—I wanted him to find Saunders for me. He didn't want to, but I coaxed him. Villers took me to a German place in Corlears street and told me to stay there till he came. He promised not to tell Plon and went to look for Saunders. It was night before he found him. Saunders hardly knew me when he came, I was dressed like a lady. The moment I got him alone, I flung myself at him. I told him he was my husband and I'd go with him and do anything if he'd help me out of my present trouble, and if he didn't, I'd end by killing myself. He saw that I meant it. He asked me what I wanted him to do, and then I told him what I had done, but I did not tell him what Plon had agreed to give me. He sat down in front of me, and said I was the craziest d—d fool and the best looking one he knew. I told him I must get that cup out of that grave and send it back or I'd die. He said with an oath that he wasn't a grave robber. I coaxed, I wheedled him and I begged him. Then I pushed him away and told him to make up his mind for I was desperate. So he finally promised to try and get someone to do the job; but he wasn't to lose sight of me. That's how it came about. I was awfully afraid of Plon and I hung to Saunders as a kind of protector. He got a rough fellow on the twenty-fifth and he went with us in a coach to the depot. We got out at Bradford's at nine o'clock at night, hired a conveyance, got the shovels somewhere and started across country for the cemetery, in the dark. Then Saunders told me that it would cost a hundred dollars, and asked me if I had any money and I gave him my purse. It had a hundred and sixty-five dollars in it in bills. Some of it was wages from Mrs. Enniston and the rest was what I had left of Plon's money. I never suffered so in my life as I did that night. Saunders had brought a bottle of whisky with him and the two men drank continually. Before I had gone half way I began to be scared. We lost the road several times, and we didn't want to ask anybody. It was one o'clock in the morning before we found the cemetery, and a big storm was coming on. We left the wagon in a grove and got over the fence, and hunted for the plot. The men were reckless and cursed and swore in a loud voice, and I trembled at every step we took. At last I found the place, and the men went to work shoveling. After awhile Saunders came and sat down on the curb alongside of me and began making love. He said he had had some pretty rough picnics but this beat 'em all I begged him for God's sake to be quiet, but he was rough and passionate and tipsy. All at once the man in the grave called out: 'Hist—there's somebody coming, I can hear the footsteps here. Get in here both of you.' Saunders caught me roughly by the arm, and before I knew it, I was standing on the dirt by the grave. He jumped in and held out his hand to me. 'Don't be a fool,' he said, 'there's nothing else for it.' Before I could get down, there was a flash of lighting lit the place. The next instant the three of us were crouching in the hole. You could hear the heavy step of some one coming. It was like a throb in the earth. My heart stood still. If we were discovered, Saunders would commit murder. I knew he was armed. The steps came closer—we could hear the twigs snap under a heavy foot. The two men were close on either side of me and their whiskey breaths blew in my face. I hope I may die before I go through it again. The steps seemed to pass very near us and then die away. We never knew what it was. It sobered Saunders companion a little, for he said in a whisper: 'Now let's get through this d—d job as soon as possible, I'm getting tired of it.' They got the cup out somehow. Saunders took the napkin off and threw it in the dirt and then lit a match and examined the cup. Then he shoveled back the dirt and we started away. I felt better already, but a new difficulty worried me. Saunder's kept hold of it, and I did not know how to get it back to Mrs. Enniston's without running the risk of arrest. Before we got back to the city Saunders was stupidly drunk. The moment he got to his room he fell down in a dead sleep. I bundled up the cup and went out of the house to find Mr. Evans. It was the butcher in Stanton street who told me he was living in Nineteenth street dreadfully poor. I told Mr. Evans at once that I had been, I knew, a very bad woman, but that I had not forgotten all his goodness; I had come to him again in trouble. I frightened him a little with my manner and wild looks, and he laid his hand on my head and said in a trembling voice, 'Therese, Therese, my poor girl, what has happened to you?' Then I told him that I had a cup that had been stolen from Mrs. Enniston's house, I wanted it returned, and I wanted him to send it back for me, I was afraid to do it myself. We talked it all over and he promised. Then I wrote Mrs. Enniston's address in an old blank book that he gave me and left the cup with him. I went back to Saunders' because I was afraid of Plon. At first I was afraid to go out, but after awhile I went out with him to the theatre, and for awhile we got along very peaceably together. I made one more visit to Mr. Evans, and found he had not returned the cup, but it was because he had forgotten where he put the address. He was very feeble, and had forgotten where I wrote it. He promised me again to attend to it. When I was coming out of the house I saw, or thought I saw, McCune watching me from the other side of the street. I was so frightened that I started on a run and did not stop till I got into a First avenue car. I had a notion come into my head that Villers had told Plon and he had put McCune on my track, or that he had hunted up Saunders and poisoned him against me or bribed him. I was dreadfully frightened and was very anxious for Saunders to come home. He did not get back till late in the afternoon. The moment he came in I knew something had happened. He shut the door and locked it. He looked fierce and pale.

"'What did you do with that cup?' he said.

"'I sent it back where it belonged,' I answered.

"'I don't believe it. You have lied to me.'

"'Bill,' I said, 'I haven't lied to you. I told you the truth. Plon has lied to you because he wants to be revenged on me.'

"'Do you know,' he says, 'what it's worth? You've thrown away a fortune with your d—d superstitious nonsense. It's worth five thousand dollars hard money this minute, and I want you to get it. Do you understand that?'

"'I can't get it, Bill,' I said. 'Don't let us quarrel about it. There's nothing but bad luck goes with it.'

"'You can't get it?' he shouted. 'Where did you take it that morning when I was asleep? Come, it's no use, by _____ I'm going to have it. You can't play me like all the rest of 'em.'

"I saw he was in one of his desperate fits, but I was determined. I looked him in the face. Says I: 'You can kill me if you want to, but you can't make me get you that cup.' Then he took to coaxing, and when that failed he was worse than before. He ordered me to put on my hat and come and show him where I had taken it. He dragged me to the door, and when I resisted he struck me and I fell down insensible. He went off, and when I came to I was so afraid that he or Plon would find out that old Mr. Evans had the cup and get it away, that I determined to go down and warn the old man, in spite of the danger of being followed. I went to the house in Nineteenth street as soon as it was dark. Just as I had got up to the fourth floor, where Evans lives, and was about to knock at his door, I happened to look at the other end of the passageway, and there stood Plon talking to a woman. He had a light in his hand, and the end of the hall was so dark where I stood that he could not see me. I turned and ran down again as fast as I could and got away. But I was bound to warn Mr. Evans. So I wrote a note and got a boy and sent it, and told him I'd give him fifty cents if he brought me an answer. I begged Mr. Evans to restore the cup at once, and told him that there was a powerful gang trying to get it, and some of them had got into his house. The boy brought me back an answer written by Manuella. It said: 'Grandpa thanks you and will be very careful.'"

CHAPTER IX.

WITHIN AN INCH OF THE CUP.

The possession of the cup worked a mystic change in Mr. Evans' character. At first he regarded it as a trust, but one day, when looking over an old copy of the *Herald*, his eye fell upon the advertisement signed by Carteret. His weak mind began to frame the most illusory advantages that were to follow the return of the property to the owner. He explained the name of Carteret easily by the supposition that he was Mrs. Enniston's agent in the matter, and he said to himself that half the reward would satisfy him and enable him to make a handsome present to Manuella. He put the cup carefully away in his closet, and then began to refer mysteriously to it when talking to his granddaughter. It was some time before she got a clear idea of what had happened, and when she understood it all she was inclined to look upon her grandfather's new object of interest with the leniency that she always showed to his harmless whims. Mrs. Sitwhite knew nothing of the cup. Therese had called there when she was out of the house, and Mr. Evans had not told her of the event.

But the cup had not been in his possession three days before Plonski moved into the front suite. Such an event would not escape the persons on the fourth floor. He had accosted Mrs. Sitwhite familiarly at once, giving her to understand that he was a doctor, and would fix her influenza up for her as soon as he got to rights.

Two causes had delayed Mr. Evans in sending word to Mrs. Enniston that he had the cup; he could not find the address and he had a dotard's desire not to part with the property hurriedly. He put it away in the closet in his dark room, to take it out when nobody was around and examine it with curious interest. He had never seen anything like it before. The silver was tarnished and the smooth inner surface was cloudy with a reddish hue. Its exterior was covered with carved and chased designs, some of them exceedingly minute, that baffled him. Hieroglyphics innumerable were woven into strange symbolic figures and geometric lines. For some reason, as even Mr. Evans could see, the most exquisite and patient skill had been exercised in its unintelligible ornamentation. The mystery of its purpose and the unusual manner in which it had come to him, unconsciously affected his wayward imagination. A childish notion took possession of him that in some way it was to be a providential means of improving his own and Manuella's condition. The accidental discovery of the reward offered, only heightened this delusion. On the fourth day after Therese's first visit, Mr. Plonski had moved in a table, a few chairs, a narrow shake-down bed and a few other articles of furniture and had got to rights. His hall door was always ajar and he was always peering out like a rat.

On the morning of that day, the Sitwhite family were all assembled in their largest room at dinner. John Sitwhite and his wife sat opposite each other at a table upon which was spread a hearty but somewhat coarse meal, and between them were the two children. Manuella and her grandfather were at the open window, it being an understood arrangement that the Sitwhites should always eat their meals first and then let Manuella attend to her grandfather in her own way, after John had gone off to smoke his pipe and the two children had been turned into the kitchen. The contrast that the girl at the window offered to this group was notable. Not alone her radiant beauty, but an indescribable air of being out of place must have struck the attention of any one. She was sewing at some article of apparel, occasionally looking up at the evening picture hung for her alone between the brick walls and the gas tanks. Her grandfather was dreaming with his eyes half closed behind his spectacles, an old musty news-paper lying on his knees, an exact reproduction in vacuo of a twenty-five years habit in better times with the *Evening Post*.

The conversation had evidently been about the new tenant, for Mrs. Sitwhite with an empty tea cup in her hand and her two elbows on the table was saying, as she turned and tilted the cup to get some kind of a figure into the tea leaves at the bottom,

"Anyway he's a gentleman and he takes an interest in our family. I noticed that, the moment I clapped my eyes on him. He knows we don't belong in this kind of a place any mor'n he does."

"Now, you let the place alone," said John, as he put a spoonful of some kind of stew on his boy's plate. "If we don't belong here, where do we belong? Dang me, if I don't think it was just made for us. I guess he's interested in the Princess," giving his head a sidewise nod toward the window, without looking that way.

John was in the habit of referring to Manuella as "the Princess," and she had grown accustomed to it. She had indeed never resented it for the simple reason that the compliment and the contempt of it were too evenly mixed for her to bother with the separation.

"I don't like the looks of the new tenant," she said quietly, without looking up. "It seems to me, he's too stealthy and none of us can ever go out without his watching us. I think he takes a deal too much interest."

"O it isn't in you," retorted her aunt sharply. "Don't get that into your head. It's me this time," and she turned the cup round to John and held it for his inspection of the tea leaves. "There's a silver goblet—on a counter—no—it's a coffin. See it?"

John was used to these tea cup divinations and was a little reckless in his interpretations. "All right," he said, "there's two piles of coke on each side of it—that's where we find our silver goblets."

"Silver goblet?" exclaimed the old man suddenly. "Where?"

Mrs. Sitwhite got up and went over to him and with one arm round his neck, held up the cup with the other for him to see.

"There it is, pop, just as natural as life. Can't you see it?"

"Yes, yes," replied Mr. Evans with tremulous eagerness as he adjusted his glasses. "So it is—so it is. What's it mean?"

"Luck, pop. Don't you remember that night that Ella saw an urn in her cup and in walked Castleton?"

"Sure enough," murmured the old man. "It's a silver one, isn't it?"

"Silver fiddlestick," said Manuella. "I don't see what you want to put such rubbish into his head for?" and she pushed the cup that Mrs. Sitwhite held for her contemptuously, but gently, away with her hand.

"It's very strange," the old man muttered. "A silver goblet. It is very strange," he repeated to Manuella in a subdued and confidential tone. "I've known these strange things before. Yes, it's good luck."

"There's more good luck, Grandpa," said the girl, "in a cup of good tea than in all the washed leaves in the world and, I'm going to make it for you."

She then got up and began making preparations to get his meal.

John Sitwhite stretched himself back in his chair, teased the boy for a few minutes by moving his plate beyond his reach; laughed heartily at the youngster's vicious resentment of the interference; lit his pipe and sauntered out, leaving a flavor of tobacco behind him. Mrs. Sitwhite generally followed him to the hallway, and either filled in a half hour of digestive good humor in leaning upon the hand rail of the stairs and looking down the well hole, or in an hour's sociable gossip with Mrs. Squinch on the fifth floor front. On this occasion she combined both amusements by leaning upon the hand rail and waiting for Mrs. Squinch to come up. Manuella was thus left to her grandfather in peace. She spread a clean napkin over the soiled tablecloth, made him a fresh cup of tea, cut him a few thin slices of bread, brought out a little jar of some kind of preserves and in a few minutes, the rather disordered board was metamorphosed into daintiness.

While this was going on, Mr. Plonski had come up the stairs in company with a rather stout and florid middle-aged man, who panted a good deal at the exertion required and who did not appear at all charmed with the interior of "O'Reardon's Terrace." He was somewhat elegantly dressed in dark clothes, showing a great deal of shirt-front, upon which were two diamond studs, and he held his silk hat in his hand as if to allow the extra animal heat to escape. Seen thus in that murky light, one instinctively felt that he was a man utterly unused to the scenes that he here met and not used to hiding his disgust and impatience at whatever interfered with his comfort. As Plonski reached the hallway of the fourth floor Mrs. Sitwhite accosted him with her most winning amiability.

"Good evening, Doctor, I hope you're as good as settled. You know if there's anything we can do to give you a lift in getting to rights, you mustn't be backward in calling on us."

Plonski bowed with the utmost politeness and even lifted his German cap. All he said was: "I thank you, madame. You are very kind," and passed on to his door. The moment he and his companion were inside the room, the latter, who was making the most futile endeavors to fan himself with his silk hat, which he worked between his palms on the principle of an oscilating engine, exclaimed, "I say, you hav'n't got any icewater or anything, I suppose."

Plonski shook his head, while he carefully shut the door.

"I go down to the beer saloon when I want a cold drink," he said. "You don't need that gas lit, do you? It makes this place hotter than a sugarhouse."

"No," said the other, who was looking round the room as well as he could. "Let's get through as quick as possible. I want to get out into the air."

He had a flabby voice, of large vocal dimensions, but without vibration. It was one of those masculine voices that denote plenty of muscle; but rather relaxed. He continued talking as Plonski pulled two chairs to the open window and they sat down.

"You say you have traced the cup to this house?"

"To this very floor," replied Plonski. "That is why I am putting up with this somewhat barbarous place."

"Have you discovered how and why it came here?"

"Not entirely. The girl Therese brought it here. I am morally convinced of that."

"Well, well, don't let us waste any time with unnecessary mysteries. If it is here, can't we get it?"

Plonski smiled, somewhat contemptuously and the uncertain light from the street made it slightly ghastly.

"I didn't say it was here. I said it came here. What do you want to do—take it by violence?"

"I want to get it without any more infernal nonsense. It seems to me, and I'm a practical man, that if it is here, we ought to get it immediately. If we can't get it in one way, I suppose we can get it in another."

"How much personal risk will you take to get it?" asked Plonski.

"Personal risk?" exclaimed the other. "I've personally risked ten thousand dollars to get it. Don't you think that's something?"

"No, in your view of returns, a mere bagatelle. Do you want to risk your neck?"

His companion started a little. "You hav'n't got a fan in this hole have you?"

"No, I'll get you a paper," said Plonski.

"I hope you don't mean that we've got to go into that sort of business to get the thing."

"What sort of business?"

"Well, to put it plainly—murder. I hate the word."

"It seems to me that that sort of thing has been gone into already," said Plonski. "You don't believe that story about Enniston falling on a knife, do you?"

"Why man, you don't mean to say that he was—."

"I mean to say, I don't believe he was killed by accident. Our woman was in the house at that time and she disappeared with the cup almost immediately and didn't come to us. I don't profess to be a practical man, only a reasonable one. I think we'll have some trouble to prove that our conspiracy was not responsible for Enniston's death, if that French woman has been bought up. You see, Mr. Chanfleur, it is necessary to go discreetly here, very discreetly. I don't want to imperil your life, whatever I may do with my own, which I expose to typhoid fever, smallpox and various other discomforts in this place to accomplish our purpose."

"Yes," said Chanfleur, fanning himself violently with the newspaper. "I don't see why you couldn't have met me at a hotel or the Maison Doree, instead of dragging me down here."

"Because," replied Plonski. "I don't intend to take my eyes off these people next door to accommodate your good taste. There's such a thing as being too practical, I suppose."

"Is it possible to find this Therese?"

"I must tell you," said Plonski, "of something that has occurred to make us specially careful. The insertion of that advertisement in the *Herald* was a mistake. An inspector from the Central Office got hold of it and went off up to Coe's Grove to nose the thing. How much he has learned I do not know. McCune says he has been up there three or four times. I am told that he is the cleverest man in the business."

"Well now," said Chanfleur, "what are you going to do here and how long will it take you to do it?"

"I am going to make a very careful attempt to get that cup. I'm not going to trust to third parties this time. I shall probably know in a day or two why it came here, if you let me alone. At present it is a mystery. McCune is looking for Therese and I have seen a lover of hers—one Villers."

"Have you heard from Miramon?"

"Not within a week. He was in Pueblo; waiting for orders at last advices. I don't mind telling you that my notion is—the cup was put in this out of the way place to throw us all off the scent."

"Have you found out why Ackerman went away and where he is?"

"No, I have heard nothing in that direction. That was one of my instructions to Therese when she went into the Enniston house and of course I cannot tell what she learned. It has occurred to me once or twice that he may have been here ever since Enniston's death, keeping out of sight and watching us. You must see yourself by what is constantly occurring that we have got powerful and secret enemies to dread."

"Why remind me of that?" said Chanfleur getting up. "The question is, who are the most powerful—they or I? I wish you'd come down stairs to the coupe with me—and do push the thing along," he said as they walked to the door. "Here's a whole year's work—prodigious work too, upset by a kitchen maid."

"Not upset I hope," rejoined Plonski, who put his hand on the door, but did not open it. "If patience, tact and untiring energy will avail us, I think we will get possession of the cup yet and once in my hands, I shall take good care that the series of mysteries ends."

"You haven't told me who these people are," said Chanfleur making a motion of his head toward the Sitwhite apartments.

"Common laboring people," replied Plonski, "but they have an old man in there and a remarkably fine looking girl that I don't understand. You'll have to let me work it out my own way. Rest assured of one thing; if the cup is on this floor, it isn't going to get out without my knowing it. But it will not do for me to be seen going and coming too much. I'll send a cipher dispatch to you the moment anything occurs and McCune is always within call. I shall stick it out here for a few days and get to the bottom of the mystery if possible. We shall probably trap Therese to-morrow or next day. I have seen her husband."

"Very well," said Chanfleur, going, "don't forget that I am in a constant fever and shall be till we have got the thing in our possession, and the sooner I hear from you the better."

Then Plonski slowly opened the door, first looked out cautiously and then followed his companion to the stairway where he bade him goodnight.

Coming back to the room, he sat down at the window and gave himself up to silent reflection for nearly an hour, first pulling down the sash, for the noise irritated him more than the heat. At the expiration of that time, he got up, lit the solitary gas jet and going to the narrow room which had once been the inner passage and where there was placed a shakedown bed, he practically disrobed himself, turned down the gas to a spark and threw himself on the rug which did service for bed clothes. His head came close to the thin pine partition on the other side of which was Mr. Evans' dark closet, and so it was that he finally went off to sleep thinking how he could get possession of the cup, and the cup itself was within an inch of him, and hidden from him only by the wall paper that covered the great seams in the partition.

CHAPTER X.

MR. PLONSKI SHAKES HANDS WITH HIMSELF.

The secretiveness of Mr. Evans was peculiar to an old man who is satisfied that a new generation cannot understand the profound advantages of having lived in the past. Childish as he was at times, there was also a doting cunning in his little plans. He wrote to Mrs. Enniston without consulting Manuella. He had but one idea—it was to secure all the advantages possible, that the possession of the cup promised for his granddaughter, and he did not want that idea disturbed or his intention frustrated. He felt instinctively that the girl would in some affectionate way, oppose him. He was in the habit of taking a short walk on sunshiny mornings of a block or two, and Manuella nearly always accompanied him. There was a little stationary store on the First avenue near Twenty-second street where the newspapers and cheap novels were sold by a woman named Holbrook, who had been a nurse in former years and had been employed in the Evans family. She was now a widow with a lively and over-developed son of eighteen who helped her in her business. She had a kindly regard for Mr. Evans and his granddaughter. The old man was in the habit of stopping at the store and Mrs. Holbrook, large, wholesome and hearty, would place a chair for him to rest, talk with him pleasantly about old times and give him a paper when he went away. She always called him "grandpop," and when he wanted to write a letter, she furnished him with pen and paper, put a stamp on the envelope for him, and made Bob Holbrook post it.

Bob had a trick of detaining the old gentleman as long as possible by the most subtle acts of courtesy. He would get out the picture papers, spread them open and tell him all about the events that were illustrated, for when Mr. Evans stayed away too long, Manuella was pretty sure to come looking for him. When they first came to the Terrace, she had let him go in the mornings without much fear, for he received the kindest attention from all who knew him in the neighborhood. But of late he had shown signs of weakness that made her more solicitous. She noticed too that he was peculiarly sensitive on this point. He did not want her to think that he could not take care of himself and he slipped out from under her eye whenever he could.

It was at Mrs. Holbrook's that he wrote the letter to Mrs. Enniston, and Plonski who had watched him go out of the house, had also followed him and saw him through the door of the shop, seated at Mrs. Holbrook's little table at the rear end of the counter in the act of inditing it. Waiting on the other side of the avenue, he saw Manuella come after him and when they had disappeared together, he crossed over and entering the little shop, purchased several weekly papers of Bob Holbrook. While picking them out, his quick eye looked over the place. Then he asked the young man if he might put wrappers on them and address them. This was not an unusual request and he was permitted to sit down at the little table. There, lying in front of him, was Mr. Evans' letter with the address plainly visible—"Mrs. Oliver Enniston, Coe's Grove." Young Holbrook watched him closely and after addressing one or two papers, Mr. Plonski went away.

But this discovery increased both his interest and his watchfulness. It was impossible for him to conceive what link it was that connected Mrs. Enniston and this poor old man. Then he began a systematic attack upon the weakness of Mrs. Sitwhite. She fell an easy prey to his wiles, for he bought presents and gave them to the children, and he adroitly flattered the mother. In the course of a few days, he was on excellent terms with her and managed to get into her room when Mr. Evans and Manuella were out. It did not take him long to find out the relationship and condition of Mrs. Sitwhite's lodgers, but it was a week before he had made any discovery that enlightened him with regard to the cup. Innumerable questions cunningly put, had satisfied him that Mrs. Sitwhite was profoundly ignorant of a silver cup; but he learned in listening to the woman's account of her better days and her father's home, that Therese had been an inmate of their house.

Once Manuella returned while he was in Mrs. Sitwhite's apartments, and to his polite attentions, she made so cold a recognition, and gave him so unmistakably to understand that she disliked both him and his manner, that he beat a retreat.

Then a little scene occurred between the sisters.

"Such airs as you put on," said Mrs. Sitwhite. "Why, the doctor was acquainted with our people before you had long dresses on."

"Our people?" Manuella repeated with a little surprise.

"Yes. Don't you remember Therese? He knew her well."

"Do you call her one of our people?" asked Manuella, a little shocked. "She isn't one of mine, I'm sure."

"No, you won't have any people. What's the matter with Therese, I'd like to know? She thought enough of you."

"Cynthy," said Manuella, "what has that man been asking you about our family?"

"Nothing impertinent. I don't have to go out of the family to find that," snapped Mrs. Sitwhite.

"I wouldn't have anything to do with him, if I were you," said her neice. "I never go out of the house but he follows me."

"That's your imagination. He's got something else to do."

"What is it?" asked Manuella, quickly, but calmly.

"Don't snap me up that way. *You* shouldn't say anything against people who have nothing to do."

At this turn in the dialogue, Manuella became silent. She felt the reproach, nevertheless.

The very day of this conversation, Mr. Evans received Mrs. Enniston's letter virtually presenting him with the cup. He read it over and over a score of times. He did not perceive the sneer in it. The more he thought about it, the more distinctly two facts grew out in his memory. Therese had told him to write to Mrs. Enniston, and Carteret was the name in the advertisement. Gradually the notion got possession of him, that Therese must have made a mistake in the name. He could reconcile the facts in no other way. He should have written to Carteret. When, in the course of three or four days, this conviction had grown into a fact with him, he went off to Mrs. Holbrook's and wrote a letter to Carteret. This letter, brought up by Barney from the office to Mrs. Enniston at Coe's Grove with several others directed to her while Carteret was away, was put into another envelope and redirected by her to Colin Carteret, Tenth street Studio, New York, and remailed. Arriving at the place and not finding Carteret, it was taken in charge for him by Otis Chapman, the artist in the studio adjoining his, where Carteret's letters were always left when he was away. Then Otis Chapman locked his studio up and went off on the Sawmill River to make some color studies, and the letter laid there among water colors, old brushes and cigarette stumps until he came back.

But in that week several events had occurred at the Terrace. Plonski had pushed his intimacy and investigations to good advantage. He had learned from some outside quarter, enough to confirm his suspicions, that Therese had brought the cup to Evans, though why, he could not yet tell. He had bribed and flattered Mrs. Sitwhite without her knowing it, into subserviency, and by degrees he had led her to believe that in spite of appearances, he was a man of wealth, with no one to assist in the world, and that he took such an interest in her family, that he would like to do something for John, her husband. As there were no conditions mentioned, it looked quite disinterested, and Mrs. Sitwhite began to have a few fancies of her own. She got to sending tea into his rooms at night, for Plonski was a great tea drinker; but he had to have it iced and insisted on paying for the ice and sending home packages of extra oolong, so that the Sitwhite family began to revel in luxuries that John had not been accustomed to for a long time. When he had established confidence, Plonski began to push his enquiries, and one day he told Mrs. Sitwhite under pledge of secrecy, that Mr. Evans did not treat her quite right in keeping from her some of the things that were going on in her house. "For example," said Plonski, "he should have told you that Therese had been here to see him several times." Mrs. Sitwhite could hardly credit it, but Plonski assured her that it was true, and that he knew the object of her visit. Having planted the germ of curiosity in her mind, he let it fructify for a day before he proceeded any farther. As is usually the case however, with such plans, the results were twofold, and the unexpected became a factor. Mrs. Sitwhite immediately taunted Mr. Evans and Manuella with having kept Therese's visit a secret. She added out of her suspicions, several accusations that were both superfluous and ignoble. The result was, the old man became alarmed. Added to this was Therese's note of warning about the cup and the mysterous intimation of danger in the house. The effect of all this upon Mr. Evans could not have been foreseen. Instead of making explanations to Mrs. Sitwhite, or consulting with Manuella, he began to consider with the secretive craft of an old man, how to hide the cup from the unknown enemies who were trying to get it away from him and Manuella. He had come to look upon it as in some way a sacred trust for his granddaughter. He tried to explain Carteret's delay in answering his letter by the most far-fetched theories. He grew more stealthy and taciturn to the Sitwhites, and more mysteriously hopeful and self-important to Manuella, his language to her, at times, making her unexpressibly sad. "Keep your courage up, my dear," he would say with a kindly twinkle in his watery eyes, "and trust your grandfather. He'll protect you from these bad people."

Manuella and her grandfather had both gone out for a walk one morning and had stopped at Mrs. Holbrook's. Manuella had left the old gentleman there, while she went up the avenue to make one or two little purchases for herself. Bob Holbrook had offered to go with her, but she had said to him with a peculiarly sweet smile, that she expected him to look after the old gentleman till she came back and he immediately declared that he would be a father to him if she didn't stay too long.

The moment she was gone Mr. Evans made Bob sit down by his side and then add there had a long and confidential conversation which ended in the young man's pulling out from under the counter a small wooden box which had formerly contained chalk crayons. They examined it and turned it over, and the old man approved of it with assenting nods. It was then rolled up in paper and he put it under his arm. Not long after this, Manuella returned and hurried him away. She did not know what had passed between her grandfather and young Mr. Holbrook.

While this was going on, Mrs. Sitwhite was sitting in close consultation with Mr. Plonski in the back room and the cup was standing there in the dark corner of Mr. Evan's closet. Mrs. Sitwhite was in a state of unnatural excitement. Her eyes needed constant wiping, owing to her influenza and not to her emotion. Her mouth was slightly parted and she leaned eagerly forward, for Mr. Plonski was saying to her:

"Now, my dear madame, what I have told you is true. You have the means of making a good deal of money by an honest act. Suppose you go and look in the old man's room now. I'll wait for you. You see a feeble old man who isn't right in his head, shouldn't be left to an inexperienced girl. He needs a woman like you, Mrs. Sitwhite, to look after him." His voice betrayed his anxiety as he spoke, but Mrs. Sitwhite was too excited herself to notice it.

"O, dear," she said, "you have made me so nervous that I'm all of a tremble," and she wiped her nose and eyes with a great deal of superfluous energy. "The idea of pop keeping a silver cup and not saying anything about it. I can't believe it."

"Well, well," said Plonski, "he'll be back here presently. Why don't you go and look for it and satisfy yourself. Shall I hold a light for you? He does not always lock his door, does he?"

"Yes, he does when he goes out. He's so afraid somebody will disturb his old books, but the key of Manuella's as room fits it."

"Does it?" exclaimed Plonski. "Then go at once and look for yourself, How will you ever believe me if you don't?"

"Yes," she said, "I'll go," and she got up, took Manuella's key from the door, rattling it a little as she pulled it out. "Yes, it's too bad to have such goings-on in one's house, right under one's nose. I always hated secret doings of any kind."

Plonski understood that this was said with the endeavor to excuse her conduct and he helped her on.

"The straight forward way is always the best," he said. "You are the mistress of your own house and you only want to satisfy yourself that I'm telling the truth. I'll go back to my own room. If you discover anything, come in and let me know."

They both looked over the handrail, down the wellhole, when they got into the hallway, with the same precautionary action, but without saying anything. It was that time of day when the male inmates of the house were at work, the children at school or on the street, and the women occupied in their rooms. It was the auspicious moment for being unobserved. Mr. Plonsky, however, thought it best to go into his room and push his door almost shut, leaving the usual gap of reconnaissance. Mrs. Sitwhite put the key in Evans' door and opened it. The room was. dark, but there was a dirty square window in it of four small panes, that looked into one of Plonski's bedrooms, about seven feet from the floor, and as Mrs. Sitwhite stood there prepared to strike a match, a stream of pale light suddenly came through, for Mr. Plonski with admirable consideration, had opened not only his shutters, but his bedroom door. Thus illuminated, the miserable room presented a narrow bed scrupulously made up, for Manuella attended to this every morning; a chair or two and several trunks. The doors of the closet at the end of the room ran down to the floor, and the head of the bedstead was close against them. Mrs. Sitwhite pushed the obstruction away easily and quickly opened the closet. The shelves were heaped with rubbish, old wearing apparel, discarded hats and old papers. She could not see distinctly, but she ran her arm in eagerly and encountered the old ledgers. The amount of lumber rather discouraged her, but she rooted at it spasmodically and at last pulled out something wrapped up in an old waistcoat. She unrolled it eagerly and going to the light saw that she had a silver cup in her hand. Her agitation was very great as she turned it over in wonder and held it up in the ray from the little window; to be sure that it was not an illusion. Her first impulse was to rush into Plonski's room and show it to him. She went as far as the door, but she had no sooner reached the knob and pulled the door open, than she heard the voice of Manuella on the stairs below. She then, with marvelous dexterity, threw the old waistcoat around the cup, thrust it back into the closet, gave the bed a shove and issued from the room as quickly as possible, barely escaping into her own apartment before Manuela and Mr. Evans reached the landing. She was so excited at her discovery, that she avoided them both and went into the kitchen where her children were playing noisily. She stood there a moment undisturbed by the racket, with her finger on her chin, leaning against the open window and trying to think it all over. Then she slipped noiselessly out into the hallway, rapped on Mr. Plonski's open door and disappeared.

Before she had done so, Manuella had thrown off her bonnet and pushed a chair up to the window for her grandfather. "Sit down," said the girl, "You look tired. Let me take your bundle. What is it Grandpa?"

"It's nothing but a box," he said. "I do feel a little tired my child. I think I'll go and lie down on my bed for a while. It's the stairs that do me up in my knees."

"Do," she urged. "Take a nap. I've often asked you to do it. I'll come and call you by and by when it's quiet and I've fixed you some lunch."

He got up. She accompanied him to the door and saw him go into his room. Then she seated herself at the window and looking through the gap in the walls to the East River, went off into a pensive reverie.

Mrs. Sitwhite had meanwhile opened Mr. Plonski's door, stepped inside, and, closing it, stood with her back to it, looking at Plonski who was walking the floor.

"Well, my dear woman," he said, stopping short and noticing the expression of her face. "Well, well, what have you got to say?"

"Yes," she said, pointing with her hand toward Mr. Evans' room, "it's there, sure enough; I saw it."

"Where?" asked Plonski, almost authoritatively.

"In there; he's got it in his closet."

He regarded her a moment with mute surprise. Then going to the open chamber, he said, "Do you mean that it is that room next to mine?"

She nodded her head affirmatively several times while he was speaking and then said, "but they came up while I was looking at it and I had to slip out, you know."

Plonski walked to the window. She saw, notwithstanding his back was to her, that one of his hands was wringing the other. It did not occur to her that this was a kind of self gratulation. She noticed that he pulled his black moustache almost fiercely. His manner was changed and it robbed her of her volubility, but she could not interpret it. Suddenly he turned about.

"Mrs. Sitwhite, sit down," he said, with an effort to be polite, "where is Mr. Evans now?"

Before she could answer, there was a rap at the door. Mrs. Sitwhite started a little and turned to go.

"One moment," said Plonski in a whisper, "let me see who it is."

It was a messenger boy with a note. He slipped inside. Plonski took the note and said to Mrs. Sitwhite:

"Don't let Mr. Evans out of your sight till I see you, do you understand?" and held the door open for her.

She assented mutely and hesitatingly and went out.

Then he opened the note and read it.

"Send me word if you have learned anything. I can lift the market by buying Erie and make a revolution in the street, but I want to know what luck you have had.

CHANFLEUR."

Plonski immediately wrote the following answer:

"Buy. Have got the bird in the next room. Will send you word to-night at hotel by which time I hope to be in possession. Telegraph to Miramon and send this boy for The Mink. I want him here at once.

PLON."

CHAPTER XI.

"TWIXT THE CUP AND THE LIP".

Mr. Plonski was now in a visibly agitated condition. He walked the floor, looked out of the window anxiously and examined the partition. He kept his door leading into the hall ajar, and peered out whenever he heard a footstep. He pressed his hand against the partition and it bent under his push. Then he examined the square window in the other room. Getting upon a chair, he found that it was closed with an ordinary swinging sash, buttoned on his side. He looked at his watch repeatedly, and although only an hour had elapsed since Mrs. Sitwhite left him it seemed much longer when McCune arrived.

This personage came into the room with a quick, springy step and shut the door after him. Plonski immediately opened it.

"I don't want you here," he said. "You can go down and wait around. Keep an eye on my window."

"Give me a match," said the man, and Plonski pointed to the mantel.

McCune stepped over and helped himself. He was a young man, probably not twenty-five; a slim and wiry fellow, with narrow shoulders, a rather long and sinewy neck, small features and a mouth that reminded you of a rodent. His face was heavily freckled and his pug nose had been flattened by a blow; his hair, which was light, was cut close to his head, and a short, yellowish moustache bristled on his upper lip. The general expression of his face was that of cunning and cruelty.

When he was gone, Plonski renewed his impatient walking. Nearly another hour had slipped away in uncertainty; then he went into the hall. No one was about at the moment. He walked softly to the Sitwhite door and listened. All was quiet except an occasional yelp from the Sitwhite cub in the kitchen. As he came back toward his own room he tried Mr. Evans' door. It was unlocked. He opened it and looked cautiously but hurriedly in. Dimly lit as it was, he could see that it was empty and the bed undisturbed. Someone coming up the stairs, he shut the door and went back to his room. He was evidently undetermined how to act. He pulled his moustache spasmodically and wiped his forehead with a blue handkerchief. He waited some time impatiently and then went to the window and, leaning out, beckoned. In five minutes McCune was back in the room.

"Look here," said Plonski, "the thing I want is in the next room. Come here and look at the partition." Then he led the way into his narrow bedroom. "Help me move this cot out of the way," he said. The two men then took hold of the bed and carried it easily into the next room. McCune examined the partition. The boards were nailed to a narrow strip at the bottom.

"Can you get in there," asked Plonski.

"Yes," said McCune; "a chisel and a hammer will do it."

"No hammer," said Plonski.

"Then a chisel big enough will pry 'em off without much noise."

"Go and get it," said Plonski, giving him a bill. "Put it under your coat." The moment the man was gone again a new idea occurred to Plonski, for he went out and knocked at Mrs. Sitwhite's door. She opened it herself.

"I wish to speak to you a moment," he said. She stepped out into the hall. "Where is Mr. Evans?" he asked. The woman pointed to the dark room. "He's taking a nap," she replied. Plonski moved his position slowly so as to look Mrs. Sitwhite in the face. His expression startled her a little. It was singularly intense. "Mr. Evans is not in his room," he said. "Don't you know it?"

"He went in there to take a nap just after I came into your room," she answered, stepping back a little as if his steady look annoyed her.

"Isn't he in there?" asked Plonski, with a sharp eagerness, pointing to the room from which Mrs. Sitwhite bad just come.

She shook her head. He put his hand on her arm.

"Mr. Evans is not in there. Are you sure the cup is? Suppose you show it to me. Come, let me see it."

He moved to the door of the dark room and threw it open. He looked somewhat ghastly as he did so, and his whole action had an authoritative air that frightened Mrs. Sitwhite a little.

"I am sure, Doctor," she said, "it isn't worth being so anxious about."

"But it is. If old Mr. Evans has gone out with it, he will be murdered. I tell you what I know. See if he hasn't taken it; be quick."

Thus appealed to, she made an exclamation and hurriedly went into the dark room. In a moment they had pulled the bed away, for Plonski did not hesitate to follow her and she was searching in the closet for the cup. A few minutes' search convinced her that it was not there. She pulled out the rubbish and Plonski, in his excitement, helped her. But in vain. The cup was gone. Suddenly she picked up something from the bed and held it up. "See," she said, going to the door to let the light fall on it.

"What is it?" asked Plonski.

"It was wrapped around it," replied Mrs. Sitwhite, and she threw the old waistcoat back into the room.

"Mrs. Sitwhite," said Plonski, "you must find your father instantly. If you value his life, tell your niece at once. I'll get a cab for her; be quick."

The woman flew to her room in alarm. McCune came up the stairs at the same moment and Plonski hurried him into his apartment.

"Never mind that," he said, as the man showed him the chisel. "The cup's gone out of the house. Go and get a cab. Damnation! What do you stand like that for? Get a cab."

Plonski was now in an almost pitiable state of exasperation and impatience. He ejaculated unintelligible words at intervals that were not unlike moans. Before McCune had got to the stairs Manuella had hurried with alarm to the dark room, followed by Mrs. Sitwhite, who was wiping her eyes and nose assiduously and was becoming each moment more dishevelled. Plonski met the girl in the hallway.

"Your grandfather is in danger," he said. "We must find him at once. I have sent for a cab. Put your hat on and waste no time."

"Where is he?"Asked Manuella, with pale uncertainty, not knowing exactly what she said.

"You must know his haunts and habits better than anyone else," urged Plonski. "Don't stand here—every minute is precious."

A recollection of Therese's mysterious and warning note came to her. She uttered a little cry of dismay and fled into the room. All her suspicion of Plonski was now forgotten in her anxiety for her grandfather. With no definite idea except that she must find him and that this man might aid her, she thrust her hat upon her head, gave her hair an automatic sweep and reappearing had started down the stairs followed by Plonski and Mrs. Sitwhite.

At this stage of the little crisis, all three stopped suddenly and for a moment stood mute with their hands on the rail; for there, on the hallway below, just turning to mount the same flight, was the object himself of all their concern. He came bent with fatigue and empty-handed, slowly up. Manuella rushed impetuously down to meet him and catching him round the neck, astonished him with an assault in which loving violence and tears were mingled.

"O Grandpa," she sobbed, "where, where have you been?"

The old man brought an extra breath or two, released himself from her clutch and looked at her with a self-satisfied sagacity.

"A little business, my dear—business. It had to be attended to. You shall know all about it in good time," he put his trembling hand under her chin and chucked her patronizingly. "As you get older, my dear, you'll understand these things better."

It was in vain that they led him to the window, put him in his chair and plied him with questions. He parried them with a simple craft and defended himself with a mental weakness that Plonski more than once thought were assumed.

But the latter was in no condition to sympathize or sophisticate. He knew that it was necessary to find out without delay what the old man had done with the cup, before he could make another move and he saw that any exhibition of interest in the matter was likely to make Mr. Evans more guarded and reticent.

Both Manuella and Mrs. Sitwhite were asking questions that elicitated no information and Mr. Plonski only intensified the general inquiry when he said:

"Mr. Evans, can't you tell us where you have been? It will allay our anxiety very much."

Mr. Evans looked up at this with a flush of offended dignity.

"There is a great deal of anxiety about my personal affairs," he said. Then with a relapsed expression and a tremulous wave of his hand, he added. "You confuse me—I am tired."

That brought Manuella to his rescue. "You are worrying him," she exclaimed. "Come and lie down. I will sit by the bedside."

Chagrined and silent, Mr. Plonski saw her lead him from the room.

The cup was now out of the house. In spite of Plonski's sleepless watchfulness, the feeble old man had outwitted him. To add to his perplexity, there was nothing to build a theory upon. If he had sent it to Mrs. Enniston, he must have employed an agent or used the express company and it seemed more probable that Mrs. Enniston would have sent a responsible person for it. He inclined to the belief that he had taken it to some friend for safe keeping. How to make him disclose its whereabouts and if possible give it up before a new claimant appeared, was the immediate question to be decided. Plonski was aware in an uncertain way, that Wilder was already on the track of it. His whole anxiety now was to get possession of it before that person appeared upon the scene, and at this moment he was farther from his object than he had been for weeks. It maddened him to think, that night after night, he had been lying within half an inch of the precious object of all his work, devising the most tremendous but futile schemes to secure it.

Plonski was a sagacious man. Disappointed, outwitted, chagrined, he did not lose his discretion. He knew that if he was to retrieve his loss now, it must be by the most prudent course. It would not do to frighten Mr. Evans and his granddaughter and make them appeal to the sympathy of the other parties. It was not prudent to let the possessors of the cup know what efforts he was making to get it. He must double his craft and begin again.

He wrote a letter hurriedly and sent it off to Chanfleur by McCune. It was indicative of his purpose and character.

"I am compelled to inform you," he said, "that the object of all our hopes and labors has again slipped out of my reach at the last moment. The details of the matter I will personally explain. It is enough for me to say now, that it has been taken out of the house under my very nose and in spite of all my precautions. I do not yet despair of accomplishing my purpose. Much of the present move is involved in mystery. I am inclined to think, however, that it is accidental and the result of a dotard's cunning and not part of our enemy's plan. I shall have to stay here until I learn something. But every effort must be made to find out if it has gone back to Enniston's. Someone must be sent up there so as not to lose time. I hope you will control your impatience. The stakes are too enormous in this game to admit of discouragement.   PLON."

"P. S.—If you have any suggestions to make, send McCune back with them. But I beg of you not to waste time with complaints and not to let your pique say anything on paper that your interests forbid.

P."

It is now necessary to explain what had taken place while Mrs. Sitwhite was revealing to Plonski the discovery of the cup in the next room. Mr. Evans had left Manuella and gone to his room avowedly to take a nap. Mrs. Sitwhite had closed Plonski's door, and he, in listening to her announcement, had let it remain closed until the messenger knocked. In reading and answering Chanfleur's note, at least fifteen minutes were consumed. Mr. Evans instead of going to bed, closed his door and, with unusual celerity of action, opened his closet, got his cup out, saw or thought he saw that it was not in the place he had put it, which only increased his nervous action. He threw the old waist-coat with which it had been wrapped upon the bed, placed the cup in his box, stuffed some bits of cotton that he pulled from the closet, down the sides of the box, pressed down the lid, the little nails still in it slipping easily into the nail holes, and then looked cautiously out into the hall. Plonski's door was shut, so was Mrs. Sitwhite's. In a moment he was slipping stealthily down the stairs. He went straight to Mrs. Holbrook's, where he was joined outside the door by Bob Holbrook who had a much larger bundle under his arm carefully wrapped. They got upon an uptown car, talking in low tones, confidentially. Mr. Evans appeared to have some difficulty in making the young man understand where he wanted to go. He insisted that they were to get out at "Turtle Bay," on his old friend, Martin Cruger's property. "Everybody," he said "knew Martin Cruger's property, he bought it during the panic of forty two." But alas Bob had never heard of Turtle Bay or Martin Cruger. By the merest accident, the young man saw when they had ridden a long distance, and the empty green lots were becoming plentiful, a big building near the river with an enormous sign on its roof, "Turtle Bay Brewery." As they got out of the car, Mr. Evans looked around in a vain endeavor to recognize his old friend's property. They stood for a moment on the southwest corner of the avenue and the cross street. A beer pavilion with an American and an Austrian flag lazily flying from the roof stood on the opposite corner. Chairs were scattered about on the elevated veranda and "Kaiser Beer" was announced in bold letters on the canvas awning. An orches-trion was droning inside. Not another building was visible on the entire square. A rickety board fence enclosed the three acres down to the next avenue and behind it was a depressed area with here and there picturesque outcroppings of- gneiss, inhabited only by dirty goats that ruminated amid the scraggly thorn apple and plantain that made the little wilderness green. They crossed this lot in a northeasterly direction and found that beyond was an outlaying district not even fenced. Heaps of rubbish shot down from the highways, made a ghastly circumference to an inner jungle of weeds, rocks and puddles. On the corner of what would very soon be the First avenue, but was now an unpaved roadway, rose a mass of rocks green with confervia and smooth with time. A little board on a stick bore this announcement. "These lots 25 by 100 for sale. Enquire of Martin Cruger's Sons, 51 Canal street." They climbed the rocks. Sloping eastward was a great tract of wild land, covered with weeds and promontories of rock. In the distance toward the river, were a few scattered houses.

Mr. Evans made Bob wait for him. "If Manuella should come down this street looking for us," he said, "you must be on the watch for her. I'll go down and find a spot. Give me the shovel. Mind you must look out for her."

Then with his box under his arm, he strolled off down into the great wild field, looked back once or twice to see if Bob was watching him, and finally disappeared behind one of the rocky hillocks. There, selecting a spot that seemed peculiarly isolated and out of sight, he dug a hole and put his box containing the cup in it. Then he stood a moment trying to impress the features of the immediate landscape upon his mind, and his childish task was accomplished.

CHAPTER XII.

THE ARREST OF MANUELLA.

Mrs. Sitwhite felt deeply hurt at the mystery in which her lodgers had plunged her. "To think," she said, "that a woman's own neice would do such a thing, when I never kept anything from her in my life, and I a-struggling and scraping from morning till night to keep 'em both comfortable."

All her efforts to make Manuella unbosom herself were vain. The girl kept her own counsel, whether it was because she suspected her aunt of acting in Plonski's interest or because she did not think her grandfather's vagaries worthy of so much investigation, let us not enquire. But from the hour of Mr. Evans return from his uptown exploit, a new chasm opened between the two women and the place grew daily more unbearable to Manuella. To add to her distress, Mr. Evans was too ill the next day after his adventure to get out of bed and when Plonski was called in to attend him, he found that the old gentleman had a slight fever and wandered a little in his mind. He immediately set about giving him his whole attention, and much as Manuella disliked the man, she had to acknowledge that his interest and fidelity were admirable. He bought medicines, ice and delicacies. He came into the dark room every hour and often sat by the bedside of the patient holding his hand.

His patience was heroic. But when nearly a week had elapsed and the old gentleman was convalescent, he had learned nothing. He began to get desperate. Word had come from Chanfleur that the cup had not been sent to Mrs. Enniston's and Plonski resolved to make a final effort to get the truth. He told Mrs. Sitwhite that she must force Manuella to disclose the facts. He so worked upon the woman's weakness that she entered unwittingly into his scheme. He invented a plausible story which won her sympathy and excited her cupidity. She grew to feel under his sophistry, that Manuella had wronged her deeply and deprived her of advantages that the cup would have secured. Before she was aware of it, her treatment of her neice grew into a petty persecution. In reply to the proposal that she should find out what her grandfather had done with the cup, Manuella flatly refused and said it was none of her aunt's business nor Plonski's. Then Mrs. Sitwhite accused her of being a treacherous, stuck-up and lazy-good-for-nothing; and Manuella reminded her that she was paying for her grandfather's board with her own money. In a moment of spite, Mrs. Sitwhite declared that they would all be happier if she would go away and support herself. As for her father, she and John could take care of him.

Manuella cried a good deal in secret over the unkindness of this, but she very soon found that Mrs. Sitwhite had a new air of independence. "If I wanted boarders," observed Mrs. Sitwhite, "I guess there are better people with more money and less airs than girls who are too big for their clothes."

This was unmistakably pointing at Plonski, and Manuella found that the man had influenced her grandfather also, who now spoke of him as a gentleman with correct notions of business. She saw that between them they meant to separate her from her grandfather if possible. Even John Sitwhite who had always preserved a coarse respect for her, now made open allusion to Princesses being in the way.

Mr. Evans, she suddenly noticed, had recurring spells of weakness and took to his bed in the dark room without any known cause, where he was shut up with Plonski for hours. Then it flashed upon her, that this man was exerting some kind of malign influence over the feeble old gentleman. She could not rid herself of the feeling. Plonski avoided her. He had embittered her aunt against her. He acted at times as if he was afraid of her clear, frank presence. The more she thought of it, the more convinced she became that they were in some way becoming involved in this man's toils and he and her aunt wanted to get rid of her so that they could carry out their plans. She tried to think of some one to whom she could go and explain all her fears and suspicions and ask for help. She could not fix upon anybody but Mrs. Holbrook.

It was a bright Sunday morning. She sat at the open window listening to the church bells. The sun was lying on the Long Island hills. Everything was unusually calm and bright without, and she thought of the many mornings when she had gone blithely, hand in hand with her grandfather to church. He was now lying in that miserable dark room, feeble and helpless. She got up impulsively and went to him. Plonski was already in the room.

"Grandpa," she said, "it is Sunday morning and the sun is shining. Can't you get up and sit at the window with me?"

"No," said Plonski. "He must not get up to-day. I forbid it."

"He shall get up if he desires it," replied the girl, resolutely but calmly. "This room is enough to kill him, without your assistance."

Plonski was too discreet to bandy words with an excited girl. He bowed and went straight to Mrs. Sitwhite.

"My dear," said Mr. Evans, in a faraway voice, "why, they told me you were going away, and I thought you had gone; I couldn't believe that you would go without seeing me. Yes, I'll get up and go to the window. What day did you say it was? Sunday?"

She put her arm about him and raised him up in the bed and kissed him.

"Don't believe them," she said. "I am not going away from you. Nothing shall part us, unless—" and she hesitated a moment as her hand felt the poor bones of his emaciated body; "unless you refuse to get well, Grandpa. You don't want me to go away, do you?"

He got hold of her as he replied and pulled her close to him.

"No, my child, but we can't have what we want. Both you and your aunt are unhappy together and I cannot have you unhappy."

"Then we will go away where we can be happy," she said. "I mean you and I."

He shook his head. "I cannot leave Cynthy," he mumbled, "she has no head for management."

The girl grasped him tightly. "Do you know what you are saying, Grandpa?" she asked almost piteously.

He fondled her a moment. "Yes, yes," he said, "but you confuse me so. You all confuse me. Everybody confuses me except the doctor. Where did Manuella go? Don't you know I want her? Yes, yes, my dear; never mind. We'll go and sit by the window." Then he began to weep.

A yearning tenderness came over her. She hung on him a moment in pathetic silence. A sense of loneliness and helplessness that was entirely new may have made her add a girlish tear of her own. She threw an old dressing gown over him, that enveloped him from head to foot, and assisting him to rise, he tottered towards the door leaning upon her.

There they were met by Mrs. Sitwhite in an unusual state of inflammation.

"Miss Castleton," she said, "it seems to me that you forget that this is my house and that's my father. Are you going to walk over us all?"

"No," replied Manuella, mildly, "I only want to get Grandpa to the window. I should think even you would like to see him come out of that room this beautiful morning."

"O, it doesn't make a bit of difference what I want or the doctor wants; you are going to have your own way, I suppose. Now, I just tell you I'm tired and sick of your ladyship's airs. Do you understand that?"

Manuella kept on her way with her grandfather and had reached the door of the sitting room. She shrank from a scene in the hallway. Mrs. Sitwhite caught hold of the old gentleman. "Pop," she cried, "you must go back to your bed. The doctor says you are to lie still."

"Cynthy," replied the old man, "how violent you are; I want to sit by the window." And, Manuella opening the door, they stepped into the room. John Sitwhite, in his shirt sleeves, was standing in front of the mantle with his feet wide apart, smoking his pipe. His two children were entertaining him with their athletics on the floor. Mrs. Sitwhite came into the room bristling. In this slight contest she had not had her way, and no one knew better than her husband that she had set out to have it when she left the room. A cynical smile was on his face as he saw Manuella quietly lead her grandfather to the window and seat him in his old place.

"John Sitwhite," exclaimed his wife, "will you stand by and see me walked over in my own house? The domineering airs of this creature are too much for human nature to put up with. It's come to this—one of us has got to leave this place."

"Cynthia," said Manuella, "you are excited and unreasonable. Do you want to throw me into the street?"

"I guess I'll have to if I ever get rid of you. I'm sick and tired of your airs and innocence. You're entirely too good for us. Why don't you take a hint and go?"

"What is it, my dear—what's the matter?" asked the old man. "You'll go, I'm sure, if Cynthia wants you to." And he caught hold of her as if afraid that she would take him at his word.

"It's nothing, Grandpa. Cynthy's got one of her spells. She'll get over it in a minute."

"Will she?" screamed Mrs. Sitwhite. "John Sitwhite, put that young lady's trunk out into the hall."

John looked at the ceiling and puffed a long column of smoke in that direction. Then he peered through the wreaths at Manuella, and it occurred to him that she looked a good deal like something he had read about, but he was not sure whether it was a princess or a saint. She was pale and composed. Her hand rested on the old man's shoulder, her dusky golden hair fell in luxuriant disorder about her neck and shoulders, her big beautiful eyes stared with helpless wonder at her aunt and turned expectantly upon John Sitwhite. Something in her helplessness or her beauty touched a masculine cord in the man and it gave out a gruff tone of magnanimity.

"Sis," said he, "don't be a fool. What do you want to throw the princess into the street for?"

"What for?" exclaimed Mrs. Sitwhite. "I tell you I'll have to, if I'm to have anything to say in my own house. It don't become you to call your lawful wife a fool, John Sitwhite, and if I am a fool I know how to look out for your interests when other people would rob you of your rights under your very nose."

"Robbin' be blowed," said John sententiously but emoliently. "Who's a robbin' me?"

"I don't think you are in your right mind, Cynthy," said Manuella. "I never tried to rob you. When you get over your passion you will regret your unkind words."

Mrs. Sitwhite had by this time got herself fairly between the sting of reproach and the lash of reprimand. Instead of having her way she invited attention to her unreasonableness. As was usual, this made her not only more unreasonable but more violent.

"Go on," she cried. "I'm a fool and I'm crazy. I'll be put out of my own house presently, I suppose. No, I won't. Don't you get that notion into your head." And then leaping from one insane accusation to another, she cried, as she shook her finger at Sitwhite, "It would be a nice accommodation for you both, wouldn't it, if I was? Do you s'pose I don't know what you want?"

At this Manuella uttered a little cry of remonstrance and John Sitwhite allowed a broad smile to extend over his face as if the suggestion were a happy one and had a promise of peace in it, if nothing more.

"Pop," continued Mrs. Sitwhite, her temper suddenly going off at a tangent as she approached her father. "That girl has put all sorts of bad notions into your head. Do you hear what I say? You've taken property out of my house that did not belong to you and I want you to go and bring it back, and John and I will go with you."

The old man was nervous and deprecating. He held up his hands in protest against his daughter's tone and manner, but his voice was weak and coaxing as he said, "Cynthy, Cynthy, my dear, don't talk that way. Everything will be explained in time. Don't you see you are making my little girl cry? You don't understand about the cup at all. Somebody has deceived you."

"I should think so," exclaimed Mrs. Sitwhite. "You ought to be ashamed of yourself for allowing it. The best thing for you to do now is to go at once and bring back the cup. I'll get a carriage and go with you. In fact the doctor's got one and it's waiting now."

The old man was helplessly patting the back of one hand with the palm of the other. "Yes, yes," he said musingly. "I suppose I must. I suppose I must."

"Then let me put your clothes on you, and do it at once. There will be no peace here till you bring it back."

He obediently made an effort to rise. Manuella, whose hand was still on his shoulder, pressed him gently back.

"You cannot go, Grandpa," she said; "you are not strong enough. Cynthy just now told you that you were not strong enough to get out of bed and sit by the window."

"Yes, yes," said the old man, "that is true too, but you all of you confuse me dreadfully."

"Come," said Mrs. Sitwhite catching hold of his dressing gown. "Go back to your room and get your clothes on."

Manuella was now bending over him. One arm was about his neck and her hair fell like a golden shield around him. Her face burned with indignation and shame—shame at the vulgarity of the contest.

"My grandfather shall not go out," she said resolutely, and with an appealing look toward John Sitwhite. "He is too weak and ill and I am sure you will not insist upon it, when you have got over your anger."

"Come," repeated Mrs. Sitwhite, pulling at him. and disregarding her neice. "The doctor is waiting. We must go and get the cup."

The two women were now almost touching each other over the old man. Mrs. Sitwhite's anxiety and determination were so much greater than the occasion called for, that even Manuella saw that something was behind all her pique and passion, pushing her on. What it was, she did not clearly understand, but she felt that to let go of her grandfather now, was to be separated from him perhaps forever. She did not reason upon the matter. Her affection acted through its own impulses. She got down on the floor and encircled him with her arms. "Grandpa," she said, "you must listen to me. I don't know what they want to do with you, but I love you and I do not want you to go out. Tell them that you will stay here."

Mrs. Sitwhite stepped back a pace or two. She was flushed about the eyes and pinched about the mouth.

"It's come to this," said she, "that either you or I must be mistress here and we might as well settle it now."

Mrs. Sitwhite was unconsciously dramatic. She drew herself up and pointed to the door as she said—

"I want you to leave my room."

Manuella stared at her a moment with the new curiosity of innocence, for the first time confronted with the cruelty of her own sex.

"I cannot leave the room, Cynthy, for I have no other room to go to, and I shall not leave my grandfather, for I feel that he needs me now more than he ever did before."

This was said mildly, almost beseechingly, but it utterly failed of its purpose.

"You won't," Mrs. Sitwhite exclaimed harshly, "you'll have your way to the last, will you? Well, we'll see about it."

Then in a purely feminine paroxysm of imbecility, she flew to the little chamber Where Manuella slept, tore the door open and seizing the little trunk that contained all of the girl's scanty wardrobe, she dragged it by one of the handles into the room, making a great deal of unnecessary noise in her demonstration and ripping up the carpet. For a moment, she stood with one hand on the knob of the hall door and the other holding the trunk, a fine picture of weakness trying to assume the air of strength. The old man had caught hold of Manuella and the two were locked in each other's embrace, making a futile but very pretty protest without words. John held his pipe suspended half way to his open mouth. In another instant they expected to see the innocent trunk hurled into the hallway. The angry woman had gathered all her energies for the act and it was to be typical of Manuella's ignominious expulsion. But just at this present crisis, there came a loud and somewhat imperative rap on the door which Mrs. Sitwhite was holding.

In her present mood of impetuosity she turned the knob, threw the door open, and in walked Mr. John Wilder and Colin Carteret.

It is doubtful if these men, in their varied experiences as officer and artist, ever before came suddenly upon a tableau of more incomprehensible picture sequences and vivid details. The interrupted emotions of the group were still burning, and there at the window, at once the focus and the finish of the picture, stood beauty, rising out of this suspended brawl like Cordelia herself, mute and statuesque with shame and surprise, but pensively beaming withal.

Wilder, who was in advance, took in the odd situation with his quick eye, and then deliberately shut the door before he said a word. With his usual celerity of judgment he cleared away all explanations, dispensed with apologies and prevented delays by announcing himself as an officer of the law, and letting Mr. John Sitwhite get a glimpse of his official badge under his coat. Mrs. Sitwhite's anger faded at once into a mute amazement and Manueella's surprise bloomed into a royal astonishment.

"Officer," repeated John Sitwhite mechanically.

"Yes, sir, we have come to see Mr. Eben Evans on a little private business."

"About the cup?" asked Mrs. Sitwhite with something like a gasp.

Wilder looked at her and at the trunk by her side. "Madame," said he, "is Mr. Evans your lodger?"

"He's my father. If you'll sit down, gentlemen, I'll explain everything. The old man's a little confused in his head and" dropping her voice, "I have a great deal of trouble in managing him."

"Is this Mr. Evans?" asked Wilder, pulling up a chair towards the old gentlemen, and then a moment later he said to Mr. Evans himself, "This is Mr. Carteret, who has come in reply to your letter."

"Yes, yes," mumbled Mr. Evans; "you are quite welcome gentlemen. This is Manuella. I forget whether I mentioned her in my letter or not."

"You have a cup in your possession," continued Wilder, as Carteret, who had bowed mutely, took a position on one side and made a rather awkward effort not to look at Manuella too steadily. "We have come to ask you a few questions about it. Where is it?"

"It's safe—quite safe, sir," replied the old man, with a chuckle. "I've taken good care of it. You know there was a large reward offered for it?"

Carteret ejaculated something, but Wilder gave him a nudge which was meant to imply a desire to carry on the conversation himself.

"That's just it," broke in Mrs. Sitwhite; "he's taken it away out of the house, in spite of me. I was trying to get him to go and bring it back when you came in. But this young woman interfered and now I suppose it's gone forever."

The indifference of the two visitors to the possible loss of the cup, struck Mrs. Sitwhite as somewhat strange. But as the officer tilted himself back in his chair as if disposed to listen to all she had to say, she went on. "My father does not know the value of it and he's old and a little forgetful," significantly tapping her forehead with her finger for the enlightenment of her visitors.

"He wrote to Carteret," said Wilder, "informing him that he had the cup. I understand you to say he hasn't got it now."

"You see he took it out of the house when my back was turned," replied Mrs. Sitwhite. "What he has done with it, the Lord only knows."

"When your back was turned," repeated Wilder.

"Why, yes, we have to watch him," dropping her voice, "he's getting old."

"Can you get the cup for us, Mr. Evans?"

"Gentlemen," said Manuella, "my grandfather has been very ill, I took him out of his bed to sit by this window. He is not strong enough to go out. He has never been a well man since that cup came into the house."

"But why did he take it out of the house?"

"Yes, answer that," said Mrs. Sitwhite, "that's what I want to know."

"I suppose," replied Manuella demurely, "that he was afraid it would be stolen here."

"Stolen," exclaimed Mrs. Sitwhite; "who is the thief, I'd like to know, in my family? John, did you ever hear anything to beat that?"

"I think," said Manuella, "he took it away so that the doctor could not get it."

"Well, I never," gasped Mrs. Sitwhite.

"Doctor?" asked Wilder, "who's the doctor?"

"Dr. Plonski," replied the girl.

"Doctor Plonski," repeated Wilder, letting his tilted chair came to the floor with an audible crack. "Did Doctor Plonski want the cup, Mr. Evans?"

"Dr. Plonski is a gentleman," said the old man apologetically.

"To be sure he is," added Mrs. Sitwhite energetically.

"Well," remarked Wilder with a slight smile, "who is it that refuses to believe it?"

Mrs. Sitwhite assumed an air of quiet reticence, which plainly said, "Now it is coming without my assistance." She looked at her niece with what was intended for calm, but ruthless justice, and thus assailed, Manuella said:

"Cynthy, I don't know what you mean, but you never treated me unkindly until the doctor came here, and if these gentlemen had not come in, you would have put me out of the house, because I love my grandfather and try to protect him. Then I should have been separated from him and I do not know what would have happened to him."

"Does Dr. Plonski live in this house?" asked Wilder.

There was a simultaneous assent.

"On this floor?"

Manuella nodded her head.

"He moved in," replied the accommodating Mrs. Sitwhite, "just before pop was taken sick."

"Yes," assented Wilder, reversing the statement, "Pop was taken sick just after he moved in. Did Dr. Plonski want to buy your cup, Mr. Evans?"

"Mrs. Enniston gave me the cup," said Mr. Evans. "I've got her letter. Ella, where is that letter?"

"Yes, yes, I see," interrupted Wilder "Mrs. Enniston gave you the cup, but did Dr. Plonski offer to buy it?"

"Tell him, Grandpa," said Manuella, "Dr. Plonski had tried every means to get possession of it and you hid it away, because you were not quite sure it was your property."

"Yes," said the old gentleman. "You know Mr. Carteret advertised for it?"

"Yes, yes," broke in Wilder again, and effectually preventing Mr. Carteret from making a blunt denial. "Then you can get it for Mr. Carteret if he should want it?"

"O, yes," replied Mr. Evans with a chuckle. "It's quite safe, I assure you."

"We'll get him to bring it back," said Mrs. Sitwhite," as soon as he is able to go out. He's too weak now; then when you come again we'll have it for you safe and sound."

"You don't think it would be safe for him to go for it to-day?" remarked Wilder.

"O, dear, no."

The officer looked from the aunt to the niece as if expecting the latter to say something, but Manuella only wore a subtle look of intelligence.

"That's the way to settle it," said Carteret. "We'll call again when the old gentleman is in better condition. We're only annoying him now."

"Thank you," said Mrs. Sitwhite, "and we'll try and have it here for you. He'll be stronger in a few days."

Wilder watched the two women. One was trying to close out the interview at that stage; the other was nervous and undecided as if she had something she would like to say.

Wilder astonished everybody by getting up, addressing himself to Mrs. Sitwhite and saying, "My dear madame you are very kind, but I have a disagreeable duty to perform. Your father is what we call a receiver of stolen property and his granddaughter is an accessory. There are great interests involved in this cup and I must arrest him and the young lady. If you will see that he is properly attired as soon as possible, I should like it. I propose to take them both with me and I don't want any objections made, and will not have any interference."

The effect of this was startling. Manuella was holding fast to her grandfather with sympathetic tenderness and staring at the speaker.

Mrs. Sitwhite took a step backward as if to get out of the way of authority, and Carteret, jumping up, exclaimed:

"O, come now, the d——d cup isn't worth it; I protest. What possible use can it be to arrest these people?"

John Wilder walked over to the young woman at the window and said to her in a low tone: "Do as I tell you and I will prove your friend." Then in a louder tone, as he laid his hand on Mr. Evan's shoulder: "Come, sir, you and your granddaughter must go with me."

Mrs. Sitwhite appeared to be somewhat stunned by the *coup*. She repeated the word, "arrested" several times as if trying to comprehend it, and then bolted suddenly from the room.

Carteret was the most excited person of the group. He asked Wilder if he insisted on taking these people into custody. Wilder replied calmly that he most assuredly did.

"Then," said Carteret, addressing himself to Manuella with a deprecatory manner, "I wish to disavow all purpose or responsibility in the matter. I should not have consented to come here, had I known the intention of the officer, and I am bound to tell you that, considering it a piece of unnecessary interference on a most trivial pretext, I am ready to stand your friend in anything that may occur."

The young lady made a slight bow of acknowledgment, that was all the more fascinating to Carteret on account of the trepidation that was mingled with it.

"If you will permit me, I will go with you," continued Carteret, who found it a difficulty to bring his one-sided conversation with the girl to a sudden close.

She expressed her thanks only with her eyes as she assisted her grandfather to rise.

"Do you understand, Grandpa," she said, "that we are to go with these gentlemen?"

"Yes, yes;" said Mr. Evans. "I understand; I must go with Mr. Carteret and get his cup for him. But, my dear, you must not go. You don't understand these things."

"I shall go with you," she replied. "I know you will be comfortable if I am with you."

Carteret looked on with pity and admiration as the girl led the old man back to his dark room. Then he took to walking up and down the room with a great deal of suppressed indignation in his arms and face, utterly ignoring Mr. Sitwhite who had sat down upon an overturned chair, and disdaining to speak to John Wilder, who walked out into the hall and leaning on the handrail, pretended not to watch the dark room and the door next to it.

In half an hour he was assisting Mr. Evans slowly down the stairs, and Carteret who was close behind him with Manuella, was endeavoring to cheer that young lady to the best of his ability.

There was a coach waiting at the doorway for Mr. Plonski. Some little parley with the driver took place and then the quartette got in and went rattling up the street, to the intense interest of a group of boys and men who had witnessed the departure.

They had not been gone ten minutes when Plonski reappeared upon the scene. He had been round to Holbrook's, but had evidently learned nothing.

CHAPTER XIII.

A RETURN FROM THE DEAD.

It is necessary to return now to the Samaritan Hospital in Philadelphia. When John Wilder left the bedside of Kate Haviland the woman was in a pitiable state of nervous excitement. The act of confession was to her a finality. Now that the world would know her shame and guilt, and her name must go back to her poor old mother associated with a terrible crime, she wanted to hide away in death. She would make an hour's sensation in the papers and be forgotten. But even that was a more terrible thing to contemplate than she had anticipated, now that it was an irremediable fact. Her condition grew worse and worse as she dwelt on the result. She tossed and turned on the bed and groaned. The awful consciousness that she was now an exposed murderess, grew with every moment to something of the nature of a continuous fright. Her heart beat violently, her cheek fluttered, her mouth was parched. She wanted to scream, and when she made the effort, she found that she had no power over the vocal cords. The matron came and found her gesticulating mutely and staring wildly about her. "I am dying," she whispered hoarsely: "I'd like to see the doctor just once more."

He had gone to New York and would not be back until late at night or the next morning.

The matron tried to soothe her. She got down and passed her hands softly over the throbbing temples and spoke to her with a woman's instinctive adroitness and tenderness.

"What is it you are thinking about?" she said. "Don't you want to tell it to me?"

The girl did not heed her but writhed and moaned piteously.

"Let me tell *you* something," said the matron, "try and listen to me. An awful accident had occurred; the New York officer who was here has been killed."

"What, do you say?" exclaimed the patient, clutching at the attendant.

"I say the officer who was here has been killed. One of the stone windlasses fell upon him as he was passing the new wing. I have just heard of it. It must have happened immediately after he left you, for the janitor told me he came straight from the main entrance. Don't stare at me that way, for God's sake, Miss; here, let me lift you up."

But Miss Haviland's stare grew stony and set. Something like a ghastly smile settled upon her mouth. The matron seized her hand and rubbed it. When she released it it fell to the bed. Then, alarmed, she went hurriedly to a bell pull and summoned medical aid. In a moment or two, one of the subordinate members of the medical staff came in. He was a young man with a self satisfied and perfunctory air. He picked up the hand of the patient, felt the pulse and dropped it. "Well, you expected it, didn't you?" he asked.

"I did," replied the matron, "but not so suddenly."

The doctor walked away, looked out of the window, and casually asked when Dr. Sanger would be back. He then turned, drummed a moment on the pane, came back, put his hand carelessly under the chin of the unconscious woman and turned the face upward, for it had fallen over. "Handsome girl," he remarked, taking an artistic view of the face as he held it. "Any record?"

The matron shook her head and presently the doctor sauntered out. He was met at the door by the janitor with a message from the Coroner. Somebody was required to attend the inquest of the dead officer. He growled and said he supposed he must go, but he didn't know anything about it. He didn't see why Sanger couldn't stay at home when disagreeable things occurred.

The inquest was held the next morning. Wilder was there and it was from this young doctor that he learned of Kate Haviland's death. At about the same hour, Dr. Follen Sanger arrived at the hospital from New York. He met the matron in the main hall. "I've brought Dr. Ferris with me," he said, "to see Number Six." Miss Haviland was thus designated in the hospital. "He will be here presently. I want you to make him as comfortable as possible."

"It is too late, Doctor," replied the woman.

"What do you mean?"

"She died last night."

He started a little, hesitated a moment and then asked, "Where is she?"

"I haven't moved her yet," said the woman. "She asked for you. She can go out to-day, I suppose. We want the bed."

He brushed passed her without replying; went straight to room number six and entering, closed and locked the door behind him. There lay the beautiful white figure as the matron had composed it. He stalked to the bedside with more eagerness than tenderness and stood staring at the pale face with an air of intense disappointment.

Doctor Follen Sanger was not a man of acute sensibilities. The vital nature asserted itself in him defiantly. His strong florid face was healthily handsome, and the glossy black whiskers only added to the air of strong masculine will that was apparent in his almost imperceptible eyelids, his erect figure and his general executive manner. That he was affected in some way by the sudden death of the woman was plain, but it was less grief than pique and indignation, as if he had been robbed. He could not have been more than thirty and as he stood there over the corpse, he might have been summed up by an observer as a man of action, not reflection, who might save a patent, but could scarcely consider him.

He appeared to be in doubt about something. He turned and walked the room several times and coming back to the bedside, bent down and kissed the white face on the cold lips. He drew back his head a few inches suddenly and then repeated the kiss. The lips were not as cold as he had expected to find them. In an instant he had torn open the white dress, regardless of all else and run his hand in upon her heart. He turned his head in an attitude of intense application. He put his ear down hard upon her bosom and listened. The concentrated mental effort appeared to relax a little as if with disappointment. Suddenly he strode to the bell, pulled it violently, unlocked the door, and then returned to the bedside. "Bring me a stethescope and a lancet case from my room," he said, as the call was answered, "and send Dr. Ferris here the moment he arrives."

He had taken off his coat, thrown it on a chair and was unbuttoning his cuffs when the attendant returned.

"Cloths and water?" asked the man, as he looked at the bed.

"No. Lock the door and stay here," said the doctor gruffly.

"Suspended animation?"

"Perhaps. Get her sleeve up. Cut it—cut it, where's your scissors, man?"

The methods of the two men were wholly unlike. The attendant lifted the long stiff arm. with gentle care and ran his knife under the sleeve deliberately and daintily. The other tore away her dress and pushed the stethescope down upon the heart with an eager rudeness that may have sprung from intensity of interest or from inconsiderate vehemence of manner. His was not the precise and patient process of the trained and experienced practitioner.

Suddenly he threw the instrument upon the bed and took up the case of lancets. Both men were intensely engrossed in their work. Doctor Sanger pulled the inanimate form over on its side to the edge of the bed. He threw open the blinds at the window violently and got down upon his knees as his companion held the rigid white arm, which even in death was round and beautiful.

At the first puncture of the lancet, the white flesh seemed bloodless and as the two men breathlessly watched the wound, you could have heard the heart of one of them beating. It was, doubtless, that of the attendant who was of a highly nervous organization. They bent their heads down close to the flesh of the helpless woman. A single drop of blood oozed sluggishly from the cut, stood like a bead on the edge of the wound and then trickled in a red course across the surface of the arm and rolled off. Another followed. Then slowly, like bubbles, the crimson drops came one after the other.

The younger of the men gave an audible gasp.

"Quick," said Doctor Sanger, getting up. "Get all the ammonia there is in the pharmacy and send Mrs. Pendleton, the nurse, with hot water and cloths."

When the young man had disappeared, the doctor drew the form of the young woman back into the bed, and while he was affixing a piece of adhesive plaster over the cut in the arm, Doctor Ferris arrived.

He was a middle-aged man, thin, white faced, reflective and precise; with a soft thin voice and correspondingly soft thin sidewiskers of iron gray color, fine intelligent features and a rather dreamy blue eye. Doctor Sanger's manner to him was one of respectful deference. He made a few words of explanation, and Doctor Ferris, putting on a pair of spectacles, went to the bedside and lifted the eyelid of the patient.

"Humph," he said. "You've had a lancet into her,"

"Yes," replied Dr. Sanger, "I thought it was the most decisive."

"It wasn't necessary," said Dr. Ferris. "Why didn't you look at the pupil. Have you got a battery handy?"

From this moment the preparations went on with deliberation and nicety. For hours the two men of science stood over the inanimate form trying to snatch the life back from the mysterious middle ground of catalepsy. At last there were some faint rewarding signs, and finally there issued a long, low moan from the woman's mouth—a tremor ran through her and she opened her eyes.

Dr. Ferris sat down and fanned himself. "It's a fine case of hysteria, Sanger," he said. "If I were you I'd get good brandy down her. I'll go now and get some of the railroad dirt off."

By four o'clock Kate Haviland was able to speak, and the first words that Dr. Sanger, who was alone with her, said, were:

"You must make up your mind to live."

"O Doctor, she moaned," in a low voice, "what shall I live for?"

"For me," he said, coming very close to her, "if you hav'n't anything else. I desire it and insist on it."

She tried to turn her face away, as if the idea tired her, but he put his hand against her cheek and prevented her.

"I'm not going to distress you now," he said, "with my conversation, but you must understand that you cannot die. My will is stronger than yours. I've pulled you out of the jaws of death."

"Cruelly," she murmured.

"No, don't say that. I wouldn't have done it if I hadn't thought I could make life a little pleasanter for you."

She shook her head and he said, "There, don't worry yourself about me. I'm going to cure you and then, if you'll let me, help you. Don't talk to the nurse and I'll look in in an hour."

The simple fact was that Dr. Sanger was irremediably in love with his patient. Mrs. Pendleton had suspected it for some time. He had never shown such anxiety about any of the other inmates of the hospital. He had gone all the way to New York to fetch Dr. Ferris to this case, Dr. Ferris being his last resort in all emergencies. His solicitude had grown to a deep concern that betrayed itself to his staff and was by some of the younger members commented upon as unprofessional. Up to the time of Kate Haviland's recovery from the cataleptic attack, he had avoided all direct reference to his feelings, in the many sittings he had had with her at the bedside, but now he did not hesitate to let her know that his interest was extra-professional. It was done indirectly and solicitously; but he more than once intimated to her that he had saved her life and had a claim on it. She had replied to him on one of these occasions, that it was not worth saving, and he told her that if she valued it so lightly she ought not to hesitate to give it to him, "for you cannot know till I have shown you, how much I prize it." So she got to know very speedily that the man loved her and was willing to marry her when she recovered her health. At first she refused to listen to his indirect proposals, and told him she had no heart and no love for anybody; and once she went so far as to tell him, that if he knew her story, he would pity and despise her. This was when the first flush of convalescent color or of shame had come into her cheeks and made her handsomer than ever.

"I do not care for your story," he said, "and do not want to hear it. Let your past be buried and make a new life for yourself." His strenuous passion could not be rebuffed and his obdurate will overcame all her objections. "As you must live," said he, "it will be better to live under the protection of my name."

This argument was the most effective of all. She thought it over long and seriously and grew to contemplate the proposal with a cold complacency.

And all this time a new treatment, suggested by Dr. Ferris, who had stayed long enough to see its efficacy and had then gone back to New York, was carrying her farther and farther from the possibility of dying. She got so she ate her toast and tea regularly and bit a piece of rare steak under orders. On Dr. Ferris' theory that it was a case of hysteria aggravated by some powerful mental excitement and needed an iron will and gentle moral nursing, Dr. Sanger was really pulling her upon her feet in spite of her own protests. Although love was impossible for her, he succeeded in diverting her attention somewhat from her own miseries. She was too weak and indifferent to oppose him with any vigor and she was too much of a woman not to feel pleased at his strong masculine devotion. Three weeks of this strange courtship and convalescence passed. She sat up and spent the hours with the doctor, pensively listening and wondering. She had thought over all the circumstances of her life and tried to penetrate the silence and mystery that had followed her rash act. Wilder, supposing her to be dying, had told her enough to make her believe that he was the only person who had guessed her secret, and Wilder she now believed to be dead. If she were to resume her place in the world, what more desirable than to change her name and all the conditions of her life by marrying the doctor? If there must come an exposure at some time, would it not be preferable to have one protector and friend who was devoted to her? Then came the inevitable repugnance to a life of deception and constant fear, and she asked herself if it would not be better to make a clean breast of it all to the doctor. But she could never bring herself to lay the crime, at which in her normal moments she now shuddered, on the altar of this man's affection. She shrank from turning the unreasonable passion that had taken possession of him into a pitying horror, and there was, too, a weak fear, let it be acknowledged, Of losing the only thing in the world that had come to her in her desolation with a strange, self-sacrificing, protecting tenderness. She confessed to herself as she listened to the doctor that, perhaps, if she had met him before another man had crossed her path, she might have loved him, but now she could only submit to him with esteem. He wholly lacked the soft and winning graces that had first caught her. There was no sentiment or moonlight cadences in his affection, but there was a strong, self-reliant, admirable and indomitable will, to which she paid a woman's unconscious deference. All the feminine helplessness of her nature, enhanced as it was by the circumstances, was inclined to lean upon him restfully and unquestioningly.

As for Dr. Sanger, he had made up his mind to possess her, and if fear on her side had its own set of impulses and reasons, desire on his furnished its subtle sophistries and illusions. He would not believe her past was clouded by any event that could darken his great passion or interfere with his great purpose. He would redeem and own her. That was enough.

One day as she sat at the window, he told her that he was going to marry her. She looked at him with a placid expression which said: "I have tried to prevent you and I have failed."

"You no longer object as you once did," he continued, "and I believe you are growing to like me a little." She made no reply and he kept on, becoming confidential and earnest. "I have never told you much about myself, my ambitions and purposes. Are you not interested?"

She nodded her head languidly. "I'm out of place here," he continued. "I was not made to study morbid human nature, but to deal with events. I'm going to leave Philadelphia."

"Are you going abroad?" she asked with sudden interest.

"No. Do you want to go abroad?"

"Yes, above all else."

"Marry me at once," said he abruptly, "and I'll take you abroad."

"To live?"

"That would be impossible. Listen to me and you will understand. My father is one of the most influential politicians in the State of New York. He has made and un-made governors. I have just been on to see him and he has promised me the position of Health Inspector of the port of New York. It is one of the richest political gifts in the possession of his party. It makes my future secure against all the mishaps of life. You will marry a man of influence and means and not a struggling doctor. To run away from this chance would be madness."

"New York," she repeated vaguely.

"Yes, it is the one place for me."

"And you will be honored; you will go into society; you will lead a gay life. What kind of a wife do you think I would make for such a position? I who dread society, who have no education, no accomplishments, no name even—"

"It is enough that I want you for myself, not for society. If you insist, you shall be a recluse. I am not asking for education or name or accomplishments. You are good enough as you are to be my wife. Will you?"

She made no answer.

"I have never asked you," he said, "about your past. Tell me now if there is anything to prevent you marrying me. I mean anything aside from your disinclination."

"Nothing," she replied promptly, "except the knowledge that you will be disappointed in me."

"And if you were assured on that point, every obstacle would be removed?"

His persistency made her smile in spite of herself.

"Tell me," he continued getting very close to her, "you do not belong to anybody else?"

"No," instantly.

"There is nobody to whom you have belonged?"

"No," unconsciously drawing a little away as he almost brushed her face with his black whiskers.

"And there is nobody," he kept on, carrying the subject a point further into the possibilities, "to whom you ought to belong."

With a woman's discernment, she seized the idea that was behind these questions.

"Doctor Sanger, there is nobody on earth but my mother, who ever professed to love me. In that direction there is nothing that I can be ashamed of."

"Enough then," he said, "I ask you now again to be my wife. As to the rest, I will never question you of your past. It shall be buried forever. Only consent to become mine, and my great love will protect and help you."

She let him take her hand and after a moment's hesitation she said: "Doctor, if a woman who does not love you as she ought to love you, who is every way unfit to be your associate, is worth having, you may take me."

He stood up and pressed her hand. Then he kissed her on the forehead. He was too much occupied with his own emotions to notice that there was water in her eyes.

One week later they were married quietly and Kate Haviland set out for New York as Mrs. Follen Sanger.

CHAPTER XIV.

MR. PLONSKI OUTWITS WILDER.

The coach containing John Wilder and his prisoners rattled away from the Terrace in the direction of the Third avenue. Its occupants were silent save when Mr. Carteret made some inquiry of the girl who sat next him, relating to her comfort or intended to be an expression of sympathy.

They had gone some distance up the Third avenue, when the young man rather gruffly wanted to know where Mr. Wilder was taking them. But that personage only grunted something that was unintelligible in the rattle of the vehicle. They stopped at an old fashioned hostelry on the corner of Twenty-fourth street, known as the Bull's Head, where they were detained nearly an hour in an upstairs parlor, while Wilder was telegraphing in the office. The coachman was discharged and about two o'clock another arrived. They were then taken into the fresh vehicle and driven to a large house in Fifteenth street near Irving place.

Mr. Evans and Manuella were silent and passive, but Carteret was suspicious, indignant and outspoken. The party were met in the hallway by a stout and comfortable looking woman who saluted Wilder familiarly.

He introduced his Prisoners. "Put them in the nicest rooms you've got," he said, "and take the best care of them. I may want them at any moment."

Manuella looked about her with a girl's anxiety and fear. She did not understand it. A confused suspicion was growing in her mind that she was in some new kind of toils. Wilder's reticence did not reassure her, and unconsciously she looked to Carteret.

"Trust me," said that young man in a whisper to her. "I do not like this any more than you do, but I shall not leave you without protection."

She gave him a grateful look that went to his heart and thus encouraged, he pulled her on one side while Wilder was conversing with the landlady, and added:

"I want you to understand that this annoyance is not of my seeking, and the whole business is against my earnest protest. This man has no right to take you out of your home on a mere trumpery suspicion and without a warrant, and I do not intend to stand by and see the injustice committed, if there are any means of preventing it."

He could say no more, for Wilder interrupted him, and Mr. Evans and his granddaughter were taken upstairs. When they had disappeared he looked at Wilder as if expecting an explanation, and as there was no disposition on

Wilder's part to make one, Carteret said, "I don't like this affair at all. It seems to me altogether irregular and unwarrantable. Why don't you take these people before a justice and make a complaint?"

Wilder smiled. "They'll be very comfortable here till I want them, and you can look after their comfort. Are you going my way?"

"No, I don't like your way. I shall stay here and find out about this house."

"Do so, but don't, I beg you, undertake to remove my friends without consulting me."

The men then bowed and separated, Carteret wearing an expression of virtuous indignation and Wilder smiling.

The officer crossed Union Square and was just turning into Broadway, when some one hailed him from a coupe. It proved to be Dr. Wollendorf.

"I've been looking for you," he said. "Can't you get in? I want to talk to you."

"If you will drive me to East Nineteenth street," replied Wilder, "I will get in."

The doctor looked at his old-fashioned watch. "I want to catch that four-thirty train—how long will it take me?"

"Fifteen minutes."

"Get in."

"Affairs at Coe's Grove," said the doctor, when Wilder was seated and the vehicle had started, "have got to be exceedingly interesting for me—thanks to you and your Toltec Cup. I am regarded as a phenomenal combination of pariah and ghoul. The finger of rural scorn is pointed at me if I go outside my own fence. The entire community believes that I am actuated by a devilish spite against the memory of the late Mr. Enniston. Dr. Flockton last Sunday, a week ago, preached a sermon on the fate of those who ruthlessly assail the reputations worthy men have left behind them. The villagers would like an excuse to ride me on a rail."

"I wonder what those same villagers would say if they knew the late Mr. Enniston's story and his tragic fate," Wilder thought musingly. "I don't see what I can do for you, Doctor; I can't allay village gossip. If I were you I'd go to Mrs. Enniston and tell her what you already know, and get her to stop the tattle."

"That's what I want to consult you about," said the doctor. "I don't want to sacrifice my property and move out. In the first place I am attached to it, and in the second place that would be a corroboration of their nonsense. On the other hand, if the truth gets out, I shall be mixed up in the investigation most unpleasantly."

"It seems to me," said Wilder, "that you are not half so much of a coward as you would make me believe."

"I'm a lover of peace and quiet," said the doctor, "and the town would never forgive me if I helped to upset their idol."

"Have you heard anything more about the cup?" asked Wilder.

"Confound the cup," ejaculated the doctor. "I was in hopes you had given up that *ignus fatuus.*"

"I intend to find it," replied Wilder calmly.

"Well, I wish," said the doctor, "that your valuable services were better employed. If you will come to Coe's Grove, I will engage you at better employment."

"I will run up in a few days," replied Wilder, "and see if I can give you any assistance. This is my place to get out."

He shook hands with the doctor, who left him standing once more in front of O'Reardon's Terrace.

Without any delay the officer went up and knocked at Plonski's door. It stood ajar and opened as he rapped. Mr. Plonski was in Mrs. Sitwhite's apartment, so John Wilder without hesitancy, walked in and sat down by the window.

He must have waited fifteen minutes before Plonski appeared at his own door. Wilder did not get up and Plonski walked in and regarded him with some astonishment.

"I need not ask you to make yourself at home," he said, shutting the door and turning the key, "but you came rather sooner than I expected."

"You knew I'd come!"

"I did, of course."

"And you probably know what I came for?"

"I certainly do."

"We shall get rid of a good deal of explanation," said Wilder.

"You might have saved us both a great deal of trouble if you had come to me in the first place," rejoined Plonski, seating himself in front of Wilder, who had settled into a patient attitude.

"You think I have come for the cup?"

"Nonsense, I'm the last man you would come to for that. You came to me to learn if you could, what it is that makes a Toltec Cup so valuable."

Wilder smiled and nodded his head. "Are you prepared to tell me? I acknowledge that a cup that instigates murder, grave robbery, conspiracy, and prompts a gentleman of your good taste to live in this place, must be of extraordinary value."

"Inspector," said Plonski, with great deliberation, "you are conceded to be a very clever man in your line. I never disputed it till now. You must have found out by this time that murder and grave robbery are no part of my endeavor to get the cup."

"You'll tell me presently that you didn't put Therese in Enniston's house, and that the cup wasn't stolen immediately after Enniston's death."

"No, I'll not. If you'll permit me, I'll tell you the exact truth and would have done so at the start if you had come to me. It is no part of my scheme to involve myself with the police in trying to secure possession of the cup"

"Was there no way of getting it honestly?"

"Pardon me, we claim to be owners of the cup, and cannot very well steal what is our own."

"It seems to me," said Wilder, "that I've got a pretty good case of theft and conspiracy against you."

"I dare say it does. Why didn't you arrest me instead of taking that old man and his granddaughter?"

"That's an idle question. They've got the cup and you haven't."

"But what will you do with it when you get it?"

"Focus the conspiracy on myself and then I shall be better able to handle it."

"I see," said Plonski, "that I shall have to make a clean breast of the whole matter to get the idea of conspiracy out of your head."

"You will, indeed," replied Wilder.

"Then have a little patience and I will tell you as briefly as possible the story of this cup. Of course you must know that its value is not an intrinsic one."

Plonski leaned one arm on the little table near him and spoke deliberately and slowly. Wilder neither assented nor dissented to anything he said in his narrative.

"This cup," he continued, "was brought from Mexico to Spain during the Spanish conquest by Don Varges Monteleone, one of Cortez's officers, with a great deal of other plunder. It remained in the Monteleone family for several generations, and, according to their traditions, had a curious family history. It was blessed by a papal nuncio during the reign of Phillip II, and its possession by a son of the original Don appears to have brought him the most extraordinary good fortune, for he acquired vast estates in Catalonia. During the reign of Charles II, and while the disastrous war was waging with France, the cup passed by the marriage of a daughter into a rival branch of the family, at the head of which was the Count Don Lucas Cortina, and it is said that the fortunes of this impoverished count began to change the moment he became possessor of the cup. However exaggerated these family stories may be, it is nevertheless certain that a distinct superstition was associated with the cup. It remained in the family of the Cortinas until the abdication of Charles IV, when it again passed over by the Spanish system of inter-marriage to the decendants of the original Don, still living in Saragossa. The feuds and intrigues for the possession of the cup would make a bulky romance. Both families claimed it. In 1847, I think it was, the cup was carried out of the country by a profligate and reckless young man, who was an officer of Queen Isabella's and had incurred her displeasure. He died in Mexico or Louisana in 1860, and his personal effects were confiscated for debt; but a servant of his secured most of his valuables and sailed from New Orleans to return to Spain. The vessel was wrecked in the Gulf of Mexico, and the survivors picked up by an American captain. Among those who died on the way to New York was the servant, and he gave the cup to the captain.

"The efforts of the two Spanish families to recover the cup took definite shape about a year ago. Both were anxious to recover what they regarded as a sort of talisman, and being in Paris I accidentally met the agent of the Cortina's, who offered to pay me a very handsome sum to undertake its recovery; but he warned me that the Monteleones were also searching for it. I need not tell you that the return of the cup will be worth a good deal of money to me, but all my endeavors to secure it have been made to appear like a conspiracy, simply because I had to guard against the knowledge coming to the agents of the rival house. I have here all the documentary proof of what I have told you. I am willing to pay you a fair share for possession of the cup, and I need not tell you that it is comparatively valueless except to these Spanish families, who invest it with a superstitious charm. I ought to say to you also that from the moment you went to Coe's Grove I had to be more than ever circumspect, for I did not know for some time that you were not employed by the rival house."

Wilder listened to this tale without any visible signs of emotion. When it was completed he said:

"What do you estimate the cup to be worth to you?"

"I'll be frank with you," replied Plonski. "I might squeeze eight or ten thousand dollars out of one of the estates if I had it in my possession. There is no limit to the superstition of those people. Have you ever been in Spain?"

"What will you give this old man if he puts it in your hand?"

"I'll tell you what I'll do," replied Plonski, "if the old man will bring it here at once I will give him a thousand dollars for it, and if you don't think that is enough I'll make it more. My profit is prospective, but I know the Spaniards so well I am willing to take the risk. Where have you got the old man?"

"I think I'll send him back," said Wilder, getting up. "There's one thing more I want to ask you, did you put the advertisement in the *Herald*?"

"Yes. You see I was completely baffled by Therese's failure to return to me with the cup. I naturally supposed that she had fallen into the hands of my rivals or been influenced by some of her low associates. I thought the advertisement would help me to determine this, for if she had not met with the Spanish agents her companions would snap at the reward. To my astonishment you were the only one that responded to the invitation. The extraordinary adventures of the cup after leaving Enniston's house almost converts me to the

Spanish superstition. It appears to bring ill luck or good luck to all who meddle with it."

"One other question. The young woman in this family here opposed all your plans to get the cup?"

"The poor child got it into her head that I was a necromancer and exerted some kind of evil influence over her grandfather."

"But you made a warm friend of the other woman."

"I did. I had to. There was no other way. The old man is in his dotage and very hard to deal with. I was quite willing to pay Mrs. Sitwhite for her services."

"And to accomplish her purpose she had to get rid of the young woman?"

"They did not agree, of course. The granddaughter has a small annuity which pays for her grandfather's board, and I offered Mrs. Sitwhite a sufficient sum to make up for the loss."

Wilder got up and moved toward the door.

"I suppose," he said, "that we shall run across each other again somewhere. The thing seems to make plenty of work for us."

"So far as I am concerned, I shall have no objections," said Plonski. "You have the means of interfering with me seriously; but I can't see that you will have any motive, for I will pay all I can afford to get the thing into my possession, and that ends it. If there's any other claimant I'll meet him and adjust matters. It's hardly a case for the police and wouldn't have been mixed up with illegal acts if I had been able to control my agents."

A few words more were spoken and Wilder sauntered out; the two men nodding to each other rather distantly.

CHAPTER XV.

MR. CARTERET BECOMES A KNIGHT.

Mrs. Joliff Hannige who kept the house in Fifteenth street had a professional hatred of women. It was confined to women who lodge; women in the abstract did not worry her, but in their capacity as lodgers, she abominated them. Her house was pretty well filled with what she was pleased to call "the sex that didn't make any trouble."

The moment John Wilder left the house, Mr. Carteret started to go upstairs in search of Mr. Evans and he met Mrs. Hannige coming down, very proprietary and *bouffant*.

"Well, young man," she remarked with a tone of severity that was utterly belied by her round, good natured face. "Do you want anything in particular?"

"I want to see the old gentleman a moment," said Carteret.

"Do you? You are quite sure it's the old gentleman."

Carteret looked at her indignantly, but there was a matronly smile on her face that was irresistible.

"Yes," he said. "I'm quite sure, and he's too old to ask him to come down again."

"Don't you think you'd better let the young lady tidy herself up? See here, you go and sit down in the reception room. I'm going to send them up some lunch in a few moments and I'll tell them you are waiting to speak to them."

"It's not a bad idea," said Carteret. "I'll do it."

"Now the trouble begins," said Mrs. Hannige, as she went beamingly down the kitchen stairs. "I've got a woman in the house."

Half an hour later, she went up to the third floor and found Manuella sitting at the open window with her hat on and Mr. Evans not far off with his head bowed on his stick.

"Bless my soul," she said, "are you going to sit there like that? Isn't my place good enough to stay a while in?"

They both turned to her with inquiring looks of helplessness. "We are waiting for the officer," Manuella meekly suggested.

"Well, you'll wait a long time. He may not come back here in a month, and I've got orders to make you one of the family till you go home again. I hope you won't frighten me out of my seven senses by acting like that. The young gentleman's waiting down stairs for you to get your things off, and your lunch is coming up."

"Are we to stay here?" asked Manuella.

"Well, it looks like it," said Mrs. Hannige, "but perhaps it isn't good enough."

Manuella got up and took her grandfather's stick and hat. "This lady says we are to stay here Grandpa. I don't understand it, but she's very kind and says we are her guests. We are to have our lunch in this room and Mr. Carteret is waiting to come up."

"Yes, yes," said the old gentleman. "I have some business with Mr. Carteret, now we are alone."

"That's right," remarked Mrs. Hannige, going toward the door. "Do try and make yourselves at home. It gives me the newraliga to think folks are uncomfortable and want to go."

Then she thought of something and came over to Manuella. "My dear, you are the only woman in the house and Jack told me to treat you like a daughter. The bathroom is on this floor and there's the wardrobe. I'll send the young gentleman up."

When she was gone, Manuella began to take some interest in the room. It was a large and handsomely furnished apartment with heavy carpet and old-fashioned mahogany furniture. In one corner stood an upright piano. She opened it and touched the keys. The rear windows looked out on the great walls of Irving Hall and the Academy of Music, with glimpses of Fourteenth Street between and green gardens below, flower bespangled. A mocking bird was whistling blithely somewhere.

"Grandpa," she said leading him to the window. "This is very pleasant. I wonder what we were brought here for."

"I must prove, my dear," he said, "that Mrs. Enniston gave me the cup. They must examine us—that is all."

"Then we are not arrested?"

"Ah, there is no disgrace in being arrested, my child. We have committed no crime."

She had seated herself at the piano with girlish delight and was running her fingers lightly over the keys as Carteret came in.

"I could not leave you," he said, "without giving you a crumb of comfort. This is a most respectable house. I met a friend of mine downstairs who lodges here. Mrs. Hannige is a very worthy widow and you ought to be comfortable in her keeping—so I would take it easy and to-morrow I'll have you out. I'm not going to let this officer do exactly as he pleases."

"It's very strange." said Manuella.

"True, but we'll make the best of it. There's such a thing as habeas corpus, I believe. We're not going to let officers or anybody else rob you of your property or your liberty, Mr. Evans."

"I have Mrs. Enniston's letter," said Mr. Evans. "Ella, what did you do with the letter?" He began to wring his hands. "We've left it behind us. Dear me, how unbusiness like—and the reward for the cup—it was published in the paper."

"The reward," said Carteret, "purported to be offered by me, but as a matter of fact it was bogus. I never owned the cup and never offered a reward for it. There's been a great deal of fuss made over the thing, and between you and me I don't believe it is worth it. If I were you I wouldn't worry my mind any more about it."

Manuella sat at the piano, her eyes on the keys she was lightly fingering with one hand, but she listened to Carteret's words with interest. His remark coincided so exactly with her own views that she turned and looked at him and betrayed in her expression how readily and entirely she agreed with him.

Thus encouraged he went on quite confidentially. "You see, the cup is mixed up with family scandal and a lot of disagreeable things and I suppose these people who are trying to get it are more or less blackmailers. I'm sure that so far as I am concerned, I wish I had never heard of it."

"So do I," said Manuella, softly.

It was late in the afternoon before Carteret got away. Mrs. Hannige had served a dinner in the room. To make it more sociable he had stayed. There was a nice bit of roast lamb, some very creamy mashed potatoes and a most appetizing game pie with a salad. It was indeed a choice little banquet and Carteret had got into a most interesting genealogical conversation with Mr. Evans, in which that old gentleman had traced out a distinct acquaintanceship with Oliver Enniston's father, and had grown quite communicative and cheerful as he talked of old times.

There was some kind of charm in the place and he found it difficult to tear himself away. While he conversed with the grandfather, Manuella was gliding about the room pretending to be occupied and only adding a monosyllable at intervals; but the young man's eyes followed her covertly as she made pictures round the apartment. He had been for some time trying to invent an excuse for coming back to see them, and when he left them Manuella naively reminded him that her grandfather would be anxious to hear from him as soon as possible, and he had replied that he would look in with all the news he could get. Then she thanked him and it had all come about naturally and easily.

The young man went away in an exultant state of mind that surprised even himself. He was whistling loudly and cheerfully on the Street, a thing he was not in the habit of doing, and keeping brisk step to the melody. It's astonishing what effect real beauty has upon the artistic temperament. He went to his studio, lit the gas and began making a sketch from memory of a girl's head. He kept at it till midnight and then tumbled into bed with the same picture running though his brain. It was notable how accurately he recalled all the glances, poses and attitudes; the little looks of amazement, helplessness and solicitude; the flush of gratitude and the modest reminder that her grandfather would be alone till he came again. He hurried to his easel in the morning, and as he saw the sketch he exclaimed: "By all the masters, that's the best thing I ever did. I'll put it in color when I get my breakfast," and then, instead of getting his breakfast, he dallied over it till nearly noon. Then he threw down his crayons and rushed out of the studio.

A general idea had taken possession of him that he must in some way defend Mr. Evans and his granddaughter from Wilder. The more he thought about it the more he resented the officer's interference. It was a burning outrage to drag that sweet girl out of her home without the shadow of a pretext and keep her against her will in a strange house. By Heavens, he'd see a lawyer. It was time such high-handed proceedings were put a stop to. He hunted up a legal acquaintance, put the case hypothetically and wanted to know what ought to be done. His friend said it was a good case against the police: "Summons the officer; demand the release of the abducted parties; kick up a row; rouse public opinion; heavy damages; great public lesson." The two young men grew very indignant over the case, looked like Champions and talked like defenders of the faith. Full of importance, Carteret then flew to Fifteenth Street. He would see Mr. Evans and then proceed at once on his own responsibility. He had not been in Mrs. Hannige's sitting room five minutes before Wilder let himself in with his own key.

"So," says Carteret. "He has the run of the house. We'll see about this business."

Wilder saluted him pleasantly. "How are the prisoners?" he asked.

"I've taken legal advice in this matter," said Carteret, with a rather forced air of determination, "and I might as well tell you at once that unless you make a charge against these people or send them back to their home, I shall commence proceedings against you. I came here with the intention of taking them back myself and I propose to have you arrest me also."

Wilder looked at the young man a moment most benignantly. "Carteret," he said, "I gave you credit for having a good deal more artistic instinct than you have shown."

"I may not have much artistic instinct," said Carteret, "but I've got an American's sense of justice and that's enough for this occasion. I'm not going to stand by and see an innocent girl dragged around for some mysterious purpose of your own."

"I've got about twenty-five minutes," said Wilder, looking at his watch. "I'm going to Coe's Grove this afternoon. I'm not in the habit of making excuses for my conduct, but I'll give you a brief explanation if you desire it. I never should have brought those people here if I had not felt sorry for them. I supposed you understood the situation in their house, but you didn't. Let me explain it. This girl was on the point of being thrust into the street when we broke in on them. Her aunt at the dictation of the man Plonski was trying to get rid of her, so that he could control the old man. Their object was to separate the grandfather and the granddaughter, and the girl put up with everything rather than leave him in their clutches. She was helpless and I guess heartbroken when we got there. I solved the whole difficulty by pretending to arrest them. They could not oppose that. It kept the old man and the girl together; it took them out of the clutches of the aunt; it baffled Plonski. I brought them by a roundabout route to my sister who manages this house. They are comfortable here and they have a valuable friend in you. They can stay here as long as they please for the same money they were paying before and they can go back at any moment. I am quite willing to wash my hands of the affair. I never in my life let my feelings interfere with my duty, but I had some monitor like you rise up and upbraid me."

"I didn't understand it, you see—I mistook your motive. Confound it—you amaze me," stammered Carteret.

"What will you do—take them back or let them alone?"

"I hardly know what to do now. I wish you had explained yourself before."

"I thought it was plain to you. It was a question whether Plonski or I got that cup. I wanted to keep my eye on the old gentleman for a few days and get him out of Plonski's reach, but I've changed my mind since and think the cup is hardly worth so much trouble. At all events, its recovery will not benefit me."

"Mr. Wilder," said Carteret grasping his hand, "I owe you an apology. I suppose you have made up your mind that I'm an ass. I don't blame you. What would you do now if you were me?"

"Will you do what I tell you for once?"

"Yes," hesitatingly.

"Go up and look after the old gentleman—I want to talk to Mrs. Hannige a few moments—then go to Coe's Grove with me."

"Coe's Grove," repeated Carteret with just a tinge of dismay. "I've got work in my studio."

"Let it wait a day. I want your company."

Manuella let Carteret in when he knocked at her door. Mr. Evans was taking a nap in an adjoining bedroom. She saluted him modestly but with evident pleasure.

"I've got some good news for you," he said, "and so I took the liberty of calling."

"Good news?" she repeated bringing her hands together with an involuntary and girlish gesture.

"Yes. You are not to worry a bit. Everything is all right and Wilder's a brick."

She was looking at him with surprise and he felt that he was in danger of being effusive. "Sit down," she said, "and explain what you mean."

He took a seat near the window and she sat down quite close to him with undisguised expectation.

"You see," he began, with a rather comical effort to be complacent; "the idea of your being arrested was all nonsense. It was a ruse on Wilder's part to get you and your grandfather away from that dreadful place and out of Plonski's clutches. You can go back at any moment. Now that's more comfortable I'm sure then being arrested."

The girl made no other response than to repeat the words—"Not arrested."

"No; Wilder couldn't arrest you when you hadn't done anything."

"But what is his interest in us?"

"O, it was the cup. He didn't want Plonski to get it and he wanted your grandfather to be his guest till it was all nicely fixed up for the old gentleman. Take my word for it, it's all right. I was terribly indignant at first myself, till I understood it,"

"Always that dreadful cup," she said musingly.

"Not altogether perhaps," continued Carteret. "Why may he not have desired to get your grandfather into more comfortable quarters, where he evidently belongs. It seems to me that would be only natural."

She was thinking of the cup. "I wish, Mr. Carteret," she said, "that you would tell me plainly about it. I do not understand it at all. I am sure that my grandfather is innocent and does not want to do anything that is wrong. Where did the cup come from and what makes everybody so mysterious about it?"

"I have asked myself these questions repeatedly," said Carteret. "I suspect that it is mixed up with some disagreeable events in the life of the woman Therese, who has had a strange career and she has unwittingly made your grandfather an innocent victim in some of her schemes. The whole subject is a disagreeable one and mixed up with a terrible accident at Coe's Grove and with detectives and crime. I sincerely hope that your grandfather will give it up and that you and he will cease to think about it at all."

"It's dreadful to think that we ever had anything to do with it," she replied. "I feel quite sure my grandfather does not know the nature of the business and has been guarding the property in hopes of getting the reward."

"It's very unfortunate," said Carteret, "because the advertisement offering the reward was never authorized by me. I did not insert it and have been terribly annoyed by it."

"Then, why did you come with the officer?"

"Because he wanted to find Therese and I could identify her, don't you see, for I had seen her at Enniston's. He insisted on my going with him, but I had no idea of what would take place. I don't regret it now, for I may be able to serve you."

"O, Mr. Carteret," she said with an impulsive sincerity," if you can help my grandfather! He is old and ill and has nobody in the world to advise him but me and I scarcely know what to do."

"Of course," exclaimed Carteret, "we must help him at once. It's a perfect shame to have that old gentleman pestered and badgered when he out to be getting all the rest and peace that is possible in his declining years. We must get him to restore the cup and forget it. Where do you suppose it is?"

"I have no idea," replied Manuella, "He has hidden it somewhere, because the man Plonski wanted to get it, and he had an idea it belonged to you and you would pay the offered reward."

"Alas," said Carteret, "I am unable to pay the reward. I am only a poor artist and you must see that such a reward for a silver cup, is on the face of it absurd. But tell me, do you wish to go back with your grandfather to your home, because I can take you back at any moment."

He was looking at her and she was staring dreamily with her lustrous eyes out through the window. He thought as he regarded her that he had never before seen anything so beautiful as her face, in its frank perplexity and transparent helplessness.

She got up while he was looking at her and went to the adjacent window where she stood a moment with her back to him. The idea of going back brought with it all that was odious in the Terrace. She saw the dark room and mysterious face of Plonski, the unreasonable persecution of her aunt. She turned her head and there through the open chamber door, she saw her grandfather sleeping quietly in the sweet white bed. The sun was shining into the room through the plants in the window. The mocking bird was whistling somewhere and the soft strains of the organ in Irving Hall came mellowed to her ears.

Go back, she said to herself. To what? Poverty, gloom, imprisonment, persecution, helplessness. Surely there must be some other and better place to which she might take her grandfather.

Carteret could only see her back, but something in the lines of the beautiful figure as she leaned thoughtfully against the casing, betrayed the character of her mood. Then as if the silence must be broken somehow, she turned and though her head was partly averted, he saw that there was water in her eyes. She moved to a distant part of the room with the pretence of doing something, until she could recover her composure, and then suddenly feeling that her efforts were obvious, she came over and stood in front of her visitor.

"Mr. Carteret," she said, "I don't know what to do. I'm only a child, but I love my grandfather and if he goes back there he will die."

"Then he doesn't go back," said Carteret impulsively.

"I hav'n't a soul in the world," she continued, "to tell me what to do, but you have been very kind. Perhaps I shouldn't talk to you as I do, but there is no one I *can* talk to. I am an orphan and I scarcely know which way to turn."

He saw her lip quiver. He saw the whole struggle of helplessness and pride and girlish modesty. Everything that was generous and impulsive, went out to her in a moment. He sprang up and came toward her. "I am an orphan myself," he exclaimed. "Sit down and talk to me as you would to a brother and let me prove to you that I can respect you and treat you like one."

So impulsive was his manner that she took a step backward and a pink danger signal began to flutter in her face.

"Pardon me," he said, "but it isn't often that a woman makes such an appeal to all that is best in a man, as you have made. If you do not command my poor services, after such an appeal, it must be because you cannot trust me as I deserve. Pray sit down; I only want to tell you that you need not be afraid of my patronizing you, for I am too poor and I cannot offend you for I am too deeply touched by what you have said. Tell me plainly if there is any way in which I can help you and your grandfather."

They were both a little nervous now. She sat down. "I hardly know what to say to you," she said; "can't you come to-morrow evening when my grandfather is up? I cannot talk any more now."

"Yes," said Carteret; "that is better, you are agitated; I have so little tact myself that I feel I have not helped you a bit."

As she got up she dropped a little handkerchief and he sprang to pick it up, and, when he left her at the door, there was an unconscious gallantry in his manner that was new even to him and that she never forgot.

"To-morrow evening," he said to himself in the waiting room. "It was her invitation."

Half an hour later, he and Wilder were on their way to the Hudson River depot. "Stop a moment," said Carteret as they were passing a florist's. "I'm going to send some flowers down to that old man to cheer up his place a little."

"Don't do that," said Wilder, "he's got a royal flower, send 'em to the poor girl."

Strangely susceptible is the artist temperament. This young man heard a mocking bird whistling, and caught the mellow strains of an organ above the rattle of the train during that ride to Coe's Grove, and the cadences seemed to be inextricably woven with a head of golden hair and to come strangely mingled with tears in beautiful eyes.

CHAPTER XVI.

IT MUST BE ONE OF THOSE MAGICAL CUPS.

As usual Dr. Wollendorf's establishment was wide open and apparently deserted when John Wilder arrived there. So he walked through the lilac bushes up the broad steps and across the long room to the rear veranda, several pigeons running out ahead of him as they had done once before. He sat down on the wooden bench. Everything was deliciously serene and restful, and in soothing contrast to the jar and anxiety of his city experience. He was not in a buoyant mood. Somehow a great conspiracy had resolved itself into a commonplace bargain and a vicious woman's jealousy. He felt that he had been letting his imagination run away with his judgment and had about made up his mind to acknowledge to Dr. Wollendorf that a working hypothesis didn't work, when the doctor poked his smoking cap through the doorway.

"Bless my soul, Wilder," he exclamied; "you here? Why I was just going to send for you."

"Here I am," said Wilder, rather languidly. "I'd like to stay here a week and watch the pigeons. There's something like medicine in this stillness."

"But it wasn't the stillness that brought you up, was it?" asked the doctor. "What have you done about the cup?"

"Confound the cup," ejaculated Wilder. "I've about come to your opinion, doctor. I've run the cup down only to find that it wasn't worth the trouble."

"Run it down. Do you mean to say that you have got it?"

"I can put my hand on it, but I don't know that I shall exert myself to that extent. The fact is, Doctor, you were right and I was wrong. The cup isn't worth wasting much valuable time over. So let us come to other business. How's your pigeons?"

The doctor looked at Wilder intently. Then he came and stood in front of him. "Tell me," he said, "what have you learned about the cup?"

"Its is a long and dry story and the conclusions do not warrant its recital when a man is tired. In a word the cup hasn't 'panned out' as we say, and I've made up my mind not to bother with it. What's new in your affairs? They hav'n't tarred and feathered you yet, I see."

"Pardon me," said Dr. Wollendorf. "Do you mean that you have relinquished your search for the cup?"

"I mean," replied Wilder, "that I have lost my interest in it. So long as it was a mystery, I wanted to run it down—now that I know what its value is, and why certain persons want to get hold of it, I don't take the slightest stock in it."

"You know its value, you say?"

"Yes."

"Who told you?"

"That fellow Plonski."

"Plonski—Plonski. Who the devil is Plonski?"

"Plonski is the chief conspirator."

"See here Mr. Wilder," said the doctor with unmistakable concern in his manner; "there's some kind of mistake. Did Plonski tell you what the cup was worth?"

"Yes, he made a clean breast of it. The cup is worth about eight or ten thousand dollars if the Superstition of a Spanish Family is to be relied upon and I don't think it is."

"Did Plonski offer you that amount for the cup?"

"Offer me? Certainly not. He expects to make it himself; but he is perfectly willing to pay me a fair price to recover the property so that he can place it in the hands of the owners."

"And you believed this fellow Plonski?"

"Why not? What he told me was a more reasonable explanation of the value of the cup than anything I have heard. In fact I may say it's the *only* reasonable explanation I have heard."

"I'm glad you came up—I am indeed. For a man who can make a hypothesis, you've got more credulity than I gave you credit for. You don't seem to understand what the thing is worth."

"O, yes I do," said Wilder. "It's worth fifteen or twenty dollars as old silver."

Dr. Wollendorf was exhibiting a good deal of excitement for so phlegmatic a man. He walked about, uttered a good many broken exclamations and thrust his hands repeatedly into the pockets of his smoking gown, presenting rather a ludicrous picture, as several pet pigeons waddled alter him and took the same turns that he did on the veranda.

"You don't appear to be in a very calm state of mind to-day," said Wilder, who was regarding him with considerable interest.

"No," replied the doctor; "the fact is, I'm considerably flustered by what you tell me. I may say I'm amazed. Did you know that Capt. Ackerman had returned and is here?"

"No, I did not."

"Yes, he's here. That is—he's over at Enniston's just now. Would you mind waiting while I send for him? It would be better to see him here than at that house. I'll go after him myself if you'll wait. It's only a step across the fields."

"I hav'n't the slightest objection to seeing Capt. Ackerman, Doctor," said Wilder, "and I can wait comfortably here. Go and fetch him by all means. We'll settle the cup business thoroughly before I go back."

"Yes," muttered the doctor; "yes, yes," and throwing off his flowing gown and putting on a rusty sackcoat, he started down the steps and went through his back gate across the fields towards Enniston's.

John Wilder lit a cigar and sat there watching the pigeons in thoughtful indolence.

"So," he said to himself, "the doctor is more interested in the facts of the cup than he is willing to acknowledge. He seems to have reasoned himself into the general superstition."

While he was listening to the drowsy crickets in the grass and the cooing of the innumerable birds, some one came up the front steps with a heavy tread, entered the open door and a moment later, looked out upon the rear veranda. It was a soil begrimed giant in a woolen shirt and loose jacket. Wilder looked up and recognized the man who had charge of the cemetery. He remembered his gruff and rather contemptuous greeting when they had first met and he nodded carelessly to the fellow's recognition.

"You here?" growled the man. "H'm, well, I thought we's got through with you. Looking for more buried people in the wrong place?"

This was said with undisguised rural contempt for a city man, who was easily duped when he got among the sagacious fellows of a quiet hamlet, and he rounded up the speech by asking: "Where's the doctor?"

Wilder took him in deliberately. He saw the type of man that Shakespeare has drawn in Dogberry and his associates; an ignorant, bullheaded, opinionated, rustic authority, who had a profound contempt for any form of intelligence not acquired by his experience.

"You're the man that let me dig for Enniston's body after you'd removed it. Eh?"

A cunning twitch of the man's mouth betrayed something of a sarcastic smile and showed a row of large yellow teeth.

"You didn't ask me anything 'bout the body," he said; "yer only asked me to let yer open the ground. I let yer."

"So you did," said Wilder, "and I'm much obliged to you. I didn't get the body, but I got what I wanted. I meant to have come and thanked you, but I hav'n't had time."

"O, I don't want no thanks. You're welcome to all you got. I don't ask any thanks for knowin' my business, I don't. You can just stir round in my grounds much as you like. You can't worry me. I'm too old a hand at my trade. Where's the doctor?"

"The doctor," replied Wilder, "has gone over to Enniston's. He'll be back here in a few moments. Are you in a hurry?"

"Well, I don't waste much time on bad grounds, I don't. He's got some business with me, *he* has."

"No," said Wilder, "you're a man who makes no mistakes. You're the only one I've met up here. I noticed it the first time I saw you. Anybody can see that by taking one look at you. Wasn't there a grave robbery three years ago in your cemetery, that made a sensation in the papers—the Wrexford case—I believe they called it; the thieves carried off the remains under your very nose."

"O, no," replied the man with an easy self-superiority. "O, no. That was before I had charge of the place. Nobody has heard of any thieving on them grounds since I've been there."

"No?" queried Wilder. "Well, I didn't want to steal anything."

"Of course you didn't. It wouldn't have made much difference if you had. I'd heered about you afore you came. No sir, there aint nobody walks my grounds without my knowin' it—'cept the ghosts. You can jist take your oath to that."

"Ghosts," repeated Wilder, musingly. "Yes, that's the worst of graveyards—there's always ghosts around after dark. I shouldn't like to trust myself in such a place when the sun's down. I 'spose I was born that way, but I always did have a dreadful fear of a graveyard at dark—but then such a courageous man as you are never thinks about these things."

"That shows how much you know about it. Ghosts," he repeated, with a hard grin, "them's sperit's, eh? I guess I've seen more sperits than the best o' 'em, but they don't worry me. I always lowed that a man could see sperits anywhere if he only wanted to. I spose you know so much about it that you call that all lying baby-talk about seein' 'em, hay?"

"Yes, I 'spose it is nonsense and superstition," said Wilder.

"No, it aint. That's where you're too smart. You can just see anything you give way to. I've seen more sperits than anybody in this country, but it never took my appetite away—no, it didn't."

"Good heavens," said Wilder, "what an extraordinary man you are. Real spirits?"

"Yes, sir, a settin' on their graves in their shrouds a mumblin' and gnashin' their teeth. I got so I enjoyed it."

"Pshaw,' said Wilder, "you don't mean it."

"Yes, I do. You'd better look out and keep clear o' that cemetery after dark if you don't want to get a round turn. Yes sir," he added a moment later, "I don't mind giving you a square warnin', don't fool round the Enniston's plot, that's a favorite place for 'em."

"O, you're trying to frighten me," said Wilder.

"Say," continued the fellow, "mebbe there aint much in it any where else, but if I didn't see the regular spook there, I hope I may never throw another shovel. Now this is dead straight: one night last July, there was a big storm come on and I was afraid the water'd wash down from the crick over the new part of the cemetery and so I gets up when it was a'pourin' and lights my lantern and takes a pull of Medford and goes up through the grounds to look after the freshet. I guess 'twas one or two in the mornin'. Well everything was all right and I'd started back and was comin' down through the brush towards the Enniston place, when there was a flash o' lightnin' and what do you think I seen? Why, over there on the Enniston plot, I seen the Enniston grave and if there wasn't a man's head a lookin' out of it, I hope I may be burnt and never rot in the grave. That's a fact. Says I, 'O, you can kin just have your own fun at that, I'm goin' home to get my wet cloths off and I aint got no time to be foolin' with sperits, you grin and roll round in that mud as much as you like.'"

"That was the night of the big storm in July," said Wilder.

"O, it wasn't such a big storm for these parts. It split the doctor's elm out there and killed some of his pigeons, but 'twant only a thunder clap. You just flight shy o' that cemetery if you want to sleep well."

"Yes, I will," said Wilder. "I'm much obliged for your warning."

The man then seeing the doctor returning across the fields, went to meet him unceremoniously and a few minutes later the doctor and Capt. Ackerman came up the steps of the veranda without him.

Both men wore serious and even anxious faces.

"This," said the doctor, "is Mr. Wilder—Mr. Wilder, Capt. Ackerman." They shook hands formally. The captain wore a rough corduroy jacket and a broad brimmed hat. He presented a curious mixture of the English squire and the retired whaling captain.

"The doctor has spoken of you," he said to Wilder, "and I've been very anxious to see you. He has told me what you said about the cup. Can you get it at once?"

"I have the man who holds it," said Wilder, with his usual caution. "The old fellow is poor and will sell it. It came into his hands honestly; in fact, Mrs. Enniston gave it to him."

"If he will sell it, all right," said the captain; "but it never belonged to Mrs. Enniston and she had no right to give it away. Where is it now?"

"It is in the keeping of this old man; the girl Therese brought it to him. He has promised to produce it for me and I have him safe under my eye, but I must tell you that he saw the advertisement in the *Herald* and expects the reward."

"That's right, that's right," said the captain eagerly. "He shall have the reward. When can you go and get it?"

Wilder smiled. "I shouldn't like to promise anything precisely about that cup. In ordinary circumstances and with anything else, I should say I could produce it in twenty-four hours, but I have learned to be wary of this particular utensil which appears to baffle everybody. If the old man has not passed it out of his hands—"

"Passed out of his hands?" exclaimed the captain. "That mustn't be. Where has he got it?"

"I don't exactly know. The fact is when I learned the history and real value the cup, I lost interest in it, except that I should like to help the old dotard who has it."

"The real value?" said Captain Ackerman. "You say you learned the real value?"

"Yes," said Wilder. "The man Plonski made a clean breast of it, as I told the doctor."

There was a moment's pause after this. Captain Ackerman appeared to be in doubt what to say.

"Sit down, gentlemen," said the doctor, "sit down; we'll come to an understanding. There is some misapprehension. We'll have to be frank about it. Sit down."

"The fact is, Mr. Wilder," said the captain, as he seated himself. "Plonski has deceived you evidently, with the hope of getting possession of the cup. He has not told you the true history or mentioned the correct value."

"In which case," said Wilder, "I look to you for the true story. Is it worth more or less than he has stated?"

The captain hesitated. He and the doctor exchanged glances. Finally he said, "I am not ready to give you a full account of the affair. What I am ready to do, is to employ your services to recover it."

"You must at least convince me that it belongs to you," rejoined Wilder.

"What was it Plonski told you?" asked the doctor. "Suppose you repeat it to the captain."

Wilder willingly assented and with marvelous accuracy told Plonski's story of the cup. He had got half way though the narrative when the captain impolitely stopped him.

"You needn't go any farther with that," he said. "It's a made-up yarn from beginning to end. Not a word of truth in it. Not a syllable. I can prove it to you." And then the captain got up and began to pace about, evidently in great doubt how to proceed.

"Very well," said Wilder, not showing his feeling of humiliation and pique at having been fooled by Plonski. "I'm willing to compare his story with yours. The cup seems to breed good stories."

"I can prove to you, sir, that it is my property, and was stolen out of my room," said Captain Ackerman, with considerable vehemence. "I'm not a conspirator—not an outlaw. I am simply trying to get back what belongs to me."

"In which case," said Wilder, "you have a plain duty. All you have to do is to go the authorities, make a complaint, take the proper legal steps and defy conspirators and outlaws."

At this the doctor dashed a brown, hairy fist into the palm of his hand with a vexatious protest, and took a few extra turns of perplexity on the veranda.

It was instantly apparent to Wilder that the captain feared publicity. He saw the two men walk to the other end of the long veranda and confer. He saw that the captain was vehemently objecting to something the doctor was urging. When they came back Dr. Wollendorf said:

"Mr. Wilder, I don't think that you will hesitate long between the captain and Plonski, in making up your mind to the truth. Plonski has no claim upon the cup, and my friend here has—but he wishes to avoid publicity for the present. The immediate question is, can he retain your services in securing the property?"

"Gentlemen," replied Wilder, "in the dilemma which you have made, I see but one course for me to pursue. Plonski has told me a straight and plausible story and offered the reward to the old man who has the cup. You have given me no evidence that it does not belong to him, and as I do not intend to be a go-between or to give my services to a scheme of which I am kept in ignorance, I shall go to the authorities, turn over my information and then you can all fight out your battle your own way. One moment, Doctor," he said as that gentleman was about to interrupt him. "I should like to tell you why I have not adopted this course before. Your cup has involved conspiracy, family reputation, sacrilege, and is associated with murder."

"Murder?" exclaimed both his listeners.

"Yes, Mr. Enniston, I am bound to tell you, was stabbed in his own shrubbery, and I have talked with the person who killed him."

"Good God," exclaimed Capt. Ackerman, with genuine and painful amazement. "Ol Enniston murdered—what are you saying?"

"Simply that he was stabbed twice that night of the party."

"Then," said the captain in some bewilderment, "I suppose our first duty will be to hang the man who killed him."

"It was not a man," said Wilder calmly, "and the woman who did the deed is dead."

"Woman? Killed by a woman? Are you quite sure, sir, that you know what you are saying?"

"Quite sure," said Wilder. "I have her confession. In the ordinary course of events, my duty would be to make the whole matter public. Consideration for your sister and the knowledge that publicity would not further the ends of justice, have kept my mouth shut. I came up here to consult with Dr. Wollendorf, and determine if it would not be a politic step to give the truth to the public in order to save him from further village persecution."

"In the name of heaven," cried the doctor in alarm. "Don't save me that way. No, no, Mr. Wilder, your better judgment will, I am sure, counsel you against such a course. I should go mad."

"Perhaps," said Wilder; "but there may be other considerations than your personal comfort."

"Personal comfort—personal destruction. What is there to be gained by it?"

"The truth," replied Wilder. "That is sometimes a consideration with a man of science. By the way, Doctor," he added a moment later, "what do you suppose became of that dagger?"

"What dagger?" asked the doctor with surprise.

"The weapon that killed Mr. Enniston."

The doctor shrugged his shoulders as if disgusted with the officer's irrelevancy. "I don't know. I never thought of enquiring."

"But does it occur to you, that its history after it passed out of Enniston's hand is of great importance?"

"Doubtless," replied the doctor, musingly. "Yes, yes, from your point of view that is an interesting enquiry." He dropped his voice and came a little closer, "What do *you* suppose became of it?"

"I suppose Mrs. Enniston got it and locked it up," said Wilder.

Captain Ackerman broke into this colloquy. He was still plunging about in a most anxious and distressed condition. "Poor Ol. I always felt there was something wrong that night. In his own shrubbery, and that d——d French woman—"

"It was not the French woman. See here, Capt. Ackerman, I suppose you ought to know now that the woman Therese was put in that house by Plonski to get the cup, and she got it out of the house by putting it in the coffin on the day of the funeral, when you were called downstairs for a few moments."

The captain had stopped walking and both he and the doctor were staring at Wilder with unmistakable interest.

"But you may not know what occurred afterwards. Doctor, you remember that July storm that split your elm and killed some of your pet birds—what was the date of it?"

"Never mind that," cried the captain.

"Excuse me," said Wilder; "it is much better to get these little things straight. Do you remember the date of the storm?"

"It was the night of the twenty-fifth," said the doctor.

"Very well," continued Wilder. "On that night, the girl returned to the grave with some of her pals and recovered the cup. While they were working at the job in the storm, that old ass who has charge of the cemetery saw them in a flash of lightning and mistook them for ghosts. He has just been here and told me so. Instead of taking the cup to Plonski, the girl was so overcome by her superstitious terror, that she carried it to an old employer of hers by the name of Evans, with the request that he would return it to Mrs. Enniston and when he wrote to Mrs. Enniston about it she told him to keep it. This old man has held on to it in spite of Plonski so far; but if I had not captured him and under pretence of arrest, carried him off out of Plonski's reach, that man would have undoubtedly had the prize before this. That is, in substance, all the information that I possess concerning the cup itself and I place it at your disposal. I should advise you to go to New York at once and see the old gentleman before Plonski finds him. But I warn you that he may have got to him while I am away, in which case you will have a difficult job to recover the property, and as for myself, I positively refuse to go on with the case unless I am put in possession of all the facts. I tell you this because I do not intend to risk my reputation by working in the dark. If Plonski has deceived me, as you claim, it is because you have not been frank with me."

"Mr. Wilder," said the captain, who was visibly distressed, "any explanations that I should make to you without documentary proof, would not be believed. What do you suppose that cup represents in money value?"

"I have only Plonski's valuation. He put it down at eight or ten thousand dollars, which may have been extravagant. I thought so at the time."

"My dear sir, he could well afford to pay that sum for it." Here he looked round and lowered his voice. "It represents between one hundred and fifty and two hundred millions."

Wilder listened to this with undisguised amazement. "Two hundred millions," he repeated. "Why it must be one of those magical cups we read about in the Arabian Nights. Are you quite sure it will not turn out to be a lamp?"

"Incredible as this sounds," said the doctor, "I dare say the captain can convince you of the truth of it, but the thing to do is to secure the cup at once, and I propose that you go immediately to the city and see this old man before it is too late."

"Yes," said the captain. "I was going to propose it myself, but I want Mr. Wilder to understand that I appreciate his candor and his services and when the proper time comes, will place before him all the proofs, for I may have occasion to use his services. Poor Ol! Poor Ol! If you will tell me all about that affair, I shall be obliged."

CHAPTER XVII.

OFF WITH THE OLD AND ON WITH THE NEW.

Very beautiful was the Enniston estate in the late autumn glow, and there on the green plateau above the river, at the edge of the deep-dyed maples, on a rustic seat, sat Rosamond Enniston on the afternoon that Wilder was talking with the captain in Dr. Wollendorf's study. A few feet away, with his face in the dried grass, was Colin Carteret, indolently whipping the turf with a switch. His position was such that he could not look into her face without rolling over. She was dressed in black, for the family was still mourning, but she wore a jaunty little chip hat that gave her a piquant air. Hers was a strong, handsome, intelligent face; viewed sidewise, the chin came out prominently and there was a good deal of meaning in the slight arch of the nose. Her eyes were very black and piercing.

"Why don't you turn round and look at me?" she asked, a trifle sharply. "I've been talking to you for half an hour and you act as if you didn't want me to see your face."

At this reprimand, the young man rolled slowly over on his back, pulled the straw hat over his eyes to shield them from the afternoon sun that came slanting through the trees, and began regarding her demurely from under the brim.

"You promised to come up yesterday and I waited at the Station for three trains. Where were you?"

"Where could I be?" he replied. "Are you afraid of my conduct or my companions?"

Instead of answering his question, she looked at him intently a moment and then said:

"Something has changed you. What is it?"

"We've had enough to change us. The events of the past six weeks would make anybody but a girl serious."

"Events don't change people's hearts, do they?"

"I didn't say they did."

"You implied it."

"No, I didn't. Were you talking about hearts?"

"I don't believe you know what I am talking about."

"Yes, I do. You were trying to scold me and not having any cause, you got it all muddled up."

His flippant manner irritated her. She gave her head a toss and turned it away. "Now *you* can do the talking. I've tried it for half an hour and you've made it a failure."

He laughed a little. "You're in an awful humor to-day, but I'm not going to quarrel with you, even if you do get jealous."

"Jealous of whom?" she asked, with a suddenness that almost startled him.

"I haven't the slightest idea. Can't we imagine somebody to fit the occasion?"

There was a moment's silence after this; then he got up and came and sat down beside her. "We haven't done much else but quarrel and make up, Rose, ever since we've known each other. I never imagined that love was such a suspicious, querulous thing, did you?"

She patted her little foot on the grass rapidly. Then she took the chip hat off and began to swing it by the long ribbons.

"What do you want me to do?" he asked, coming close to her.

"I simply want you to act in your old manner. A woman notices these little things. Something has changed you."

A look of annoyance and surprise came into his face. It was less surprise at the accusation than at her discernment.

"At all events," he said, "nothing has happened that can make me break my word. You have got my ring on your finger."

"And I'd tear it off and trample on it this minute," she said, with flashing vehemence, "before I'd have you regard it as a fetter."

"There you go. You might tear off my ring, but you can't tear off my obligation. You'll leave me a little honor I hope."

"Bah, for honor," she exclaimed. "Did you come up here to tell me that you are compelled to love me with your honor? You used to do it with something else. Didn't I tell you you were changed?"

"Rose," he said, "what is the matter with you? What have I done to you?"

With a sudden impulse she put up her arm, caught him around the neck and in a burst of passion exclaimed:

"Dear, I'm jealous, awfully jealous. When you are away my mind is filled with all kinds of fears. I'm left in this dreadful place all to myself. I have no one to talk to but Dr. Flockton. Why don't you speak to me as you once did?"

"Because," he said, "I supposed we had got over all that and were sailing in the clear, calm water of the inevitable."

She caught at the word with a woman's fine sense." Why do you say inevitable? Do you mean irremediable?"

At this he broke out into a laugh. "Now, upon my word," he said, "this is carrying suspicion into etymology. You've spoilt the beautiful afternoon with it and now you'd poison the honest English. Don't you think it is time we began to act like reasonable beings? I always thought that when matters got as far as a ring, things settled down into calm and contentment. You see I don't know much about it."

"I hav'n't got any calm and contentment," she exclaimed. "I'm getting to hate the words. An occasional earthquake or a murder would be a relief. I wander round these grounds counting the hours. My mother crushes me with her equable severity. She has made a recluse of herself and expects me to imitate her, and when you come, you talk of calm as if I wasn't suffocated with it. What I want is excitement. I feel sometimes that it would be a mercy to my nature to do something desperate."

He regarded her with surprise and anything but admiration as she poured out this complaint.

"O, I could be awfully wicked," she continued. "It's in my blood and I can't hold it. They'll drive me to it."

"Heaven!" exclaimed Carteret; "how pat you've got it. That's what they all say."

"Who?"

"The wicked women, you know."

"Well, I must talk it all out to somebody. You're not angry and disgusted with me, are you?" and she put her cheek close against his.

"I'm not angry," he said.

She drew her cheek quickly away. "But you *are* disgusted—is that what you mean?"

"O, rubbish," he replied with a laugh.

"Now I'm done," she said. "How long are you going to stay this time? I want you to-morrow all to myself."

"O, but I must be in the city to-morrow. It's important."

Her whole countenance changed in an instant. "Is it more important than my request?" she asked.

"My dear Rose—"

"Now you are going to make some trumpery excuse. You can at least be frank. Who are you going to see tomorrow?"

He got up, sauntered off a little distance and came back. He could not quite conceal his perplexity. He hated to be compelled to lie and knowing how unreasonable she was, he disliked to tell the truth. While he was considering, she was watching him.

"Well," she said, "have you got the excuse framed? How much trouble you might save yourself by telling the truth plumply."

Nothing she could have said would have nettled him as did this unerring precision of suspicion. The two or three words that he uttered were haltingly contradictory.

She stood up with a sudden impulse. "Honor bright, Mr. Carteret be a man for a minute at least—are you going to see a woman?"

Come at in this style, he flushed a little, looked into her black, flashing eyes and answered—"Yes."

She let out a wicked laugh, whose tones were strangely like the gleam of her eyes.

"Pull yourself together," she cried. "I shall not hurt you and you can't hurt me. I assure you I can stand it. I'm going to be calm and contented. You were afraid I'd make a scene. What nonsense. You shall go and see her—not only to-morrow night but to-night. Go at once. Here, give her this," and she began pulling at the ring upon her finger.

"Rose," he cried, dismayed at the violence and recklessness of her words and manner. "Listen to me," and he came towards her. But she stepped backwards and getting the ring off, threw it at him with spiteful force. It struck him on the cheek with a little sting and fell into the grass. For a moment he stood speechless at her exhibition of passion, then he cried to her again—"Rose, I swear to you—"

She interrupted him. "Go," she said. "I'm done with you. If you do not want me to insult you, leave me. I've been fooling you all the time. Go and keep your promise to one woman."

He lifted his hat. A look of pity rather than of indignation was on his face. He bowed and turning, strode slowly away toward the gravel road and was presently lost to sight.

The girl stood there until he had disappeared. Then as if coming out of a trance, she staggered back to the rustic seat and dropping upon the ground, limp and heavy, rested her head on the gnarled bench and broke into convulsive sobs.

The sun had gone down behind the hills. The cool breeze came up from the little bay and fluttered her black hair. The tinkle of the bells on the returning cows out in the highway came to her. The dew began to gather on the grass around her. Suddenly the voice of Barney echoing in the woods as he called for her roused her. She sprang up and looked around, then falling on her knees in the grass, she began feeling for the ring, but it was too dark to find it and she started for the house on a full run. Half way there, she encountered Barney. "Quick," she said. "Get the mare out with the phaeton and go to the depot and catch Mr. Carteret. Bring him back with you. Don't stand Barney, for God's sake—do what I tell you. I must see him."

"Indade miss," says Barney. "I'd rather ride the mare, than be harnessing her. Sure I can send him back on her and walk up myself."

"Anyway, but be quick. That eight o'clock train will not go before you get there—it mustn't."

All this after-desperation of penitence was, however, of no avail. Carteret had taken the seven-fifteen, while Rose was having her hysterics on the bench.

When Barney brought her word, she was pacing the veranda impatiently. Then she accused Barney of delay and indifference and spite, which he was apparently accustomed to, for he made no reply and the girl went to her room and getting a quire of note paper on her knees, sat down on a cushion and penned the following letter to Carteret.

"*O, My Darling:* How can you ever forgive me? I was insane with jealousy. Forget all my rash and bitter words and come back to me. I promise you never again to let my foolish passion master me. O dear, what must you have thought of me and you so good and patient. I am here alone in my room. My heart is breaking at the thought that I have sent you away forever. I shall die if I do not get some word from you. I shall have your ring on again in the morning—I shall find it if I have to hunt on my knees all my life. Can you forgive me, my darling, and love me a little as you did in the old times, in spite of all my wickedness?

God bless you my own.   ROSE."

It was too late to send this that night and in the morning after a restless late sleep of a few hours, she had changed her mood. Her first thought when she arose and looked out at the clear blue sky was, that this day which should have been hers, was to be given to another woman. Then she read the letter of the night before and trampled it under foot with scorn.

After she had swallowed some coffee, she got her pen and paper and wrote another letter which ran as follows:

"COLIN CARTERET—*Dear sir:* In our sane moments it is idle to refer to the childishness that is past. A girl must ever look up to a man for guidance. I have asked God to forgive me—Can you? I have replaced your ring, because knowing you as I do, I dare not break the pledges of months with the foolishness of a moment. The girl of yesterday is the woman of to-day and will hold you to your promise because she loves you.

Yours,
ROSAMOND ENNISTON."

This appeared more dignified. She read it over many times and then sent Barney to mail it.

Meanwhile Colin Carteret, confused and perplexed with conflicting emotions, had got out of bed in New York, and the first glad thought that came to him was that he would see Manuella that evening. He did not quite satisfy himself with his reasoning on the matter. He had known Rosamond for a year; they had made love and quarreled and made up again through the summer and winter at Coe's Grove, but he had grown to believe that the love was all a mistake. Now he knew it. That he would have kept faithfully every pledge made to Miss Enniston had she not flung them all in his face there is no reason to doubt.

Even now, released as he was, a tender feeling came over him as he recalled the romantic hours spent in her company—but it was a regret shaded with pity. "After all," he said, "it was not an affection that could stand the test of time, and no woman who really loved a man would whistle him down the wind in that manner. I would have married her, I suppose, but her own temper has saved me from itself forever. Well, we had many pleasant hours on the old place. I wonder who'll pull her on the little bay now, and sketch her in her picnic dress, and write verses on her black eyes."

While he was painting Manuella's face Rosamond's letter arrived. This was a better test of his inclination than all his sophistry and resolves. He read it with amazement. Then he said to himself that he would answer it, and laid it open on a pile of tube colors, where it remained for a week and Rosamond was watching every mail.

CHAPTER XVIII.

"BUT WHAT DID YOU DO WITH THE CUP,

GRANDPA?"

Save for one or two things, Manuella's life in Mrs. Hannige's establishment would have been a pleasant one. The uncertainty of her position and the growing helplessness of her grandfather worried her. Her surroundings were in marked contrast to the squalor and vulgarity of the Terrace. Mr. Evans breathed the pure air and got plenty of sunshine. Mrs. Hannige was as attentive in her kindness as if Manuella had been her own daughter. But the girl was not altogether at ease. Wilder had asked her to stay indoors, as he did not wish Plonski or his agents to discover her whereabouts, and it was evident to her that he had given Mrs. Hannige some kind of instructions, for with all that lady's motherly affection Manuella saw that she watched her closely. The mystery of the cup and the strange effect it had upon her grandfather was a continued and inscrutable annoyance. Her absolute dependence, her ignorance of the practical world and a growing fear that something might happen to the old gentleman at any moment made her think at times that she ought to be with her aunt, disagreeable as the Terrace was and unjust as Mrs. Sitwhite was sure to be.

In her loneliness it was not possible to reject the little proffers of intimacy that Mrs. Hannige made. Busy as the landlady liked to appear, she found opportunities in plenty to run into her lodgers' rooms, and her harmless gossip about her house and its inmates, in the absence of any one else to listen to, served to amuse Manuella and sometimes to interest her. There was a hearty practicality about Mrs. Hannige that was very likely to win the admiration of a dependent girl, and it was not long before the younger began to tell some of her perplexities to the elder woman, and the little confidences were followed by a womanly gratitude on one side and womanly sympathy on the other.

Mrs. Hannige's establishment was not unlike hundreds of others of its class in New York. Lodgers came and went away all through the year. They were artists, actors, bachelors of leisure; some of them brought their traps with them and left them when they disappeared, so that, in the course of time, Mrs. Hannige had a vast collection of antique furniture and canvasses and a most unique museum of ornaments. She had learned to discount her losses in all calculations for a season and also to offset them with little extras. The most genial young men who flattered her and made the most prodigal show of money on the slightest provocation, she had learned by experience, were the young men most apt to suddenly disappear and write her letters afterwards, pointing out that a temporary embarrassment, a death in the family or a disaster in the firm had called them away for a while; but that they considered the balance that was unsettled a debt of honor, etc., and Mrs. Hannige would receive a remittance in a few days or as soon as affairs were straightened out; would she mind taking charge of the trunks and few effects left behind, which of course represented a much larger sum than the balance, etc.? Mrs. Hannige had also learned by experience what this meant, and her method of taking charge of the trunks and effects was promptly to open the one and take possession of the other. There were two or three lodgers in the house who had "stuck by her," to use her own phrase, "through everything." One of these was Otis Chapman, the artist, known in the Tenth Street Studio as "Oats." He differed from most of his fellows in the possession of a good deal of commercial tact, which enabled him to sell his landscapes. To this was added a talent for unconventional color and a weakness for what he called "spells." He painted assiduously for weeks, piled up canvases and lived a recluse life in his studio. Then he locked his door and went off for a fortnight on a "spell." During that time he mingled conviviality and commerce with prodigality and tact. He belonged to the Century and Halcyon clubs, and when he made his appearance in either of them it was understood that a "spell" had commenced. In the Century it was regarded with mild deprecation; in the Halcyon, it was hailed as an "aesthetic toot." It was said he spent in one club what he made in the other. During the continuance of this recuperative racket he bought wine, argued schools of art, made wagers, struck up acquaintances with patrons, was seen at the opera, outstayed the owls who never left the club till morning, and generally manifested the freedom and loquacity of a Bohemian with the prodigality of a man about town. Then it all suddenly stopped. He returned to his studio penitent and taciturn, and as Liebman had remarked, "scourged himself and good taste at the same time for weeks with his own brushes." Oats' appearance depended entirely on his spell. During his hibernating period he wore a dishevelled air. There was very apt to be flake white on his trousers and Prussian blue under his finger nails. His thin face got haggard and his gray eyes looked hungry. His tall, lank figure bent slightly, his red hair got long and matted and his red beard gave him an inflamed look as if he were internally consumed with ennui or dyspepsia. But when the spell changed he was another man. No one wore better clothes. His tall figure was erect and aristocratic. A gleam of humor played around his gray eyes. His red stubble disappeared from his chin and cheeks. His tone was cheery and ebullient and his actions absolutely vivacious. No one knew the precise moment of change better than Mrs. Hannige. When the man who had for weeks come sullenly and quietly in every night at dusk and stole to his room without noticing anybody, and as quietly and regularly stole out in the morning, was heard at an early hour singing boisterously in his room and making a great clatter with the toilet articles, she knew that Oats was not going to the studio—that he would come noisily downstairs into her kitchen before going out and chuck the maids under the chin and ask Mrs. Hannige herself if he shouldn't send her home a good bottle of Otard from the club. Then the two of them would chat pleasantly for a while, Mrs. Hannige calling him "her bad boy," and Oats insisting on addressing her as "Mommy," reminding her how he had stuck to her and pretending to be very jealous of that old wheelwright, Stonybrook, on his floor.

Mr. Stonybrook was Mrs. Hannige's pet lodger. He had followed her from place to place. She had adapted herself to his bachelor whims, and respected most of his crotchets. It was understood in the house that he was "well fixed." He had at some time made a good deal of money on a patent that he had bought cheap, and had invested the money judiciously. He was at least fifty-two or -three years old, but quite hearty and his slightly portly figure, his iron gray hair, and his precise and dignified manner, gave him the appearance of a man of affairs. Mrs. Hannige was doubtless under many obligations to him. In some of her modest speculations he had been a valuable friend, as, for example, when she wanted new carpets for her parlors, and had got her mind set on a particular pattern she had seen at Stewart's, Mr. Stonybrook had come to her assistance by advancing the money and allowing her to pay it back on the installment plan. On another occasion when she had made up her mind to move into a larger establishment and enlarge her business Mr. Stonybrook had cleared away all the difficulties with the landlord by becoming responsible for the rent. It is doubtful if Mrs. Hannige understood clearly the character of her lodger, and it is still more doubtful if a clear understanding of it would have changed their relationship. She did indeed apprehend in a general way some of his weaknesses, with a woman's instinct, but she never thought much about them, except perhaps to gloss them over. She had always paid up her indebtedness with scrupulous regularity, sometimes at a great sacrifice, so that whatever may have been her opinion of him, it was never suffered to change her public treatment of him. She always felt that with Mr. Stonybrook in the house she had a fund of reserve power against the usual lodginghouse contingencies. She knew better than anybody alive that he was vain of his personal appearance, that he did not regard women from a chivalrous point of view, that he devoted his life mainly to his personal pleasures, most of which were of a trivial kind that most men regard as beneath their notice. But it is more than likely that if any one had told her that Mr. Stonybrook was a methodical voluptuary who preferred her house to a hotel simply because he could buy indulgences and cover his selfishness and vanity with a genteel exclusion she would have denied it all with vehement indignation.

It was not possible for a beautiful girl to become domiciled in an establishment of this kind and not exert a subtle influence on all its inmates. Glimpses of her were sure to be had at unexpected moments. There was a presence in the atmosphere like a fragrance and the male inmates knew there was a bouquet somewhere, although they could not see it.

Oats encountered the new condition of affairs rather unexpectedly one morning as he came blithely down the stairs arrayed and straightened for a spell. He almost ran upon Manuella at the turn of the stairway in the dusky hall, and as he took his hat off to apologize and she looked up startled, a ray from the skylight fell across her beautiful face. For an instant the artist stood speechless with his hat in his hand, then Manuella backed away in phantom style and disappeared through a doorway, and Oats went down stairs rubbing his hand across his eyes as if they had been strained. However, his emotion was caused not so much by admiration as by astonishment. He appeared in Mrs. Hannige's kitchen door a moment later. That lady with a feather duster over her shoulder like a bayonet was watching the preparation of a cup of French coffee, and timing the boiling of an egg for Mr. Stonybrook's breakfast.

"O, ho," she cried with a broad smile on her face, "so your time's come, has it? Don't you want a cup of coffee before you start in?"

"Mommy," says Oats, beamingly. "I was following the aroma of it downstairs when I got such a turn. Who's her royal highness? You didn't tell me a word of it. Do you think it fair? And you know I'm an artist, too. I'm astonished at you."

"You're a bad boy," replied Mrs. Hannige, swinging her duster at a presumptuous fly that was hovering over Mr. Stonybrook's tiny cream jug. "You're a very bad boy and I'll have to keep an eye on you."

"You do—you do," says Oats, "you're a model of maternal solicitude, and there's only one thing you don't do. You don't tell me who she is and how she got into your family without the favored members knowing anything about it. O, it isn't spoons," he cried, "it's curiosity, pure professional curiosity, for if I didn't see a portrait of that young lady on Carteret's easel I hope I may lose my cunning and have things cleave to the roof of my mouth."

Mrs. Hannige held her duster suspended in the air a moment and looked at her lodger with inquisitive eyes. Then she went on with her preparations. "Better let me brace you up with a cup of this," she said. "You've had a shock. It will steady your nerves. Bridget pour a cup of that out for Mr. Chapman."

He stood leaning against the door post with the cup and saucer in his hand.

"I don't question your right to violate all precedent and bring a good looking girl in here to destroy forever the quiet and trustfulness of our domestic haven, but by Jupiter, Mrs. Hannige, I object to having this dream of beauty and mystery dropped on me unexpectedly in the hallways and on the stairs without knowing whether to do the conventional thing or drop on my knees like a Pagan. I think the oldest and solidest members of the family are entitled to some consideration."

"How do you like that coffee?" asked Mrs. Hannige.

"It will ruin your house, Mommy, sure," replied Oats. "It will get round that ghosts walk on the landings and vanish through the walls. No man who's got an ounce of blood in him will stand it. I give you warning."

Finally she pushed him considerately out, and he went away chattering and looking up the well hole of the stairs, to come back in half an hour with the pretence of having forgotten something.

Mr. Stonybrook's experience was somewhat different. He had seen the vision innocently pass his half open door twice, and he made ingenious inquiry of Mrs. Hannige, learning a great deal more than she would impart to her harum scarum artist. With affected indifference he had said: "Sometime you may introduce me to her father; as we're neighbors we might as well be friends," and Mrs. Hannige remarked, "Yes, and they need friends, too."

How far her feminine tact was exercised in bringing about the introduction will never be known. It all appeared incidental enough to Manuella. Mrs. Hannige took her through the house mornings, when all the men were supposed to be out, and with an allowable pride of vocation pointed out some of her quaintest relics and furnished facts about their acquisition. Her stories of the various orders of lodgers had a gossipy charm of newness to the girl, who listened with interest to phases of character and eccentricities of demeanor that let her into a new world. They had come to Mr. Stonybrook's suite. Mrs. Hannige went through the formality of knocking first and then pushed the door open. The lodger was out. His empty coffee cup stood upon a little gilded table by the head of the bed, but his egg was uncracked. Manuella hesitated at the door.

"Come in, my dear," said Mrs. Hannige. "There's nobody here, and I want you to see his pictures."

The girl timidly followed her guide in and looked round at the luxurious furnishing with surprise. No other rooms in the house could compare with these.

"O, it's his own," remarked Mrs. Hannige apologetically. "I couldn't begin to afford it. He's got loads of money and nobody to spend it on but himself."

"How dreadful," said Manuella involuntarily.

The floors were carpeted with heavy velvet—a great grey llama skin spread out before the bed. A heavy rosewood buffet was crowded with decanters and cut glass of the finest Bohemian pattern. An immense wardrobe, the polished doors of which seemed to be pressed open with the wealth of garments within, reached across one side of the sleeping room. A malachite centre table was loaded with French novels that formed a circle round a magnificent Limoge lamp, and by its side was a luxuriant easy chair with foot stool, in which one might recline with drowsy ecstasy. The toilet stand was covered with costly appliances of personal comfort, and the walls were decorated with paintings, etchings and engravings. Over the mantel hung a great picture in oil of Hermes and his mountain-nymph mother, Ilaia, just issuing from the Arcadian cavern. It was what the artists called a "study of the nude." Manuella looked at it side-wise without knowing its significance. On either side of it were etchings of the long limbed myths of Ætolia and bisque statuettes of the vuluptuous Diana and Venus.

The effect of all this upon a girl of Manuella's youth and innocence was not unlike that produced by a museum. She stared at the works of art with sim-ple curiosity, and listened to Mrs. Hannige's rhapsody over the furniture and enthusiasm over her lodger with one deep abeyant wonder why a man should take so much trouble to shut himself in with luxuries that no one could enjoy but himself.

While they were thus engaged there came suddenly to the open door a mid-dle-aged gentleman who looked in with a significant smile. He was rather ele-gantly dressed in the English style and held his hat in a hand that was decorated with a heavy diamond ring. His somewhat massive face wore a soft indetermi-nate and conventional look of affability that was habitual, and he pulled at his long and slightly gray side whiskers with his disengaged hand as he stood bow-ing somewhat deprecatingly, as if he had intruded. The first impression made by this face and figure upon Manuella was a vague one of alarm. She could not have interpreted or even described it. At the best it was an unconscious instinct that the owner was not of the same class and order as herself. But whether he was better or worse or only different she could not tell. His elegance, his easy self-command and his prompt arrival after they had got into his room alto-gether struck in her a timidity that was delicate but inexplicable even to herself.

"Dear me," exclaimed Mrs. Hannige, "why, we thought you had gone out for the day, and so we could look at your pictures. Miss Castleton wanted to see them, and I took the liberty. This is Miss Castleton, Mr. Stonybrook. She's a neighbor of yours."

"Don't make any apologies, ladies," he said, holding out his hand to Manuella. "I'm sorry I wasn't here to welcome you. I'm afraid the pictures need explanation. Most of them are classic subjects." He was holding the girl's hand while he spoke, and she was looking into his face with the deep uncon-scious scrutiny of a woman. Then she gently withdrew it and by an almost impreceptible movement placed herself the least bit behind Mrs. Hannige, still looking him in the face. She could not have told why she did this. As well ask why the *Mimosa pudica* shrinks at the touch of a human hand.

"It's too bad," he continued, "that I hav'n't time to entertain you properly. I've got to go out of town, and only came back for a satchel. Allow me to offer you a glass of wine, ladies," and he took down a decanter from the buffet and began pouring out the liquid. "I trust you will not stand on any ceremony with my bachelor rooms. I so seldom have company that I ought to thank you for the visit. I hear you have an invalid father, Miss Castleton. Will you take my respects and say I shall be honored to make his acquaintance? That is a very light and delicate wine. Here's to his better health and our better knowledge of each other."

His self-possessed and affable manner seemed to reassure the girl. She said something meant to thank him, took a sip of his wine and then the women withdrew. But Mrs. Hannige dwelt exhaustively on his merits, his breeding and his wealth, when they were safe in the little reception room, and she emphasized all his good points with her duster. He was such a gentleman, and he had been such a good friend to her, and he was so particular about everything. "I tell you," she said, "he must have lots of good women setting their caps for him."

The very next day Manuella found him in her room holding a most persuasive conversation with her grandfather, and she knew that Mrs. Hannige had brought it about. Then he met her on the stairs and always insisted upon shaking hands in a paternal manner and evincing the tenderest solicitude for her grandfather. Finally the old gentleman found his way into the elegantly furnished rooms, and there being a back-gammon board there, Mr. Stonybrook utilized the antique game to win Mr. Evans' confidence. So without any apparent design the lodgers became neighbors in an incredibly short space of time— for such occurrences are helped on amazingly when there is a woman like Mrs. Hannige in the background, and she had the satisfaction of seeing her guests on the best of terms in less than a week. On the day that Carteret was to make his call, Mr. Stonybrook sent for Manuella to come down in the sitting room. The moment she appeared, he took her hand and said: "Only a word of advice, my child—we must get your grandfather out into the air. I saw him going out with a gentleman and it relieved my mind very much, for I was going to suggest a change of scene for him. I presume he has gone to ride with a friend."

Manuella assented without explanation. The fact was Mr. Evans had gone with Wilder to get the cup, and she did not care about discussing it; but Mr. Stonybrook made her sit down and he talked so sensibly about her duty to her grandfather that she was drawn into a conversation, and while thus engaged, Carteret arrived. Mrs. Hannige gravely informed him that the young lady had company and he would have to wait. When he asked for Mr. Evans, he was told that he had gone out. Restless, impatient and already jealous, he walked the parlors and gave very little heed to Mrs. Hannige's endeavors to entertain him. Finally, when his patience was exhausted, he walked boldly into the reception room to find Manuella and an elderly gentleman in earnest conversation.

The moment he came in, the girl got up with undisguised pleasure in her face and gave him her hand. "I have been waiting half an hour," he said, with the slightest possible petulance of a man whose rights have been overlooked.

"I'm sure I did not know it," replied Manuella, truthfully. "You know I expected you. Mr. Carteret, this is Mr. Stonybrook."

The two men bowed formally. There may have been some foregleam in their souls of the contest they were to have. It may have been only the antagonism of two male animals when a beautiful female is between them, but they were not cordial. Mr. Carteret was the franker; Mr. Stonybrook was the cleverer. The latter got up with great politeness. "I beg your pardon," he said, "for having detained you. Remember what I have said." He took her hand respectfully. She was thankful for his behavior and treated him graciously.

"I shall not forget," she replied, and with a bow Mr. Stonybrook was gone. In spite of himself, Carteret was nettled. Somehow he had got the impression that he had found a nugget and the world did not know it. He now had a suspicion that some one had found it before him. But it was impossible for his boyish jealousy to last long. Manuella was in extraordinary spirits. "Mr. Wilder has been here," she said, "and he has gone with Grandpa to get the cup. You cannot know how glad I am that the whole business of that dreadful cup will now come to an end. It has haunted me and I have wanted several times to ask you what it meant."

"Miss Castleton," said Carteret, "I am just of your opinion about the cup. The less we have to do with it, the better. Where is it?"

"I cannot tell. Grandpa has placed it somewhere for safe keeping; but he has taken Mr. Wilder to get it and is to receive a large sum of money for it. It was almost pitiable to see his childish delight as they went away. He kissed me repeatedly and said all our troubles were at an end; that a good angel had come at last. I was hoping that you would come before they went away so that you could go with them. I am afraid of that man Wilder and if anything should happen to Grandpa—"

"Nothing will happen," said Carteret, reassuringly. "Wilder is a much better fellow than you suspect. The idea of your being arrested and a prisoner is all nonsense. There was no other way for him to get you away from Dr. Plonski's influence and keep you and your grandfather together. He didn't want to argue with you and Mr. Evans and Mr. Sitwhite, so he cut the knot by pretending to arrest you. I hope you don't regret it now."

"It was a strange proceeding," she replied musingly, "and all about a cup. I can't understand it."

"Well, so long as it all turns out happily, don't try to. Who is Mr. Stonybrook?"

"He is a friend of Mrs. Hannige's and has a suite of rooms in the house. He has been very kind to Grandpa."

A slight touch of contempt on Carteret's face, as if it were no merit to be kind to her Grandpa, was unobserved. She wasn't thinking of Mr. Stonybrook or of Carteret's suspicions.

"I want to ask your advice," she said with a little effort, "I have no faith in the dreams of my grandfather and if he should die," with a little pause, "I shall have to earn my own living."

"Is that what you want to ask my advice about?"

"Yes; I must get counsel from somebody and it seemed to me you could tell me what I want to know."

"Well, I don't think it will ever be necessary for you to earn your own living," said Carteret, gallantly and vaguely.

She looked at him demurely. "You don't think my grandfather will die?"

"No, that's not it. I mean that there will always be plenty of brave and good men willing enough to work for you."

She laughed. "But I don't want a brave and true man to work for me. I only want from him a little homely advice about something I am woefully ignorant of."

This slant compliment tickled him a little. "Well, why don't you ask it? Can't you see I am burning to give it?"

"Mr. Carteret," she said, with charming hesitancy and many little breaks, "if you had a sister about my age who wanted to be quite independent and earn her own living, how would you advise her to set about it in this big city? Thousands of girls do it, you know."

"If I had a sister like you," replied Carteret, firing up a little at the noble idea of such a thing. "I'd take her away as far as possible from this city and lock her up to prevent so dreadful a thing. I would indeed, and I'd keep her under lock and key so long as I was able to work for her."

"Then," said Manuella, "you can't give me any advice. I made a mistake. You'll pardon me for having mentioned it." This was said with a genuine air of disappointment, and the young man, with the elasticity of youth, immediately jumped to another conclusion.

"I beg your pardon," he exclaimed. "On second thoughts I probably wouldn't do anything of the kind. A man's impulses do not always agree with his acts. If she were a stubborn little sister like you, I'd very likely find out what she could best do, and then help her to do it with all my might; because if she were my sister, you know, she'd be poor like myself and I could sympathize with her."

She got up suddenly, walked to the window and looked out.

He waited a moment. Then he said plaintively, "Have I offended you?"

"No," she replied, softly, "I wish—"

He waited again. A cold fear came over him that she would wish him to go away. "Well," he said, "you wish?"

"I wish, Mr. Carteret," she said, "that I were your sister."

Then as his heart gave a bound, she turned about boldly.

"Try and understand me," she said. "I am so helpless that I am forced to overstep a girl's diffidence. I must have employment not only because I must have something to occupy my mind, but because I must protect myself."

"Yes," he assented. "You must protect yourself—from what?"

"From all the humiliations and annoyances that a helpless girl is subjected to. I appealed to you because I thought you could help me without adding to my annoyances. I don't know why I thought so. That I have to talk to you this way is proof enough how helpless I am," and here she began to cry.

This was too much for Carteret: He sprang towards her with the impulse of great pity. She put her arm up as if to warn him back,

"Miss Castleton," he said, making an effort to demean himself with patience and decorum, but evincing a good deal of eagerness in his tones, "you have expressed a wish that flatters and agitates me. The first thing for you to do is to act as though you meant it. I think you were quite right in appealing to me, for our circumstances are near enough alike to make us understand each other, and I am enough of a man to be honored by your confidence, and too much of a man not to place all that is best and noblest in me at your service. I am willing from this moment to make you my sister sacredly. It is for you to tell me how I can best execute the trust."

Here his breath was out. He often wondered afterward by what kind of inspiration he made that speech. It took him a long time, as it takes a long time for all of us, to learn that a deep and sudden emotion is the most powerful of inspirations.

She had lifted her eyes and was looking him in the face as he concluded. It is doubtful if the words appealed to her understanding. As tones lie deeper in the soul than articulations, something in the man was hidden under all the phrases, visible only to the divine instinct of a girl.

"Thank you," she said, with an exquisite little impulse of sincerity. "You have seen how I am placed. My grand-father is helpless, almost childish, and everything that I do for him or for myself must be done in opposition to his affection for me. The best and only friend I have got is my worst enemy without knowing it. Can you understand me?"

"I think I do," said Carteret.

"He is the victim of all kinds of people. He looks upon me as a child. He has plans and schemes for my future which it will break his heart to frustrate and he is miserably poor. I must earn my own living. I cannot go on this way, subject to everybody. You must tell me how I can get employment—I, who have no talents and no skill."

"I see, I see," said Carteret, reflectively. But what he saw was a picture of this beautiful girl transformed into some kind of an operative, coming and going with a crowd of women, doing some kind of ignoble drudgery in a factory, all the bloom rubbed off by exacting monotonous toil. He had already poised his ideal on a rosy pedestal with the summary fancy of an artist, and to pull it down at her bidding into the dust was not possible. He was perplexed and lost in conjecture. So she went on.

"How I shall ever manage to take care of Grandpa while I am employed away from home, I don't know. He depends upon me for everything. You see, Mr. Carteret, I can only mention difficulties."

"O," cried Carteret, with a flash of wisdom, "you must have employment at home, you know."

"If I only could," she replied, with girlish eagerness. "But I can't do anything. I can't even sew well enough to earn anything."

"Heaven be praised," cried the young man, "don't you know that sewing women are always celebrated for what they don't earn? We'll escape that proverbial misery, anyway. There must be something. How about music lessons? By George! you play. It's genteel and quiet. I'll get Oats and we'll drum up a lot of pupils and you can charge 'em bang up prices."

The idea seized him so completely that he got up to let a little of its surplus energy escape in action. "Do you know," he said as he strode about in the narrow room, "I'm convinced that's the providential trick. There's nothing like it for heavy returns if you get pupils enough—and Oats can get them."

She was shaking her head musingly, and the shake interpreted, meant to say, "The notion of my teaching anybody would be something like imposture."

But he paid no attention to her mute protest and rattled on. Now that the germ of a scheme had dropped into the warm soil of his imagination, it began to fructify and start all the other unsuspected germs. Suddenly he stopped before her where she had sunk upon a sofa.

"Can you draw?" he said with the comical air of superiority that a young man assumes when suddenly weighted with a delicate responsibility.

"Yes," she said with a quiet smile. "I was considered very good at it when I was at school."

"And you told me you had no skill or talents," he cried with admiration that tried to make itself sound like reproach. "Why, you've got your independence in your own hands. Listen to me a moment," and he assumed the attitude and used the gestures of an intensely practical man. "Instead of being helpless, you are independent. Your grandfather will come back here with a fortune in his pocket. A thousand dollars—why it's princely. You'll take a quiet little place where you can have your grandfather all to yourself. You'll have your little boudoir with a Chickering piano in it and an easel. In three weeks I'll teach you how to paint horse shoes, silk skirts, velvet and all the rubbish the town's running mad over. All I'll have to do will be to sell it for you. Don't you shake your head—the more amateurish it is, the better it will sell. Don't you run away with the idea that merit gets the market. I'll make Oats take hold of you and your brother will die contented if you're independent, even of brothers, and are happy."

Enthusiasm is more infectious than practical sense. The rattling earnestness had its effect. She was young and hopeful herself and the glimpses of independence and comfort combined, however illusive, fell in with the desires of her heart. Nobody painted such pictures for her and she said to herself, "He is a man and ought to know. How good he is."

To Carteret it was all plain sailing. "You will free yourself at once from the Wilders and Plonskis and Hanniges," he said, "and even the Stonybrooks, if you want to," at which she smiled archly; "you will be your own mistress and make your own circle as a lady should. It's my advice and I'm willing to do a brother's share of work. Haven't you got any drawings to show me?"

She thought she might have some in her trunk, but they were such dreadful crude sketches, she was ashamed to show them. He insisted and she ran upstairs with many buoyant protests to get them. He walked up and down while she was gone. She would be a pupil of his. He would sit beside her and guide her. They would be intimately associated in a beautiful employment. She would learn to trust him, perhaps to—he tried to calm himself. What kind of mirage was this rising on his horizon? He heard her coming down the stairs rapidly and humming a song as if her heart were light. A deep involuntary unspoken prayer went out of him, "Heaven help me now to help her."

Then she sat down beside him on the sofa without hesitancy and together they turned over the few little sketches, blurred and stained, that she had saved. They were so close together that her hair brushed his cheek at times as they bent over to examine some hardly legible marks and she explained what they were. Of course, he praised them honestly. The clumsiest lines seen through one's mist of sensibilities may take on the sweep of Giotto's pencil and turn to Hogarth's curve of beauty. She blushed with pride at his admiration, not because it was effusive but because it was discriminating. The sketches that she deemed the worst, he selected as the best. "What I admire in them," he said, "is not the execution so much as the idea, but then nobody but a born artist would have drawn that geranium and stem with that free sweep." How long they would have sat over the bits of cardboard had they not been interrupted it would be difficult to say. The vague sketches somehow grew into flowers of promise and an art phantasy seemed to convert them into garlands that entwined both of them.

A coach rattled up to the house and the bell rang violently. Manuella with a little start, went to the window. She saw Wilder helping her grandfather, very limp and wretched, from the coach. Instinctively she knew that something unpleasant had happened. She ran to the hall door, followed by Carteret, just as Wilder reached the entrance with Mr. Evans. He hurriedly gave the old gentleman into their charge and went down the steps. Then, as if some explanation were necessary to the surprised persons who were looking mutely after him, he turned, "I'll be back in an hour or two. Look after the old man. He's lost his head," saying which, he sprang into the vehicle, slammed the door and drove off rapidly in the direction of Irving place.

"What's the matter, Grandpa?" cried Manuella holding him by the arm, and bending over to look into his face. "What has happened? Did you get the cup?"

He shook his head mournfully and his lips trembled as he murmured something.

"Let me lead him in here," said Carteret, assisting her, "he appears to be weak."

They got him upon the sofa, where he sat, a picture of imbecility, wringing his hands and moaning. She thrust a cushion behind him and getting down in front of him, clung to him beseechingly. "Can't you tell me," she said," what has happened. Where is your cup?"

"Gone," he said, looking vaguely around, "gone, gone." Then seeing Carteret, he added: "I assure you, sir, I have not deceived you. I am a man of strict business integrity. What I tell you is true—quite true. You shall see if you will get me my books." His voice sank to a thin and plaintive key. "Nobody will look at my books. They have not been brought up from the Terrace. My dear, we must send for the books. Mr. Wilder must see the books. Do you understand, my child?"

"But what did you do with the cup?" Manuella asked as she stared at him with wet pity in her big eyes.

"Yes, the cup," he said, "it is so strange. The cup's gone and Martin Cruger's gone and Turtle Bay is gone. Everything is gone, my dear. But I am honest, I assure you I am honest."

Carteret looked at this mental wreck and at the heartbroken girl, and the impulsive nature that a few minutes before had breathed a prayer, now uttered a curse on the cup and all its belongings.

They tried with questions to elicit something, but in vain, and when he put his hand on his head as if in pain, Carteret begged her to desist. "We'll get the facts from Wilder," he said, "and meanwhile we must get your grandfather to his room and let him rest."

Mrs. Hannige coming upon the scene at that moment, they carried him away between them, and Carteret came down and renewed his walk in the parlor while he waited for Wilder.

Hour after hour passed—he heard Oats come in and go upstairs humming a war song and presently go out again. He thought over all that had occurred in a few hours—asked himself with secret satisfaction why Manuella should have come to him for advice when she had the fatherly Mr. Stonybrook to appeal to; wondered if that accursed cup had reduced all his plans to ashes, and then arriving at no solution in his impatient mind, he went across the street to the Century club and asked for Oats. He was not there, but some one asked Carteret in and he sat for another hour at an upper window watching Mrs. Hannige's house. It was dusk when he saw Wilder come back, and hurrying across, he caught the officer in the reception room and not in the most amiable of moods.

"The matter is simply this," he said in reply to Carteret's impatient question. "I've been fooled again with that cup. That old man promised to return it, but he had got rid of it and tried the thinnest kind of ruse on me."

"I think you are mistaken in the old man," Carteret ventured to say.

"I'm not mistaken in the facts. He took me uptown to show me where he had buried it—"

"Buried it?"

"Yes, and there was a block of buildings on the spot. Then he went all to pieces, cried and whined and broke all up. Either he is a softheaded old fool, or a pretty sly old fox. It isn't easy to believe that he went up there and dug a hole and put that cup in it, and if he did it isn't likely that his granddaughter is ignorant of it."

"Then you think—?"

"I think that he has sold out to Plonski and has tried a boy's game on me."

Carteret shook his head. "You are dead wrong," he said, "if the old man said he buried it, you may depend on it, he did. Idiotic as it all is, it is not as unreasonable as to suppose him capable of a deliberate deception. What are you going to do now?"

"Don't ask me any questions," said Wilder, "you will hear in good time. I am going to see the young lady alone. There is no use in your waiting."

CHAPTER XIX.

THE RESPONSIBILITIES OF A BROTHER.

Carteret was now earnestly in love for the first time in his life, and as is usually the case with artistic temperaments, the new sentiment took full possession of him and wrought its effects not alone in his conduct but in his work. A new enthusiasm stimulated his mind and got into his eye and his wrist.

He was up at daybreak, and instead of dawdling over his breakfast or spending hours dreaming and gossiping at Pizanni's saloon on the Sixth avenue, which was the headquarters of a knot of young artists like himself, he was at his easel; and he did not fail to notice the new facility of execution. He dashed in color boldly and rounded forms exultantly. A kind of inspired impatience made his work broader and fuller of meaning than ever before.

Chapman came in one morning and showed a good deal of surprise as he looked at a color sketch on the easel.

"By the gods, Carteret," he said, "that doesn't look like your work. Let it alone. Don't spoil it by finishing it. Nothing is so fatal as completion. If you put another dab on it, you'll ruin it. Hang me, I didn't believe it was in you. You've been coloring sonnets with the point of your brush—now you've forged a Greek strophe. Let it alone—let it alone."

Carteret was so full of ideas that he used up all the canvasses and academy board in his studio. He threw in color with frenzy and then stood the sketch against the wall and began another. It was altogether a departure from his old puttering.

He was thinking of his pupil continually and during these happy days, watched the hours for the time when he could rush off to her.

He had put up an easel in Manuella's room and transformed himself into a tutor. His patience with her was a surprise to himself. His admiration of her poor little attempts was a noble hypocrisy that he never suspected.

They were thus drawn together in the most natural and dangerous manner. The steps of the intimacy were so small that they mounted over them to confidence without knowing it. Every afternoon he sat just a little behind her pretending to watch her work, but really, if it must be confessed, admiring the beautiful curve or her wrist and the matchless contour of her neck. Never had he experienced such a piquant delight as the birth of hopes, and the pride of achievement in this girl, gave him. Never was his skill so precious or the imparting of it so delicious. He had to teach her the names of the colors; he had to show her how to hold the palette. They laughed together over her awkwardness and ignorance while Mr. Evans dozed at the window.

At first his behavior was a little formal, as the responsibility of his charge and the duty of a brother would naturally make it. He went a little out of his way to be polite and preserve the dignity and superiority of a tutor, and showed the firmness of experience and knowledge. It was, "Now then, Miss Castleton, are you ready for work? I must not waste time you know," and Manuella would say, "O dear, yes, what a lot of time I do waste in talking. I wonder if all pupils are as giddy as I am."

Just at what point this frostwork of cold propriety melted away and left the lover uncovered, not even Carteret himself could tell. But certainly it didn't take many lessons to establish little points of mutual confidence. Funny little experiences occurred that nobody on earth could understand but themselves. Little phases of character that nobody else could know, were made apparent to each other. Trivial incidents, too small to be recorded, knit their confidence secretly, as when the momentary weakness of her grandfather took her from her work and then Carteret found himself assisting her in her attentions to the old gentleman. It was impossible to be so much together without learning a great deal of the weaknesses of Mr. Evans and of the trials of the girl, that she never told to anybody, and it was natural that sooner or later Manuella would talk to Carteret about those things of which she must know he was cognizant.

One day they wanted colors and Carteret suggested that she should go the next day and purchase them herself. "You might as well get familiar with the business at once," he said, "you will have to do it sooner or later."

"But I don't know anything about it," she said.

Then with the most natural impulse, he cried: "I'll go with you and teach you the ropes. Do you know, Devoe's ought to sell some of your work for you. We'll go down there together. I'll introduce you to Seaver and he'll sell you what you want at a discount. You meet me to-morrow morning and we'll explore their establishment."

So it came about that one pleasant morning they met and got into an omnibus when Broadway was in shadow and nicely sprinkled, and rode down to Fulton street together. It was one of those impromptu excursions that leave their lucky sunshine in the memory forever.

Carteret was as proud of her as a boy could be. He noticed that men turned to look after her. He said to himself: "How much more beautiful she is in her simple homely dress and little chip hat, than all the women that I see."

The great establishment of Devoe in Fulton Street astonished and delighted her. There was such a deal more in the art world than she had ever dreamed of. They spent an hour or two looking at all the collections. "What a deal Carteret knew about art." They turned over all the portfolios. They sat at each counter and wondered at the devices to make amateurs happy with paint, and Carteret bought nearly everything that the girl admired.

When they came away, it was at the busiest time of the day downtown. The streets were choked and noisy, men ran against each other in their inconsiderate haste.

Just as they reached Broadway some kind of a labor procession, with a band, was passing and the street was for a moment in possession of a mob that surged along the sidewalks.

Suddenly jostled by the rude throng, Manuella, startled and timid, unconsciously caught hold of Carteret. He seized her hand as she did so and pulled her arm through his and for the first time, he had her close in a protecting grasp.

Drawing her out of the crowd into the doorway of a convenient shop, he held her until the street was passable and then without releasing her he said:

"New York is a big rude place for one's sister, did you ever know just how big it is? I mean, did you ever get a bird's-eye view of it? How would you like to look down on it from the clouds?"

The girl timidly looked up at him and gave her arm a protesting little pull, as if she were afraid he was going to propose a runaway in a balloon. He held her fast however. "What a nervous little creature you are for a sister," he said. "I don't believe you have much confidence in brothers after all. I was only going to say, there is Trinity Church spire just over there. Suppose we go and climb it before you go back. I'd like you to see the town you've got into. They say artists live in the clouds and here you've never been any higher up than O'Reardon's Terrace."

"O, but I must get back to Grandpa—remember, I've been away all the morning."

"Nonsense," said Carteret; "Mrs. Hannige will take care of him till we get back. I gave her special instructions myself and I'm sure you did also. Let's walk over there and then I'll rattle you home in a cab. Unless you get some oxygen occasionally, you'll lose all your own vitality and I'd like to know what Grandpa would do then. The greatest kindness to him is to look out for your condition. It don't need a wise man to see that. Come along," and in spite of her declarations that she shouldn't, he took her over to the churchyard and a few minutes later they were panting and climbing the zigzag stairs in the spire.

From that day a new and indescribable relationship existed. It was as if the event had committed them to a new companionship, without betraying the sentiment that was growing up.

It was the very next day, that sitting together in Mrs. Hannige's room, Manuella gave way to her girlish delight over the things that had come home from Devoe's, and went through the affectionate comedy of explaining everything to her grandfather, who evinced a sleepy enjoyment that was a mere reflection of the girl's high spirits.

When she was seated before her easel and Mr. Evans with a handkerchief over his head was feebly snoring in a rocker, Manuella with her back to Carteret, said:

"You have told me so much that I didn't know that I'm afraid to ask you one question that is in my mind."

"What is it?"

"Have you got any other pupils?"

"Not a blessed one," said Carteret, with an unnecessary amount of earnestness.

After a moment's pause, Manuella, as if with a sigh, remarked, "Then you are not a teacher after all. What a disappointment."

"Not a teacher?"

"Certainly not. If you were, you would have more than one pupil."

"Well, I suppose I can get more if you think it is necessary. I'll put an advertisement in the papers to-morrow if you desire it, for female students."

"Somehow I don't think you ought to give all your valuable time to one pupil."

"Not if she is a sister?"

"No."

"Why not?"

"Because it makes her appear dreadfully selfish."

"But it makes him appear awfully self-sacrificing and—good. Two noble qualities in the family offset the mean one. Don't let us quarrel about that."

"But I must. The arrangement gives you all the good."

"But I would not be good and noble if you had not made me. You appealed to me. It was you who converted me into a brother. It was you who insisted on my no longer remaining a selfish recluse and on my becoming a self-sacrificing tutor. Look at me—I'm your work, I ought to ask if you have any more pupils. There, you are doing that wrong. If you put that light on first, how will you get your shadows in?"

"It's because you confuse me. My hand shakes so this morning, I can't do anything. I don't think I'll work any more," and she laid down the brush. "I want to talk about something else."

"All right," said Carteret, considerately. "Never force your mood. What shall we talk about?"

At that moment Mr. Evans, whose head had fallen over on his breast, gave a deep groan. It was a mysterious, inarticulate moan—the saddest, weirdest of all human sounds. Both the young people turned towards the sleeper and as they did so, he lifted his thin wrinkled hand and said:

"Patience, patience, my friends, I have lost my books and I can prove nothing at present; but I am an honest man, believe me, as you shall see when I get my books back, they were buried and built over, but then will come back to me and then all will be right—if—" and his voice sank to a tremulous plaint, "if my heart doesn't break in the meanwhile."

"Grandpa," cried Manuella, springing towards him in an impulse of tenderness and pity. "You shall have your books. I will go and fetch them myself."

"What is it?" asked Carteret, with some surprise.

He had to wait for her filial mood to pass before he got his answer and he walked to the window and looked out while the girl hung upon the old man, who in spite of her caresses did not awaken, but continued to mumble inarticulately in his sleep.

Presently she came over to the window and laid her hand on Carteret's arm. Carteret only looked at her expectantly without saying a word.

"The loss of Grandpa's books appears to have caused him more unhappiness than anything else. When he had them he was cheerful. I think I ought to go and get them for him."

"Of course you should," said Carteret, "if you can. But as I don't know what books you are talking about or where they are, I cannot advise you."

"They were left behind at the Terrace," said Manuella, "they are his ledgers and cash books. He prizes them beyond all reason and has never ceased to lament their loss. We left the place so suddenly and so strangely that they were not thought of. I am sure Cynthy would give them up."

"Suppose we go and get them," said Carteret. "I am sure that great comfort to you grandfather is worth our little trouble. Put on your hat and we'll run round to the Terrace and demand them."

"How good you are," said the girl, looking up at him. "But do you think it is safe for me to go?"

Carteret answered this naive question after a moment's thought by saying, "I will go myself," and picked up his hat.

"How impulsive you are. I am sure my aunt would not give them to you," exclaimed Manuella.

"Then suggest something besides a dilemma that I can do," said Carteret, helplessly.

"Give me some advice. Do you think it is quite safe for me to go back there—I mean if you went with me?"

"I do not quite understand what you are afraid of?"

"That man Plonski. If I go, my aunt will be sure to find out where I am living and tell him."

"And if she does?"

"I cannot tell what will happen—but I fear for my grandfather if that wretch finds out where he is. Your friend, the officer, asked me to keep out of his way."

"Oh!" says Carteret, jumping at her suggestion. "Why not get Wilder to fetch the books."

The next day he brought word to Manuella that Wilder was out of town and they would not or could not tell at the Central Office where he had gone.

Meanwhile she told her grandfather that the books were to be restored, and it had so encouraged him that when Carteret informed her of Wilder's absence she said: "Then I will go myself and you shall go with me."

In an incredibly short time she had her hat on and was ready, and together they started for the Terrace.

Whether intentionally or not, Manuella went up the First avenue, and when at Twenty-first street said she wanted to call at Mrs. Holbrook's, who would be anxious to hear about her grandpa. Bob Holbrook was on duty there, and greeted her with unmistakable delight.

"Couldn't think what had become of you. Spliced, eh?" looking at Carteret. "Gone and done it, I'll bet, haven't you? No? Honest? How's the old man? Got a new soda fountain in since you were here. Don't you want to sample it? What'll you have—sarsaparilla or lemon? Same for you, sir? Lord, what a lot of people's been asking for you."

"Who?" asked Manuella with a foaming tumbler under her nose.

"First, there was that girl, Clianthe Mignon, who lives in the top of the Terrace. She's been here three times."

"What did she want?" asked Manuella with some surprise.

"Wanted to find out where you had gone. She's a dizzy one; she wouldn't give herself away to me. Then Mrs. Sitwhite was here and an old rooster with a hook nose and a red scarf pin. But they come to the wrong shop. I didn't know anything, and wouldn't have blowed if I had. Now, try the vanilla."

All this frightened Manuelia a little, and she began to hesitate about going to the Terrace.

Carteret saw it, and immediately suggested to her to stay there in the stationers' and he would go alone.

Bob Holbrook eagerly seconded this proposition, and after some hesitation Carteret set out alone and Bob took the girl in the little back room out of sight.

"What have you been doing, anyway?" he asked as soon as Carteret was gone. "Heard you was arrested. Couldn't make it out. Mrs. Sitwhite, she comes here and said the old man had left some stolen property with us and she wanted it. My old woman came nigh firing her out. They had it quite hot. Where are you living, anyway? You ought to tell a fellow that. Can't I serve you with the papers? There's a big story running in 'The Girl's Own' now; have you seen it?

I've got all the back numbers. I can tell you the first chapters in five minutes, so you can catch on without wading back, if you want me to."

"I'm sure, Bob," said Manuella, utterly disregarding his garrulity, "that if Grandpa left anything here with you would tell me."

"Of course I would," said Bob, "but he didn't. I always done what you told me, didn't I?"

Manuella tried to remember, with a smile, what she had ever told him to do, and said, "Yes," graciously.

"I've done lots of things for you that you didn't tell me to do."

"Oh, have you indeed?" said his companion, lifting her eyebrows.

"Lots; but I'm like that feller De Lancy in Mrs. Southworth's new story; have you read that? It's gay. Wait a minute, there's somebody in the store."

When he came back she said: "I can't imagine what that girl Mignon wanted with me. Didn't she tell you anything?"

"Not a word. They all seemed to have an idea that I had the old man concealed somewhere. Why, I never saw him after we buried the dog."

"After what?" with new amazement.

"After we buried the dog—your pet. Didn't he tell you?"

Manuella looked at him a moment as if undetermined whether this was one of his figures of speech or a revelation.

"No," she said, "he didn't tell me."

"Well, what a sly old rooster. He didn't want to see the dead pet put in an ash barrel; he knew it would hurt your feelings. So I gave him a box and we went up to Turtle Bay and had a funeral."

"When was that, Bob?"

"It's two weeks and more ago. You remember the day. You left him here and came back for him. He had the box under his arm when you went home."

"And he came back here for you, and you went with him and buried it?"

"Yes, I did. What makes you stare at me that way? Wasn't it all right?"

"I'd like to see the spot," said Manuella, still staring dreamily at him.

"Well, I'm the boy that can show it to you. I can just put my finger on the grave, and we'll take a wreath and go up and decorate it. Wait till the old woman comes back and we'll snatch a horse car."

Manuella had become very thoughtful. Bob rattled on, but she gave little heed to him, and while he was telling her the plot of a new story in the "Fireside Delight" Carteret returned.

On the way home he told her of his ill success. "Your aunt, I must tell you," he said, "was insulting and brutal, and she did not hesitate to accuse you of all manner of sins."

"Oh, dear," cried Manuella, "what a deal of annoyance I am making you suffer."

"Annoyance!" he replied with genuine surprise. "Nonsense, what is any annoyance by the side of your misfortune? I'd go back there a score of times if it would do any good. If I tell you the exact truth, don't think I am complaining. Mrs. Sitwhite said you had taken her father away; that between you she had been robbed. She threatened, accused, denied and wept. She said she had burned the books up for old lumber, and then said if you wanted them you would have to come yourself, and finally said she'd bring them to you if I'd give her your address; and when I declined to do it she abused me like a pickpocket."

"I suppose we shall have to let them go," said Manuella rather disconsolately.

"Not a bit of it," replied Carteret, "they belong to your grandfather, and he must have his property. Suppose we go this way. I'm afraid that she or some of her friends will follow us. If they should find out where you live there will be no end of annoyance for you."

Then he hurried her off the avenue, and they walked so fast she could not tell him until they arrived at Mrs. Hannige's what had occurred at Holbrook's.

"It seems that Grandpa did bury the cup after all and took that boy Bob with him."

"What an unaccountable freak," said Carteret. "I'm awfully glad he did though, and I hope he buried it deep enough."

They had sat down on the lounge in Mrs. Hannige's reception room.

"Wait a moment for me," she said, "I must run up and see that Grandpa's all right. I'll come right back. I want to say something to you seriously," and then she flew upstairs, leaving him wondering what the serious thing could be.

She was gone exactly an hour by his impatience and precisely six minutes by the little ormulo clock on Mrs. Hannige's mantel.

"Sit down here," she said. "I want to ask you not to be a brother any more."

"Not a brother? What shall I be?"

"Nothing. Don't look offended. It's going to tax you too much to put up with my whims and I've no right to expect it."

"What do you mean, Miss Castleton?" blankly asked the young man.

"I mean that I am a capricious, exacting girl, but I have moments of good sense when I can be severely just to myself and considerate of others. This is one of them."

"It is infamously false," cried Carteret. "You are the most considerate, the most modest and kindhearted woman I ever met."

"When I'm serious as I am now," she replied; "you cannot be a brother of mine."

"Cannot? Perhaps you will tell me why, in your modest mood."

"Because I expect too much of you."

"Is it more than I can do? Are you sure that you have tried me? Perhaps," he exclaimed as he got up from the lounge, "you want some other brother—Mr. Stonybrook, perhaps?"

She patted her hand on the lounge significantly for him to sit down again.

He obeyed the gesture without being conscious of her quiet exercise of authority.

"Don't be foolish," she said. "Suppose that I said to you—Brother, I want the moon."

"By heaven," said Carteret, "I think I would commence immediately to do all that man can do to get it for you. Could a brother be more insane than that?"

"But would a sister be worth all that trouble?"

"Some sisters would."

"Then you insist on being a brother with all that it entails?—consider."

"I refuse to consider. I insist on being the only brother. I don't want two in the family."

"But you don't ask me what I want."

"Yes, I do."

"Listen then. I want that cup and I want those books."

He was about to get up again but she held him by the coat sleeve. "Don't jump about in that way," she said, "if you were to ask me why I want them, I couldn't tell you exactly—or I wouldn't like to at present, but I may some day. Don't ask me now. You have been the best friend I ever had, Mr. Carteret, and I blush to appear so unreasonable to you, but I shall think a thousand times more of you if you will say you'll help me in this just because I want it."

"Miss Castleton," said Carteret, "I believe that cup is accursed. I believe it will bring misfortune to everybody who meddles with it, but I'll help you get it because you want me to."

Her hand dropped upon his. He felt her warm clasp. No thanks she could have uttered would have gone deeper or seemed to him more exquisite.

"Come to-morrow," she said, "and we'll talk it over."

CHAPTER XX.

ROSAMOND GOES INTO ART, TOO.

The next day Carteret was for the first time in weeks too abstracted to paint. He had brought over to the studio quite a collection of little toy picture frames, fans and miniature easels, that it was his hypocrisy to say Manuella had painted, but which, to tell the truth, he had in great part executed himself. They stood all round the room in quaint array, decorated with pansies and autumn leaves and peach blossoms. He was wondering how he could sell them. There were also conspicuously in sight two bold likenesses of Manuella, painted from memory. One was as he remembered her with her golden hair down, the first day he saw her at the Terrace. The other was the same girl piquantly attired in rather a Watteau style. At intervals his eye rested on them and he went off into a reverie. But he could not keep his mind long in any definite line of thought. It ranged over the eventful yesterday with vagrant zest, and generally shot out into his own indefinite future with a tinge of anxiety, at which point he would invariably rush at his easel and begin painting with renewed vigor.

It was his custom to leave the key of his studio in Chapman's room when he went away. Letters came sometimes to the place and picture buyers sometimes wandered in. Chapman obligingly kept an eye on several of the rooms whose occupants were away.

On this particular day Carteret locked his door in a buoyant state of mind, took the key into Chapman, and praised that artist inordinately out of his own happiness, and then set out for Mrs. Hannige's.

He had not been gone half an hour when a vehicle drove up to the Studio Building and a richly dressed young woman got out. She stood a moment in the entrance way looking at the occupants' names and numbers on a big panel, as if trying to recall the location of a particular room, and then went up the stairs slowly and through the corridor to Carteret's studio where she rapped several times with her parasol and then tried the knob. Failing to receive any answer, she sauntered along the passage until she came to Chapman's door, which stood ajar, and here she stopped and again applied her parasol, evoking a gruff "walk in" from somebody.

She then pushed the door open and entered. Chapman, who was seated at his easel with his back to the door, did not turn round, but went on painting most unconcernedly.

"I beg your pardon," said the lady. "Can you tell me when Mr. Carteret is in his studio?"

Chapman then turned slowly round on his stool and saw a handsome brunette, whose black eyes flashed with health, and whose projecting chin arrested his artistic sense of character.

"Carteret," said he, "works in the mornings only, now. He has been gone about half an hour. Will you sit down? I can show you his studio if you wish to see his work. His key is here."

"You are very kind," she answered. "I would like to. I am an admirer of his work; but I must get my breath first."

She sat down and looked about the room at the various pictures, with self-possessed and rather critical interest. "Has Mr. Carteret been doing anything new lately?" she asked.

"O, yes," replied Chapman, as he put a dab of paint on his canvas. "He's been working very steadily and has come out in a new style, quite broad and Frenchy. He's got a canvas ready for the fall exhibition. It's been very much admired."

"Does he have many visitors?"

"Not many. The fact is we don't any of us have as many as we'd like. Do you care for landscapes? Here's a composition of mine I've just sold to David Home, the banker."

Chapman then pulled round a big canvas, rubbed it off with a rag and stepped back to get a look at it himself.

"It's very beautiful," said the lady. "Do you know where Mr. Carteret lodges?"

"I believe he has a room at the Revere," replied Chapman. "Perhaps you like smaller pictures," and he put his hand on the canvas to remove it.

"Please let it remain a moment," she said quickly. "Mr. Carteret has been making studies, has he not?"

"Not that I know of. I think he has been steadily at work for weeks. He used to go off in the country and loaf for a season, but he's given it up. It was a waste of time."

"Did he say so?"

"I think he did say something about having lost a whole summer. There's a sketch of Lake Saranac. How do you like that?"

"Very much indeed. What is the price of it?"

"It's sold. It was in Schaus's window and was bought by Dr. Follen Sanger. He gave me a hundred dollars for it."

"It is not customary I suppose," said the visitor, "for ladies to visit the studios alone."

"O, yes," replied Chapman, promptly. "We've outgrown that long ago. There are so many lady artists and amateurs, that they could not wait for company. O, no, indeed, why there are several lady buyers who purchase on commission;

they wouldn't think of having gentlemen escorts when they are attending to their business. Are you purchasing?"

The young lady smiled. "I may be," she said, "but only for my own pleasure. I always had a fondness for studio life and I dare say it was on account of its freedom from straight laced nonsense. Some people are born Bohemians and I've often thought I must have had an artist forefather."

"Then you do a little in paint yourself?"

"No, not that, but I'm always hanging round where it is done, and have always from a child had the good fortune to be thrown among artists. Will you show me Mr. Carteret's work?"

Chapman laid down his palette and brushes, took the key and led the way to his friend's studio.

The moment he threw the door open, they were confronted by Manuella, and her golden hair gleamed like a spot of sunshine in the dusty and disordered workroom.

The visitor exclaimed at once: "O, its Godiva."

"No," said Chapman; "I think its Cordelia. 'Tisn't bad, either. Between you and me, I think it much the best thing Carteret has done."

"Is it from life?"

"Well, it's what we call an ideal, but the fact is all ideals have to have a model."

"Ideal? Does Carteret call it his ideal?"

"Of course. If it's a Cordelia it must be an ideal, don't you see?"

"Why, that's another of the same woman. She's got a chip hat on—is that an ideal too?"

"I suppose so," said. Chapman, carelessly.

"There must be more of them," said the lady, walking about the studio peeringly.

"Studies, perhaps," assented Chapman, turning over a number of canvasses and pulling out several sketches in color of the same unmistakable beauty, which he put in a row on the floor under the Cordelia.

The lady stood in front of them attentively. "They all have the same features and the same expression," she said.

"That's a sure evidence," replied Chapman, smilingly, "that he had the same model."

"You said," remarked the visitor without ceasing her survey of the pictures, "that Carteret had come out in a new French style, did you mean these pictures?"

"Well, yes. They are the best he has ever done. I can show you some of his old work and it doesn't compare with this."

Then he went poking about, making a good deal of dust as he examined the canvasses that were standing against the wall, and finally he pulled out a head somewhat less than life size, and removing the dust from it, placed it beside Cordelia on the same easel.

The visitor gave a little start. But Chapman, who was looking at the picture and rattling on, did not notice it. It was a labored, full-faced sketch in oil of a black eyed and passionate girl, handsomely dressed. She had a gipsy hat hanging to her arm, and back of her was a clump of chestnuts, through which gleamed the blue water of a little bay. The handsome face was rather formal, and what the artist had intended for piquancy of expression had a slightly fierce look.

It was a picture of the woman who was now looking at it, and it was a sufficient criticism of its excellence that Chapman did not notice the resemblance, but talked glibly on as he rubbed the surface with an oiled rag to bring out the dead colors.

"There," he said, "he worked at that a long time, and the more he worked the worse he made it. I don't think he had any heart in it. You've got to have heart in your work, now, I tell you. See the labor on it. It's hard, conventional and unsuggestive; it doesn't throb, as you might say, with color and life like the other."

"No," assented the visitor dreamily.

"In fact, one is done *con amore*, as we say," continued Chapman, "and the other isn't."

"I don't agree with you exactly," said the lady after a long pause. "It seems to me that one face was beyond the artist's grasp. It had too much purpose and character for his brush. There is a determination in one woman that he couldn't understand. The other is mere form and color, and he got that. Is that Cordelia for sale?"

"I think not," replied Chapman. "He's going to send it to the next Exhibition."

"How about the other?" pointing with her parasol to the same face under the chip hat.

"Really, I don't believe Carteret wants to sell them, at least he hasn't said anything to me about it. He's gone into this sort of thing for the trade," and he pointed to the decorated trumpery on the floor.

"Since when did he become so independent?" she asked.

"O, he isn't independent; far from it."

"You are a friend of his I take it," said the lady, turning slowly about and regarding Chapman.

"I am, most certainly."

"So am I," she rejoined. "I'd like to help him. I'll give you my name and address at the proper time, but you can serve his interests and mine by keeping my secret at present. Tell me now," and she pointed her parasol with just the slightest air of contempt at the Cordelia, "is that the portrait of a professional model or a theatrical beauty?"

"O, nothing of the sort," cried Chapman, "'pon honor. We don't like to give away these professional matters, but I don't mind assuring you on behalf of my friend, that she is a poor but highly respectable girl in good standing. O, I'd hang that picture in my parlor over my family altar, that is," he added, "if I had a parlor and kept my family altar in it."

"Poor but highly respectable," repeated the lady with a tinge of irony, as she patted her boot on the floor vexatiously; and then, as if recalled to the fact that she was betraying herself, she got up suddenly with an entire change of manner.

"Well, well, Mr. Chapman, that is your name, isn't it? I think I shall have to buy some pictures of both of you. But do try and keep my visit quiet for a few days. I think we understand each other," and she tapped him on the shoulder familiarly with her parasol. "People do try to patronize artists without letting them know it, don't they sometimes, to save their pride?"

"O, yes," said Chapman with ease. "They like it."

They looked into each other's faces and laughed, and at that moment someone called Chapman loudly from the corridor. He looked out the door and then saying, "Excuse me a moment, take a seat—I'll rejoin you in a second," disappeared.

The moment he was gone the girl looked hurriedly about the room. There was a little cabinet at the side of the easel full of tiny drawers. She pulled them out with a quick, deft jerk and looked in. They were filled with dried and partly used tube colors, mouthpieces of pipes, matches, empty phials, broken brushes, and they emitted an odor of dead turpentine. On the table was a similar accumulation of debris and out of it stuck the tinted edges of a note. She pulled it forth with an eager snatch. The envelope was gone. It was her own letter and she read the last line with her teeth clenched. "The girl of yesterday is the woman of to-day, who will hold you to your promises because she loves you."

Her letter had been thrown there carelessly for any chance eye to see. She turned it over. He had used the blank page for memoranda. There were the figures on it in pencil:

Paid Revere $2.90
Loaned Chapman 1.50
Bought paint, etc., for Manuella 5.00
$9.40
Balance 60

A bitter, contemptuous curl of her lip showed itself as she read this and it was followed by a wicked glance round the room. Her eye then fell upon a waste basket in the corner. She listened a moment as she passed the door and then with stealthy desperation, turned the receptacle down so that the contents came out upon the floor. There were paint rags, old envelopes, one or two dirty collars, old gloves, cigar stumps, bits of paper and one little packet of bills or memoranda tied with a piece of wire from a beer bottle. As she heard Chapman approaching, she thrust this with the crumpled letter into some convenient harbor of her dress.

They stood at the open door and conversed half chaffingly and half in earnest a moment, and her last words to him were, "Mind, I want that picture, and if you've got another as good as Lake Saranac, I'll buy it. In a day or two I'll drop in and see you with a lady friend; but remember," and she pressed the amber handle of her parasol upon her lips, crushing a significant smile into a symbol of silence.

"Honor bright," said Chapman. "Glad to see you any time. Ever so much obliged. Good day." And he stood bowing till she reached the end of the corridor, where she threw a farewell gesture to him and disappeared.

The moment she was out of sight, her manner relapsed to a natural moodiness. She went down the stairs with her hand on the rail as if she were too busily engaged in thinking to trust herself to the steps. There was a cold, set look in her face—very vindictive and willful. She stopped at the doorway and looked at the name in the list of artists: "Colin Carteret." Then she got into the coach, telling the driver to go to Mrs. Hardynge's and the moment he started, she pulled out the note and turning the blank side, repeated several times, "Manuella, Manuella."

CHAPTER XXI.

LOVE SEARCHES FOR THE CUP.

The first thing Manuella said to Carteret when he arrived that day at the house was:

"O, I've got some good news for you. Grandpa's got his books."

Her eyes were full of sparkling pleasure as she greeted him.

"How did he get them?" asked Carteret with honest surprise, as he admired her expression.

"Why, it seems he had told Mr. Stonybrook all about it that day we went to Devoe's, and this morning he went with an officer and a search warrant and Cynthy gave them up at once. I'm chiefly glad because it will save you all the annoyance, don't you know."

"As if I wanted to be saved the annoyance," said Carteret reproachfully. "Mr. Stonybrook is very considerate."

"Yes," she replied, "of Grandpa. They are in there now and Mr. Stonybrook is going to have an expert—I think that's what he called him—examine the books. He was in here looking at my work."

"What did he say about it?"

"Well, to tell the truth, he laughed at it. I believe he's a connoisseur."

All this nettled Carteret in an inexplicable way and he only said: "Shall we go on and give him something more to laugh at? He hasn't discouraged you, I see; you've been at work this morning."

"I have been unusually industrious," she replied, "because I wanted to take a little jaunt this afternoon. I was going to ask you to go uptown. I want to see the place where Grandpa buried the cup."

His anticipations of pleasure were a little dampened by the after knowledge that Bob Holbrook had to go along to show them the place; but he could not quite divest himself of the notion that it was the desire to go out again with her tutor and not the idle curiosity to see a vacant lot uptown, that influenced her.

Manuella put on her chip hat and after some little coaxing and sparring with her gandfather, she accompanied Carteret to Holbrook's, and having picked up Bob, the three started uptown in a horsecar. It was a pleasant ride when once they had passed the denser portion of the city, and, although the garrulous Bob did most of the talking and made a boyish show of gallantry, Carteret understood from Manuella's glances that she was more amused by him than interested. He took them over the same route that had been traveled by Mr. Evans, and before they had reached the sign of "The Turtle Bay Brewery" he had told Manuella, with the utmost particularity, all the events of that day. Carteret listened with indulgence and some weariness and wondered at the patience of filial interest in what seemed to him to be the mere vagaries of senility.

They got out at the cross street, saw the beer pavilion with the American and Austrian flags flapping lazily, followed the board fence and came to the Martin Cruger estate. Here they again picked their way up the rocks and when on the summit, Bob Holbrook, who was ready to point out the very spot where the box had been buried, struck an attitude of helpless wonder and exclaimed:

"Well, if I aint jiggered. I hope I may die."

He pointed eastward to a row of houses in the course of construction not a stone's toss away and which had already reached the first story. Men were going up and down the ladders; processions of horses and carts were coming and going; the shouts of the drivers and the ring of trowels reached them in a continuous din of labor.

"That settles it," said he. "They've put a house on top of it."

"Where abouts was the exact spot, can you tell now?" asked Manuella.

"Why, yes. Do you see that sharp rock this side of the mortar heap? There's a goat on it; well, the old man told me to stay here and he went down to that rock and stopped a minute and looked round. I was watchin' him, but he didn't know it. Then he went about twenty feet, just about where that brick wall is now, and I slipped down these rocks and saw him dig a hole and put the box in it."

Manuella was pensively listening to this with her eyes on the piles of bricks that had sprung up on the spot.

"I was thinking," she said, as she saw Carteret looking at her wonderingly, "of the cruel disappointment and helplessness of Grandpa as he saw the result of his childish efforts. Your friend, Mr. Wilder, must have been very angry with him, and possibly unkind. You could not make him believe that Grandpa told the truth; and now you see that Grandpa was right."

Carteret led her one side. "I don't exactly know what is in your mind," he said, "but whatever it is we do not need to make this boy a confidant. He may be very loyal and discreet, but remember he has already told you that several people have been inquiring for you, and if he once understands what the nature of your search is, we have no assurance that he will not tell it. My prudence tells me that we had better go back and complete your plans when we are alone."

Put in this way, it made Manuella suddenly timid and she wanted to go back immediately. Carteret was not averse to a course of excursions with her and he did not much care whether the hunt was for a cup or for painting materials.

The result was that they went back, and on leaving Bob, Carteret, in a rather princely manner, remarked as he put his hand in his pocket, "Well, my boy, we can't expect you to lose your time for nothing."

To which Bob said, "He didn't know as he was hiring out when a lady went with him on a picnic."

The next day Carteret proposed, somewhat to Manuella's surprise, that they go back and make some further investigations. The simple fact is that he rather liked the idea of getting Manuella away from the house, and one pretext was as good as another.

She turned round from the lilies of the valley that she was painting on a piece of velvet, and said with girlish innocence:

"Why, what more is there to investigate? It's gone."

Thus forced to find a plausible excuse for his pleasure, the inventive art of love came readily to his help.

"O, I don't know about that. Bob's idea that a house is on top of it is very juvenile. They have to excavate for louses, and the men who excavate are poor drudges. They would be sure to find the cup and pretty sure to give it up for money."

"And you think," she said, looking at him earnestly, "that we might find it?"

"I think," he said, "that we might try, as you told me my brotherhood in some way depended on it, and your friend Stonybrook has robbed me of the other task."

And so with the beguilement of duty they began a course of excursions that led to the most extraordinary results and which, sunny enough with the October days, were nevertheless fretted by new and unexpected complications.

Their second visit to the suburbs was made on a Thursday afternoon. They picked their way over the rocks and came down to the waste of building material with no definite purpose. In truth they talked about everything but the ostensible purpose of their journey, until Carteret finding himself and his companion in an uptorn and choked roadway, standing on a narrow plank and surrounded by mortar beds and piles of brick, asked a laborer who was working at a steaming bed of earthy plaster with a hoe how they could get out, and got for an answer, "How the divil did yes get in?"

"Look here, my man," said Carteret, "I'll make it worth your while to be civil for five minutes. Did you ever earn any money that way?"

"Be gorry, I niver earned any that wasn't honest, for I didn't earn it with me tongue," replied the man with a chuckle, and without looking up from his mortar bed.

"What is it?" asked a burly, red shirted fellow who stepped out from a pile of bricks.

"I want to find the man who has charge of this work" said Carteret.

"What work," asked the burly individual, taking in the two figures on the plank with easy amazement. "Do you mean the mason work?"

"Isn't there somebody in charge?" asked Carteret.

"Charge of what?" snarled the man.

"Let's go back," said Manuella.

"Wait a moment," suggested Carteret, "I don't think we can get back without a guide. Those carts appear to have cut off our retreat. Are you the boss?" he asked at a risk of the man who stood staring at him.

"I'm the boss of this gang of helpers. Do you want the overseer or the superintendent or the contractor or the architect or the owner?"

"Any one of them will answer my purpose," said Carteret, "if you will kindly point out the best way to get to him."

The man pointed his arm without turning his head to some distant part of the chaos. "The superintendent is in that house where the steam is, or if he ain't he's round there somewhere," and with that he moved off.

The house where the steam was proved to be a shed extemporized for tools and donkey engine. By many devious and dirty ways they reached it and the superintendent, a young man with a blank book in his hand and marks of black lead on his face from pencil sharpening, involuntarily lifted his hat as they appeared at the door, and said, "Want to see me?" in a rather loud voice, occasioned by the noise of the engine.

"Just a moment," replied Carteret. "I want to ask you who was the contractor that did the excavating for this job?"

"Did you come from the Street Department?" asked the young man, who had evidently not complied with some ordinance.

"No," shouted Carteret. "If I had anything to do with the Street Department I'd have paths made so that a lady could get down here without losing her life."

The young man smiled and turning to somebody said, "Timmins did that work, didn't he?" to which a nod of assent was given. "John Timmins, Third avenue and Forty-Second Street, is your man."

"Thanks," said Carteret. "That's all I wanted to know."

"Well," remarked the young man, "you could have found that out without coming here. Is there anything else I can do for you?"

"Only direct us how to reach the avenue with the least labor."

He called some one to guide them out and touched his hat to Manuella as they disappeared.

In spite of all the petty difficulties of this little adventure both Carteret and Manuella got a good deal of enjoyment out of it. What indeed were the discomforts and annoyances of the way? Did he not have to lead her in many places by the hand? Did they not both laugh at the rough answers and uncouth manners? Did not the very bricks and mortar have a new interest?

When they got out upon the avenue, he saw the Austrian pavilion and suggested that they sit on the veranda and rest a moment and drink some cool Kaiser beer.

To Manuella the idea of drinking Kaiser Beer seemed preposterous, but the veranda was deserted and cool and she thought there could be no harm in seeing him drink it if he desired.

Often enough afterwards Carteret thought of that hour with all its trivial and homely incidents, magnified and softened by a growing sentiment.

Other scenes were grander and more beautiful; other experiences were rich with character and events; but somehow a charm of recollection hung about that happy October afternoon on the veranda of the beer saloon, when the dusty roadway, with its weeds and goats, and the barren lots, rubbish-crowned, seemed like outlying fields of enchantment. It is doubtful if ever after in life other and worthier occurrences gave him half the delight that Manuella's attempt to drink the Kaiser beer out of his glass then gave him. How delightful were her grimaces and little sputterings. How noble was her attempt to drink it because he requested it; how admirable was her failure.

The slant October sun shone through the awnings; the hum of the great city, like a vast nest of bees, came to them softened and drowsy. What were Toltec Cups or conspiracies to them? They possessed the talisman that converts the roughest roadway into a garden and sets the flying hours to music.

And yet not a word of love had been spoken.

To have spoken it then would perhaps have brought the delicious fantasy to earth as if one should insist on waking up and enacting a dream.

Carteret knew well enough by this time that Manuella was happy in his company. She took no pains to conceal it. Her confidences were the best evidence that she trusted him. Her willing companionship was proof that she preferred him.

They sat there and chatted about a thousand unimportant things in low tones, and laughed at their own sallies and rehearsed their joint experiences, already making a private record, until the shadows crept over the veranda and a frog or two in the pools by the river began to croak faintly. Then Manuella jumped up, and Carteret, as if it were necessary to refer to their mission occasionally, said "Tomorrow, ho—for John Timmins."

But on the morrow, when Carteret came to the Hannige establishment, Manuella ran down to the reception room to meet him, instead of sending for him to come up, and there was a slight shade of annoyance on her face.

"Grandpa has asked me not to go out with you to-day," she said, "and I ought to obey him—occasionally."

"Did he ask you not to bring me up?"

"No," hesitatingly, "but I thought it better not to. You must remember that an old man is crotchety and whimsical and ought be humored."

A pang of jealousy shot through the young man. It was a new and sharp sensation. "He hasn't interdicted Stonybrook, has he?" he asked.

The girl looked at him with calm frankness, but there was a light blush of color in her cheeks.

"Do you think I ought to go with you to-day?" she asked.

"Yes, I do," he replied with unwarranted directness.

"Then I will go. I am my own mistress. But we must not stay long. Wait a few moments and I will be ready."

The instant she had disappeared, he wanted to call her back and tell her he was an inconsiderate wretch. But he did not, and it may be doubted that the masculine mind fairly understood how much more consideration she had for him than he had for her, or that it stopped to think how much more she sacrificed to please him than he had thought of doing for her.

John Timmins, Contractor, had an office on upper Third Avenue. Carteret easily found his name in the directory, but he and Manuella walked past the gold sign in the window, too busily engaged in conversation to notice it. When they reached Fifty-ninth street, the sounds of a string band playing one of Meyerbeer's torch dances arrested their attention. It came from Terrace Garden. The entrance way was up a few steps; there were trees and flowers at the top. "Let us go in and sit down a moment," said Carteret, "where it is quiet. The music will refresh us." They presently found themselves at a table under an ailanthus tree. A few orderly Germans with their wives and children were scattered about and the band in the pavilion went on with Strauss and Lanner. "I wanted to say to you," said Carteret, "that I think the jolliest and the most sensible thing we could do would be to take your grandfather off into the country for a breathing spell. I know a quiet spot up on the Pocantico where I have sketched many a summer, but this year I've given my vacation to my pupil and haven't had a sniff of nature. If we could get him up there and feed him on fresh cream while we painted, it would do him good."

Manuella shook her head dreamily. "O dear, no," she said: "that's an idle dream for me. How kind you are to Grandpa."

"Idle? Why it would be your first real effort at art. You've got to get acquainted with nature sometime if you mean to paint, and I'd like to introduce you, for we are intimate. One week out of this city would be sufficient. I'm going to write to old Manser about it. There will be two or three weeks of the most delicious autumn weather."

She listened to him but no longer objected in words. He painted the rural retreat with the blue October skies and flying white clouds, the peace and seclusion and beauty, as only an enthusiastic young artist can, and it all mingled with the sounds of "The Blue Danube" from the band, and Manuella in a reverie shook her head.

Her mild firmness piqued him a little. He felt now that he had some right in her, but he could not explain to himself how much.

Suddenly he said, "Manuella, is there anybody you would rather go with than me?"

"No," she said softly, "I don't know of anyone."

He had to pause a moment as if he wanted to turn this answer over in his mind and get the full relish of it Then like an epicure, he had to paraphrase it.

"That is to say, you'd rather go with me than anybody else."

"I suppose so."

"But you will not."

She shook her head. "Pray don't," she said with the mildest little appeal, and then suddenly, "O dear, we've quite forgotten what we came for."

"Yes," said Carteret, "John Timmins——"

"Yes, sor," said John Timmins, "I tuk the dirt out for Cruger's Row, exoictly. Take a stool, ma'am. Where are yes goin' to build?"

John Timmins was a portly Irishman, with a florid face and short, red side-whiskers. He wore a loose navy blue coat without any vest or necktie and a scrupulous silk hat. The moment Carteret met him, he suspected that he was a politician and perhaps an alderman.

Carteret undertook to explain that he wanted to find out, if possible, where the gang of men were who did the excavating, as a piece of valuable property had been lost on the spot, which they wished to recover.

The moment Mr. Timmins heard this, his interest died out.

"Sonny," said he, "you must have it wrong. I don't superintend the work myself, but I can gamble on it there wasn't a load of rubbish taken out at Cruger's. It's all dumped on the other side of the lots. Me secretaree can tell ye that. Patsy, attend to this gintleman. I'm goin' on the road for a droive."

With that he lit a cigar and started out.

Carteret changed his tactics with Patsy, who was a young buck of an Irishman and had been eyeing Manuella from the doorway.

He presented her formally as Miss Castleton and said, "I only come to open the way for the business. I am sure you and the lady can fix it up some way."

Patsy drew up a chair and said he'd do anything to assist the lady.

Carteret then explained that what Miss Castleton wanted was to find out who the men were that dug for the foundations, as one of them had found a valuable piece of property on the place when the work was begun.

Patsy then addressed himself to Manuella entirely and ignored Carteret, as it was intended he should. He explained to her that this happened to be one of the jobs that had been sublet. There were two men had the work and they were to take out the soil at so much a square foot. They had hired their own gangs.

Carteret had walked away with an air of indifference and Manuella thanked Patsy with much sweetness and asked him for the names of the two contractors. He went to a big book, hunted them up, wrote them on a bill-head with their address and coming back, said, "It'll be no easy job to catch 'em, Miss, for they work all round the city, but I think we might hunt 'em down if it's worth the ride."

She thanked him again and said she thought it might be worth while, whereupon Patsy gave her a wink and said, "You know where to call if you want any help," and the visitors came away.

When they were on the avenue, Carteret looked at the paper and said, "Ho now, for Tim Burns and Michael Grady."

CHAPTER XXII.

MISS ENNISTON HAS A SPASM.

No two young women could be more unlike in temperament and training than Grace Hardynge and Rose Enniston. One was equable, self-possessed, methodical, and temperate in her desires and her actions. The other was mercurial, unrestrained, wayward and apt to be intemperate in her likes and dislikes. But they had remained fast friends in spite of many quarrels, owing in great part to Miss Hardynge's discretion and moderation. The acquaintance and friendship which had been formed at boarding school had ripened into an intimacy and Miss Enniston made Grace's house her home whenever she came to the city.

Col. Jack Hardynge, as he had for years been called by his most intimate friends, had retired from active business with a mild crop of gout and an income of twenty-five thousand dollars a year, but he had by no means retired from society. A generous, liberal, sagacious man in all other respects, he had one hard side and it was political. He believed that the war then raging had been brought about by what he called the "damned doughnut eating, psalm singing, abolitionists," and that the South would inevitably conquer a peace. Events so far had not brilliantly sustained his opinion, but they deepened his bitterness on this one subject. He always referred to the conflict as the "fratricidal war," and stigmatized the loyal efforts of the Government as the "bloody frenzy of bigotry." Naturally enough, he drew about him a coterie of similarly disposed fellows whose sympathies were with the South. They were mainly social and political veterans who had lost the power of adaptability to events, but who drank any quantity of brandy and water and were brim full of admiration for the past of the Republic. The eulogies of Jackson and Calhoun that were heard in Col. Hardynge's dining room were fervid with Southern eloquence and Northern wine, and in singular contrast to the dull, unending tramp of soldiers going through New York to the front.

The Colonel had dabbled considerably in the local politics of New York, with a shrewd business eye. His investments had been made uptown with a pretty good knowledge of what the unscrupulous ring authorities were about. Before boulevards were surveyed, the favored ones had their chance at the adjacent wild lots and before court houses were built, the quarry men and brick makers and lumber dealers put in their political claims and made their "deals."

The Colonel had been assessed heavily for several elections, but he had drawn his check promptly and in the inner circle of the ring he was counted on as one of the faithful. His reward had been handsome, not only in real estate, but on the tax list assessment.

In these quiet operations he had been indebted very largely to his particular friend, Judge Sanger, father of Dr. Follen Sanger, and for a long time member of Assembly from the Colonel's district in New York, but now a sort of Albany Warwick, given mainly to wirepulling at conventions and the apportionment of rewards after elections. Judge Sanger and Col. Hardynge were both bitterly opposed to the war and as it was not politic or comfortable to express their sentiments publicly, it was a great relief to come together and mingle them privately over the Colonel's brandy.

The only difference in them was that the Judge carried his convictions into action and worked incessantly in a covert way to antagonize loyal sentiment; to hamper and perplex the Government and to create popular dissatisfaction and distrust, while the Colonel was content to embody his conviction in private denunciation and ridicule and never ventured to meddle in the contest.

The political influence of Judge Sanger in local politics was something prodigious and would be inexplicable to any one not familiar with the organization of the dominant party in New York at that time, and with the other fact that a great proportion of the voting population was divided into clans with recognized chieftains who owed allegiance to these political masters and carried their hordes with them to the polls.

With an unexampled memory of men and details, a singular gift of sophistication and good fellowship, and a rugged mathematical facility in getting at results, Judge Sanger knew and remembered every ward politician in the city and every wirepuller in the State, and no one with paper and pencil could so accurately forecast the results in majorities of any political contest. Bets depended on his tip and editorials changed by his wink.

He had planted his son, the doctor, in one of the most lucrative offices in the gift of the commonwealth. In fact his son's position had been made a condition of the appointment of a certain police commissioner, and when his ambitious nominee had come to New York with a handsome wife and set up in a magnificent establishment, as a political doctor, it was understood in an incredibly short space of time by the whole social political circle that whatever might be the doctor's medical skill, there was no denying his political power.

He had one advantage over his father and it lay in the fact that he had not been led by a long series of local successes with unstable factors of society to underestimate the great normal possibilities of public sentiment, and he therefore was very reticent about the issues of the war, and while he led the Judge to believe that he fully sympathized with his views, he took good care not to antagonize those who did not.

Grace Hardynge had been brought up with most of the advantages that wealth and indulgence can confer. She had been liberally educated among a set who entirely differed in their views from her father, and she instinctively felt that he was on the wrong side of this question. But she had an ardent affection for him and kept her suspicions and fears to herself as became a dutiful daughter.

On the afternoon that Chapman was exhibiting Carteret's pictures to his unexpected visitor, Judge Sanger sat at the mahogany table in Col. Hardynge's study, in conversation with that gentleman, who sat on the opposite side of the same table with his leg pillowed in a supporting chair. The two men were about the same age, probably fifty-six or seven; but the Judge was much the more rotund, vital and vigorous. He had an abundance of flossy white hair that blew at the slightest current of air in picturesque disorder over his forehead and heightened his massive rubicund face. He sat erect with his arm resting on the table, not for support, but for convenience and emphasis, for there was a glass of brandy at his finger ends and he occasionally used it for pointing his remarks, by knocking the bottom of the glass on the mahogany. He was dressed in easy fitting broadcloth and a broad white vest shown under the rather jaunty cutaway coat. His language and manner of expression were those of a man who had fallen into the habit of talking for effect. You could detect the flavor of the stump, so to speak, in his ideas, and he used the trite, sonorous sentences that mean the least, but sound the most effective.

"Pardon me, my old friend," he was saying, "I am not a prophet nor the son of a prophet, but I can see through a stone wall. In less than three months, if this barbarous waste of life and treasure goes on, in the insane hope of forcing sovereign States to give up their inalienable rights, the North will rise as one man and light a fire in the rear that will sweep forever this administration and its black Republican supporters from the continent, with the besom of a whirlwind. Yes, sir" (striking the tumbler on the table), "the besom of a whirlwind—mark me."

"I hope not, Judge," said the Colonel mildly, "there's whirlwind enough now. I'm a peace Democrat. In three months I hope that defeat and disgrace will have convinced the North of its expensive error. What are you going to do with your park property? I suppose Siddell will kill that improvement with a commission."

"He can't kill it, if we get the commission we want. I've had the slate made up for a month. The Governor's weak on one point. He's afraid of riots in New York and martial law. I had a talk with him on Sunday and he said nothing would please the war fanatics so much as a popular outbreak and martial law with a provost marshal. It would spike our guns certainly. I told him I thought I could handle our district and then I referred to the park commission. He came down at once like Captain Scott's coon and asked who I wanted and I whipped out my slate. He's too much of an old fox to commit himself, but he gave me a look and said my knowledge of men was a great help to him. If you can only keep the sword of Damocles over a man's head, it's astonishing how much he will do for you. I can bust the Governor's little game for next term and he knows it."

"You must have a pretty good slice of that Boulevard property, Judge," said the Colonel, suggestively.

"No," replied the Judge. "I put the Doctor in there; he wanted to make an investment and I wanted to tie him up. It's all in the family, you may say. The doctor's cutting a wide swathe, eh? Sprang to the top of the ladder at one bound."

The Colonel assented and said he had heard he was driving a double team in the district.

"Social, social," said the Judge. "Can't do our work, Colonel, with gloves on. I'll have him on that Sanitary board next year and twist some of them property owners on the East side into line with their tenement houses. By the way, you're coming over next Thursday, of course."

The Colonel didn't know. He didn't go much into society now. What kind of a reception was it going to be?

"He wants to trot his wife out. She hangs fire awfully. But she'll pace high enough after he gets her started. You'd better come over and bring Grace. We must enter him with some tone. Besides, you are both in the Boulevard boat."

While they were talking, a carriage drove up to the house and Grace Hardynge, who was watching for her at the parlor window, saw Rose Enniston jump out and run up the steps.

Meeting her in the hallway, Grace in her stately way exclaimed, "Why, how flustered you are—what has happened? I believe you've been crying."

"Come upstairs," said Rose, "I'll tell you all about it. I've had the greatest adventure."

"Dear me," thought Grace, "What has she been doing now?" and followed her impetuous companion leisurely up.

Once in the privacy of a boudoir and the key turned in the lock to keep the maids out, Rose began in her headlong way both to remove her apparel and to unload her mind.

"What do you think that man has done?" she asked, rather viciously, with her elbows in the air at right angles to her neck as she untied the strings on her throat. Without paying the slightest attention to her companion's exclamation of ignorance and curiosity, she went on: "After hanging round and following me for a year; after asking me to marry him; do you see that?" holding out a finger with a ring on it, "after putting that on my hand; after all kinds of promises—what do you think he was capable of? O, you can't guess. It isn't in human power. Don't mind picking up those things, dear, sit down on the sofa and listen to me. You know how I loved that man. Everybody must have seen it—more shame to me—"

"In the name of mercy," said Grace, without the least eagerness, but with blank wonderment, "tell me what it is."

"It's this—only this. He has deceived me—abandoned me; thrown me off as he would a dead buttoniere and trampled on me."

"How you are running on," remarked Grace. "Have you seen him?"

"I don't want to see him. But I saw her. I went to the studio. She was there in all her brazen impudence. She's the person I want to see," and Rose's teeth clicked audibly and a couple of hairpins fell to the floor.

"I wish you'd try and be reasonable," said her companion. "Who is she that you saw at the studio and having seen, immediately wanted to see?"

"I saw her picture, don't you understand—a pink and white minx, with saucer eyes and stage hair. She's a devil—O, I believe it. She's robbed me and I was fool enough not to suspect it. But it's all out now."

"Did you have a quarrel with Carteret?" asked Grace.

"Why didn't he let me alone?" continued Rose with her hands in her hair and her eyes in the glass. "What did he come to Coe's Grove a year for? Ma warned me against him."

She put the comb in her mouth for a moment, but continued to mutter unintelligibly. Then taking it out, she stared suddenly at Grace and said: "Do I look like a girl who can be whistled down the wind in that way? Do I?"

"Well, you don't look like a girl who would go traipsing round the town after a man who had offended and snubbed you. You look as if you had too much spirit, to say nothing of good sense, for that."

"Yes," said Rose "I've got too much spirit—that's my curse. If I were like some girls, I could be reasonable and indifferent and insensible and become a sainted old maid at twenty-five. You never had your heart broken and your pride crushed and your self-respect wounded all at once. I'm the most wretched, miserable creature on earth and I haven't got a single friend left."

At which point Rose sank down with her head on the sofa and burst into a flood of tears.

It was with great difficulty that Miss Hardynge succeeded in calming her sufficiently to get a clear statement of what had taken place, and when at last Rose had told her what she had done, Grace naturally came to the conclusion that her jealousy and her suspicions together had unduly exaggerated the whole affair. But as she reasoned with her companion and the hysteria subsided, she was pained to see that vindictiveness took its place.

"Yes," she said, "her name is Manuella," and she hissed the word as if it had come down the century freighted with the odium of a Borgia—"I hate her.

I could take her life. O, you can shrink away from me. I know I'm not good enough for you and hypocritical and weak and false enough."

"Why don't you write to Mr. Carteret and ask him for an explanation?" inquired the direct and plain sailing Grace.

"Why don't I?" exclaimed the ebullient and captious Rose. "Because I did and he never answered it and I found my letter full of love and tenderness lying open for every one to read, where he had flung it in his studio. That's why." And she pulled out the letter and held it up.

"Let me read it," said Grace.

Rose folded it up and replaced it in her dress. "It's been read often enough," she said.

"Carteret must be a poltroon and a sneak," remarked Grace, reflectively. "I don't see how you can afford to waste any more thought on him."

"O, you think so, do you? You saw a good deal of him at our place; did you ever notice that he was a sneak?"

"No," said Grace. "It isn't what I noticed, but what you tell me."

"Well, I tell you, some designing, unscrupulous woman has got hold of him and changed his whole nature. I've got to find her and tell her my mind."

At this Grace lifted both her hands and said: "Don't. In fact," she added, "I know you will not when you have thought it all over and cooled off. You have had quarrel with Carteret; you know how impulsive you are, and he hasn't got over it yet. Don't, I beg of you, be rash, and above all, don't be stupid."

The next morning Rose was in another mood. "Grace," she said, "Carteret is poor. He has had to give lessons. I'm going to buy all his pictures, and I want you to go with me to the studio. I am determined to heap coals of fire on his head. What do you think of that for revenge? Isn't it something to know that he's depending on me. I'm going to buy all his bric-a-brac and send it up to Dr. Flockton and Ma. They like trumpery, and I'll keep the saucer-eyedgirl in my room where I can stamp on her."

This vein of badinage gave Grace some hope and she promised to go to the studio with her, but suggested that it would be better to send an agent to make the purchases.

"That's a dear," replied Rose. "Go with me, and in return I'll go with you to Dr. Sanger's party. Now I think of it, who is Dr. Sanger?"

"He's one of Pa's friends, that's all I know about him, and Pa is responsible. I have heard that he has a pretty wife who keeps very close. She's a Philadelphian, I believe. I never saw her."

"What kind of people will be there?"

"How can I tell? The doctor is the Health Inspector of the Port and a man of great influence. I suppose we shall meet the Mayor and a lot of official people, who are generally great bores."

CHAPTER XXIII.

CARTERET GOES TO THE OPERA.

Carteret's next visit to the Hannige establishment—and his visits were now made with great regularity—was attended with unusual elation. He came across Union Square with an elastic step and hummed a rat-a-plan air that kept time with his buoyant motion. Mrs. Hannige, in a large white apron and armed with her feather duster, stood in the open doorway watching the opposite portals of the Century Club. He greeted her with the familiarity of a regular visitor, and, as was his custom, asked after Mr. Evans' health.

"He's quite picked up lately," she replied, without taking her eyes from the club house. "Quite smart. They're all gone off somewhere on important business."

"They?" repeated Carteret, following her steady gaze, and himself looking over at the club house.

"The young lady and Mr. Stonybrook," said Mrs. Hannige unconcernedly. "They've got some one now who can straighten out his affairs, if they want 'em straightened. Was Chapman at the studio to-day?"

"I did not see him," replied Carteret. "Where have they gone?"

For such an impertinent question as this Mrs. Hannige had her own evasive contempt.

"That boy," said she, "has started in to-day for a fortnight's rampage. What fools some young men are."

"Did Miss Castleton leave any word for me?" asked Carteret.

"Yes," said Mrs. Hannige. "There he is now," and she stepped down from the door-sill to the stone and began beckoning with her duster.

Chapman, who had come out in front of the club dressed in a new fall suit, had a cane under his arm and a tooth pick in his mouth. He stood there a moment pulling on a russet glove and then sauntered obliquely across the street.

"Halloo, Carter," he cried, before he had reached the curb. "I say, Mommy, people will think I'm in arrears if you shake that duster at me in that way. What's up?"

"You're a bad boy, Oats," she replied. "Come up here, I want to talk you before you start in."

Oats winked at Carteret and came up the steps. "It's all right," he said, "I haven't got any money. If I had I'd leave it with you, honor bright, yes I would. But I haven't got any. I'm going to borrow some of Carter, who's flush, and I'll be back in my bed ready to be tucked up at nine o'clock as trim as wax works. So let up."

"Did you say there was a message left for me?" inquired Carteret, as incidentally as he could.

Mrs. Hannige made a motion over her shoulder with the duster. "It's on the mantel in the reception room," she said, and went on talking to Oats.

Carteret went in and found a letter delicately addressed with his name and standing up against the ormolu clock.

He tore open the envelope eagerly. It was in her hand. There was her name at the bottom. It was the first time he had ever received a line from her. It was indeed the first time he had ever seen her name written out by herself. What a singularly pretty name it was: "Manuella Castleton."

"*My Dear Mr. Carteret,*" it said. "It will be impossible for me to take my lesson to-day. Mr. Stonybrook, who is kindly examining Grandpa's business accounts, has insisted on my going to witness a paper before a Notary—that's what he called it. I'm real sorry to miss a lesson, but you, I am sure, will not be sorry to escape for one day from your stupid pupil and your

Always grateful friend,
MANUELLA CASTLETON."

Carteret was keenly disappointed. He wanted to see Manuella for some urgent reason. He read the simple note over again with a lover's desire to discover some hidden meaning that might have escaped him. "'Always grateful friend,'" he said to himself, "that's guardedly formal, as becomes a girl who does not wish to betray all her feelings. 'But you, I am sure, will not be sorry to escape for one day from your stupid pupil'—that's to say she would be sorry if I was. Damn Stonybrook!"

He thrust the letter into his pocket and rejoined Oats, who was still chaffing Mrs. Hannige.

"O, I'll hang on to Carter," said Oats. "He's in luck; struck a swell buyer. Got all the society girls running to his studio. Mashes 'em first and scoops 'em afterwards. Don't you, Carter?"

"Don't be a fool," said Carteret with dignity. "Come over to the club; I want to write a letter."

"What the deuce did you mean by that speech?" Carteret asked, when they were in the club house.

"I meant that you were in for a fat thing—regular female bonanza—if you only paint fast enough and work it for all it's worth."

"How do you know it's a female?"

"Because nobody else would buy that kind of truck," said Oats.

"Perhaps you're right," Carteret said, musingly.

"Of course I am. Write your letter and I'll wait for you."

Carteret then proceeded to write the following letter to Manuella:

"Dear Miss Castleton: I am sorry I did not see you to-day, as I have some good news for you. Try and see me tomorrow early. I will call at noon. Meanwhile I shall hunt up Tim Burns and Michael Grady.

Your friend,

COLIN CARTERET."

This note he dispatched to Mrs. Hannige, and Oats, who had sauntered out, coming back, proposed that they make a day of it.

To this, Cartaret, with a moral sense that was new to himself and a superiority of manner that Oats had never noticed before, replied: "Simply impossible, my boy, I'm too poor to do it. I've got to husband my resources and work like the devil."

"Husband 'em?" cried Oats. "When did that word get into your vocabulary? I'll wager you a bottle of wine you weren't going back to the shop to-day. Own up, now."

"You're right, but it was because I had something else to do."

"I know, you've made an appointment with a woman. It's that big-eyed Hebe* at Hannige's. That's the size of your poverty. You sell out everything in your studio, or I sell it out for you, and then you put on miserly airs with an old chum. Lord, what a fall from good fellowship when a man begins to talk about husbanding it. I wouldn't have believed it of you, old fellow, damn me, I wouldn't."

"What do you want to do?" asked Carteret, a little touched by this way of putting it.

"It's three o'clock," replied Oats, "let's take a turn on the road, come back to the club for dinner at six, and go round to the Academy at eight. The Opera opens tonight. All the girls will be there. We can see who's in town and keep ourselves green in their memory. I know three or four that's sure to walk the plank this winter, and then they'll want pictures. My dear boy, it's impossible to husband honey unless you rove the fields occasionally where the blossoms grow."

Thus enticed, Carteret went off with his companion, who got a team at Brady's and drove him out to Fordham. They came back to the club, ate a rather luxuriant dinner, with wines, which Oats insisted on paying for, and then went to the Academy. It was the first night of the season and La Grange was singing the Casta Diva when they entered the house, for the opera was Norma.

---

* Hebe: an ancient Greek goddess of youth, daughter of Zeus and Hera.

There was a resplendent assemblage present, for although the land was filled with the sounds of woe, and the hearts of the Northern people were sad with unending lists of the killed and wounded, the opera went on, and it may be that many of the richly attired in the horseshoe's glittering curve were all the richer for the conflict. Certain it is that many of them found relief in the sensuous music of Bellini from the stress of war times and the anxieties and uncertainties of the hour.

Among those who saw and recognized the two young men as they entered the parquette was Rose Enniston, who was in Col. Hardynge's box with Grace and her father. She called her companion's attention to them with a touch of her arm, and there was just the least bit of proprietary pride in the toss of her head. If the thought passed through her mind could be fairly expressed, it would be a sly triumph at her patronizing revenge. Carteret was in evening dress, and both the young men were in excellent spirits after their dinner, and Miss Enniston could not help thinking that she was the unseen goddess who had enabled him to enjoy himself.

"If they see us," said Grace, "they will come to the box after the act."

"They will not see us?" replied Rose, somewhat interrogatively.

"Why not, if you lean out in your light dress that way?" observed Grace.

To which Rose rejoined, "How absurd you are. I'm not a bit more conspicuous than the rest of the circle."

Grace noticed that for the rest of the evening she was nervous and abstracted. Grace did not, however, know that Rose was saying to herself: "If he does see me and does not come up, it will be because he wishes to avoid me," and she kept her gaze fixed upon the two young men, as if determined that she would put him to the test.

At the end of the act Chapman scanned the house with a glass and presently discovered Miss Enniston. He then gave the glass to Carteret and Rose turned her head slightly and tried to assume an indifferent look as Carteret slowly put the lorgnette to his eyes and apparently at Oats' request, directed it toward the Hardynge box.

A moment later the two young men got up and left the parquet.

Rose now felt sure that Carteret was about to visit the box. It was impossible for her to conceal her feminine anxiety from Grace. She went to the mirror in the box and looked at herself, while she talked rapidly and somewhat excitedly in what was meant to be a careless manner. Several acquaintances came in and chatted about the music and the social prospect of the season, and at every step in the corridor, Rose's heart gave a little jump in her throat. What should she say? How receive him? Was not the old way, as if nothing had happened, the best way? Would he act formally and distantly as if she had put a barrier between them? Had Chapman told him about her visits to the studio? That would make a difference. She looked at his ring on her finger—he would be sure to recognize that. She felt somehow that her self-sacrifice in putting it back ought to melt him.

A thousand questions ran across each other in her agitated mind. Col. Hardynge had gone down in the stockholders' room where he smoked a cigar and gossiped with Col. Ebbins about the American yachts and the production, of American talent at the Academy.

Rose looked at the equable Grace, over whose chair were leaning two superbly dressed young men with their crushed hats under their arms, talking the platitudes of such occasions with genteel profundity, and she wondered how some women could be so cold-blooded.

The whole house was engaged in that silken flirtation peculiar to the entract of the opera. A confused hum of voices and swish of fans made the air voluptuous. The animation and color and soft excitement of it appealed with strange force to the nature of Rose, so long shut off from the allurements and coquetries of social life.

She seemed to feel instinctively, without thinking much about it, that she was floating in a sea of delicious intrigue with the sensuous music of Bellini still luxuriously wafting everybody. She knew that the belles of a season were looking over their fans at their cavaliers. She compared herself with them and asked if she were not as brilliant and as beautiful as they. And then a quick unbidden recollection of her dismal winter home in the country, with her mother's unsympathetic and austere companionship, the dreary visits and pragmatical conversation of Dr. Flockton, the long, lonely hours with not a creature to worry or to pour out her hot soul to and not one to quarrel with but Barney the gardener.

But the orchestra came back. The lights of the great chandelier were turned down, the stragglers were returning to their seats, the curtain went up and Carteret had not come.

A sullen bitterness fell upon her. Somehow she felt that she was grievously wronged. Her vanity was hurt. It was impossible to disguise from herself that Grace had read her hopes and her disappointment and now knew that she had been deliberately snubbed.

They sat awhile. Carteret and Oats did not return to their seats. Then Rose could sit still no longer. She complained of a headache and the party left the house quietly, much to Col. Hardynge's comfort, he holding to a private notion that all operas ought to be restricted to one act.

Oats, who knew almost everybody in the boxes, had been calling off the names to Carteret with comments, when his eye lit on Rose Enniston in Col.

Hardynge's box and he saw that she was watching him. He gave the glass to Carteret with the remark, "There's a fine looking girl in the first row next to the proscenium, who has been watching us for some time. See if you know her."

Carteret did not need to use the glass. He recognized Rose without it. But he made a show of scanning the circle, and giving it back to his companion, said, "Let's go out and take a turn in the foyer, the house is insufferably warm."

They found the foyer full of people standing in groups or winding in and out, a rather dense and Babel-like mob of musicians, gilded youth, Italian connoisseurs and teachers, army officers in full uniform, musical critics and middle aged stockholders. They talked about the price of gold, the Port Royal expedition, the winter's masquerades, the deals in cotton, the attitude of the Governor toward the Government, the new brands of champagne, the dresses of the women in the boxes, and everything in fact but the opera—except to remark occasionally that it wouldn't pay.

Carteret was pulled about annoyingly. Bradshaw of the rowing club was glad to see him back in the world once more; Comstock of the Eighty-fourth buttonholed him in a war group; Sanderson of the Manhattan asked him if he knew Miss Enniston was in the house; Finley, of Finley, Broks & Hodgson, cloak importers, asked him if he had been sick, and Jack Mumford, the assistant district attorney, wanted to know if he was going to the Sanger party.

Oats fairly sparkled in the cross purposes of this crowd. He knew everybody and had a tireless adaptability that was both garrulous and politic. But it exhausted Carteret and he wanted to get away from it. "Come over to the club," he said. "I'm as thirsty as a desert and as hot as a simoon."

As the club house was on the next block, they crossed the street with the intention of coming back, but when they reached it, an incident occurred that prevented them and that led to the most serious consequences afterwards.

"Look here, Carter," Oats was saying, "you are a better artist than I am, but as a diplomat you're no good."

He had hold of Carteret's arm and was quite patronizingly superior.

"You actually snubbed Bradshaw and he's chairman of his club's house committee. They want to furnish their new rooms this winter. You could have worked Bradshaw for a three hundred dollar job, for he likes you. Then I cracked you up to Finley as a coming man and you made him feel as if cloaks were a badge of dishonor. You're too gifted and imperious to make money."

"You're right. I'm afraid I haven't got genius enough to be sycophantic," replied Carteret.

"Or prosperous," added Oats, "as if keeping posted on the market and buyers were sycophantic. What an awfully perverted nature. What's the matter, young woman?"

This sudden question was addressed to a girl who, as they approached the club, stood close against the iron railing of an adjacent house, looking up at Mrs. Hannige's, in whose second story a bright light was burning. She had stepped out upon the walk so as to get a good look at Carteret's face as he was passing.

"Is your name Carteret?" she asked.

Both the young men stopped and looked at her curiously.

"Seems to me this business is getting confoundedly personal," said Oats.

"My name's Carteret," said his companion. "What do you want?"

"I want to speak a word to you."

"And you want me to go on. I'm too innocent. Who'd'a' thought you had so much consideration for guileless youth," said Oats. "Say Lillian—your name's Lillian isn't it, or Maud—you've got things upside down. I'm the hardened villian you want. This is my country cousin."

"Let her speak to me," said Carteret, and Oats went on to the club steps where he waited, whistling.

"What is it?" asked Carteret.

"You are looking for a cup, ain't you?" said the girl.

"What do you know about it?" he replied evasively.

"I know where it is," she replied.

She was a rather good-looking young woman, somewhat flashily dressed and, as nearly as he could see in the poor light of the street, with a pert, precocious look and a subdued manner that was evidently assumed.

"How did you know my name?" Carteret asked somewhat guardedly, for in spite of himself his suspicions were awakened.

"I live in the Terrace," said the girl. "On the top floor. I knowed you and a young lady was looking for a cup. It aint no matter who told me. I kin put you on the track of it, sure."

"Where is it—can't you bring it to me, if I pay you for your trouble?"

"No, I can't, but I kin take you to the gent as has got it."

"Did he send you to me?"

The girl hesitated. "Yes, he did—if I seen you I was to tell you as he'd got it; mebbee you know where it is."

Carteret caught the inquiring look that accompanied this question. "Why don't you tell me who it is?" he asked.

"I kin take you to him."

"Now?"

"Yes."

"Where is it?"

"It's at the Liverpool Boordoor."

"The what?"

"The Liverpool's in the Bowery. I sing there. I aint working to-night. I kin introduce you to the gent what's got the cup."

"How much does he want for it?"

"I d'know. You aint afeered of me, are you? You kin bet I'm a lady; ask the Sitwhites."

Carteret's first impulse was to go with her and see what would come of it. Then his reason told him to consult Oats.

He told her to wait a moment, and rejoining his friend, narrated to him briefly that he had been in search of a piece of lost property for several days and that this girl wanted him to go with her to recover it.

"You must be a country cousin indeed to think of it," said Oats. "The Liverpool is one of the vilest dives in the Bowery; you don't know the girl and you don't know what kind of a trap is laid for you. If you insist on going, I'll hunt up Charley Roach and we'll all go together."

The girl had come up while they were talking. "If you can't go to-night," she said, "come to-morrow night and when I git through I'll come round to your table and find the man for you, if you want the cup. If you don't, I wouldn't waste the time. You'll see me for I'm on for a dance at nine."

Saying this she hurried away toward the Fourth avenue and, after standing a moment on the corner to see that she was not followed, she got upon a Fourth avenue car going downtown.

The young men then went into the club, and soon growing confidential, over claret and ice, forgot to return to the opera.

CHAPTER XXIV.

LOVE TRACKS THE CUP TO THE SILVERSMITH'S.

The moment Carteret saw Manuella the next day, he said to her, "Well sister, I've sold all your work and there's the money; fifty good dollars and true," and he handed her an envelope that was rounded out with the bills.

Her girlish delight was very pretty to see. "Did I really earn all this?" she cried, spreading out the money on her knee. "O, it can't be possible. You must be telling me a fib."

"No fib, little woman. Somebody wanted that kind of stuff and sent an agent who bought the whole of it. Have you got any more ready? I told him I could supply it by the ton. That's the good news I had for you."

"And I have so much to tell you," she said, forgetting the money in an instant and becoming absurdly serious.

She had come down to the reception room to meet him and as she got up and closed the door, it was a graceful preliminary of confidence. "I don't want Mr. Stonybrook poking in," she said, as she seated herself on the lounge by his side and turned round so that they were facing each other. "In the first place, you musn't scold me for what has happened, for it was your fault. You know what you told that young man at Timmins."

"Do you mean Patsy?"

"His name is Patrick Brady," said Manuella, "and he's quite an Irish gentleman. He has called to see me twice since I saw you."

"That wasn't my fault, I'll be bound," said Carteret.

"Yes it was, for you told him he and I could attend to the business. You remember you were quite independent."

"Yes," said Carteret laughing, "so I was—well?"

"He came down to tell me that he found the two contractors and they never heard of anything being picked up."

"Well, there wasn't any cup found," said Carteret. "It wasn't necessary for him to come twice to tell you that. I could have told you that at the start."

"Wait a moment. The cup was found."

"What?"

"Yes, indeed. O, it's too curious for anything, and I was so impatient to tell you that I couldn't sleep last night."

"Bless your dear little soul," said Carteret, inaudibly, and without moving his lips.

"It's so confusing," continued Manuella, "that I had to write down the names." With that she unrolled a bit of paper on which she had made memoranda. "Mr. Timothy Burns didn't know anything, and Mr. Michael Grady said there wasn't anything valuable dug out of those rocks, because if there had been, he'd known it. This is what he told Mr. Brady, and I was so disappointed when Mr. Brady told me, that he said he'd go and see the foreman of Grady's gang. But he had died with delirium tremens. Then off goes Mr. Brady to find the foreman of the Burns gang, and he was working at Prospect Park, Brooklyn. O, I tell you, Mr. Brady is a jewel. Then back he comes, and says he, I've got it, Miss. A green hand by the name of Seely (here she referred to her memoranda), O, no, Seely comes later, the green hand is Fallen, see? I marked it G.H. Fallen did dig up a box, says the foreman. He put it in his dinner kettle and threw his coat over it and took it home to his shanty on—wait a moment— Limerick Rocks on Sixty-fifth street. The foreman heard this afterwards. Then up goes Mr. Brady to Limerick Rocks and sees Mrs. Fallen. I wish you could hear Mr. Brady tell it. He's the funniest man I ever heard talk."

"Yes, but then you know Mr. Brady isn't funny unless he's present," says Carteret. "Leave him out."

"O, I can't," says Manuella. "That would be impossible. He did everything. You'd like him."

"No, I wouldn't," insisted Carteret "He saw Mrs. Thingamy—"

"Fallen; and what do you think she said?"

"Haven't the remotest idea."

"She said—"

"O, I'll tell you what she said," exclaimed Carteret. "That the box contained a dead cat."

"She said," continued Manuella, "her man found the cup and they got up a—wait a moment—they got up a raffle, and Seely, Tim Seely—that's where he comes in—won it and he sold it to Martin Shay, Yes, Martin Shay, liquor dealer, see, I marked it L.D., on the corner of Third avenue and Forty-ninth street, who wanted it for a prize for a—what was that?—a target shoot, you know what that is. Wait a moment, I made Mr. Brady write it down. The Martin Shay Homeguard, and Martin Shay sent the cup to Dittmar & Kleinbacker, silversmiths in Lafayette place, to have an inscription put on it. Here's the inscription. See? I made him write it. 'Second prize presented by Martin Shay to the second best shot made by the Martin Shay Homeguard.' That's on the cup now. There, what do you think of Mr. Brady now?"

"I think," said Carteret, "that he ought to get out a new version of the Arabian Knights."

"You don't believe his story?"

"Do you?"

Their eyes met. There was a moment's pause. Hers wore an arch expression that added to their beauty.

"Mr. Brady seemed to me to be the soul of honor," she said. "I was really charmed by his manner."

This was too much for Carteret. Her girlish attempt to make him jealous of Brady on whom she evidently had not bestowed a thought, was a piece of delicious flattery entirely incidental to the subject that charmed him. Her beautiful face was within a foot of his, and it wore a quizzical expression of annoyance at his want of appreciation of Brady. So strong was his impulse to catch her in his arms and kiss her, that he had to get up and walk the room once or twice.

"I'll tell you how we can settle it," he said. "Put on your hat and come to the silversmith's. I've a serious reason for knowing if this story is true, which I will tell you as we go. It's only a step from here."

"I'd like to see the cup, wouldn't you?" she exclaimed.

"To tell the truth, I wish I had never heard of it," he replied. "It is the most mysterious and eventful cup the world ever dreamed of."

During the walk to the silversmiths', the girl was in unusual spirits. "I feel," she said, "like a millionaire. I've got money enough, now, to take Grandpa in the country for a week."

"Yes," remarked Carteret. "I feel worried about Grandpa. If we could only get him away from all these people for a few days, where it is fresh and calm, I think it would make a new man of him. We really ought to make an effort. I've got a letter from my friend Manser at the Gate House; his arms are open in every line."

"You said you would tell me why you wanted to satisfy yourself of the truth of Brady's story," suggested Manuella, and then Carteret told her accurately what had occurred the night before. He confessed he was puzzled completely. "Can these people have got possession of the cup?" he asked. "And if they have, why should they come to me? I don't understand it."

Manuella stopped suddenly. She had one of those intuitonal flashes that are peculiar to her sex, and that do the work of a man's reason in a twinkling.

"I'll tell you," she said. "They wanted to find out if we had the cup. That's all. Don't you know all record of it ends with Grandpa's leaving the Terrace. He was suddenly taken away, and we have been with him ever since. I know the girl. She is a saloon singer and lives in the Terrace. That man Plonski's employed her to find out where we are and if we have the cup, or have disposed of it. O dear," she said, "what is it gives this cup so much importance?"

Carteret looked at her with admiration. Something told him she was right, and this explanation had never once occurred to him. But he was not in a mood to think profoundly or continuously of the matter. Another idea had suddenly taken possession of him.

"You really ought to run away yourself," he said, "before this delicious weather ends. Manser has got a great rambling old farm-house, locked in by hills that are intoxicating with color just now. I'd like to have you and your Grandpa go up there for a few days. Do you know, I'd work better here if I knew you were both enjoying the country."

"But where would be all my instruction—my introduction to nature that you promised—if, don't you know, if you were here?"

"Well, I leave that all out. You seemed to want it that way when I first mentioned it.

"No," she said vaguely. "How dull men are. I didn't want it; that was the trouble. It seemed to me to be too delightful to be right."

"I know what you mean," replied Carteret. "I can clear away your difficulty—but not here on the street. This is the silversmiths'."

Dittmar & Kleinbacker was the firm name on an old fashioned, three story brick house in Lafayette place. It was not a pretentious shop and there were no showy warerooms. The sign was small and unobtrusive, and the entrance way, through the basement, was not inviting. But it was nevertheless one of those establishments which do a great deal of work quietly for the large silverware firms of the country. Mr. Dittmar, a wiry, nervous old gentleman with a white apron over his trousers and a pencil behind his ears, met them in the doorway and, looking at them over his spectacles, with politeness and anxiety combined, asked what they wanted, very much as if he feared their questions would drive some more important consideration out of his mind. He was evidently a slightly overtaxed old gentleman and had a great deal on his mind, for there were several messengers and agents in waiting, and their general air was one of impatience at his old-fashioned way of doing business.

Carteret explained as briefly as possible that they had come in relation to a cup that was sent to be engraved.

"O, you will have to go upstairs and see Adolph," he said. "He takes charge of that sort of thing; I don't bother with it. You can go upstairs there. I guess he's on the next floor. Ask for Mr. Kleinbacker," and Mr. Dittmar actually pushed Carteret gently toward the doorway, and without paying any more attention to him turned to somebody else and said: "Are you sure they were to be ready to-day? Bless my soul, it must have escaped me."

Carteret and his companion went up the steps of the house and rang the bell. A young workman with some kind of tool in his hand and a silver plate under his arm opened the door.

"I want to see Mr. Kleinbacker," Carteret said.

"He's in Europe," replied the man, without relinquishing his grasp of the door. "Mr. Dittmar's down stairs."

"But Mr. Dittmar sent me up here to see Mr. Kleinbacker," said Carteret. "Adolph, he called him."

"O, Adolph," exclaimed the workman. "I guess you can see him. He's the young man." Whereupon he held the door open until they came in, pulled a wire that was in the hallway and unceremoniously disappeared, leaving the visitors looking at each other and listening to the sound of hammers and the ring of metal in a rear building.

Presently a boy looked over the stairway rail and said, "Hi, what is it?"

"Hi," responded Carteret. "Tell Adolph a lady and gentleman wish to see him."

"Why don't you come up then?" said the boy. At which both Carteret and Manuella began to ascend the rickety stairs.

Mr. Adolph Kleinbacker was the son of the junior partner of the firm. He was not quite twenty-four, and his father had made a place for him in the house to keep him out of mischief. The young man was a spoiled favorite of a weak mother. He had been expensively but superficially educated, and after a short but extravagant and profligate career had come into the house of Dittmar & Kleinbacker under a threat from his father that he should never have another cent unless he earned it. He was not devoid of a shrewd intelligence, and had shown at times an errant but unmistakable aesthetic instinct, but frivolous associates and habits of social dissipation among a crowd of young pleasure seekers, together with the indulgence and mistaken patronage of a foolish mother, who in moments of frankness often acknowledged to him that he was handsome and bright enough to marry a rich wife and not slave as his father had done, had made him diverge very far from the methodical and industrious life of his German father. Adolph Kleinbacker did not, however, seriously contemplate marriage. That step was associated in his mind with a total abnegation of everything that just at present made life a summer picnic. He was not handsome, but his vanity and his mother's assurances had created a well-satisfied conviction that he was. He dressed himself with fashionable care, rather showily. He oiled his flat, black curly hair and scented his black moustache and waxed its ends religiously. But at his best there was a jaunty suspicion of want of weight. He was slender and nervous in build and narrow and peering in countenance. He could play the piano in a rattling manner with his long fingers and imitate any number of actors with a shrill and rather feminine voice. He knew a great many young women of the stage, and had managed to get up harmless flirtations with several of them which lasted just as long as he kept up the airs and the expenditures of affluence. One or two affairs had occurred which were not to his credit. He had got in debt and had paid off the claim afterwards by borrowing the money of Mr. Dittmar by a specious and heartless falsehood and a pitiable request that the loan should be kept from his father; and he had bought some jewelry for an actress of one of the large firms that dealt with Dittmar & Kleinbacker and given his note for it, which his father had been obliged to take up. This led to the old gentleman's putting his foot down with unusual severity.

He declared to Mrs. Kleinbacker that he had long suspected their son of being a scape-grace, but now he found him to be a scamp.

Adolph was genuinely penitent and profuse in protestations of reform. He promised to do anything that his father desired. He'd go into the army; he'd apprentice himself in the shop. Then it was that his father, after a long and disagreeable consultation with his partner, made a place for him in their establishment. Most of their work was what was called contract work, and came from large dealers, but they had of late years received a great many special jobs from private sources and it was to take charge of this work that young Kleinbacker was assigned.

Mr. Dittmar, an old fashioned gentleman, whose German prejudices had not died out, had very little faith in the boy. "He's been spoiled by his mother and the ruinous American notions of fine appearance," he said.

But Adolph went to his position with a grave and honest determination to show both his father and Mr. Dittmar that he had something in him. "I'll work up the private trade of the city," he said, "and ring all the swell purchasers to our shop. The old man's got sterling qualities, but he's too slow for the age."

He fitted up the little room on the second floor quite tastily, and in strong American contrast to the rest of the establishment. He had a patent desk of polished cherry and a luxuriant chair. He put two or three antiques on the wall and hung a fine photograph of Ristori over his desk. His waste basket had a bunch of colored ribbons on the side and his inkstand was a fine specimen of the work of the establishment.

Manuella and her companion were ushered into this room where they found a young man in a loose silk jacket, seated at the elegant desk upon which he had just laid a sporting paper that he had evidently been reading. He got up politely and they saw a slim, rather boyish person with a narrow, triangular face that seemed to vanish in the sharp point of his chin, and whose central object of interest was an unusually large and unusually black moustache.

Carteret explained as briefly as possible that they had come to obtain some information about the Martin Shay cup, which they were anxious to see.

Believing it was the intention of having similar work done that had prompted their visit he treated them with instant and easy politeness.

"There was a cup," he said, "brought here by Mr. Shay; it was to be cleaned up and engraved for a prize. It went home two days ago. I think the trial was to be made to-day."

"Then," said Carteret somewhat superfluously, "you have not got it."

"Why, no; did you want to have one made like it? It was a very curious affair."

"So curious," said Carteret, "that we should very much like to recover it. It was a memorial belonging to this lady and was lost. It fell into the hands of some laborers who sold it to Mr. Shay, and he offered it as a prize. We would be willing to pay a fair price for its recovery."

"Might I ask you where the cup came from? It was a most extraordinary piece of repousse work," said Kleinbacker.

"My dear sir, the story is too long and we do not wish to take your time," replied Carteret. "It is not of great intrinsic value, but as a memorial; what would you say it was worth intrinsically?"

"Eighteen dollars and sixty-four cents," said Kleinbacker promptly. "I weighed it. It's possible that the man who wins it would sell it for a small sum; these people are generally poor."

"Very likely," remarked Carteret, rising; "we are much obliged to you, sir, for your information," and he was about to go.

"Wait a moment," said Kleinbacker. "I'm sure I saw the rifle contest advertised in one of the papers. It might be possible to recover the cup. How much would you like to pay for it?"

"A good fair price; a good fair price," rejoined Carteret, with a resonant liberality that was meant to cover up a vagueness of quantity.

"Would you go a hundred dollars?"

"O, dear," cried Manuella, "I couldn't afford that."

Kleinbacker, with what was meant to be a winning smile, instantly said, "Ah, you lost the property, madame?"

"It belongs in her family," remarked Carteret, coming to her rescue.

"Her family is not his family," thought Kleinbacker; "what a stunning girl."

"Would you go fifty?" he asked. "You see if I knew your margin I might negotiate for you. It would be quite in our line."

"I think I could pay that, couldn't I?" Manuella asked of Carteret and thinking of her earnings.

"I don't think it would be worth it," said Carteret. "You must remember these people have had their inscription put on it and that cheapens it. Don't you think we have taken enough of Mr. Kleinbacker's valuable time?"

She moved to the door with him. "You forget," she said in a whisper, "that Grandpa was to get a large sum of money for the cup. He had built a great many hopes on the promise of that money. I think I'll give the getleman my address. He might near something."

"Just as you please," said Carteret indifferently, who was beginning to feel an insane jealousy of the cup.

She came back and approaching the young man so closely that he felt her warm breath as she spoke, she said, "I'll give you my address and if you hear of it, you can let me know."

Carteret sauntered into the hallway. Mr. Kleinbacker said, "O, thank you," and jumping up asked her to sit down and write it. He spread a piece of paper before her, selected a pen and put it in her hand, touching her warm fingers as he did so. He had filled the pen overflowingly with ink, and at the first attempt to write it made a big splash, at which they both laughed and the young man, begging her pardon, gave her another which failed to write at all, and after one or two attempts she held it up despairingly and looked at him with an arch help-lessness. He gave her another and after she had written her name, she moved her head back to look at it and said, "Gracious, what a hand; did you ever see anybody as awkward as I am?"

What Mr. Kleinbacker thought was that he had never seen anybody quite so graceful.

"You write a lovely hand," he said. "I can read it. Take your time."

"There," she cried, getting up. "Really, Mr. Kleinbacker, I don't know that I ought to do it, but you will keep my address private, I hope."

"As secret as the grave, on my honor," he replied in a low and confidential tone, at which she gave him a thankful smile and ran out.

He went to the window afterwards and watched her until her figure was lost in the distance. Then he went to the mirror that hung in a closet and spent some time musingly twirling the end of his moustache and looking at himself.

The more he thought of it the more firmly he was convinced that he had impressed the girl. Her coming back; her by-play with the pens to gain time; her determination to give him her address in spite of her companion's protests, and her pledging him to secrecy, to say nothing of her expressive glances and low tones to avoid being heard, were cumulative evidence to Mr. Kleinbacker that she had been struck by his personal appearance and wished to cultivate him.

It was not possible for him to conceive of all this as the ingenuousness and frankness of a girl who had no schooling in duplicity. His experience of women forbade any such nonsense.

CHAPTER XXV.

LOVE IN THE PARK.

After leaving the silversmiths', Carteret's seriousness was in marked contrast to Manuella's gaiety. He did not feel quite warranted in complaining of her undiscriminating affability to everybody and the unexpressed desire to do so made him reticent and quite solemn.

"You have lost all your spirits," she said to him as they reached Union Square. "What is it; have I offended you?"

Come at in this direct way he immediately executed what may be called a tangent of deceit.

"I'm annoyed," he said, "when I think of how much I have to say to you and of the many trivial things that interfere with my saying it. First, it's Stonybrook, and then it's that infernal cup. Here we are nearly home again and we've given all our time to a cad in a smithy."

"You haven't acted as if you had much to say," rejoined Manuella, demurely. "Can't you say it to-morrow or next day?"

"I'd rather say it now," Carteret insisted. "With our helplessness you never can tell what a day may bring forth. What were we talking about when we got to the silversmiths'?"

"You were talking about how happy you would be here when Grandpa and I went into the country for a week," and then the minx actually hummed a few notes of a song as if that matter were disposed of forever.

"So I was," he said, as if it required her prompting to bring it all back. "Suppose we sit down here in the park a moment—there are not many people here at this hour—and talk it out?"

"Can we talk it all out?"

"Yes, we can settle it in ten minutes. We're not children, Manuella, and it's only five o'clock."

She became timidly silent and he led the way to a deserted bench out of the main path under a catalpa tree. The moment she was seated he began in his impetuous way.

"I said we were not children, but we have been, Miss Castleton, and it's mainly my fault. I really thought that I could be a brother to you and I have led you step by step into a dilemma that I must clear up. I can't serve you any more; I've done everything that I can do. After to-night I must stop, unless—" here he paused and Manuella, who was looking down at the tip of her boot as if it had suddenly gained some extraordinary interest by contact with the asphalt pavement, said nothing.

"I say," he repeated, "that to-night is the last of my friendship and the end of the brotherly dream unless—Do you hear what I say?"

"Yes," in a soft voice; the most indeterminate and noncommittal and barren "yes" that is imaginable.

"Do you want it to stop?"

"O, Mr. Carteret, why do you ask me that? Why do you talk in this way? Please let me go."

"I talk so because you put your case in my hands and I wouldn't be a man if I didn't. We must shake hands here tonight and say good-bye, unless—"

She turned around, looked at him suddenly and said with genuine wonder, "Unless what?"

"Unless you promise to be my wife. Why do you start like that? You knew it must come if I were a man. I don't ask you to be my wife now. I only ask you to promise if you can and to tell me plainly if you cannot. I want the right to visit you and protect you. I don't want the intimacy any more without the assurance. Don't get nervous, my dear. I started in to teach you but you've taught me a lot of things I never knew. You've taught me that I could love somebody so deeply and grandly that I couldn't rest while there was a possibility of somebody else getting her. There are other things but that's the most important. Now my dear, it can't go on this way; it isn't fair to you in one sense and it isn't fair to me in another. I ought to know now where I am before I get any deeper."

He stopped a moment. She said nothing. But he could hear her breathing for he was very close to her ear and his arm was on the back of the seat behind her in a half encircling position.

"Do you understand what I am saying to you, Manuella?"

"Yes," with a faint little gasp.

"I'm asking you to be my wife sometime, when I am worthy and able to have such a treasure. I'm asking you because I love you and want you forever, not because I have a single claim of ability or position or means, but because I will have, if you trust me and help me and give me the great encouragement of your promise."

Poor, innocent little heart. This was the first time it had had the Æolian music of love poured into it. It was so strangely sweet and new—it was so sudden and so unlike the selfish harshness of her past experiences—that it flooded her with an inexplicable emotion and she burst into tears.

This manifestation was incomprehensible to him. He felt that he had either hurt her feelings inadvertently or that her sympathy for him in view of the disappointment that must ensue, had overcome her.

"Manuella," he said. "Don't cry. I beg of you. Whatever you say I shall always, I hope, be your friend. You don't like me well enough to be my wife, do you?"

"You know I do," she said suddenly and with a self-assertion that was almost accusative. "You know I do. I couldn't hide it from you if I tried ever so hard," and then she turned completely away, as if her excess of emotion shouldn't be enquired into.

"I thought I had made you unhappy," he said in soft tones but in a major key now. "You are not unhappy, are you?"

"No, no," she said with a sob or two and wiping her eyes. "I'm only a little fool, but I'm not—no—I'm not unhappy."

"God bless you, my darling" he said. "Rather than make you unhappy for one instant, I'd take myself out of your sight forever. Do you remember what I was asking you a minute ago?"

She waited a moment. She had to wipe her eyes and get over her emotion. He waited too. The cars tinkled dreamily along the Fourth avenue, a hand organ down some side street was playing "the Blue Danube," the yellow mists of the afternoon shone in long shafts across the park and the shadows lay invitingly on the grass. He heard in that interval the faraway newsboys crying the afternoon papers and he wondered at the calm, happy aspect of the city.

"Mr. Carteret," she said softly and slowly, "I hope you will not think I am a child. I was crying because I am so weak and inexperienced and unworthy, and because you are so good and noble and kind and you tried to make me think—poor little me—that I was conferring some kind of honor on you, when it's all the other way; you know it is, and if you were to go away and I shouldn't see you again, I'd die—yes, I believe I would now; and then you were so mean as to threaten it, you did, indeed, and pretended you wanted me to send you away, when you knew I couldn't and you've so upset me, I'm a perfect fright and I ought to go back this minute."

They got up simultaneously and she put her arm through his with that mute but subtle acknowledgment of a new relationship that only a woman can make.

"But we haven't said one word about the trip to the country," said he.

"I shall have to talk Grandpa over, you know," she said, "but I want to go," and he felt her give his arm a little involuntary squeeze.

"We shall have to be quick about it," he urged. "No one can tell how long this weather will last."

When they arrived at Mrs. Hannige's she let herself in with a key and they both went into the little reception room—the Lord knows why.

"To-morrow," she said, "we'll settle about the jaunt. Come early, will you not?"

"Yes," he replied, imitating her cooing tones and looking her in the eyes. "The earlier the better. To-morrow is ages away."

"But not too early, what will Mrs. Hannige think?"

"Think?" Why, that I have got the right at last," and he caught her suddenly and kissed her and she ran up the stairs with a gurgle that may have been a flying protest or only a wild fragment of a laugh.

Carteret acted like a madman that night. He hunted up Chapman. He fairly amazed that ebullient fellow by his high spirits. He bought wine for a whole party at the club. He beat Chapman at billards, an unprecedented thing.

"Look here," said Oats, bringing his cue to a ground-arms and leaning on it, "what's the matter with you anyway? I've seen men before who didn't want patrons, but they preserved a decent melancholy, they didn't break out in this style and insist on singing 'The Blue Danube' between every shot."

"Oats," cried Carteret as he made a double carrom. "I am the happiest man in New York. If I should die before tomorrow I charge you to see that the proper thing is put on my mausoleum, died of an overdose of ecstasy."

"Have you been taking nitrous oxide gas, or did that moth last night turn out to be a Maecenas?"

"I'll tell you some day. I can't let any of it go now," replied Carteret.

Manuella returned to her grandfather to find him in consultation with Mr. Stonybrook. She kissed him with unusual warmth and although he chided her for staying away and looked unusually severe, she was not to have her spirits dampened.

The next morning Mr. Stonybrook again made them a visit. He had taken a deep interest in Mr. Evans' affairs and Manuella noticed that he had come to believe in her grandfather's theory of the books. She listened for the sound of the bell and wished he would go. Once or twice she looked over the stairway expectantly and there was a new glow in her cheeks and a fresh sparkle in her eyes. At last she heard the tinkle. It was a peculiarly vigorous ring and she recognized it. One of the maids called up the stairs, saying, "There is a gentleman to see you, Miss." She hurried to the glass and arranged several little details of toilet and went down the stairs to the reception room trying to calm herself. She stopped a moment in the hall as if to get a little composure and then with a glad face, entered.

She found Mr. Kleinbacker with his hat in his hand waiting for her.

"You see I have found you," he said. "I s'pose you expected me;" and he advanced to shake hands with her.

She passively allowed him to take her hand.

"You're looking splendid this morning, Miss Castleton—quite radiant. I think we can work our little game our own way. I went to work at it right off."

She withdrew her hand and was looking at him with curious wonder.

"Well, you are a scrum girl, aint you?" he said, taking a survey of her. "I can tell a thoroughbred when I see one. O, you let me alone. How's your friend?"

"Did you call to see me on business?" asked Manuella, beginning to shrink away from him unconsciously.

"O, that'll keep. Everything's all right. I'll manage that and keep it to ourselves too."

"Sit down, Mr. Kleinbacker. What is it you think you can manage?"

"O, pshaw," said Mr. Kleinbacker. "Don't you beat round with me that way. I'm no chicken. When a girl asks me to do a confidential thing, I do it up to the handle, you can bet. Sit down here. Nobody'll come in here, will they?"

Manuella went to the window. "Why don't he come?" she said to herself. Then she sat down in a chair helplessly.

"'Twasn't just the regular thing in our house," continued Mr. Kleinbacker, who had thrown down his hat and posed himself with a little yellow cane in his hand, the large silver head of which he rubbed along his upper lip at intervals as if to keep the black moustache from interfering with his captivating utterance and at the same time to preserve its symmetry of form. "But I tackled it. So would any gentleman when a lady like you made it a special thing. But that's all right. You're nicely fixed here," and he took a survey of the room with his little black eyes rolled up and sidewise, but without turning his head. "Swell quarters. The cup's an old curio. Don't wonder you wanted to get it back."

"Mr. Kleinbacker," said Manuella, "I don't think I quite understand you."

"Of course not. It's my deuced way. There's too much hustle about me for a girl at first. But that's all right. You'll understand me better when you come to know me. You ask any girl if the grass grows under me. You just slip on your shawl and things. I've got a coupé at the door. We'll take a turn up town and I'll show you the cup."

In spite of herself a smile came over her face at the easy impudence of Mr. Kleinbacker, which Mr. Kleinbacker interpreted to be an expression of pleasure.

"You put on your togs," he said, "and I'll smoke a cigarette. Don't dally and get yourself up too fearfully, you know—just medium. The old woman will let me smoke here, won't she?"

Anything like indignation had now faded in the girl's mind to an amused wonder at this fellow's effrontery. An innocent desire that he would stay there until Carteret could see what a fool he was and enjoy it with her, took possession of her, and at the same time she felt a woman's curiosity to know what he had done with reference to the cup. Out of all this grew a shy tolerance of him.

"I am afraid I cannot go with you this morning," she said, "but you may tell me what you have done."

"That's all right," he responded glibly. "We'll take the ride some other time. You get a good ready and I'll tell you about the goblet. Did you ever go out to Pawlison's?"

Manuella shook her head. "I never did," she said.

"Well, I wouldn't have thought it, to look at you. You don't know what you've missed. It's the best place on the road now for a small party. Bang up table; A number one wines; no crowd; no questions asked. How are you on soft shell crabs?"

"Mr. Kleinbacker," said Manuella with a beamy kind of contempt manifesting itself on her face, "Will you please to tell me what you have done about the cup?"

"Of course I will'; you're not in a hurry, are you? Don't expect anybody, do you?"

"Yes, I do."

"That's all right. You won't find me unreasonable. I can take my turn. Can't have everything your own way at the first clash, eh? Can you, now? But the cup's all sound. You see it wasn't a first, only a second prize. Lord, what the Shay Sharp Shooters don't know about sterling ware would stock a wareroom. They had a plated pitcher for first prize and that solid cup went second and, by jove, Miss Castleton, Dinnis McElroy, who never owned a shaving mug, plumped it and pawned it before the smoke cleared away. 'Come on my boy,' says I. I'll buy your tickets.' 'Be gorry, me little man,' says Dinnis, 'buy me a dhrink.' 'I'll go you councillor,' says I. 'Let's go Shay's, he's got the democratic poison.' I set up the whole gang—that's all right—washed Dinnis off his pins. 'Barrin' the crook in your nose,' says he, 'you're a thrue man.' 'I hope I may die if I aint,' says I. 'Let's take another h'ist. I'm the man that made the mug and you're the boy that won it. Why didn't you swipe the pitcher while you was about it—the mug wasn't worth nothin' except to sell again. I'll give you twenty dollars for the paper, bet you a hat you didn't get ten on the thing.' Did I get 'em. Well, you gamble I did."

And Mr. Kleinbacker took out a handsome wallet from his breast pocket, opened it and held up a piece of dirty yellow paper. "That's the certif.," said he, "O! I don't go to sleep when loveliness is on deck."

At this moment the door bell rang. In a minute Manuella was at the window. To her utter amazement she saw Mr. Patrick Brady in the doorway.

"O, dear!" she exclaimed unthinkingly, "I can't see him now."

Mr. Kleinbacker coincided with her easily. "That's all right," he said, "You're out; ha! ha! It won't hurt him much. O! I've been there. I noticed yesterday he was one of the soft kind. They get over it quick."

The girl looked at him with a quick flush in her cheek which he mistook for annoyance at the interruption, but even then her indignation crossed by an irresistible sense of the ludicrous and a desire to hear what he would do with the cup faded into an expression of impatience.

"You may say I cannot be seen today," she said to the maid who passed the door as she closed it.

"Thanks," cried Kleinbacker.

"I suppose you have brought the ticket for me and want the money."

"I'm not that kind of a commissioner," said the young man. "You just leave the business to me and I'll close it out. I don't do things that way. Have you seen Maggie Mitchell in Fanchon?"

"I do not go anywhere," she replied, "I have a feeble grandfather who takes all my time and I ought to be with him now."

"O! that's all right. What ails the old man? Let me send him over some High Rock spring water. It's a great toner. I take a swig of it every morning. It's immense after a racket."

"I'm much obliged," she said, "but I don't think I'd bother."

"It goes either way; Blaine and Trivette keep me supplied; I've got lots of it. Well," he added as she moved towards the door, "you've got to go, haven't you? I'm awful sorry, but it's all right. You leave the cup to me. Don't you worry. When's the best time to catch you alone?"

"I'm nearly always alone," said Manuella with her hand on the knob.

"Really? I wouldn't have believed it. Tell the old man to brace up. Don't forget Pawlison's. I'll run in on you whenever I get a chance."

All this left the poor girl in a state of bewilderment approaching hysteria. She sat down on the lounge after he was gone and laughed and cried alternately and in that condition Carteret found her.

"I want to get away from these people," she said.

"Everything is ready, my dear. All we have to do is to get aboard the train with a satchel. We can get off in half an hour if your things are packed."

"Packed," she replied, "I haven't bought them."

"But you can buy them to-morrow morning and be ready by five o'clock. Have you coaxed your grandfather?"

"I have told him that I was going to take him in the country for a week and he at first objected on business grounds. Mr. Stonybrook discouraged it, but I think I can manage it. Mr. Stonybrook is going to Boston in the morning and we can slip away before he gets back."

The moment it was decided to take this flight, they both had enough to do. Manuella who had for some weeks been fitted and fretted by a dressmaker, had to hunt up that dilatory personage. She also had purchases to make and her grandfather's traps to pack up. It was indeed to her an event of great importance and much bustle, altogether the most important in its anticipations and its independence of any she had encountered.

Carteret packed his kit of tools, told Chapman that he was off for a week and presented himself in a carriage at Mrs. Hannige's the next afternoon. He found Manuella transformed. She was arrayed in a most becoming dress and wore a little beaver turned up at the side. He regarded her with pride and wonder and thought he had never seen anything so beautiful.

"Let me look at you," he cried with artistic privilege, turning her round so as to get every line.

"Isn't it becoming?" she asked. "You don't think it too full, do you?"

"Full," he said. "Yes, of the sweetest, dearest creature on earth."

There was a pleasant confusion in the hall. Mrs. Hannige and her maids were bringing down the trunk and satchels and all talking at once, when who should arrive but Mr. Kleinbacker with a parcel under his arm.

He stepped into the hall with a brisk self-importance, and was accosted by Carteret coldly. They passed some words and Kleinbacker said: "Excuse me, I have a little business with the lady," beckoned to Manuella to come into the reception room.

"It isn't necessary to tell our business to everybody," he said, jerking his head significantly toward the hallway when they were in the little room and at the same time unrolling the package. "I've got the plunder. Told you I'd capture it. Why didn't you introduce me to the old man? Changing your quarters?"

"No; I'm going to take Grandpa into the country for a day or two," said Manuella, with her eyes fastened on the package which he had most elaborately wound with brown paper.

"Where is it? Long Island? There," and coming at last to the contents of his bundle, he lifted out an elaborately ornamented cup and holding it up, said: "It's a prize and I'm proud to have rescued it from the hands it had fallen into." Manuella who was staring at it with something like awe in her face and with her hands clasped in a pretty attitude of curiosity immediately called out:

"Mr. Carteret, come here."

The young man came at once to the door of the room, but he did not know that he was followed by the inquisitive Mrs. Hannige who looked over his shoulder and caught a glimpse of the cup which Mr. Kleinbacker was holding up.

Carteret a moment later pulled the door shut after him without regarding Mrs. Hannige, and she went back to Mr. Evans and her maids.

Manuella was pointing with her finger at the odd piece of silver which Mr. Kleinbacker held up and turned round for them, as a salesman would exhibit a piece of similar ware.

"Isn't it perfectly wonderful," exclaimed the girl, drawing close to it with genuine admiration, no doubt colored by a mysterious dread.

"It's unique," said Mr. Kleinbacker, supplying the trade word.

Carteret looked at it a moment wonderingly and then said, "But we have no time to waste on it now, if we want to catch the train. Put it in that big satchel. We can discuss its beauties afterwards. What is the amount, Mr. Kleinbacker, that we are indebted?"

"Excuse me," said Mr. Kleinbacker; "O, that's all right, but if you've no objection, I'll close out the business with the lady."

Manuella put up her hand involuntarily as Carteret was about to say something, and he caught the appeal on her face. "Very well," he said, "but time is short," and he went back into the hall.

"No eye for the beautiful," remarked Mr. Kleinbacker, as he began wrapping the cup. "Now then, Miss, the bill's all right. I'll make out the damage before you get back. It's all right. You leave that to me, we do these things in a regular way. But I want to say to you," and he dropped his voice, "that if anything should turn up about that cup, you let me know and I'll tell *you* something about it that no other living soul on earth knows. Don't you forget that. When are you coming back?"

Manuella really couldn't say, and after a few words of semi-confidential platitudes Mr. Kleinbacker put the cup in her hands carefully wrapped and took his departure.

It was then hurriedly packed in a satchel and for the time being forgotten in the more joyous and important details of departure. Mr. Evans was carefully lifted into the coach, the luggage was piled up under the driver's seat. Mrs. Hannige was on the steps. "You'll be sure to be back by the twelfth, won't you?" she cried.

Carteret leaned out the coach door. "To-day's the seventh. If the weather holds, I don't think we will. Goodbye."

Mrs. Hannige took off her slipper and threw it.

"Gracious," said Manuella, all blushes and smiles, "the neighbors will think it's a wedding party."

CHAPTER XXVI.

MRS. FOLLEN SANGER GETS A SHOCK.

The Sanger reception was given on the night of the eighth in the big mansion on Gramercy Park.

It was the doctor's scheme entirely. His wife had invented all kinds of objections in vain. His strong will overcame them all.

"You seem determined, my dear, to be a recluse. I shall not have it. I can readily understand that there may be, and no doubt are, some reasons which are more valid than those you have given me, but that makes no difference with me. I married you with the idea of making you my wife, and I intend to make the world recognize you as my wife. So you might as well get over all this retiring nonsense, and adjust yourself to the situation," and he gave her a kiss on the forehead as a kindly token of authority.

The stately woman wore a delicately resigned look, but the shade of helplessness was too fine for his robust sense.

"You've got to come out of this shell of timidity. I insist on it, and I'll take care of the consequences. You leave all that to me."

Many times before this conversation Mrs. Sanger had regretted that she had not made a clean breast of it and told him everything. But the longer she delayed the more difficult it became. She was now occupying the position of a lady. She was talked of, if not much seen, as the wife of a proud man of influence. She had not the courage to destroy or even to disturb the strange dream of affluence and affection that had grown up around her. The doctor's love for her was one of those strong proprietary passions that such natures alone are capable of. It usurped every faculty without modifying or ennobling it. He was uneasy if she were not somewhere about, but he generally left her to her own pensive resources when she was. All his endearments were touched with a color of ownership. He thought she was the most beautiful woman on earth, and he dressed her in the most expensive robes and decorated her with the most costly jewels; but he immediately wanted to exhibit her, and that was the one thing she was continually begging him not to do.

She was surrounded by all the luxuries that an imperious devotion and splendid income could supply. Her boudoir was oriental in voluptuous comfort. She had her own maids and her own equipage, and the whole circle of the politico-social people was ready to flatter and receive her. But for weeks she clung to her room, excused herself when visitors came, pleaded indisposition when her husband asked her to drive, and shunned even her own maids; and withal, there was a woman's craft that kept one eye on the effects of all this, and prevented her husband from seeing the real cause of her actions.

When alone she had moods of despair, terror and remorse that followed each other with grim regularity. One feeling alone was permanent and invincible—it may be called a consciousness of coming exposure. That was the phantom that kept step with her everywhere. She tried with morbid introspection to picture how and when this phantom would step out into the blazing light and point its terrible finger at her trembling and jewel-bedecked person. Then she would summon all her reason and resolution to prove to herself how idle were all these fears and how excusable had been her mad exploit. There was no one alive who knew her story save that man Elkins and he knew it only in part. Where was Elkins? Had he ever coupled Enniston's death with her disappearance? Had he ever tried to find her after that night? Pshaw! he was implicated in Enniston's crime and self-interest would seal his mouth. No one save the dead man had seen her insane act; and then when all that reason could say had been said, there stood that ghastly terror waiting for her with a cold, inexorable patience, and so phantasmal are the fears of a guilty, perturbed mind that this effigy of her terror sometimes took bodily shape and the cold, patient face was that of the officer who had looked down into her soul and heard her confession on that terrible day in the hospital.

To pull the woman out of the apathy into which these moods plunged her, required all the will and determination of her husband. She generally complied with his requests in the end, but compliance only heightened her secret dread and fear.

When a month had gone by and he had insisted on her appearing in public with him, she began to complain of her eyes, and, with a feminine ingenuity that was admirable, succeeded in making him believe that the optic nerve was affected and that she suffered intense pain when exposed to a strong light. The result of this was a pair of clouded spectacles which in some slight degree disguised her, and which she wore whenever there was danger of being recognized. The doctor ridiculed them a great deal, but put up with them because they removed one excuse for her retirement.

Doctor Sanger was not in any sense a man of extraordinary acumen and like most masculine natures rather enjoyed the petty deceptions of a woman he admired. He knew perfectly well that several members of the profession were aware that he had taken his wife from a hospital and that her record was obscure. He knew also that an officer from New York had called to see her there while he was away. But with plausible skill she had explained that and he believed that the officer had been killed by an accident. But as he looked at most matters through his will, he believed that his relationship to the woman closed out all further discussion of her antecedents. At some future time, when she came to be more tractable, she would no doubt tell him her story and he would chuck her under the chin and tell her that that all belonged to a foolish past, before she knew him, and wasn't worth talking about.

She had looked forward to the reception with dread, but the preparations for it went steadily on. Several times she had made him name over the people who would be there and had scanned the invitation lists with intense interest, fearing that the name of Elkins was lurking somewhere. It never occurred to her that Elkins might be an assumed name as Ennis had been and that he would sometime stand before her with another.

All that she knew was that the list of names was of people that she had never heard of and that there was a reasonable chance they had never heard of her.

"My dear," the doctor said, "it's the regulation, hum-drum thing. All you'll have to do will be to smile—I know it's hard for you to smile—and bow, and say a few gracious common-places and retire with honor. Any woman of average tact can go through it and come out with flying colors. I'll be at your side, we'll make a show of receiving them and then let them have things their own way. There will be a crowd of sycophants, political aspirants, officials, scheming Brummagen dowagers, with a sprinkling of solid men, fast boys and precocious girls. Your old Knickerbocker who saved his pennies up in a stocking and burnt candles, would call it a vulgar mob. Your live man of affairs, who keeps abreast of public opinion in this day, understands that the vulgar mob makes and unmakes events and men. I've got to put up with it or I'll be forgotten in the scramble. I don't ask you to hob-nob and let them paw you. You can do the quiet, superior sort of sufferance business, and say a word to everybody, and I want you to wear that new, white corded silk."

Dr. Sanger's description of the party was not inaccurate. It was one of those affairs in which totally unlike people come together by attraction of policy, vanity and envy, and stand round and make remarks about each other or discuss their several weaknesses and ventilate their prejudices.

A great many municipal dignitaries were there, for they had a distinct idea that Dr. Sanger was a coming man. The Mayor came alone, stayed half an hour and went away. There were commissioners, assemblymen, judges, lawyers, editors, hotel-keepers, operators, contractors, manufacturers and one police captain. Some of them brought their wives. All these were men of local affairs. But there was another set, consisting of younger men of the town, ambitious, restless and spirited, who wanted patrons, or having them, kept in their wake; young lawyers with political aspirations; scheming artists, and a sprinkling of the fast fellows whose fathers made money enough for the whole family.

The general air of the assemblage was democratic. Dr. Sanger was more anxious to obtain power than to secure social distinction, and there was an absence of vulgar display about the affair that made it entirely unlike the shoddy receptions of many of his acquaintances who were vastly wealthier, and there was also a hearty simplicity observable in most of the men, in spite of their Celtic accent and slightly over-dressed appearance, and in contradistinction to their loud tones and inelegant English, which made one feel that they had not in their rise to importance and independence either reached or cared to reach that plane of elegant hypocrisy and correct duplicity which often marks what New York calls its "best society."

At nine o'clock the parlors of Dr. Sanger's house were somewhat uncomfortably choked and the entire absence of that order and repose which one might reasonably look for in a private party of this kind was due in great part to the constant arrivals and departures of people who owed it to the doctor to put in an appearance and were compelled by their duty elsewhere to get away as soon as possible. One felt instinctively that the great proportion of these people was too deep in the whirlpool of human endeavor; too deeply engrossed in the struggle for success to waste much time with the superflous conventionalities. But there were a few old New Yorkers with their families who gave something of a social back-ground to the reception. One or two bankers who handled the city's money, a retired speculator whose daughters were women of the world, a group of property owners who were at the mercy of rapacious aldermen, genteel old ladies of irreproachable social standing and Knickerbocker blood, but without fortunes and whose husbands depended on a party for positions, and several old time acquaintances of Judge Sanger, who came out of their retirement at his beck and lent the flavor of their presence at his request.

To this latter group must be assigned Col. Hardynge, who had brought his daughter Grace and Rose Enniston with him. They stood together at the end of the rear parlor overlooking the crowd while Grace's father, not far away, was one of a group that was conversing with the conspicuous and handsome host, whose wife, in a corded silk, stood near him, pale and reserved, a pallid object of interest in this informal and intensely vital concourse.

"It reminds me," said Grace to Rose, "of a reception at the White House that Pa took me to once, where everybody seemed to be coming and going, and crowding, and everybody had to talk very loud to be heard. Don't you think Mrs. Sanger is a beautiful woman?"

"Is she an invalid," Rose asked, "or an aristocrat? I've watched her for five minutes and havn't seen her move her lips."

"Wait a moment, we'll get presented and then we can find out."

But that opportunity did not come immediately. Several acquaintances came up and spoke to the young ladies. Among them was old Mrs. Pettigrew, in white curls, with the hoop of her heavy gold spectacles sunk deep in the pulpy little nose. She had been waddling about in black silk for half an hour wherever the crowd was densest, to complain of the heat and the exertion, and to remind everybody inopportunely that "we have to do it, you know."

"Well, girls," she said, fanning herself furiously, which kept her pudgy pink face in the centre of a dance of white curls. "You can stand it at your age, I s'pose, but look at me. It comes tough on us veterans. I fancy you think it's fun, don't you. Well, I used to. It's business now."

"There's a chair Mrs. Pettigrew," said Grace. "Sit down awhile."

"No," said Mrs. Pettigrew. "I've got to make hay while the gas shines. You sit down, dear. I've got to catch Blogget; you know Blogget when you see him, don't you? He's clerk of the Board. I'm afraid he'll slip in and then slip out before I know it—I mean the School Board, of course—how should you know?"

"If you stay here," said Grace, "you will be sure to see him. He will come to Dr. Sanger. We want you to tell us who these people are."

"Yes," said Rose with less delicacy. "First tell us who Mrs. Sanger is."

"There you go," replied Mrs. Pettigrew, striking at Rose playfully with her fan, "just like an innocent girl. She's Mrs. Dr. Sanger. That's all I'm entitled to know. But you, you delicious little outlaw, you can ask anything. I wish you knew Blogget. I'd get you to ask him some questions that I dare not."

"Do you mean to say that it is not allowable to ask where Mrs. Sanger came from?" persisted Rose.

"No, it's allowable for such freelances as you, and it's perfectly delicious to hear you. There's nothing so precious as the ingenuousness of youth; I dote on it."

"She's a lady, at all events," said Rose, "Any one can see that in her dress and manner. I think her reserve and dignity are just charming."

"I'm glad you admire reserve and dignity, my dear," said Mrs. Pettigrew, making another dash at her with her fan. "When a girl begins by admiring them, she ends by acquiring them. I wish you'd ask the doctor where his wife came from. There's so little of the frankness of youth in these crowds that I think it would tickle him."

"What a hideous old cynic," said Rose, as Mrs. Pettigrew passed on to distribute her irony.

Among others who drifted to the young ladies as they stood there was Otis Chapman. He had the tact to be presented formally and then to say that it was perhaps superfluous. He knew everybody and immediately began a spirited running description, per capita.

"I expected my friend Carteret to be here, but he went off suddenly with one of his pupils for a sketching jaunt," he said.

"Where did he go?" asked Rose with her usual disregard of concealment and with a rash eagerness.

"'Pon my honor I couldn't tell you. It was a sudden freak. What do you think of the hostess? Quite a mediæval vision in this full blooded company, isn't she? A sort of St. Cecilia, only she doesn't patronize music, or painting either, for that matter. I'd like to get the doctor to let me have a sitting or two. If you get a chance you can drop a hint for me."

"Who is the tall, dark-visaged man with a French air?"

"That's Veilé, the pianist. He's been trying for a year to work a scheme on the School Board for a musical superintendency, at a salary of five thousand dollars. He could buy all the pianos for the public schools, stand in with the manufacturer and make five thousand more. He furnishes the music for all the big wire pullers. When he begins to play, all the men who want to talk business will go into the billiard and smoking rooms. He belongs to what they call the tumultuous school of music."

"How interesting," exclaimed Rose.

"Who's the large fluffy man he is talking to?"

"I believe his name is Chanfleur. I don't know much about him except that he is a speculator in Western mining lands, or something of that sort. I don't think by his cut that he'd interest you. That's Colonel Stillingfleet, who raised a regiment of his own and lost his arm at Pittsburg Landing, and the man he is talking to is the handsome Brannagan, Commissioner of Charities and Correction. Mrs. Stillingfleet in the steel silk is, I believe, a literary woman, and has written a book or two. You can tell it by her sinewy neck; I don't know why it is, but literary women all have sinewy and long necks."

"That is her daughter, I suppose, who goes about talking to all the men so earnestly. I've tried to follow her for a minute—she's like a fluttering moth and that absurd cape looks like wings."

"That," said Oats laughingly, "is our Miss Humphreys. I say *our* because that's what we call her in the studios. She's a fashion reporter on one of the papers. She goes everywhere with a mad faculty for getting people's names and clothes and making an erroneous catalogue of them. If your see your name in print to-morrow with an inaccurate description of your wardrobe, put it down to Humphreys. Here comes the Sanger party."

And Oats stepped aside as Colonel Hardynge and Dr. Sanger and his wife turned and slowly made their way toward the young ladies.

"Let me present my daughter Grace, and this is her friend Miss Enniston of Coe's Grove," said the Colonel.

A cold, quick shock went through Mrs. Sanger. She had extended her hand to Grace with an extra welcome when the name of Enniston was pronounced and Miss Hardynge felt the spasmodic impulse as the woman turned with a quick start and stared at Rose.

The crowd was close about them and the clamor of voices made the little gasp inaudible. But Mrs. Sanger was a woman by this time too skilled in managing her nerves to give way to more than an involuntary start. Her wits were too keenly alive to her danger to be caught without a struggle. She gave her hand to Rose and with a supreme effort managed to conceal her emotions.

"You are a resident of the city?" she said.

"Hardly a permanent resident," replied Rose, "but I expect to spend much of the winter here."

"We're going to keep her," said the Colonel, "and bring her out properly. Her mother has been educating her for a convent."

"Hardly that," Rose rejoined, laughingly. "I shouldn't be surprised if Ma came to town herself this winter."

"We can show you plenty of life here," said the doctor, "and I hope you will both consider us among your old friends and not wait for receptions. Your father is almost as bad as Kate here; he seems to have a dread of being pulled out of his shell. I want you to get as intimately acquainted as possible."

Saying which, he turned and was soon in conversation with a group of men that was waiting for him.

"If you will give me that chair," Mrs. Sanger said to Col. Hardynge, "I shall be grateful. The heat and light overcome me."

Two or three pairs of hands were quick to obey her and she sat down with her back to the chandelier. Grace was standing in front of her and Rose bent over her. The Colonel had gone for a glass of water.

"You are ill, Madame," said Rose. "Would it not be well to retire? This room is a dreadful trial to the nerves."

Mrs. Sanger was listening to the tones of the girl's voice and did not immediately answer. There was an awful reverberation in them of tones heard once before; their vibrations seemed to light with an electric flash the terrible memories of that night and the face hanging over her with sympathy seemed to be saying, "You are the murderess of my father. You can't hide from me for I have his eyes."

"Pardon me," she said with a hollow voice, "I was trying to get my breath. I am not ill, but if I retire at the first opportunity I am sure you will forgive me. Have you met any of your acquaintances here?"

"O yes, several." said Grace.

"And you?" asked Mrs. Sanger, looking furtively at Rose.

"I have so few acquaintances, Madame," replied Rose, "That I should have to look a long time to find them. I hope to enlarge the circle this winter."

At that moment Dr. Sanger returned to the group with a gentleman in his wake and in his gusty manner threw him at the whole party and then went off again with his head bent down to the ear of a henchman who had been following him for some time. The newcomer proved to be one of the young men who had a stock of small talk, and the moment he opened it Mrs. Sanger got up and moved away. She passed through the crowd speaking to several persons and smiling and nodding to others with a hostess's impartial graciousness. When she reached the hallway she had to encounter another set, but with an assumption of patience and delight that she did not feel, she got to the stairway and slowly mounted to the second floor. The moment she reached her room and had locked her door she broke down.

"My God," she said in a husky, supressed tone, "I cannot endure this, I cannot, I cannot," and she strode up and down wringing her hands, her white dress making a sharp swish. "I shall kill myself if it goes on. That is what it will come to."

She went to the closed door and listened. The murmur of the voices was quite audible and the movement of the crowd imparted a slight vibration to the floor. The sense of multitude appeared to intensify her loneliness. She strode indeterminately and then fell on her knees by her bed in an involuntary attitude of prayer, exclaiming, "O heaven, if you do not give me some one to tell this to, I shall die."

Her head sank into her hands imbedded in the rich, soft counterpane; an overwhelming sense of self-pity supervened, and she began to sob.

Quite as suddenly she sprang up, went to the glass and began to smooth her hair. A sudden fear of her husband, whom she knew would instantly miss her, made her desperate in quite another direction. She dashed some kind of spirits on her face, unlocked the door, and was rubbing her eyes with a towel when her husband knocked.

"Come in, is that you, Follen?" she said with a sudden sprightliness.

He opened the door. "What's the matter, Kate?"

"My poor eyes," she said. That's all; I had to come up and bathe them. I'm going right down again. Has the Hardynge party gone?"

He came over and looked narrowly into her face. "I believe you have been crying," he said.

"No, no, not so bad as that. If it is, I will not go down."

He continued to stare at her and then kissing her on the forehead, he said, "Poor girl, don't come down if it distresses you."

She actually coaxed him to permit her.

"You go back," she said, "I'm coming right down. I want to see the Hardynges before they go. Everybody will miss you. Go along, do."

She was hoping now to delay her return until the Hardynge party had gone. The one definite purpose in her mind was to prevent if possible a growing intimacy with the Ennistons.

While this scene was enacting, others were taking place in the several rooms open to the company.

Rose Enniston had captured Oats and got him into the conservatory, there escaping from several young men who bored her insufferably.

"Now tell me," she said, "for you know, who is it Carteret's gone off with?"

Oats began to protest.

"You know perfectly well, it's that Manuella."

"Why, do you know her?"

"Do you think I would ask questions if I didn't? I thought you were going to be a friend of mine."

"O come now," said Oats. "I'm a friend of Carteret's. You don't think I'd talk about his affairs behind his back, do you?"

"No, not affairs of secrecy or confidence. I'm surprised, Mr. Chapman, that you suspected me of asking you to betray your friend. I want to help him. I've proved that. He doesn't take pupils secretly, does he?"

"He might for all I know about them. I'm not going to get him into any trouble by meddling with his affairs."

"O, you think it would get him into trouble by telling me who his pupil is."

"No, I don't think so, for I don't know anything about it. I said I wasn't going to get him into any trouble."

"But you'd help to get him out of trouble, wouldn't you?"

"Yes, but to tell you the truth, I don't believe he's in any just now. I never saw him so happy before. He used to go moping around last summer like a man under a sentence, but lately he's been bubbling over with the most consummate and unprofessional cheerfulness, I had to warn him that people would think he'd given up painting."

Rose winced a little under this, but she was persistent. After a moment's pause, she said: "I think you ought to trust me. I wish I could convince you that my object is not one of mischief, but of assistance. Can't you understand that if he suspected it my whole purpose would be frustrated? It's to your interest to help me."

This was adroitly put. Chapman had a keen commercial sense, and he knew that Miss Enniston could make herself an invaluable patron if she chose. He did not like to throw away such a chance.

"Well, I'll tell you," he said, "I don't believe Carteret is doing anything he is ashamed of and he hasn't put me under any pledge of secrecy. He is instructing a very beautiful young lady who lives at Mrs. Hannige's. I believe her name is

Castleton. All I know is that she is poor and very worthy, for I live at Hannige's myself."

Rose turned her hand over and looked at Carteret's ring. A very bitter feeling was in her heart. There was something of her habitual disregard of consequences in her betrayal of herself as she said:

"Is she so very beautiful?"

Chapman saw the jealousy of this. "She is certainly a good looking young lady. It would be useless to deny it," he said. "But it don't follow that he's in love with her except as an artist. You don't know how beauty catches the artist's eye."

She did not follow his thought at all. "She is beautiful and worthy," kept ringing like a reproach in her mind.

She looked up and found Mrs. Sanger, who had returned to the room, regarding her from a distant group with a steady, searching stare.

This incident called her out of herself, just as Grace Hardynge joined them.

"Mrs. Sanger is a most extraordinary woman," Rose said. "She affected me strangely. Did you notice anything unusual about her?"

"Her unusual nervousness," said Grace. "She's all starts and moods. She keeps looking about while you are talking to her as if she dreaded an accident. I think she has had a shock to her nervous system."

For an hour or two the Sanger mansion blazed and reverberated with slowly diminishing radiance and noise. The more conservative guests had gone home and taken the ladies with them. By degrees the remaining men, nearly all politicians, fell into groups in the several rooms where they smoked cigars, drank wine, and discussed party affairs with the freedom of a late hour and an exhilerated condition. All formality was relaxed. The front door stood open and men with spring overcoats on their arms went up and down the steps and the sound of vigorous "good nights," and "take care of yourself, old boy," mingled with gusty laughter might have been heard for some distance in that quiet and respectable neighborhood, if everybody had not been asleep for hours.

It was nearly one o'clock when a man on the sidewalk, who was wrapped in a blue military cloak and had been in conversation with several of the departing guests who were waiting for their carriages, slowly went up the steps to the entrance way. There were no servants at the door and he easily slipped into the hallway among the men who were engaged in conversation. Just as he had passed the vestibule, he came face to face with Rose Enniston who was in advance of the Hardynge party, with her skirts on her arm and a good night on her lips to somebody. She looked up and found a dark and wiry man with a beaked nose and a bald head bowing with his hat in his hand as he stepped aside for her. She remembered for a long time his piercing black eyes and the red stone on his throat. He looked after her as she went down the steps and then glancing about at the people in the hallway who paid not the slightest attention to him, he threw off his cloak, put it over his arm and with his soft hat in his hand, sauntered peeringly into the front parlor. If any one noticed him, he was mistaken for a confidential servant, a secretary, or a tutor, sent to escort some young lady home or to look after a son who was apt to stay too late. His dress was one of genteel but not fashionable black and his manner was slightly obsequious, as if he meant to heighten this natural mistake. Unobserved, he ran his eye over the men who were standing about until he saw Chanfleur at the end of the saloon in conversation with someone, and then he mingled unobtrusively with the crowd until he got an opportunity to whisper in his ear:

"Get away as quick as you can. I've something important to tell you."

Chanfleur looked at him with surprise. "You here?" he said.

"Yes, I walked in *sans ceremonie*, at this hour, because I could not wait. Have you talked to the doctor?"

"Yes. He's anxious and agreeable. You'd better let me introduce you, now you're here."

"That'll keep, that'll keep. I've got something that will not. Suppose you get your coat and hat. I'll go to the entrance and wait."

"Did you know Miss Enniston was here?" asked Chanfleur.

"Met her going out," replied the other.

The two men walked down the room during this conversation. Suddenly Chanfleur said: "Very well, wait for me. I've got to say good-night to the host," and they moved apart.

It was nearly an hour later when Chanfleur came to the street entrance with his coat on his arm and looked down inquiringly into the street for his friend.

A cold moon was coming up over the Gramercy hotel and the morning was chilly.

He buttoned the coat about him and went down. A voice hailed him from a coach window.

"I got in here," he said, "to escape the night air and I didn't want to be seen." A moment later they were driven away.

Neither of them had noticed a man half hidden by one of the Park trees opposite, who had been watching them from the shadows.

It was John Wilder.

CHAPTER XXVII.

ROSE ENNISTON GOES ON THE WARPATH.

An event occurred just after John Wilder had returned with Mr. Evans from the unsuccessful visit to Turtle Bay, which diverted him for several days from the search for the cup. Chagrined, and disgusted at the trivial events which turned all his efforts to disappointment, and undetermined whether Mr. Evans was honestly senile or had already disposed of the cup to some other parties, he went straight in search of Plonski. Here again he was baffled. That individual had disappeared and this gave weight to the suspicion that the wily old man had outwitted him and carried off the prize. All efforts to find him in the city were vain. After writing a letter of explanation to Dr. Wollendorf, he was about to undertake the thankless task of endeavoring to worm the truth from Mr. Evans, when he received a summons from the Central Office to go in search of an absconding bank cashier who was supposed to have gone to Denver by the way of Chicago. He caught the man in the latter city, but the feat consumed time, and before he got back Plonski, who had never for one moment rested in his search, and who had at first believed that Wilder had got the cup, satisfied himself that it was still in the possession of Mr. Evans or that he knew where it was. His means of espionage were better than Wilder's, for he employed a number of unscrupulous agents and Wilder was alone in his search. He found out by the most patient prying that the cup had not reached Mr. Ackerman at Coe's Grove, which it must have done had Wilder secured it. He wormed Bob Holbrook's secret from him and got upon the track of Manuella and Carteret in their excursions uptown.

His indefatigable patience and persistence during these weeks were marvelous. He had to keep out of sight and make others do most of his work. But he had servile accomplices in The Mink and others of his class, and he counted the girl Mignon and Mrs. Sitwhite on his detective staff. No one could have been aware of the tireless ingenuity of method and the sleepless shaping of every figment of fact into consecutive information without feeling that the man was working for some extraordinary prize.

On the day before the Sanger party, he had so far followed his clues as to reach the establishment of Dittmar and Kleinbacker and through some of his agents to reach approximate facts from the lips of Adolph Kleinbacker himself. The information that Mr. Evans and Carteret had left the city came close on the heels of conclusive facts. The Mink was dispatched at once to Coe's Grove with instructions to send word immediately, for Plonski had not the slightest doubt now that the cup was on its way to Mr. Ackerman and on the night of the party, unable to remain idle, he went in search of Chanfleur.

Driving uptown in the coach, Plonski told all this with many curious details, here omitted, to his conspirator, who smoked a cigar and listened with intense interest. At the conclusion he said, "What do you propose to do now?"

"If the thing gets back into that safe, we've got our work to do all over again," he said, "but this time, it ought to be done without any delay or nonsense. There's nobody in that house but Captain Ackerman, Mrs. Enniston and two servants. We mustn't permit Ackerman to get away with it."

"I should say not" remarked Chanfleur emphatically. "Have you heard anything from your man?"

"Not yet. I've given him a code to telegraph by. I'll probably get word in the morning. Meanwhile, I've got to watch that house in Fifteenth Street. There's one chance in a hundred that Evans hasn't gone to Coe's Grove, and he may come back at any time. The woman who keeps the place is as close mouthed as if she were in the game."

"Now then," says Chanfleur, "about Dr. Sanger."

"Well, as I told you," replied Plonski, "I want his influence at headquarters. That man Wilder is our great danger, and the doctor carries one of the police commissioners in his pocket, I am told. It looks as though we'd need all the political influence we can command before we get through. His father is a rabid copperhead, and is making speeches at the new constitutional leagues that have been formed uptown. I shall have about two hundred sore-headed patriots to-morrow night at Brannagan's Hall, and Judge Sanger is one of the speakers. He's got an idea which has been carefully pumped into him that I can pull about three hundred votes in his district against the war democrats, and what I can't pull I can smash by the aid of heelers. You'd better come over and hear him talk."

"No, I thank you," said Chanfleur. "You'll have one of those United States marshals running you all in to Fort Lafayette, if you are not careful. It's a perilous piece of business."

"Well, it's my opinion," said Plonski, "that if the Judge and the rest of them succeed in getting the sub war elements of the city, which are mainly Irish, organized, there'll be a little civil war here, and the Mayor will run a municipal secession flag. The Judge said to-night that this ought to be a free city."

"Did he? I wouldn't have believed the Judge was such a damned fool."

"Let us congratulate ourselves that he is," said Plonski. "His main idea is that the opposition to a forced levy of men for the war is so wide spread that it can be made a local issue in politics."

"It's an issue that will be swept out of sight the moment it's made," replied Chanfleur. "Don't you make any mistake about the temper of the North. The

war is going to be fought through to the bitter end, and there's only one outcome of it. The South is going to be impoverished, licked and subjugated. I'm
getting very sick of the whole thing, and I wish this infernal cup business was
closed out. I'd go to Europe."

"It's very absurd to talk as you do about closing out and going to Europe,
unless you mean to sell out," said Plonski. "The risks and the results are too
enormous to be treated with impatience. I'm content to work five years with a
reasonable chance of success, seeing that there is nothing else within the grasp
of human patience that can possibly pay so well. As for the war, it is the most
fortunate of all circumstances for us, as you must see. The attention of the
Government is absorbed in it, and the public mind so filled with it that a million
individual iniquities, that at any other time would fill the papers and convulse
the community, are unnoticed. The best time to rob a house is during a riot."

"Plonski," said Chanfleur, "you will never rob a house. You're too much of
a philosopher. You'd mingle with the crowd and make speeches."

"I might," replied Plonski. "It depends on how many interests were involved.
If I had followed your advice with that cup, Wilder would have had me in jail
before this on some old charge, just to tie my hands up. I could have got possession of it by violence, but I ran the risk of bringing the whole conspiracy
before the public and ruining our chances forever. What I want to say to you
now is that you must hold yourself in readiness from to-night to act instantly
the moment you hear from me. Every hour that we are in New York after I have
possession of that cup is a suicidal risk, and remember that possession of it
may entail some consequences that are not comfortable. I've a very disagreeable notion that that man Wilder will jump in on us at any unexpected moment,
and he not only has my record, but he holds a grudge against me. I'd give up
part of my interest in this thing to know just where he is now and what he's
up to."

"You're sure he's not at Coe's Grove?"

"No, I am not sure at this moment of anything, except that the cup has gone
off in the keeping of that old man and his daughter. If it has gone to Ackerman
and Wilder is not there I'll have it in twenty-four hours, if I have to burn the
house. If he is there, I've got to guard against this being one of his traps. But it
is useless to speculate now. I've got to hear from The Mink first."

"Can you trust that man?"

"I don't trust him. He is ignorant of the value of the cup. He is in my power,
and he is paid handsomely for placing what to him is a worthless piece of property in my hands. The Mink is a villain, but I drew his teeth before I employed
him."

"Suppose," said Chanfleur, "Wilder makes a straight cut, arrests your man,
threatens him with State's prison, and he should squeal?"

"If Wilder opens that kind of war on me, I'll break him. That's where Judge Sanger and his son come into our game."

"But he'll have the cup?"

"Not necessarily. Ackerman will have it, and he had it once before. It only means a bigger campaign. The safest way to look at it all is that way. We may have a year's work ahead, but we've got some heavy political wires laid now. Ackerman is a slow moving old fool, and thinks he is hidden securely away at Coe's Grove. Once get Wilder out of the way, and the trick is ours. To put the thing in a nut-shell, it's a question after to-morrow whether Wilder breaks my neck or I break his back. It's astonishing what little things upset us. If I hadn't put that advertisement in the *Herald*, he'd never been heard of. I feel like taking myself by the throat whenever I think of it."

The morning after this conversation John Wilder was at Mrs. Hannige's. He had arrived in town the day before, and tired as he was he had gone to Gramercy Park on the strength of some information at headquarters and stood under the trees for two hours watching the place to see Plonski go in and afterwards come out and wait for Chanfleur.

Mrs. Hannige knew enough and told him enough to convince him that something had occurred in the history of the eventful cup while he was gone to warrant his immediate action. That Mr. Evans had recovered it was certain, for Mrs. Hannige had seen it in Kleinbacker's hands. But where they had gone she did not know, for Carteret with a lover's craft had determined this time to have the Evanses to himself, and had said to Mrs. Hannige that they had not decided on the place, but he would write and let her know as soon as they found a cottage.

Wilder's immediate thought was the same as Plonski's, and it was that they had gone to Coe's Grove. But a telegram to Wollendorf brought the prompt information that they were not there, which was equivalent in purport to the following dispatch received at the same time by Plonski from The Mink, but which was sent from a little railway station north of Coe's Grove:

"Property no good. Rent too high. No Sig.," which in Plonski's code stood for "Not here; haven't been here."

Wilder's deductive process was, however, surer than Plonski's. After a long and inquisitive talk with Mrs. Hannige he came to the conclusion that the lovers had been mainly intent on their picnic, and would probably give very little thought to the cup until they returned. They were not aware of its mysterious value and Carteret had regarded it as a baleful nuisance. Anything like a troublesome attempt to restore it was not likely to be made by him. The only point worth considering was did Plonski know of their possession of it and their whereabouts.

The result of all this was that Wilder very expeditiously made up his mind to devote his attention to Plonski and wait for the return of the Evanses or for some word from them.

There was one turn in the conversation with Mrs. Hannige, however, that led to results that Mr. Wilder could not anticipate.

"It looks," said he, "as if Carteret was making love in dead earnest, doesn't it?"

"Dead earnest," exclaimed Mrs. Hannige. "He's dead gone to pieces."

Wilder smiled. "I wonder what he's done with the other one," he said.

"O," said Mrs. Hannige, with a true woman's interest fired up at once, "is there another one?"

"Yes, there was," replied Wilder musingly. "I thought it was a match, but don't you go and mix yourself in that, Molly. Let things alone."

"Well, I declare; mix myself—I like your coolness. Have I got to be such a miss myself, without a head on my shoulders?"

"You're a sensible woman, Molly. So don't bother with this. Does the girl care for Carteret?"

"Care for him? He's got her so wound up that she don't think of anything else. I've watched her. I can tell by the set of her mouth the days he's coming, and when he don't come the house can't hold her. I'd have shut the door in his face if I'd known there was another one."

"Well, that's the reason I didn't tell you," said Wilder. "I think he's a gentleman."

"Is the other one a lady?" asked Mrs. Hannige.

"Yes, but I suppose they fell out, and the affair was declared off. I like Carteret's rapidity. He's made good use of his time."

"Well, I don't know about its being good use. I like that girl, everybody does. She's simple and weak, but she's sweet as she can be. I don't think you ought to lend a hand at any nonsense with her, John. I feel now as if I'd put a rope round her neck myself in letting her go off with him. 'I really don't know exactly where we are going,' he said; why, it's simply outrageous."

"Perhaps they've gone to get married," suggested Wilder.

"I should hope not," replied Mrs. Hannige, almost bristling. "She hasn't got a cent and he's as poor as a church mouse. Why, she could marry a fortune. There's Stonybrook would take her tomorrow and set her up like a lady on that third floor; he's told me as much, and you know he's a gentleman."

John Wilder smiled at the thrift that lurked in his sister's moral sentiments. He only said, "If I were a girl, Molly, I think I'd prefer Carteret to Stonybrook, even if I had to take him without that third floor."

This conversation took place in Mrs. Hannige's basement. John Wilder had got up to leave, and his sister followed him up the basement stairs to the first floor, talking the while. When they reached the landing the hall bell rang and one of the maids opened the front door and a handsomely attired young lady stepped into the hall, and was shown by the servant into the reception room. John Wilder and his sister were looking down the hallway and saw her plainly. Wilder simply said, "Damn it," and his sister asked, "Who is it?"

"It is," replied Wilder, putting his hands in his pockets, "the other one"

"Good gracious," observed Mrs. Hannige, "I wonder what she came for."

"I know her," said Wilder, "I'll go and speak to her. If she desires it you can see her afterwards."

Mrs. Hannige was in the habit of obeying her brother and she, therefore, made no objection, although her curiosity and impatience were obvious.

Miss Enniston was very much surprised and nonplussed to see the officer walk into the reception room. But Wilder said with straightforward tact:

"I beg your pardon. I saw you come in. Mrs. Hannige, who keeps the house, is my sister, and I wanted to ask you if you knew where Cartaret is. I telegraphed to Coe's Grove for him, but he was not there."

Miss Enniston flushed a little, and she was rather chilly in her recognition, as if she had been caught in an act that was not to be discussed. Wilder thought of her mother and his memorable reception as he saw the girl draw herself up and throw her head back.

"I do not know where Mr. Carteret is," she said.

"Thanks," said Wilder. "Did you wish to see Mrs. Hannige?"

"If you please."

He then bowed and passing into the hall, beckoned to his sister, who was waiting at the stairs, and telling her that he would come in again in the morning, went away, saying to himself, "To manage that woman and her mother, it is always best to give them rope enough."

Mrs. Hannige, having smoothed her gray locks and adjusted her collar, then entered the reception room.

"Are you Mrs. Hannige?"

She looked at the questioner who stood in the middle of the room and remarked that she was a handsome and determined woman.

"Yes," she said. "Won't you have a seat?"

"I will only detain you a moment," Miss Enniston said as she sat down. "I want to get some information about a young woman by the name of Castleton. Is she living with you?"

"Yes, but she has gone into the country."

"Ah, how unfortunate. If you will give me her address I will write to her," and she took out a card case.

"It's too bad." said Mrs. Hannige, "but I can't do it. I don't know it myself. She went away quite suddenly and did not know exactly where she would stop. I expect a letter from her every moment."

"That's somewhat unusual, isn't it, for a young woman?"

"O, I don't know. Are you acquainted with her?"

"No, but I want to be."

"It's a very easy matter when she comes back."

"When will that be?"

"Really I couldn't tell you. Miss Castleton is studying to become a painter and has gone on what they call a sketching jaunt. You'll like her very much. Everybody does."

"Indeed."

"I'm sure of it. Are you interested in painting?"

"Yes. I buy pictures when I like them."

"You'll like hers. People say they are uncommonly good. Perhaps you know her teacher."

"Who's he?"

"Mr. Carteret, the artist."

"Yes, I know him. I've bought his pictures."

"Have you known him long?"

"Quite a while. Does he live with you?"

"O dear no. But he's a great deal with Miss Castleton, you know."

"Ah! teaching?"

"Yes," (doubtfully). "You know him intimately?"

"Why do you ask?"

"Because I would like to find out something about him and his character."

Rose Enniston stared at her companion a moment searchingly. Then she said:

"Madame, I ought to know him. I'm engaged to be married to him."

Mrs. Hannige's astonishment was great.

"Heavens alive, Miss, you don't tell me so?"

"O, yes. That's his ring," and she held up her finger.

"Well, upon my word, you take my breath away."

"Is there anything unusual in that?" asked Rose with something like a grim smile of unconcern. "It appears to astonish you."

"Yes, it does," says Mrs. Hannige, still regarding her with wonder. "So you expect to marry him?"

"Expect to? Didn't I tell you we were engaged?"

"Did you come here to see Miss Castleton?"

"Yes."

"What for?"

"I take an interest in the girl and Carteret is a foolish boy. That's all."

"You will tell her that you are engaged to him?"

"Really, madame," said Rose, "you speak as if I ought to keep it a secret. There's nothing clandestine about it. He has been a constant visitor at my mother's for a year. I was told that you were a mother to the girl."

"I love her like my own child," Mrs. Hannige said.

"And so I thought I might come to you in her interest. Carteret is thoughtless, that's all. It seemed to me to be straightforward and honest to tell the girl the simple truth without having any words with Carteret. What do you think?"

"Yes," replied Mrs. Hannige, "I think so too."

But she was really thinking of how Manuella would take this and if it would not break her poor little heart; and if after all it were not an interposition of Providence in behalf of Mr. Stonybrook and that third floor.

"As you have the girl's interest at heart," continued Rose, "it might be well if you would let me know when she returns, and I'll have a quiet interview with her. These things can always be managed easily by such women as you and I, Mrs. Hannige, and the quiet woman's way is always the best. I live at Coe's Grove when I am at home, but I am stopping in the city with Col. Hardynge. There's my name and address. Your brother knows Mr. Carteret and will vouch for the truth of what I tell you."

They then got up and Mrs. Hannige asked if she would not like to look at some of the young lady's work. This took them upstairs and led to a more familiar conversation, so that an hour later, when Miss Enniston came away, the two women were quite intimate and confidential and shook hands at parting.

Reticence, as will be observed, was not one of Rose's characteristics. She told Grace Hardynge what she had done.

The look of puzzled surprise and displeasure on that young lady's comely and dignified face meant a great deal more than she could put into words. Had she been able to formulate her instinctive summary of Rose's conduct, it would have corroborated the experience of all time in these words—You may cajole, you may create, you may destroy love—but you cannot coerce it.

All that she did say was:

"Rose, I think you have been a very foolish and undignified girl."

CHAPTER XXVIII.

A PREMONITION OF THE RIOTS.

Brannagan Hall was over a feed store in Avenue A, next door to the corner. Immediately opposite was McGloin's, and round the corner was O'Reardon's Terrace.

On the night after the Sanger party men began to assemble in the room noisily. They came in couples and had to knock at an upper door for admittance, which door had a wicket in it and was opened by McGloin himself when he was satisfied of the soundness of his applicants. The men who came were of the roughest class, unshaven and soil covered or smeared with coke stains from the gas works.

McGloin accosted most of them in a familiar way. "Yuz hav' a fine crop of hair on yuz, Mike, for a terrier. Is that you, Barney? I heerd you was licked for lettin' another man kiss yer gerril. I ask yer pardon, Mr. Murphy, by the color of your eye I tuk yuz for a black Republican. Say, Patsey, did yuz bring yer bull dog?"

Most of these salutations were answered in coarse style, meant to be witty and amicable, as "Ah, shwaller your head, Mr. McGloin, and choke yourself," or "Your spache is as bad as your rum, me bye," or "Hould your whist, yez divil's cub."

The meeting room at the head of the stairs was about fifty feet deep and was provided with a platform and wooden benches. At eight o'clock there were about fifty men in the place, standing about in knots, discussing the war and local politics. Among them was Mr. Sitwhite, who had brought two or three of his fellow laborers from the gas works.

The meeting had evidently been called by private means, and care had been taken to have only those present who were opposed to a prosecution of the war. Plonski had learned from Sitwhite that nearly all the laboring men in the employ of the gas works were "down on the whole fight," owing to a belief that if the "Black Republicans," as they termed all loyalists, succeeded in overcoming the South, negro slaves would over-run the North and underwork all white unskilled labor. He had therefore asked him to bring as many of them as he could to the meeting.

All these men were ignorant and intensely opinionated. Most of them were Irishmen—though a few were Poles and Germans—and it is notorious that in New York City the Irish furnished both the most ardent defenders and the most bitter denunciators of the government in its efforts to suppress the rebellion.

The class of Irishmen who afterwards made up the great bulk of the riot-ers of sixty-three were no doubt not yet Americanized in the better sense—an operation which it appears requires two generations. They brought the pugnac-ity, the incorrigibility and the bigotry of a peasant class, but they had not yet learned the American lesson of tolerance, of obedience to law and of submis-sion to authority.

The assemblage in Brannagan's was made up mainly of these men. They talked loudly and coarsely and defiantly. One stalwart ruffian told an admiring group how he and five others had taken a policeman's club away from him and beaten him senseless with it. But he made no mention of the fact that four of his companions had gone to the State's prison. Another told of a colored woman driven out of his tenement with blows, but he said nothing about the unfortunate negress being a mother who had appealed in vain to her remorse-less persecutors, with her child in her arms, and had seen it trampled under their cruel heels. His recital excited only admiration, and the only criticism offered upon the performance was that it "served the black divil roight, ahny way."

Here were present, if not the worst, at least the most dangerous elements of society; more dangerous at times of civil discord than the mere outlaws, for bigotry and intolerance allied to brute courage and an honest but mistaken sense of wrong, have always been the fire-brands that sophistry and unscrupu-lous political craft have thrown into the heart of the commonwealth, while vice in any attempt to organize itself is met with coercive and summary measures not only by the civil power but by the protective sense of the community.

Most of these men were more or less sufferers in their homes or in their persons from the war, for the drain upon the country was being severely felt in many directions, and they were strangely ignorant of the American sentiment which perpetuated and warranted the struggle. They saw only the concrete effects in their privations, and heard only the iniquities in the lists of killed and wounded or the threat of conscription. They wore sullen looks not unlike ani-mals whose instincts warn them of a danger they do not know how to oppose, but whose natural means of defense are all ready to be exerted.

It was nine o'clock when Mr. McGloin mounted the stand and called the meeting to order, at which signal the assemblage with much noise of hob-nail shoes and heavy boots knocked their short pipes out the windows and scram-bled into their seats.

"Fellow citizens," said McGloin in a loud voice, "we have met here to orga-nize a citizens' protective constitutional league. I nominate Patrick McCaffrey president *pro tem*."

Mr. McCaffrey, a middle-aged and rotund man without any collar, but with a hard, red face and short red side whiskers, climbed upon the platform and proceeded to inquire what the pleasure of the meeting was. A few preliminaries of electing a secretary and other officers over, Mr. McCaffrey called upon Mr. Phil Farley to explain the objects and nature of the Citizens' Protective Constitutional League and sat down in a chair and fanned himself.

Mr. Farley, a respectable but somewhat rusty old gentleman with a bald head, set into a black stock, and a precise but foxy face, placed his umbrella against the table and in a dry, precise and deliberate manner proceeded to inform the assemblage that the league was meant to give American citizens a chance to discuss the issues of the day, and to stand by each other in a lawful and constitutional attempt to express their opinions about the government and its policy. He then went into a dreary statistical enumeration of what he called facts, made a long and tiresome explanation of the purpose and scope of the leagues, and perplexed his hearers with some socialistic theories and a few hypotheses of political economy and States' rights.

It was a methodical statement that proved very wearisome, but it was listened to with a dull respect by men who had a superstitious regard for what they could not quite grasp.

While he was speaking in his hard and halting manner, Judge Sanger, accompanied by several robust politicians, had come upon the stage from a rear door. Their entrance made an immediate buzz of excitement. McGloin whispered to McCaffrey, "Ha, ha, he'll wake 'em up," and then smilingly nodded his head to several of the boys in front with an expression that plainly and triumphantly said, "It's all right now; here's our big gun."

Judge Sanger with the broad lapels of his light overcoat thrown back and his flossy white hair flying, his portly mien and authoritative air, gave a new aspect to affairs. The men that had come with him found places on the rear platform, and among them was Plonski, who kept well to the rear and peering about inquisitively, found an unconspicuous seat and sat down.

Mr. Farley gave way immediately, and McCaffrey took pleasure in announcing that the "Imminent Judge Sanger, who had been the poor man's friend so many years at Albany, was prisint and would addhress the meeting. All I've got to say, byes, he's a good one, and you kin bet your bottom dollar every dhrop of blood in him's Dimicratic."

This burst of crude fervor was hailed with a shout of applause, at which McCaffrey shook his head in emphatic sympathy, and looking round at his fellows on the platform with an unmistakable "How d'ye like that?" sat down and resumed his fan.

Judge Sanger, who was what they called an old "Democratic war horse" at this business, took a minute to get his light overcoat off. He deliberately threw it over the back of a chair, took a drink of water from a tumbler, pulled down his coat sleeves, but left his immaculate cuffs and their gold studs conspicuous, and with one hand on his elegant fob, came down to the edge of the platform and said:

"Friends and fellow citizens:

"In all free countries, the right of the people to meet and calmly discuss the affairs of their land and the acts of their rulers, has never been questioned, and it was never questioned in this free land until a chief magistrate was thrust upon us against the protests of one-half of the country, and used the power thus unlawfully conferred to subvert the law and drench our free States in blood." (Applause.)

"It has been our privilege and our custom, as it was the privilege and custom of our fathers, to criticise and condemn the acts of the rulers we had chosen. But it is not our privilege, it seems, my friends, to criticise and condemn the acts of these rulers we have not chosen. Today the United States marshal and the Provost marshal walk our streets. There are bayonets at our doors and at our ballot boxes. Our forts that were built to protect us from foreign invaders, are turned into prisons for innocent citizens.

"And for what, my friends?

"I will tell you what for.

"It is to subjugate a free people and turn loose upon us millions of slaves to compete with the free labor of the North. For that the constitution is disregarded; the law is broken and civil rights are invaded; the writ of habeas corpus suspended; the price of bread doubled; and our husbands and sons torn from us and sent to die their bloody deaths for an unjust cause in an invaded land.

"It is high time, my friends, that those of us who have been educated to free speech, should stand together and demand that our voices be heard above the thunder and rattle of this inhuman strife. We demand the same choice in assembly that we have at the ballot box. That's all. We demand the right to protect ourselves by association, in the expression of our opinions, that's all. We want our right to labor for our little ones in peace held inviolate. We want the laws of the country observed in time of war as well as in times of peace; we want the horde of contractors and speculators who are piling up fortunes and shedding blood—the best blood of our land—told, thus far and no farther. We want it because we know that no free people like our Southern brothers were ever subjugated. We want it because we know this war will drag on for twenty years, draining us of blood and treasure to enrich the unscrupulous few, and will be no nearer an unrighteous victory then than now.

"What have we gained so far?"

This question was greeted with a shout of derision, and the speaker then reviewed the events of the war in his own sarcastic way, saying that whenever they—our sister States—have met us squarely, they have licked us with fewer men and worse equipments. "Do you know why? It's because they are right and are fighting for their homes and their country. But what are we fighting for? Let, me tell you. To preserve a broken and separated union; to force men at the point of the bayonet to lay down, not only their guaranteed rights, but to lay down their opinions and think as we do; to establish a centralized military government. That's what we are fighting for. Now, my friends, I don't know that we can stem this mad deluge of bigotry and hate; I don't know that we can do anything by our actions that will help to restore peace and prosperity and good will. But I'll tell you what we *can* do in this great metropolis of New York. We can organize ourselves under law, and present a solid phalanx of opinion and protest that will make the tyrant of black republicanism and all his satraps pause before they undertake to enforce a conscription here." (Great applause.)

"We have got a Governor who knows what the rights of a sovereign State are, and who if his hands are strengthened, will use the whole power of his office to defend us. I council peace. I would not have any man raise his hand in violence at this time. Lawful protest is a mighty weapon if it is only strong enough. Organize, organize. Come here next week with your sons, your friends, your acquaintances. Enroll yourselves as freemen, not for aggression but to show a solid front to the aggressor. Do that and our city will be saved from the humiliating sight of a draft, and you will not be torn from your loved ones to die in Southern graves.

"If you do not do it, the results will be upon your own heads. You will have placed your necks under the heel of the new tyranny, and, my friends, I warn you that the same bigotry which to-day has risen up in the puritanical meeting houses of Massachusetts and demanded of nine million free men that they shall abandon their convictions, forsake their opinions and under penalty of the bullet and the firebrand and against the guarantee of the constitution, shall give up their most cherished institutions, will to-morrow, if successful, make a similar demand of you. The intolerance to-day is political fanaticism; to-morrow it may be religious fanaticism. It may be then that you will be asked to lay down the religion of your fathers and conform to the psalm-singing laws of New England and take the black race into your temples and homes and see him put into your workshops as foremen and your pulpits as priest."

Indignant cries of "By God, never," were elicited by this burst of eloquence, over which rose one clear voice, saying: "It's a damned lie, every word of it." There was some confusion. Several men jumped to their feet and angry threats were heard. But the speaker went on:

"I do not assert," he said, "that this will take place—far from it."

"No," said the voice. "You are only trying to bring it about."

"My friend," remarked the speaker, dropping from his oratorical key to a colloquial tone, "if you'll get up so I can see what State you came from, and feel satisfied that you're not one of those traitors from abroad who sold his own country out first for money and then came here to sell his countrymen again, I'll give you a fair show."

This renewed the confusion. Cries and laughter broke out in a gust.

"Keep quiet, my friends," said the Judge, extending his hands beneficently as if his sophistry always carried a benediction with it. "This is a place of free speech. Every man has the right of his opinion, but we want to know that he is a man and not a nigger."

A thunder-clap of admiring approbation followed this coarse but applicable treatment, and when it subsided, there slowly rose up, to the astonishment of everybody, a gaunt, sun-browned giant in a back seat. He looked like a man who had worked very hard all his life, but there was a calm intelligence in his gray eye and his cool demeanor that lifted him immeasurably above the imbruited men about him. There was a tinge of gray in his dark locks and a slight stoop to his shoulders as if he had long dug his subsistence out of the earth with patient bending.

Immediately there were fierce cries of "Down with him!" "Foire him out!" mingled with obscure epithets that have no place in written language.

But Judge Sanger was equal to the emergency. He knew his advantage and he was not considerate in the use of it. The man folded his arms and looked calmly but not defiantly round at the turmoil he had created.

"That will do, my friend," said the Judge. "You can sit down. We've all had a look at you, and there isn't any danger."

But there was something in the attitude and expression of the man that nettled him. It was as if truth herself had risen up and given him the lie with unanswerable and incommunicable eloquence. And so, as the man sat down, he turned the whole battery of his humor and malignity upon him. He pictured the Irish informer and spy who betrayed the comrades and patriots of his bleeding country; he said that there had never been an honest effort made by Irishmen to throw off the British yoke, but some traitor rose up in their midst and sold them out; and he ended with a glowing peroration in which he warned them against tyrants without and traitors within, and then seizing his coat and hat, he escaped in a dignified manner by the rear door, followed by Plonski and the heelers who had accompanied them, leaving the assemblage in an uproar.

Then occurred one of those scenes which, for brutal extravagance and incomprehensible cowardice, have oftenest been seen in New York, but at no time so often or so memorably as during the war.

It was in vain that Mr. McCaffrey pounded and bellowed for order and told his friends that the meeting had not adjourned. His friends were standing up all over the hall in knots and all talking at once. Jargon of blasphemy and vengeance filled the air. The man who had interrupted the meeting stood up at bay against a pillar with his brawny arms folded over his great breast, and looked at the threatening ruffians who had closed round him and were accompanying their opprobrium with their fists in his face.

All he said was, "I'm an American. All I've got I owe to the United States and I'm down on any man who tries to stab the Government in the back when it's fighting for its life."

"You're a liar. He's an Orangeman. He's a British spy. Pull the head off him. Throw him out the windy," were a few of the phrases that reached him above the general melee.

"I'm not a British spy," he said. "The man that says I'm an Orangeman is a liar," he added protestingly. "Man to man, I'm as good as any of you,"

At that moment an arm reached over the heads of those nearest him with a terrific swoop. It was loaded with the only weapon at hand, a heavy iron-bound shoe, held by the ankle and wielded like a sledge. It struck him between the eyes, the nailed heel making an instant gash that deluged his face with blood and blinded him. With the instinct of an animal and the force of a giant he struck out wildly right and left, but he was hemmed in. A ruthless fist fell with a soggy sound and crushing effect upon his face, another from behind struck him under the ear and staggered him. He fell back against the post and slid down upon the floor. A wild, demoniac cry accompanied his fall and a half score of heels were planted in his face. The sight of his helplessness seemed only to intensify their violence. Men who were behind fought with their fellows for a chance to get one kick at the quivering and bleeding form. The greatest triumph for every one of these infuriated wretches was to be able to say that he "got one kick in," while the man was down.

Insensible, disfigured, a mass of wounds, they pulled the body over the benches while the more craven continued to rain blows and kicks upon it. They dragged it with curses and yells to the door and the stairway. A frenzy of sub-ter-human hatred seemed to have possession of them, and it was in vain that McGloin pushed and fought and screamed to rescue the man. Some of the more desperate hauled the unresisting body down the stairs, thrust it into the street with utter disregard of the consequences, and then leaving it with one or two parting kicks, returned to the hall, ready in their delirium now to fight with each other at the slightest provocation or without it.

Mr. McCaffrey, who, during this broil, had carried on an unperturbed conversation with Mr. Farley on the platform while he fanned himself, seeing the men returning into the room, got up and said:

"Well, boys, yuz had your amusement and yuz are in too excoited a sthate of moind to purshue the business of the evening, I suppose. I'm going to adjurne the mating. But I want you all to be here on Monday evening and don't you forget it, neither."

This summary process closed out all formal proceedings, and Mr. McCaffrey and Mr. Farley went off with McGloin to get a drink, leaving the disorganized crowd to bellow and gesticulate in the hall for an hour later.

Mr. Sitwhite had been an observer of this disgraceful scene and to some extent participator in it. The man so cruelly beaten was his friend. He had brought him there and he had received no inconsiderable mauling himself in his efforts to extricate him. He found himself on the street now in the centre of a new mob of men and women attracted by the sight of an apparently murdered man and the chance of a row. Whatever other virtue he may have lacked, he had the common virtue of loyalty to his friend, and he was for a moment puzzled by the duty of standing by him, and the fear that a policeman would turn up and carry him off as an accessory or a witness.

In this dilemma, Clianthe Mignon put her head through the crowd, and recognizing Mr. Sitwhite, asked him who was killed.

"There ain't no one killed," replied Sitwhite. "Dan Sully's been mauled in a row, that's all. If I could get him off the street I'd save him from the peelers."

This woke an instant sympathy in the bystanders, whom nothing so quickly united as a project to beat the police.

"Whar' d' you want to git him?" some one gruffly asked.

"Take him over to the house," Clianthe suggested, and the suggestion seemed to be instantly seized upon by half a score of hands. In a moment he was laid on a couple of shutters and carried across to the Terrace, followed by the inevitable crowd of idle men and morbid boys, Clianthe taking the greatest interest in the transfer and giving all kinds of directions for his comfortable transit over the curbs and upstairs.

Once in Plonski's room, now left to Mrs. Sitwhite as a reward for faithful services, and placed on Plonski's mattress, Clianthe got water and cloths and John Sitwhite summoned his wife and went for the nearest doctor.

Meanwhile two opinions were being expressed on the events of the evening.

Judge Sanger, who had stopped in to see Col. Hardynge on his way to the Manhattan Club, threw the lapels of his light overcoat jauntily back and said:

"Colonel, I've just addressed a meeting of anti-war Democrats in the Eighteenth precinct. They represented the yeomanry of our emporium. I never saw so much enthusiasm and such a clear intelligence of the vital issues of the hour. We expect to have two hundred leagues formed before next summer. The work goes bravely on and once organized I think we'll have a reliable political machine that even the Federal Government can't break."

Mr. Plonski, at the New York Hotel, was asked by Chanfleur what he thought about the meeting, and he said:

"I think that these politicians—and Judge Sanger is the leader—are sowing the whirlwind. I want to get away before the storm sets in."

CHAPTER XXIX.

LOVE TAKES TO THE COUNTRY.

Somewhere about thirty-five or forty miles north of New York City, the old Croton aqueduct crosses the valley of the Pocantico on an immense and solid structure of stone, pierced only by one great arch, through which the brook sings lazily in dry seasons, making the enormous vault and its vast abutments appear altogether disproportionate to the work they have to do, but which in times of freshet, thunders through in a roiled and noisy current.

The old aqueduct stretches in a half curve of wall and glacis like an enormous serpent across the valley and is then lost in the side of the opposite field. Its half mile of visible surface is level and green with a well kept sward, and from this sequestered promenade you may look down into the larch groves of the Pocantico through which the little river flashes and winds its way to the Hudson, whose misty surface, with the profile of the Palisades, makes a phantom picture in the distance.

It is a dreamy place where the phoebebird and the bobolink are undisturbed, and the chipmunks run all day among the blackberry vines on the stone water way. Except for an occasional pair of lovers from the village on a Sunday afternoon or a stray artist, held by the carmines of the maples or the vermillion of the sumac, or perhaps some boys chestnutting in the timber to the north, the place is hardly ever visited, and save for the gate-keeper's white house, there is not a cottage to be found till you come to Mrs. Tucker's, a mile down the stream below, still snuggling away in the browning sunflowers as when Wilder visited it.

Mr. Manser has kept the gate house for six years or ever since Mr. Tucker died. He is a hard-working, simple-minded rustic, whose only son was killed at Chancellorsville, and whose wife makes the best butter and raises the best herbs in Westchester County. He is about fifty years old, and when not at his work is content to sit on the little white porch that is covered with Virginia creeper and wild rose, and discuss the war, in which he takes the deep interest of a patriot, and a father who has made a most precious investment in it.

His duties are peculiar but not exacting. He has charge of a section of the aqueduct, and besides cutting the grass and watching the culverts and glacis, has to superintend the gate by means of which the water in the section above him is let out into the valley, when it is necessary to inspect or repair the conduit.

This conduit is nine feet in diameter, and runs full of water, deep down in that long stone serpent. When he shuts one gate and opens the sluice, a torrent leaps forth and tumbles with roar and foam down the sides of the valley and leaps with a shout through the astonished glades into the Pocantico.

To this spot Carteret had brought Manuella and her grandfather because of its seclusion and beauty, and because the Mansers, with whom he had spent many summer hours, were sure to provide just the homely comforts that he desired, without charging exorbitantly for them.

To Manuella the trip was one of unalloyed delight. Every rod of the way to her fresh sense had its vision of loveliness, and all the familiar and over-described features of the lower Hudson were lit with hope and soft with the romantic atmosphere of love. Mr. Manser came down to the Scarsdale station with his team to meet them, and what a ride it was in the sunset shadows over the hills on winding and grass-grown old roads, through orchards whose fruit hung in the glow like golden pippins, and filled the air with a dainty fragrance. On the top of the highest hill the driver stopped, and the lovers stood up while Carteret pointed out some conspicuous and well known points in the land-scape. There was Haverstraw Bay, like the Bay of Naples, at their feet, and there was the long peninsula of Croton Point lying like a sleeping beauty robed in dyes upon the blue depths. Far north, where the rolling summits grew indistinct, he knew that Coe's Grove nestled in the elms and junipers, and he pointed that way as if she knew enough of his experiences to take a special interest in it. Then down the valley, dewy and shadowy, past the rustic homesteads with the families drinking their tea in the summer kitchens; along the banks of a little river, seen only at intervals as it came upon them with sudden curves, or dashed away for the time being, down some rocky glen. The air was heavy with autumn incense, and vocal with the evening sounds from the river banks. It was the most delicious ride imaginable, and ended by their driving up to Mr. Manser's gate where Mrs. Manser in a extra cap and apron came out to greet them in a motherly way, and what with the heartiness of the old folk and the exuberance of the young, they made the quiet spot more animated and vocal than it had ever been before.

Mrs. Manser kissed Manuella on the forehead at once, there being certain intimacies of the sex that are inscrutible and independent of time.

"Now how hungry you must be, my dear, ridin' over from Scarsdale. You just come in and take your things right off, and we'll have tea. I'd let them horses stand, Dan, till after. Why, Mr. Carteret, it does seem a long spell since you was here, and you ben't a day older in looks. You've been well, I s'pose?"

Carteret declared jocundly that he was a little overworked and had come up to get some fresh air and find some quiet for Mr. Evans, and then this little family party all went into the house to find tea waiting; and so unreasonable are young lovers that Carteret never noticed the spotless linen or the golden butter or the late hollyhocks in a pitcher, or thought of the benign old lady at the head of the table, or praised her preserves, or took the slightest interest in Mr. Manser's conversation with Mr. Evans about old times; he only ate slice after slice of homemade bread, and home-cured ham, and drank his tea down scalding hot, and exhibited undue impatience to get out on the aqueduct with Manuella before the twilight faded. He had so many things that were a private possession of his memory that he wanted her to share.

But Manuella, utterly without the proper impatience that the occasion demanded, said the most commonplace things in the most deliberately gentle manner to Mrs. Manser, and seemed determined to praise all her edibles in the most tedious formula possible, and Carteret had to whisper to her to hurry or they'd miss the twilight.

He was almost impolite with his impatience. What did he care about the growth of Westchester County, or the history of the Croton aqueduct, or a schedule of the well-to-do Mr. Manser's tons of hay and bushels of potatoes. He had a thousand things in his memory that he wanted to show Manuella, and nobody else could possibly care for them. He succeeded in carrying her off in the gloaming, and keeping her on the grass till the stars came out, and then he had to put his arm around her when they came back, because in the night she was a little timid on such a high narrow path as the aqueduct. Then he was beautifully magnanimous about accommodations. "Don't mind me, Mrs. Manser," he said. "I can sleep anywhere—on the grass or on the floor. I'm an old campaigner. You just take care of Mr. Evans and his granddaughter, and I'll drop down somewhere."

And Mrs. Manser, holding up the kerosene lamp, and looking at him wonderingly over her "specs," said, "Land sakes, man, drop down somewheres in my house—you must be out of your head."

She utterly refused to gratify his hardy instincts, and thrust him into a "yarb" scented and white-washed chamber, where the luxury so overcame him that he went to sleep in a kind of Oriental ecstasy, and never woke up until one of the "hired men" pounded on his door and said breakfast was waiting. Then he whistled himself into his clothes and went down to find them all at the breakfast table, and Manuella in some kind of a muslin robe that he had never seen before which made her look very crisp and dainty, and he kept admiring her so obviously that she got quite nervous.

He was amazed and delighted to see how quickly the poor girl of yesterday had come out like a lady. She had been transformed under his very eyes, and he could not tell how. There was a new curve to her body and a new line in her shoulders, and although her hair was dressed in a new way, and as he thought, more *á la mode*, it never occurred to him that her dressmaker had revealed some graces that he had not suspected.

It made him feel like a good angel to observe her high spirits and to watch the blithe independence of her grandfather.

"I'd like to get a cheap cottage up here somewhere," Mr. Evans was saying as Carteret came to the breakfast table. "I s'pose I might buy a modest one for two or three thousand dollars."

"Two or three!" exclaimed Mr. Manser, "you can pick one up for fifteen hundred, big enough for your family."

"Yes," resumed the old gentleman. "I like the air. I think the city air affects my head, I do indeed. I must look about Mr. Manser. My little girl ought to have a home in the country and as I am about, to settle up my business, I don't think I could do better than invest my money in a home for her, do you?"

"Indeed I don't," Mr. Manser answered heartily, and Manuella gave Carteret a well known look of deprecation and began to talk of something else.

"Now you are to go to work," she said, "remember your promise. Let me get your box of paints. I'm going with you and carry some of the traps."

"Of course you are going with me and you are going to paint, too."

"No, not at first. You know very well that is absurd. What can I do with nature? I'm going to sit beside you and watch you," she said cooingly, "that is if I don't bother you. I want to see how you do it."

"But, my dear, we can't walk out with a load of implements and wander all over with them. We must go first and prospect and find the place. That's the proper way. Studies do not lie all around loose; you have to hunt for them and when you've found them you go straight to them with the tools. Come along."

So it was a ramble after all in the Paul and Virginia style in which they did an inconceivable amount of hard work without knowing it and saw so many studies that they retained only a confused recollection of them. They had the whole day to themselves. It was the first time the delicious sense of freedom and confidence had been theirs and it was quite natural that it should lead to sentiment. His tender solicitude and his admiration of her atmosphered her with a romantic witch light. The day was like a dream and the scenes were enchanted. They sat down on the flat capstone of the abutment with the brook singing and dancing at their feet, surrounded by the deep dusky coverts, and under the shade of "melancholy boughs" drifted with the waters into the old, old story. He must have told her his past history minutely, for they sat there a long time and a peeping observer would have seen that she was a listener.

Mrs. Manser came out on the aqueduct and called them. One of the hired men went the wrong way to look for them and if he had gone the right way, he would have arrived in time to hear Carteret say, as he picked the girl's hand up:

"Now, my darling, all I want to ask you is, do you believe me?"

And Manuella, gazing into the stream, murmured "yes," and it seemed to float down the little river as if she had dropped a rosebud of promise into its music.

"I haven't forgotten what you said to me in the park the other night. But when I look at you and think of myself I feel so unworthy, that I'm afraid you'll slip away in some incomprehensible, but poetic manner. You never will, will you?"

She was thinking of something else. The music and not the meaning of the words reached her this time and she said, "No," promptly, at which he began to laugh.

"That answer came from your soul and not from your sense," he said. "I'll prize it."

"What a silly little fool I must have been that night in the park. I was thinking how good you were not to laugh at me."

"My dear, you were not silly, but you may have been mistaken. Did you mean what you said or would you like to take it back?"

"No," she answered softly, "I would not take it back. It stands for life with me. I was thinking that I might have said it differently. It's only a few nights ago, but I was a girl then."

The next day he planted his easel on a bank and went to work. Manuella, who insisted on helping Mrs. Manser with her housework, stole off during the morning and came to him softly.

"You see I couldn't stay away," she said, "but it's the picture I'm interested in." And then she sat down on the bank and patiently watched him until the sun drove them both off.

One morning she called him to her chamber door and throwing it open, pointed to the recovered cup standing on her mantle. They had forgotten all about it.

What was more noticeable, Mr. Evans took very little interest in it now. His new mood engrossed him and it dwelt entirely upon his former business accounts, which he insisted had been adjusted and would make him comfortable for the rest of his days. To his constant references to this, the young people gave little heed. They assented to everything he said and straightway forgot it.

"I didn't tell you," said Manuella, "why I wanted you to recover the cup, and you have never asked me."

"I often thought of doing so," said Carteret, "but I wanted you to tell me without asking."

"Can't you guess now?" and she actually blushed, "there was a big reward offered for it. I thought if I had some of the money"—she dropped her head on his shoulder—"I thought I could make myself better fit to be an artist's wife."

"My darling," he said, "you couldn't make yourself better fit. There isn't an artist on earth that's good enough to think of you."

They went down and sat on the little porch. "I want you to do something to please me," she said as soon as they were seated.

"Name it."

"I'm going to the city to-morrow."

He looked at her with surprise. "You don't mean to say that you think it necessary to ask me to go with you as a favor?"

"No, but *not* to go. I'm going to run down on an early train and come back in the afternoon. Mrs. Manser wants to do some shopping, and the old lady hasn't been to the city in so long a time, she's behind the age. Besides I have some little things to get myself. I want you to keep on painting."

"Why cannot I accompany you?"

"Because it would be a waste of time. We shall be on the go all day, and it would be a bore to you."

"I suppose I must submit to my fate."

"Will it be so awful hard?"

"Manuella," said he seriously, "is it safe for you to go alone? I have an idea that this is one of the cases in which I ought to kick against fate. I'll not have a minute's peace while you are in the city."

"Don't be foolish. I'll go to Mrs. Hannige's for lunch. I've got to—there is something there I have forgotten to bring, and you shall come down with Mr. Manser and meet us at the five o'clock train. Think of that ride back. Besides you know, I would not have a moment's peace myself if Grandpa were left here alone."

Thus beguiled, he was forced to smother his protests, and after a night's preparation, Manuella and Mrs. Manser went off next morning early to the city.

Carteret then heroically set to work, but he soon found that everything went wrong. The wind annoyed him; the flies pestered him, and the sun baffled him. It was his mood and he thrust it upon nature. He laid down on the grass and looked up into the sky. An eagle was sailing in circles like a mote far up in the ether. It oppressed him with a sense of loneliness. The glades were ominously still and even the brook had lost its voice. He upbraided himself heartily for being a fool, but watched the leaden hours for five o'clock. Going back to the house, he wondered at Mr. Manser's equanimity. He threw himself on the bed and tried to sleep. Failing in that, he hunted up Mr. Manser again and tried to interest himself in the gate house.

"They're goin' to shut off the section above in a day or two," said Mr. Manser, "and I'll be lettin' the water out. It's worth seeing."

"I dare say," said Carteret.

They went into the gate house and looked down at the black swirling current that writhed like an enormous serpent noiselessly.

It was only the sweet, beneficent stream on its way to slake the thirst of a million people.

But Carteret shrunk at the sight of it. It reminded him of Lethe.

He never spent so weary and so inexplicably melancholy a day in his life. Finally he saw Mr. Evans dozing on the little porch, and he went and sat down by his side.

"Mr. Evans," he said. "Mr. Evans."

The old gentleman opened his eyes and looked about blinkingly.

"Bless me," he muttered, "I thought I heard Manuella calling for me."

"Do you think, Mr. Evans, it was safe to give Manuella commissions to execute in the city? Why didn't you send me?"

"Commissions? Safe? Yes, yes, I see. She hasn't come back. O, she's safe enough. I told her to take a message to Mr. Stonybrook. He'll look out for her. Mr. Stonybrook's a very prudent man, sir. You've met him, haven't you? If she doesn't come back today, it's because he wanted her to stay over. Perfectly safe—perfectly safe man," and Mr. Evans dozed off again in serene ignorance of a yellow jacket that was trying to effect a lodgment on his bald head.

At four o'clock Carteret asked Mr. Manser if he wasn't going to the train.

"Certainly," replied Mr. Manser, "but I don't want to go an hour before hand. I can drive there in twenty minutes."

This restlessness increased unreasonably until they rode away, leaving Mr. Evans under the eye of a hired man, benignantly and comfortably musing on the porch.

The five o'clock train was ten minutes behind time. The little depot had very few people in it and Mr. Manser left Carteret to himself while he talked with them. He heard the whistle at last and went out on the platform. The train came up. They saw Mrs. Manser get out with her bundles, assisted by a neighbor who had come up with her. Manuella was not on the train.

In reply to the headlong questions that fell upon her, the old lady somewhat confused and surprised said:

"Lands, Mr. Carteret, I thought she had come up ahead o' me. The child was to meet me at the train. Dear me, I hope nothin's happened to her."

This maddened Carteret. "What did you do with her? Where did you leave her? How were you separated?" he asked in one breath.

"Me?" said Mrs. Manser looking placidly at the young man. "Me do with her, Mr. Carteret? I guess she just missed the train, that's all. You see," she continued, addressing herself to her husband, who was picking up her bundles as fast as she dropped them. "Mr. Baxter, here, went down with us and we all went to Percy & Stivers on Sixth avenue. I had to go there to get them pillow slips and she wanted some braid and things and then Mr. Baxter asked me to go over and see Jane Morgan, who's alivin' in Twenty-fifth street, and is down low with her old complaint. Law, Dan, you remember Jane, and you wouldn't know her now if you was to see her. She's all skin and bone. 'Well,' says Miss Castleton, 'you go on with your friend and I'll run over to Mrs. Hannige's'—I think that's what she said—'just you don't bother with me, and I will meet you at the five o'clock train,' says she. I was all turned round when I found she wasn't there." And then she added with an utter defiance of reason that at any other time would have made Carteret smile, "It was lucky I had Mr. Baxter with me, for the Lord knows how I'd got along with all these things."

Carteret did not wait to hear more. He went immediately to the telegraph office and sent an imperative dispatch to Mrs. Hannige.

"Where is Miss Castleton? Answer at once."

Then he came back. "I'll wait here for the next train," he said, "and get a conveyance to bring her up. You go back and don't tell Mr. Evans on your life."

"My sakes," said Mrs. Manser as her bundles were handed into the wagon. "There isn't much peace where that young man is. He's flustered me so, I expect I've left all my things behind."

But Carteret had gone back to the telegraph office. "Did you rush that?" he asked through the wicket of the young woman. "It's important."

"It's gone," she said with great equanimity, as she put her gloves on, "but you can't get an answer to-night"

"Cannot? Why?"

"Because I close the office at seven."

"But you can wait for that dispatch, can't you, if I pay you for your time? It may be a matter of life and death."

Carteret had yet to learn that life and death were mere syllables to a female operator in a small office who wanted to get home, and that things in a country station were not adjustable to large emotions or great events. He coaxed, threatened and pleaded through the wicket and finally the girl with an air of personal injury, said she'd hold on a white but it was "agin the rules."

He walked the depot floor in a state of helpless impatience, looking in to the wicket occasionally to see that the young woman had lit a lamp and was reading a novel with her hat and gloves on and preserving the haughty indifference of personal wrong, subdued by personal pride.

It was an hour before he got an answer and that was marvelously quick. Another train had come up and gone and he had watched with growing disappointment the half dozen passengers get out. Then he heard the click of the telegraph instrument.

"Don't stop to write it; read it off," he said, "if it's for me."

This was the message slowly drawled out for him.

"Colin Carteret,

"*Scarsdale Station.*

"Miss Castleton left here to go to five train at three o'clock. Haven't seen her since.

HANNIGE."

He threw down a bill and rushed for the time table. It presented to his impatience a whirl of meaningless and confused figures that maddened him. The station master was out on the bank watching some boys swimming.

"When is the next train down?" he shouted.

Nine-thirty," said the man, without taking his eyes off the boys. "Them lads don't mind the chill. It's gettin' late in the season fur it. I remember the time when I no more thought of—"

"Are you sure there isn't a train before that?"

"Sure? Well I ought to be. It's my business to be sure, what d'you take me for? Jerry, come out o' that now, you've been in long enough." Then he turned to walk away.

"I shall go mad before that" said Carteret. "It's seven-fifteen now."

"Well, I couldn't alter the schedule if you did," said the man, turning and looking at him for the first time with some curiosity. Carteret's distress evidently touched him for he came back.

"You want to get to the city?"

"Yes, immediately."

"There's the Chicago express goes through here in twenty-five minutes. She stops at Tarrytown for water. If you had wings now, you could climb her at Tarrytown."

"Hoofs will do it," exclaimed Carteret. "Give me a team, I'll pay you five dollars."

"You couldn't fetch it. She'd be there before you got half way. The road runs three miles out o' the track, unless—" he said, stopping to consider.

"Yes, yes, unless—" cried Carteret "Don't waste time considering."

"Unless," said the man, "she wore half an hour late. Wait a second."

He went back from the platform and looked up the track. A hand car with two laborers was coming toward them.

"Hold on a minute, Sackett," he shouted. "Get this man to Tarrytown ahead of the Chicago express and he'll give you five dollars."

"Yes," cried Carteret, "speak quick."

The two men stopped and consulted inaudibly a moment. "How much time we got?" one of them asked.

"Twenty minutes," said the station master; "but she's likely to be ten or fifteen minutes late. All the South through trains have been."

Both the men had their coats on, "Come along," said one of them and then they both took their coats off.

Carteret jumped upon the little car.

"Lay to it boys," he cried, "you can do it."

And away they went. It was a straight stretch with no grades, of a little less than five miles. The two men bent to their work silently. Not a word was spoken. It had grown so dark that in some of the cuttings he could not see their faces, but he heard the regular puffings of their lungs. The shadowy banks shot past. They flew over the culverts. He saw in an indistinct way the lapping waves on the shore and the reflected stars in the pools beneath them. A train thundered past them with blinding glare and deafening crash. The swirl of wind almost swept him from the little platform and the dust filled his eyes and nostrils. But the steady throb of the men as they toiled was not intermitted.

Their faces were turned to watch for the headlight of that Chicago express, but they never stopped to rest. Ten, fifteen, twenty minutes were up. The express was due. He almost held his breath as he listened for the whistle and he almost gasped as he encouraged the men. He looked ahead. It was dark. He wondered how much father off the station was and if after all he would be left behind. What, O what was happening to Manuella while this wretched machine crawled its snail pace toward her?

"There she is," said one of the men. "Jump quick."

Before he could realize it, they were all on the ground and his companions were lifting the car from the track.

"My God," he said helplessly, "we're too late."

"All right," said the men. "Here's the tank. She'll haul up here. Where's the money?"

He gave them the bill, ran across the roadway and saw the station lights, until then hidden by an overhanging rock.

"You've done it," cried one of the fellows, "but a tenner wouldn't buy it over. There's your train."

Two minutes later, Carteret had boarded the Chicago express and ten minutes later was flying at the rate of forty miles an hour towards New York and blaming the road for its miserable speed.

CHAPTER XXX.
THE ABDUCTION OF MANUELLA.

Mrs. Hannige was a woman of large heart and an active brain. She not only desired to see people comfortable, but she devoted a good deal of her time to scheming for that end. There could be no better subject than Manuella. That poor girl needed just such a practical and experienced woman to shape her career and ensure her success. Mrs. Hannige felt this instinctively. That the girl, if left to her inexperience would throw herself away before she knew it on a poor artist, was plain enough. That it was the duty of an older and wiser head to prevent it in the girl's interest, was one of the kindly conclusions that Mrs. Hannige came to without the least trouble. It never occurred to Mrs. Hannige that her own interests influenced her conduct. Mr. Stonybrook was, in her estimation, a worthy man of character and unlimited means. His long residence under her roof had convinced her that he needed only one thing to be a consummately happy and profitable lodger and that was a wife. He had not disputed this when it was thrown at him in Mrs. Hannige's moments of intimacy. He had taken the precaution to protect himself from any possible personal advance of Mrs. Hannige herself by saying, "Yes, my dear woman, but she must be a *young* wife." It did not take his landlady long to ascertain that Manuella had caught his eye, despite his wary and self-possessed manner, and she was not slow in using the many little devices and privileges of a woman in her position to throw them together. Once entered upon, this indefinite impulse soon shaped itself into a definite purpose. Events, no less than her interests, fashioned her endeavor and the most important and determining event had been the visit of Miss Enniston and her disclosure. Rose had come back the next day on the plausible plea that she had left her card case there, and was persuaded to stay to a quiet little lunch over which the two women grew confidential. They assisted and abetted each other in the most charming manner.

"I'm so glad," said Mrs. Hannige, "that I know this. It relieves my mind of a great responsibility. That girl worried me a good deal—she's such a child you know. But of course now she'll have her eyes opened and I shall be relieved. Why, Mr. Stonybrook would marry her to-morrow if she'd say the word."

"You think?" said Rose, interrogatively, "that she is a simple-minded creature who has drifted along without knowing where she was going?"

"I know it. She's nothing but a child. Anybody can twist her round his finger. But she's as good as she can be. All we've got to do is to open her eyes."

"Well," said Rose, "we'll do that summarily. But I don't want a scene."

"No fear of that. She'll cry a little and worry for a day or two, but it will fix it. I don't see what Mr. Carteret's thinking about."

"Oh, young men at his age don't do a great deal of thinking," Rose observed, with easy wisdom. "They have to have somebody to do it for them. But they generally preserve a definite notion of their immediate pleasures, I'll give them credit for that."

Mrs. Hannige speedily understood that Miss Enniston was a young woman of social position and independence and she as speedily convinced herself that her own task was as much to Carteret's advantage as to Manuella's.

"Young people do get into the foolishest scrapes," she said, "before they get wise heads on 'em, when they haven't got mothers to look out for 'em."

She very easily and promptly grew to view the work she had set about as the most natural and proper of undertakings and its results as a foregone conclusion. "But I can't help feeling sorry for the little fool," she said. "When she finds her young man put where he belongs and she loses her doll."

On the day of Miss Enniston's third visit to the house, Manuella came to the city from Scarsdale. She had gone with Mrs. Manser and Mr. Baxter to several stores on the Sixth avenue and Broadway, arriving at Percy & Stivers' about twelve o'clock, considerably annoyed at the imbecility and mental confusion of the old lady, who had no definite idea in the chaos of objects about her what she wanted or where she was to go. To her great relief Mr. Baxter, while at Percy & Stivers' patiently following them about through the crowds of purchasers, proposed to Mrs. Manser to make a call on an old friend who lived in the neighborhood. Manuella readily consented to let her go. Her own wish was to run over to Mrs. Hannige's and her time was short and the old lady was very timid and slow. Besides it was then one o'clock and she had not found the articles she was desirous of purchasing. It thus came about that they were separated, Manuella saying, as the old lady went away, that she would be at Stewart's at three and then go straight to the five o'clock train.

She walked hurriedly across to Fifteenth street and arrived at Mrs. Hannige's while Rose, attired in her fall walking suit, was conversing with that lady in the little dining room.

Florry, the maid, was in the hall when she let herself in and Manuella was already on the stairs, when Mrs. Hannige came out and called to her.

"Oh, my dear, is that you? How glad I am to see you. Wait a moment. Have you come back so soon?"

"No," replied Manuella, as Mrs Hannige came up the stairs and kissed her affectionately. "I've only run in to do some shopping. I've got to catch the five o'clock train. How are you?"

"It's too bad to fly in and out that way. How's your grandfather and Mr.

Carteret? I'm so glad I caught you before you got up. There's somebody here wants to see you. It's a lady. Come down a moment. I think she's in a hurry to go. How fresh and lovely you look, to be sure."

"Who is it?" asked Manuella, in hesitating wonder.

"Come along, my dear. It's a surprise for you. Oh, you don't know her, but I want you to."

And she caught hold of her hand and gently pulled her down the steps, still mingling compliments and questions in an ejaculatory stream, until they came to the door of the room in which sat Miss Enniston very erect and slightly pale, with her back to the light and her arm resting on the table.

"My dear," said Mrs. Hannige, "this is Miss Enniston. She wants to talk with you. Miss Enniston, Miss Castleton. Sit down, Miss Castleton. Ladies, I'll leave you for awhile, as I've my rooms to look after."

But she left them only so far as the adjoining room, shut off by a heavy curtain and from which room she could both see and hear what took place.

At the name of Miss Enniston, Manuella who was still standing in the centre of the room staring at the woman in front of her, whose face was made indistinct by the glare of the light behind her, started a little and looked involuntarily at the door by which she had entered and which was now closed.

"You are the young lady they call Manuella," said Rose, with just the slightest air of cold superiority.

"My name is Manuella Castleton," replied the girl, in a half timid tone that in its softness and fulness sounded pleasantly against the hard articulation of the other. "What did you want to see me about?"

"I wanted to speak to you about Mr. Carteret," said Rose slowly, and still staring at her companion, whose beauty had an unpleasant and bitter fascination in it. "I merely wanted to have a few frank words with you and if you will permit me, put you on your guard."

"Dear me," Mrs. Hannige was saying to herself on the other side of the portierre. "We've all got to go through these things some time, but she'll be better for it when it's all over."

Manuella glanced timidly around as if about to call Mrs. Hannige back for support. But she said nothing.

"I must explain to you, Miss Castleton, at once," continued Rose, "that I am Mr. Carteret's affianced wife; that ought to spare me the trouble and annoyance of any further explanation, but as you are represented to me as an innocent and inexperienced girl, I think it is due you to say that I have come here as a friend merely to open your eyes to Mr. Carteret's foolishness. I have known him a long time and can make every allowance for his artistic capers, but I did not think it was fair to you to leave you in the dark as to the true state of affairs. I am engaged to be married to Mr. Carteret, and was sure you did not know it.

I wish you'd sit down. We can have our few words of explanation without any unpleasantness."

Manuella was leaning slightly forward with her hands clasped and her big eyes fixed upon Miss Enniston with a dreamy stare. But still she said nothing,

The situation was that of strained dignity on one side and innocent bewilderment on the other. Miss Enniston felt sure that she had to deal with inexperience and timidity, and the slight hint of arrogance in her manner was not affected.

"I have surprised you," she said, "you never suspected; Mr. Carteret never told you, of course?"

"Yes," replied Manuella, softly, "he told me."

"O, did he? Did he tell you that he had been a visitor of mine for a year; that I wore his engagement ring?"

"More," said Manuella.

"Ah, that he made love to me on his knees, made me promise to marry him; that the honor and manhood of a gentleman were pledged and could not very well be forfeited."

"Yes," said Manuella, "and more."

"What do you mean?"

"He told me that after all this, you flung him off; told him that you did not love him; that you were fooling him; that you threw his ring at him and drove him from you with taunts and sneers and bade him never come back. That is what he told me."

"And you believed it?" asked Rose with a new pallor in her face and a new pitch to her voice as she started to her feet.

"Yes," said Manuella, calmly. "I believed it. I never knew him to lie. You said you were done with him forever. You would not listen to him. He did not leave you; he was driven from you and he did not know that you would come whining after him. You can never be his wife."

Miss Enniston came a step toward Manuella. Her mouth was slightly parted and the tips of her teeth gleamed. Her black eyes flashed and her chin appeared to grow hard and prominent.

"So then," she cried, "it was you who led him into this. You are the creature who taught him to lie, and lured him into deceit and shared his iniquity with him. The scheme was yours, was it?—and you stand here ready to defend your paramour."

"Miss Enniston," replied Manuella, deliberately and softly, "I do not know what you are talking about. I only know that you cannot be his wife, for he could not love you."

"So he told you that?"

"No, it is not necessary to be told it, now that I have seen you. The only lie he ever told me was when he said you were a lady. He has told me everything. I believe him. I do not believe you. Is there anything more you wish to say to me?"

"Only this, Miss Castleton; it is such abandoned and brazen creatures as you that only need exposure to end their careers; you, with an old man upstairs and a young man on the town, with Mr. Stonybrook by one string and Mr. Carteret by the other; with your demure face and your hypocritical tongue, you expect to have your own way with everybody. I'm going to teach you a lesson in life that you hav'n't learned."

She had her arm lifted as if she meant to strike with it. Her words almost hissed, not with virtuous indignation, but with passionate spite.

Manuella did not wait for her to finish the speech. She went to the portierre and held it back disclosing Mrs. Hannige, who stepped into the room as unconcernedly as if listening were one of the regular privileges of the house.

"I do not think you can teach me anything," she said. "The woman who insults a man to his face and maligns him behind his back, would be very apt to go about exhibiting her passion and her humiliation at the same time. I knew long ago that Mr. Carteret did not love you and now I know that it is impossible for you to love him."

Miss Enniston made a step toward Manuella that was almost a spring, but Mrs. Hannige who was boiling over interposed.

"See here, Miss Enniston," she said, "This is altogether more than I bargained for, and if I'd known that you meant to use such language in my room I wouldn't have let you in. I want you to understand that this is a respectable house and Mr. Stonybrook and Miss Castleton are my guests. I don't believe you know what you are saying or doing. I don't, upon my word."

"Madame," rejoined Miss Enniston. "I don't know anything about your house, except that you permit young men to come and go when they please and do what they like and take the part of any adventuress who pays you for it. You can save your temper with me. I ask no favors of you."

Manuella did not hear this; she had gone out with silent and dignified contempt and then ran upstairs. Once in her room she broke down and began to sob and walk the floor in pitiable distress. But this little burst of emotion over, she began to bustle about, gathering some little articles that were forgotten when she went into the country and then smoothed her hair and her face at the glass. She hurried down the stairs, for she had to go to Stewart's and then catch her train.

Mrs. Hannige who was about to put her motherly hands on the girl's shoulders, reconsidered the act and desisted. She was conscious of a new admiration of her lodger but she could not have given a reason for it.

"You are a woman indeed, and as for that person, I've no patience with her. I never was so scandalized in my life, and to think that I just threw you on her claws, but I had no idea upon my word, Miss, not the faintest conception. Are you going straight to the train?"

"No, I'm going to Stewart's to get some lining for that cloth mantle. Goodbye."

Manuella walked very fast on her way down Broadway. It was the tumult of her feelings rather than her haste that quickened her steps, although she had a strong desire to get away from the city as soon as possible.

She found the store choked with people, it being the hour at which the great thoroughfare was thronged with women, most of whom spent no small portion of their promenade wandering in an out of the larger shops. It was some time before she succeeded in making her purchases and she had come back to the entrance way through the groups and was standing at the doorway, indeterminately watching the brilliant concourse of customers, when a young woman somewhat jauntily attired came up and spoke to her.

"Well, d'you know, I knowed I couldn't be mistaken. You don't remember me, I'll bet. I'm Clianthe, you know. I lived on the floor above you at the Terrace. Lord, how gay you look, anyway. How's the old man? Your aunt was talkin' 'bout you only yesterday; whyn't you come down and see the folks?"

Manuella shrank back a little and making some involuntary remark of recognition, asked if her aunt was well and was about to pass on, when a man with a whip in his hand entered the door, looked around a moment and then taking off his glazed cap, spoke to Manuella.

"Beg pard'n, Miss," he said, "I guess this is for you," and he handed her a note which was written in pencil and hurriedly folded.

"*My dear Miss Castleton,*" it read. "You hadn't been gone half a hour when an important dispatch came from your grandfather. I don't dare to send it by this man because I don't know if he'll find you. You'd better get in the coach and come right away. I'd come myself only it would take half an hour to dress.

MRS. HANNIGE."

Manuella uttered a little half suppressed cry.

"I was to bring you over in the cab," said the man.

She was bewildered and hesitated

"What is it?" asked Clianthe, "Something happened?"

"I'm afraid so. I can run over as quick as the cab can go," and she moved toward the door.

"No, yer can't, neither, Miss, at this time o' day," said the man.

"Are you afeerd?" asked Clianthe, "I'll go with you. Come on," and they passed out upon the sidewalk.

"Here you are," said the man, holding the door of the cab open. "I'll have you there in a minute and a half."

Time was everything now. Clianthe had got in and after a moment's irresolution Manuella followed her.

The door was slammed with a loud report; the man sprang into his seat and the vehicle shot away.

"O, you know, I've wanted to see you fur a long time," began Clianthe, "I wanted to tell you of lots o' things that's happened at the Terrace. We don't have such gayeties as you did. What was that young man's name as come with the officer? Carteret, wasn't it? Where's he now? He was a sport, wasn't he? Is he all right? Lord, you can't hear me one bit fur the rattle, ken you? Why don't you come down and see your aunt? Did you know the old doctor was gone? O, he aint there now and she aint very smart neither. She kinder thinks you've gone back on your old friends. What a rum go that was about the cup, wasn't it? O, your aunt told me all about it and how smart the old man was."

Clianthe kept this meaningless tattle going with a great deal more earnestness than was necessary and she accompanied it by animated gestures that were evidently intended to hold Manuella's attention. But they signally failed, for that young lady suddenly exclaimed:

"Where is this driver going? This is not the way to Mrs. Hannige's," and she caught at the handle of the door at the same time as if to open it.

"He's gone round, I s'pose, to get out of the street jam," said Clianthe unconcernedly, "but I wanted to tell you what I heard about that cup."

Manuella paid no attention to her now. She was looking eagerly and anxiously at the passing houses in a vain endeavor to ascertain in what direction they were going and she still clung to the handle of the door.

The cab had been driven down Thirteenth street in a westerly direction towards Sixth avenue; the neighborhood was unfamiliar to her, and the vehicle was going at a headlong rate. Every breath the girl took as she held her face against the glass added to her suspicion, and every ill defined suspicion grew into alarm. She began to tug at the door desperately. Clianthe caught her by the arm. "What are you goin' to do?"

"I want to get out," said Manuella, with a gasp. "Open the door or I'll break the window and scream for the police."

"Are you crazy?" exclaimed her companion, "do you want to break your neck, what's the matter with you?"

"Open the door," she cried, and her look of terror and desperation as she turned and gave the woman at her side a quick glance, startled even that creature for an instant.

"Don't, for God's sake," almost screamed Clianthe, "I don't want you to kill yourself."

But without heeding her the girl made a sudden spring at the door on the other side of the vehicle, and so energetic was her grasp and so vehement her impulse that it gave way and Clianthe heard her cry and saw her spring and knew that she had leaped from the vehicle before it had fairly occurred to her to prevent it. With a cry of alarm herself she looked out and saw that the girl had fallen on her face, and was lying in the roadway some few rods behind. The driver was pulling up his horse and shouting. Several witnesses of the affair had already run into the street and were holding the girl up as Clianthe reached her, slowly followed by the vehicle that had with some difficulty been turned about.

"Look here," said a brawny fellow who had picked Manuella up, "what's this mean? What the devil are you tryin' to do, hey? What are you thinking about, anyway? You've killed her. Call a policeman, somebody."

"O, what the matter with you?" said Clianthe, who saw that Manuella had struck her head on the pavement and was insensible. "What are you going to do with the p'lice? She's my sister, that's all. We girls was on a little toot and she got too much on. Help me git her in the cab and get her home. I told you she'd jump out, Johnny. She aint got no head when she's loaded. Come on, don't leave her here; haven't you got any feelings, man?"

"You mean to say she's your sister?" asked the man, looking from one to the other.

"I just do," said Clianthe, "would you like to dispute it?"

"O, that's all right," chimed in the driver, "I know 'em both. That un's a little wild when she's on a tear. I was takin' her home and she lowed she'd have another dash," and he began assisting Clianthe to get her into the coach.

The man fell back with the remark, "Well, if she's your sister there must a' been two sets o' parents, that's all I've got to say. There aint no smell o' liquor on that one."

There was quite a crowd of men and boys in the street, but Clianthe's business like self-possession produced the impression that an accident had happened to a reckless girl of the town, and they had no inclination to mix themselves in the matter.

And so poor Manuella's attempt to escape, oddly enough, brought about the very conditions of successful abduction. She was hurriedly put back in the coach, and the driver hastily whipped up his horse and made as speedily as possible for the river. Ten minutes later he was rushing up Tenth avenue at a clattering pace.

Clianthe with some difficulty held the girl in her arms. Whatever her purpose she had a woman's sympathy for her, and felt some anxiety about her condition. For half an hour they sped up the avenue. The houses grew wider apart, and the passers-by grew less. Great spaces in which was no help began to yawn on either side of the road. The five o'clock train shot by them on the Hudson River road bearing Mrs. Manser and Mr. Baxter homeward, and still the man urged his horse northward.

Between Forty-ninth and Fiftieth streets there was at this time long piles of rocks and heaps of the rudest building materials, with a little old-fashioned house on the northern corner which had once been a cottage, but had been since used as a saloon and later as a storehouse and dwelling of some squatter, who kept his eye on the material in the neighborhood. There was not another house within half a mile. The rocks above shut off the road from sight, and the straight stretch below being unmacadamized and too rough for light vehicles was frequented only by laborers' carts and truckmen whose gardens lay in the sunken lots beween the piles of gneiss. Manuella though unconscious was breathing irregularly and had responded to the rude jolting of the vehicle with occasional gasps, which satisfied Clianthe that she was only stunned. The girl held her as carefully as possible to protect her from the sides of the cab, and as if to relieve her own conscience poured out in a crooning way her sympathy and her regrets.

"What d'you go and do it for, you aint goin' to be hurt. Nobody aint goin' to kill you, do you think I'd stand in with that? Why don't you come to, anyway? You've only knocked your head, you'll git over it bime bye; say, I'm here with you. What's the use of goin' on like this? I tell you it's all right, nobody aint goin' to touch you. They can't, you know."

When they came to the little solitary house the vehicle slackened its pace and drew slowly up. The driver did not stop his horse, but walked him past the place and looked cautiously about as if in search of some one. He had gone but a few rods above the house when the door opened and a man with a light surtout overcoat on and a muffler round his throat, that with his soft felt hat pulled low down on his face left little of his visage but the black whiskers to be seen, came out. The cab stopped, and the man looking up and down the road came up to it.

Clianthe threw the door open and he leaned forward to look in.

"We've got her," said the girl, "everything's all right, only she jumped out and struck her head."

The man drew back a little.

"Is she hurt?"

"Not much. She'll be all right. You've got to git her somewhere, she's knocked her head. How am I goin' to git back?"

"Come out," said the man gruffly, "and don't chin."

"Look here, Curly," insisted the girl, "you aint goin' to have no rough treatment, are you? She can't stand it. She'll die on your hands. I didn't go in for that."

"Are you goin' to stand there and keep this up?" asked the driver savagely. He was twisted around in his seat and looking down the road. "If this is business, why don't you git in? Damn me if I don't let you drive yourself, if you don't look sharp."

"Come out, will you?" said the man at the door, as he put one arm in and caught hold of the girl. "What are you thinkin' about?"

She got out, protesting all the while, and he took her place in the vehicle without saying a word. The moment the door was pulled shut, the driver started his horse with a fierce cut of the whip and the cab with a sudden jerk went off up the road leaving Clianthe standing there looking after it.

"If they touch a hair of her, I'm blessed if I don't blow the whole of 'em," she said. "Lord, wouldn't she pull money in Slocum's afterpiece with that hair. I'd like him to see her."

Manuella, limp and dishevelled in a corner of the vehicle, the motion of which in her semi-conscious condition had bent her hat and shaken her golden hair into pitiable disorder, presently opened her eyes with a cry. The man had grasped her, not rudely and was endeavoring to hold her in something like a comfortable position.

Her first impulsive action was to throw off his hand; her next to make a desperate attempt at the door with a new terror in her face and a new alarm in her movements.

He caught her instantly by the arm and pressed her back in the seat.

"See here, lady," he said in a coarse, but not unkindly voice, "yer tried that once. Don't do it agin, it's no use. If you'll be quiet, I'll take care o' yer like a gentleman. Anyhow I aint a goin' to let you do that."

"Who are you?" asked the terrified girl, shrinking into the corner and staring at her companion, who kept his face partly averted and held his head down in the folds of his muffler. "Where are you taking me?"

"I aint goin' to do you no damage," he said. "I'll take care o' yer like yer own father if yer behave, and I'll land yer safe and sound with your friends when you tell me where that cup is; that's all yer got to do, and if I don't put yer back where yer belong, I hope to die. An' I'm jist a goin' to keep you till you do. That's the straight of it."

All this to the girl was an incomprehensible horror. To her shattered faculties, it seemed that Clianthe had been transformed before her eyes into this foreboding and implacable wretch. Her head was cruelly aching; she could not straighten the whirl of events sufficiently to apprehend the real danger or to act with intelligent precaution. A cloudy sense of terrible wrong and terrible danger oppressed and confused and alarmed her. She shrank with instinctive delicacy, no less than with natural terror, into her corner, but her eyes were fastened on the man beside her. She tried to command her faculties sufficiently to reason it out, but the concussion she had suffered and the nervous shock under which she was still laboring made this a difficult task.

"You needn't go into spasms with me," said her companion. "When I say I won't damage you, it goes. I ain't a goin' to tech you, an' I'm goin' to take you back safe nor sound when you tell me where that cup is; now what's the use puttin' on all these frills! We've got you this time and no mistake, an' if yer went and hurt yer head it wasn't my fault, I wish yer hadn't."

She could see by the occasional turns of his head made by her efforts to adjust herself to the motions of the vehicle over the rough road that he was a squarejawed, black whiskered man with enormous shoulders upon which his head sat with no intimation of neck and that from under the edges of the felt hat protruded short, flat, black curls of hair. But she had no clear idea of his purpose or connected recollection of what had taken place. The fraudulency of the message brought to her and its part in this chain of occurrences was not yet apparent. The first impression made was that something had happened to her grandfather and this had deepened into an acute feeling that she was being taken from him at a time when he needed her most. That she was in the power of a person unscrupulous in character and repugnant in speech and appearance, she clearly perceived; but farther than this her reason in its bewildered condition did not at the moment go. To the first frantic desire to escape, succeeded a pitiable helplessness without cowardice. She would have kept her lips closed to the end of the journey in shame and contempt, but that the man said to her:

"Why don't yer speak? I don't want the bother of holdin' on to you for the rest of your life. It would just suit me to waltz you home this minute and hand you over to your old man without a look at you—yes, it would. I ain't no womanstealer, but I've got to have that cup and you can tell me how to get it. There's them as ain't so reasonable as me and we're goin' straight to 'em."

It then began to straighten itself out in her thought. She was a victim of a conspiracy to get the cup. A gleam of hope shot into her mind.

"I'm sure," said she, "you can have the cup and welcome, if you take me home at once. Stop the cab."

"Where is it?" asked the man quickly.

"It's many miles away from the city."

"How many miles? What's the place?" So anxious was he that he turned squarely around and bent forward to catch the answer.

"Stop the cab," she said, "and take me back; I'll tell you where the cup is."

"Why can't you be sensible? I'll just take you where there's a place to fix yourself up a bit and then you won't give me dead away to the first man you meet. I ain't a fool."

She crouched back in her corner and for some time there was not a word spoken.

She heard the vehicle rattle over a long bridge and she saw the gleam of water. Some instinct told her that they were going rapidly north and she saw plainly enough that they were already in the suburbs. Thoroughly frightened, she still had the courage of desperation and had there been the least chance of success, would have again attempted to throw herself from the cab. But at the slightest move, she became aware that the man was watching her closely.

It was dusk when the vehicle turned into a lane eastward, and the noise of the macadamized roadway, gave place to a softer sound as if they were traversing a grass-grown thoroughfare. Not long after they were driven up to a cottage in which lights were burning and two or three people came out, one of them being an elderly woman, and Manuella was carefully, if not tenderly, conducted into the house.

CHAPTER XXXI.

CARTERET STARTS IN SEARCH.

It was half past ten when Carteret reached the city. He jumped into a cab and at eleven o'clock was at Mrs. Hannige's door.

In answer to his vigorous summons on the bell that lady came into the hall, wiping her mouth with a napkin to see Florry let him in.

"Dear me," she said, "You'd wake the dead. Is anything the matter?"

"Miss Castleton has not returned," said Carteret. "I am afraid something has happened to her."

"What an idea," replied Mrs. Hannige. "You don't know that girl. She can take care of herself. Would you like a bite of supper? I was just pulling a lobster to pieces. Come in and sit down. I said, when I got your telegram, something's up, sure enough."

"You said in your despatch that she left here at three. Did she go straight to the train?" Carteret asked as he followed Mrs. Hannige into the room.

"Why, no. She had to go to Stewart's for some basque lining. Do set down, Mr. Carteret, and have a cup of tea. What makes you think something's happened to her?"

"Because," said Carteret who kept walking impatiently about, "she was to come back at five o'clock and she would not have staid away from her grandfather without sending us word."

Mrs. Hannige suddenly became very reflective. Her attitude with a lobster claw in her fist and her mouth open was one of inspiration somewhat heightened by appetite.

"Good gracious," she said, "I wonder if that woman could have—It would be just like her."

"What woman?" demanded Carteret, coming to a halt and regarding Mrs. Hannige with a painful curiosity. "What is it you are talking about?"

"Yes," remarked the lady, as if trying to convince herself by her own tone. "I do believe she is capable of anything."

"Mrs. Hannige." said Carteret, quite impressively and coming close enough to make her her chair back an inch or two. "If you have anything to tell me, I wish you would out with it without any nonsense. I am not in a condition to put up with a great deal. Who is it you are talking about? What has happened?"

"I'm talking about Miss Enniston. She was here to-day in a great tantrum and met Miss Castleton."

"What?"

"Yes, and they had it out tooth an' nail."

"Well, well, they met? What do you mean by having it out? What was said and done?" Then he started off at a stride and with something like a groan, swinging his arms and striking his fist into his open palm, saying, as if to himself. "That reckless and unscrupulous woman would say anything. Poor girl, why could not I have spared her that?"

"She's a wild cat," said Mrs. Hannige "and I wouldn't have let her into my house if I'd known the kind of tongue she carries. You can depend on that."

Then Mrs. Hannige took a sip of tea and began helping herself to more lobster.

"Were you present at the interview?" asked Carteret.

"Was I? She abused me like a pickpocket and called that child everything that's filthy and mean. I'm sorry I didn't fetch a policeman and put her into the street. I believe that woman's capable of anything. Why, she went on like a highway robber and threatened to do something, I don't know what."

"She is a passionate, revengeful woman," said Carteret. "What do you know or suspect? Go on, tell me exactly what occurred. Poor girl, poor girl, what did she say? She was astonished, of course, humiliated, overwhelmed. My God, what a misfortune."

"No, she wasn't. She acted like a lady. Don't you make any mistake, and she stood up for you, young man, like a heroine. 'I believe him,' says she, looking at her with them big eyes of hers, 'and I don't believe you. He never lied to me but once and that was when he told me you were a lady.' Yes, she did. Them's her own words and then out she walks like a princess and didn't even slam the door."

"And you say she threatened? Can it be possible? Pshaw, it's too absurd. Threatened what? Why didn't you send to Stewart's when you got my despatch?"

"What, at that time o' night?" said Mrs. Hannige. "You've lost your head," and she spread a piece of bread. "When you say anything mean is impossible to that woman, you're making a mistake."

"Do you think that Manuella could have been taken sick, fainted or—"

"No, I don't. She isn't the fainting kind. I think something else has happened to her, but I don't know what it is. Where are you going?"

"I'm going to Miss Enniston," replied Carteret. "I can't stand here. I must learn something. Where does she live?"

Mrs. Hannige smiled. "If I were you," she said. "I'd try and be cool. You don't want to go flying round to-night like a hen with her head off. You wouldn't find anybody at this hour and in the morning you'll feel better like work. I don't know exactly where she is. She's stopping at Col. Hardynge's.

I think it would be a great deal better for me to go over there in the morning and make some inquiry. John will be here to-morrow and if there is any deviltry, he'll get to the bottom of it."

At the mention of Wilder, Carteret jumped headlong in another direction. "Where is he? I'll find him to-night. Why didn't you say before that he was here?"

"If you'll take a cup of tea," said Mrs. Hannige, "it'll steady your nerves. I dare say Miss Castleton will turn up all right in the morning. That girl has got a head of her own and knows what she's about. Women have their own way of doing things. Sit down and be reasonable, and I'll give you a bed. You needn't leave the house to-night. We'll find out all about this matter in the morning. I haven't told you half. I can't, the way you go on."

Carteret threw himself into a chair helplessly with the remark, "But while I'm wasting time here, what may not be happening to Manuella?"

"I guess that woman has found some way to keep her over. She could do it with a lie and she wouldn't stop at anything. I don't think it's any worse than that. I feel it in my bones. Bad as she is, I don't believe she'd go any further than talk and threats. Her kind sputter and swell a great deal and get tired out before much damage is done. If you'd seen Miss Castleton handle her, you wouldn't be afraid of that girl's taking care of herself. She's a cool one."

Mrs. Hannige not only succeeded in detaining Carteret, but she even led him to believe as she did, that Miss Enniston's spiteful and reckless behavior had in some way interferred with Manuella's return. It was a great relief to feel that matters were no worse and he unwittingly tried to take that view of it. The longer he listened to Mrs. Hannige, the more plausible her theory became, in spite of two or three insuperable objections to it. Little by little the staring fact that Manuella had no place in the city to stay over night but Mrs. Hannige's was softened down until it became indistinct. "She could go to her aunt's," said Mrs. Hannige. "She could take a late train. I shouldn't wonder if she was up there with her grandfather now, sound asleep while we're worrying ourselves to death over her." And Mrs. Hannige handed Mr. Carteret a bottle of Bass's ale to open, with the incidental remark that it had stood so long it must be warm.

The result was that Carteret went to bed late; slept little and got up early—so early that he was at a loss how to fill the time before he could get his breakfast. He sent two dispatches to Mr. Manser—one directed to Scarsdale and the other to Tarrytown, being uncertain which would be delivered, and at ten o'clock he was at Col. Hardynge's house ringing the bell urgently.

He was ushered into a reception room by a servant who did not conceal her astonishment at the untimely hour of the visit, but took his card saying, "The ladies most likely aint dressed yet," to which, Carteret with reckless indifference replied, "Tell the lady it is urgent business and not to stop to dress."

When Miss Enniston received the card, she was in a morning languor, half reclining in an Oriental chair and lazily polishing her finger nails with a little brush. She sprang up instantly. "Is there a lady with him?" she asked.

"No'm," said the girl. "The gent is all alone."

Whereupon Miss Enniston dashed into Grace Hardynge's room, all in a flutter, thrust the card into her friends hands and began to talk rapidly and disrobe herself violently.

"Are you going to see him?" asked the imperturbable Grace.

"Why not?" exclaimed the vehement Rose. "If he has any explanations to make, there's no harm in hearing them, is there? Lend me your swandown wrap; it's longer than mine. Dear me, my hair's hideous. Come in dear and help me a moment, do. All my things are in a heap. I had no idea he'd call; did you?"

"If I were you," said Grace calmly, "I wouldn't see him."

"Well, I just will—there," retorted Rose. "All I want is to see him. I could do anything I pleased with him when I had him under my eye. Bring your pins and come into my room and do try and be sensible for once in your life."

Carteret meanwhile worked himself up into a condition of impatience and nervous excitability that was pitiable. The maid had brought word that Miss Enniston would be down right away, but a half hour passed while he was waiting, and every moment added to his perplexity at the situation. He tried to arrange in his mind what he would say, and, as is usually the result in such cases, came to the conclusion to trust to the impulse of the moment. His anxiety to hear of Manuella almost obscured his anomalous relationship to Miss Enniston, and the suspicion that she had in some way interfered with the poor girl, gave him a sort of protective indignation.

When his patience was almost exhausted, Rose appeared at the door in gorgeous morning attire, just a trifle flushed, but radiant with smiles. She hesitated a second, gave her head a little toss as if throwing off the last lingering hesitancy and came toward him with her hands extended, saying:

"Colin."

The young man took one of her hands rather formally and said:

"Miss Enniston."

"Don't treat me that way," she said. "Let by-gones be by-gones now that you have come back."

"Miss Enniston," he replied somewhat surprised, "I came here to ask you about Miss Castleton. She was to have returned to her friends yesterday and they have been unable to hear of her or trace her since she was in your company."

He said this with an intentional implication that Rose was in some way responsible for Miss Castleton's disappearance. But his companion's indomitable vanity made her suspect that he might be using the Castleton matter as a plausible excuse to make this call.

"I'm surprised," she answered, "that you should for a moment think I could know anything of the girl's whereabouts. It's absurd on the face of it. I am not interested in such people."

"But you called upon her and, I understand, had a scene with her, which to say the least, was unusual and unbecoming. I believe you threatened her."

"O, you heard about that little encounter, did you? It was not pleasant. She called me a liar among other things. Don't you think"—and she leaned a little toward him and held up her hand so that he could see the ring on her finger—"Don't you think I had some excuse and some right to see her?"

"No," said Carteret. "After what passed between us I cannot conceive of any mad impulse that would make you so far forget yourself."

She drew herself up and stepped back. He politely offered her a chair, but she only put her hand on its back and remained standing.

"No?" she enquired. "Cannot you conceive of a woman, after a year's promises feeling a little reckless when they are all broken in a moment? Can't you understand that perfidy, deceit, and wrong make a woman desperate sometimes?"

"Miss Enniston," said Carteret, "I did not come here to argue our past with you. I called for no other purpose than to get some information concerning Miss Castleton. It is idle and useless for us to upbraid each other now. If you know where Miss Castleton is, or what became of her after your interview, I beg you to tell me that I may send word to her grandfather."

"Mr. Carteret," she replied, "nothing that you have ever done compares with the impudence of coming to me for such information. You must know that it is an insult. Was it your deliberate purpose to insult me in that woman's behalf?"

"Far from it," said Carteret quickly and earnestly. "You had a violent scene with Miss Castleton yesterday, and you threatened her. She has not been seen by her friends since. I came straight to you and ask you as courteously as possible to give me such information as you can. Nothing could be farther from my purpose than to reproach you for your conduct or to—"

"Reproach me?" she interrupted with an admirable gesture and expression of contempt. "Reproach me? For what? Was it for listening to you a whole year when you were at my feet, pretending to love me and asking me to be your wife? Was it for discovering that you were making love to another woman at the same time? Do you want to reproach me for being hurt and indignant at the time, and then like an idiot beseeching you to come back to me and be forgiven?"

"Rose," said Carteret, somewhat pricked by the small point of justice in this speech, "what you are saying is not true. I did not love two women at the same time. You were very unjust in your charges, and you are still in the same temper. I only loved one."

His manner softened her in an instant.

"Why didn't you answer my letter?" she asked, with something like a tone of tenderness.

"Because," he replied, "you had told me with an insult that you were done with me forever. I took you at your word."

"Don't you think," she said, as she dropped her eyelids, "that you were a little hasty in taking me at my word in a moment of jealousy, when I had taken you at your word during all the serious moments of the year?"

"Rose," exclaimed Carteret, with just a trifle of annoyance, "it was your fault. In a moment of bad temper you undid the work of a year. It is irrecoverable. Let us remain friends."

"Yes," she said, "we will try. I will not believe that all the vows and pledges of a man's honor can be so lightly thrown away in a moment. If your words to me mean anything they mean that you are mine still—that no mere fancy of the moment can disturb the affection of a twelvemonth. O, Colin, why don't you say what is in your heart? You don't love anybody as you loved me, do you?"

She had come toward him as she said this, and he had moved backward a step and was holding his hand up deprecatingly.

"Miss Enniston," he said, "I shall always have the kindliest feeling for you. I want you to remain my friend; but I—pardon me—I don't think we can renew the past."

She felt that there was a repulse in his manner even more acute than in his words. She paused. The quick blood flushed into her cheeks.

"Look at me," she said, with an ominous effort to be calm, "is there no pity in you for me? Is there nothing in my face that makes that past a living truth?"

"Rose, I think we both made a mistake."

"Do you?"

"Yes, we thought that two such natures as ours could be happy together. You were the first to discover the mistake. You have spared us both a life of misery and mockery. I think we shall be far more comfortable as friends."

He moved toward the door. "I shall have to leave you," he said; "I did not come here to renew our old quarrels, and I must go and find Miss Castleton."

"Stop," she cried, "you shall not go that way," and she sprang to the door and interposed her person. He knew from past experiences with her when he was more tolerant of her, that some outburst of passion was pending. He tried to avert it.

"Miss Enniston, Rose, I beg of you to calm yourself and be reasonable with me. This is not the time to lose our tempers. I have an urgent task on hand. Surely if we must go over this matter we can find a better opportunity. Let me pass."

She put up her hand in her impetuous way and pushed him back. "You think you can go away and avoid the truth like a sneak," she said.

Carteret shrugged his shoulders and turned away from her. His actions indicated his effort to be indifferent to her worst mood.

"Do you suppose," she went on, "that all the feelings and passions that you labored so long and so patiently to create in me can be annihilated in an instant to suit your convenience? They must go on in some direction. If I cannot love you I must hate you."

"As you please," replied Carteret. "I can no more command my feelings than you can, but I can command my speech."

He said this without turning to look at her.

"You will make a devil of me," she cried. "If a woman ever tried to do right I have. You found me a trusting girl; you have made me a vindictive woman. I hope to God the love which could not hold you will have the power, now that it is turned to hate, to destroy you. Go."

He looked at her with admiring amazement a moment as she stepped from the door, and with flashing eyes and distended arm ordered him out.

"I will try," he said with a bow, "to think better of you than you deserve, so long as your malignity is given wholly to me. But when you bestow it upon an innocent and unfortunate girl I hope that I will have the means and the right to defend her."

This was the bitterest speech of all. It turned the last drop of prudence she had into desperation. He had passed her and was on his way to the street.

"Ah, ha," she cried, "how can you defend her when you do not even know where she is now?"

He turned about. To be able to hold him even by the wretched pretence of having committed a desperate act was something.

"O, now you are interested, are you? You'll be much more interested before you are done with me."

If there was an insane hope in her chaos of passion that this unwomanly threat would bring him back begging, it was disappointed. He looked at her with an eager and curious perplexity and then, making another bow, took his departure.

It was a long and uneventful but anxious day for him, and it was not till nightfall that he received a dispatch from Mr. Manser sent early in the morning and saying, "Miss Castleton not returned."

It was nine o'clock before he found Wilder, who had come to Mrs. Hannige's and he immediately began a recital of all the foregoing events, unconsciously coloring them with the implication that Miss Enniston, insane with jealousy, had made away with Manuella. Wilder listened patiently and then said, "Miss

Castleton has been abducted, but Miss Enniston is as innocent of it as you are. She had no means or disposition to do it. Drop that notion. The girl has been carried off to obtain information about the cup. She will probably give it to get out of their clutches and get back to her grandfather. We must go straight to where the cup is and wait for them."

"They might use violence to extort their information," said Carteret in distress.

"Hardly," replied Wilder. "Threats will answer and violence will be risky as I know the principal in the game. They will take all the risks up to that stage. Miss Castleton will be returned but they will get the cup. You are quite sure that Miss Enniston doesn't know any of these people?"

"I am not at all sure," said Carteret. "Why do you ask?"

"Because two of them were at the Sanger party and she was there also."

"You see" cried Carteret, "that woman is at the bottom of it."

"I don't see," rejoined Wilder calmly. "I suppose you left that cup lying round loose."

"It is on the mantle in her sleeping room."

"An open country house, eh? With the men all away during the day."

Carteret assented to all this mutely and with impatience.

"Why didn't you leave it here in a place of security?"

"Because I only got it as we were starting and wasn't going to waste the time."

"It would have saved a good deal of trouble and time," remarked Wilder thoughtfully. "That eleven-forty train does not stop at Scarsdale. Could you manage to catch the ten-thirty? It's ten now. If you get there ahead of them, you will save the cup."

"Damn the cup," cried Carteret. "I'm anxious to save Miss Castleton. I can't sit here and think that she is in the hands of ruffians and I can't go off into the country and leave her behind."

"You will not go up to-night, then?"

"No; don't ask me to do anything impossible."

"Or reasonable?" suggested Wilder.

"I'll do anything that a man can do to save her. But to run away to secure that cup would be folly."

"But don't you understand that it is the cup they want and not the girl?"

"No, I don't understand anything of the kind. The girl would be a temptation and a prize that no ruffian would treat with consideration."

"Well, my boy," said Wilder, "I suppose we'll lose that cup again. I don't feel like going to Scarsdale to-night and walking five miles in the woods, but we can find out something about the people who have had a hand in this."

"We never will, if you sit here and let that Miss Enniston slip out of your clutch."

"What a vindictive young man you are," observed Wilder reflectively. "You don't appear to understand that an unscrupulous gang of miscreants are moving heaven and earth to get possession of that cup and one of their moves is to get possession of Miss Castleton and frighten her into revealing its whereabouts. That's all there is to it. Now if you'll dismiss Miss Enniston from your thoughts you may be of some service to me."

"Go on," said Carteret helplessly. "You'll ask me next to dismiss Miss Castleton from my thoughts, and good God," he exclaimed, jumping up, "she may be murdered by this time. You remind me of an unscrupulous gang and expect me to have patience. Of course there's a gang; there's no end of disreputable people, and it all comes of that poor girl's living down there in that tenement house. Why, one of them stopped me on the street one night and asked me if I didn't want to get the cup. She looked like a street-walker."

"You never told me about it."

"Didn't I? Well, I didn't think it worth telling. She said if I'd come to the Liverpool Boudoir, she'd show me a man who'd get it for me."

"When was this?"

Carteret then described his little adventure with Mignon in front of the Century Club and Wilder listened to it attentively.

"That's all there is to it," said Carteret.

"There's a good deal to it," remarked the officer. "That girl is what we call a 'pal' of the man McCune. But I had never thought of connecting her with the affair. If McCune is absent from New York on this abduction business, she will be apt to know as they have made her one of their agents by your account."

"What did she want me to go to the Boudoir for?"

"My boy," said Wilder, "I suppose they wanted to abduct you and failing, they caught at the girl. I don't think they would have treated you so tenderly. Get your spring overcoat. We'll find Betsy Wood, if she's at the Boudoir."

CHAPTER XXXII.

THE DESCENT INTO HELL.

Owing mainly to a professional reticence, John Wilder did not communicate his suspicions and inductions in full to Carteret. Indeed he had only consented at the last moment and at the urgent solicitations of the young man to take him with him.

He believed that Plonski's two agents, Curley Samson and The Mink, would be the most likely men to undertake such a job as the abduction of a woman. He knew that they would act very quickly when once they found out the hiding place of the cup, and he knew the chances of reaching it in that hiding place, before they got there, were small. So he determined to find the girl Clianthe if possible, and get what information he could, and if his suspicions with regard to these men were sustained, to put the machinery of the Central office in operation and take them with the plunder in their hands.

It was a plain sailing task and he merely told Carteret on their way downtown, that the first thing to do was to find Clianthe whom he believed to be acting in some way for Plonski. They arrived at the Liverpool Boudoir at half past ten. It was at that hour when the lower Bowery is in full swing. Three great theatres immediately adjacent were pouring their crowds upon the sidewalks during the intermissions of the performances. The lights of the great beer gardens came through the open doors and the sounds of orchestras and singers floated crosswise upon the ear from half a score of places. Men and women were crossing and recrossing the roadway. All the denizens of the dance houses and bagnios were on the street. The gayest, jauntiest and most abandoned girls were flirting, sky-larking and promenading with their admirers and victims. The curbs were lined with the noisy venders of pork pies, hot corn and waffles. Costermongers were crying their goods from their carts and groups of sailors and soldiers jostled each other and passed their rude salutations loudly. Anything more animated, more heterogeneous, or more reckless, could not be seen in the city at that time, than the lower Bowery at eleven o'clock at night. The vast Atlantic Garden held its thousands, the adjoining Bowery Theatre with its great portico throbbed with life, and across the way the still larger Stadt Theatre like a hive, held its buzzing and intermingling swarms.

Just below the Stadt Theatre, on the East side, where the crowd was thickest and noisiest, a canvas sign across the upper windows of an oldfashioned brick house, showed the inscription, "Liverpool Boudoir and Philharmonic Concert Saloon. All the best talent nightly engaged. Admittance free."

This place, known to its habitues as "The Boodaw," occupied the whole of the first floor. A vestibule, choked with men and boys, led directly to a bar-room, thick with smoke and clamorous with excited voices. People crowded each other at the bar, and two men in their shirt sleeves were rapidly serving drinks across the wet counter. A screen of green blinds shut off the concert room proper, but once behind it, the audience was seen seated at little tables, drinking and smoking and watching listlessly the performance on a tawdry stage at the end of the room.

The character of the people here assembled was obvious enough. The greater part of them were rough idlers out of work by compulsion or by choice, seeking the excitement of an evening, and finding it in the irritant atmosphere of the place and in the contact with men and women made effusive and congenial by liquor. Save a few who sat stolidly at the tables, the occupants appeared to be contiually coming and going. They sauntered in and out in search of companions or novelty. Bedizened women, louder and more vivacious than the men who pulled them about, came in continually from the street, stood around a few moments in the crowd, and then slipped out again to visit some other adjacent resort, it being their custom to work all round this orbit of the lower Bowery every night in search of pals, adventures and prey.

Wilder had told Carteret briefly that he wanted to find the girl Clianthe; that he suspected her of complicity and that he had brought him along to identify her as the woman who had spoken to him that night on Fifteenth Street. What he did not tell him was, that if the man known as "The Mink" was in town, he would be hanging round the girl Clianthe, and that if he was not there to-night, the chances were that he was out of town on Plonski's job and the girl would know of it.

They passed through the crowd at the entrance of the Boudoir as unobtrusively as possible and entering the concert room, seated themselves at a table close against the wall. There was a great deal of confusion in the place; men were coming and going, and most of them talking loudly. Wilder and his companion were, therefore, not objects of attention. A stratum of tobacco smoke lay motionless-on the close air, save where the gas jet drove it up in little eddies. The curtain that shut off the narrow stage was down, and during the lull of the performance several young women, who were not uncomely, but were anything but modest, went about with trays and took the orders at the tables for drinks.

Without paying the slightest attention to the place or the inmates, Carteret asked his companion with an impressive earnestness the moment he was seated, if he was going to sit there and enjoy the performance.

"I don't know exactly what I shall do," replied Wilder, "and if I did, I'm not sure that I would tell you. If you'll just keep your eyes peeled, as they say here, and tell me if you see that girl that spoke to you on Fifteenth street, you'll help me out."

There was just a slight hint of gruffness in this answer and Carteret, impatient as he was, concluded to put up with it rather than be left out of the scheme, whatever it was, to get on the trail of Manuella. But while he determined to accept Wilder in any mood, he could not, at the same time, refrain from asking questions.

"What do you suppose," he said, with an almost comical effort to appear unconcerned, "is the mystery of that precious cup?"

Wilder's answer was somewhat irrelevant: "Do you suppose you would know that young woman if you saw her again?" he asked.

"Very likely," said Carteret, "but what has she got to do with the cup?"

"That's what I want to know," replied Wilder.

"In plain English, you don't know any more than I do," observed Carteret.

"It's doubtful if I knew as much, up to date."

While they were carrying on this absurd conversation, the girl Clianthe, who was on the stage, came leisurely to the curtain that shut her off from the audience, and closing one eye, put her head down and looked through a hole in it at the assemblage on the other side. She had a quick glance, and the lights in the house had been turned up. Wilder was at that moment standing up and facing the stage, endeavoring to get a view of somebody who had come in and had gone down the centre aisle. She saw him almost immediately, and a moment later recognized Carteret at the table. With a half audible exclamation that sounded like an oath, she turned from the curtain, stood scarcely a moment in thoughtful perplexity, and then ran off through the narrow wings, down a still narrower stairs and plunged into a stall-like room that was one of several uniform compartments. Pulling the door shut quickly, she, with incredible speed, kicked off the dirty white satin slippers from her feet, dropped the short, gaudy skirt in which she was dressed and tore the artificial flowers from her hair. It took her but two minutes to snatch a dress of common material from a peg and pin it round her waist, to pull on a pair of elastic gaiters, and then, seizing a hat, she clapped it on her head at a little mirror and ran out and along the paved alley way of the cellar toward the door that led to the sidewalk.

Some one shouted to her before she reached the steps. The noise of feet on the floor above made the summons unintelligible, but she stopped a moment, and a man in his shirt sleeves ran after her. She put her hand on his mouth as he came up to her to warn him not to shout.

"Where are you going?" he asked angrily.

"For God's sake, don't stop me now," she said in a rapid manner. "If they want me, say Leary's—don't forget—Leary's."

"What the hell is it?" he asked with some astonishment.

"Tell yer to-morrer," she said, and then opening the door hurriedly and with some difficulty, owing to her haste, she sprang up the steps and, looking up and down the street, ran through the crowd as fast as she could towards Chatham Square.

She had scarcely got away from the place before the curtain rose and a blacked-up performer came out with a chair and proceeded to entertain the noisy assemblage with a banjo and a song, the refrain of which was:

"For Little Mac is still in front,
And the people say he'll stay."

But the audience were not disposed to put up with Little Mac or the minstrel either. They interrupted him, hooted him, swore at him. It was some minutes before it was apparent what caused the disapprobation, and then it was shown in the cry of: "Bring on your girls," at which there was a howling chorus of assent.

"Aye, aye, where's the women? Trot out the maidens," and one young man in a blue army surtout cried, "Clianthe, Clianthe," at the top of his voice, at which there was a fresh burst of assent.

The minstrel with great good humor picked up his chair and bowed himself off. For some time the stage was left empty, but the jeers and laughter of the audience continued, and clearly above it all was heard the voice calling for Clianthe.

Presently there appeared upon the scene a man with a light overcoat thrown over an acrobat's flesh-colored apparel, his pink legs sticking out beneath. He was to do some tumbling in the course of the evening, but at this moment appeared as an apologist.

"Say, gents," he began; "the manager says if you'll giv' 'im a show, he'll giv' yer yer money's worth." As nobody had paid to come in, this appeared to strike the audience as a fine piece of humor, for it laughed ironically. "Mamsell Clianthe Mignon, the champion double kicker, ain't here, bein' called to the painful bedside ov a sick mother. Ther manager hopes yer'll hav some decency on ther mother's account, an he'll show yer the Australian knife swallower, who has been secured at a fabulous expense at the court ov the Australian Emperor."

Wilder did not pay the slightest attention to the satirical laughter that followed this attempt to be witty; he jumped up suddenly and went out into the corridor, followed by Carteret. Working his way through the crowd with considerable more energy than when he had come in, he presently found the proprietor of the place, a shabby-genteel Jew, in beer-stained broadcloth and shining silk hat cocked on one side of his head, and with a heavy gold chain dangling across his stomach.

"Was Betsy here to-night?" Wilder asked summarily.

The man evidently knew the officer, for he held out one hand without removing the other from his pocket.

"Hallo, Captin, been inside? 'Eard you vas away; come and take suthin'; 'o's your friend?"

Wilder caught him by the arm and drew him away to the doorway; once there, he withdrew his hand from the man's arm and placed it on his shoulder.

"Where's the girl?" he asked.

"If I knows, I 'ope to die. She aint the same girl as she was, no how; 'av' a bottle of wine, Captin?"

"Take me on behind," said Wilder, "and look sharp about it." They moved toward the sidewalk, Wilder partly conducting him.

"So 'elp me 'eaven," said the man, "I didn't know she'd been up to anything—right down this 'ere way, Captin."

The moment they were inside the doorway at the foot of the steps, the man in his shirt sleeves met them. Wilder repeated his question, "Was Betsy here tonight?"

Thus addressed somewhat imperatively, the fellow looked from one to the other, and getting no sign from his employer, he answered, "Yes."

"How long has she been gone?"

"Not ten minutes."

"Was she on the stage?"

"She'd just come off of it when I seen her goin' out."

"And she was in a hurry, wasn't she?"

"She said she was agoin' to Leary's and I wasn't to tell anybody."

Wilder and this man looked each other in the face for an instant, then the officer turned and retraced his way up the steps at the top of which Carteret stood waiting for him. "What did he mean by Leary's?" asked Wilder. "Is that the Madison street sty?"

"Sandy Leary's," replied the proprietor of the saloon. "Sandy's dive, that's where her man hangs out."

Wilder did not stop to hear more. Without speaking to Carteret, he started across the street and turned down towards Chatham Square at a brisk walk, followed by that young man. When they reached the Square, he hailed a cab and after a few hurried words to the driver, which were inaudible to Carteret, he turned and said:

"I don't think you had better come."

"If you don't object," said Carteret, "I'd rather. It's life or death to me."

Wilder smiled. He held the door of the cab open. "Get in," he said.

Scarcely a word was spoken in the vehicle. Both men were anxious, one was impatient almost to madness. But Wilder sat with his head partly out the cab window, watching the people on the sidewalks as they passed him, and he did not invite conversation.

In less than ten minutes the vehicle had pulled up, as the driver had been directed, at the corner of Pearl and Madison streets, and the men got out and walked down the slight declivity to the place known as Leary's.

It was a still lower grade of dive than the one they had just left. A noisy crowd of sailors, 'longshoremen and negroes hung round the doorway. A long wooden bench upon the curb was crowded with them. The music of a discordant band issued from the place and a troop of dirty and noisy boys and girls was dancing to it in the street.

Wilder unceremoniously pushed his way into the house. It was not unlike the Boudoir, save that it was noisier, dirtier and narrower and contained a greater and more dissolute crowd, drinking beer, smoking and singing the popular songs of the time.

He ran his eye quickly over the inmates. It was anything but a pleasant spectacle, and several of the roughest women shouted at him and one or two came up and caught hold of him. To escape from them he got upon a chair so as to overlook the crowd, and several of the inmates gathered round him. Among them was a lad not over twelve years old. As Wilder stepped off the chair, the boy spoke to him.

"Are yuz lookin' fur somun?" he asked.

The officer heard him but paid no attention to him. Going over to the entrance way, he spoke to the policeman who was leaning against the door post. Carteret saw them in a whispered conversation, but heard nothing until the policeman said:

"There's lots of 'em here must know her," and then seeing the boy who had come up behind Wilder, he continued, "Say, Shorty, you must know Betz Wood, hey?"

"Well, I knows her bettern my own sister. What's ther matter with Betz?"

"Is she here to-night?"

"You bet she is. Didn't she gimme a postal stamp ter see whether her feller was over in Oak street?"

"Where is she now?"

"Oh, she's on deck. Say, is he one ov her lugs?"

This part of the conversation was loud enough to be heard by several persons in the immediate neighborhood of the speakers, and a man neither of them had noticed, broke in:

"Betz's down t' other end th' floor; go fetch her, ye thief, what yer bitin' at?"

At this the boy went nimbly off into the crowd, Wilder looked at the man who had spoken to him. He was sure he had never seen him before and equally sure that he would know him anywhere again.

He wore a loose tweed suit that hung on his brawny frame in indifferent folds. His face was surrounded by black whiskers that contrasted strongly against his sallow skin and made his small, cold, grey eyes seem strangely out of keeping.

"Who is he?" asked Wilder of the policeman.

"I guess he's a Katy-did," replied the officer, "and hives with the Dry Dock gang."

While they were talking the boy returned. He made an absurd show of panting, as if he had been exhausted in getting from the rear of the room.

"She's gone up to ther Cave to find her feller," he said. "She didn't stop here mor'n a minnit; hey, Susey?"

"That's so," remarked the young woman he had appealed to, and who had to take a tumbler from her lips to respond. "I seen her and she lowed she was worried."

At this the man with the zinc eyes said, "Ov coorse, that's where he is if he's in ther city to-night, cos there's a scrap there bettween Hooley and ther Navy Yard Terror."

All this transpired in about five minutes. When Wilder reached the street, followed by Carteret, he was reserved and thoughtful, which did not, however, prevent him from walking very briskly toward Pearl street, where his cab was waiting.

"I wonder," he said to himself, "if that girl saw me from the stage, and is trying to save McCune?"

"Well," asked Carteret, as they got into the vehicle, "what have you got to say? What's to be done next? We're losing an awful lot of time."

"Of course," said Wilder. "The only thing we can keep is our patience."

They were now on their way to the Dry Dock, and traversing a portion of the city which Carteret was entirely ignorant of and of which Wilder knew but little. It was half past eleven o'clock, but the streets were alive with vagrant crowds, and the vehicle appeared to be passing through a continuous bacchanalian orgie.

At this time, and for a long time after the war, the Dry Dock was probably one of the worst neighborhoods in the city. It was not only the rendezvous of a class of longshoremen who were densely ignorant and bitterly opposed to the war, which had ruined their vocation, but it was infested with the Katy-did gang, a band of ruffians existing under some kind of organization of outlawry, who were a terror to the police and who had received the name by which they were known from their peculiar call or signal on the streets to each other. The gang has since been broken up and its ringleaders sent to the State's prison; but during the years of the civil war, owing in great part to the relaxed condition of civil authority and the concentration of public interest upon the safety of the Federal Union, it became the curse of the inhabitants in a large district of the East side.

The Cave, as it was called, was an old warehouse on Water street that had been turned into a dance house, where sparring exhibitions and balls were given, and public meetings held upstairs, and some kind of rough entertainment went on nightly in the cellar, where a notorious woman had established a sailors' dive, and here congregated a noisy rabble of both sexes and all colors and all nationalities, and here were always present some of the most notorious members of the Katy-did gang. Wilder knew the reputation of the place well enough, but he also knew that McCune was, at one time, a member of the Katy-did gang, and that when the police wanted him they looked in this place for him. He therefore hoped to learn something of his whereabouts.

When the two men arrived at the Cave it was at the flood tide of its orgies. Wilder, as before, left the vehicle a block away, and failing to induce Carteret to stay in it till he came back they together entered the dance house.

There was a mob of men in front of the old warehouse, and groups of rough and noisy people were scattered about the neighborhood and upon the adjacent wharves. The sparring exhibition in the hall, which had been attended by a vast concourse of idlers and roughs, had disgorged its spectators upon the sidewalk and roadway, and a great many of them had drifted into the Cave below. To the elements thus forming the usual components of the place was added on this occasion part of the paid-off crew of a United States man-of-war from the Navy Yard across the river.

It was plain to anyone who came upon the scene that it was turbulent and mischievous, owing to causes back of mere idleness and dissipation, residing in the political and social upheaval of the times, and to the accidental mingling of elements that were bitterly antagonistic. An extra number of policemen were visible at different points, stolid, grave and watchful.

The two men had some difficulty in forcing their way through the half intoxicated sailors and 'longshoremen who blocked the passage and were chaffing each other in anything but polite language. A hot air assailed them on the steps as they went down; it was loaded with an indescribable din of blasphemy, laughter and ribaldry.

Once inside and past the two stalwart policemen, who stood like buttresses at the foot of the stairs, Carteret found himself in an enormous room that was choked with men and women. It appeared to stretch back a hundred feet to something like a platform where four or five musicians were going through the motions with their instruments, the sounds of which were lost in the din of the place, and where a number of people had climbed to shout and gesticulate to their fellows in the crowd. The ceiling of the place was very low and dirty, and it had sagged on one side, as if the duties of the storehouse had subjected it to a great strain at some time, with cotton and tobacco.

The inevitable barroom was hidden from sight by a throng of clamorous men and women who were singing, quarreling and gesticulating.

In the centre of the room was some kind of a dance going on, as could be seen by the bobbing figures, and the inner circle was watching them.

The outer mass was heaving about in a dense whirl. Familiar as Carteret was with city life, he had never come face to face with anything so multitudinously reeking and riotous as this. He stood for a moment near the door surveying the scene with Wilder. He saw at a glance that into this cesspool had drained all the worst elements of city life. He looked into the gin-soaked faces of the women with something like a shudder and remarked the stolid, leering, treacherous countenances of the men. The language of both sexes was the kind that knows no restraint without a muzzle. Much of it struck the ordinary sense with its unbridled obscenity and blasphemy, and the vocabulary was copious. Men, half intoxicated, were mingling with black and white wenches, no more sober than themselves. Open traffic of lust went on, interrupted by the hilarity of quarrels of others. Occasionally there were screams from some part of the dense company, and there would be a visible movement of the throng in that direction. The two policemen would prick their ears mechanically and grasp their truncheons, but a gust of laughter coming after indicated that the occurence, whatever it was, had taken the direction of comedy rather than tragedy.

Wilder had worked himself through the crowd with the intention of reaching the platform from which he could get a survey of the faces. He had got as far as the edge of the dancing circle, and saw that a party of Jack Tars had recklessly captured the best-looking women couples, and were pulling them round in a waltz, while the crowd jeered and taunted them. He knew from the situation that it would end in a fight, and, looking back to see where Cartaret was, he hurried on through the crowd toward the platform. It was at that moment that he became instinctively aware that some one was following him. There was an overturned chair in his way and he stepped suddenly upon it and looked back. As he did so, he saw, or thought he saw, the face of the man he had met at Leary's. A pair of wild, grey eyes were fixed upon him in the crowd, and the moment the man saw Wilder looking at him, he ducked his head. As if struck by a sudden suspicion, Wilder then jumped from the chair and made his way with a new determination to gain the platform. He had scarcely reached it when a wild yell went up in the middle of the hall, and the rhythmic dance was drowned in the confused stamping of feet and the shouts of enraged men. Someone had been stabbed. The musicians had ceased playing and were standing up staring into the *melee*, and men and women were climbing upon the platform for safety.

Jumping upon it himself, Wilder looked over the scene with his quick eye. In a moment the whole assemblage had been turned into riot and panic. He saw that the 'longshoremen and Dry Dock gang had fallen upon the sailors and that a desperate fight was going on in the middle of the room. He heard the catcalls of The Katy-dids all around the hall, saw that the 'longshoremen were fighting in a murderous manner with their short cotton hooks and that the sailors had knives. It was an indiscriminating and desperate affray, in which men were turned into wild beasts and women fought like tigers. While standing thus, probably not more than a minute, he saw a man pointing toward him from the crowd and beckoning to some one at a little distance. He even heard a gruff voice say, "There he is," and saw the desperate efforts of several men to get to the platform in obedience to the fellow's information. At such a moment a man thinks very rapidly and some truths, not before suspected, flash upon the mind. Wilder, who was a brave, cool-headed man, set his teeth, jumped from the platform and began fighting and pushing his way through the crowd toward the entrance with the certain knowledge that at least half a score of men were doing the same thing in pursuit of him. He heard above the hellish din of the place the signals of the gang passing all round the room. By fighting, dodging, and at times almost crawling, he got well round the hall toward the door, reaching that part of the room where the ceiling sagged lowest and had been propped at some time by an additional post. What was his surprise to see in the midst of this pandemonium of excitement that a man with an axe was endeavoring to chop this post away. Wilder was quick, skillful, sinewy and not unfamiliar with crowds. Once, indeed, he had to draw his pistol and thrust it down the throat of an open-mouthed ruffian who caught him by the arm, and once a blow was directed at him from some unseen fist that nearly knocked him off his feet.

Just as he had reached this corner of the room he was struck by a heavy bottle in the grip of a brawny arm that reached over the heads of the crowd. The blow fell slantingly upon his temple and stunned him slightly. He staggered a little, but by a powerful effort of his will, retained both his feet and consciousness. He knew perfectly well now that he would have to fight for his life, for he was in a trap and more than one desperate outlaw was there to kill him and take the benefit of the general *melee* which they had probably precipitated for this purpose. He glanced quickly about. There was no use trying to reach the front entrance. The police would be there in force presently. If he used his pistol, its report would concentrate the vengeance of the immediate crowd upon him. He was hemmed in on three sides. The way back to the platform was comparatively open. With a sudden and irresistible plunge he turned and threw himself with all the celerity and force of desperation against two men who blocked the way in that direction. One of them fell headlong and Wilder leaped through the gap like a cougar. For a minute it was a hand to hand fight, but he reached the edge of the platform. In front of him and standing on this platform was a great raw-boned, herculean man in his shirt sleeves. In his hands he held the neck of a bass viol that had been smashed to pieces. It was an efficient club and the fellow leaned forward with it as if waiting to use it on the heads of the men below. Wilder's first impulse, as a last desperate resource, as he encountered this new obstacle, was to shoot the man, spring upon the platform if possible, and keep his pursuers at bay with his weapon until the police arrived. He put his hand upon his pistol and the man shouted to him above the din, "Here, come up here. What are you thinking about? Quick!" and he actually extended a hand to him. Wilder seized it and partly leaped and was partly dragged up, the bludgeon in the hand of the man falling with a sharp splintering sound upon the head of the ruffian who was nearest in pursuit.

"Now, then," said the fellow, "be quick—this way. I'll get you out. They want your life."

The platform was full of men and women, and the man dove into the crowd followed by Wilder. They reached its other extremity where there were three steps and at the bottom a little door in the wall through which those most familiar with the place and anxious to escape were crowding in a noisy jam.

Wilder's new guide was neither considerate nor slow. He pushed his way over every obstacle, thrust Wilder ahead of him into the doorway and held the crowd back while he entered.

On the other side was a dirty little room looking like a cellar way and heaped with broken chairs and lumber. Thirty feet away there was the dingy light coming down from the side street. In less than a minute they were on the sidewalk. Wilder turned to the man and asked, "Who are you?"

"I'm Dan Sully, and I want to tell you something. Your name's Wilder, ain't it?"

"Yes. Don't stand here."

Wilder then started for the front of the building, followed by his new friend. He was chiefly anxious at this moment about Carteret, but when he got to the entrance of the cave he found that a battalion of police had possession of the hall, and after some little searching, he picked up Carteret considerably disarranged, but unhurt.

As they hurried back to the vehicle, Carteret allowed his disgust, his disappointment and his bitterness to escape.

"Good God," he cried. "What a waste of time. What did we want to go to that hell-hole for? We've fooled away the precious hours and Miss Castleton may be out of our reach."

Wilder made no answer, and just as they were about to get into the coach, the man who had followed them put his hand on Wilder's shoulder.

"O, yes. I had forgotten you; come and see me in the morning, can't you? I want to talk to you," said Wilder. "I've got a job on hand now. Here—meet me at ten o'clock," and he gave him a card, "Good night."

"Get in quick," he said to Carteret.

A few moments later they were tearing up the First Avenue at headlong rate.

As Wilder did not volunteer any remarks, Carteret, after gnashing his teeth in silence for a few moments, broke out again:

"I don't see why you should be so taciturn," said he, "simply because you didn't find that skunk there. I never expected to find him."

"Mink," said Wilder, with a smile. "You need not mix his natural history up because you have lost your head. If we had found him there he could not be in the abduction business."

"And you think, because he was not there, he is in it?"

"I think," said Wilder, "that he was not there, because he has got a big job on hand that keeps him out of it, but I was not looking for him."

"No?"

"No. I was looking for the girl and I fell into a trap."

"You mean you walked into a trap, but you must have known all about the place before you searched. The only thing worth thinking about is that you did not find her."

"No, but I found something much more important."

"Did you? What was it? Why did you not tell me at once?"

"The girl had not been there, nor at Leary's."

"And that is what you call important! If you felt as I do, you would regard it as child's play."

"Perhaps it is, but a man has to be guided by the light he can get and perhaps I have got a little more than you think; I don't know."

"Then I wish to heaven you would turn it on; we have wasted the whole night; nothing is done, and I am crazy with disappointment. Damn it, man, put yourself in my place, every minute is eating my heart out."

"That whole business at the Boudoir was a stall," said Wilder. "Betsy never went to Leary's, nor to the Cave; she was told to steer me that way and her pals stood in with her, as we say, to get me up into that cellar; do you know what for?"

"I don't understand you," said Carteret, with his eyes very wide open. "How did she know you were looking for her?"

"She saw us from the stage at the Boudoir. They intended to kill me at that cellar; they were cocked and primed for it and the opportunity was a good one in that fracas, but it has not worked well, you see. The chances are the girl went straight to her room in O'Reardon's Terrace and I intend to take her there. That is my theory; it may be wrong, but I have to depend on off chances in this business. I suppose that you can see that the girl wouldn't have run away from us the way she did on a mere whim. She must have known something about what is going on, and to my mind had a hand in it. I think you ought to see, too, that they would not want to make away with me at this time, if there wasn't great danger of my interfering with something."

"And you expect to catch the girl tonight?"

"Well, I never go as far as expectations; I'm going to make a big try for it. Here we are now; stay in the coach, please, this time."

Wilder jumped out in front of O'Reardon's. The ordinarily noisy neighborhood was quiet now. Save the voice of some belated but jolly young man, in the distance, who was bawling "Dixey" at the top of his voice, there was scarcely a sound to be heard. The officer took a whistle from his pocket and blew as he stepped upon the sidewalk. It was five minutes before the patrolman responded to it and came up.

Carteret, who was looking out of the coach door, saw the two men in consultation and he heard Wilder say: "Keep your eye on the door and snatch her if she comes out." After which he went in at the open entrance and mounted the stairs.

There were no lights on the upper floors and Wilder ejaculated several forcible and inelegant remarks as he came in contact with trunks, wash-tubs and coal hods. Arriving at last at the fifth floor, he found the door he was in search of and struck several resounding raps upon it with his fist, sending an echo through the deserted passages. He had to repeat this operation several times and each time he did so, he flattened his ear quickly against the panel of the door and listened. Presently there was a stir inside and the glimmer of light, then a shrill woman's voice asked:

"What's the matter? What d'ye want this time o' night?"

"Open your door. I am an officer," said Wilder.

He heard some faint signs of trepidation and a rustle as if two persons were moving about and making motions in dumb show. Presently the same voice said with a slightly more constrained tone:

"Who are you looking for? I am here alone and can't let a man in."

"Open your door," said Wilder, "or I'll break it open," and again his ear was pressed to the panel.

"Holy Mary deliver us," said the voice. "Wait till I git me clothes on."

He was almost certain that he heard hurried whispering.

After a few monents' delay the door was unlocked and cautiously opened.

Wilder pressed himself gently but quickly inside to see an old woman with a red shawl over her head, from beneath which her gray hair in scanty disorder stuck out in all directions. She had placed the lamp upon a table and had her hands clasped ready, as he suspected, for the wringing.

"Where is Betsy?" he asked.

"The Lord knows, not me; she's not been in her bed these two nights. Shure it isn't Betsy yer wantin'?"

"Who's in that room?" asked Wilder, pointing to the only closed door of the several that were visible.

"Indade thin, 'tis me own bed-room and yer not the man to say Oi 'ud hev ehnyone in it."

"Very well, open it," said Wilder.

At this the old woman began to wring her hands and mutter and wail.

Wilder sat down and laid his arm across the little table by the side of the lamp.

"See here, old woman," he said, "if there is anybody else in that room I don't want to see who it is, but I'm not going away till I know Betsy is not there. Let her come out, I want to talk to her."

A fresh outburst of lamentation was the only response she made, but while she was wailing and wringing her hands, the door of the room opened cautiously and Betsy appeared. She stepped out and carefully closed the door behind her.

"Stop yer yowlin!" she said to the old woman with an assumption of bravado. "What d'ye want to lie fur?"

Wilder looked at her calmly a moment.

"Well, young woman," he said, "you've been in some pretty bad jobs, but I didn't think you'd mix yourself up in an out-and-out murder."

"What?" exclaimed Betsy. "You don't mean it?" and she started forward with her hands up.

"Don't you know it—don't you know what they've done? Young woman, you're in for it this time, and no mistake."

"Yer don't mean they—I don't know what yer talkin' about."

"Well, I just mean they've done it; that is what I'm talking about. I wouldn't have believed you'd have tripped yourself in an out-and-out hanging scrape. I've come for you this time because you wasn't smart enough to get me out of the way—Leary's didn't work. Now just put your hat on nicely and quietly. I've got two men at the door below and we needn't wake anybody up."

She was staring at him eagerly and confusedly. "Murder," she repeated several times; "did they murder her?"

Wilder smiled. "You had better read the papers in the morning," he said.

"Well, I didn't hev nothin' to do wi' it, I swear I didn't.

"Granny," she said, turning to the old woman who was wringing her hands in speechless misery and wonder; "I swore ef they touched a hair of her head, I'd blow the whole gang—I did, I did."

"If you didn't have anything to do with it, you'd better make a clean breast of the whole thing to me," remarked Wilder. "Out with the whole of it and mebbe I can befriend you before you get there. There's nothing like looking out for your own interest in such a bad scrape as this. Now, then, was McCune in it?"

"No, he wasn't; I swear he wasn't. They told me they didn't want to hurt her; they only wanted to find out suthin'."

"Yes, they wanted to find out where the cup was. You piped it to the house in Fifteenth Street and tried to trap Carteret to the Boudoir."

"I'll take me oath I dunno—killed her, well, I'm—Curly said they only wanted to hev her show 'em where 'twas."

"Curly, was it, took her?"

"Yes, I rode up to the Boulevard an' he took her. I hope I may die ef I know enny more. Oh Lord, O Lord, she was sich a sweet un."

Then she sat down and began to sway herself, holding her head in her hands as if to help her comprehension of it.

"I didn't go fur to do ennything as bad as that, I didn't." Then she began to cry.

"No, I don't believe you are as bad as that, Betsy," said Wilder; "but you gave me that steer to Leary's. Now, then, who put you up to that?"

She made no answer for sometime, but kept on sobbing, and finally the old woman broke in:

"'Tis all that old Jew who's made the trouble. She's not had a day's honesty since he took to paying her. O Lord, O Lord, what'll become of us now?"

"Get your hat on," said Wilder, "and be lively; you'll have to come along, but if you behave yourself I'll stand your friend."

"Indade, sir," said the old woman, "she's as good a girl as the best of them, ef they would only let her alone; she is, now, and wouldn't go for to do sich a thing, no she wouldn't." Then both of them joined in a wailing chorus, Betsy mechanically getting her things together as she snivelled and protested. She had to go into the little room to complete her attire, and she pulled the door carefully after her. When she came out with her hat on, Wilder got up and before either of them could interfere, he had opened the door of the little room and looked in. It was empty. A moment later they were going down the dark stairs, Betsy's gasps sounding at intervals as they made their way to the street.

Carteret was asked to get up with the driver, and then they rattled away; the vehicle making a strange clatter at that time of night.

Wilder drove straight to the Eighteenth Precinct Station House on Twenty-Second street near Second avenue, and after a few moments' consultation with Capt. John Cameron, left the girl in his keeping, saying he would make a charge against her when he came back, and asking him to keep the arrest off the blotter till he heard from him.

Carteret then got into the coach with Wilder and they both went to Mrs. Hannige's.

It was nearly two o'clock in the morning when they stood in the hallway and Mrs. Hannige, who had evidently been lying awake with anxiety to hear from them, came to her door on the landing and called down to Wilder, "Did you find Miss Castleton?"

To Carteret's amazement, Wilder, with something of a cheery voice replied: "Yes, I have found her; she will be home tomorrow'. Have you got a cold bite in your refrigerator?"

"There's some cold duck and some cold meat pie," replied Mrs. Hannige, in a hoarse whisper. "If you want ale, you'll have to go into the cellar—don't forget to shut the refrigerator."

"What are you going to do?" asked Carteret.

"Get something to eat," said Wilder. "I'm as empty as a dime novel."

Carteret went into the little dining room, sat down and waited for Wilder, who was heard below, knocking over bottles and making considerably more disturbance than was usual at that time of night. Presently he came up with a dish in his hand and a bottle under each arm. Placing the cold duck upon the table, he proceeded to extemporize a lunch with utter indifference to Carteret's anxiety and impatience, which could not long be restrained, for he burst out with:

"What the devil do you mean by saying you have found Miss Castleton? It seems to me, Wilder, that you are treating this awful subject with a levity that is almost disgraceful."

"Young man," replied Wilder, as he proceeded to carve the cold duck, "are you superstitious?"

"Hang superstition; what the devil are you driving at?"

"I am beginning to believe that I don't know myself. I believe that I am getting superstitious. Do you know that we have both escaped to-night with our lives by a hair's breadth? A conspiracy, broad and powerful, had determined upon putting us out of the way to-night, and we have escaped by the merest chance. Have a piece of this duck?"

"Why should any conspiracy want to get us out of the way? Yes, you must be getting superstitious."

"Well, you eat a piece of this duck, and you will begin to see things a little clearer. Let me give you some ale. You might as well eat, for you can't sleep, and I've not got anybody but you to talk to."

Wilder then filled a glass and pushed it towards his companion.

"I'm beginning," he said, "to feel that my head is turning. This cup has baffled me at every turn. I want some one to tell me how and why a cup of any kind can induce men to enter into conspiracies and risk their lives for its possession. That, my dear boy, is becoming the nightmare that never leaves me. In another fortnight, if I don't solve this riddle, I shall go to a lunatic asylum."

"What beats me is this, that you think more of the cup than you do of the life or honor of an innocent young girl," said Carteret.

"No, but the life and honor of an innocent young girl are only incidents in the mad pursuit of this cup. These people do not want Miss Castleton's beauty; they want to extract from her by threats some knowledge of the whereabouts of that goblet; she will have told them before this, and is probably now sleeping quietly in her bed at Scarsdale. Drink your ale."

CHAPTER XXXIII.

MR. MANSER OPENS THE WATER GATE.

When Mr. Manser got word that he was to let the water out of his upper section of the acqueduct, he knew that the superintendent of the Croton board would be coming along for an inspection, and for several days he assumed an unwonted air of authority over the two hands, and even put on an extra dignity with Mrs. Manser. The place had to be cleaned up, the gate house whitewashed, the paths cleaned, the iron work oiled, and the roadway straightened; for every keeper on the forty miles of water way knew that keen eyes would note everything, and written reports would be made to the board.

It was a warm, bright morning, and Mr. Manser was down at the gate house with his men. The sun was pretty well up, and it was probably eleven o'clock, for the long green shadow of the aqueduct had crept up close to the stone work and almost disappeared.

Mr. Evans was alone on the little porch, with a newspaper on his knees. The drone of the locust and the drowsy air had proved too much for him, and he had gone to sleep. But his kindly old face wore an expression of anxiety, in spite of his peaceful nap. The house appeared to be deserted. All was as still and secure as if that spell could keep away danger as well as annoyance.

Away off, down the long curved level of the great green bank, and just where a white wagon-gate marked the intersection of a country road, two men were standing, one of them leaning on the stile, and both of them looking up the road to where Mr. Manser's house shown modestly through the larches that grew-on the flat reaches that lined the aqueduct. One of the men was stout, heavy jawed, short necked, and wore a slouched hat, from beneath which flat, black curls projected. The other was younger and slighter. His figure gave you an idea of litheness, and his face, save that his nose had been flattened by a blow, was not unlike a terrier's in its alertness. Both men were roughly but not suspiciously dressed. The heavier of the two wore a gray surtout, and the other a rather heavy jacket. Their clothes were dust soiled, and the younger had turned the bottom of his trousers up over his hob-nailed shoes.

"That's the bower, sure," said the latter, in a sharp voice. "It don't swarm. 'Taint worth waiting till dark for."

"Waiting?" said the other, who had his heavy jaw down on the rail of the fence and was contemplating the prospect. "I don't wait till dark round no sich place as this."

"That *would* be lonesome," said his companion, looking about him. "I'll flip yer who beggers 'em."

The other did not remove his head from the rail or turn round, though his companion took a coin from his pocket and, after tossing it in the air, caught it in his hand and covered it with the other palm.

"How many of them, do you think?"

"Two," answered his companion, "an' they're in the bush."

"An' one old woman?"

"That's what they said."

"I'll work the vet dodge on 'em and see how the coop looks inside. You ken sneak the bush on the side. If I git into ther room, I'll chuck the mug to yer. If I don't, I'll ketch yer in the clump down there." And he pointed to a dense portion of the timber on the other side of the aqueduct.

His companion gave the penny another toss into the air, put it back into his pocket unconcernedly and said;

"The dogs'll spring yer if yer work the path, better wade in the trees."

These men, who had evidently been on many similar expeditions, and had always carried their lives in their hands, were curiously reticent in making their arrangements. A few grunted sentences and they appeared to understand each other perfectly. Having arrived at a clear knowledge of what they were to do, and what share each was to take in the transaction one of them whistled and took off his shoe to empty the gravel that had evidently annoyed him, and that declared the length of their journey, the other said gruffly, "Does she go?" To which his companion somewhat mechanically, as if he had gone though the ceremony often before, replied:

"She goes. Two stiffs but no blab." A form of pledge which in ordinary English would be, "Both of us may get kilted but we do not betray each other."

Then one of them produced a flask, they took a drink, shook hands, and slowly started down the slope that led to the timber on the east of the aqueduct.

They had the cunning if not the woodcraft of Indians, and picked their way slowly and carefully though the grove with their senses alert. The attempt to reach the vicinity of the house without arousing any dogs that might be on the place and that would be sure to attract the attention of the men, was successful. They appeared to know that a dog lying upon the ground can detect the vibration of a footfall that is started at an incredible distance, for they put their feet down as softly as if they had worn moccasins and avoided as much as possible the dried leaves. Stealthily crawling along in this manner, they came to the gentle declivity of the green aqueduct where it has not yet entered the valley far enough to show stone-work, and both men got down upon their knees and climbed slowly to the top, where their heads just showed though the dried grass of the level.

Not twenty feet away from them was the east side of the house, and they could not, of course see, Mr. Evans asleep on the little south porch. The Virginia creeper, now scarlet and russet, still hung in flaming festoons from the eaves. A riotous locust was strumming clamorously, and the chintz curtain in an upper chamber window, moved lazily out and in with the soft breeze.

The younger of the two men, after they had cautiously surveyed the scene for a moment, lifted his hand and pointing to the window, said with a whispered oath:

"By—Curley, look at that."

They were so close to the house that when the wind lifted the curtain, they could see into the room, which was apparently lit by an open door or window on the opposite side, and the swaying curtain was not more than fifteen feet from the ground.

"There's the bloody skillet on the shelf. I cud skin up the vines and lift it; if I couldn't I'm d—d."

And this was true, for as the curtain was lifted by a puff of wind, they both saw the silver goblet standing on the end of the little mantel, close to the window.

The eldest of the two men was much the coolest. He made no answer, but got upon his feet, and walking deliberately out upon the level that surrounded the house, listened a moment and then went slowly to the front and passed out of his companion's sight.

The moment he turned the corner of the house, he saw Mr. Evans and stopped, for the old man had put the newspaper over his head and face. In another moment he was assured that the man was asleep; he then went slowly up to the open door and rapped with his knuckles on the casing, peering at the same time into the empty hallway. There was no response and he stepped inside cautiously and listened. On one side of the hall was the open door of Mrs. Manser's parlor, with its two pink china dogs on the rug, facing him. From that room opened another door that led to the dining room, and beyond was the kitchen. As he listened, he heard the sound of crockery, as if some one had struck a plate, and he knew that the kitchen was occupied, Then he rapped on the parlor door and waited a moment. The sounds from the kitchen continued at intervals. He shrewdly suspected that there were not very young ears in the vicinity, or they would have heard his rap. He stepped into the parlor. A sketching easel stood near the window with one of Carteret's unfinished landscapes on it. A wide-brimmed gypsy hat, trimmed with pink ribbons, hung carelessly on its top and a bunch of dried grasses was stuck in one of the peg holes at the side. He went slowly towards the dining room door and again listened. Some one was moving softly about in the little kitchen. There was an oldfashioned sideboard in the dining room, and standing on it were two bottles of old Bourbon whiskey that Carteret had given to Mr. Manser. One of them had never been opened. The window in the room looked out through the vines upon the bank where The Mink was hidden. The thief, as he now stood, reflected that if he waited a moment, the person who was in the kitchen and probably at work there, would in the course of her duties, pass the opening and he would see her. In this he was quite correct, for a moment later, Mrs. Manser in a clean white apron, with her sleeves rolled up and her spectacles on her nose, came plainly and unsuspectingly into view. In one hand she held a fowl by the legs. Her other hand was covered with flour paste. He knew then that she was dressing a chicken and preparing a meal, a task she was not likely to assume if she had any help. With that he edged away, got back into the hall, listened an instant and said to himself: "if there's a maid up there, I'll chance it and mebbe she'll git choked." He then went quickly and lightly up the stairs.

In this humble and honest home, where the family had never been disturbed by tramps, and the doors were scarcely locked at night, everything was open and unprotected. Manuella's chamber door stood wide, and the moment he reached the upper hall, he saw the cup. It was but a moment's work to glide into the room, seize it, and leaning cautiously out the window, to toss it to The Mink who caught it dexterously in the grass. The whole operation scarcely consumed a minute, and the man then slipped down the stairs as rapidly as he had come up. So far everything had been in his favor. But it was just like him "to push his luck" as he would himself have phrased it. He remembered the bottles of whiskey on the sideboard, and the apparent desertion of the house to an old woman, led him to believe that he could capture that prize also without risk. It was the temptation and the decision, as the reader will see presently, that brought the whole scheme to naught. He was thirsty and reckless and so he went back to the dining room, He encountered no one. The window was open. He seized the bottle of whiskey by the neck and looking for a soft place in the grass, he threw it out and then left the house as he came. He got round to the side, found the bottle unbroken in the dried grass, and as he picked it up and went off down the slope, he gave vent to a series of chuckles. Once or twice he broke out in rough exclamations, as if his feelings were too much for him. "Why then, a wench could a' done it. Damn my eyes if I don't feel ashamed o' the job; I'll be agoin' out to hair dressin', I do believe, afore that old hook-nose gits through with me. If it wasn't fur this rum, damn me, I'd write to the old snag and make him apologize."

The distance from the aqueduct house to the little river at the bottom of the valley was probably not more than three thousand feet, but the slope was wild, uneven, and densely wooded, save where the trees had been cut out sparsely by Mr. Manser for fire wood. In places the sassafras and dogwood made an almost impassable jungle, and in others the dry water courses, where the stream of surface water had come rolling down during the heavy rains had bared the shale and lime-stone in smooth patches. Curly Samson had not gone very far into the thicket before he found The Mink waiting for him, partly concealed behind the trunk of a heavy chestnut tree, and hugging the cup under his coat.

He was evidently impatient to get away, for he said to his advancing companion, who was taking it very easy, "there ain't no good stayin' here now, is ther'? Yer don't want to hang round till they invite yer to dinner, do yer?"

"What in — do we want to hurry from?" asked the other. "I ain't seen nothin' to hurry from. I'll go back, I b'leeve, and get that tother bottle." And he held up his prize to the surprise and delight of The Mink. "Nobody's got no hard feelin's to us, my bloomin' sweetheart, 'cos nobody ain't sot eyes on us. If yer'll wait a few minits we'll have the family a comin' down to thank us for liftin' the bloody mug. They won't know it's gone till ther' gal comes back."

"Where did yer swipe that?" asked The Mink, regarding the bottle, which the other held up in plain sight.

"Present, so help me, fer takin' the mug. Would yer kindly haccept this same, says the governor, fer takin' the blessed mug out of this? Would I, says I, well yer just make it a bottle every time, says I, and I'll take the blessed roof off yer heads, if I don't I'm —."

Then both the men laughed coarsely, and Samson began digging the cork out of the bottle with a jack knife.

The ground over which they had come was rough and thickly overgrown, and the spot at which they met could not have been more than fifty feet from the Pocantico, but the intervening space was a dense mass of underbrush and tangles, wiry vines and saplings. Samson, who had succeeded in partly extracting and partly inserting the cork of the bottle, had put the liquor to his lips and said, with an unprintable oath: "Take ther mug and fetch some water, we can finish ther bottle better on our backs."

He looked around; the thicket closed them in; an old water course, dry and grass grown, showed a few green bowlders. A flat surface of lime-stone, dry and smooth, invited them to a platform that was free from the bush. Behind it rose a little precipice, six or eight feet high, on the top of which the dried grasses and the scarlet sumach made a heavy curtain. Samson sat down on the flat stone with his back against the rock and the bottle between his legs. The Mink objected.

"Come on," he said, "we can finish it on the road. Yer doan't want to stay round here."

"Yes, I do, too," replied Samson; "if yer'll squat here, I'll go back and lift a roast chicken. There ain't no good in standin' round here starvin', is ther? A workin' man's got the right to a little peace an' comfort—fill yer mug, I want ter chin yer."

The Mink looked at him a moment, disapprovingly, but he appeared to be in the habit of obeying him. So he leisurely went down along the line of bowlders to the stream, filled the cup with water and came back.

"Say," said Samson, when he had returned, and had placed the cup on the flat rock, "what do yer make out ther d—d thing to be?" and he pointed the bottle at the silver flagon, curiously glistering with the water, and presenting a silver contrast to the gray wilderness of the surroundings. "You've been on the lay longer'n me. What's it worth?"

"O, kill me, if I ever got it dead to rights," answered The Mink. "Pass ther rum?"

"What's it worth to us?"

"O, shoot that. We can't do no business agin' old Beaky."

"Why can't we?"

"Give me a swig, how in — do yer expect me to be doin' business if yer doan't start square?"

"Who's a goin' to stop us if it doan't go back?"

The man thus appealed to put the bottle to his lips, took several swallows of the liquor, and replied,

"You allers wuz too d—d anxious fur yer own good. Now yer'd smash yer head agin ther old man. It's no good. I'm tellin' yer and I know him."

"O, he ain't such a blazin' d—d fool as to smash anything when he ken pay fer it. We've just got the dead grip, old man, don't yer go fer to ferget it."

The Mink shook his head disapprovingly. He understood perfectly well what was passing in the mind of his pal. Something of the same sort must have passed through his own at moments of temptation. Aware, as they both were that some kind of mysterious value attached to the cup, and that two parties were scheming and conspiring for possession of it, it was only natural to a character like Samson's, that having the property in his hand, he should begin to consider which party would pay the most for it. Instinctively, The Mink seized upon his thought and met it with an unexpected protest.

"You're too anxious, that's what yer are. I allers told yer. You an' me doan't want that d—d thing. Coz why? It's unlucky. Ther' bloody thing's cursed."

"Well, may I be —," said Samson, with a leer of unutterable contempt. "Come out ov a church, hey?"

"No," replied The Mink, "it come out ov a coffin."

The look of contempt on the face of the elder man melted into one of incredulity. "Out ov what?" he asked.

"Out ov a coffin. I wouldn't keep it over night fer a bank."

Samson continued to regard the cup for a moment with dull curiosity, then he returned to the subject that was uppermost in his mind.

"How much could we strike him for?"

"He ain't good at bein' struck."

"Cos he never had the right blokes ter work him," said Samson. "What's ther' use o' chuckin' off a big chance when we've got the dead twist, anyway? It ain't business."

"Look here, Curly," said The Mink, "you're pipin' the wrong idee, so help me you are. It'll turn our luck, or I'm a liar. Doan't yer chase that. There's more shadders' and ghosts round the burnin' mug than's healthy fur us."

"What kind er slob are yer talkin'?" asked Samson, whose stubbornness appeared to be intensified by the whiskey. "Yer ain't got no head fer a good turn. I allers said it."

"I ain't served as long at college as yer have yerself," said The Mink, "but I know 'nuff to keep out ov such devil's luck as that thing totes round—what's that?"

Both men listened. A peculiar sound was heard, not unlike a distant but steady gust of wind. They both looked up. Not a leaf stirred.

"It's a train," said Samson, and he rolled over on his stomach, carelessly, and regarded the cup. He took a heavy drink from the remaining stock of whiskey, and added, "What do yer say, old man, do we stick?"

Both men were looking in each other's faces, and there was an instant's pause. They were listening.

"What ther bloody hell is that, anyway?" said The Mink. The sound had grown nearer and louder, and it did not intermit as a breeze will. And the sense of something inscrutable and unseen, rushing steadily towards them, made both men pause with the guilty instinct of danger; and then as McCune, who had raised himself on his elbow, was staring about him, they both heard the rush of what seemed to be a winged host, and suddenly there leaped from the top of the little precipice under which they sat, a torrent of muddy water, with roar and splash and hiss, carrying with it stones and drift-wood and turf. Samson, who had his back to the rock, received the full blow. McCune, who had sprung up, partly escaped, and with his accustomed alertness, made a leap out of the torrent to the bank, and then seeing Samson floundering, confused and helpless, against the bushes at the foot of the flat rock where the water had swept him, he seized him with great difficulty, and pulled him upon the bank, where a moment later both men stood in ridiculous amazement, and both of them staring at the stream, now roaring with the violence of a cataract over the stones.

It was at least a minute before their astonishment had sufficiently subsided to allow them to think of their own affairs, and McCune was the first to speak.

"B—," he said with a start, "the mug."

It had been swept away, and there was now boiling and leaping through the trees a mad, noisy river that wet them with its spray as they stood there.

Both men simultaneously started on the jump, and with desperate haste hurried along the edge of the torrent, running against the trees, stumbling over the stones, entangling themselves in the vines and briars, and with equal desperation, if not equal dexterity, fighting their way down to the Pocantico in search of the cup.

But it was nowhere discernible in that swirl of angry waters. It was scarcely possible to get near enough to the torrent itself, which they now found was tumbling downward in a natural gully, and was shut in for the greater part of the way by an impenetrable thicket, to make the search thorough, but they worked resolutely and even recklessly for some time.

When they reached the Pocantico they found that usually lucid stream turbid and foam-covered. It was no longer possible to see what its contents might be.

For a moment they stood there looking at each other. McCune's face was scratched and bleeding and Samson's clothes were hanging in wet folds. As is the habit of such men when baffled, they both began to curse. Presently McCune had kicked off his shoes and was wading vainly about in the shallower pools of the river in the hope of finding the lost treasure with his feet. The water swept round him in little yellow whirlpools. He stèpped upon sharp stones, and emitted continuous blasphemy; he staggered about and finally falling down, scrambled and jumped back to the bank and gave up the attempt.

The cup was gone. Of that there was no longer any doubt. It had probably been swept into the Pocantico and how far down the stream it had gone, or how far it could go, they had no idea.

There was something grotesque in the baffled and angry expressions of the men. At intervals they looked back up the hill with speechless wonder, and then, unable even to guess by what unknown power water had been made to gush out of the dry earth, they fell to cursing again.

The explanation was simple enough.

Mr. Manser had opened the water gate in the aqueduct.

CHAPTER XXXIV.

OFFICER WILDER REACHES THE END OF HIS ROPE.

The next morning Carteret, at Wilder's suggestion, started for Scarsdale with instructions to telegraph immediately. He could not have lost any time, for at ten o'clock Wilder received a dispatch as follows: "Miss Castleton here. Scoundrels abducted her. Hunt them from the face of the earth. I will help you. The cup is stolen. You were right as to the men."

The officer, although not in a pleasant mood, smiled as he read this characteristic message. Then he sat with it in his hand for some time in a deep reverie.

The truth is, he was sore perplexed. The incidents of the night before staggered him a little. He could not fail to see that some lawless power was trying to get him out of the way. Turn it in every way he could, his conviction remained the same; that the only motive for this attempt was to prevent him from getting the cup. It had indeed occurred to him more than once that Mrs. Enniston might be at the bottom of the conspiracy, but he had dismissed the thought almost immediately. Whatever might be Mrs. Enniston's fears or foolishness, he did not think that she would resort to such extraordinary means merely to prevent a family scandal and he had seen and heard enough to convince him that she knew nothing about the mysterious cup beyond the fact that it had been stolen and had brought about a disagreeable scene with Job Ackerman and a letter from Mr. Evans. Every train of thought with its freight of experiences brought him somehow to Plonski and then there remained in his mind the one blank, unanswerable question—why does this man scruple at nothing to get possession of that cup? With what inscrutible value is it invested that money, brains and desperation insist on hunting it through violence and crime?

It was plain to him now that two of the vilest villains had been employed to abduct and frighten Miss Castleton into a confession of its whereabouts. He felt that her life would have been a small impediment had it stood in the way of their success, and that she had returned in safety was to him proof that they had no further use for her. The cup had at last fallen into the hands of the indomitable man who had schemed so long for its possession.

It was quite within the power of Wilder, on the basis of abduction, to put the machinery of the law in motion, send out a general alarm and take Samson and The Mink, if he acted at once, for they could hardly have reached the city yet in their roundabout and skulking method. But if he arrested them, would he secure the cup, and of what advantage would the conviction for abduction be? Would not such a step lead to just enough publicity to make all the principles in the game withdraw from sight? Above all things else this man disliked to give up his pursuit of the mystery for the sake of punishing a pair of worthless agents. He was conscious that under all these vulgar details of crime was some great animating purpose and it was that his professional pride urged him to keep in view, even if he missed one or two opportunities for incidental triumph.

So, after an hour's hard thinking, it suddenly occurred to him that he had told the man Sully to come and see him, and then as if a new idea had actuated him, he started off for the Central Office.

He had not been at headquarters ten minutes, before that brawny giant was brought in. Wilder looked the fellow over in his quick comprehensive way and beckoned to a chair.

"I understood you to say last night," he began at once, "that you knew there was to be an assault made on me. How did you know it?"

"Well, boss," said Sully, "That's some'at that I can't tell yer in a second. Yer see, I'm a coke shoveller in the gas works and most of our men belong to the new ward s'cieties that are agin' the Government and I had a row there one night and got set on by the whole gang, cause I wasn't agin the Government They took the wind o' me what with their hands and their fists. I was broke to pieces and somebody carried me over to the Terrace in Nineteenth street—you might know it—where I was dumped into a room as was empty. I was there on my back for three days, and I heard some o' the gang in the other room puttin' up the job without knowin' me near—to get you out o' the way. That's it for short."

"Who took you to the Terrace?" asked Wilder.

"A mate o' mine who's foreman o' the shovellers."

"What's his name?"

"Sitwhite. He had a room."

"A front room?"

"Yes. There was a bed in the closet. I guess the gang must 'a' hired the room before and didn't know Sit had put me in the closet."

"Do you know who the persons were that came there?"

"Only two of Rem. One of the parties lives in the house, t'other one was Big Casey, as hit me with a shoe. I heerd Rem talkin' and all I could make out was that somebody had put Rem up to kill an officer at the Dry Dock Cave and I says to myself, I'll go there and see it if my jaw gets well."

Wilder listened to this with intelligent interest. He was not slow to see what it all meant and by dint of questioning he arrived at the conclusion that Plonski had let these men meet there unaware that Sitwhite had put the wounded man in the small room, and fortunately they had not looked into it and discovered him. But no cross-questioning could elicit any information as to why they wanted to kill Wilder, and his inference was that Plonski had made the men believe that the officer was inimical to their schemes, thus hoping to get rid of him. And even as he drew this conclusion, he acknowledged to himself that it seemed very farfetched, for why should a man go so far out of his way and adopt such a deep laid scheme to be rid of what was a mere hindrance or annoyance?

What perhaps astounded him more than anything else was to learn that Plonski had been at that anti-war meeting, for Wilder made the man describe all the men on the platform and all that took place, and he did not fail to recognize Judge Sanger and Plonski. From all that he could gather, he made up his mind that Plonski was in some way dabbling in the dangerous elements that the war evoked and he saw that the man Sully was an honest, illiterate fellow who placed no credence in the noise of the mischief-makers, and it occurred to him that he could use him to good advantage. The man had a simple, blunt admiration for the United States, although he was an Englishman, and a certain stolid shrewdness that was unmistakable.

"I'll tell you what it is, my man," Wilder finally said, "you have done me a good turn and I may be able to do you one."

The moment Sully was gone, Wilder went to the department telegraph office and in ten minutes a score of messages were flying over Westchester county. When he had completed the task, he went straight to the office of Burton & Dunn. He walked into the inner sanctuary where Mr. Albert Burton was sitting in his heavy chair and closing the door behind him, deliberately sat himself down in front of the expectant but undisturbed lawyer.

Mr. Burton was scrupulously dressed, his white shirt front was singularly calm and expansive and the musk-pink in his button-hole was dewy and fresh. He had a reflective habit in the court room of taking this flower from his coat and sniffing at it in moments of the keenest forensic eloquence.

"Well, Wilder," that gentleman said, "something unusual, eh?"

"Very," replied Wilder, "the most unusual of my experience."

"Murder?"

"Yes, and everything else. The fact is, Mr. Burton, I come to you because I am at my wits end. To use a Western expression, I've bitten off more than I can chew."

"We all do at times," said Mr. Burton invitingly. "What kind of a case is it?"

"It will take an hour to state it runningly. Have you got the time?"

"Is it worth it?"

"Yes, I think you will say it is. I confess myself utterly baffled and completely mystified. Besides the secret grows in magnitude at such a rate that it is necessary I should have a confidant."

"Very well. State the case. My faith in your judgment of such matters makes me anxious to hear what has baffled you."

Mr. John Wilder then began a narration of all the events given to the reader of which he was cognizant, beginning with the advertisement cut from the

Herald and ending with the interview with Sully. It was broken only at one place and that was by Mr. Burton's exclamation of astonishment and dismay when he heard that Ol Enniston had been murdered in his own shrubbery. After that he preserved a placid listening attention, occasionally asking a pertinent question to make some minor point clear to his legal mind. When the narrative was concluded Wilder said:

"Now Mr. Burton, the magnitude of this conspiracy has not baffled me so much as the mystery. I am confronted with some kind of a human motive of which I am ignorant and that motive is associated with a cup. I have exhausted my inventive faculty in trying to find a theory that will explain the value of the cup and warrant such indefatigable labors and such vast operations as this man Plonski is carrying on to secure it."

"It is," said Mr. Burton, "the most extraordinary case that I ever heard of in the whole course of my professional experience. I know of nothing like it. I cannot help feeling that a great deal of it is romance."

This nettled Wilder, who instantly said, "Pardon me Mr. Burton, but you ought to know me too well to say that. I am not given to romance and I have told you only the facts that came under my own eye."

"Very extraordinary—very—very extraordinary," repeated Mr. Burton, sniffing at his flower absent-mindedly and not heeding Wilder's little show of annoyance. "Doesn't fit into our times at all." Then he fell to cross-questioning his visitor who stood the examination heroically and with marvelous patience, answering every inquiry with day and hour and making explicit and pointed explanations. It all ended by Mr. Burton saying once more, "Very extraordinary this, Mr. Wilder. Now then, what do you want me to do? Join in this preposterous hunt?"

"I should like," replied Wilder, "to have you explain in some way how a cup can be worth all this trouble. To do it requires a range and kind of knowledge that I have not got. I am going to have that cup if it is on top the earth, but it would help me out prodigiously if I had a working theory."

"Well, I'll tell you," said Burton, "there is one aspect of your case that interests me deeply and it is the political side. If this man Plonski is an active agent in stirring up the ignorant populace against the Government, I mean to circumvent him. The citizens' committee of safety has just been organized and I am a member of it. It is our purpose to prevent such firebrands as Judge Sanger and his tools from making too much of a conflagration in the rear of the Government. It is just possible that our purpose and yours can be joined. I wish you'd bring that man Sully to me. He's just the fellow the committee can use."

Wilder got up. He was a little disappointed. It looked as if Mr. Burton only cared for one feature of the affair and took little interest in the extraordinary cup.

"I'll come and see you again in the course of a fortnight," he said; "if I hear anything that will help the committee, I'll let you know."

"Rubbish," said Mr. Burton "you will come here to-morrow at three o'clock sharp, without fail, and I will give you a theory about the cup. You don't expect me to jump at such a case on the instant, do you? Let me sleep over it. I always do over every good case, and I tell you again this is the most extraordinary tangle of circumstances I ever heard of. Meanwhile my dear fellow, don't let that man Sully out of your sight."

John Wilder knew perfectly well that Mr. Burton was one of the ablest men in his profession. Scholar, jurist, analyist, philosopher, and patriot, he felt sure that once interested in this mystery, he would bring to it a knowledge and a sagacity far broader and maturer than his own. He therefore said as he left him, "You are the only person that I have confided in and I shall be guided hereafter by your advice. I hope you will think it all over and give me the benefit of your conclusions."

"I will, John, I will," said Mr. Burton, who shook hands with the officer at the door. "By the way, are you sure that woman died in the Philadelphia Hospital?"

"She was dying when I saw her," replied Wilder, somewhat astonished at the question. "One of the doctors from her ward was at the post mortem of officer Sergeant Odell the next day and he told me she was dead. He was going South to join a yellow fever brigade of physicians and stopped at the inquest on his way."

"You don't remember his name?"

"Yes, I do; it was Calhoun—Archibald Calhoun."

"Humph," said Mr. Burton, "try and look in to-morrow about three. I shall be in court all the morning."

With that they separated.

Wilder found half a score of telegrams waiting for him at headquarters. They were from the local constables in Westchester, who were watching the stations on the Hudson river and New Haven railroads and the general tenor of them was, "Your men have not shipped here. Cannot pass without our knowing it."

Wilder then took an official map of Westchester county which had all the highways marked on it and studied it carefully. Then as if he had reached the only conclusion possible, he got two of the best men in the special service and set out to run Plonski down with the conviction that the cup had not yet reached him and that by getting between him and his agents, he could intercept it.

Not half an hour had elapsed before he was at the Eighteenth Precinct Station House in search of Clianthe.

To his astonishment he found that she had been released. The only explanation offered him by the sergeant was that orders from headquarters demanded it and the captain had to obey them.

When Wilder tried to learn who had sent the order, the sargeant said good humoredly, "It's no use, John. We let you have a pretty good margin in detaining people who are not on the blotter, but when they have a pull at headquarters, we've got to stick to the letter of the law."

"You don't mean to say that girl has a pull?"

"I mean to say that a message was received here early this morning from one of the commissioners, which said, 'If there is no charge against the girl brought in by officer Wilder, release her.' I don't see why you didn't make some kind of a charge if you wanted to hold her. We couldn't keep her with nothing agin her. You know that."

"Who is the commissioner?" asked Wilder.

A sly look stole over the Sargeant's face as he said, "O, now look here, John, you'd better see the captain. We can't go into that and I don't think you want to."

It was now clear to Wilder's mind that if he was to pursue this complicated and dangerous game, he must have sagacious legal advice. That Plonski had some kind of political influence was certain and Wilder knew that it would be folly to antagonize the Central Office. His discretion told him that in order to get at all the ramifications of this conspiracy, he must avoid a public charge and he felt that the proofs of Plonski's complicity in all the strange events were not yet strong enough. If he could arrest Plonski with the cup in his possession a definite purpose would be attained. To arrest him on a charge of conspiracy or even of abduction, would not necessarily result in the possession of the cup or the secret. Both would pass into the keeping of other people and Plonski would get the benefit of political influence in a trial in which he could suborne all kinds of witnesses.

It was therefore with a good deal of reluctance that Wilder made up his mind that at this stage of the game, discretion was much the better part of detective valor and that he would wait until he had got Mr. Burton's advice before precipitating matters. Meanwhile he would, if possible, keep Plonski under the closest surveillance. The only immediate interference with this sagacious scheme that he anticipated, was from the rash Mr. Carteret who would in all probability insist upon a prosecution of the men implicated in the abduction.

For the next twenty-four hours Mr. Wilder's perplexity and anxiety were not at all lessened. He received a note from Mr. Burton making an apology for not being able to keep his appointment owing to his having been called out of town, and Wilder somehow received the impression from the tenor of the note, that Mr. Burton was making excuses for a want of interest in the case. It is true the letter said that he would expect to see Wilder at the end of the week, but to Wilder's mind this looked like an evasion.

To add to the annoyance this occasioned him was the fact that he could not discover the slightest trace of Plonski nor of his agents, The Mink and Samson.

CHAPTER XXXV.

O, COLIN, COLIN, THIS IS NOT LIKE YOU.

Colin Carteret arrived at the gate house early in the forenoon very impatient and very nervous. Mr. Evans had just come out and taken his accustomed seat on the little south porch. His pleasant and cordial greeting of the young man betrayed none of the anxiety which a knowledge of all the recent circumstances must have occasioned and Carteret knew instinctively that these circumstances had been kept from him.

But it was very different with Mrs. Manser, who drew the young man into the kitchen, closed the door and with awe and suppressed eagerness in her voice and face, proceeded at once to treat the subject with all the importance that it assumed in her uneventful life.

"Did you ever in all your life hear of such a thing?" she began. "Why I wouldn't have believed it possible. It is just dreadful, Mr. Carteret."

"Yes, yes," said Carteret; "but Miss Castleton—where is the young lady? Have you heard from her?"

"Why, yes. She is in her bed this blessed minute if she has not got up, and I asked her not to, because she was that shaken up, but it's just like her to pay no sort of attention to me. I'll go up and tell her you've come. She'll be relieved, I know."

"Yes, do," said Carteret, "I want to see her at once. It's a highhanded piece of business. You're quite right. There go along and tell her I'm here. When did she get back?"

"She came home yesterday afternoon, poor thing," said Mrs. Manser, as she cautiously opened the door. "I hope to gracious, Mr. Carteret, you don't think it was my fault. If I thought—"

"O no," replied Carteret, gently pushing her out of the door. "Let her know I am here safe and sound and want to see her at once."

Anxious as Miss Castleton was to see Carteret, she managed to keep him waiting some time while she stood at her mirror and went through an elaborate process, trying to eradicate all traces of her fall in the street. When at last he rushed up the stairs, she met him at the door of Mrs. Manser's room exclaiming, "O, how glad I am that you have come."

"The danger's all over my darling," exclaimed Carteret as he caught hold of her endearingly.

"Yes," she said. "I hope so, but it isn't that. The old people here do not know. I did not tell them. They would not understand the mystery about the cup and our entanglement with it, so I did not tell them anything except that I was detained and maltreated by ruffians and excaped."

"Very well, you have escaped, that is the main thing," and taking her face in his hands, he saw the marks on her temple and cheek that had been caused by the New York cobble stones.

"Heavens," he exclaimed, "what did they do to you?"

"Nothing," she answered assuringly. "I was more frightened than hurt. I jumped from a conveyance and scratched myself. But, you know, the cup is gone. It was taken before I got here."

"I don't know anything," he said, "and I want you to tell me everything. I promise you never to rest until I have brought the miscreants to justice," and he kept looking at the scratches on her beautiful face with amazement and wonder.

Manuella then told him all the reader already knows, Carteret listening with many exclamations of indignation.

"Yesterday morning," she said, "the woman with whom I had been left, came and told me that the men were miscreants and that she was going to take me home. She got a buggy and drove me herself to the road that leads into this valley and left me. That is really all there is to it, and now that they have the cup, let us hope we shall never hear of them again. But I did want to see you so. It was all so strange and terrible to me and I could not tell Mrs. Manser."

"Why not?" asked the impulsive Carteret.

"Because, dear, don't you understand; it would be difficult to explain to her that the girl Clianthe had not been an associate of mine, and that there was not something wrong behind it all. She would ask me about the cup and what could I tell her? When I think it all over, it seems so incredible and unreal that I hardly believe it myself. It would worry the poor old woman and make her regard us with suspicion. I thought best, for your sake, to say nothing about it till you came."

These words of confidence and unabated trust, after all that had happened at Mrs. Hannige's house, so filled him with tender thankfulness, that for a few moments he gave way to his feelings and so loaded the young lady with endearments that she had to put in one of those gentle protests without words which are in themselves a caress.

"And you did not believe one word of what that woman told you at Mrs. Hannige's?" he asked.

"No," she said. "You do not love her. I don't think you could. She is a revengeful, unscrupulous person. Now you are excited."

Carteret was walking up and down.

"Yes," he said, "I am. You have been in danger of your life. I can't even think of it and sit still, but that isn't all, I have been in danger myself. Nobody, I am sure, would have gone through that ordeal at Hannige's and had a woman tell you that I had promised to be her husband and then acted as you have done."

"What have I done?" exclaimed Manuella with a little start.

"What have you done? You have shown for the first time in my life, what simple, pure faith and trust and loyalty are; you have made me understand how precious it is and how ennobling. When I think of you I tremble for fear that at some thoughtless moment I will not be worthy of such trust. That's all. But as for those miscreants, I'll have them hunted from the face of the earth."

"O no, don't," pleaded innocence. "We have something else to think of. They have got the cup and they will not trouble us again."

"Yes, they got it. They stole into your very bedroom. My God, they could have murdered you with impunity."

"No," said Manuella; "you forget, they took it before I got here. It was gone when I arrived."

"And where, I should like to know, were the men of the house?" exclaimed impulse. "Is that the way they take care of you when I am gone?"

At this futile attempt of affection to find fault, Manuella laughed outright "My dear," she said, "I have worried all I intend to about it. I'm here safe and sound and you are back and we must finish those two canvasses down stairs. I'm not so dreadfully marred, am I?" and she began to look at herself in the mirror.

He stared at her admiringly. "Marred? No," he said, "but I feel as if sacrilegious hands had been laid on you. Are you sure you would know that rascal if you saw him again?"

"Yes," she answered; "anywhere. His hideous face was too close to me in the coach ever to forget it. I felt as if I was suffering with a horrible nightmare."

Then this girl with a charming assumption of indifference, made light of her troubles, insisting that it was all a scare and that some adhesive plaster and two good days in the sunshine would fix her all right. And Carteret, manlike, never suspected that she was hiding from him her nervous terror—her shock—her apprehension and a new set of alarms that went off in her mind at the slightest provocation. He never knew that for many nights afterwards she woke suddenly with a start and saw the heavy jaw and the short, flat, black curls of Samson against her window pane and heard the noise of the darkness turned into his gruff voice by the illusive witchery of the fancy.

He only knew that her dire experience in some way endeared her to him and that he was the only person to whom she had confided her trouble and who shared with her the full knowledge of all that had occurred.

But it was not possible for the recollection of this mishap to quite cloud the sunny days at the aqueduct. Carteret's task to pursue the ruffians from the face of the earth was postponed when he got his easel set upon the slope in the clear autumn brightness, and Manuella was sitting by his side on a campstool watching every stroke of his brush. His fierce resolves to see that justice was executed sobered down in the halcyon hours that followed, especially as Manuella never sympathized with them or assented to them. He promptly sent word to Wilder as he had promised, and then with a sudden ambition resolved to get his two pictures done for the winter exhibition at the Academy. One of these pictures had grown almost to completion in the sunshine of the season and of love, there on the green slope above the Pocantico, with the dreamy murmur of the water in the artist's ears and the sweeter murmur of the woman he loved in his heart. It was indeed a child of love and romance. He had called it half a score of mythological names, but it was always Manuella standing in the dappled field, swathed by all the dreamy irridescence of the fall. He had painted her as he first saw her, with her hair down and a look of wonder, reproach and anxiety on her face. He had taken an artist's liberty with her drapery, but he had not transcended the living beauty and splendor of the girl who stood beside him to inspire him, and who saw with almost childish wonder and admiration this picture grow into something that to her eyes excelled all the other pictures that had ever been painted.

The season waned. The October nights were getting cold. Mrs. Manser lit a fire in the evenings in her little parlor. The *cicada* had been strumming now something more than six weeks before frost, and there they were on the aqueduct day after day while the sunshine lasted, and Hi Tucker, who came up the stream at odd times with a boy's fish-pole in his hand, sat on the abutment of the aqueduct and watched them, occasionally joining in the conversation or running willingly to the house for Carteret on small errands. Nearly a week sped by in this uneventful and happy way, and then came one of those little incidents that so often shatter in a moment the hopes of a season.

Carteret had worked hard to get his picture done in time to enter it at the winter Exhibition, and the moment it was finished he was anxious to get the canvas to New York. One Saturday morning, after much fuss and loving care in packing it, and a solemn assemblage of the little household, he started in Mr. Manser's wagon to take it to the train. Manuella, who was almost as nervous as himself over it, went down to see him off, and her last words to him were: "Don't stay longer than Monday. I shall come down to the morning train to meet you." The very next day who should drive up to Mr. Manser's with a spanking team but Mr. Stonybrook, looking very elegant and beaming most generously. Manuella, who was sitting on the little porch with her grandfather, under the few late morning-glories that the frost had not killed, considering whether she would go to church with Mrs. Manser or stay with her grandfather, saw with something like offended astonishment this sudden apparition dash up over the gravel. But Mr. Stonybrook, attired in a fashionable suit and a faultless silk hat, sprang undaunted from the vehicle, and, doffing his hat, grasped Mr. Evans by the hand warmly, and as he pulled at his whiskers with the other said: "I got your invitation, you see, and here I am. I bring you good news, Mr. Evans. Miss Castleton, I'm delighted to see you once more, and if I could find the right adjective in an instant I'd try and tell you how superb the country sunshine has made you look."

He stood gazing at her with undisguised admiration. She was no longer the slightly pale girl that he had seen at Mrs. Hannige's with her eyes cast down. There was color in her cheeks and a new sparkle in her eyes, and even the man of the world could see that she had a new bearing.

"Your grandfather invited me up," he said in explanation. "You know now I undertook to straighten out his books and look into his business settlements. It was important that I should see him, as something has come of that affair which is to his advantage. What a delightful little Swiss retreat you've found here. It puts me in mind of one of those vales in the Carnatic."

Manuella listened to all this and then determined to go to church with Mrs. Manser The instant she had made this feminine resolve she became very polite to Mr. Stonybrook, bringing him out a chair and begging him to sit down by her grandfather. She only regretted that she could not enjoy the conversation with him at that time, as she was going to church.

It was in vain that he offered to drive her to her devotions, as he called it. She went off across the fields with Mrs. Manser, and he saw her figure for a long time as he sat there, paying very little attention to the maundering of the old gentleman, and watched it with unabated interest as it went in and out at the curves of the road, and finally disappeared in the hazy distance.

That Sabbath morning had for Manuella a sort of holy quaintness that she never forgot. The little old church, built in 1699 by Holland burghers, with its high-backed pews, its sounding board still unremoved, and its Flemish communion service on the altar table, the simplicity of the service and the sincerity of the worshippers, most of them rural workers, seemed to carry her to some far-away country that she had read about. She sat as if in a spell. The drone of the preacher somehow interwove itself with the drone of the insects that came through the windows, and the village choir, in ribbons and straw hats, sounded like that song of the maidens in Faust that her imagination had set to music when Carteret read her the poem. The sleepy hush, the subdued mellow tone of everything and the homely earnestness and picturesqueness caught her fancy and she kept saying in her heart: "How Carteret would enjoy this. I must bring him down here and let him hear these girls sing and show him those old time-stained beams. How his artist soul would revel in the curious old place, and how he would laugh at Hi Tucker perched up there beside his mother with a washed face and brand new jacket on."

And then, when she came out, conscious that all the village beaus were looking curiously at her as she marched demurely by the side of Mrs. Manser in the throng, there was Mr. Stonybrook, with his spanking team, and her grandfather waiting in front of the church for her.

It was useless now to refuse him. He insisted on driving her home, notwithstanding that he had to take Mrs. Manser in with her. Nor was it possible to treat him with a chilly reserve when he began to tell her what he had done for her grandfather. "Why, Miss Castleton," he said, "your grandfather had a partner in the coal business who swindled him. His name is Rankin. I have set an officer to look into his record and there is proof enough to convict him of conspiracy. I intend to make him restore part of his money to Mr. Evans, for he is well to do and fears exposure. The fact is, your grandfather has always been perfectly right about his books. They show a clean balance in his favor."

She was sitting beside Mr. Stonybrook as he told her this. Mrs. Manser and her grandfather were conversing about the Dutch Reformed Church, on another seat. She could not suppress a feeling of gratitude as this news of her grandfather's good fortune and honesty was imparted to her, and all her suspicion and timidity vanished in a sense of satisfaction that Mr. Evans might now be placed above the humiliations of abject poverty for the rest of his days. She became very affable and tried to point out to Mr. Stonybrook some of the beauties of the country with which she had grown acquainted under the guidance of an artist's eye. But Mr. Stonybrook didn't care for the beauties of the country. He only said, "Yes," indifferently, to her outbursts and asked her how she liked the team, or if the loneliness of the place did not wear on her.

Then he insisted on driving her farther up the river road toward Croton Point, and Mrs. Manser had to be left behind at the house, for she had to get dinner before they came back, and so Manuella went spinning up the highway with Mr. Stonybrook in spite of all.

In certain circumstances this would have been a most exhilirating drive. The road, for three thousand feet, runs along the edge of a natural terrace, and observers suddenly come upon Haverstraw Bay, blue at this season and banked with azure hills like Lago Maggoire. Croton Point with its vineyard lies like an island on the surface, and above it the gates of the Highlands stand wide open. The girl stood up and clapped her hands with animation. Mr. Stonybrook regarded her, with admiration. "By Jove," he said, "how you would enjoy Lucerne or the Mediterranean. Miss Castleton, you'll have to keep some of your enthusiasm for the real thing."

There was a tone of superiority in taste about this speech that her quick sensibility detected and she felt that it might be provincial to praise the Hudson River. In brief, Mr. Stonybrook quite chilled her natural impulses and insisted on talking about the country as if it were a hardship. "I hope," he said, "when you come back to the city, you will let me show you some of the world-famous scenes. We hardly class the Hudson among them now. They belong to the Washington Irving stage of development." After that she was a little afraid that she would show Mr. Stonybrook how little she knew and she began to suspect that he was one of those superior persons who never descend from criticism to feeling.

The drive proved much longer than she had intended it should be, and they stopped at a summer hotel ostensibly to let Mr. Evans stretch his limbs and before Manuella was aware of it, Mr. Stonybrook had ordered a dinner and there was no escape. His profuse directions and his extravagant banquet, did not please her. She felt that the sumptuous show of wine was in some way out of keeping with the guests, especially as she did not drink any herself. But her grandfather seemed to enjoy the diversion so heartily that she put up with everything except Mr. Stonybrook's views of art. Connoisseurship was something Manuella did not understand, and Mr. Stonybrook's easy superiority to anything like art endeavor and his ready deprecation of the drudgery of an artist's life, when one had the chance of enjoying art as an onlooker, made her resolve to tell Carteret what a strange creature this personage was and how little he knew of the delights of painting. But Mr. Stonybrook was too crafty to let her get into an argument. He talked fluently and cleverly and led the conversation back to her grandfather. "Now," he said, "Miss Castleton, we have got this affair on hand, we must not neglect it till it is all settled up and he is made comfortable. I expect your coöperation for his sake. We must do this and we must do that," and finally they were confidants in what was a very creditable piece of work, and she had forgotten in her interest in her grandfather all that was objectionable in Mr. Stonybrook.

It was late in the afternoon when they got back to the gatehouse and when Mr. Stonybrook left them, it was with a frank intimation that he was coming up again in a day or two to talk the matter over with her.

The only clear idea which the girl had as she thought herself to sleep that night was what a lot of things she had to tell Carteret about Mr. Stonybrook.

But it so happened the next day, when Carteret came up, and they had heard all about the picture, that she had forgotten most of the disagreeable things about Mr. Stonybrook and was mainly intent on telling Carteret about the good services that he had done for her grandfather. In her candor and innocence, she unwittingly spoke of Mr. Stonybrook's visit with what appeared to Carteret like ardor. He was astonished at once, that the man had come there. He was not at all relieved to hear that her grandfather had invited him, and when Manuella told him of the ride and the dinner, he was amazed. Jealousy stood out in every lineament and gave a little impulse to every tone.

"You don't mean to tell me," he said, "that you went driving on Sunday with this man and stopped at a hotel to eat his dinner?"

She looked at him wonderingly. She had never heard this tone exactly, from him.

"What have I done?" she asked, "Nothing so very wrong, have I?" She came close to him and looked bravely into his eyes, "You don't think I did anything wrong do you? You don't think I could, do you?"

He turned away. "I don't know what to think, Manuella," he said. "The moment I leave you, something happens. It may be that this man with his ready money and his airs is all that you claim for him, and he may be a great and powerful friend. I only know that a helpless, penniless artist who cannot gratify your tastes, must be very selfish to stand in your way."

These words were incomprehensibly painful to Manuella. Her native honesty and innocence told her they were unworthy. Their mistrust wounded her. Their injustice touched her pride.

"I am sure," she said rather helplessly, "that I do not like Mr. Stonybrook for his money or his airs."

"But you do like him," replied Carteret, quickly, "you are candid enough to acknowledge that."

The girl looked at him reproachfully. There was water in her eyes. Then she turned and walked away a little distance. It was the impulse to avoid what was to her a most disagreeable dilemma. The young man in his unreasoning mood of jealousy, interpreted it instantly to be an acknowledgment that he was right.

There they stood on the green sward in the cool morning, all at once separated by a phantom. There was a space of ten feet between them. One was irresolutely swinging her parasol to and fro through the dried grass. This was undying loyalty with her back to love. The other with indignation in his eyes, and something of proprietorship in his attitude, was jealousy, holding the door of his imagination open for real trouble to come along and pop in.

The girl stood thus a moment or two. Should she tell him she did not like Stonybrook, that at heart she despised him? What a concession to stupid, exacting stubbornness. If he did not know it beyond all doubt, then she was disappointed in him. No; she would not humiliate herself by such an abject confession. It was not worth talking about. Colin would come to her and beg her pardon for his momentary forgetfulness.

At the end of an awkward pause, nothing being said, she moved towards the house, without looking back, but expecting at every step to hear his feet in the dried grass, and to feel him at her side clutching her eagerly, and with one word closing up the gap. And at each step she made, the gap widened.

Carteret stood there, staring after her with a numb pain, until he saw her disappear in the house. Then with a bitter tone he said, "So it is true of her like all the rest. Love cannot compete with money, and fidelity is no match for ostentation with a woman. What a revelation!"

He started down the bank, his mind in a whirl of absurd and contradictory impulses, and threw himself on the grass where his easel had so long stood, and where he had worn a little spot with his feet while painting.

Carteret had very little experience with his own emotions, and now that they were running riot, his judgment disappeared from view. He felt that he was injured, wronged, duped. Stonybrook had doubtless been paying his impertinent attentions to Manuella for a long time, and the grandfather had abetted him. All at once, a hundred insignificant things flashed through his mind in corroboration.

Altogether Mr. Carteret worked himself into a supreme condition of groundless misery, and in half an hour began to look upon himself as the best-abused man alive. He would go back to the city and let Manuella see that it was a serious matter with him, and thus with pique and impetuosity, rather than acknowledge his folly, and face the protesting looks of the woman he loved, he wrote a note for her, and went off to the depot and took a train to the city.

Manuella cried a little as she read the missive written with an artist's pencil on a crumbled piece of paper. "Of course," it said, "it is not pleasant for me to stay here to-day and run the risk of meeting that man. So I have thought it best to go to the city and look after my humble affairs there."

She said nothing, but her heart mutely repeated its own misery. "O Colin, Colin, this is not like you."

The moment folly lets down the bars of common sense in such cases, circumstances stand ready to break into the domain of peace. Hardly had Carteret been gone an hour before a letter came to Manuella from Stonybrook.

"My dear Miss Castleton," it ran. "In your grandfather's interest, I think you had better come to the city at once. His presence is necessary here, and it is better that you should be with him. Mrs. Hannige is anxious to have you back, and the country must be getting disagreeably cold. If you will telegraph me when you start, I will meet you at the train with a conveyance."

There was a little grimness in her beautiful mouth as, laying this note on her mantle, she said to herself, "Yes, I suppose I must go to the city, too, and look after my humble affairs."

She kept up a brave heart that day. Mr. Stonybrook was doing what nobody else had thought it worth while to do. He was vindicating her grandfather's character, and securing for him a competence. She would not be so ungenerous as to treat him with discourtesy while he was working for her. And after all, was not Mr. Stonybrook a discreet man of experience and broad views? Would he waste time in idle accusations and boyish suspicions? She even asked herself if a girl might not be happier with a man of his age and settled opinions than with an artist who was all impulse. Once having admitted this comparison into her mind, she was a good deal more miserable than she knew, and what with worry and anxiety, towards evening she had a sharp headache, so Mrs. Manser made her a cup of green tea about nine o'clock. "There was nothing like a cup of good strong tea for a headache," and at ten o'clock Manuella went to bed to toss and think, and count one thousand, but not to sleep. After several hours' futile endeavor to shut out her perplexities, she sank into a fitful doze and then awoke suddenly with a start, out of a fearful dream. She thought she had seen the swarthy face and black locks of Samson pressed against her windowpane. Her heart was beating violently, and the full moon was shining into her little window. She got up, threw on a wrap and sat down with her elbows on the casement and looked out. It was a splendid night. The valley was bathed in radiance, and a million stars twinkled above her. The peace and beauty of the actual world soothed her. Mr. Manser's old mastiff, kept chained all day, was walking up and down on the aqueduct path, and throwing an absurd shadow on the green sward. She called to him, and he wagged his tail and barked at her good-humoredly, as if to reassure her that all was safe and serene. It was so still, she heard the clock on a church tower across the river strike the hour in faint, faraway tones. She seemed to be gazing upon enchanted ground. Every familiar spot sacred to romance and love's young dream stood out in the magic of the night, clear, soft and invitingly, and old Towse, the dog, seemed to say to her as he looked up, "Can't see why people want to sleep such a night as this, when they can sleep all day."

Something wooed her out. It may have been that the room and her thoughts were what she wanted to escape from; it may have been that she thought a turn in the air would not only restore her nerves but dispel the effect of the dream by reassuring her of the solitude and safety of the place. At all events, she put a shawl over her head and stealing softly down, went out through the little porch upon the aqueduct, the dog welcoming her with all sorts of gyrations and antics. She noticed how strongly impregnated the night air was with the odor of mint and wondered why she had never smelt it before. The stars twinkled and danced. The larches whispered softly. A late whip-poor-will called plaintively from the grove. The great stretch of the waterway with its steep walls was so shut off from the valley that she felt safe upon it. No one could reach her that did not approach from either end. She patted the dog on the head and walked slowly out upon the pathway leading toward the roadway and white gate half a mile south and now shining distinctly in the distance. The mere novelty of her action, with its solitude and night-freedom, served to relieve her mind and she strolled unsuspectingly away out to where the embankment makes its turn toward the hill and has decreased in height so that the stream on one side and the thick grove on the other approach to within fifty feet. It was here that she stopped and leaning on the rail watched the dog which had begun to scent something. "What's the matter Towse?" she said. "What do you see?"

But the dog had his nose to the ground and was looking steadily down into the adjacent grove, his tail quivering and the hair on his back bristling.

Following the direction thus indicated she began to scan the mysterious depths of the foliage which swept up the incline to within fifty feet of where she stood. Suddenly she gave a start and a little cry and clutched the rail convulsively. There, almost close enough, it seemed to her, for him to jump upon the stonework, standing upright in the brush and looking straight up into her face, was the square form, the massive head, the thick neck and the unmistakable face of the man who had carried her away in the coach. There could be no mistake. She saw him move and even thought she saw him make a gesture of warning to some one hiding behind him.

Then with a cry like a frightened animal, she ran with all her strength toward the house and darting into the hallway, held the door half open a moment to hear the dog barking violently in the distance. Then she closed and bolted it and with frightened eagerness, pounded at Mr. Manser's chamber and presently had the whole household aroused.

CHAPTER XXXVI.

ON THE EDGE OF THE MYSTERY.

Wilder waited. The weather was getting cold. People were coming to town. The season of outing was over and the crisis of the civil war had arrived. Little else was heard of but the news from the front and little else was discussed in the newspapers but the operations of the armies in the East and the West. Events of local importance which ordinarily received attention in the daily press, were now lost sight of in the crowding of national affairs. So true was this, that in New York the organization of the Knights of the Golden Circle was effected without a murmur of opposition. Its lodges held meetings in most of the wards and violent opposition to the Government was manifested in speech and action and very little public attention was given to the dangerous elements thus brought together and fanned into cooperation.

In his search for Plonski, John Wilder had learned a great deal of this state of things and he felt naturally piqued at Mr. Burton for having failed to keep his word. That the lawyer had other matters to attend to and did not care to interest himself in the matter of the cup, was the conclusion Wilder came to, and after the failure to find Plonski or to track the two men who had abducted Miss Castleton, he had just settled down to the conviction once more that the Toltec Cup had been carried off by Plonski, who was probably out of the country and that the affair had now reached a point where it must die a natural death, when he received word from a local officer at Scarsdale that Samson had been seen hanging around in that vicinity for three days. He had been seen in the Pocantico woods by several persons and some of Mr. Manser's people at the gatehouse had been alarmed by his prowling round there at night.

This information revived in an instant all the professional heat of the officer. He thought this looked as if there had been another miscarriage of the cup, for he could not conceive of a sufficient motive to induce the man Samson to remain in that vicinity, if he had secured the object of his visit, unless it was to prevent Plonski from obtaining it.

Scarcely had Wilder received this news when there came a summons from Mr. Burton. It would not do to wait and consult the lawyer. He must have Samson at once. He therefore got a warrant and sent a reliable officer to Scarsdale to take him on a charge of abduction.

It was three o'clock and a cold afternoon, with signs of snow, when Wilder entered Mr. Burton's office. That gentleman was walking up and down with his trim cutaway coat buttoned over his breast and smelling at his spice pink.

"John," said he as the officer came in, "this is the first case in twenty years that I have done any real hard work at without being retained. Take a chair. What have you done with your man Plonski?"

"Lost track of him entirely," said Wilder as he sat down.

"Humph," grunted Mr. Burton reflectively, as he continued to pace the floor. "You haven't lost sight of the cup, I hope?"

"I'm afraid I have," said Wilder, "at least for the present. But the fact is, it is impossible to hazard any kind of a guess with regard to it. It doesn't follow the ordinary course of events. It may pop up to-morrow somewhere."

"Let us hope it will," said Mr. Burton, who was still walking up and down. Presently he stopped. "John," said he, "that cup if it is worth anything at all, is worth one or two hundred millions. You asked me to look into the matter. I have. Try and follow me. The two little points in that advertisement that I had to fasten on, were 'Toltec' and 'Hieroglyphics.' It was pretty plain that any great value could only be represented *on* the cup, not *in* it and that fitted 'Hieroglyphics.' They might contain a secret. The only secret that can express intrinsic value is the secret of treasure and the moment you arrive at the idea of treasure—Toltec suggests hidden treasure."

He had been walking up and down as he said this, delivering himself in a short incisive manner, very much as he did when he was arguing a case in court. He stopped a moment and looked at Wilder.

"Perhaps I go too fast for you. Let me explain. The Toltecs were the primitive race of Mexico—the precursors of the Montezumas. Theirs has always been a land of treasure and a land of revolution, and such a land is always a land of hidden treasure. I have taken the trouble to go into this matter and I find that one of the Toltec customs perpetuated by the Montezumas was that of making memorial cups, commemorative records of great events which were deposited in the royal treasury or in the temple. Having arrived at this, my next step was to ascertain if possible, what kind of an event, treasure event, so to speak, would be worth commemorating. There are three handed down by Mexican tradition. The one which bears most strongly in favor of my hypothesis is this: When Cortez invaded Mexico the capital was the depository of treasure that had been accumulating for centuries. Nearly all the gold mines which have since been so successfully worked by the Americans on lands acquired from Mexico were known and worked by the Mexicans themselves before the discovery of America. Most of this treasure flowed into their capital in the shape of bullion and gold dust and was accumulated in incredible quantities in their treasury and in their temples. There is ample evidence of this in the records they have left, but it is well known that when Cortez reached the Capital, he found to the infinite disappointment of his soldiers, comparatively little treasure and that, says the Spanish record, was of a memorial character.

I have now to tell you that there has been in Mexico ever since the Spanish invasion, a legend that Montezuma, unable to prevent the approach of Cortez, secreted this vast wealth somewhere in the mountains north of Mexico and if you will permit me I will add that there is a reasonable supposition in my mind that the deportation and hiding of that treasure were, according to custom, recorded our a memorial cup which was deposited in the Temple of their God of War. If we now add that the cup contained in its graven hieroglyphics the exact amount of treasure there hidden and the exact place of hiding we have an adequate explanation of the value of the cup.

"So much for the hypothesis. Now for the facts. I had to go to Washington last Tuesday to argue a case in the Supreme Court. It gave me an opportunity to make some investigations. The best Mexican archaeologist in the country is a Spaniard, who has long been retained at the Mexican Embassy. His name is Almonti. I had an interview with him. He is a scholar, an antiquary and a linguist. I had not fairly broached the subject before he began to laugh. 'What,' he said, 'are you looking for that cup?'

"'Then there is a cup?' I asked with some surprise. 'There ought to be two,' be answered. 'It was the custom of those people to make one for the Temple of Huitzitopotchli and one for the Royal Temple of Records. Both these cups are supposed to have been carried off during the Spanish invasion. One was lost sight of, the other has something of a record and is traceable for a century in Europe. You will find an allusion to it in the Mendoza Codex, the most valuable of the collected Aztec manuscripts. It is also mentioned by Dr. Robertson in his history of America published in London in 1796, which is quoted by Prescott in his "Conquest." Why,' said Signor Almonti, 'there has been as much time wasted looking for that cup as has been spent in the search for the philosophers' stone, but with far more reason, for it was positively known to be in existence as late as 1861.'

"'And I suppose,' I said to Sig. Almonti, 'that the search had been instigated by a chimerical tradition of buried gold, after the manner of the searchers of Kyd's treasure.'

"'On the Contrary,' replied Sig. Almonti, 'nothing is better attested by tradition and corroborative records than that the priests secreted the enormous treasure that had been accumulated in their capital. A knowledge of this tradition entered into the schemes of the French Invasion and was at the bottom of the well known Donophon Expedition. There was in this department during the administration of Franklin Pierce a clerk named Miramon who became something of a monomaniac on the Toltec researches. He had spent considerable time both in Spain and in Mexico and had accumulated a vast fund of information. He was a competent scholar, but dishonest, and being accused of tampering with the official records in the State Department, resigned. I have heard since that he was acting as the agent of a stock company interested in the recovery of this treasure.'"

Here Mr. Burton stopped walking the floor and looking at Wilder said: "Have I furnished you with an adequate theory to account for the value of the cup?"

"You have indeed," said Wilder, "but will you explain to me why operations for the recovery of the cup should be carried on in secret?"

"For several excellent reasons," replied Mr. Burton. "In the first place, under the common law of England, which usually governs us in such cases, this is a case of 'treasure trove,' and the government can put in a claim if it is shown that the treasure was hidden with the expectation of recovering it at some future time. It may, too, be on government lands; possibly on a reservation. In the second place, to divulge the existence of such a vast amount of wealth would excite the cupidity and arouse the dishonesty of all sorts of people. In the third place, if there are two parties aware of the value of the cup and searching for it, they would not, for obvious reasons, be apt to let each other know what operations were being carried on. The possessor of the cup in this case, if it points out the hiding place and he can keep the secret, is also the possessor of the wealth. There is still another reason that is not without weight and it is that a person having a knowledge of all these facts will find it very difficult to obtain credence, from a listener at the outset. The story would be very apt to excite laughter and the narrator would be regarded as having gone wild over one of the most incredible fictions of history. This consideration would be apt to deter any man from talking about the scheme carelessly, for few sane men exist who would not rather be unsuccessful than be laughed at."

"Did you ask Almonti what the buried wealth was estimated at?"

"I did. He said that the last descendant of the Montezumas died in New Orleans in 1832 and was accredited with being the depositary of some of the original secrets of the Montezumas. This personage had written a letter during his last illness to the U.S. Consul in Vera Cruz, in which he said that the Mexican Government had buried about three hundred millions of treasure in the Saguache Range. The whole statement was so incredible that the State Department to which the document was forwarded, paid no attention to it. It purported to give a narration of the manner of disposing of this wealth, which was in the shape of gold bars, utensils and ornaments. It had been loaded, so the account said, on the backs of three thousand slaves and carried north under a guard of priests and soldiers, all of whom were afterwards sacrificed to keep the whereabouts of the treasure a secret. This letter was for years buried in the State Department, but disappeared during the administration of Franklin Pierce. So you see there is a pretty fair basis of facts for my hypothesis. In what manner Mr. Job Ackerman became possessed of the cup, what interestOl

Enniston had in it, and whether it is the cup in question, are matters that now rest with you to determine. If you will let me go a little farther with my theory, I believe the man Plonski is acting as the agent of an organized company with the intention of selling them out at the last moment. It would not be unlikely that a company banded together in such a scheme of secrecy as this would employ the most crafty person, especially if that purpose was to defeat a rival organization, and I must say that the rational inference is that this company is in possession of some facts in regard to the cup of which we know nothing, because men do not nowadays risk capital, perfect organizations, and carry out wide and dangerous schemes on a basis of superstition or fanciful returns."

"Is it then possible," asked Wilder "to indicate on the cup the exact spot where this wealth is hidden?"

"It is quite possible," replied Mr. Burton, "to indicate it with sufficient exactness to lead to its recovery. The Toltecs were well advanced in astronomical observations and had a geometrical system of their own, which they could apply to topography, and there is no more difficulty in reading their symbols than there is in deciphering the cuniform inscriptions. M. Le Plongeon has already gone quite as far as Grotefend in this direction."

"Then," said Wilder, "if I understand you, there is a strong probability, not only that the two hundred millions is still buried somewhere and that the secret is inscribed on the cup, but that the possessor of the cup will be very apt to obtain the wealth."

"That the wealth was hidden," replied Mr. Burton, "appears to be a historic probability. That it has ever been discovered is not likely, for such an event could hardly be kept from the world. But that the cup in question is the one that contains the secret, or that the possessor will be able to read its riddle and secure the treasure, are conclusions entirely aside from any deduction warranted by facts. There is a great deal more to be learned before we can jump at any such results. My advice to you is that you go at once to Mr. Job Ackerman and advance this theory, not as a theory, but as your knowledge of the value of the cup, and ascertain if possible, what ownership he can establish in the cup. If he has a clear claim, it would be well for him to retain both of us to secure it, for if it is the authenticated cup, it has a clear value aside from the question of who gets the treasure, in the fact that the possessor of the cup can sell it to the Mexican government. Once establish Mr. Ackerman's ownership and we have a case. He must be in possession of some facts that are of great value in clearing up the history of the cup, but I am bound to tell you that I suspect his title is a precarious one and his possession complicated with some circumstances that are at least doubtful, for I cannot otherwise understand why he has remained hidden away up there at Coe's Grove without making a vigorous and determined fight to recover his property. I remarked to you, John, when you first told me this story, that it was the most extraordinary series of events I ever heard of. I have to tell you now that a patient investigation of it has only increased my astonishment. Even as it stands, it makes the Diamond Necklace romance puny indeed and throws the Count of Monte Cristo back to the childish era of the Persian fictions."

"What amazes me," said Wilder, "is that the possibility of such an enormous amount of treasure, so easily shown to be a historic fact, and such a conspiracy to recover it, can be kept within the councils of a few conspirators."

"The enormity of it," replied Mr. Burton, "makes the incredibility. If there is anything that excites the humor and contempt of the American people it is a search for hidden treasure. This is quite natural in a country like ours where there is no background of wealth and revolution, and everything has been achieved by labor. The feeling of incredibility has been heightened by the numerous absurd attempts to recover Captain Kyd's buried doubloons. But we forget that the conditions and probabilities are all changed when we come to Mexico. There we have a land of treasure where records reach far back into myth and whose people were driven out or conquered by invaders, and who, in perils of sudden revolution and cruel war, instinctively hid their wealth from invincible foes, only to perish with their secrets.

"The American people are, at their present stage of national development, more afraid of chimeras than of foreign foes. You can frighten them much more easily with a scheme than with an invasion. They are moved by events, not by principles or probabilities. If they were not we should not now be shooting each other down by the thousand. Why, sir, we are at this moment, standing in this municipality, on the edge of a social crater, if you will permit me to use that figure. We have information at the headquarters of the Committee of Safety that there is a deliberate scheme on foot, backed by Southern capital and Northern perfidy, to organize the very worst elements of this metropolis into an army of cutthroats to take possession of the city. Every form of ignorance, old-world prejudice and hatred of law, every race antagonism and imbruited desire, is used to this end, and it needs but the spark of occasion to touch off the whole inflammable material and to see our homes and our temples in flames and our streets choked with rapine and carnage.

"But in the face of this awful shadow the community sleeps on in security, nor can anything but the event itself arouse the conservative forces of safety."

Mr. Burton had warmed up to oratorical fluency and was walking and talking at a forensic pace. He suddenly stopped and smiled as if remembering that he was not in the court room.

"But enough of this, John," he said; "I feel deeply on the national side of this crisis. Let us come back to the case in hand. You propose to arrest the fellow Samson?"

"Yes, if I am to keep track of the cup. It looks now as if something had occurred to prevent the delivery of it to Plonski. If it is in the possession of Samson, I think I can bring pressure enough to make him squeal."

"I have little faith in the proceeding. It seems to me that you are wasting time with details. You had better begin with Ackerman and Plonski, and above all, fix, if you can, the ownership of the cup."

"It appeared to me that the summary way of doing that would be to get it in my possession."

"Very well, but you are going to meet with opposition from a quarter you least expect."

"You mean from the Central Office?"

"Yes. Have you any idea who it was effected the liberation of the girl Clianthe?"

"I have a suspicion that it was brought about by one of the commissioners."

"Very well, the same influence will liberate Plonski. These men have in Judge Barnett a ready tool. He will issue a writ of habeas corpus, your man will be out on bail and jump it before you can get a fresh paper served on him. No, no, there is but one way to hold that fellow under your thumb, and it is to get him into the clutches of a United States marshal. Once in Fort Lafayette, he will have his claws cut, and that is where he belongs, and in this you can count on my full cooperation. Go and see Ackerman. Get, if you can, a history of the cup from his lips—"

"But, in the meanwhile, Plonski may escape with it."

"Well, of that, you will know more when you have Samson. By the way, if you should get your hands on the cup, let me see it by all means. It has aroused my curiosity to an extraordinary degree."

This conversation somewhat dampened John Wilder's ardor of pursuit. He was not, perhaps, conscious that the removal of the element of mystery had much to do with it. He felt that an ingenious lawyer had been appealed to for a theory and had brought all his learning and fancy to the task of constructing one.

Nevertheless, as he obtained no news of Samson that day, he started the next morning for Coe's Grove once more, and about noon dropped in upon Dr. Wollendorf, shrewdly suspecting that he would find Capt. Ackerman there. In this he was right. The two men were sitting before an ample fireplace in the doctor's big room with a jug of hot spiced rum on a little table before them, for it was a sharp day and the wind whistled through the locusts with a shrill premonition of winter. After a few desultory remarks, Wilder informed the captain that he had come up to see him on his own affairs and desired to have a talk with him, whereupon the doctor got up, saying he had something to do, and went off to his pigeons, leaving them alone.

"Now, then," said Wilder, coming directly to the subject, "I am here again about the cup. I have got to the bottom of it."

"What do you mean?" asked the captain in some surprise.

"I mean that I have learned all about its value, the treasure it represents, its origin and much of its history. It belongs to the reign of the Montezumas in Mexico, and represents the hidden treasure which the last of those monarchs concealed in the Saguache mountains, from Cortez."

"Where is it?"

"The treasure?"

"No, the cup."

"Of that presently, Captain. The first thing is to learn from you if you really desire to recover it, and are willing to take the proper and direct means."

"I'll give ten thousand dollars for it," exclaimed Captain Ackerman. "That's what I'll do, if it takes every cent I've got. But I won't be beaten or black-mailed. How did you find out about the thing?"

"Captain," said Wilder, "if you have a notion that I want to take advantage of you with the knowledge I have, dismiss it. You are perfectly welcome to all my information, but as I am an officer and cannot enter into any of the con-spiracies to get the cup I want to be satisfied as to your claim to it and then you can command my services to the full extent, even if I am not paid for them. It is necessary to get this right at the start. I don't think you quite understand that the search for the thing has already worked crime enough to convict half a dozen men and women."

"I know, I know," said Captain Ackerman; "but I haven't anything to do with that."

"Yes, you have. If you are the owner of the cup you can take me into your confidence and possibly baffle these people. What I want is something like a legal foundation to work upon. I make this condition before we do anything else."

"Do you know where the cup is now?" asked the captain.

"I told you that I was willing to put all my information in your possession, but I'm not going to waste time with a man who may have no sort of claim in the matter. How do I know that the man Plonski has not a better right to it than you have? How did the cup come into your possession, Captain?"

Captain Job Ackerman got up and took a turn or two, with his hands locked behind him. He was evidently in something of a quandary. Suddenly he stopped and said, "What will you take for the cup, cash?"

Wilder laughed. "I don't want to deceive you in any respect," he replied, "I haven't got it. If I had it and knew you to be the owner of it I'd turn the prop-erty over without making a bargain. But as I haven't got it, and the securing of it involves not only expense but personal risk, I think I am justified in having some kind of assurance from the person who claims it. What is more, I've got to have it immediately for by to-morrow I hope to know if the property has passed out of New York. See here, Captain, why don't you call you friend, the doctor, into this consultation. You have evidently confided in him, and he knows me better than you do. Is there anything you don't want him to hear?"

Captain Ackerman walked up and down reflectively, Then he said, "Just wait a moment," and went out of the room.

Wilder knew that he had gone to consult with Dr. Wollendorf, and he occupied himself in trying to coax a lame pigeon from the corner of the room. Just as he gave up the attempt the men came in.

Both of them were nervous. The doctor made a great noise and show of filling his German pipe and the captain poured out a tumbler half full of the spiced rum, and spilled some of it as he drank it. Wilder watched them unperturbed, and was just trying to make up his mind how much of their uneasiness was owing to his official and representative character, and how much to their implication in something that they did not want discovered, when Capt Ackerman said:

"Mr. Wilder, I'm a plain sailing man, and I never had any dealings with the police, never wanted any, for I've led a pretty clean life and I haven't got anything to conceal, but the fact is this business is such a mixed up affair, and there are so many rascals hunting after this cup, and such a lot of innocent people who are liable to be jugged into scandal and trouble as soon as the thing gets out, that sometimes I feel like washing my hands of the whole affair. I'd rather take ship and clear out for good than face the courts and get into the newspapers, and have the whole gang about my ears. That's why I've kept still and out of the way. I aint used to this sort o' thing, but I'd tell all I know from beginnin' to end to any man who stood on the side of decency and had some regard for the feelings of respectable families."

Wilder nodded his head in assent to this evidently labored speech, but said nothing, and Captain Ackerman went on. "You see, Mr. Wilder, if I've got to get into a public row over the thing I'd rather let it go, much as I want my property."

Wilder felt but did not betray impatience at this weak conclusion. "Captain Ackerman," said he, "the secret of the cup has passed out of your hands. As an officer I tell you that I have sufficent proof to bring the whole matter to a public tribunal. I do not see that it is obligatory to do so at present. I simply want to prevent an unscrupulous gang from carrying off the property by the most highhanded means. If you will convince me that you have a rightful claim to the cup you can count on my discreet assistance. My main incentive, up to within a few days, I might as well acknowledge, was curiosity. My main desire now is to outwit one of the craftiest rogues I ever encountered. I don't think that you can make me the depositary of any secrets that are more scandalous or terrible than those I have encountered accidentally in my search so far."

"Yes, yes, I know," said the captain, as he took another drink of the hot rum. "I know. It's got to be a monstrous mess."

"How did the property come into your possession?" asked Wilder somewhat abruptly.

"It was placed in my hands," replied Captain Ackerman, "by the owner of it on his dying bed. I've all the documents in my safe."

"One moment," said Wilder, "were the documents in your safe or Mr. Enniston's safe on the summer night that Enniston's house was entered by thieves?"

"No, they were temporarily deposited for safe keeping in the city."

"Before you go any farther," said Wilder, "let me ask you what the nature of those documents is?"

"They are," said Dr. Wollendorf, "letters, drawings, translations of Toltec inscriptions and transcriptions of Spanish official papers. Perhaps it would be better, Captain, to have the documents brought down here."

"No," said Wilder, "I should like to see them, but it would be better not to risk their removal. We will go there. Is Mrs. Enniston in the house?"

"No," replied the captain, "she is in the city."

Ten minutes later the doctor had on his frieze overcoat, the captain had put on his pea-jacket, and the three men were crossing the fields in the direction of Enniston's, and shortly thereafter the captain let them in the back door and Wilder found himself once more in the room where the extraordinary events that had grown out of the cup, had occurred. There was the safe as Therese had described it. There were the wire frames screwed into the sash, and there was the leathern lounge upon which they had placed the bleeding body of Ol Enniston. To a person of morbid sensibility the place in its echoing solitude and dreary association, must have had an uncanny effect. But neither Wilder nor his two companions, gave any heed to their fancy. The captain opened the safe, making a creaking noise as he did so, withdrew therefrom a bundle of papers carefully rolled up, put them upon a little table which he drew up to the window, placed two chairs for his guests at the table, took his pea-jacket off and as Wilder and the doctor seated themselves, walked up and down and began his narrative.

CHAPTER XXXVII.

CAPTAIN JOB ACKERMAN'S NARRATIVE.

It was somewhat amusing to observe that Capt. Ackerman in spite of all his previous reticence and protests, went at the work of explaining his interests in the Toltec cup as if it was a relief to unbosom himself.

"You see," he said slowly, as he stood up in his shirt sleeves between the two men who had seated themselves, "as I told you, I am a seafaring man. That cup was handed over to me in the Carribbean Sea by a Spaniard we picked up in an open boat. They were five days adrift and we hailed them in 14 degrees east longitude. It was the worst case I ever heard of. There were three of them alive and four dead in the boat with not enough life between the lot of 'em to roll a baby over. They proved to be the captain, mate, two passengers, and three sailors, of the barque Santa Clara, consigned to the Mexican government, with a cargo of Spanish vines for an experimental vineyard. She had sailed from Lisbon and taken her passengers on at Marseilles. She had sprung a leak in a tornado and the crew had taken to the boats. The survivors were the mate and two passengers. The mate was alive but he had received fatal spinal injuries by the fall of a yard and died soon after we got him on board. The other two, it seems, were mortal enemies and nothing but the mate's pistol kept them from tearing each other to pieces while in the boat. One of them was a Spanish gentleman on his way to Mexico in charge of official business, a slender, weakly fellow at the best and a mere skeleton now. He died two days afterwards of exhaustion in spite of all our efforts. I treated him as kindly as I could, gave him my cabin and offered to put in to Caracas and get him a physician. I also kept the other man out of his way, for I did not like his looks. But it was too late to save him. He sent for me on the second day and in very good English told me that he was going to die and that he attributed his death to the fellow we had saved along with him. Then he told me that he was on his way to Mexico as the secretary of a government agent who had died on the passage under the most suspicious circumstances, that this agent had left in his keeping a lot of private papers and a box which he had managed to save in the boat. He had also told him that he had been poisoned by the evil eye of their passenger, who it seems, had also tried to rob him, and the captain had threatened to give the fellow over to the first magistrate they reached. The papers and the box were made over to me in the presence of two of my men and I never examined them until my chests were opened in New York. But while at Key West, I discovered that our surviving passenger had been caught in my locker overhauling my things and I put him ashore there. His name was Miramon."

"What?" said Wilder, for once allowing his surprise to get the better of him.

"He called himself Miramon, but as likely as not it was assumed," said Capt. Ackerman. "I had intended this to be my last voyage in the South American trade, and had made arrangements to invest what money I had in a speculation with my brother-in-law, Mr. Enniston, and shortly after my arrival in New York I came up here to this place to spend the summer with my sister. It was at least a week later before I told Enniston about the stuff I had in my trunk and he proposed to me to examine it. It's there just as I received it with the exception of the cup. The moment we began to examine the papers, Enniston became deeply interested in them. The first thing we did was to pull out that cup, done up in heavy canvas double-stitched and packed in a metal box. We both looked at it with curiosity. He had never seen anything exactly like it, but I had seen the same sort of thing in Yucatan, cut on the Maya idols. We went carefully through the papers and discovered that the owner's name was Valladares, a direct descendant of Don Joseph Sarmiente Valladares, Count of Montezuma, and that the man Miramon had been employed by him in some kind of clerical capacity and discharged. The Count was on his way to Mexico with this cup and was accompanied by Miramon, who tried to get the cup away from him. You will see enough to show that, if you examine the papers. There are letters of Miramon's."

Capt. Ackerman now untied the packet of papers and they fell loosely apart, a collection of curiously stained documents, written on vellum and on antique letterheads, several of which bore a crest. "This," said he, unfolding the largest of the papers, "Enniston and I made out to be memoranda of the history of the cup, although it does not expressly say so. You will see that it alludes to a drawing made of a Mexican representation of the cup in the Museum of Antiquities at Cordova and this, we concluded, was that drawing." Saying which, the captain spread out a stained ink sketch of one face of a goblet that was covered with hieroglyphics, and which showed by a pen mark that the original drawing had been mutilated. "The memorandum says that the drawing, of which this is a copy, was bequeathed to the museum by one of the Mexican priests who was brought over to Spain after the conquest and converted to Christianity. With it was deposited in the museum the manuscript called the 'Legend of the Chalcas Journey,' which is an account of the burial of the king's treasure. You will notice that the hieroglyphics on the drawing are all numbered with a fresher ink than that of the drawing itself, as if some one had used this copy in a hard job to make out the meaning of the signs. And fastened to this by a piece of wax was this list of treasure." And the captain laid before Wilder a yellow and much folded scrap of parchment, which he read with some difficulty, as follows:

AXAYACATL.

200 Itztili plates .... 2,000 pesos.
100 Plumaje (perishable).
250 Cholula cups .... 8,000 pesos.
150 X O Chimilco ingots.. 1,500 pesos.
1500 Chalco ingots .... 150,000 pesos.
200 Chimilco cups.. 220,000 pesos.
87 Royal fans (perishable).
90 Royal wands (perishable).
135 Gold Chafing dishes .... 9,000 pesos.
398 Gold Ixilmtli cups.. 40,000 pesos.
1500 Quills of gold dust .... 110,000 pesos.
139 Gold wheels (estimated) .... 2,000 pesos.
194 Silver goblets .... 800 pesos.
127 Tlascala bracelets... 6,000 pesos.
200 Golden axes from the Temple of Huitzilopotchli .... 1,900 pesos.
360 Golden knives from the Temple of Huitzilopotchli.... 1,900 pesos.
90 Chronological wheels .... 18,000 pesos.
410 Tezcotzinco anklets... 7,700 pesos.
392 Tezcotzinco bracelets.. 6,110 pesos.
270 Silver bars .... 3,980 pesos.
1288 Azcapozalco ingots... 229,600 pesos.

MONTEZUMA.

200 Cups of gold grains.. 3,000 pesos.
600 Skulls gold dust .... 300,000 pesos.
890 Chalcos ingots .... 700,000 pesos.
500 Chimilco ingots .... 350,000 pesos.
1670 Quills of gold dust .... 3 3,870 pesos.
200 Gold chains... 800 pesos.
1270 Gold plates (Cholula) .... 900,000 pesos.
900 Gold plates (Chalco).. 500,000 pesos.
200 Crysoberls.. 100 pesos.
100 Emeralds .... 4,000 pesos.
530 Panaches (perishable).
330 Gold goblets.. 1,250 pesos.
178 Iztapalapan necklaces .... 1,890 pesos.
2 Casques of gold dust.. 20,120 pesos.
700 Tobasco ingots .... 750,000 pesos.
190 Silver plates .... 20,000 pesos.

900 Gold bars .... 91,000 pesos.
830 Cuitlahuac ingots .... 675,000 pesos.

ROYAL TREASURY.

1,800 Gold bars (Chalco) .... 164,000 pesos.
1,700 Gold bars (Cholula) .... 150,000 pesos.
1,650 Gold bars (Chimilco) .... 148,000 pesos.
900 Gold ingots (Ixihuitl) .... 145,000 pesos.
1,000 Stamped Chalco coin .... 110,000 pesos.
100,000 Castellano .... 100,000 pesos.
2,750 Silver bars .... 140,000 pesos.
8,000 Stamped Cholula coin .... 110,000 pesos.
50,000 Stamped Chililco coin .... 20,000 pesos.
75,000 Stamped Iximitli coin .... 13,000 pesos.
400 Gold cups .... 1,450 pesos.
300 Silver cups .... 500 pesos.
1,000 Gold plates .... 2,100 pesos.
3,000 Quauhtitlan ingots .... 250,000 pesos.

John Wilder looked at this extraordinary list with real concern. "That," said he, "appears to represent a fabulous amount of wealth. What is a pesos?"

"A *peso de oro*," said Dr. Wollendorf in a prompt explanatory manner, "is worth about eleven dollars and sixty-seven cents of our money."

Wilder ran his eye down the column of figures again with the slightest incredulity on his face. "Have you footed it?" he asked.

"Yes," replied the doctor; "It amounts to seventy-six million dollars."

Wilder smiled. "I'm not surprised," said he, "that Mexico has been the poorest country on earth ever since the death of Montezuma."

"And," remarked the doctor, "probably the richest country on earth before."

"There are three letters," broke in Capt. Ackerman, "which show that Miramon and Valladares were at one time on terms of intimacy and cooperation in this job. They are from Miramon. This is the first one and is dated Paris, June 27, 1859." Dr. Wollendorf put his hand on the stained paper to keep it from curling up on the table and Wilder read it with difficulty.

"*Senor:* I beg that you will forego the perilous attempt to proceed through Mexico. The condition of the country is one of constant revolution and outside of the capital it is infested with banditti. In addition to this, the inhabitants of the provinces are superstitious, ignorant and suspicious. It would be almost impossible to organize such a party as you will need to proceed north without exciting the attention and jealousy of a factional Government and arousing the fears of the people themselves. The United States is the proper basis of operations and the route lies over what was once the Santa Fe trail, now almost abandoned and leading to within at least two hundred miles of the district which I believe to hold the spot we are in search of.

"There are other and equally weighty considerations in favor of this, one is that there are several archaeologists in the States who can be depended on to complete the interpretation of the Toltec symbols, now that you have the cup itself, and in case your expedition needs money and enterprise, the men can be found there much more readily than elsewhere. I urgently desire that you should see the necessity and propriety of going to the States with me, as I urged you from London and as you gave me to understand that you would. I think the ultimate success of the enterprise depends upon that. I shall expect to meet you in Marseilles on the 30th as agreed.

MIRAMON."

"The second letter is dated Paris, July 6th," said the captain as he laid down another paper which Dr. Wollendorf kindly spread out.

"*Senor:* Your letter of the 28th is incomprehensible to me and there is only one conclusion to be drawn from it. You desire to evade your contract with me, now that I have enabled you to get possession of the cup. You will not find it as easy of accomplishment as you think. I hold in my possession, as you know, means both of authenticating and means of interpretation which you do not. I ought also to say that as the operations can only be carried on in the United States, I have influence and means at my command there, which, if you were prudent, you would hesitate to array against yourself. Were your title to the cup a clear one, our positions would be different and you must see that you do not possess any right in it which I do not share. I hope that you will meet me at Marseilles prepared to carry out our original plan, as I shall insist upon accompanying you whether you go to Mexico or the States. The delay in the sailing of the Santa Clara is, on the whole, fortunate, perhaps, as I have not completed all my arrangements here.

MIRAMON."

"The third letter is a mutilated fragment and without date. It is written with pencil apparently much earlier than these two, but is in the same hand. Here it is:

"The importance which I attached to the lost first letter of Cortez, written to the King of Spain, has not been overestimated. Prescott spent a great deal of time in the museum and library of Madrid looking for it and then gave up the search. Had he gone to the Royal Library at Vienna he would have been more successful. I unearthed that document there after the most inconceivable labor and opposition, and although it disappointed me in not having any allusion to the memorials in question, it contains a direct reference to the priesthood of Mexico and the importance of converting as many of these priests as possible, because says the writer, 'in them are lodged the secrets of the empire and the knowledge of the vast treasures which have been hidden under their directions with pagan rites, to preserve them from the Christians and your Gracious Majesty, to whom they rightfully belong.' That several of these pagan 'Prelates,' as Cortez calls them, abandoned their ancient religion after the fall of the empire and went to Spain, is made certain by the Spanish records. But that they carried with them some knowledge of the great secret and of the symbols which could alone interpret it is beyond all doubt, and had Estrada given over the clues furnished by Bernal Diaz and instead of hunting in the dust of the Spanish libraries gone to the few monasteries in Toledo and Navarre which have escaped the suppressive decree of 1837 and which have been for five centuries the depositaries of monkish lore, he would have arrived at my conclusions, for it is there that the traditions and the secrets of the perishing Toltec dynasty found their last lodgment.'"

When Wilder had read this letter, Dr. Wollendorf said: "This man Miramon appears to have spent the greater part of his life in pursuing the cup. I do not have a very high opinion of his character, but I am bound to respect his ability and his knowledge."

"We had not been in possession of the property two months," continued Capt. Ackerman, "when we both knew that Miramon was working to recover it, but Enniston was so well convinced that we had a fortune in it, that these attempts only made him the more determined to hold on to it. He worked out the secret his own way in this room and we entered into a kind of partnership. I had invested a good deal of my money in Buenos Ayres and I finally, at his request, went there to settle up my business and withdraw my money. We were to invest an equal amount each in the working of the scheme to recover this treasure. The sudden death of Ol Enniston put an end to our partnership and together with other things that happened, gave me a kind of superstitious dread of the cup."

"Do I understand you to say," asked Wilder, "that Mrs. Enniston knew nothing of all this?"

"Nothing whatever; there were several reasons why Enniston could not take his wife into his confidence. In the first place they were about as unlike as any two people could be. Ol was a generous, liberal and somewhat careless fellow who liked women and was inclined to speculate. Mrs. Enniston is a pretty hard-fisted, old-fashioned woman of New England type, just as true as steel and about as stiff in her notions, and she managed to run her house her own way. In the second place, Ol had been married before and Mrs. Enniston did not know of it. It was a foolish and not very creditable affair, and the woman was dead, but she left a son that Ol took good care of. This was a sore spot with him and he wouldn't have had Jane know it for the world, for she had a way of lording it over him that wasn't pleasant to a man. So we concluded to keep the thing to ourselves. Well, sir, when Ol was lying on that lounge and the blood was running out of his scuppers as if he had had a shot amidships, he said to me, 'Job, I'm done for. Jane is well fixed. If there's anything in that cup, I want it to go to my boy. Give me your hand, old friend, and your promise,' and I did."

"Where is Enniston's son?" asked Wilder.

"I don't think that family matter properly comes into this talk, Mr. Wilder," said the captain. "Do you?"

"Perhaps not," replied Wilder.

"You see," continued the captain, "Jane may be a pretty severe woman, but she's my sister and she's got a clean record. I want to spare her as much as I can and I don't see that it will do any good to stir up Ol Enniston's mistake now. Let her have the benefit of her belief in him. It won't hurt anybody."

Wilder made no response to this magnanimous appeal. He only assented to it by changing the interrogations.

"There are several other papers here, Captain."

"Yes," replied the captain. "There are two or three in Spanish that have not been translated and there are two in French which do not appear to have any bearing on the cup. They are marked; let me see," and the captain put on his glasses and examined the papers which were indorsed in pencil marks. "Yes," he said half musingly, as he looked at one of the documents. "I remember the night Ol wrote that line on there, you see it isn't finished, for we had been sitting up pretty late in this room, going over these things and just as he started to write that line, he said: 'Job, there's somebody at that door. I've heard a footstep several times,' and he got up suddenly and opened that hall door and looked out. When he came back, he said: 'I saw that French girl's skirts on the stairs. You don't think she could have been listening, do you?' I remember we talked about it for some time and he forgot to finish the writing that night and never got another chance."

"Let me ask you," asked Wilder. "In the investigations that you and Mr. Enniston made, did you ascertain what interest the man Plonski represented in the search?"

"I'm coming to that, sir," replied the captain. "You see the matter required a great deal of expensive and tiresome work and we had to be very careful in every move and not take in any confidants. Ol Enniston got carried away with the idea of so much wealth; he was more easily worked on than I was. Well, he went to Washington and tried to find out about Miramon, and there he learned, after a lot of hard work, that there was an organized stock company, including a governor of a northern state, a retired capitalist who had been a tobacco merchant and a well known Massachusetts Senator who had invested largely in a scheme to furnish funds to the Mexican Government to fight the French, and in return were to receive an enormous tract of land in Southern California somewhere on the peninsula. The terms called for a settlement in lower California as a consummation of the agreement and there had been a meeting of the stockholders at Harrisburg, Pa., to organize an expedition to the California peninsula, at which meeting the man Miramon was present. All attempts of ours to get at the secret of this expedition have failed, but we both came to the conclusion that Miramon was in some way playing a double game and, while effecting this company to purchase the land upon which the treasure was supposed to be buried, was in reality leading the stockholders astray, for his own documents point to the Saguache mountains and not to the California peninsula. That, I say, was our conclusion and it was Enniston's purpose to have made a thorough and systematic investigation. We had just about got our scheme perfected when he died and the cup disappeared."

"It is your suspicion then," said Wilder, "that Plonski has been employed by the company to recover the cup?"

"We believed him to be an agent, but whether employed by the stock company or by Miramon it is difficult to say."

"And you think the success of the stock company depends upon the recovery of the cup?"

"That was Enniston's conclusion. I did not agree with him always. You see, Ol was a good deal more impetuous than I am, and we squabbled a good deal over the matter. One thing is tolerably certain, this syndicate has no more claim to the cup than Plonski. The last owner was Valladares, and there does not appear to be any direct claimant in his behalf. It was part of Enniston's plan to send to Spain and trace, if possible, the history of the cup and his rights in it. All this required money, and, as I told you, we agreed to invest an equal amount to carry out the investigation. Now suppose we look at the rest of these papers. Here are some facts secured by Enniston in his search.

"This is an extract from the official report of Major General Haven, made to the government, of a topographical survey of portions of Southern Colorado in '58. Just read that, Doctor, will you?"

The doctor put on his spectacles and taking up the paper read as follows:

"Extract from report of Major General Haven to Secretary of War, 1858. Page 408:

"An interesting incident occurred while our scouting party stopped at the old Spanish Monastery in the Lareau Pass. They showed us there, among other curious Toltec relics kept in a secure and quaint little museum in the Padre's parlor, an ingot of gold stamped with an old Toltec mint mark—Ixihuitl. It was estimated to be worth at least eight hundred dollars, and had been kept religiously for many years in this monastery as the sacred property of the church.

It was picked up on the mesa, about ten miles south of the Pass. The Padre, who is an intelligent old priest, and quite conversant with many of the ancient traditions of the country, told me that it must have come from the City of Mexico, where the royal mint and treasury were situated, and he could only account for its presence so far north by supposing that it had been carried off at the time of the Spanish invasion. I looked at the interesting treasure with much curiosity. It had been forged by a hammer, for the marks of the tool were visible, and I learned from the Padre that there was a Spanish tradition that enormous quantities of treasure were brought into this country and buried during the time of the invasion. There are several curious Aztec relics at Fort Garland which would seem to corroborate this romantic idea. They are Toltec anklets and castellano coin which have the Royal Montezuma Treasury mark on them."

When the doctor had read this paper and laid it down Wilder betrayed by his question that his mind had been traveling in another direction.

"Have you ever encountered the man, Plonski?" he asked.

"No," replied the captain, "but Enniston received information which put us on our guard against him, and when the cup was taken out of the house I suspected that he had a hand in it. This other paper is from the secret service reports of the War Department, and relates to what was called at the time the Santa Fe Anabasis, or the Donaphan Expedition. This expedition was conceived by Governor Edwards, of Missouri, in 1846, at the time of the Mexican War; its objective point being Northern Mexico and its route the Santa Fe trail, as it was called. The command, about 1,800 men, mostly mounted, started from Fort Leavenworth about the middle of May of that year and fought their way to the Sierra Madre, where they were in November. The expedition was under the flag of the United States, and the men had been sworn into the United States service, but you will see by this paper, which is a report made by an agent in the secret service of the government to the War Department, that the expedition had been conceived in Missouri with some other purpose than the triumph of the government. Will you read that, Doctor?"

Once more the doctor readjusted his glasses, and in a round, deliberate voice read as follows:

"In pursuance of orders I proceeded on the first of November to the sources of the Puerco, where I found Lieut. Col. Jackson with about one hundred and fifty men encamped on Bear Spring and surrounded by Navajos, under a chief named Sandoval. There were no signs of hostilities, and most of the men were off duty prospecting in the neighboring ravines. Col. Armijo, the well-known Mexican vaquero, arrived here on the 29th of October, and on the 30th went with a squad of Jackson's command into the mountains looking for gold. The explanation of this is furnished by the statement made by Armijo, who, after a dispute with the command, left here on the 6th under a threat of his life. There is undisputable proof that he was hired by some kind of organization which accompanied this expedition to furnish certain information in his possession concerning treasure supposed to be buried in the Sierra Madre range. The dispute arose over his declaration that the treasure could not be located unless the company got possession of a certain cup, for obtaining which he wanted five thousand dollars and a share of the plunder. He was killed on the 8th while crossing a stream on his way south. A brass bullet was found in his neck. There is no reason to doubt now that this detachment was sent here in pursuance of a scheme concocted in St. Louis and elaborated among some of the officers at Fort Leavenworth who had been connected with the exploring expeditions in the far West."

"It makes a magnificent romance, doesn't it?" said Wilder, when the doctor had finished. "I am bound to say that your story is far superior to Plonski's. But I should advise you to postpone any farther consideration of the papers at present. I've got to catch a train. I've a great curiosity to see the cup, and I may lose the opportunity if I remain here too long."

"But I want you to tell me all about that affair of Ol Enniston's," said the captain.

"I'll do so," replied Wilder; "but you'd better come to the city with me and discuss this matter of the cup. I can tell you about Enniston on the train."

CHAPTER XXXVIII.

A PAPER HUNT.

The memorable winter of '62 now had set in, and the carnage of Antietam was to be followed by the disaster at Fredericksburgh. It was to be a winter of doubt, discouragement and gloom for the nation, and of wild and feverish incertitude for New York. But just as Wilder's eventful chase began to assume the importance and dignity of a legal inquiry and of rational purpose, all clues and knowledge of the object of pursuit suddenly ended. Beyond the fact that the cup had been taken from Mr. Manser's house by one of Plonski's agents, nothing could be learned. The attempt to arrest Samson failed, for he could not be found. All that was known was that he had been seen hanging around the Pocantico for several days after the robbery, but when a search was made for him he had disappeared. The keenest detective scrutiny could not discover a trace of him about any of his city haunts. Nor could Wilder, by the most diligent search, come upon any traces of Plonski. There was but one reasonable conclusion to be arrived at in this dilemma, and it was that they had secured the object of all their plotting and had left New York. It was with a deep sense of humiliation that Wilder, after days of incessant and fruitless work, had to acknowledge this to himself. It was the most momentous, and by all odds the most prodigious, job that had ever fallen to the lot of an American detective, and he had been beaten dead, to use his own words, by the man, Plonski. Just as he had come to the conclusion that the affair must be relinquished, and would probably remain an unsolved mystery, something occurred which, trivial in itself, revived in a flash all his hopes and all his interest.

To explain what that something was, it is necessary to go back and narrate what occurred after Manuella saw the face at night in the aqueduct grove.

Her condition the next day after that alarm was one of pitiable terror. She had reasoned herself into a belief that she would never see or hear of the ruffians again, now that they had secured the mysterious cup, and to come suddenly upon one of them skulking about the place filled her with an indefinable dread. Mr. and Mrs. Manser, who had been unable to discover any cause for her alarm, were of course entirely unable to reassure her and she was thus left shut up, as it were, with her own terrible fancies. Then there came over her an irresistible desire to get back to the city at once, and remembering only that Carteret had brought her to this place, and that he alone could understand the cause of her alarm, she sat down and wrote him the following letter, in which the appeal of affection and helplessness left no room for reproaches.

"*My Dear:* I expected you to come back to-day and you have not. I suppose you are detained by your picture. But something dreadful has occurred and I write this to you in hopes that you will come up immediately and take Grandpa and me to the city. I saw in the wood last night the man that stole the cup. He is hanging round the place and I cannot stay here. Of course, Dear, as the Manser's are your friends, you ought not to leave me with them without some explanation and now that I have told you there is danger, I am sure you will not. Please come up at once. MANUELLA."

This letter was written on Tuesday morning about eleven o'clock. Once in the mail, it should have reached Carteret in time to take a late train up. But it was rather too much to ask Mr. Manser to harness his horses and drive five miles to mail a letter, and she had to wait till the team went to the village at three o'clock. This delayed the letter till the six o'clock mail and it was not delivered at the Tenth street studio till nine o'clock the next morning and, as was so often the case with Carteret's letters, it fell into the keeping of Otis Chapman, who was just getting ready to shut up his place and go off on a week's "toot." He took it with the most generous intent, put it on his pile of tube colors with the best motives, wondered when Carteret would be back to work, and then locked up his studio and went over to the Century Club. He did not see Carteret till Thursday, that being varnishing day at the Academy, and when he strolled in there to look after a Saranac Lake picture that he expected to sell, he encountered his friend in a group of artists, all standing before a large canvas conspicuously placed on the line, and all praising Carteret. The moment Chapman looked at the picture he recognized the girl at Mrs. Hannige's, but recognition gave away to admiration of the work and he began praising it himself. "By jingo," he cried, "you've been born again, hav'n't you? I did not believe it was in you. Look here, I don't know as I ought to be so familiar with you now, but there's a letter from that very girl over at my studio or I'm a house painter. It's marked Tarrytown and it came Tuesday. I'd'a' put it in my pocket if I'd known I was going to fall over you here."

"A letter from Manuella," Carteret repeated to himself and his heart gave a jump. After that, the praise of his associates was of little importance. Nothing would do but he must go and fetch it at once.

"All right," said Chapman; "here's the key. You can leave it for me at Mrs. Hannige's."

It was about two o'clock when he got it. Amazement, alarm, self-reproach, impatience, beset him as he read it. It was written Tuesday. It was now Thursday afternoon. It would be six o'clock before he could reach the gatehouse, use what speed he might. And then, muttering all sorts of abuse of himself, he flew around, knocked down canvasses, mislaid the very things he wanted, packed his hand-satchel with the wrong articles, swore at himself immoderately, as young men will, and about half past three was flying up to the Thirtieth street depot at a headlong pace, entirely forgetful of the promise to leave Otis Chapman's key at Mrs. Hannige's.

This proved to be a fool's errand. Never was impetuosity so shorn of his strength as when Mrs. Manser said to him, "Law me, the young lady went to the city this morning, bag and baggage. She and her gran' father and the gentleman she sent for."

"What?" said Carteret, somewhat dumbfounded.

"Yes," replied the old lady, "and didn't you know it? Why, Mr. Carteret, you look cold. Come in and get a cup of tea."

"No, I thank you," said Carteret, vaguely. "I've got to get back, you know. I didn't expect she and the gentleman would get away till to-morrow."

"Well, you can't walk back without something in your stomach, I'm sure, this cold weather. So she didn't send you word? Well, well. The fact is, Mr. Carteret, the young woman's got some queer notions into her head. I tell you, girls ain't brought up as we were, now-a-days."

Carteret, disconsolate, suspicious, indignant, and generally out of humor, got back that night about nine o'clock. It now occurred to him that the most pressing duty and responsibility, was to leave that key of Otis Chapman's at Mrs. Hannige's, and nothing did so much to restrain him from rushing off there at ten o'clock as the consideration that Mrs. Hannige's guests would probably be abed, and that it would be proper form to leave it till the next morning when people were up and around and not likely to be disturbed.

So the next morning after eating his breakfast at seven o'clock, and wondering what the deuce he got up so early for, and feeling quite elated at the mention of his picture in the morning papers, he went to Mrs. Hannige's and met that beaming lady in her hallway armed with her feather duster. There was the usual good-natured flourish. Mrs. Hannige as keeper of the casket, could afford to be patronizing to these young gadflies that tried to get a look at the jewel.

"Well, I s'pose you know that the folks have come to town. Isn't it pretty early to be making a call?"

"I came," said Carteret, with considerable dignity, "to leave Mr. Chapman's key. He asked me to leave it here for him."

Mrs. Hannige was not hard-hearted. She felt in her woman's breast some sympathy for Carteret now; so she said: "I'm going up. I'll see if any of the folks are about. See?—and I'll holler down to you. You just wait a few moments in there."

Then she climbed the stairs and Carteret sauntered into the little reception room, rather nervous and undecided.

But Mrs. Hannige found Mr. Stonybrook in Mr. Evans room with a lot of papers spread out and she wasn't going to break in on a tete-a-tete that promised so much for her. So she backed out saying to herself: "That young man can just wait. It'll do him good," and went off to flourish her feathers in Mr. Stonybrook's room. Carteret waited half an hour, then he looked out of the window and seeing Chapman standing on the club steps across the way, he went over and the two sat down at a front window where Carteret could see the Hannige mansion. He had not been there ten minutes before he saw a coupe drive up and Adolph Kleinbacker spring nimbly out and go up the steps in fashionable furs and riding gloves. That young gentleman was shown into the reception room by the maid, whom he chucked under the chin with the remark that she'd have a house of her own in six months if she didn't take a tuck in that smile. "O, that's all right, my dear," he added, as the girl stared at him. "Don't mind me. You tell her Royal Highness that her cup-bearer's here. She'll know. That's enough; no cards. I'll dawdle round while she crimps, hey? You understand. Say, I'll bring you over a silver bracelet one of these days; it'll make the hair curl on the man you marry. Go on now."

Rather overloaded with this message, the maid met Mrs. Hannige on the upper floor and told her there was a young man in the waiting room; to which Mrs. Hannige said: "Well, you go down and get the lobster shells off that back room carpet and let him wait. Do you understand?"

It is very doubtful if the maid did quite understand to her dying day. But she obeyed, and by and by when Mr. Stonybrook came out of Mr. Evans' room, Mrs. Hannige went in and quite incidentally said: "Miss Castleton, there's a young man down stairs who says he came over to leave Mr. Chapman's key, but as he's waiting I guess he must have some other business."

Manuella, without paying the slightest heed to the subterfuge, cried out at once: "It's Mr. Carteret"; and Mrs. Hannige with what she thought was a most subtle wit, remarked: "Well, well, I wouldn't have believed you could guess it so easily."

In an incredibly brief space of time, Manuella was tripping down the stairs and before she was well aware of her own actions, she was standing face to face with Mr. Kleinbacker, taking short breaths and staring somewhat indignantly at that young man.

"Your most obedient servant," began Kleinbacker, "took you on the fly, didn't I? O, that's all right. Just looked in to see if you had got through with the rural and to leave you a city bouquet. Everybody's in town; thought you must be. How's everything? Anything new in cups? Say, you won't mind my remarking privately, will you, that you're just stunning. It's true, you've doubled up on your looks. How's the old gentleman?"

As it was impossible for the astonished Manuella to decide instantly which one of these questions it would be the most discreet to answer, and as she stood irresolute, staring at the questioner, he started off again: "Don't mind me, Miss

Castleton. That's my way. I just wanted to run in, don't you know, as I went by and ask after the folks. Had a good time, I suppose?"

"Yes," said Manuella, "I enjoyed my visit very much."

"And glad to get back, I'll bet a hat. Country's great for a dash, but wearing for a regular thing. How's the cup? O, that's all right; I'm mum. But don't forget if ever you want a pointer on that cup, I'm your man. Just walk right over to me."

"I am indebted to you already," said Manuella. "I haven't paid you for the cup yet."

"My dear Miss Castleton, don't you go off on that. If there's a bill in our establishment, it will come round right. I wanted to serve you and it was awful good of you to let me. I s'pose you'll go out some this winter? It's going to be lively. You don't shut yourself up, do you, all winter?"

"I don't go out a great deal, Mr. Kleinbacker, on account of my grandfather. I'm sure I'm much obliged to you for your kindness."

"O, pickles. Cut that. You want to get a little life now and then. Why can't you let me take you and your grandfather to the Sanitary Fair? It's a big thing. We've got some cups there that would interest you. You're one of them girls that has to be coaxed, ain't you?"

"I am afraid it would be a waste of time to coax me," she replied.

"O no, it wouldn't. You let me coax you, and I'm satisfied."

At this she laughed, and Kleinbacker said: "All right. I'm not offended. I'll just keep you on my list—see?—and kind o' enquire after you now and then. How many have you got now?"

"I don't understand you," said Manuella. "How many what?"

"Fellows. What's become of the one that carried the cup for you? He don't like me. O, I noticed it. But that's all right. He'll get over it. Say, does that cup really belong to you or to the old gentleman? I want to know. I'll tell you something about it one of these days, if it is your's. Do you know there isn't anything like it in this country? Why, it's worth a hundred dollars."

"I believe," said Manuella in the most noncommittal manner, "that it is very rare."

"What did you do with it?"

"I put it on the mantel in my bedroom," replied Manuella.

"Good enough. You keep it."

"Yes," said Manuella vaguely.

"And if you go in for that sort of thing, come to me when you want the genuine article. Don't forget. Good bye. Take care of the old man, won't you? That's right; I can open the door, and if you say that you'll go over to the fair, I think the old man would enjoy it. O, don't mind that. Good bye."

And Mr. Kleinbacker opened the hall door and ran down the steps, leaving Manuella staring after him with wonder and perplexity, and holding a very large bouquet of late roses in her hand.

She stood a moment wavering between indignation and disappointment, and who should come up the steps but John Wilder.

He accosted her courteously and said: "I want to see you a moment, Miss Castleton. Come into the reception room. You had a very disagreeable experience."

"Yes." she replied, "but I am fortunate that it was no worse."

He then made her tell him all about her detention in the house on the road and the woman who attended her, Manuella taking occasion to tell him how kind and considerate she was in assisting her to get home, to which Wilder remarked: "I would not waste any gratitude on her if I were you. She belongs to the same gang, and only obeyed their instructions to get rid of you when they recovered the cup. It was the next morning, wasn't it, when they went over to Mr. Manser's?"

"I suppose so. The man appeared very anxious to get there at once, and I heard his voice till late that night, so I don't think he started till morning."

Wilder considered a moment, then he said: "How long did it take you to drive over?"

"About two hours and a half."

"Did you go slowly?"

"Yes; the horse was lame and old, and the driver seemed to be in doubt about the road."

"Well, that's all I want to know about that; but I saw Mr. Carteret just now, and he told me about your seeing the same man at night. Are you quite sure you recognized him?"

"O, quite sure. The moon was shining bright, and he was not farther away from me than—than—the street is."

"What was he doing?"

"He was standing by a tree. He had one hand on the trunk and something in the other that looked like a net."

"A what?"

"A fish net. It was a pole with an iron ring on it and some kind of web. At least that was what I thought it was; and when he saw me, he turned half way round, as if he was warning some one in the wood to go back, and made a motion with the net."

"What time of night was this?"

"It must have been at least two o'clock in the morning, for the moon was way over in the west. You see, I couldn't sleep, and went out to get the air."

"Yes, I know, and you alarmed the house."

"Yes, I was frightened, and Mr. Manser and his man went out and looked all round, but they did not see anybody."

"How far down the stream was it where you saw him?"

"O, quite a ways down. You don't know the place, do you?"

"No," said Wilder. "Was it half a mile?"

"O dear, no, not so far as that. I only walked a little way from the house.

"And you are quite sure you did not see the other man?"

"The other man? What other man?"

"The one he warned back?"

"I wasn't sure there was one. I only thought he acted as if there might be."

"Yes, I understand. You think you would know him again if you saw him?"

"I am sure I would; but I hope I never shall see him."

"I'm afraid you'll have to at some time, Miss Castleton," said Wilder.

This conversation set the officer thinking, and not an hour afterwards he suddenly took a train, got off at Scarsdale, and drove over to Mr. Manser's.

Once there, he undertook to explain to the old man that he was an officer come up to see about the men who had scared Miss Castleton. At which Mr. Manser's good natured contempt knew no bounds.

"It's a great waste of good time," said he. "Why, the girl's young and giddy. I've lived here nigh onto ten year, and I never seen a tramp nearer than the railroad over to the river. Why, we don't even lock our doors at night. The girl was a-dreamen'."

In spite of this honest incredulity, Wilder managed to interest the old couple for half an hour and, by dint of adroit cross-questioning, to learn something about the place and the domestic conditions at the time of the robbery. It did not take him very long to ascertain that neither Mr. Manser nor his wife knew anything more about the cup than that such a thing had stood on Manuella's mantel in her bedroom and of course they did not know of the motives of her abduction. He could readily understand the girl's delicacy in burying all this in her own bosom rather than excite the suspicions and fears of these simple-minded people. When he therefore asked permission to look at the room Manuella had occupied, Mrs. Manser very proudly and promptly offered to show it to him, though she could not for the life of her understand what interest the officer took in it, and why he looked out the little open window and examined the vines that hung leafless now on the side of the house.

But Mrs. Manser was a hospitable and an indulgent old lady, and when Wilder asked Mr. Manser to show him over the place she said that so far as the house went, there wasn't much to show or to offer, but as it was a pretty cold afternoon, "p'raps the gentleman would like something warmin'," and then the trio went into the little dining room and the garrulous hostess began to apologize as she took; down the whiskey bottle from the dresser.

"There ain't such a deal of it left," she said, as she dusted of the bottle with her apron, "put perhaps there's enough to warm you up a bit. I don't see what could have become of that other bottle, Dan, do you? I'm sure it ain't like Mr. Carteret to take it without saying nothing and it don't stand to reason that Miss Castleton would touch it."

"You forget, Mrs. Manser," said Wilder, good-naturedly, "that there have been strange persons seen hanging round the place."

"Lands, man, there ain't been no strange persons in here without my knowin' it and a thief wouldn't take one bottle and leave tother."

"When did you miss the bottle, Mrs. Manser?" asked Wilder, who had gone to the window and looked out.

"Why, I missed it on the afternoon after Miss Castleton came back. She was nervous like and I wanted her to take a little. I was aputtin' away the dinner things. It would have stood there a lifetime for all of us. Dan don't tech liquor 'cept when there's company. I never knew Mr. Carteret to drink anything, did you, Dan?"

"O, there's no telling what young men do nowadays when you're not lookin' at REM," said Mr. Manser, sipping his whiskey.

Both the old people grew communicative while in the hospitable act of furnishing refreshment and Mr. Wilder continued to ask questions.

"I should think," said he, "if there had been anybody hanging round your place, you would have known it."

"Sure," said Mr. Manser. "Why, I got up and went down to the crik and looked all round that night, and the next day I went all over the woods and I didn't see nothin' but that scap net somebody left leanin' agin' a tree."

"A what?" asked Wilder.

"A scap net. Some youngster forgot it."

"Where is it?"

"What'd you do with it, mother?"

"I left it standin' there in the hall," said mother, "and I told Mitchell to take it in the barn, but he didn't," and then Mrs. Manser, with a feeling that such unimportant matters were unworthy of their guest's attention, added: "You see, sir, we don't bother 'bout vagabones and beggars up here. There ain't nothin' in this holler to lure REM on and there's a law agin' trespassin' on the water works."

"I wish you'd let me see the net," said Wilder. "I'd like to look at it."

"O, it's a common scap," said Mr. Manser. "There ain't nothin' you want to see 'bout it. Would you like to see the water gate?" and he sat down as if that matter was disposed of effectually. But Mrs. Manser went into the hallway and presently returned with the article in question which she handed to Wilder, saying, "They use ʀᴇᴍ to catch bait."

Wilder took the implement. It was a seven foot ash stick with a hoop of iron at the end, covered with stout netting that made a widely-meshed bag. It was what is known to sportsmen as a shrimp net, and Mrs. Manser was right in saying it was used to catch bait, but it instantly occurred to Wilder that it was not made or used for any bait that might be found in a mountain brook, and as it was not new, it must have been brought from one of the river towns where such nets were in constant use at low tide. He examined it with a particularity that brought a smile of contempt to Mr. Manser's face.

Never seen anything like it afore?" remarked the old man.

"O, yes," replied Wilder. "It's a shrimp net—used them when I was a boy. But you don't find shrimp in fresh water creeks."

"You find bull-frogs; that's enough for the youngsters," said Mr. Manser with a quiet superiority.

Wilder was examining the handle of the net carefully. There was a mark burnt into it and he showed it to Mr. Manser. Neither of them could make out what it was.

"The net belongs to one of the men on the river who let boats and fishing tackle," said Wilder. "What's the man's name at Tarrytown who has the place by the ferry dock?"

"'Pears to me," said Mr. Manser "t'aint worth talkin' about."

But Wilder thought it was and after walking all round the grounds and making a personal inspection of the harmless Pocantico that was now gurgling innocently enough among the stones, he persuaded Mr. Manser to let him carry off the net and it was thrown into the wagon that jolted him to Tarrytown.

Once there, he learned that the man who let the boats was Lem Dutcher, the brother of Cob Dutcher the constable. In fact it was Cob Dutcher who told Wilder this, and who went with him to the boat house. Cob was already known to Wilder for he had something of a reputation as the thief taker of Westchester. He was a rugged, long-limbed, big-boned, good-natured fellow and felt especially honored to be associated with the celebrated inspector from the Central Office.

Together they went to see Lem Dutcher and it was late in the afternoon when they got to the boat house down by the ferry dock, where they found Lem, battened in, as it were, for the season and smoking a short pipe over a red-hot monkey stove.

He disowned the net. Nobody had got a net of him and he hadn't lost one. He hadn't owned but two shrimp nets for a year and they were in the corner.

The clue ran into the ground here, and Wilder after a few futile questions, came out of the boat house and stood upon the float with Cob Dutcher, about to give him some instructions about keeping on the lookout for the men he wanted.

The ferry dock was not thirty feet away, and several people were waiting for the last boat to come from Nyack. A couple of hack drivers shivered in the chill air, and the scene was altogether anything but an inspiriting one. But it is certain that Wilder, half screened by the projecting boat house, suddenly became intensely interested in it. He looked at it so intently that Cob Dutcher, who had asked him a question and got no answer, did not repeat it. Wilder was looking at a man dressed in a heavy overcoat that fell to his heels and the collar of which came up over his ears. This man had come slowly upon the dock and in trying to reach the darkest spot had crossed the roadway so that the dying Western light fell for a moment across a part of his profile. Wilder knew it in a second. It was Plonski.

Self possessed and steady nerved as the officer was, he experienced a little throb of astonishment and surprise at this discovery.

Mr. Cob Dutcher stood close beside him. Wilder drew him on one side and pointed to the object of interest. "Cob," said he, "there's my man. The whole thing's in a nutshell, now. I mustn't lose sight of him."

"Do you want to take him?" asked Cob, impassively.

"I may have to," said Wilder, "but the main thing is to shadow him and find out his lay and his pals. I'll do that. Do you think you can get a wagon and find me after I start?"

Cob thought and then said, "Yes, if you paper it.'

Wilder who did not take his eyes off the man on the dock, said in a quick sentence: "What do you mean by paper it?"

"Don't you know what a paper hunt is?"

Every second counted now. If Plonski left them, Wilder would have to follow him. There was little time for explanation when an understanding must be had at once. But Cob Dutcher was aggravatingly patient and deliberate.

"A paper hunt," said he, "is a hunt where one party starts out on horses over and round the county, and slings bits of paper as they go, and the other party has to find them by the bits of paper. Our swells are up to it every summer; it tickles the women riders."

"Very well," said Wilder, between his teeth; "any way you like, I may want you."

"All right," replied the man. "'Nuff said, you shadder him and let my boy Hank keep you in sight. I'll get there. He'll do the paperin'. Wait a minute, I'll get the old man's togs for you."

He then went into the boat house and returned with a gray and greasy surtout and red woolen muffler and a soft felt hat, much the worse for wear, and Wilder, without taking his eyes from Plonski, put them on with Cob's assistance. It was but a few seconds before he was fairly well disguised, and Cob hurriedly said to him, "Hank will hand you a pair of pepper and salt face blinkers, you'll have to come up the street. Your man won't stay on the dock and the boat doesn't go out again to-night."

Wilder nodded his head without entirely comprehending the meaning of what was said to him, and Cob started off.

Plonski was indistinctly seen standing almost skulkingly against a warehouse and peering about guardedly. He was evidently on the lookout for somebody on the approaching ferryboat, and he was evidently impatient and cold, for he moved about restlessly and kept his arms and feet in motion as if his circulation were benumbed.

The ferryboat came in, three or four people came ashore, the hackmen drove off leisurely and presently the dock was deserted. Then Plonski moved along in the shadow of the warehouse, and as he disappeared up the road, Wilder followed him at a discreet distance.

It was growing dark. The twilight had faded out and a still cold gloom had settled over the river and the town. Here and there the lights from the shop windows threw their feeble rays across the road, and down the railroad track the signal lights gleamed wan and far off. Wilder pulled his loose surtout about him and set out on a chilly chase, without a clear idea of what it would lead to.

When he had reached the open space made by the Hudson River railroad tracks and was cautiously working his way across, Cob Dutcher came out of one of the little houses on the main street followed by a boy who may have been fifteen or sixteen years old, and who was baggily dressed in a jacket that bulged all over him, as if it had been made for his father. On his head he wore a much too large fur cap, out of which peered a sharp, precocious and somewhat pinched face. Cob pointed in the direction of Wilder hurriedly, and the boy started off.

CHAPTER XXXIX.

WILDER TAKES HIS LIFE IN HIS HANDS.

Plonski was toiling along in a skulking but alert way, wholly unaware that the man of all others that he dreaded was on his heels. He kept out of the light of the village shops, turned off the main street at the first opportunity and began ascending the hill on a parallel, but much less frequented road, with Wilder cautiously following him. It was not an easy task for the officer to keep him in sight. It was growing dark and the roads were not only miserably lit at long intervals, but were masked by trees and shrubbery and the walks were treacherously uneven. Several times he stumbled over the roots of trees or stepped into an unexpected hole, and he had to exercise the utmost caution not to be seen or heard by the man he was pursuing, for he knew perfectly well how suspicious and crafty he was. In spite, however, of all the difficulties of the undertaking, he kept him in sight, having made up his mind that he would not lose him this time if he had to make himself known.

When Plonski had toiled along the road half way up the hill upon which the village is built, he came to the great river highway that is known all along the Hudson as Broadway, and here he turned north, Wilder doing the same, after peering round the corner and seeing him indistinctly.

About a half minute later there emerged from the shadows of the trees on the same corner, the figure of a bulgy boy in a loose fur cap and bare feet. He ran out into the middle of the highway and taking from his pocket two pieces of white paper about the size of an ordinary envelope, he tore them into little squares and threw them upon the roadway. There was no wind blowing and they lay upon the macadamized surface in white spots, plainly discernible even in the gloom of the night.

Then he took to the walk and ran noiselessly northward close to the hedges and fences that lined the private grounds.

It may be well to explain here that Cob Dutcher had invented and imparted to this boy a very simple and very safe code of symbols by which he could track him over all the familiar roads of the county. The lad was provided with a quantity of white and deep yellowish brown paper. When Cob Dutcher arrived at the crossing of these roads, he would know by the bits of white paper that he was to go north. Had the main road upon which he found them run east and west, he would have known by the same sign that he was to go east. At the crossing of the two roads there would, of course, be four corners or angles and Cob would look for the colored paper held down by a stone on one of those corners to indicate his course. There were many other devices and combinations in the code which it is not necessary to explain, but it had all grown out of a local pastime which Dutcher had correctly called "a paper hunt."

Plonski, having taken to the highway, went northward for about a mile with Wilder at a varying distance behind him. Then he turned eastward into a road that ran over the hills and began laboriously to climb his way along the rough path. Once or twice he stopped and listened so suddenly that Wilder barely escaped coming upon him. It was just possible that his quick ears had caught, on the clear cold air, the sound of Wilder's footstep. It was in one of these pauses that Wilder became aware that Plonski had somebody with him. He indistinctly saw two figures instead of one and he could just make out that one was much larger than the other. While he stood crouchingly peering between the cedars that lined the road, he heard their voices and saw that they were coming down the declivity toward him. There was a rough stone wall beside him composed of bowlders from the adjacent field and it took him but a second to slip over it and huddle himself close among the dead brambles and vines at its bottom. He heard the approaching voices and footsteps of the men who presently came abreast of his hiding place and stopped. With the utmost caution he drew himself up and peered over the wall. He could see them plainly enough now through the cedars and he saw that Plonski's companion was Samson. Then the man spoke and he recognized his voice.

"You ain't goin' all the way down the bloody hill, are you? Can't you see there ain't nobody in sight?" said that personage, in a gruff and complaining tone.

"I was sure I saw somebody," replied Plonski.

"Well, you can't expect the inhabitants all to move out to accommodate us, ken you? S'pose there was some one, what of it? I'm bloomin' cold, that's a fact, and I don't want to walk all over this d—d county to see if anybody's in it."

"Listen," said Plonski.

"Yes," responded the other, "that's the gruntin' steam car down there on the railroad."

Both men were then silent a moment and it occurred to Wilder that Plonski would insist upon retracing his steps down the hill, in which case he was likely to run across Dutcher's boy and perhaps detect his work in the road.

To his great relief, they presently turned about and went back up the road, and climbing over the stone wall, he again set out after them. About half a mile in the ascent, the men in advance came to a road that ran down into a broad open valley toward the northeast, and when Wilder a few minutes later reached the intersection, he could indistinctly see their shadowy forms on the dull, sombre gray of the roadway. His task was now more difficult than ever, for if he allowed too great a space to intervene between himself and the object of his pursuit, he would lose sight of them in the deepening gloom and if he approached too near, he would be observed in the open roadway if they looked round. But in spite of these difficulties and dangers, he kept on with a determined purpose to discover, if possible, what they were up to. As near as he could calculate, they walked two miles into the valley and then he found that they had reached one of those extemporized settlements made by Italian laborers and who in this instance were employed in excavating a great ditch and quarry, either for a railroad or for some hydraulic scheme. He saw that there were rude hovels at intervals on either side of the road and in one of them he heard the patois and laughter of the Italians who were evidently gambling. There were no signs of life outside. Here and there a sickly gleam of light came through the chinks of a shanty, but the unexpectedly cold night had driven the foreigners indoors. The miserable abodes terminated in a cheap frame house of some pretensions and Wilder rightly enough guessed it was the contractors' boarding house where the more luxurious of these imported novices were pillaged by the man who hired them. It was at this place that Plonski and his companion stopped. Wilder, skirting one of the hovels on the other side of the street, peered round the rear of it at them and saw them knock at the door of what appeared to be a temporary addition or shed, and a moment later he heard the door open and alter a stamp or two of Samson's heavy feet on the steps the door was closed and all was still. Wilder tried to make out in his mind what it meant. The only reasonable solution was that these men had taken lodgings in the house to be near their new scene of operations or to hide away from pursuers. Could it be possible that the cup was in that house? If not, what were they doing there? In thinking it over vainly, his curiosity made him reckless in the determination to discover, if possible, what it all meant, and he stole carefully out of his hiding place to make a reconnoissance. He was conscious of the danger he was now running. These ignorant and superstitious Italians, if they discovered him prowling about, would raise the hue and cry and become dangerous assailants. They could be easily induced by Plonski or Samson to make away with him. But this knowledge did not deter him. He recognized but did not stop to consider the risks he ran. There was a possible chance of finding out where the cup was and he accepted the risks.

The night had grown steadily colder and it was that kind of still and bitter cold that made all ordinary night sounds doubly sonorous and sharp. He stole round to the road and listened. He could distinctly hear men's voices in conversation, and there came to him on the crystaline air the faraway rumble of wheels over the ground and the voice of some belated yokel singing the then popular refrain of "When Johnny comes home from the War." He went a long way round to get to the rear of the boarding house and saw that it was a hastily constructed frame building built "balloon" fashion. At the back was a "lean to" shed used for wood and coal, which reached up to the bottom of the second story windows, and through the chinks of the closed shutters glimmered the thin pencils of light. He stole up close to the shed and could distinctly hear the voices of a number of men in conversation in the room. There was no doubt in his mind that these were the persons whose secret he wished to discover. He put his hand on the boards of the shed. It was roughly built but firm, and it was not a difficult matter to creep up its hemlock roof to the window, and the darkness of the night and the desertion of the place favored the attempt. The chances were in favor of his hearing something if he could get his ear against that shutter.

Without further thought he got upon the shed. It cracked and swayed under him and was certainly not as strong as he had supposed. But by the most careful exertions he threw himself along its incline close to the main building and pressed his ear cautiously down on the shutter. As he suspected, the sash was not very tight and the sounds of the voices became instantly intelligible. Several persons were talking together and the words confused each other, but a moment later there was a pause and then a voice, deliberate, clear and sharp, though in a low tone, said:

"These Italians can make more in one day by this job than they can make in a week here. I'll pay them three times as much. I must have the property and the only way to get it is to drag the river. If you'll give me five or six of your men, I'll pay you five hundred dollars, but I want the thing done thoroughly." There could be no doubt of it, this was Plonski's voice. Some one with a slight Celtic brogue replied:

"Damn it, man, you'll have the whole country on you thinkin' you're after a corpse. Sure it must be a pot of gold that would make a man drag a river such weather as this."

To which another voice said gruffly: "O, bedad, thin, I'll do it for a hundred dollars without asking the weather, barrin' the bloody risk of a job that no one knows anything about. It's easy enough if you have the tools and no wan stops yer, and the money's sure."

"The money is sure," said the voice of Plonski. "The article I want to recover belongs to me. It was lost in that stream. It's of no value to anybody else. I'll put the money in the hands of any man you say is reliable, but I want the work done to-morrow."

In spite of Wilder's professional and emotional experience and discipline, he heard his heart beat as he listened. He did not, it is true, give any thought to the examinaton of his own feelings after the manner of psychic literary experts, but he could not fail to notice the effects on his involuntary system of the revelation that was being made. The cup then had been lost in the stream. How?

he asked himself. Were the men that had been sent to get it drunk, or were they deceiving Plonski? He pressed his ear so hard against the shutter that it hurt him, and he heard a confused murmur of voices and then the same Irish voice say: "All right, boss. I'll get the men to-morrow afternoon. It can't be done in the mornin'," and Plonski said, "I'll go with you. Keep your mouth shut and everything will be safe and sure. My men know where to look and it isn't much of a stream." This speech ended in a fit of coughing and some one said, "There's too much baccy smoke in here for him: Open the windy."

Wilder heard the sound of the chairs moved, and before he could get away, the sash rattled as if a hand had been laid on it. Without a moment's hesitation, he backed away from the window and began hurriedly to slide down the shed of the roof. In his anxiety to prevent discovery which would inevitably put them all on their guard and alter their plans, he let haste overcome discretion, and just as he reached the overhanging ends of the boards that made the roof, one of them that was insecurely fastened tilted with his weight and sank under him. the upper end rising in the air. He fell about three feet and the board dropped to its place with a loud crash, just as some one at the window with the sash in his hand exclaimed, "What in — is that!"

He looked up from the ground where he had fallen, saw in a flash a group of rough faces in the light of the window and one pale and anxious countenance peering in the background over the shoulders of the others. Then, without a second's delay, he plunged into the darkness and ran as fast as he could, stumbling and colliding as he went.

He must have gone in this blind manner about two thousand feet when he stopped to take breath and listen. He heard a commotion behind him. Somebody was calling. There was a sound of doors opening and shutting and a confused murmur of voices. Then there rose above it all, the deep, long bay of a dog and the faint sound of a chain rattling. His knowledge of the animal told him it was a blood-hound, and he put his hand involuntarily on his pistol. It was almost impossible now to see more than ten feet ahead, but he started off again in what appeared to be a southerly direction and with such speed as the uneven and stony ground would permit. He ran until he came to a stone wall. The moment he had surmounted it, he found himself once more in the highway and once more he stopped to listen. The alarm was out, that was certain. He saw the lanterns swinging and heard the eager baying of the dog more plainly than ever. It was an uneven chase he knew. The pursuers were ignorant and ruthless men and Plonski, in this crisis, could easily use that ignorance to make way with an enemy. All this he was conscious of in a flash as he listened an instant, and then in strange contrast to it all, there came on the still, clear air the sonorous tones of a hearty voice somewhere singing lustily, "When Johnny Comes Home from the War." In such a condition as Wilder was, at this moment, the inductions are not apt to be rational, and a half conscious notion shot through him that this was one of those beguiling illusions of the sense that meant to entrap him. He heard the voices down in the valley and they had grown nearer while he listened. The men were on his trail, that was evident, and it was almost inevitable that they would overtake him before he could reach the confines of the village. But he started up the road as fast as he could, actuated less by fear than by an overpowering desire not to be discovered. He had not gone five hundred feet when he saw a dark object blocking the roadway ahead of him and at the same moment he heard the bay of the hound behind him startlingly near and evidently crossing the very field over which he had just come. He was between two fires, so to speak. He could now indistinctly see that the object ahead of him was a horse and vehicle. There was no time to consider. He put his hand on his revolver and determined to pass the object ahead of him. The moment he set out again, a voice hailed him. "Is that you, Inspector? I've been singing myself hoarse hopin you'd hear me."

"Quick," said Wilder, running up to the vehicle. "They're out with a dog. How's your horse?"

"Forked fire," said Dutcher. "Leave any cablegram behind you ever sent. Now then, lively there. Sling yourself up behind, Hank."

Wilder grasped a hand and bounded into the light vehicle. There was grating of iron as it came round in the road and then they started like a bolt and with an impulse that nearly threw the officer out behind. In another second they were flying like the wind through the valley.

CHAPTER XL.

LOVE PASSES UNDER A CLOUD.

It is doubtful if Colin Carteret would have sat very long in the Century Club even under the spell of Otis Chapman's vivacious eloquence, had it not been that his effusive companion managed to interest him with some accounts of the situation of affairs in the Hannige establishment.

Chapman, as the reader already knows, was a rattle-brained, good-humored and often inconsiderate talker, and Stonybrook's name having been mentioned, he immediately launched forth in a tirade against that gentleman. He abused him roundly for getting all the favors from Mrs. Hannige. "Why," he said, "she hasn't time to attend to anybody when he's about. He runs the house, pays the rent, puts in the furniture, and tells her who to fire out when the board's due. This is bad enough, of course, but on top of it all he patronizes everybody and looks at you in a way that means to imply that you couldn't stay in the place unless he gave the tip. Now, I'll tell you something if you'll promise not to fly out and act like an idiot. Hannige is trying to steer that girl that you're so sweet on into his arms."

"O, pickles, Chapman, cut that. What do you mean by steer? Talk sense, please?"

"It don't sound sensible, does it? But it's a solemn fact and I'll tell you why she's trying to do it. You see if Stonybrook married your Venus, they would probably settle down on that third floor and go to housekeeping and then Hannige could pay for a new set of furniture for her parlors and clean off some of her old debts."

"O, well," responded Carteret, with an affectation of carelessness; "that may all be and I suppose it is in the line of a calculating boardinghouse keeper, but she'll find that the young lady herself doesn't take kindly to that kind of a steer."

"How do you know? She's like all young ladies, ain't she?"

"No," shouted Carteret, rather emphatically, "she isn't."

"What's to prevent her? She's poor and Stonybrook's well fixed."

"Nothing," said Carteret, "except that she's promised to be my wife."

At this Chapman emitted a long whistle and remarked, "well, I'm blowed. You don't say so? If I'd known that, I'd have kept my jaws still. Why didn't you tell me before?"

Then changing his tone and manner, he said, as he put his hand on Carteret's shoulder, familiarly. "See here, old chap, if that's the case, I'm blessed if I wouldn't bring it to a head. I saw her come home yesterday with Stony and they were just as thick as pie. You know you can tell when a girl's sweet on a fellow by the way she balances her chin and turns up her cheek and drops her eyelid and kinder purrs at him with every feature. I take it Stony is a professional masher and not one girl in ten has got constitution enough to warn him off when he sets in strong. It's none o' my business, old fellow, but I can't help saying to a partner like you, that if I had made up my mind to marry that girl, I'd just marry her, that's all there is to it. She's too good looking to leave round loose on promises."

Carteret, annoyed and surprised at this information, got up and walked away from Chapman, partly to hide his own feelings and partly to avoid what was both impertinent and well meant. But Chapman was not the sort of man to be avoided in that way and he followed Carteret up and rattled on, only making the matter worse. "See here, Carter, I hope I haven't offended you. I am brutally candid, I know, and in these matters, candor is worse than the leprosy; but I'm your friend and you can count on me against Stony."

"Well, don't talk about it any more, please. I'm going over to make a call on the young lady and it isn't very pleasant to have one's mind poisoned in advance. Mr. Stonybrook would be a great ass if he didn't admire a handsome girl living in the same house with him. You talk too much, Chapman, about things you don't understand."

"Do I?" said Chapman, "if there's anybody that understands old Hannige any better than I do, I wish you'd trot him out. I'll bet you a dinner at the Maison Dore that Stony will buy your picture at the Academy when he sees it."

"I can't prevent him, can I, if he pays my price?"

"No, you can't, and if he does, perhaps it will keep the picture in the family."

"You talk like an idiot this morning, Chapman," said Carteret. "You're getting to be a frightful bore."

"But I know something about your customers, for I've dealt with the people who like your work before this."

"And I suppose you think that the favor you did me gives you the right to be impertinent."

"No," said Chapman. "It only gave me the right to be confidential. I thought I was giving you a valuable tip on Stony. I'm sure if a chap was to come to me and say, 'Look here old fellow, there's a swell blackguard trying to carry off your goods,' I'd say, 'Thank you, old boy, I'll punch him in the eye and come back and go to lunch with you.' But you put on more airs than a photographer, and I do believe feel like punching me. I suppose I've got to put it down to the eccentricity of genius since you've painted that picture and it's awfully rough on a common workman like me to have to associate with genius and get snubbed and sat on and kicked around in this humiliating fashion, simply because I can't lie like old Hannige and spend money like Stony. Where are you going?"

"I'm going across the street," replied Carteret, without turning round.

"Well, come back here when you get it all fixed and go to lunch with me. I'll wait for you, and don't be a disagreeable prig."

Carteret made no response but went down the steps of the club, crossed the street with a rather grim face and pulled the bell at Mrs. Hannige's.

When Florry opened the door he said with a degree of importance and dignity that was new to Florry, "Tell Miss Castleton that Mr. Carteret is here and would like to speak to her." Whereupon Florry with the most placid promptness replied, "Miss Castleton has just gone out with Mr. Stonybrook and said she would not be back in an hour."

The tone of voice with which Carteret said, "Ah, indeed," was so ghastly that Florry gave a little involuntary start and added: "It's true, sir. She hain't been gone ten minutes, but Mr. Evans is hupstairs. P'raps you'd like to go hup and wait."

"Yes," said Carteret, with a rueful firmness, "I think I will go up and wait."

When he arrived at Mr. Evan's apartment, he found that old gentleman sitting by a grate fire with a rug across his knees and a most beaming expression of satisfaction playing upon his countenance. His emaciated fingers formed a contemplative pyramid in front of his face, partly to shield it from the glare of the fire and by his side in a chair lay one of his open ledgers.

"Ah, yes. Bless my soul, Mr. Carteret, so it is. Why, how do you do, Mr. Carteret? I was asking Ella about you yesterday and Mr. Stonybrook thought that you were too busy to call and see your old friends. I am pleased to see you, sir, I am sure. Will you sit down? It is a very cold day. Ella has gone out to attend to some business of mine. You see, Mr. Carteret, I cannot attend to my business affairs as I used to. I regret it very much for I am a businessman and my affairs demand constant attention. You know how it is, Mr. Carteret, when business affairs get complicated, it's very difficult to straighten them out."

"I called, Mr. Evans," said Carteret, "to see Manuella and make an apology for not getting her letter. I did not know, of course, that she intended coming to the city so suddenly or I would have fetched her myself."

"O, Mr. Stonybrook came up and took care of her. It was very kind and thoughtful of him and he was very attentive. Mr. Stonybrook is a gentleman of great business capacity, Mr. Carteret, and I feel very thankful that Ella has interested him so much. She needed the advice of a businessman like Mr. Stonybrook. Won't you take a chair?"

At this repeated invitation, Carteret sat down rather suddenly.

"I am very glad, Mr. Evans," he said, "that you have found in Mr. Stonybrook such a valuable friend."

"I knew you would be," continued Mr. Evans; "he is a very rare gentleman and I am sure you will like him when you come to know him as Ella and I do, and now that there has been such a change in our circumstances, I hope to be able, Mr. Carteret, to invite you to meet him here and show you some of the hospitality which you know our circumstances hither-to would not permit us to extend. You must not think that because my business affairs have been adjusted, that we are changed in the least. You know that I have always had Ella's interest so much at heart that I regretted my inability to place her in that position which I am sure she would adorn."

"Mr. Evans," said Carteret, with a very formal and slightly anxious tone of voice, "I am very glad to hear that your circumstances have changed and that you will not allow them to change your granddaughter's character."

"O, dear no. I wouldn't permit that. Ella will always have the greatest respect for the friends she made when she was somewhat unfortunate, but Ella is a Castleton, Mr. Carteret, and she will now assume the social position which my temporary embarrassment deprived her of. It is Mr. Stonybrook's desire as well as mine, that she should at once take that place in the world which her beauty and her talents should command for her. Did you find it growing much colder out, Mr. Carteret?"

"Yes," replied Carteret, "it has been growing steadily colder for an hour, but it is very comfortable here. Do you expect Miss Castleton to return shortly?"

"She said she would be back in an hour but dear me, Mr. Carteret, you never can tell how long a girl will take when she goes shopping and you don't like to hurry her either, so I said; 'Go along, my dear, and take your time. I shall be very comfortable till you come back.' You see she and Mr. Stonybrook went to the notary's for me, but Mr. Stonybrook wanted her to go to the dressmaker's afterwards and so they killed two birds with one stone."

"I suppose," remarked Carteret, quite meekly, "that Manuella—Miss Castleton—will have to relinquish her art studies now that she is going to assume her proper place in society?"

"O dear, yes," replied Mr. Evans, with a maddening look of complacency, "it will no longer be necessary for her to think about earning her living. A girl like Ella, Mr. Carteret, is really intended for but one thing in life as you know, and that is marriage, a proper marriage, Mr. Carteret, and you can have no idea what a weight of responsibility has been lifted from my mind now that she will have the opportunity to marry properly."

Carteret was fast losing what little patience he possessed by nature. There was a patriarchal imbecility about Mr. Evans with which he was perfectly familiar, but the cool disregard of the intimacy which had grown up between his granddaughter and his visitor and the sudden assumption of superiority, nettled Carteret to such an extent that it was with the utmost difficulty that he preserved the formal courtesy which was so habitual to Mr. Evans.

"My intimate acquaintance with your granddaughter," he said, "and my association with her during your recent struggles and hardships, entitle me to hear from Miss Castleton's own lips what her views may be with regard to her change of circumstances and change of conduct. I have always found her so frank and honest and so loyal, Mr. Evans, that I feel assured no change of circumstances will make any material change in her conduct or character."

"O, dear, no. Certainly not. I couldn't permit that. Ella was always very obedient and considered my wishes before she considered her own. You will find, Mr. Carteret, that she is just the same that she always was, and just as ready as ever to be guided by a man of business habits like myself."

"I am very anxious, sir, to hear her say so with her own lips and to learn from her if Mr. Stonybrook's views of life and of conduct are the same as hers."

"O, they are, they are, I assure you they are," said Mr. Evans. "Mr. Stonybrook is a very discreet man of affairs and it is a great satisfaction to an old man like me, sir, to feel that his child will have the guidance of a man like Mr. Stonybrook when she has lost her natural protector, and I can't expect, Mr. Carteret, to live forever. I know perfectly well that I am getting on in years and with all my business training, I cannot look after affairs as I used to."

"Perhaps," said Carteret, who had now reached that crisis of feeling which generally resulted in an explosion. "Perhaps you think of marrying Miss Castleton to Mr. Stonybrook?"

The old gentleman turned partly round in his chair, and the look of complacency deepened into an expression of senile craft. There was a momentary gleam in his watery eyes as he said:

"Ha, Mr. Carteret, you are such a friend of the family that I can talk these domestic affairs to you without committing any impropriety. I am pleased, sir, to see that you agree with me. I have thought the matter over very seriously—"

"But I don't agree with you at all, sir," exclaimed Carteret.

"Certainly not. O, dear, no. It don't stand to reason, sir, that we should have precisely the same view. My business training—"

"Your business training, Mr. Evans, is all very well, but you will excuse me from expressing any great admiration for Mr. Stonybrook, for I don't know anything about him. I dare say his business training is equal to yours, but as I have never been able to find out what his occupation is, you must not expect me to have as high an opinion of him as you have formed somewhat hastily, and as your granddaughter is of age it is just possible that she may have some views of her own quite independent of business training."

Having fired off this somewhat farfetched and slightly opaque expression of his views, with a conviction that it expressed as much as he felt, Mr. Carteret got up, as was his custom when a little excited, and began to take rapid turns up and down the room.

But whatever may have been the purpose of his words, they utterly failed to have the desired effect upon Mr. Evans, whose complacent benignity of countenance had settled into a half ecstatic and wholly dreamy imbecility.

"Just so," he murmured; "I quite agree with you, Mr. Stonybrook, and we shall all agree much better when we get these things fixed on a business basis—a business basis, sir. As I have told you, Mr. Stonybrook, I leave these matters in your hands, because you understand business—business. It's—It's great comfort, my dear, to, have things go on in a business—business—business—"

Here his voice died out in an inarticulate murmur. His head sank on his breast, and as Carteret advanced upon him with an impetuous remark, he saw that the old man had gone to sleep. Then it was, for the first time, that an acute consciousness of the situation was experienced. Mr. Evans was in his dotage, and Mr. Stonybrook was assuming all the rights and privileges of a guardian and adviser in his place.

He walked to the window and stood looking disconsolately upon the familiar roofs and walks of the neighborhood. There, in the corner, stood Manuella's easel, still holding the canvas upon which she had tried to trace, under his loving guidance, the lilies of the valley that he had brought her. It was dust-covered now and neglected, but it woke in him a train of recollections inexpressibly tender; for it was there that he had sat with his face but a few inches away from her ordorous and radiant hair, and guided her nervous little hand in its art endeavors; and even while he stood there, as if to enhance the associations, there came from Irving Hall, where someone was rehearsing, the deep mellow notes of the organ, and he caught once more the strains of "The Blue Danube."

This reverie was broken into by the flinging open of the door and the entrance of Manuella herself, who burst in wholly unconscious of a visitor, followed by Mr. Stonybrook, whose arms were full of paper parcels.

Glowing with exercise and radiant with excitement, the girl rushed to her grandfather, kissed him on the forehead, and then saw Mr. Carteret standing in the window. With the same ingenuous impulse she went immediately to him and held out both her hands, exclaiming, "At last. It seemed as though you were never coming to see me any more."

And to this frank expression Carteret responded by giving her one hand and bowing with almost an icy dignity.

If the girl was sensible of his somewhat chilling demeanor, she gave no other sign of it than by a slight lifting of the upper eyelids, as if an unconscious surprise had expended itself in an almost imperceptible and evanescent stare.

"I'm so glad you came," she said, without a change of manner, "for I have got so much to tell you. Of course you didn't get my letter in time."

"I got it," said Carteret, "with reasonable promptness and answered it in person with unreasonable haste."

"You didn't go up?"

"Yes I did, of course."

"What a shame," exclaimed the girl with genuine consideration. "Grandpa," she added impulsively as she turned about, "Mr. Carteret went all the way to Scarsdale to come back with us," and then seeing that her grandfather was busy listening to Mr. Stonybrook, she addressed the rest of the sentence to Carteret in a lowered tone of voice. "And you were just too late, and had your journey for nothing."

"Yes," said Carteret.

Then as she instinctively moved close to the window and Carteret followed her, she said softly, "You are annoyed. You are angry at me."

And come at it in this blunt and honest way, Carteret could only frame a compromise between his pride and his love and say, yes he was—as if it was the inalienable right of a lover to pout a little and be coaxed back.

"But you mustn't be at me," said this straightforward piece of honesty as she dropped her lids. "I couldn't think of staying up there without you, don't you know, and you were so busy with your picture. O, tell me about the picture. When are you going to take me to see it?"

"Somehow I got the idea," replied Carteret, "that you were going to give up your art studies, change your masters or something. I think your grandfather said as much. I can't expect you to take as much interest in my poor efforts as you once did."

She hesitated a moment, then she said, "I thought you understood Grandpa better. I don't think you understand me at all, Mr. Carteret."

The little bit of pride that now made her draw herself up was so unlike the generous outburst that had preceded it, that Carteret was sorry in an instant that he had made this speech.

But the tete-a-tete could not be carried on any farther and the girl's tact saw perhaps that it was not prudent to prolong it. Turning, she said. "You have met Mr. Stonybrook before, I believe, Mr. Carteret."

The two men bowed, Carteret rather formally, and Stonybrook rather carelessly. Manuella then gave herself to the impartial duties of hostess, treating her two visitors with equal courtesy and Carteret very speedily felt that he had brought about his own punishment in some hardly distinguishable way.

It was impossible for him to avoid seeing and feeling that Mr. Stonybrook treated him with a careless courtesy which was meant to say that he was of no consequence, and no effort of his, however subtle, could make Manuella indicate by word or look that there was any difference in her guests.

Mr. Stonybrook assumed the easy familiarity, not only of an honored friend, but of a domestic confidant, and said those little things which were meant to give Carteret to understand that he and the family had some confidences.

It was not in the nature of the impetuous boy to put up with formality very long, and so when he had endured as much of it as was possible he picked up his hat, and bidding the old gentleman adieu, was about to make a stiff, ceremonial exit with a distinct hope that Manuella would rush after him to the door and he could get her alone for a final pout in the hall.

To his inextinguishable disappointment she bowed to him from the middle of the room with a ceremonial dignity equal to his own, and he went out with a well preserved majesty that lasted till he reached the stairway. Then it began to collapse, for there was nobody but himself to regard it, and somehow it went to pieces under his own scrutiny.

The result of his visit was painfully unsatisfactory, for several reasons. He had encountered Manuella under new conditions and his innocent protegé had shown the new tact, the new reticence and the formal courtesy of a woman. Besides, he had assumed the position of a wounded lover openly and she had not responded with a lover's anxiety, but had drawn herself up and let him come away without explanations. As he thought this over his pride rebelled and he rashly determined to be as careless and defiant as possible. He could stand it if she could. So he went out of Mrs. Hannige's slamming the door rather more viciously than he intended, and crossed the street whistling somewhat vehemently, as if Miss Castleton could hear him.

"See here," said Chapman, who came down the club steps to meet him, "you'll forgive me, old fellow, but I wouldn't whistle like that if I were you. I'd hum it, don't you know. It isn't so transparent."

"I thought," replied Carteret angrily, "that you'd stop being an infernal fool if I came back. If you can't cut that, say so at once and I'll leave you. I'm not the sort of fellow to put up with a guying companion."

Chapman, entirely undaunted by this reception, slipped his arm through his friend's and walking close beside him said: "Don't get mad at me, old chap. The fact is that you're annoyed at something that's happened. It sticks out all over you. I could read it in the curve of your back without waiting for that absurd whistle. You don't know how you trot all your feelings out. I don't want to pry into your affairs, Carter, but when you hang them all on the front fence I can't help taking notice of кем. Can I? What's happened?"

"Nothing," said Carteret with heroic emphasis.

"Has that old beau of Hannige's got the field? Why don't you treat me like a friend? You haven't got many who'd do as much for you; and look here, old fellow, perhaps I could do a good deal more than you suspect. I live in the house.

Besides, you don't want to go into the blues. You've made the hit of the season at the Academy. Hang it, the whole town will be talking about you in a week."

Carteret listened moodily. They crossed the park and he turned to look at an empty bench under a bare catalpa tree.

"Come on," said Chapman. "What are you stopping here for? Let's go up to the Academy and see who's there."

CHAPTER XLI.

AN ENCOUNTER IN THE ACADEMY.

Manuella made up her mind that Carteret would call the next morning when Mr. Stonybrook was away. She was a little annoyed at his manner, but her woman's instinct told her it was all owing to his jealousy of Mr. Stonybrook, and she knew so well that he had no cause to be jealous of that person that she did not give herself any unnecessary discomfort. But she watched for his ring the next morning, and as the hours went on and he did not come she felt disappointed. Then for the first time the thought crept into her mind that perhaps Mr. Carteret was fickle. How could he think he loved one woman for a whole year to discover his mistake afterwards, without being in danger of doing it again? But this ungracious thought only made her the more anxious to see him. It was one o'clock and he had not come, but instead Mr. Stonybrook arrived. He came in quite familiarly now, and after his usual courtesy to the old gentleman he said, "Miss Castleton, there's a picture of you at the Academy. Don't you want to see it?"

She instantly clapped her hands and said, "Yes, I do," and as immediately regretted that she had been so impulsive.

"Then," said Mr. Stonybrook, "get your new dress on and we'll go up and look at it. I believe the town is talking about it, and if it does you justice we'll buy it, don't you know."

This consideration decided her. "Yes, of course," she said to herself, "I'll get Mr. Stonybrook to buy it. Why didn't I think of that before? What a surprise for Carteret. Besides, he should have called. It would just serve him right to go off and do him a favor and not be in if he should be so mean as to wait till the afternoon before he came."

So Mr. Stonybrook went to his room and she began to array herself in her new winter garments with a girl's pride, and by and by when she went down the stairs with Mr. Stonybrook, Mrs. Hannige, who was lying in wait, rushed out and said: "Come in a minute, my dear, I want to see how your dress looks." And the girl had to be turned round several times in Mrs. Hannige's back parlor and listen to the crafty colloquy that went on without appearing to be aimed at her, "You're the handsomest girl now I ever saw my dear. What a difference clothes does make. You never looked like yourself before. You must take good care of her Mr. Stonybrook. I'm afraid she's a little wild and needs an experienced protector. There, go along, my dear. You ought to be as happy as a lark. I declare I never saw a handsomer couple then you two do make."

Manuella was not over praised on this occasion. She was becomingly and even attractively dressed in a new winter silk and cloak and bonnet which her grandfather's improved circumstances had warranted and Mr. Stonybrook felt very proud of her as he handed her out of the coach at the Academy.

They arrived there about three o'clock, at which hour in the afternoon the place was frequented by the fashionable crowds. Manuella had never been in a gallery before and she was all surprise and delight. She felt, as she stood in the south room among the throngs of elegant visitors, that she had entered a new kind of existence in a new role. And there was Carteret's picture on the line with a crowd of buzzing admirers in front of it. It quite dazzled her, poor girl, familiar as she was with it, for she had never seen it in a handsome gold frame, properly lit and nobly associated with so much honor and beauty. She looked at it with a charming girlish enthusiasm and in her little outburst forgot that she was praising herself.

How well she knew every touch on the canvas. Did not that delicious stretch of dried grasses on that bank recall the the afternoon when Carteret painted it with Hi Tucker sitting there on the abutment? Did not that fold in her dress bring back the hour he spent in posing her and the lover's despair that he put into a compliment when he declared no one could ever hope to do her justice, and that flying lock of hair on her temple, did it not bring back the thunder storm when they laughingly gathered the canvas and tools and went scurrying along the aqueduct in childish glee to escape the rain, and then sat on a little porch and saw the black clouds roll over the hills and empty themselves away out over Long Island Sound.

Why, she felt that she knew the picture better than anybody on earth. How many times Carteret had painted out that hand and gone at it all over again, and how many times he had pretended to study it and had held it in his own and forgot all about the picture, and they had been roused out of their lover's dream by Mrs. Manser calling them with her bell in her hand to come to tea.

A thousand memories, gentle and tender, flooded her as she looked at the work, and over and above all was a half conscious pride in herself that she looked so handsome, and a wholly conscious pride in Carteret that he was such a great painter.

In the fullness of her heart she expected Mr. Stonybook to put some of her ardor and admiration into words. But that gentleman was looking at the picture critically and without any ardor.

"My dear Miss Castleton," he said in reply to her exclamation of "Isn't it beautiful?" "it's a beautiful subject but it requires a master to do it justice. I'm afraid that young man undertook too great a task. A Tadema or a Bouguereau might have done something with it. It strikes me that it lacks fluency and breadth. Like all the American attempts in that direction, it is a trifle hard and unsuggestive."

Nothing that Manuella had ever heard struck her as so unjust and unwarranted as this speech. To her it was simple jargon. For the first time she felt indignant and rebellious and a little color flashed into her cheek. She heard a lady who stood near her say: "It's the gem of the exhibition and has brought to the front a new genius. I understand he is quite a young man." Manuella looked at Mr. Stonybrook with a triumphant little flash of her eye and toss of her head.

He smiled. "You musn't let the opinions of these people weigh with you," he said. "As a rule they know as much about art as they do about social distinctions. We all grow out of these things if we cultivate our taste and our knowledge. We'll take a turn round the rooms and come back to it after we have seen the best canvases; then you'll get a clear comparative view."

While they were talking, Otis Chapman, who was sauntering about the room, felt some one tap him on the shoulder in the throng, and turning round, he found himself face to face with Rosamond Enniston. She was accompanied by Dr. Wollendorf, whom she introduced and immediately dismissed, saying: "Now Doctor, you walk round and enjoy the pictures for a little while. I want to talk to Mr. Chapman." At which the doctor goodnaturedly moved away and Miss Enniston, catching hold of Chapman's arm, said: "Sit down here on this sofa. I want to talk to you."

They both sat down on one of the sofas in the middle of the south room and dropping her voice, she said with her usual impetuosity: "Do you see that lady and gentleman standing before Carteret's picture?"

"Yes," said Chapman, "that's Miss—"

"Yes, I know. Who's the man?"

"That?" said Chapman, "Why that's a fellow by the name of Stonybrook."

They were sitting directly in front of Chapman's Saranac Lake picture and at that moment no passing figures hid it. She pointed to it significantly. "Is it sold?" she asked.

"No," he replied.

"But you want to sell it?"

"Do I? You don't think, Miss Enniston, that I painted it to accommodate these old fogies of the Academy, do you?"

"Very well," she said, "now tell me, is Mr. Stonybrook—is that his name—is he paying his attentions to that woman?"

"Well," replied Chapman, "so far as my casual observation of the subject goes, I should say he was. Do you want to buy the Saranac Lake?"

"Where does she get the money to dress like that?"

"Like what?" asked Chapman a little surprised.

"How much do you want for the picture?" asked Miss Enniston.

"Well, I ticketed it at 500, but I'll make a discount for cash of course."

"You understand me, Mr. Chapman. I'm a good deal more of a woman of the world than you give me credit for. Does Mr. Stonybrook pay for her clothes?"

The commercial instincts of Mr. Otis Chapman were now in a slight quandary. He understood perfectly well that Miss Enniston meant with almost brutal distinctness to have him understand that she would buy his picture if he told her what she wanted to know. He was inclined to gratify her as much as he dared without being false to his friend Carteret. He hesitated a moment, so she asked another question.

"Is he an admirer of her's?"

"O, of course," said Chapman promptly. "Who wouldn't be?"

"Don't trifle with me. He's her lover?"

"Upon my word, Miss Enniston, just how far his admiration goes in the matter of ardor or wardrobe—"

She interrupted him again.

"You know what I mean," she said, "why don't you tell me? You live in the same house. You are aware of what is going on. Does Mr. Stonybrook want to marry her?"

"At a risk," said Chapman, "I should say he did. But he don't confide in me."

"What's his occupation?"

"That's a puzzle. I don't believe he's got any."

"Has he any money?"

"He makes a show of it."

"Does the girl like him?"

Chapman laughed. "Miss Enniston," he said, "You flatter me. I don't deserve it. I don't know half as much as you give me credit for."

"I wish I *could* flatter you," she said, "You are not as clever a salesman as I thought. I ask your pardon for making the mistake."

She got up, bowed rather stiffly and moved away

"Well, well," said Chapman to himself as he looked after her, "I should hate to have her love me. There's five hundred dollars gone in to the abyss of discretion and sentimental nonsense. O, phantom sensibility, how much you *do* cost me."

The young woman's action had been so sudden and was so ill-advised that he sat for a moment regarding her with astonishment.

"It would be just like Carteret to come in here now," he was saying, "and I wish he might. It would let a light in on Stony."

Meanwhile Manuella and Mr. Stonybrook had gone off into one of the other rooms and were moving about from picture to picture, presenting quite a contrast of connoisseurship, and Miss Enniston was watching them with a keen, observant eye.

Slowly they traversed the whole suite of galleries, the girl listening closely to Mr. Stonybrook's criticisms and secretly disagreeing with them all, and finally they came round to the south room and to Carteret's picture once more.

"Now," said Mr. Stonybrook with a rather rash confidence, "you will see that your friend, clever as he may be, has a good deal to learn." An elderly gentleman was standing in front of them with a catalogue in his hand and was audibly expressing himself to a younger companion. "My dear sir," he said "I regard that as not only the freshest but the most promising piece of work in the room. It has less affectation than anything in the exhibition. It shines from the inside—the rest of ʀᴇᴍ have to be lit. I'm surprised at it, for I know the young artist very well, and, although I regard him as a noble fellow, I didn't think he could do it. I was in hopes I'd meet him here and be able to congratulate him."

"I wish he was here," said his companion. "I'd like him to hear your opinion of his work. There are so many prigs who don't understand it, and will not have anybody who cuts away from the cup and saucer business that it's a luxury to hear you talk."

Manuella's heart gave a little jump of triumph. The old gentleman had long, iron-gray hair and a massive, intellectual face, and she felt sure that he was an artist himself, and that at all events he was an intelligent critic. She glanced up at Mr. Stonybrook slyly to see how he would take the eulogium, but that gentleman presented a cynical composure.

"Miss Castleton," he said, "you have a personal interest in the picture. That is a sufficient reason why I should buy it, and I have a personal interest in not having you hung up in public in that style."

But you must not buy it if you do not like it," she said, "there are so many that do. I don't think you take interest enough in it to purchase it."

"But I take interest in you," he said.

"Not in that way, I hope," she replied. "I wouldn't buy it if I were you."

"But don't you think I ought to help a struggling genius?" he asked. "They need help as a rule."

While he was saying this an attendant came in front of them and slipped a card into the frame of the picture. The moment he moved away they both saw the bold black letters on it, "SOLD."

"O, I wonder who's bought it," exclaimed Manuella, with impulsive satisfaction.

Then a young woman who had stood behind her moved a step or two forward and said, with a curious, mixture of defiance and contempt, "I have."

And as Manuella caught hold of Mr. Stonybrook's arm and turned away Miss Enniston glared after her as if she had inflicted a mortal injury.

When they had gone down the room Mr. Stonybrook found his companion's arm in his own, and she was almost clinging to him in her timidity.

"That's the most extraordinary performance I ever heard of," said Stonybrook. "Do you know the young lady?"

"No," said Manuella, with a pardonable white lie, "I am not acquainted with her."

"She must have taken us for saloon keepers," said Mr. Stonybrook, "and was afraid we wanted it for our gin palace. I never saw such an extraordinary performance."

Then they went down the grand staircase, Manuella still clinging to him, and, as they reached the first landing, Carteret, who had just come in, saw them go by.

He stood near the wainscoted wall, talking to a brother artist at the time, and the expression of his face as he looked up and caught a sudden and transient glimpse of the woman he loved sweeping past with her arm in Mr. Stonybrook's and his mouth close to her ear, was one of pained surprise. But he did not know that at the top of the staircase a pair of eyes that had been looking for him for an hour, were now fixed upon him with a sharp interpretative inquisitiveness.

Before he was conscious of his own acute surprise, Manuella and Mr. Stonybrook had swept by without perceiving him and gone out the entrance way.

The special cruelty of this incident to Carteret was not in the fact that Manuella was in Mr. Stonybrook's company, but that she had not paid her first visit to the Academy and enjoyed her first surprise with him. He had counted on that. It was the one triumph that he had hugged above all else. He had promised himself the enjoyment of pointing out his achievement and talking with her over all the confidences and hopes it had inspired. He felt that she had inconsiderately and almost ruthlessly robbed him of something that was his by right. It could not of course occur to him what motive had prompted Manuella to go with Stonybrook. He only saw and felt that she had conferred upon that man a privilege that every tender instinct ought to have told her did not belong to him, and he only remembered that she had gone out clinging to him and listening to him.

He went moodily up the stairs; a dull premonition of some kind of heart disaster weighed upon him. The woman he loved appeared to be drifting away from him willingly, and an obscure suspicion lurked in his mind that she might not be as sincere and honest as he had painted her.

His introspection was suddenly broken into by Otis Chapman, who caught him at the top of the stairway eagerly by the arm.

"O, I say, Carter," he ejaculated, "there's been the jolliest kind of a go here—come over out of the crowd, I want to post you—hang it, man, you're the only fellow that carries a sensation in train. The beauty herself was here with Stony."

"Yes," said Carteret, "I saw them."

"Did you?" asked, Chapman with a look of surprise.

"Yes, they passed me on the stairs."

"Did they?" asked Chapman, with a look of inquiry. "Well, do you know Stony wanted to buy your picture and the girl wouldn't let him?"

"What?"

"Yes; sit down here. It's true. I just heard enough of their conversation to make out that she discouraged it."

"What did Mr. Stonybrook say about the picture?"

"O, what do you care what he said? Do you know the other one's here?"

"What other one,"

"Miss Enniston, and the two women came face to face. I was on the other side of the room, but I saw Rem meet in front of your canvas."

"Are you acquainted with Miss Enniston?" asked Carteret, with an unexpected coldness.

"Yes, I met her at the Sanger party. By Jove, here she comes now."

Carteret looked up and made a sudden movement to go. Chapman caught him by the arm. "Don't run," he said, "face it out."

Miss Enniston came straight to them and stood in front of Carteret. She wore a smile on her face.

"Let me sit here a moment, Mr. Chapman, I have a little business to transact with Mr. Carteret. I shall not separate you but a few minutes."

Chapman got up with a polite impulse, and before any other protest could be made the young woman sat down in his place. The moment Chapman moved away she said:

"Colin, I've only got a few words to say. Listen to me, do. I must humiliate myself to say them, but there is no other course after that wretched scene we had. I have despised myself ever since, but you must know now that your suspicions and insinuations about Miss Castleton were unjust. Let me talk, please, just a moment," she said, as he was about to break out. "I only want to say to you that I have thought everything all over calmly, and you were right when you said we could be friends, and that the past was gone. I want to be your friend, that's all, and help you. Can't we be? There isn't any reason why we should keep up a lover's quarrel, and hate each other, when we can act like sensible acquaintances, and let love go where it pleases. We may not have been made for lovers, Colin; you may have been right when you said that, but we can at least be friends, and not persecute each other with the past. Don't you think so?"

"It never entered my head to persecute you, Miss Enniston. I have only the kindest wishes for you."

"Yes, yes," she said, not at all heeding his words. "It is so indescribably silly for two people to go and proclaim their little private squabbles to the world, and for a woman, don't you know, Colin, it's worse than a man, to have everybody pointing at her and saying she has been jilted, or she set her cap for so-and-so and made a mistake; you understand. We ought to act like sensible, grown-up persons, and not like children. You've got your fight to make in your profession, and you want all the friends you can get, and when you find out, if you ever do, how hollow and mercenary and false some of them are it will be pleasant to know you've got one who outgrew sentimentalism and all that, and was proud of you for your talents."

"Thank you, Miss—Rosamond," said Carteret, a little confused as to the logic of this speech. "I'm sure I appreciate your kind motives. There is no reason that I know of why we should not be friends."

"We'll shake hands over it," she said; "not here, but some other time. Now, come over to the picture. I want to show you something."

They got up and walked to the end of the south room and Carteret exclaimed, "Why, it's sold!"

"Yes," replied his companion; "I've bought it."

"You? Impossible."

"Why impossible? You'll get a check for it to-morrow. I'm going to send it to the loan exhibition next January."

She looked into his face. "I'm going to help you win your fight, Colin, just as a sister would, for the sake of auld langsyne and not have any more nonsense. You must come and see me at the Hardynge's just like any other acquaintance. It's only fair to me. you understand?"

"Yes," said Carteret, wonderingly.

CHAPTER XLII.

MCCUNE IS HUNTED LIKE A RAT.

The immediate vicinity of O'Reardon's Terrace two nights after Wilder's exploit in the country was alive with all its characteristic elements.

At the entrance to the middle building stood Mr. John Sitwhite, leaning against the doorpost in his shirt sleeves, utterly regardless of the cold, and smoking his short clay pipe. Close beside him stood two other men with whom he was in conversation. One of them wore the uniform of a United States volunteer, and his bronzed face and well worn clothes showed that he had seen active service. The other man was Dan Sully.

"A man's a fool," said the soldier, "who stays round here breakin' his back tryin' to earn a livin', when he kin git his three hundred dollars down, his regular pay, and have a long picnic out doors with plenty of appetite and plenty of liberty. Two months' sojerin' is likely to spile any man as has got a heart. Why, look a here, our men all last summer laid up in camp livin' on the fat o' the land, wherever we could get it, and drawin' our greenbacks regular. If I had a wife and two kids like you, John Sitwhite, I'd just hand the old woman three hundred dollars, put on the sojer clothes, say 'goodbye, old gal,' and jine the boys at the front. If anything happened, the old gal would git a pension, and I'm blowed if she ever will while you're shovelin' coke. Why, six weeks in a tent would cure that influenza of yours."

"I should say," remarked Mr. Dan Sully, "that shovelers like Sitwhite was the kind of sojers what would have the biggest pay, as most of the army don't seem to do much else but shovel."

"O, shovelin's all right," remarked Sitwhite. "If there weren't anything but shovelin', I take a hand in't. But a man can't do much shovelin' on crutches or in a hospital."

"No, some men," said the soldier, "would rather live in a hospital all their lives than risk one for six weeks. I guess sojerin' has kept more men out of the hospital than it's put in. Anyway I've seen a good many fellers come to hard health in the ranks that hadn't much to boast of afore, and if I was a coke shoveler, I'm blessed if I wouldn't change off from the smell of gas to the smell of gunpowder, if there was some fire in it. Dan's goin' to jine our regiment; you heerd of it, I suppose?"

"No, I didn't," said Sitwhite, "the more fool he for doin' of it, when he could go as a substitute if he'd wait for the draft."

"There won't be no draft," answered Sully.

"Why won't there?" asked the soldier, quickly. "You kin bet your pay there'll be one if old Abe orders it. Who'll stop it?"

"I dunno as anybody'll stop it, but it'll be tough work to force it in this ere city, and don't you make no mistake," answered Sully.

"No, I don't," continued the volunteer, "and I'd be one of fifty thousand boys at the front to make it good if old Abe says it goes."

While these men were thus conversing on the most pressing topic of the moment which obtruded itself into the thoughts of all classes, there stood, not ten feet away from them, a girl dressed in coarse but showy garments, made to project absurdly with the hoops that were then in vogue. There was an obvious mixture in her apparel, of the coarseness of her class and the finery of a professional exhibitor. She had a cheap fur wound about her form in a flaunting manner and an enormous feather drooped over the side of her hat to her shoulder. She had listened without much interest to parts of the conversation of these men whom she appeared to know, and then had given her attention to the life of the street, which even in cold weather did not intermit its variety.

As she stood there with her hand upon the iron rail listlessly watching the boys in the roadway and the passing people, a lad in the street came to the curb and attracted her attention by a number of audible signals.

She stepped from the little entrance way and went to the curb, approaching him so closely that she said in a coarse whisper:

"What's the matter with you? What is it?"

The boy, with an exaggerated grimace and a most absurd wink, replied, as he jerked his hand over his shoulder:

"He's there and told me to tell yer."

"Who?" asked the girl.

"You know; it's Ther Mink. He wouldn't come up coz he's hunted."

"Where is he?"

"He's at McGloine's. You'll ketch him at the side door coz he's watchin' fur yer."

Without another word the girl gave her furs a flirt around her neck and started hurriedly across the street, going toward the avenue. When she came to McGloine's on the corner, which was now ablaze with light and noisy with the congregated idlers and drinkers within, she opened the side door without hesitation and looked in. The moment she did so, The Mink, heavily muffled up, cautiously put his head out and after looking up and down the street, joined her.

"What is it?' she asked anxiously. "Are you hiding?"

"Hish't," replied the man warningly. "I don't want the coppers to see me. I guess they're lookin' for me by this time."

"What do they want you for now? When did you come back?"

They both moved away from the entrance to McGloine's, the man hurriedly taking her with him down the street.

"Are you hunted?" she asked.

"Don't you know?"

"Hope I may die if I heered a thing."

"Old Beaky's took and Samson with him."

The girl stopped and looked at him.

"Honest?" she asked.

"So 'elp me level, and they want me. Beaky was took yesterday mornin' on the river when he brought his gang to drag it, and they coppered Curly in the wood. I shinned out on my marrers and never gasped till I struck the town. Beaky and Curly's in quod."

"Who's got the cup?" asked the girl with unmistakable interest.

"Why, nobody ain't got the d--d mug, 'cause yer see the bloomin' river where we lost it, is froze."

"You don't say!" exclaimed the girl with surprise.

"Yes, I do, but don't stop here. Yer don't want me snatched, do yer?"

"Who worked the lay?" she asked as they both moved on.

"Yer couldn't guess if I was to give yer a coach and six. Yer'd be a thinkin' it was some officer from t'other side, wouldn't yer? And it couldn't no how come inter yer head that it was the same bloomin' d--d inspector that allers works it. O, no, yer just couldn't, could yer?"

"Then the jig's up, hey?"

"Well, I wouldn't swear it was. If Beaky ain't out to-morrer a walkin' Broadway in his long tail blue with his finger on his nose, then I'm a cow. But it don't foller that a feller like me is a goin' to be so particular looked after by his political friends as is old Beaky, so I ain't goin' to be seen if I can help mysel' till I hear from the boss."

"Where you goin' so you won't be seen, hey? Do you think that you won't be seen if you walk the streets? Why don't you come to the Terrace like a man?"

"Coz I don't want to be pulled out like a rat. That's just the swimmin' hole where he'd go to look for me. Coz why? Coz you're there. Oh, no, my honey bean."

"But you needn't come up to my rooms when Beaky's got apartments on the tother floor and nobody ain't agoin' to look for you there coz nobody would know you was in the place and I could fetch you down a hunk and a mug all the same, and you could get a night's sleep and not be skulking till daybreak. It's sense."

McCune was tired and hungry and thirsty, and his desire overcame his discretion.

"If yer kin run me in, gal, I'll go yer. Blow me if I aint holler. It takes the wind out of a man to be hunted."

"Come on, then. There aint nobody about as'll ax any questions, and it's dark on the stairs. I'll git you a light in the shoveler's and you'll have the room to yourself and I shouldn't wonder if there's a bed in it. The woman'll give me the key."

Thus coaxed, the man allowed the girl to pull him round and they made their way somewhat skulkingly back to a place on the sidewalk opposite the entrance to the middle house in O'Reardon's Terrace. There they stood in the shadows watching John Sitwhite and the soldier as they stood in the entrance way, and who presently went off together down to McGloine's to get a drink, when the girl said quickly:

"Come on, now. The road's clear."

They then crossed the street, the girl in advance, and, entering the hall-way, went hurriedly and stumblingly up the stairs. Arriving at the floor upon which the Sitwhites lived, the girl tried the knob of the front room and finding the door unlocked, she hastily pushed it open and as unceremoniously pushed McCune in, saying:

"Stay there a bit and I'll git a light. They won't look for you here."

McCune, as the reader already knows, had been in the room before and was familiar with it. But he did not know, as the reader knows, that John Wilder was equally familiar with it and knew even more of its occupants than he did himself. But at this moment he was chiefly anxious to get something to eat and drink, and in the stress of physical condition, like most men of his class, he would take more risks than his cooler judgment would prompt.

The girl had gone upstairs, and after an absence of fifteen minutes she came back with a candle, matches and a bundle of something wrapped in a news-paper. When she had lighted the candle in the room, it was seen that she had amply provided for his immediate comfort, for she had brought part of a loaf of brown bread, a sausage and a delf pitcher, and had even in her thoughtfulness included a clay pipe and a handful of coarse tobacco.

"Git that into you," she said, pointing to the food; "and I'll fetch you a pitcher of beer."

The Mink needed no urging. He fell upon the coarse food like a famished wolf, and when the girl returned with a foaming vessel of beer he put it to his lips and took a long, eager draught that plainly betokened his thirsty condition. While he was draining the pitcher the girl had opened the door of the closet where Plonski had slept, and was pointing with one hand at the bed while she held the candle up with the other.

"There you are," she said; "if you've got to be took, you might as well be took in yer bed with some sleep in, as on the street without any."

"Right you are, sis," replied The Mink, who now felt much more cheery. "Put yer glim down on the floor. I want to chin yer." He then seated himself on the boards with his back against the wall and for want of any other accomodations, the girl, after putting the pitcher on the floor in front of him, placed herself in a like posture beside him.

The scene was picturesque and unique. The bare room feebly lit by the puny flame, showed a little circle of light round these two rude lovers, who, oblivious of all discomfort and for the time being, of all the danger, were content with the temporary happiness of each other's company. The man put his arm around her, a proceeding which she did not object to, but she cut short his rough sentiment by saying,

"Now give it to me straight. How did it all happen?"

"Well, yer see, sis, I thinks as how that bloomin' perlice terrier smelt out Beaky that werry night he was a hirin' the men to scrape the river. We was asettin' up there in the shanty agettin' things dead to rights and Beaky he was fixin' the navvies to do the job, when dam me if there wasn't a cop at ther winder takin' it all in."

"Yes," said the girl breathlessly. "Did you see him?"

"Why, no but we heered him and seen him when he was makin' over the country."

"And he found out the whole job?"

"Certin. Didn't the inspector turn up in the mornin' and put the bracelets on the old man?"

"Well, I'm beat," said the girl sympathetically. "Aint it awful? What will they do with him?" Then as if remembering something, "but you didn't have nothing' to do with the job o' takin' the girl off."

"Didn't I?"

"No, you didn't. I'd swear to that"

McCune smiled grimly.

"What a shame the men slipped up that night at the dry dock, eh? That would a give you a rest, wouldn't it?"

McCune's smile lengthened into a chasm. "That was a bad job, sis. Beaky show'd his hand that night and now we'll all be hunted. What do you think the old man wants that cup for?"

"For keeps," answered the girl musingly. "It's luck."

"Then I'm d---d if I ever seen the luck of it," said McCune. "Why, it's cursed. Look 'ere gal, we didn't have it in our hands mor'n a quarter of an hour when if a river didn't come up out of the dry ground and wash us away, I hope I may burn."

"What are you given' me?" asked the girl with a leer that was meant to indicate at she thought this was a flight of fancy.

"True as if I was a priest," said McCune. "We was asettin' like this adrinkin' our lush and the sun was shinin' and we was half a mile from the river, and there was the bloody cup, just where that candle is, and blow me, quicker nor a whack, rip! and up comes the river and takes us both on our bellies and carries off the cup. If I hadn't snatched Curly by the slack of his neck, he'd been drowned. I'm tellin' yer the straight thing and you don't want to give it away, neither."

"I wouldn't tell," said the girl, "they'd put me in the 'sylum.'"

"Perhaps yer don't believe me."

"I think you be gillin' me."

"It's me dying words, all the same and square."

"What, the river cum up the hill and took the cup?"

"No, the bloomin' water works busted and dumped us. I'm scratched and chawed all over. They never would 'a' busted but fur the mug, and now the old un's took, Curly'il go up, and I'm broke. I ain't got a blessed stamp to wipe my weepin' eyes with."

"Then you'll shake the old un, and the cup biz? I would. 'Taint no good. What's the use o' bein' hunted weekdays and Sundays? A man wants a little rest, doesn't he? No gal 'ud stand it."

McCune shook his head somewhat regretfully. "I can't do it, sis," he said. "I'd rather be hunted by the perlice than by Beaky. He's the best 'un I've got, and he'll be out agin. When he is, he'll fix us, coz he wants me. He knows I've been square with him."

"He'll be your death," said the girl, "It's in my bones."

"No, he wont. Say, you don't know. If he gits the mug, I'm fixed. You wait, he's straight, and he's got more soap then all of 'em. O, he aint so crooked as yer think."

"Sh-sh," said the girl suddenly. "There's some un comin'."

There was the sound of a hand on the knob of the hall door. McCune sprang lightly to his feet, seized the candle and blew it out. Both of them stood in the darkness to hear the door slowly open, and McCune felt the girl clutch him with something like terror. There was a moment's darkness and silence, and then they could see by the dim light that came through the partly opened door, that some one was looking in. Then a voice in sharp, subdued earnestness that was like a coarse whisper, said:

"It's me—Plonski. What the devil did you put the light out for?"

McCune uttered an oath of astonishment, and began feeling in his pocket hurriedly for a match. While he was doing so, Plonski had struck a match and was holding the little flame up in the air and peering curiously at the faces that it lit pallidly.

"Give me your candle, here," he said; "be quick."

After a moment's nervous fumbling, the feeble light of the candle shone once more in the room, and Mr. Plonski, looking at the girl, and then at McCune, said, "So you've told her, have you?"

McCune began a coarse apology and protest. Plonski cut him short.

"Listen to me. You are to go back at once. Carry the woman with you if you like. Don't take your eyes off that brook for an instant. If some one else takes the thing we're lookin' for, it's your fault. I know—I know," he said quickly, as McCune was about to object, "you're out of money. You wouldn't have been if you hadn't lost the property like a drunken idiot. Here's money for you. I'll keep you supplied. You'll be taken if you stay here. Go at once. Keep out of the way and watch that stream. Do you understand?

You've got the chance of your life. It'll make or break you."

"Where's Curly?" asked McCune.

"He's out, but I don't want him. I can trust you. You know what I mean. If we don't get that property now it's your fault. We'll get it if you stick to the place and stand by me."

He had taken out a roll of money and pulled from it several bills. "Here," he said, "you mustn't stop here. Go down to Saunders at the dock. You're safe there till morning. Then start back. I'll keep you in money when you get there. Now go and keep your head or the inspector'll grab you. If we get the property you're made. You know me. I'll keep my word. There's more money for you now in being straight and silent, than you'll ever see in this world. Go on."

"Then Curly's out," said the man.

"Yes; keep away from him. If he hadn't been with you, this wouldn't have happened. Remember, so long as you do what I want, the police can't hold you. Send me word to Saunders the moment you get on the spot. There's an office at Scarsdale and one at Parks."

Then he pushed McCune out the door and the girl following, he shut it softly and turned the key.

He was in an unusual state of nervous agitation, for he put the candle on the mantel and fussed about the room in an abstracted way, striking one hand into the other and pulling at his moustache spasmodically. Presently he took the candle off the mantel, placed it in the recess between the fireplace and the closet and going to the window leaned thoughtfully against the frame and looked out into the night. The energy of his thoughts was too great for silence and he began to mutter in self relief as he stood there.

"I wonder if there is going to be an end to this. What kind of mysterious fate is it brings me back to this accursed hole. Was ever a man baffled, lured and kept on the edge of success and disappointment like this? No, no, no; let me keep my reason. I have outwitted the police, defied the authorities, escaped from the law. If ever a man earned the right to success, I have. Let me keep my head; yes, that's the principal thing. It has saved me so far. I must not lose it now."

Then he blew out the candle, and letting himself out, went stealthily down the stairs and up the almost deserted street.

CHAPTER XLII.

RESOLUTION ENDS IN RHYME.

Miss Rosamond Enniston had now adopted a new set of tactics with something more than her usual subtlety. Two or three trivial occurrences favored her, although she was not aware of it. In the first place Carteret was piqued beyond measure at what he conceived to be Manuella's inconsiderate heartlessness in going to the Academy with Stonybrook, and he could not forget the picture of confidential intimacy which she presented as she came down the staircase clinging to that gentleman's arm, nor the air of satisfied proprietorship which Mr. Stonybrook wore as he carried her carefully through the crowd. Had some superior intelligence told him with unquestioned wisdom that he was wronging an innocent nature and taking the very course, in his boyish displeasure, to bring about an abiding and irretrievable separation, he would probably have been startled and gone headlong to the girl and thrown himself figuratively at her feet. But unfortunately there is no superior and compulsory intelligence provided for these cases in real life. An impulsive young man may be a hero, but he is never a philosopher and he has to go through the devious paths that his pride, his passion, and his petulence are continually opening for him. It is only when the paths are traversed, that he can see how vainly wide of the goal they are.

He sat in his studio trying to reason with his feelings and becoming aware as he did so, how importunate and arbitrary those feelings were. He sprang up, dashed down his mahl-stick and said: "Confound it, I've allowed this thing to make a poltroon of me. It's crowded every bit of self-respect and industry and sense of duty out of me. A mid-summer madness is all very well for an artist, but a lifelong mania is more than one bargains for. A man surely ought not to let one woman make a hypochondriac of him when there are so many women in the world."

Something seemed to say to him just then in another and softer key. "But there are not so many. The truth is, there is only one, and you know it." He looked round the room. There she was in her gypsy hat and he heard the strains of the Blue Danube and saw her beautiful face close to his again on the autumn afternoon when she tried to drink the Kaiser beer. He went and turned the canvas round as if it interfered with his fell purpose of being reasonable.

"She's no doubt right. Why should a lovely creature like that marry a poor artist?" he said. "She has probably grown to be wise enough to see her own folly and to exercise a woman's caprice and craft."

He took a turn as he said this, and there she was again on one of those studies made on the banks of the Pocantico; once more they were on the stone ledge of the abutment and he heard her say, "I believe you. I would not take back the words I said in the park. They stand forever with me," and mystically mingled with this inexpressibly sweet plighting, was the music of the waters in his soul once more. He gave way to it for a few moments, then he started.

"Hang it," he said, "I'll go mad if I stay here. I'll go and make a call. I must do something." The indefinite impulse grew to a definite purpose as he put on his collar and cuffs and arrayed himself before the glass. He'd go and see Miss Enniston. It was only decent and magnanimous. She had appealed to him not to advertise to the world that he had jilted her. Love was over between them. She had acknowledged that and she was a well to do patron who had come to his rescue when others had deserted him. He repeated the final words of this strain twice, "Deserted me." They sounded so horribly dismal and discordant in his soul that he kept them echoing with the relish of wonderment.

Then he called at his open door loudly to Chapman, for he had heard him go in.

"O, I say, Oats, come in here, will you?"

"What's afire?" said that personage sticking his head in a few moments later. He was in walking costume and looked very dapper.

"Everything's smoldering," replied Carteret. "I'm going out to get fanned up a bit. Come with me and make a call on Miss Enniston. You may sell that Saranac Lake."

"I'll go with you," said Oats, "but don't talk about that woman buying my pet picture. She wants to buy me. You can't get it into her head that men are not like canvases."

"What are you talking about?" asked Carteret, carelessly, as he fussed about in completing his toilet. "You say the most reckless things of any man I know. Perhaps I can sell the picture for you. She appears to have gone into the purchasing business."

"O, she's been in it for some time. I'll tell you all about it some day. Don't tie that scarf that way, if you are going to make a call; here, let me. Do you know, there's a spot of flake white on your moustache. You've been chewing your brush, wrong end on."

"What bothers me," said Carteret, "is where she gets the money. She had some property left her by her grandfather, but I didn't know she could get at it. I shouldn't wonder if she hypothecated it. It would be just like her, if she got hold of a money lender."

"Then," said Chapman, "it becomes us to make hay while the money shines. So come on. Wait till I lock my door."

Carteret did not pause to examine his motives on his way to the residence of Col. Hardynge, but he vaguely acknowledged to himself that if Manuella chose to give her time to Mr. Stonybrook, it was a fair, tactical offset for him to call on Miss Enniston. He had relinquished a woman of wealth and position for a poor and friendless girl. If that girl now preferred a companion of more ample means than her poor artist, the poor artist was entitled to preserve the friendship of his wealthy friend.

The hollowness and absurdity of this logic could only become plain to him in some other mental mood. He did not attempt to reason about it. He went rather defiantly to the Hardynges as if he wanted to escape from himself, and as if he thought it allowable to punish Manuella in a harmless way, for going to the Academy with Mr. Stonybrook, and above all for clinging to him so, but it is doubtful if even this impulse was well defined enough in his mind to be called a determining thought.

When the two young men arrived at Col. Hardynge's they encountered Miss Hardynge and Miss Enniston in the hallway, clad in furs and ready for some kind of an excursion.

There was a suppressed look of triumph on Rosamond's face that Carteret did not perceive. Then the ready Chapman said they had only come for a formal call, not on business. "Of course," he added, "if you are going out, we shall not detain you with any of the proprieties."

"We were going," said Miss Hardynge, "to see the Follen-Sanger picture, the ordered one. It has arrived and he has issued invitations to the first exhibition of it in his parlors. It's a Schreyer, I belive."

"Yes," said Chapman, feeling in his pocket, "I got one of the cards and forgot all about it."

"How fortunate you happened to come along," remarked Miss Enniston. Now we can invite you to go with us and get the benefit of your opinions."

"Delighted," said Chapman.

"The Colonel," she continued, "who is a tyrant, issued an order that we were to put in an appearance there and we were going to obey it most perfunctorily, neither of us knowing anything about Schreyer, but now that we can have expert company, there may be more art and less tedium. I hear only good opinions of your picture, Mr. Carteret, from everyone. I really hope you will let me feel just a little proud that a New Yorker and not a Schreyer has made the town talk. I can't help being national or even provincial in these things."

She said this with a formal intimation that she intended to be precisely courteous and he need not get nervous.

"I think," he replied; "that you have earned the best right to be proud of the picture."

"True," cried Chapman, laughing. "The buyer is the only connoisseur that is worthy of the artist's respect."

At this they all laughed quietly and were presently going down the steps into the street; Carteret and Rosamond in advance, as if accidently.

It was not a long walk from Col. Hardynge's to Gramercy Park and the little party went leisurely along, conversing about the most trivial affairs in the most conventional manner; Miss Enniston taking good care not to obtrude herself or her feelings into her speech and Carteret making the most hum-drum answers.

"You appear," he said, just before they turned into the park, "to have gone into art wholly. I should never have suspected you of hunting up a Schreyer."

"O dear, no," she explained. "It's all Col. Hardynge's doings. He insisted upon our coming here to-day. The doctor has made the picture an excuse to give a little reception, I believe, and he's a great friend of the Colonel's. Did you ever meet his wife?"

"Never to my knowledge."

"A most singular woman. The Colonel insists on our cultivating her, but every time we have called, she has been indisposed. I've never myself seen her but once. I believe her husband is one of those heroes who want to get their wives into society against the wives' wishes."

Dr. Sanger's spacious mansion was at once an office, a rendezvous and a salon. He had a splendid consulting room in the wing at the end of the hall-way, the door of which opened into the hall. It was here that he ostensibly gave advice and held consultations, but in reality, saw political friends, and generally kept a secretary and a stenographer busy with his correspondence, for he was now a man of affairs. In the centre of this room stood his costly table desk, at which he wrote a prescription with a gold pen on a tinted pad, or a letter on his monogram note paper. He sat on a handsome revolving chair with his feet on a heavy polar bear skin with his face toward the hall entrance.

There were two liveried servants in the hall, who on this occasion directed visitors into the open parlor where the Schreyer, an enormous cattle-piece, was theatrically draped and lit and when Carteret and his friends entered, Dr. Sanger who was in his office writing a note for which a messenger was wait-ing, came to the door and saw them. He and the messenger entered the hallway together. The moment he recognized Miss Hardynge, he hurried forward in his breezy, hearty manner.

"Ha," he exclaimed, "You've come to see the picture, but wouldn't come to see me. I've trapped you into being neighborly, hav'n't I? Miss Enniston, I had hoped to see more of you. Mrs. Sanger has spoken of you frequently. Really, you impressed her."

Rosamond had it on her tongue to say that Mrs. Sanger's interest took the form of a sick headache whenever she had called, but somehow the reply melted into a more courteous phrase: "I've been unfortunate," she said; "Grace and I called twice to pay our respects to the lady and on both occasions she was too ill to see us. You must not think it was indifference on either side when it was only indisposition."

"Did you really?" with considerably more surprise than the speech appeared to warrant. "I'll send up for her now. She's in capital condition to-day and will be delighted to see you."

He then called one of the servants and bade him tell Mrs. Sanger that Miss Hardynge and Miss Enniston were in the parlor and, turning to the salon, he threw aside the heavy velvet drapery, saying: "Here is my prize, but I must let you into a secret. I got it through a diplomatic *coup-d'etat*—never could have paid the price for it in the world. They say it's very fine. I don't pretend to be a high art critic. Step this way, the light is better here."

Miss Hardynge and her companion sat down and while looking in the direction of the canvas, kept up a rambling conversation with the doctor, who stood with his back to the picture; and Carteret and Chapman, with genuine professional interest, silently examined the work. In a very few moments the conversation, kept up in a light and rambling way, became general and the picture was disregarded entirely. One or two persons came in from the street and the doctor bowed to them and continued talking.

"Mr. Carteret," he said patronizingly, with a side gesture, "appears to be the artist that we ought to talk about. I have read about him in the papers, but I have not had time to see his picture. He is what we call a rising young man."

"I suppose you know," said Miss Hardynge, "who bought the picture."

"No," replied the doctor, "the fact is, the picture world is a charmed domain that I am almost completely shut out of by my coarser profession. But I've made an attempt to redeem myself," and he referred with one of his gestures to the canvas behind him.

"Miss Enniston has bought Mr. Carteret's picture," remarked Miss Hardynge.

"Ho, ho," said the doctor, "Miss Enniston is a connoisseur then. I must avail myself of her knowledge and friendliness to help me out. She can give Mrs. Sanger the benefit of her advice. You see I'm going to make Kate a regular art patron. It will give her an occupation. Your father says there is nothing takes the rough edge off politics like art. I'm going to try it."

"Doctor," said Miss Enniston, "if you really desire to do something in art, you ought to seize upon Carteret and give him a commission, for he is a coming man. I suppose you know that he is the only artist who has this winter shown the ability to reproduce a beautiful woman on canvas without resorting to trickery."

"You surprise and interest me," said the doctor. "I think I must get him to take a look at Kate—Mrs. Sanger. I'll talk with you further about it, Miss Enniston."

Just at this moment, one of the doctor's secretaries entered with paper in his hand for some kind of instruction and the doctor with an apology, stepped aside; the movement brought him much nearer to Carteret and Chapman than he was probably aware of, and they both heard the hurried conversation with the secretary:

"What is it?" asked the doctor.

"It's from the Commissioner. Plonski has been released on bail."

"Good," replied the doctor, "Does he say anything about the inspector?"

"He says there are no charges."

"Very well, make a memorandum and send it to the Judge. He will furnish the charges. That will do."

Here the secretary bowed and left the room.

This conversation, having caught the quick ear of Carteret, set him wondering. But there was little opportunity for reflection as the conversation of the group became general.

The doctor made a few affable and empty remarks, and then saying he would go and fetch Mrs. Sanger, left. Miss Enniston and Carteret, and Miss Hardynge and Chapman, paired off.

"It appears to me," said Rosamond, "that with your present prospects, you ought to give your whole attention to your art. Doesn't it appear to you, this is the opportunity to take fortune at the flood?"

"Undoubtedly, but what would you suggest that I am not endeavoring to do?"

"O, I can't suggest, but it seemed to me that having got over the sentimental phase of your career, you ought to win fame and wealth, if you keep in the right path, and make the right kind of friends. You've got the entre into the best society and after all it's social distinction that helps a painter. Half a score of good patrons are worth more than all the public clamor. You ought to know Col. Hardynge and Judge Sanger. The Judge was saying the other night that it was political influence alone that secured that splendid commission from the State to Holman to paint the picture for the capital and Holman certainly did not start with half the friends you've got. You see I'm trying my best to make you independent, even of the past. I want to prove a friend who is disinterested enough to be interested."

"You are very kind," said Carteret dreamily. "I have no right to question your generous actions, but I feel anxious about my ability to repay you."

"Friendship that is disinterested needs no pay. Don't think of it," she replied. "I'm selfish enough to want a hand in the success of an old friend. If we keep our council and our heads we can win a great triumph. I am sure of it. You know well enough that I must have something to occupy my mind. It was stagnation that made me so restive and reckless at times. You didn't understand it. Now that I have got something to accomplish you will see that all the nonsense of the past will disappear."

"Rosamond," said Carteret, "there is much in our past that I do not want to forget. You do me a great injustice. A thousand recollections make us friends. If we were foolish enough to play at being lovers it should not prevent us from acting as sensible and closely attached acquaintances."

Rosamond winced a little, but she said: "Exactly, that's what we will do. You will find soon enough in your Bohemia how hollow are the flirtations, and foolish the romances, and long for a discreet and unimpassioned attachment. I know my sex better than you do, Colin. Some day you will tell me that I was right when I said a girl's love is a phantom, a woman's friendship a beacon."

While this conversation was going on Doctor Sanger had gone up the stairs and rapped gently at the door of his wife's boudoir. As there was no answer, he pushed it open a few inches and spoke through the opening with a gentle voice:

"Kate, my dear, Miss Enniston is down stairs and knows you are in. You must come down a few moments; you really must, don't you know, Kate."

A maid came along the upper hallway and interrupted him.

"Mrs. Sanger's gone out," she said.

"Impossible," said the doctor; "when did she go out?"

"Half an hour ago. She said as how she was going to the dentist's."

The doctor opened the door and looked in, as if doubting the girl's words. The room was empty. He then came down stairs rather thoughtfully, pulling on his black whiskers with one hand automatically.

His apology to the party in the parlor was made with his usual hearty sang-froid and they went away. But after they had gone down the steps he stood in the hallway at least a minute, still pulling at his whiskers. Then he went into his consulting room and shut the door.

During the walk back, Miss Enniston continued to appeal to Carteret's ambition, and adroitly managed to present to him the possibilities of a brilliant career that was open to him, and when he left her at Col. Hardynge's home, his mind was really aflame with the prospects of success. To-morrow he would have one thousand dollars. He would devote it all to his work. He would reject his Bohemianism. He would work ten hours a day. He would reform; he would become a recluse. He would win a place among the gifted and honored and famous. Yes, he would. Fortune had smiled on him. It was not time for dalliance. Henceforth hard work, practical good sense and mental discipline.

Then, as he walked his studio late at night, he stopped a moment and looked at the face that shone at him from a canvas on the floor. Then he pulled a little table up under the solitary gas jet, and with pencil wrote on a sheet of foolscap the following verses:

TO GRETCHEN.

Do you recall that day, my dear,
  Begemmed with early dew?
The autumn air was crystal clear,
  The Heaven was cobalt blue.

We saw the glory from a scene
  Of opal gladness born,
And watched the day-god peep between
  The Orient lace of morn.

And there, along that stubbly way,
  With hand in hand we rambled,
And came upon a sandy bay,
  All canopied and brambled.

Through oozy pathways, where the brook
  Sang solos on the sedges,
We reached a shadowy stone outlook
  And sat down on its ledges.

The moments moved on perfumed feet;
  The joy of absent words
Was broken only by the sweet
  Disturbance of the birds.

The sky had caught its liquid hue
  From two blue eyes below,
And cloudy ships sailed on the blue
  With phantom freights of snow.

I held your hand, my dear, my own;
  I knew not time was fleet.
I scarcely heard that chanting tone
  Of waters at my feet.

I thought you murmured sweetly then,
  Though eloquently dumb;
It must have been that cascade when
  It beat its airy drum.

I thought I pulled yon to my side,
And heard you softly sigh;
It must have been that summertide,
When it went mocking by.

Why was the autumn zephyr such
A song no mortals sing,
That I believed its gentle touch
My guardian angel's wing?

Some weeks have flown with joy and pain,
As weeks must come and go,
And still is humming in my brain
The peaceful waters' flow.

Still sweeps at times that mystic air
On memory's summertide,
And still I see you sitting there,
My Gretchen and my guide.

O, dear illusions, vague and vain,
Their phantoms come and flit;
Tis recollections mise-en-scene,
And you are part of it.

This effusion he folded up, after reading it three or four times, put it in an envelope, and directed it to Miss Manuella Castleton, No. 51 East Fifteenth street.

But he did not seal the envelope. He could not send the letter till morning, and he wanted to read the verses once more before mailing them.

CHAPTER XLIV.

MR. BURTON TAKES A HAND.

Two days—bitter, cold days they were—had gone by since John Wilder had arrested Mr. Plonski and his man Samson. He got up feeling that at last he had secured the arch conspirator, and that it was now impossible for that person to obtain the cup, if it was in the Pocantico. Though, to tell the truth, Mr. John Wilder never for one moment believed that the cup was really there. He clung to the notion that Samson had deceived Plonski. "But, in any case," he said to himself, "I've got the principal where he is helpless, and if the cup is in the stream, I shall recover it before he takes the field again."

He was on his way to Burton & Dunn's office. When he reached Broadway and Fourteenth street and was about to jump upon the step of a 'bus going downtown, he happened to catch sight of a man standing under a lamp post, on the hotel corner. It was Plonski. Their eyes met, and Plonski, with formal courtesy, lifted his hat and made a rather deliberate bow.

Wilder understood in an instant what all this meant. The man was out on bail, and had outwitted him with celerity by habeas corpus and a Ring judge.

So he jumped into the 'bus, and went straight on down to Burton & Dunn's office. As he feared, Mr. Burton was in court, and Wilder, not caring to wait, had to walk up from Trinity Building to the courtroom in the Park, and then had to wait in the courtroom, for Mr. Burton was arguing a case, walking up and down in front of the judge's bench, smelling of his musk pink, and talking rapidly on an admiralty case. It was not until the recess of the court that Wilder got his ear. "Hallo, John," said the old gentleman, what's the matter now? At your wits' end?"

"I'm afraid I am," replied Wilder.

"Humph. Come over to Delmonico's with me. I must get some lunch. I've been talking two hours and a half. You can state your case while I replenish."

"It's the cup, of course," remarked Mr. Burton when they were seated at a table in the then busy restaurant on Chambers street, and he had tucked a napkin into his vest and pulled it daintily over his buttonniere. "What's the latest twist?"

"Plonski's out on bail," said Wilder, sententiously.

Mr. Burton leaned back in his chair and emitted a soft, good humored laugh that shook him gently all over.

"I can't help it, John," he said. "It's really too good to see you baffled in this way. You'll have to give over that job to me, I'm afraid."

"Nothing would delight me more," said Wilder.

"Well," continued Mr. Burton, with the smile still on his face, "I warned you that you couldn't hold him with your machinery."

"Yes, you did," remarked Wilder. "Have you any better machinery?"

"Undoubtedly. Eat your soup. You'll have to put yourself under my orders for a few days. How will that strike your vanity?"

"Not at all, sir. I haven't any."

"O, yes, you have. I'll take him for you and hold him if you'll carry out my orders explicitly."

"I most assuredly will."

"Very well. Send that man Sully to me, at my house to-night at nine o'clock. He's a much shrewder brute than you suspect. Don't touch Plonski or Samson—keep out of their way. I'll send for you in about three days. You don't mind my being in a hurry, do you? I've got to talk another hour on that case. All you have to do is to send Sully to me to-night; don't interfere with the two men and don't fail me when I send for you. I think I'll bag your game effectually."

"In the meanwhile."

"Meanwhile, what?"

"They may recover the cup."

"I thought you said there would have to be a thaw. This weather doesn't look like it, eh? Don't bother about the cup. I'll hire that man Sully to go up there, live on the stream and watch for it like a bull dog."

"It requires a finer instinct than a bull dog's," said Wilder.

"True, true, John. I'll provide that. You just go and rest for a few days. Don't think about the cup; take a good holiday till I want you. You'll pardon me for making my meal so hasty, but the fact is I've got to finish a long plea this afternoon. Will you have a glass of wine?"

"No, thank you," said Wilder.

Then the lawyer got up, put his hand on the detective's shoulder quite parentally and said, "I never bargained to go into this, John, but I hate to see you beaten. Let me work Plonski for a while. I'm very anxious to get a grip on him."

"Very well," replied Wilder; "it shall be your way. Sully will be at your house to-night at nine."

"By the way, I may have to keep Sully up there a week or two. Can you give me a letter to some resident where he can board, conveniently to the scene of operations?"

"There's but one house in the neighborhood. I'll try and get you a letter for him."

Here they parted.

John Wilder's feeling was that Mr. Burton had underestimated the difficulties of the search and overestimated his own skill at detective work. But he set out to keep his word.

He had to find Sully, which was not a difficult task, and that accomplished, he walked over to the Tenth street studio, and to the evident surprise of Mr. Carteret, strolled into that young gentleman's studio about five o'clock.

"I was just thinking about you," said Carteret. "What in the name of wonder drew you over here?"

"Nothing important," replied Wilder, seating himself on a stool familiarly. "I want you to do me a little favor."

"No more identification business or arrests?"

"No. You don't owe the Mansers anything, do you, up there on the aqueduct?"

"Owe them?" cried Carteret with astonishment; "owe them? Have they sued me for extras? Good heavens! Why I paid them all I could rake and scrape."

"Good friends with 'em, then?"

"So far as I know."

"Then write me a letter. I want to board a man up there for a week and they'll want to know something about him."

"What's the new iniquity? Is it that infernal cup?"

"Yes," said Wilder. "I'm going to send a man up to look for it. It was lost in the woods by the men who stole it."

"Say, Wilder, I'd like to do you a service. Ask me to paint your portrait or your girl's or lend you some money, and I'll do it, but to set a man to work to find that infernal cup if it's lost, is too much."

"Don't be a ninny," said Wilder. "Do what I want. It will save me a lot of work, don't you see? Just take a piece of paper and write a good letter to Mr. Manser. You'll be wanting something of me one of these days. You've always found me pretty level headed, haven't you?"

"O, you're smart enough, but you've got that cup on your brain and it will be the ruin of you, curse it."

"See here, my boy, that cup may turn out one of these days to be a fairy gift for you—one of those talismans we used to read about. To tell the truth, it has been already. It brought you a sweetheart and it brought you the opportunity to make love to her and that brought you the chance to paint your picture. I don't think the cup ever hurt you any and I wouldn't be so superstitious about it, for whenever it comes back, I'll wager you, you'll be cooing and billing again over there in Fifteenth street."

"What do you want me to write?"

"Just a strong letter of recommendation for an honest working man who wants a place to stop for a week and will pay handsomely for it. Go ahead—his name's Sully—Mr. Daniel Sully."

When it was written, Wilder took it, read it, folded it up and said:

"Thank you Carteret. I'll do as much for you. Get the notion out of your head that the cup brings you ill luck. I could tell you something that would make you hunt for it yourself."

"Bah," said Carteret, "you mean the reward. By the way, Wilder, that reminds me of something. I was over to Dr. Follen Sanger's just now looking at his picture with a party, and I heard something that I wanted to tell you. It struck me at the time as awfully queer. You see we were all talking in the parlor with the doctor and one of his secretaries or clerks comes in with a despatch. The doctor turns round and says he, 'What is it?' 'It's from the commissioner,' says the clerk. 'Plonski's out on bail.' 'Good,' says the doctor, 'how about the inspector'? 'No charge,' says the clerk. 'Send the memorandum to the judge,' says the doctor, 'and he'll take care of the charges.' Do you know, I thought when he said "inspector," he might have meant you? What the deuce has the doctor got to do with that old rat Plonski?"

"O, it might be some other Plonski, don't you know," replied Wilder reflectively. "Are you sure he said, 'Send it to the judge?'"

"Yes, certain. It was just like me to connect it somehow with you. I s'pose that's because you've always been mixed up with Plonski. You don't think the thieves lost the cup in the woods, do you?"

"O, it isn't impossible. I'm going to make a hunt for it. Did you hear the doctor say anything else?"

"No, that was all."

"I'm much obliged for telling me. I may come in and see you at work next week. I'm going to have a holiday for a while. When are you here?"

"O, I'm going to be here all the while now," said Carteret bravely. "I'm not going to waste any more time."

CHAPTER XLV.

PLONSKI FALLS INTO THE TRAP.

In trying to follow Mr. Burton's advice and let the cup alone for a while, Mr. John Wilder found that it was impossible to shut from his mind the chain or events and the possibilities of the conspiracy. Just at the moment when the circumstances appeared to be widening out and taking in political and social complications, he had been asked to give over the strange and fascinating hunt. It was Mr. Burton himself who had, more than anybody else, convinced him that the search for a hundred and fifty millions of wealth was not altogether a chimerical hunt, and then Mr. Burton had flippantly asked him to let matters rest for a while. In thinking of this, a smile of incredulity flitted over Wilder's face. He could not quite get rid of the idea that Mr. Burton would find this business a little out of his line, and as for setting Dan Sully to look for the cup, where, in his opinion it never was, that would make any detective smile.

But John Wilder was a little overworked and needed rest. What with letters and telegrams from Mr. Job Ackerman, whose patience had been completely exhausted, and with all the other entanglements and disappointments and surprises and hard work, the cup had led him a lively dance for months and now threatened to involve him with the Central Office through the political friends of Plonski. The information furnished by Carteret was of great significance. He now saw that Plonski was operating through Judge Sanger, and the judge was using his son, the doctor, to influence the police department and even the bench. This was a grave discovery to the officer, for he had no means of measuring the judge's interest or influence with the Central Office. He knew, although it had not occurred to him before, that one of the police commissioners held his place as the result of a political deal with Judge Sanger, but just how far that influence was inimical to Mr. John Wilder, it was not easy to determine at once. There were many reasons why he didn't at this moment wish to sever his connection with the Central Office, and he believed it was policy to keep virtually out of sight of these people for a while and see what Mr. Burton would do.

The result of all this was, that he wrote a letter to Doctor Wollendorf in which he said:

"I cannot reply by letter to all the questions that you and the captain ask me. It will take some time to tell you minutely all that has happened and as I have a leave of absence for a few days, I think I will run up and pay you and the pigeons a visit. I suppose there are some quail running in your vicinity, or at any rate a rabbit or two."

While Mr. John Wilder was domiciled at Coe's Grove with two ancient and worthy veterans, going deliberately over all the facts and possibilities of the Toltec Cup amid the savory fumes of spiced rum and tobacco, something interesting was going on in the household of Mr. Manser.

That quiet circle had received as an addition, a giant of formidable appearance with a scar on his forehead and a curious imprint on his cheek bone made up of five little cicatrixes in the shape of an arch.

He had come up there and gone to live in the new stable where there was a fairly comfortable harness room, overcoming the disinclination or Mr. Manser by a letter from Carteret, and presently winning him completely by a stalwart ability to do several things that Mr. Manser could not, without him, get done.

"Goin'to look in the creek for a lost cup," said Mr. Manser with rural sarcasm. "Well, upon my word, why don't you look into the moon for green cheese, it'd pay better."

"I'm paid to do it," said Sully, "and as it pleases them as sent me and don't hurt you, there aint no good kickin', and as I pays ye fairly for keepin' of me, who's hurt? Mebbe I can give ye a turn at one o' your jobs."

"My work's all done for the winter," says Mr. Manser with the pride of a small agriculturist who has got his hay loft full and his tools all greased, "unless you can cut trees."

"Boss," replied Sully, "when I first got to this ere country I went to Michigan. I worked there two winters."

"Humph," said Mr. Manser. "Lookin' fur cups?"

"Cuttin' trees. I was a pinery hand. That's what I was. You don't want to say nothin' to me 'bout cuttin' trees. There ain't no trees round here," and Mr. Dan Sully cast a rather contemptuous glance at the bare chestnuts of second growth and the dogwood and cedar on the hillside.

This discovery, more than anything else, made Mr. Manser a friend. He had about three acres of timber that he had been trying for a year to clear, and he chuckled to think that his boarder could sling an axe.

In a day or two after his arrival, Mr. Sully had equipped himself with that necessary implement and had begun to make holes in the ice on the brook. He showed himself to be an old forester by the way he went to work and Mr. Manser, who had little to do now, came down the hill side and watched him on several occasions. A week passed away and it looked as if he had settled down to a winter's job in the country to search for the cup. He inspected every turn and pocket of the stream for a quarter of a mile below the aqueduct or to where it began to widen out in placid stretches—now glades of ice. Had he gone half a mile further down he would have come upon the cottage of Mrs. Tucker and probably run across Hi himself, though that lad was now taking his winter's schooling.

Sometimes he built a fire on the ice or on the shore, and was occasionally seen sitting reflectively over the embers with his axe in his hand. He was, of course, a good deal of a mystery to Mr. and Mrs. Manser, who had many discussions during the long winter evenings over him. Mr. Manser, when taking a final turn at night with his lantern in his hand to see if the stable was all right, had seen him more than once through the harness room window, poring over a letter held close to the flame of the little kerosene lamp, and he was well aware that he walked regularly to the village post office. But as a week went by and nothing out of the ordinary way occurred, the old people got accustomed to their lodger, who spent the greater part of everyday hanging round the still frozen Pocantico with his axe.

One day McCune, who was skulking through the wood like a grey wolf, came upon him poking with a pole searchingly into a hole he had made in the ice. He watched him for some time with keen interest and saw him go down the stream with his pole in his hand to a bend where the water in warm weather must have been deflected by a bank of stones and roots and rushes. Here the man stopped and began searching in the several holes that he had made. McCune was not such a fool as to overlook the fact that this was the most likely place to search for anything that had been carried down the stream, for the probability was that it would get caught in the network of roots or lodged in the tangle of water-grasses. He stared at the fellow patiently poking into the holes and trying to pry the ice out of the way with his lever and then he suddenly said, with his choice ribaldry of astonishment:

"Roast me soul, if he aint diggin' for the mug, I'm d——d," and then a grin of incredulity distended his rodent mouth as he thought of the hopelessness of such a hunt at this time of year.

"I'll keep me eye on him," said McCune, "and when he fishes it, I'll hit' im on the back o' the head and swipe it."

This was a mere outbreak of McCune's humor. He had expected from the first to run across somebody sent to prospect the stream and watch for a thaw, but the deliberate attempt to dig through the ice in search of the cup, struck him as being too ridiculous to be true. He continued to watch the slow operations with an expression of derision and wonder on his sharp face, that slowly grew into one of acute interest as he saw how methodical and deliberate and patient the man was. Even so obtuse a mind as was McCune's could understand that if the cup was in the stream, it was such a search as this, inch by inch, over every foot of the water way, that would find it, if continued long enough.

For two hours he kept his eyes on Sully from behind the trees, gliding here and there and suffering considerably from the cold. By and by, when the man gave over his work for the day and went off towards Mr. Manser's, Mr. McCune watched him enter the gatehouse.

The next day he came back and there was the man chopping a new hole in the ice with his axe as methodically and patiently as before. He heard the ringing strokes of his tool and the gruff tones of his voice as he occasionally sang a bit of a song, long before he saw him. There was something in the man's manner that suggested to McCune the possibility of his devoting the remainder of his life to the search, and in spite of the improbabilities, he said to himself, "That's the feller that'll find it, if it's here, as soon as the ice melts. He's doing things I'd never thought of. I'll hev to interduce myself to him and let Beaky know."

In spite of this resolution, three days passed by before McCune found the fitting opportunity to speak to Sully, and by that time he had made up his mind to a line of policy and had heard from Plonski. He found his man one morning cutting the trees in the very wood where he and Samson had been surprised by the torrent. He stood a moment admiring the swing of the axe, whose sharp blows rang through the grove and came reverberated from the opposite hill. Sully saw him and evidently took him for a tramp.

"Given up cuttin' ice, hey?" said McCune.

Sully went on chopping a moment, then he dropped his axe blade to the ground and spit upon his hands.

"No," he answered indifferently, "I ain't given it up."

"I seen yer choppin' in the stream; couldn't make it out. First I said lookin' fur a fish, then I said no, he don't ketch no fish, lookin' fur some'at else."

Sully started in with his axe again. He merely nodded his head and said: "Right, boss, lookin' for somethin' else."

"Gold?"

"No, silver."

McCune laughed. "Why don't you wait till she thaws?"

Sully leaned on his axe handle and looked The Mink over.

"Because I ain't that accommodatin'," said he.

"Ain't yer feered som'an else'll look fur it while yer choppin'?"

"No," said Sully. "Tain't no good to nobody but me."

"Is it yourn?"

"Yes, so don't you bother."

"O, I ain't botherin'. I'll help you. I ken set on the bank, can't I, and see you? Mebbe I know some'at about it."

"What do you know?"

"Well, I'll tell you after you've dug the whole bloomin' crik over. It'll make you more civil. I'll walk over and see you to-morrer; goin' at it to-morrer?"

"No, I'm goin' off fur a day to-morrow. If you ken tell anything, come the next day. I'll be down there. Do you live in the town?"

McCune nodded his head.

"I might ask you to put a letter in the office."

"All right," said The Mink, "I'll put it in when I'm goin' that way."

The next day he did not come back, but spent the time in a wild carouse over at the Italian settlement. But the day after he was on hand and found Sully wandering around the wood with his coat on as if he had not got over his holiday.

The moment he saw McCune he joined him and they walked down the wooded declivity towards the stream.

"What hev you got to tell me?" he asked gruffly.

"Not much, only you're wastin' time lookin' fur anything in that crik."

"Guess not," said Sully. "I know what I'm about."

"No, you don't. I hate to see a man fooled. I took the cup out two weeks ago. If you don't believe me, I'll describe it to you. It was that big," and he held his hands about a foot apart to illustrate, "and that big round;" he formed his thumb and fingers into a circle; "it was all over silver figgers as nobody could understand. I got paid fur doing your work. You was too late."

Sully looked at him with amazement. "You took it out?" he said.

"Dead sure. I ken tell you what I done with it and where it is. Mebbe I kin take yer to see it if you'll go. That's what made me laugh when I seen you with a pole and when yer said it was yorn."

"You got it?" Sully asked with innocent astonishment.

"That's what I'm sayin' and that's what I ken prove to you. It knocks yer over, doan't it?"

"Yes, it does," said Sully.

"Why? Coz I got up earlier than you?"

"No," replied Sully, "cause there must be two cups."

"Two cups. What are you givin' me?"

"You see," said Sully, "I told you I was a goin' to lay off yesterday, but I knowed it was comin' on warm that night and the stream 'ud break up. So I set a net half a mile down and didn't want you round. I took the cup out yesterday. You can ask the people up at the house. They seen it and it was just like yourn. There must'a' been two of em."

"Where is it?' asked McCune. "Is it up at the house now? Lemme see it." His eagerness overcame his sense of discomfiture. But Sully was deliberate and without a sign of suspicion.

"That's the d——dest turn yet. Two of 'em. Well, the stream must be full of 'em, boss," he said. "Why don't you keep on lookin' fur 'em?"

"What was it like?" asked McCune with undisguised interest.

"It was like one of them mugs they hev in the theatre; all silver and solid marks thet no man ken make out. I never seen a cup like it; must be worth ten dollars. I showed it to the old people and they said they'd never seen nothin' like it neither, except, says the old woman, 'A mug that a gal had up here last summer to put posies in.' Then I took and sent it to town fur safe keepin'. What I can't make out is how there came to be two."

McCune shot a vicious glance at him, but Sully showed no sense of irony in his brawny face.

"I'd like to see it."

"O, you've got one; thet ought to satisfy you," said Sully, "especially when they're both alike."

"Look 'ere," said The Mink, "how much did you git fur findin' on't?"

"I was paid all I want. I'll have good wages on't."

"An' you're takin' it to the man it doan't belong to."

"I am?"

"Yes, you are."

"No, I ain't. It belongs to Mr. Ackerman at Coe's Grove, but he went to Baltimore. Come up to the house. I'd like the old folks to know how many cups there is in the river."

McCune hesitated a moment. There was no one there that knew him. Then he said: "Come on," and together they went up to the gatehouse.

Everything about the place was now bleakly silent and deserted. They found Mr. Manser in the kitchen oiling his winter boots over the kitchen stove and Mrs. Manser was making doughnuts.

"Here's a chap, Mr. Manser, as says he found a cup like mine in your stream. It beats me."

Mr. Manser looked up from one man to the other and Mrs. Manser stopped the rolling of her dough.

"What kind of a cup was mine?" continued Sully.

"I didn't think there was another like it," said Mr. Manser. "Do you say he found another one?"

"That's what he said."

"Did you see it?" asked McCune of the old man, disregarding everything in his anxiety to know if Sully's story was true.

"Did I see it? Yes, I had it in my hands. It was a silver tankard—that's what it was; but if it was solid or plated I couldn't tell. They make them things so perfect nowadays. When I heered he was a lookin' for a cup in that river, I laughed at him. Yes, I did; and when he brought it up here yesterday, I said, this beats me. Now you tell me you found another. I can't make it out unless Gen. Washington flung 'em in when he skedaddled over here from White Plains."

Very little more of any consequence was said; the Mansers did not like McCune's looks; Mr. Manser was disposed to treat him as a tramp. So the men withdrew after a few minutes' colloquy, and Sully walked along the aqueduct with his companion and tried to talk of some other subject. McCune brought him back to it. But he was a little overtaxed by the dilemma he was in. He wanted to find out what the man had done with the cup, but he dared not betray his anxiety. He wanted to communicate with Plonski but he dared not lose sight of Sully. Finally he said:

"If I was dead certain yer had it, I'd tell yez sommat that would put a bag o' money in your paw."

Sully stopped and looked at him. "A bag o' money?" he said. "How much?"

"Mor'en yer ever seen," said McCune,

"I ain't seen much, that's sure. I've shovelled and chopped pretty much all my life. I'd be a fool to let a bag o' money go. But then you don't look like the kind that has 'em."

"I'll fetch you to them as has. Where is the cup?"

"Why, you wouldn't hev me lose it, would you? Show me the bag o' money."

"I can't show yer here, ken I? Where is the cup?"

"It ain't kickin' round for nobody to pick up. I ain't such a rich un as can afford to lose my chance with it. Them as wants it, pays me fur it and I'm quits; that's all I want. You don't think I want the cup, do you?"

"No more do I," said McCune. "I wants the rhino. I was offered a thousand dollars to fetch it. I'll go half if yez got it"

Sully's eyes stuck out with incredulous amazement; "a thousand dollars," he repeated; "what a liar you are."

"Hell," exclaimed McCune, "money don't lie. I'm talkin' gold. We're both on the same lay. You've got the start o' me. Put the cup in my hands and I'll divvy. My men'll put up ten times mor'n yourn will and we'll come out of it flush. T'other way, you'll get a tip and die poor. I'm talkin' reason. There ain't no lies in that. Where hev yer got it?"

"You take me for a fool," said Sully. "I ain't."

An idea suddenly struck McCune. "It's the captain as takes you for a fool," he said. "I know him. He'll chuck you a ten dollar bill when you could make hundreds. See if you wasn't a fool. He don't know you found it."

"I didn't expect to," replied Sully. "I says to myself, O, I'll go and stay round all winter and look fur it if you pay the wages. One job's good as 'nother. But if I thought I'd see it afore spring, I hope to starve. When I got it, I just says now you'll give a hundred for it or I don't know my biz. He will."

"A hundred," said McCune, with beaming contempt; "An' you call it biz? Say, if you and me stand in, we kin git a thousand apiece. O, I know what I'm talkin'. You'd better see my man afore you act like a fool."

"There ain't no man'd give two thousand for a cup. I don't look like such a luny, do I?"

"Say, what I'm tellin' yer is straight. You come wid me to the city. I'll show yer biz. If I don't, yer needn't plank the cup. You're safe nuff."

"A thousand dollars," repeated Sully, thoughtfully, as if the sum dazed him a little. "Who's your man?" he asked.

"The man what owns it, an'll pay mor'n anybody else. It was stolen from him."

"What's he want to give a thousand dollars fur a cup fur?" asked Sully with what was meant to be unanswerable contempt.

"What in h——do I care what he wants to do it fur?" exclaimed McCune with sharp indignation, "s' long as he wants ter. I s'pose a man like you wouldn't take it till yer found out. I'll bring him to you. Where yer goin' to be? Why don't yer stay here? I'll fetch him."

Sully shook his head. "I'm goin'," he said. "Now, when you show me a thousand dollars, I'll think of it. Take care of yerself," and he moved off.

"How the bloomin' blazes ken I show it to you if you don't tell me where yer goin'?"

"I'm goin' to the city," said Sully. "You might ketch me in the mornin' at the Cortlandt street Hotel—The Farmers. I'd like to see a thousand dollars onct, and I'd like to see it in the hands of a man like you."

"I'll cum, then," said McCune. "What time?"

"I might be awalkin' in front o' the house at ten."

"I'll go with you now. We ken talk it over on the cars. What d'ye say?"

"I don't care when yer go," said Sully. "I ain't scared o' you."

The men had now walked a long distance as they talked, and were through the trees and on the highway.

McCune believed that his companion only needed hard pressing to give way to the temptation, and after taking a drink of whiskey at one of the rum shops in the village, they boarded the train together and sat in the smoker with their pipes lit. Sully had no baggage and carried nothing but a heavy hickory stick that he had cut in Mr. Manser's grove. It was in vain that McCune became confidential. Sully grew communicative enough when he lit his pipe, but he would not divulge the whereabouts of the cup or what he had done with it. When he was asked how he came to be put on the job, he told a long story of his life, and how he had been doing this kind of work for years in rivers and ponds; he was sent for to find the cup and hired like any other man; he was to stay there till he got it. That was all there was to it.

When he got to the end of his rambling account, McCune said suddenly:

"Say, damned if I don't bleeve yer been grillin' me all the time, coz yer wouldn't 'a' let go of it if yer had it."

"Then why don't yer go back and look for it?" answered Sully; "I ain't goin' to interfere with yer. I'm done. See here," and he pulled from his pocket a piece of yellow paper, "what's that?"

McCune took it; he knew it was an express receipt by its appearance, but he could not read it. There was a train boy near him with a box of cigars in his hand.

"Say, sonny, read that," and he put the paper in the boy's hand.

"Ah, what's the matter wid you.?" said the boy. "That's a express recipe. Can't yer see?"

"Read it fur me, Shorty," said McCune. "I ain't got me glasses."

"One box, containin' silver cup, valyerd twenty-five dollars, that's what it says," and the boy flipped the paper back with a business addendum: "SEGARS?"

When the train arrived at the New York station, both men took a drink. Sully was friendly and communicative enough on all subjects but the cup, he talked in a lumbersome and verbose way about his past experiences, but no farther information could McCune get out of him. When they came out of the saloon, The Mink said, "I'll go with yer to the hotel—see?—so I'll know it in the mornin'."

As Sully made no objection, McCune then kept him company until they arrived at a miserable little tavern in lower Cortlandt street, frequented by canal boatmen and market men. He saw his companion put his name roughly on the dirty register and receive a carpet bag from behind the desk and then he left him, feeling certain that he would catch him there in the morning.

With all the speed he could command he hunted up Plonski, and to that person's unbounded astonishment, related all that had occurred, adding, "He's got it, sure; but he'll sell out."

Plonski was suspicious. He did not quite understand the new move and he was constitutionally wary. Then an idea struck him. He went to a telegraph station and wrote the following dispatch:

"Job Ackerman, Coe's Grove, Shall you be home to-morrow, will run up.
JOHN WILDER."

As he gave direction for the answer to be held in the office, he came back an hour later and was handed the following:

"COE'S GROVE.

"JOHN WILDER, New York:
"Job Ackerman gone to Baltimore. Will not be back in a week.
JANE ENNISTON."

It was true then, and something must be done immediately. If this man had the cup, they must not lose sight of him.

"Why didn't you put up with him and get him drunk?"

"O, say," replied McCune. "He's no goat and he carries a stick under his arm that 'ud h'ist a house. Money's the game with him, mind I tell yer now. He'll sell out if you come down heavy."

It was late that night when Plonski did an unprecedented thing. He got into a coupé and drove to the residence of Judge Sanger. That pompous but foxy politician was caught in his dressing gown. "I want to find out where Inspector Wilder is," said Plonski, "that is, if he's out of town and gone South. If you'll send a messenger to Dr. Sanger or give me the note to him, he can send to the Central Office and obtain the information. It is of great importance to me."

Judge Sanger did not stop to inquire what Plonski's motives were; he wrote the note to Dr. Follen Sanger and Plonski carried it there. The doctor put one of his clerks in Plonski's coupe and after a delay of an hour information was received from the Central Office that John Wilder was on a vacation and off gunning in the country. He communicated with the office every day and was awaiting orders. He could not go South without the Central Office knowing it.

The next morning Plonski and McCune started for Cortlandt street. Plonski kept out of sight, hiding himself in a liquor shop on the opposite side of the street, while McCune approached the hotel where Sully was stopping. He encountered the giant in the doorway carrying a cheap carpet bag under his arm and his heavy stick in his hand. The moment he saw McCune he made a mute gesture and the two men walked into the hotel and sat down in an obscure corner.

"Have you got the money?" asked Sully immediately, without taking the bag from under his arm.

"Have you got the cup?" asked McCune.

Sully put his hand on the bag significantly.

"Is it in that?"

Sully nodded his head.

"Lemme see it."

Sully looked round the place hesitatingly. There were several rough characters in the room.

"Come up stairs," he said, and got up.

McCune followed him to a little dimly lit room with a bed in it on the third floor and entered it as Sully held the door open.

"Stand over there," he said, and The Mink stepped back into the room. Sully then closed the door with his back to it and opened the carpet bag. "Keep back," he said grimly. "I'll show it to yer, but stop where yer are."

He then took out a bundle, unrolled the paper and held up the cup at arm's length.

McCune uttered an oath of surprise. It was the very cup. There could be no mistake. Dark as the room was and quick as Sully's movements were, McCune recognized the object in an instant.

There it was within five feet of him, in the possession of a slow and stupid fellow who was ignorant of its value. He could spring upon him with a knife and he was desperate enough to do it. But there was something in the giant's self-possessed manner and long arms that drove the possibility out of his mind. Before he had got over his astonishment, Sully had rolled the cup up and closing the bag, had it under his arm again.

"Now, show me the money," he said.

"Stay here five minutes," said McCune hurriedly as he moved to the door, "and I'll bring the man as has got it."

Sully caught him by the arm and turned him round roughly. "No, you doan't," he said; "you don't mean square. You said you'd bring it. Now you want to fetch a pal. Gimme the money and its yourn. You know it ain't worth that money to anybody and you ain't got no money. Your kind don't do business with money and I knowed it when you talked dollars by the thousand. You tell your man Dan Sully ain't a lame duck and is going to put the cup in a square man's hands."

Then Mr. Sully held the door open.

The Mink begged him volubly and earnestly to wait five minutes and he'd have the money.

But it was no use. Sully had lost confidence in him. "I ain't waitin'," he said; "because I'm on a train in fifteen minutes. We can't do no business."

It was in vain that McCune asked him to come across the street and take a drink. All appeals were in vain and he saw him stride off to the ferry house with his bag under his arm.

It took but a few seconds to run across the street and catch the impatient Plonski and a very few minutes more sufficed to pour out in rapid and excited manner the information that Sully had the cup beyond all doubt and that McCune could have obtained possession of it if he had carried the money with him. Plonski was even more perturbed by the news than was his agent, but he controlled himself better. They conferred in low tones for a few seconds and then both started for the ferry boat, arriving at the dock just in time to see the boat that carried Sully go out of the slip. This delayed them in pursuit fifteen minutes, but to their relief they reached the Jersey City depot just in time to board the train to Baltimore, in the smoker of which McCune had espied his man smoking his pipe and guarding his carpet bag which was in the corner of the seat.

The trip was uneventful enough and much more tedious than the reader of this book can imagine, for the transportation of troops and supplies for the army interfered seriously with the regular travel.

Plonski, wrapped in his cloak, conversed with McCune in an inquisitorial manner, asking him a thousand questions, but utterly failing to shake the man's conviction that the cup was now on the train. What exact course to pursue Plonski had not decided upon. Circumstances must guide him in a great measure. But at present it was imperative that they should not, by any negligence, again lose sight of the cup or allow their man to escape from them. No act, however desperate, would be avoided if it promised to accomplish the purpose.

So at every station, McCune and Plonski got out on the opposite sides of the train and watched. They even slept by turns during the way, so that the man in the sleeper could not disappear without their knowing it. As they went South, the stations were more and more choked with soldiers and the confusion and delay of the moving troops increased; and when they arrived at Baltimore, they were both in a condition of incertitude and exasperation. They watched Sully get out of the train and go round the station as if searching for some one, still hugging his carpet bag under his arm and acting warily and suspiciously. It was then that McCune, approaching him on the platform, accosted him.

"Hallo, boss," he said, "I tracked you down here, thinkin' you might change your mind."

"Well, I'm half a mind to," said Sully growlingly, "my man agreed to meet me here and he ain't done it."

"That's what you get for botherin' with him when yer ken do better with him as has got the rhino. Yer cud a dodged this tramp down ere if yer'd a listened to me. What are goin' to do?"

"I d'now," growled Sully, as he tramped up and down on the dimly-lit platform. "I ought to get some word. This ere ain't treatin' a feller fair, no how." Then he stopped suddenly as if struck with a new idea. "Mebbe he left word or sent it to the telegraph office. I'll go in and see," saying which, he started off in search of the office. It was a little box, partitioned off from the passengers' waiting room, and as he went in, he turned round to McCune rather fiercely and said, "Don't dog me. Stay here."

McCune remained on the platform, but he could see dimly through the frosted windows that Sully had gone in the direction of the telegraph office. Not more than five minutes went by before the man came out again upon the platform, poking a piece of paper in his pocket and wearing a reassured countenance.

"More travellin'," he said to McCune, "now it's Annapolis Junction; I'd like somethin' hot. Where's your partner?"

"I'll get him," said McCune, "he must be froze waitin' for me. Where you goin' now?"

"Goin' to the Junction. That's where my man is. He left word to keep my grip on his cup. Ha, ha, I don't see what you need come for."

"O, we'll go with you now we're here. We might buy the cup o' your man if you won't part with it, don't you see?"

"What d'you want it for?"

McCune dodged this question. "Let's go and get some rum," he said, "I'll interduce you to my man. We needn't quarrel if we don't do any business. When's yer train?"

"In ten minutes," said Sully.

The result of this was that the three men came together in an adjacent tavern and the moment Plonski got a good look into Sully's face, a haunting notion that he had seen him before took hold of him. But he could not, by any mental effort, tell where or when he had encountered that stalwart form and broad, massive face.

"So we cannot do any business, my man," he said.

"I d'now, mebbe. You'd better talk to my man."

"Your man doesn't own the cup," said Plonski; "I'm the owner, it's the cup I want, I'll give you five hundred dollars for it; prove to you it's mine and guarantee you against any damage. I'm a responsible man and can make my word good. I don't want to take any advantage of you. What's the use in going to Annapolis Junction when you can do better here?"

"O, I keep my word," said Sully. "If my man ain't there, damn me if I don't turn it over to you."

Just then the toot of an approaching locomotive interrupted the conversation.

"That's her now," exclaimed Sully. "I'm goin'. If I ain't treated square I'll come to yez when I go back. Yes, I will."

"We'll go with yer," said McCune. "You don't care. Your man mightn't be there. I don't bleeve he will."

A few minutes later they were all on the train; Sully, as before, sitting guardedly against his carpet bag, which was in the end of the seat, McCune next to him and Plonski in the seat behind him. They were now on sufficiently good terms to carry on a conversation, and Plonski eagerly but adroitly plied Sully with questions. He did not succeed in learning anything save that Sully had been hired to hunt for the cup and had found it. The man came round doggedly to this statement, in spite of his examiner.

Finally Plonski said suddenly: "Where have I seen you before?"

"I d'know," replied Sully coolly. "Mebbe it was in the Mackinaw pine lands. You see I've chopped and wrecked and worked on railroads and done most everything. I d'know much 'bout New York. Mebbe it was somebody that looked like me."

And while Plonski talked with him McCune thought over a number of schemes to get possession of the cup. If he could get the man to drink from the flask he carried might he not doze off, and then would it not be possible to get the cup and throw it from the car window at some deserted place and come back from the first station and recover it? Why hadn't they drugged the rascal?

None of his schemes came to anything. Sully did not doze, and he was not a man to trifle with, and so they arrived at the Junction without having achieved anything. The place was choked with military freight and noisy with teamsters and stragglers. The men got out upon the platform and Sully, without any heed of his companions, began to search among the crowds for his man. Plonski and McCune watched him closely. They saw him go up to a man in a sort of undress uniform and light a pipe at his cigar. He seemed to have some trouble in accomplishing his purpose, but his pipe once lit he went off looking through the groups and poking his head into the muffled faces of everybody. There was a train bound north that pulled up while this was going on, and McCune was the first to discover through the moving figures on the platform that Sully was boarding it at the far end with his carpet bag. Just as he had communicated this piece of information to Plonski a man laid his hand on that person's shoulder. He looked round and encountered the erect form of an officer in undress uniform.

"Plonski?" said the man interrogatively.

"Who are you?" asked Plonski nervously.

"I am the United States marshal for this district. I have a description of you and I arrest you. There is a file of soldiers here. Don't attempt to escape. Step this way, please. And you," to McCune, who had begun to slink away, "I want you, too. Corporal, bring your men up, and iron these gentlemen if they resist."

Plonski was a pitiable object of helpless wonder at this moment. The train for the North had moved; as he stood there the cars went by and he saw the face of Sully looking from one of the windows intently at them.

Then the whole truth flashed upon him. He was trapped in the hands of a marshal, beyond the reach of habeas corpus or local political aid. No one of his friends knew where he was. He would be sent to one of the forts. The whole business of the cup was a decoy, and he cursed his stupidity bitterly and turned all his anathemas upon McCune, when they were left together under guard. "Now, you villain," he said, "I hope to God they will hang you. This is what comes of your insisting that that d——d decoy duck had the cup."

"Say, boss," replied McCune, "p'raps I ain't as smart as you be, and I didn't drop to this lay any more'n you did, but if that feller didn't have the same cup as we took out o' the girl's room, and I seed it with these same eyes, then I hope to hang this minute. There ain't no two such mugs on this earth."

To which Plonski with savage hatred replied, "You're a liar, and I'll get square with you if I live long enough."

They were taken that day to Fort Henry, and the next morning were on their way to Fortress Monroe.

When the door of the casemate closed on Plonski Mr. John Wilder walked into Mr. Burton's office.

"John," said the lawyer, "I got along without you, but I thought you would like to know. That man Sully of yours is a trump. He ought to go on the force. Plonski's in Fortress Monroe, arrested through the Government's secret service, and beyond the reach of the ward politicians of New York. Now you've got a clear field. He straggled over into the domain of martial law. That's all."

CHAPTER XLVI.

DR. FERRIS LOOKS INTO A HEART.

And now was to occur an interregnum of months in the adventures of the cup, which was indeed all this time lying snugly under a mossy bank on a bed of dead water cresses, half full of silver sand and caught securely in the roots of a young willow. Above it now ran the singing current of the Pocantico, and now formed the ice and snow banks, and once or twice a frugal muskrat had partly turned it over with her curious paw and then left it with contempt. Once Hi Tucker had waded to within a foot of it in trying to find out where the same frugal muskrat went, but the pool where it lay was too deep and the water too cold and after marking the spot in his mind, he gave over his search until warmer weather.

Plonski was pacing his narrow casemate shut out from the world by bastile walls, unable even to communicate with McCune, who at his own request had been set to work with a gang of laborers on the glacis. For several days Plonski walked his little prison house in a pitiable state of mind. He knew too well how unavailing would be any attempt to get a hearing in the present over-burthened condition of public affairs and how perilous that hearing might be if he were tried by court martial for aiding and abetting the enemy. Worse than all, he knew or thought he knew that while he was incarcerated, Wilder and his principals would secure the cup for the recovery of which he had spent so many weary hours and upon which he had concentrated such a prodigious amount of craft. He was too shrewd not to know that Wilder did not want his life and only wanted him kept out of the way, and he believed that as soon as the cup had been recovered, there would come an order for his release. He, therefore, with admirable philosophy tried to summon all his patience and fortitude and abide events rather than beat his head against the granite walls of his prison.

A fortnight went by and the winter rains were running unnoticed above the Toltec Cup.

John Wilder had gone to Mr. Burton to inform him that he had been ordered to Chicago on a case of a bank robbery and to communicate his suspicion that the department wanted to get him out of the city. Mr. Burton advised him to go and not betray his suspicions. Just before taking his departure from Burton and Dunn's office, he had asked the lawyer how he had managed the Plonski affair, and Mr. Burton told him. "I gave the man Sully explicit instructions and he carried them out to the letter," he said: "I even provided him with a cup."

"A cup?" repeated Wilder.

"Yes; it occurred to me that I could hire some kind of a silver cup that would answer the purpose and I sent to a silversmith's, Dittmar and Kleinbacker—there's their card on the table. They sent up a young man; I told him I wanted to hire a silver flagon, something as unique as possible, for a few days and would be responsible for it and pay a handsome sum for its use. The young man said he had just the thing, if I would give him a personal bond for its security, which I did. He sent it here in a box, which I did not open and which Sully took away and safely returned when he got through. You see it was necessary for the man to make a show of having the property, in order to lure them on. The committee of safety sent word to Washington that this Plonski was one of the leaders of the Knights of the Golden Circle and he was nabbed the moment he touched Annapolis Junction. It was all neatly done and we have to thank Mr. Sully for it. I'm going to ask you to do something for him when you come back."

"You found Plonski sharper than you suspected, I think," said Wilder; "it was lucky you warned Capt Ackerman or he would have been deceived by that telegram. You can see how unscrupulous the man is by signing my name to the dispatch."

"Well, well," said Mr. Burton; "I think Captain Ackerman deserves some credit for signing Mrs. Enniston's name to his answer."

About a week after this conversation, Wilder, much against his inclination, left New York and did not return for a month.

At the very hour that he departed, Dr. Follen Sanger received word informing him of the fact. He threw the dispatch down on his table, carelessly, and turning to his secretary, asked:

"Anything heard from that fellow Plonski?"

Nothing," replied the secretary.

"Humph," said the doctor, stirring over his letters. "He is unusually quiet. Is Selden looking after the primaries in that ward?"

"Yes," said the secretary. "At least I believe so. There is nothing new."

Dr. Sanger was not a man to display nervousness, but on this occasion he was evidently perturbed and restless. The door of his consulting room stood ajar so that he could see out into the hallway and his glances in that direction showed that his mind was not fixed upon his usual clerical work.

It is necessary to explain the causes of his anxiety.

On the afternoon that Miss Enniston and her little party had called, the doctor had been disturbed by something dropped in the course of the conversation. When they were gone, he called the maid. "Let me know," he said, "when your mistress returns."

It was half an hour later before Mrs. Sanger came in and she went directly to her room. The doctor followed her up almost immediately. When he entered her boudoir, she was throwing off her furs and heavy cloak, and with his habitual attentiveness, he began at once to assist her. For a moment not a word was spoken, but she had caught a quick view of his face in the mirror and turning, she put her arm round his neck and said: "You are angry at me. I can see it in your eyes, it's in your touch. What have I done?"

"Kate," he said, without making any attempt to return her caress; "you are trying to avoid Miss Enniston. Will you tell me why?"

There was no severity in his voice, only as she thought, a portentous chill and gloom.

"O, is that all?" she exclaimed with a smile. "I was afraid I had offended you."

"It isn't quite all, Kate," he replied. "It may be that in order to avoid Miss Enniston, you think it necessary to deceive me. I don't know that even that would offend me but it would grieve me."

"Never," she said with immediate vehemence, "never," and put her arm on his shoulder where it partly curved round on his back ready to stifle with gentle force any further development of displeasure. "I will tell you why I do not wish to see her. It is because I instinctively dislike her. Don't ask me why. You promised me once that I should have my own way in some things and this is such a little thing. I suppose I could even overcome this repugnance if you really desired me to, but I thought all along that in such a trifle you would readily let me have my own way. It never occurred to me that it would be necessary to deceive you."

Her arm moved a little with an encircling pressure, half supplicating in its timidity. He caught her in his forceful way, drew her close to his breast and kissed her on the forehead. Then he held her out at arm's length and looking into her face said:

"Heavens, Kate, how your heart is beating. You look frightened."

"Yes," she said, "I thought you were angry."

"Nonsense," he replied, as he laid his hand on her bodice. "You are suppressing some kind of emotion."

"No," she said. "No, it is nearly always so. It keeps me awake at night."

"What is it keeps you awake? The action of your heart?"

"Yes."

There was an instant shadow of anxiety on his face. "Why haven't you told me?"

"I suppose it's because it's another trifle and a woman doesn't like to annoy her husband with trifles, especially when they are infirmities. I was going to ask you last week to let Dr. Ferris come to me."

"Why didn't you? He'll be here this morning," he said as he looked at his watch. "I'll send him up to you." Then he tried to approach her with his ear so as to listen, but she playfully stepped back a pace.

"There," she said. "It's all over now." He regarded her attentively a moment, then he returned to the subject that had brought him up.

"My dear, I am afraid you are attracting attention to your antipathies. Miss Enniston made a remark that sounded very much as if she understood that you were avoiding her. I wish for the sake of appearances that you would see her. It doesn't cost much to pass the empty civilities."

She was now enfolded in his arms again and her head was bent over on his breast. He waited a few seconds and as she said nothing, he went on.

"I know that you wish to avoid publicity, but you do not appear to see that the means you are taking is attracting a prying attention and curiosity. People are beginning to wonder at your retirement and, shall I say it, my dear, your fear of meeting certain persons. There was that young artist I spoke to you about, Mr. Carteret. I have made an appointment for you which I hope you will keep. You have no antipathy to him, have you?"

"No," she said; "but I have a dislike to having my portrait painted."

"But I want it, my dear. This Carteret is a rising genius and I want to patronize him. It's my wish that you give him two or three sittings."

There was just the least intimation of the man's will in this speech, but there was nothing imperative in his manner.

"If you wish it," she said, "I will sit."

"And I with," he added, "that you would see Miss Enniston. The Hardynges are valuable, and I might say, necessary friends of mine. I cannot afford to offend them, and Miss Enniston, I must say, has tried very hard to establish an intimacy. She told me she was going to bring her mother to see you."

"Did she tell you that?"

"Yes. You are surprised?"

"No, no, no, only it appears a little irregular, doesn't it?"

"Not at all. Did you ever meet Mrs. Enniston, my dear?"

Here she broke away and began rapidly to complete her disrobing; "What a lot of absurd questions you are asking," she said with a forced laugh. "Where should I meet her? You forget, Follen, that you took me out of obscurity and I warned you of this when you asked me to marry you. Do you wonder at my timidity when you think back?"

His obduracy took on a gentler air, but it did not abate. He followed her up and caught hold of her again,

"I wonder only, my dear," he said, "at your stubborn wish to be still obscure. There's no excuse for it now. You must see that if I have disregarded all your weaknesses, it was because they did not attract attention. Now that people are beginning to talk about them, I am going to ask you to have some regard for your husband's position."

This was nearer severity than he had ever come in his treatment of her and she felt it, but he did not relax the half embrace which held her. Altogether the effect was that of an affectionate will that meant to have its own way and she was sensible that in spite of the man's passion for her, the time was coming when her artifices would be of no avail. She was visibly agitated in spite of her efforts to appear undisturbed, and she knew that he was watching her with more than his usual discernment.

"Follen," she said, as she released herself, "let me get my heavy things off."

As he let her go, she moved away from him to the mirror and began arranging her apparel and removing her hat with her back towards him.

He waited a moment, then he said: "Have I annoyed you?"

No," she replied carelessly, without intermitting her task or looking round. A second later she added: "You can't—but you may let other people annoy me."

"There is no reason why they should, that I can see. Does it annoy you to adapt yourself to your position and show common courtesy for my sake?" he asked.

Then as if the speech, now that he had listened to it, were a little harsher than he intended, he went up to her, pulled her round and said:

"Kate, don't be foolish with me. Look at me. You know I am not unreasonable and you must know in your heart that you are. What makes you so nervous?"

She was delicately squirming and trying to release herself.

"I'm trying to get my things off, Follen," she said. "Please let me finish my toilet. You pounce upon me half dressed and wonder what makes me so nervous."

"Do you want me to leave you?"

"Yes, please. I must fix myself. I'm uncomfortable in my street harness."

"Very well," he said, stepping back. "I suppose I do show a man's inconsiderateness. When you are comfortable we'll talk it over." He then approached her, kissed her on the forehead, as was his habit, and was about to leave the room. At the door he turned and said:

"Are you comfortable enough to see Dr. Ferris when he calls?"

"I'm *uncomfortable* enough," she said. "Please send him up."

The moment her husband was gone, her fussy and nervous preparations ceased, and leaning with her hands upon the marble of her dressing-case, she stared at herself in the mirror musingly for a moment or two, then she walked to the window and, lifting the heavy curtain, looked thoughtfully out upon the winter scene. A few wet clouds were racing across the sky from the north-east. A vague, envious sense of their freedom of flight made her regard them with an unconscious interest. Presently she dropped the curtain and with an impulsive and indeterminate stride, walked to the centre of the room, where she stopped and looked round at the appointments. It was easy to divine what was passing in her mind. The consciousness that she was a prisoner, shut in by luxury and reserved for an inevitable catastrophe, had taken possession of her. A wild, sudden desire to fly—anywhere, so that she could escape from the everthreatening and constantly advancing danger, seized her. She ran her eye over the elegant and luxurious furniture and the costly ornaments with a shrinking repugnance. "Better," she said to herself, "to be a starving gypsy in rags, so that I am rid forever of this terror. Why should I stay here under a curse when I can escape into freedom and safety and obscurity. Why should I insanely wait for all these hungry and envious social vultures to pounce upon me and gloat over my disgrace, when I can bury every thing in some unknown wilderness. So, Miss Enniston insists that I shall see her mother...why should she insist? What does she want me to see her mother for?" Then she doubled up her beautiful hand and placed her fist over her mouth as if to stay the words that her impulse put into sound. "My God, I wonder if that woman saw me that night through the bay window?"

A rap at her door startled her out of this conceit. She evidently knew who it was, for she said, "Yes," in a permissive tone, without looking round. The door was opened and her maid, putting her head in, said:

"If you please—Dr. Ferris."

"Tell him to come up," replied Mrs. Sanger.

With admirable celerity, she threw on a wrap and when the doctor came she was in an easy chair with her slippered feet on a cushion in a charming attitude of invalidism.

He drew up a chair in his precise and gentle way to within a foot of her and as she acknowledged his salutation, she caught the calm, inquiring glance of his mild blue eye. Some instinct of sex told her that she could not deal with this man as she dealt with her husband, but she girded herself for some kind of desperate attempt and meant to go through with it.

"Follen tells me your heart troubles you," he said. "I hope it's nothing serious."

"I'm afraid it is," she replied. "It is so continuous. But I dislike to worry him about it, doctor; you know how a wife shrinks from betraying her infirmities to a husband. I mean, a petted and admired wife."

"What are your symptoms, Mrs. Sanger?" asked the Doctor. "Are you troubled when you lie down?"

"Yes, do you know, I think it's the New York air. I was here several years ago and had the same trouble. When I left New York, it disappeared."

"Pardon me, madame," said the doctor, "if you will confine yourself to the effects, I shall be able to judge of the cause myself. Did you ever suffer from an attack of rheumatism?"

"Never."

"Difficulty of breathing when you lie down?"

"Yes."

"Do you sleep on your left side?"

"No."

"Humph! Follen asked me to make a thorough examination. I think that will be the best way and I brought a stethescope up with me. Remove your wrap— on the left side, please—and I'll apply it."

He got up, went to the window and looked at the instrument and she, some-what nervously, threw back a portion of her wrap, exposing the white lace and linen. The doctor then pushed an ottoman up beside her, sat down upon it with his face toward the dark portion of the room while hers was toward the windows. She could not help noticing how precise and deliberate and delicate he was, and how different from Dr. Sanger. When he had placed the instrument on her heart and had his ear to it, he said:

"Don't give your mind to this, please. You may converse on any subject. Have you ever been abroad?"

"No."

There was a pause. Then she said:

"Aren't some kinds of climates better than others for heart disease, Doctor?"

"Yes, decidedly; low altitudes. What did your mother die with?"

"She isn't dead."

"No? Where is she?"

"She's at her home in the—in this State."

"Ever have any pain?"

"Yes; sharp, sudden pains when I exert myself."

"Humph, that's bad. Don't get excited. Haven't you taken laudanum?"

"No, never."

"Been worse since you came to New York?"

"Yes, this climate kills me."

"Yes, you don't like excitement."

"No; it prostrates me."

"You don't feel any soreness under the pressure of this instrument, do you?"

"A little, Doctor."

"Humph! *Were you acquainted with the Ennistons before you met Dr. Sanger?*"

The unexpectedness of this question was such that several seconds elapsed before its significance became fully apparent to her, and when it did, there simultaneously seized upon her several disturbing emotions. She was conscious as she fully apprehended the question, that her heart was beating more rapidly, and that no effort of her will could control it. Some kind of vague knowledge, sudden and terrible, that the doctor she had summoned was literally listening in her heart for a secret she had hidden from the world, was accompanied by the desire not to betray herself and to have the listener believe that the agitation was the result of disease. By a supreme effort she said, "There, Doctor, my heart is beating now. It starts in that manner without any cause whatever."

"Do you feel any pain?"

"Yes, a sharp prick as of a needle."

The doctor took away the instrument and rose from his seat

"You want to go abroad, don't you?" he said.

"Yes, I do," she replied. "It depends upon you. Your report will decide it with Follen. A woman with heart disease ought to have her way in some things."

Dr. Ferris was standing but a few feet away from her, and wiping with his handkerchief, the moisture from the stethescope that had been occasioned by the firm grasp of his hand. His unperturbed manner was the same, and he said with a soft voice:

"Madame, there's nothing the matter with your heart. It's sounder than mine. It isn't even functionally disturbed. It's action is perfectly normal, even when greatest, and I am bound to tell you that the emotional causes which increase its action have not been of long standing, for such increased action long continued would have thickened its walls, or, in other words, produced a slight enlargement."

She was sitting bolt upright in the chair, staring at him as he mechanically wound the white handkerchief round the instrument. It required no tedious process of reasoning to see that this speech virtually accused her of deception, and that the speaker not only did not believe a word she had told him, but had reached by an unexampled process down to her emotions, and for aught she knew, to her secret. She hated him in that minute with all the acrid, unforgiving hatred, that only a woman can feel who has had the privacy of her soul pried into and has been cajoled into confession in defiance of all her feminine arts and reticence.

Her lips were white and were drawn across her teeth as she said:

"Doctor, what report are you going to make to my husband?"

Dr. Ferris held the instrument up to his eye, looked through it to the light, put it carefully in a little box which he placed on the edge of the dressing case, closed and fastened the box, and after wiping his hand automatically with his handkerchief, he placed a chair close beside Mrs. Sanger, and in the same mild, thin tone, said, while he fastened his cool blue eyes upon her:

"Mrs. Sanger, I am bound to tell your husband the truth, not necessarily the whole truth. I shall report to him that there is nothing the matter with your heart, but that it would be an excellent plan to send you abroad."

"And why," she asked with a forced tone, "do you think it advisable for me to go abroad if there is nothing the matter with me?"

"Madame, there *is* something the matter with you. I don't believe your nervous system will escape from the strain while you are in this country. But it is not necessary to tell your husband that. What that something is, falls outside of my professional inquiry. It is enough for me to know that it is not physical. You want rest—a secure rest from your own emotions."

He got up, said something politely about the beauty of the room, and bowed himself out.

The interview and examination were tenfold more disturbing than had been her husband's indefinite suspicions. With her husband, even at the worst she could depend upon the blindness of his infatuation. But there was no deceiving Dr. Ferris. "What did he know?" she asked herself several times as her mind went back to the question about the Ennistons. It never once occurred to her in her condition of alarm that Dr. Sanger and Dr. Ferris were very confidential, and Dr. Sanger might have mentioned his wife's avoidance of Miss Enniston, upon which small hint Dr. Ferris had built his question. To her excited fancy, it appeared that he must know even more than he had divulged. But more acute than even this fear, was the one fact that Dr. Ferris had somehow looked into her heart and that she was thus brought unexpectedly to face a means of discovery that had never entered into her calculations. It looked to her as if this strange incident was meant to show her how futile it was to hope that she could hide in the recesses of her being the guilt and discomfort of her life, and she no doubt invested it with a superstitious dread, just as she now contemplated Dr. Ferris with an altogether ungovernable hatred. In the one moment that he had stood calmly regarding her, she had felt the impulse to spring at him, just as she had sprung at Mr. Enniston long before, and now that the impulse had died out, she was thinking of it with a new terror.

Altogether the woman was as helplessly miserable as a woman could be, and seeing no possible means of turning or avoiding the events which pressed upon her in this place, her mind relapsed to the one alternative of instant flight. She locked her door, and getting down upon the floor, put a key into a drawer of her dressing case and opened it softly. It was full of odds and ends of female finery, but underneath it all was a small box which she drew out and opened. It contained money, gold pieces, bills and jewels. She turned them over as if calculating their value, and sat musingly silent with them in her hand.

With some idea of being prepared for a possible emergency, she had long ere this began to hoard her little surplus pocket money, and as Dr. Sanger was very liberal with her and did not inquire how she spent her allowance, it was not difficult, with a purpose in view, for her to accumulate thus secretly, quite a sum.

The act of regarding this little hoard brought the dire contingency of flight and possible vagabondage, and nameless skulking vividly to her mind and she again looked round at her warm and elegant environment and thought of the pride and passion of her husband, and the envy and adulation of his friends. Then she set her teeth and said in a low whisper that was almost like a hiss:

"No, I'd rather be the companion of some dirty pioneer in the wilderness and have the freedom of his log cabin, than be shut in here with all this mockery."

The speech betrayed a fact and a mistake.

The fact was that Dr. Ferris may have listened to her heart, but Dr. Sanger had never touched it.

The mistake was that she believed she could escape from the consequences of her conduct by escaping from her surroundings.

Once more she was interrupted by a knock, and when she had replaced the box in the drawer and opened the door, the maid said:

"If you please, m'm, the artist," and she handed her mistress a card. On it were written the words, "Colin Carteret."

"Tell him," said Mrs. Sanger, "to wait. I will see him in the parlor."

CHAPTER XLVII.

THE RETURN OF THE PRINCESS.

It would be difficult to describe Manuella's feelings when she received Carteret's verses and read them. At first they wholly failed to touch her as he imagined they should.

She ran her eye down the lines, recognized the author and said to herself: "Why should he send me verses instead of coming to see me?"

Then she folded the paper up and put it in a sacred receptacle of her dress which brought the verses very near her heart and kept them convenient for her hand.

To such a nature as Manuella's there was less perplexity and annoyance in Carteret's conduct than Carteret himself suffered, for the simple reason that she was guileless and consequently undisturbed by suspicions and fears. She expected every day to see him walk in. It never once occurred to her that anything had happened or could happen to estrange them thus mutely and suddenly.

She did not answer the rhyming letter, and three days elapsed, during which time Carteret was wondering why his tender peace offering did not bring some token.

Sometimes when Mr. Stonybrook was over attentive and stayed too long in their rooms, she felt a little girlish resentment as she thought that Carteret had abandoned her to this entirely, instead of helping her; but it was impossible to treat Mr. Stonybrook rudely. He had deposited several hundred dollars in the bank for her grandfather, which he claimed was the result of his negotiations with Mr. Evans' former partner, and he was scrupulously careful not to alarm Manuella by any display of passion. The improvement in Mr. Evans' circumstances showed itself mainly in Manuella's appearance, for both Mr. Evans and Mr. Stonybrook managed to divert enough of the money in the direction of clothes to transform her into a young lady of comfortable position and excellent taste. While thus enjoying the advantages of independence, it had occurred to her several times with something like a pang of consanguinity, that she ought to go and see Mrs. Sitwhite. It was so easy to be magnanimous now.

The only thing that deterred her was the fear of meeting the girl Clianthe, or one of the ruffians who had been employed in the abduction.

In mentioning her desire to Mrs. Hannige, that personage had said at once:

"Why don't you let John go with you? He'll do it; he'll be here to-night and I'll ask him to go with you in the morning."

At first Manuella shrank from the idea, but as she thought it over, there was no reasonable objection to be urged against it. John Wilder was a discreet man, he would be a protector, and he was a friend of Carteret's. So it was arranged that he should take her to the Terrace the next day, and in the morning she went out on Fourteenth street and bought a drum and a gun, with mimic military trappings for Mrs. Sitwhite's boy, and a complete housekeeping outfit for the girl. She even purchased some beautiful cakes of soap and bottles of perfume and a dress pattern for Mrs. Sitwhite, for it would be Christmas time in a few days. These things she had sent over to the house in Fifteenth street, and when John Wilder came to escort her, she said:

"Dear me, however shall I carry all these bundles?" and John looking at the unwieldly parcels replied, "We'll have to put 'em in a coupe, I suppose," which task was performed with the aid of Mrs. Hannige, who declared, as the last and most important package was handed into the vehicle by John Wilder, that she looked for all the world like a fairy godmother or a real princess, and this latter title reminded Manuella that she was going back to where it had originally been conferred upon her.

There was a genuine stir about the doorway of O'Reardon's Terrace when she and John Wilder arrived. A small knot of idlers hung round the place, the two Grinch girls were at their windows, and Cokey Tim, who was trying to skate on one leg in a frozen gutter, hopped over on his other leg to the coupé door and then let out a summons, "Hi, fellers, cum mere."

Manuella, after stepping from the vehicle, stood a moment holding her garments from the slush of the sidewalk and displaying her handsome boot. She was wondering how she would get all her bundles up the stairs, and feeling delicate about asking Mr. Wilder to carry them, "O, dear," she said, "I'm causing you such a lot of trouble. How good you are."

"No trouble," said Wilder. "You just catch hold of these small ones; that's it, and I'll tackle the big ones. See? That's all right; now come along. They'll think Santa Claus has arrived."

And so, blushing and laughing, she followed him up the well known stairs, through groups of children and knots of women, well aware that every door was ajar, that the Grinches were looking up and the Pitwilks looking down, and that she was getting salutations from people as she passed, whose faces in the dark hallways were not discernible. It was amazing how good natured Wilder was. When he stumbled against a washtub full of clothes and dropped the drum, she picked it up and he laughed. When he struck the bedstead that Mrs. Gridlegrean had been cleaning in the hall and knocked down the post with a crash instead of swearing he cried out, "All right, Miss Castleton, I'm sound yet and so is my cargo;" and she arrived at Mrs. Sitwhite's door panting and blushing and wondering audibly how she ever came to put anybody to such a foolish lot of trouble, and Wilder, who saw her radiant with excitement in the dim, dirty light, said to himself, "What an unaccountable ass that fellow Carteret is to let such a girl as this slip through his fingers."

She rapped at the door and she could not help thinking, as she heard the sound of her aunt's washboard, and listened to the rough voices coming up the stairway, how much more dreadful the place was now than when she lived in it.

When Mrs. Sitwhite opened the door and stood there, wiping the soap suds off her bare arms on her dress and peering out, Manuella said:

"Cynthy, don't you know me?"

"Well, of all things," exclaimed Cynthy, "is that you, Manuella?"

"I've come to see you and the children. This is Mr. Wilder, I guess you don't remember him," and the two women kissed each other, and one of them began to cry and wipe her nose and eyes with her dress, while the other, with Mr. Wilder's assistance, began to pile the things up on the dinner table.

"You've taken me by surprise," said Mrs. Sitwhite, "and I'm sure I wouldn't have known you anywheres. Take a chair, mister. I'm a sight to be seen, Ella, and everything's topsy turvy."

Manuella looked at her aunt with pity. She was more inflamed and bedraggled than ever, and the girl began to feel some, compunction on account of her own comfortable appearance. She opened the kitchen door and let the children burst in. "How's John?" she asked.

At this Mrs. Sitwhite put her dress to her eyes and began to sob afresh through its wet folds.

"He's gone," she said in smothered gasps. "He's 'nlisted. Yes, he has."

"Gone to the war and left you?" Manuella asked.

"Yes, he has; and the chances are we'll none of us see him again."

Wilder walked to the door. "I'll wait for you, Miss Castleton," he said. "I'll stroll about while you are having your chat, but I'll keep my eye on you," saying which he went into the hall.

The moment they were alone Mrs. Sitwhite dropped her dress.

"What have you been a doing, Ella?" she asked with more curiosity than reproach. "What'd you bring him for? Are you married?"

"What an idea," said Manuella. "I just came over to see how you were getting along, and to bring the children something for Christmas. I brought him along for protection. He's an officer, don't you remember?"

Mrs. Sitwhite evidently did remember. She gave her eyes and nose a wipe as she said, "I'm sure I'd given up all idea of seeing you again, and it worried me, Ella, to think that one's own blood relations should fall out about nothing; don't set down on that, it's got molasses on it and you'll spoil your beautiful victorine; here, take this," and she gave her visitor a chair which she wiped off with her damp apron. "How's pop? I tell you what it is, Ella, it isn't right, you know it isn't, to carry him off and not let his own daughter know where he is. I call it awful; yes, I do."

"Well, I guess that's all right now Cynthy," said Manuella with vague emoliency. "I hope we'll all have better times, and not get into any more trouble. How do you manage, now that John's gone?"

"That's just it, how can a woman manage? He got the bounty, it's three hundred dollars. But what's three hundred dollars when it's gone? You know yourself it won't last forever, and most of 'em that 'nlist don't last long themselves. You know that," and Mrs. Sitwhite began to mop herself afresh.

Manuella unrolled the drum from its wrappages and put it on the neck of young Master Sitwhite. "I shouldn't wonder if John got to be a general or something," she said. "It's a great chance for him, and I'm glad he's got out of the gasworks; and I'm sure he thinks too much of his children not to be careful of himself."

While these women were thus conversing, and as it were, burying with amiable words the family hatchet, they were interrupted by several callers. First Mrs. Gridlegrean came in to know if Mrs. Sitwhite didn't want some fresh porgies, there was a man with the nicest lot she'd seen in front of the house, and while Mrs. Sitwhite was politely disavowing all desire for porgies Mrs. Gridlegrean was taking in Manuella from head to foot. Then Fanny Grinch burst in pantingly and said, "O, excuse me, Mrs. Sitwhite, I didn't know you had company, I only wanted to find out if your water runs. I knew you was washin' and ma's been particular to shut it off," and Miss Grinch, while making this speech of explanation, was enquiringly examining Mrs. Sitwhite's visitor, who went on placidly arranging little Miss Sitwhite's tea set on a soap box. Mrs. Sitwhite got rid of her visitors in her own brusque way, remarking as she shut the door on them, "Did you ever see such impudence? Porgies. Well, I never. And 'Does your water run?' They're too friendly all at once."

Mr. John Wilder had lit his cigar and walked to the end of the hall where he stood looking out of the dirty window into the street. He was thinking what a lot of time he gave to other people's affairs, and wondering at the curious fatality that brought him back to this house. While he stood there musingly an elderly gentleman came slowly and somewhat laboriously up the stairs and looked inquiringly up and down the hallway. He was wrapped in a heavy shawl, much worn by men at this time, that was wound round his neck and breast in heavy convolutions, and he wore a fur cap pulled down over his ears. His face, seen in the subdued light, was that of an alert, intelligent man of at least sixty. He stood, slightly bent, with a gloved hand on the stair rail looking about as if undetermined what to do. Then he went to the door of the front apartment and knocked. At that moment Wilder turned slowly and regarded him.

A woman with a baby in her arms opened the door a few inches and looked through with an annoyed and flushed face.

"Pardon me, madame," said the stranger, "I am looking for a gentleman who hired these rooms two or three months ago."

"Two or three months ago?" exclaimed the woman in a sharp impatient tone. "Well, he ain't hirin' em now because I'm doin' it."

"Ah," said the stranger, "I didn't know but perhaps you were acquainted with him and could tell me where he is. I'm a friend of his."

"How the devil could I tell yez? Sure the place was empty when I tuk it. Why don't yez go to the agent?"

"I beg your pardon," persisted the man politely, "are you Mrs. Sitwhite?"

"I'm not thin," said the woman, "my name's Hoolihan, an I've not been here a week, and I wish I'd never com—the divil a bit of water's in the place and what with the bugs and the noise overhead and the sick childer, it's the devil's hole complately."

Then she shut the door rather viciously, for the cold air had begun to make the sick baby cry.

Wilder watched the stranger go to Mrs. Sitwhite's door and he heard him make the same inquiries. But Mrs. Sitwhite who was at the moment engrossed with her neice, and had already been interrupted annoyingly, gave the man curt and unsatisfactory answers and he turned away at last, as she shut the door, and was about to go down the stairs when Wilder hailed him.

"Looking for Doctor Plonski?" he asked.

The man hesitated a moment and then said, "Yes, he lived here at one time."

"But he doesn't live here now," said Wilder.

"So I perceive," replied the man. "Do you know him?"

"Yes, I knew him when I lived in the house. I did some work for him."

"O, did you? Do you know where he is now?"

Wilder hesitated as if undecided how to act. Then he came over to the old gentleman and said, "Are you a friend of Plonski's?"

"Yes, I am."

"I s'pose you know then," said Wilder, "that he has some enemies and his friends don't tell everybody where he is."

"I thought I knew all his friends," said the man. "Who might you be?"

"What do you want of him?" asked Wilder.

"I want to see him on private business. Is he in the city?"

"No."

"Are you sure?"

"Quite sure."

"Then you know where he is?"

"I don't know where he is to everybody."

The stranger was trying to get a good look at Wilder's face, but the light was not favorable.

"I've come a great distance, sir, to see him," said the man, "on business of an entirely private nature. If you can direct me how to find him, you will be doing me a very great service."

"Well, the fact is," said Wilder, "he had a scheme that had to be worked very secretly and when I was living here, I did something for him and he treated me handsome. I always found the old man very square and I wouldn't like to get him into any trouble. I don't live here now. I just came over with my daughter to make a call. I'm waiting for her now."

"What is your business?" asked the man.

"I'm running a boarding house just now," replied Wilder, "have you been in the city long?"

"No."

"Well, if you want nice rooms, give me a call, there's the address, Hannige, Fifteenth street."

"Is that your name?"

"That's my name. My wife runs the house. You'll find it quiet, convenient and reasonable. If you find the doctor, he'll tell you it's all right. I've had several of his friends there. Come and look at the rooms."

Here Wilder took hold of the knob of Mrs. Sitwhite's door. Whatever else he might be thinking of, he evidently did not wish to stand there any longer and risk a meeting with Clianthe or a return of Mrs. Sitwhite, while the man was present.

He was rather thoughtful as he entered the room. Who this new personage was he had no idea, but he felt confident that he had said enough to get a speedy call from him, if the man did not come back and make inquiries of Mrs. Sitwhite or go to the Fifteenth street house before he got there.

Manuella and Mrs. Sitwhite kissed each other and Mrs. Sitwhite and her children went down the stairs with their visitor to see her off and there were a good many superfluous parting admonitions from the aunt on the lower landing, to a violent accompaniment of a drum, such as, "Now Ella, be sure to bring pop and mind you don't get your victorine against them bannisters, I think it's tar. Goodby, dear."

When they were in the coupé, the girl wanted to know if it would be safe to take her grandfather there and Wilder told her it would. "You need have no more fear of the man Plonski," he said, "and save for the annoyance of meeting the girl Clianthe; there is nothing to deter you."

When they had got out at Mrs. Hannige's, that radiant housewife was watching them from the window of the little reception room.

"John," she said as they came in, "If you'd had somebody to train you, you would have made quite a ladies' man."

"Mollie," said Wilder, "there'll come an elderly man here looking for Mr. Hannige; I'm Mr. Hannige and you're my wife. I want to see him. Do you understand?"

"No, I don't," said Mrs. Hannige, "who could understand all your goings on? Come in the sitting room, my dear. Did you see your folks?"

"O, no," replied Manuella, "I must go up and get my things off. I saw them. There wasn't a letter came for me, was there?"

"No letter," said Mrs. Hannige, "but I got some news."

"News for me?"

"I guess you'll be interested in it."

"O, tell me what it is," cried the girl, who was half way up the stairs and leaning on the handrail, eagerly.

"I guess somebody you know is going to be married."

"Somebody I know?" Manuella repeated. "Why, I don't know anybody."

"O, yes you do. Somebody that was engaged,"

Then the girl's little heart began to sink. She turned: "O, it's some foolish gossip you want to tell, I suppose," she remarked, in a changed tone and went up the stairs.

It was not fifteen minutes before Mrs. Hannige came after her. The old gentleman was taking a nap and Manuella was not in a cheerful mood.

"Oats is on one of his spells," began Mrs. Hannige. "He never talks till he has a spell. You can't get a word out of him till he starts in and then he tells all he knows. You know how he rattles on."

"No, I don't," said Manuella, "and I don't think I want to."

"O, Oats is a good boy. He's a little foolish sometimes, but he's respectful, and if Oats ever tells a girl he'll marry her, he'll do it. He was telling me about the Follen Sanger's picture, I guess you saw it in the papers, and he kept on in his way talking about the party that he went with and finally I said: 'Oats, what in the name of goodness do you mean by a party, who was it?' 'Why,' says he, 'Miss Enniston and Carteret.' 'What?' says I, 'that creature?' 'Creature?' says he, 'what do you mean by that? She's bang up.' You know how he talks. 'Yes,' says he, 'bang up; lots o' money and a great patron of the arts.' 'And Carteret went with her?' says I, opening my eyes. 'Of course,' says he. 'Why not? He called for her and took her there.' 'Well, upon my word,' says I. I suppose I must 'a been starin' at him all I knew how, for he says: 'What's the matter with Miss Enniston? Didn't she buy his picture? Ain't she dead gone to pieces about him? Do you suppose Carter's such a mushroom as to make faces long at that chance?' 'Lands alive,' says I, 'Oats, how you do run on. I thought they had fallen out.' 'They've tumbled in again, then,' says he. 'It's all right. I wish I had his chance; I'd marry her like a wink.' "

"Mrs. Hannige," said Manuella, "Mr. Chapman is a very amusing gossip, but I wish you'd talk of something else."

"But I haven't told you yet," continued Mrs. Hannige, unabashed and undeterred. "It seems that that dreadful creature has got Doctor Sanger to let young Carteret paint his wife's picture, because she goes there regularly and can meet him there."

It was impossible not to be hurt by this information, and when Mrs. Hannige had been gently put out, the girl went and sat down by the window, and taking from her breast a folded sheet of paper she spread it out and began reading it with a new interest. It was Carteret's verses. She was not aware that one only apprehends poetry with the reason and that one's moods interpret it. There was a new melancholy in the lines that she had not noticed before. They appeared to be written by some one who was paying a tribute to something dead and gone, for the memory of it. Why did Carteret talk of her as a pretty recollection? Why did he stay away from her? Could it be possible, after what had occurred, that he had gone back to Miss Enniston? After a moment's reverie she opened the paper and read the concluding lines again:

> "O dear illusions, vague and vain,
> Their phantoms come and flit;
> 'Tis recollection's mise-en-scene
> And you are part of it."

The only sense that she could at this moment get out of this was that of a tender lament, that she was part of a vague and vain illusion.

Her woman's pride rebelled at the thought that anybody could so easily shift from a reality to a fantasy.

She folded up the paper pensively, but she did not put it back in her bosom. She opened a little drawer and threw it in. Then she got up and busied herself with her grandfather until the room grew dark. She had a great deal to tell him about Cynthia, and she seated herself on a stool before the grate fire, looking very charming in the soft glow. But somehow her thoughts ran off in a sad path of their own, even while she talked with him. It had blown up cold and stormy, and the sough of the wind and the dash of the rain against the windows added to the gloom of the evening.

She was sitting thus, their conversation having lapsed into monosyllables, when Mr. Stonybrook rapped on the door and a moment later came in, with an apologetic familiarity.

"By Jupiter," he said, "how cosy you are here. It makes my dreary quarters look and feel like one of those snow sheds in the West. I've got my slippers and gown on; you will not care, will you, Miss Castleton? Its grown very cold out doors and the heater in my room is working badly. I thought perhaps you'd like a game of backgammon, Mr. Evans."

His voice sounded quite blithe and reassuring to Manuella, in her despondent mood. He had brought his backgammon board under his arm, and Mr. Evans appeared to be stimulated by the sound of his voice.

"Ah," he said, "I'm glad you came in. I was afraid you would overlook us tonight. Pull the table up, Ella, and fix the drop light."

In a moment there was a pleasant stir, and a new radiance as Manuella bustled round and lit the gas and Mr. Stonybrook, who was talking all the while to Mr. Evans, drew up a chair and seated himself at the table.

"By Jove, Manuella, this is just the night for a negus—listen to that storm—a prime Queen Anne negus."

She was pulling down the curtains, and she turned round to ask: "What's negus?"

"Don't you know?" he cried. "You've got a delightful surprise. Grandfather, Miss—Manuella doesn't know what a negus is. Now, I'll warrant you've swallowed many a one. Eh?'

"Negus, negus. Bless my soul, yes," said Mr. Evans, very chipper. "Port wine negus, to be sure. We used to make them when I was a young man and you could get the port wine, but you can't get the wine now."

"O, yes, you can. I've got some of the real stuff. I'll tell you how it is," he said, addressing himself to Manuella. "It's this way: You have a dainty little copper kettle and a grate fire, see? and when the water begins to steam and bubble, somebody that's clumsy like me puts the port wine in the glasses with a pinch of cloves and a dash of lemon and just a spoonful of sugar, and somebody that's graceful and quick like you whips in the hot water, and then everybody, young and old, has a delightful and innocent drink, besides all the jolly fun of making it."

"But we haven't got any copper kettle," says Manuella.

"But I have," replied Mr. Stonybrook. "My trouble is I haven't got any grate. I'll go and get it. You'd better come with me and fetch the wine."

Then they bustled out and went poking about in Mr. Stonybrook's cold rooms for ingredients, running against each other until he got the gas lit and coming back loaded with all the appurtenances of negus. Just before they reached Mr. Evans' door, which stood ajar, Mr. Stonybrook said: "I guess we don't want to invite Mother Hannige up," and Manuella, thinking of Mrs. Hannige's disagreeable gossip, had said instantly: "No, don't;" after which Mr. Stonybrook became very amiable indeed, and squeezed the lemon and put the napkin round the hot kettle for Manuella and stirred the mixture, the while making all kinds of harmless little jokes. And when the brew was all fixed and sending forth a spiced vapor it was given to Mr. Evans to pronounce judgment upon, and that worthy gentleman judicially sipped it and said:

"Stonybrook, I don't want to be too critical, but that's a sangaree. Yes, sir, it isn't negus. I haven't drunk a real negus since '42." And Mr. Stonybrook, making signs to Manuella, pretended to be much hurt and undertook to defend the drink learnedly, both he and Manuella being greatly amused to see the old gentleman pass his glass again and again while he was finding fault with the drink. And so the greater part of the evening passed away in light and hospitable banter, and when the old gentleman began to show signs of drowsiness, the two younger people got the backgammon board out and sat down at the table with their heads very close together over the game. It was some time afterwards, when leaning back, in his chair, Mr. Stonybrook looked at his watch and said: "Jehu, it's eleven o'clock. Well, I have been beguiled. We've had a very delightful evening, haven't we?"

"It has been very cheerful," said Manuella.

"Do you know," continued Mr. Stonybrook, "I thought when I came in you were looking horribly melancholy. I hardly dare think I have turned your evening into a pleasant one."

"I think you have," said Manuella, "I was feeling very blue."

"Incredible. Why should a girl like you feel blue? You are not in love. You are delightfully situated and make friends wherever your glances fall. But if you were blue, it is even more incredible that I should overcome it; that is to say, its incredibly flattering. If I thought it was true, I'd have something to live for. It isn't always that a girl acknowledges as frankly as that that a man's coming makes her happy."

"Cheerful, was my word, Mr. Stonybrook."

"Well, it was a dangerous admission, for when a man finds out that his coming makes a girl cheerful, he's very apt to want to come all the time. You didn't like me at first, Manuella."

"Didn't I?"

"No, you were afraid of me."

"Was I?"

"Yes, I think so. Don't you know you've got over it?"

"I've got accustomed to you."

"You mean you can put up with me?"

"Yes, I suppose so."

"How much of me?"

"How much?"

"Yes. I mean if you saw a great deal more of me?"

"Why, Mr. Stonybrook, you have always been so considerate and kind and have done so much for Grandpa, that I have grown to look upon you as the best friend we've got; as a benefactor."

"Oh, don't say that. Hang it, Manuella, that's too bad. I never wanted to patronize you. We got along very well and grandfather seemed to like me and I was beginning to think you did."

Manuella was not as nervous as the case warranted. She instinctively knew what was coming, but she had a clear conscience and no double purpose. The first five minutes with Carteret, when he had grown serious, had set every nerve jumping and every vein swelling. That afternoon in the park came back to her as she sat there, and, with all its faraway romance, was a little bitterness, as if the girl, now grown a woman, was beginning to see that there was disappointments in store for her.

"I am sure, Mr. Stonybrook, we have learned to esteem you very highly."

"Yes; I've often asked myself how highly. There's a good sensible young woman, I've said to myself. No flirtation nonsense about her; no novel reading moonshine; no sentimental folly; clearheaded, and every way practical. I wonder if I should talk good, common sense to her, how she'd take it? That's what I've asked myself. If I was to say to her: here, we've been both working for grandfather in a loose kind of way, why not make an arrangement that is permanent and proper. Let's make a home for him; I asked myself what such a girl would say? Would she esteem me highly enough to consider it seriously?"

"Mr. Stonybrook," said Manuella, "you are asking me to become your wife, for grandfather's sake."

"Not altogether, Manuella. I'm doing it for my own sake, too. In fact, it looks to me as if it was for all our sakes. The idea doesn't offend you?"

"No. How could it? I think I ought to feel proud that a man like you makes such a proposition to me. But you must not be offended when I tell you that I must think it over."

"You don't refuse me?"

"No. I consider you, Mr. Stonybrook. Give me time to get it all right in my mind and I will be as frank with you as you have been with me."

She held out her hand across the table and he took it respectfully.

"How much time does it take to consider?"

"Not very long."

He held her hand. His impulse was to kiss it, but it occurred to him that that was theatric, so he fondled it a moment and then got up. "Good night and pleasant dreams, Manuella."

"Goodnight, Mr. Stonybrook," she said.

CHAPTER XLVIII.

MIRAMON COMES ON THE SCENE.

Mr. John Wilder was not mistaken, the stranger he had met at the Terrace called at Mrs. Hannige's the same evening. Wilder found him in the little reception room, muffled up in a cloak and looking very wet and cold. He took him into the comfortable sitting room where there was a cheerful fire and tried to induce him to make himself comfortable.

"I have called," said the man, without paying much attention to Wilder's invitation to take his cloak off, "to see if I can find out anything about Mr. Plonski. I have been in the city three days and although I received a letter from him asking me to meet him here, I have been unable to get the slightest information concerning him from any of his friends. I understood you to say that you knew something of his whereabouts."

"Yes," replied Wilder, "you did, and I tried to make you understand at the same time that there were good reasons why his whereabouts should not be disclosed. Mr. Plonski has been a good deal annoyed by the police and it wouldn't become his friend to betray his hiding place, that is, if he is hiding, and he might be, don't you know."

"Mr. Plonski," said the stranger, "is not in the city. He wrote me to meet him here on very important business. Had he been here, he would not on any account fail to see me. If you can tell me anything that will lead to his discovery, I shall be very grateful. I have come a great distance and I fear something has happened to him."

"Would you care to give me your name?" asked Wilder.

"You wouldn't know it. I am a stranger here," replied the man. "It's of no consequence. If you do not wish to assist me, let us not waste time." He then got up.

"I think you are Miramon," said Wilder. "If you are, I don't mind telling you all you want to know."

The man turned sharply about, made an involuntary step toward the door and stopped.

"Well, sir," he said, "what do you know of Miramon?"

"Not a great deal. I can tell it all in a minute. If you will sit down, I'll try to."

"Well, sir?"

"Miramon," said Wilder, "was in the office of the Mexican Legation at Washington and abstracted the Montezuma letter from the State department."

"It's a lie."

"Well, that sounds like an authoritative denial from the man himself," said Wilder. "When he had a disagreement with Valladares—that was before leaving Marseilles—he threatened that gentleman. Afterwards he tried to get possession of Valladares' papers, and, shall I say, his silver. I mean, of course, Don Jose Sarmiente Valladares. After the shipwreck and when Captain Job Ackerman took possession of the Don's effects, Miramon entered into a conspiracy with Plonski and others to obtain possession of the cup. This conspiracy came to grief owing entirely to the stupid, roundabout and burglarious methods of the man Plonski, who employed an adventuress to steal the property and hired a couple of cutthroats to frighten her half to death. More than that, Plonski inserted an advertisement in the *Herald* which attracted the attention of the police and brought Inspector Wilder into the game. Of course with the usual meddling impudence of his kind, Wilder not only prevented Plonski from getting the property, but succeeded in making the principals resort to all sorts of questionable means to secure their rights without making public their secret."

The stranger nodded his head assentingly and involuntarily said, "Curse him."

"The property which Plonski was in search of," continued Wilder, "was lost by one of his agents—"

"Who the devil are you, sir?" interrupted the man with a quick tone of inquiry.

"I am Inspector John Wilder," said the officer. "I was coming to that, for I consider it the most extraordinary accident in the series of strange events which have beset this search, that you should have run into my arms in this manner, and I don't mind telling you that I am positively glad to see you and wish I could make you a little more comfortable."

After a moment's pause during which time the man did not take his eyes from Wilder, he said:

"Will you permit me to communicate with Plonski or see him?"

"I shall put no obstacle in your way," said Wilder. "But to tell you the truth, I don't think you need to see him. I can tell you all that he knows, perhaps more than he knows, if you'll sit down; shall I call you señor or mister? If you will sit down and throw that wet cloak off, I'll try and accommodate you."

"I'd like to ask you one question and it isn't necessary to sit down to do it. Have you got possession of the cup?"

"Mr. Miramon, from all that I know of the affair, and if indefatigable labor entitles a man to anything, the cup ought to be in your possession. Whether you have a better legal title to it than Captain Ackerman, I cannot tell, but one thing's certain, I have no claim to it whatever and have not got it. Your own good sense must tell you that the police have no right to interfere in the carrying out of your scheme properly to secure either the cup or the treasure it represents, and I should never have been mixed up in the affair if your agent had not employed felonious means to get the property. I think it very likely that Plonski has deceived you in some way. I have no faith in the man; his record is not a good one and he is implicated with secession schemes and seditious gangs. I have come into possession of all the facts concerning the cup—they are curious and unexampled, but of no value to me except to assist the rightful owner in obtaining his property. Understanding this as you ought to, I think it just as well that you sit down and carry on this conversation in something like a reasonable manner."

"What you say," replied Miramon, "is so surprising to me that you will pardon my apparent want of courtesy. It is quite possible that I have been misled with regard to your share in the unaccountable circumstances of the past four months, but I have no right to inquire into your official conduct."

Wilder smiled. "My attempts to clear up a mystery and gratify my curiosity can hardly be called official," he said; "they did not come within the line of my duty, which is to deal with law breakers. Your scheme to recover the Mexican treasure is a perfectly legitimate one, and if it met with some annoyance from me it was because it was foolishly involved in a series of crimes."

"You will pardon me," said Miramon, "but I understood from the first that you were acting under instructions and under pay for a rival organization, and were using all the machinery of the police department to baffle us in our attempts to recover the cup."

"So I suspected," replid Wilder. "But it is not true. I have not been hired or paid, and had I succeeded in obtaining the cup, I would have turned it over to whomever claimed to be its owner. Plonski has deceived you, and I began to see very early in this game that you would in all probability have to appeal to the police to protect yourself from him."

"Mr. Wilder," said Miramon as he came a step nearer and placed his hat on the table, "I am placed in a peculiar dilemma."

"You mean that you are afraid that I am trying to trap you into some kind of disclosure. Dismiss that idea. Sit down and I will tell you briefly the history of the cup since it left Mr. Enniston's house. You can compare my statement with Plonski's."

Mr. Miramon then sat down, throwing back his cloak from his shoulders but not removing it, and Wilder narrated succinctly all that he knew of the cup up to the time of its theft from the house of Mr. Manser. "Now," he said, "that the cup was lost in a brook, appears to me to be too absurd to think of. I made up my mind at once that the fellow Samson had gone off with it and had invented this story to gain time and enable him to command the highest possible reward for its recovery. This theory is made more probable when I tell you that I can account for nearly every day of Plonski's and The Mink's time after the loss and up to the present, but Samson was seen hanging round the Manser place for some time after and then disappeared, while Plonski kept up some kind of a search at the brook, which you will remember has been frozen over for weeks."

Miramon listened to this account with the keenest interest.

"Mr. Wilder," he said, with considerably more of a deferential tone, "pardon me if I ask you a question or two. I will explain to you, if you desire it, why I make the inquiry. Did you get from 'Capt. Ackerman a clear statement of the value of the treasure and the importance of the cup in any attempt to recover that treasure?"

"Yes," replied Wilder, "I understood that the treasure amounted to between two and three hundred millions; the schedule supposed to be taken from one side of the cup was among the papers, and the locality of concealment was supposed to be engraved on the other side of the cup."

"And did it occur to you that the persons who had worked out from the cup itself the schedule that you saw might also have worked out the other side of the cup, and that such a transcript might be in existence somewhere?"

"No, it did not. The extraordinary efforts made to recover the cup itself were sufficient evidence to me that no such transcription existed, and that the parties despaired of recovering the wealth without first getting possession of the cup."

A grim suggestion of a smile flitted round the corners of Miramon's mouth, but quickly disappeared.

"I have only to say, sir, in explanation of these questions, that you are the first man I have ever encountered who has looked into the historic proofs of the existence of this wealth and the value of the cup and preserved an indifference and an unselfishness that do honor to your character."

"Thank you," replied Wilder. "So far the extraordinary events have aroused my curiosity rather than my cupidity. The cup, I must acknowledge, appears to unbalance the judgment even of sagacious men like yourself. Why, if you believe in the existence of this wealth, you do not go at once to Capt. Ackerman and effect a partnership in knowledge and prospects, I cannot understand. There is enough wealth for both of you if your theories are correct, and so long as there is a quarrel about the ownership of the cup, and both parties employ unscrupulous agents, just so long will it be exposed to these accidents."

"What you say is on the face of it quite reasonable," said Miramon, "but there are some few facts connected with the affair that you are not acquainted with, and I hope that our further acquaintance will warrant my laying them before you. What I wish to say now is that should Capt. Ackerman recover and claim the cup he will in all probability fail to read its cabalistic signs, and will thus fail of securing the wealth. The key to the cup is lost. I have spent at least twenty years in the most toilsome search for it, and all I can say is that I have approached nearer to it than any other living man. The transcript which you saw in Capt Ackerman's possession was made by a Mexican priest not ten years after the conquest and it is by using that transcript in comparison with the signs on the other side of the cup, and by applying the knowledge which I have acquired, that anything can be done."

"In other words," said Wilder, "the cup and the transcript ought to go together, and if you have one and Capt. Ackerman has the other both will be valueless. This is only saying in another way that you and Capt. Ackerman ought to put your heads together in a practical spirit of compromise, like men employed in any other venture, and leave such agents as Plonski out of the question. I can readily guess what the other facts you speak of are. In your extraordinary endeavor to unearth this secret you have involved yourself in several questionable undertakings, and you shun publicity. But I cannot see that these considerations should deter you from taking the only straight course to the accomplishment of your purpose. Capt. Ackerman is an honest, simple-minded, frank sailor."

"Were I the only person interested in preventing Capt. Ackerman from getting the cup," said Miramon, "I should undoubtedly have been led to that course at once. But you must understand that the search for this cup has been carried on for years in Europe, and our securing of it involved a great deal of expense. There are others interested heavily in its prospective value. One overt step and the whole scheme might become public, in which case the Mexican government would effectually prevent any attempt at recovery if the treasure is on their soil, and a thousand adventurers would be looking for it if it is on the soil of the States. It is this knowledge that the announcement that such an enormous amount of wealth was waiting to be recovered would inflame the cupidity of unscrupulous men all through the West, that has led, without intention, to the series of misadventures you have narrated. In addition to this, I should tell you that for years past the possessors of this secret have become monomaniacs in their greed. The possibility of possessing such a treasure, and the growing probability of its existence as the historic proofs are obtained, have almost invariably converted the depositaries of the secret into ruthless madmen. In fact, there is a proverb in the eastern part of Spain that to look for gold in Mexico is to find poverty in the madhouse. But I had no intention of taking your time, sir, in this manner. You have not told me where Plonski is."

"I shall have to decline to furnish that piece of information," said Wilder, "but can tell you this much: He is far away from here, against his will, and I had nothing whatever to do with his absence, nor did any of the parties in this search. I only learned the circumstances of his departure after he had gone. I am positive that he has not got the cup and is effectually stopped for the present from searching for it."

Mr. Miramon had got up.

"One word more," said Mr. Wilder. "Should you and Capt. Ackerman determine upon a joint course of action, so that there would be no question of ownership, I should be glad to place my services at your disposal in any further
attempts you may make to get possession of the cup, and in that case I might
have to be paid for my time and efforts. Until that course is adopted I can
only give you this piece of advice. Find Samson. I ought to tell you that Capt.
Ackerman offered to pay a very handsome sum for the property."

"Capt. Ackerman," said Miramon promptly; "will not, I am sure, pay as
much as we will. With Capt. Ackerman the value of the cup is problematical.
With me it is a mathematical certainty. Should you feel disposed to place the
property in our hands, we are ready to pay you the required sum."

"You appear to have no doubts of the existence of the wealth," said Wilder.

"It is of no consequence to others what our facts or beliefs are, so long as
we are willing to back them up with money. I may say that I am authorized to
negotiate at once for the cup and if you desire to see a piece of private property
restored to the owner, there is a good opportunity for us to have an immediate
understanding."

Wilder shook his head. "I am going to Chicago," he said; "and shall be
gone several weeks. Let me advise you to see Capt. Ackerman and adjust your
claims. When I return I may be of some service to you. The property is unquestionably at present in the hands of some ordinary rascal who is waiting to get
the largest possible ransom for it."

CHAPTER XLIX.

LOVE ENDS IN DESPAIR.

Colin Carteret discovered a few days after Wilder was gone, that he was no longer in a painting mood. The bouyancy of mind that had imparted a freedom and an elasticity to his touch had vanished. He was moody, uncertain and at times, slightly irascible. It made him angry to see Chapman plod at the easel all day without saying a word.

"You've got to be a painting-machine, hav'n't you?" he said; "All your good qualities have drained away through your old brushes."

Chapman, without intermitting his employment, merely said in reply: "Thank you, old fellow. Why don't you drain some of yours off in the same way?"

"I'm beginning to think I hav'n't got any. That thing at the Academy was a spurt and a snare."

"Have you got your check for it yet?"

"No, I believe that's another snare. Not a word about the money. What do you think is the matter?"

"Nothing. Hasn't attended to it. She don't know how much you need it, that's all," said Chapman sententiously. Then after a moment's pause: "She must be worth a snug sum Carter?"

"What makes you think so?"

"Why, Ol Enniston was well fixed and I understand her grandfather, who took a great shine to her, left her something in her own right. Charley Brainsby told me she was independent. Her father took good care of her, too. It isn't every day that you find a girl with the brads and the brains too. How she worked that Dr. Sanger. You're a lucky dog, Carter."

"I'm glad you think so," Said Carteret, "but we never agree on these things."

"Well, I consider it a very delectable piece of good fortune to strike a female patron who is good looking, well fixed and enthusiastic. I fancy it's good luck to change a pupil for a patron. I suppose I ought to know, seeing that I never had either."

"What do you mean," asked Carteret, "by changing a pupil for a patron?"

Chapman was scumbling away at an umber morass; his brush kept on and he did not turn his head or take the briarwood pipe from his mouth. All he did was to follow with his eyes the brush that stirred the colors on his palette and then stirred them on the canvas.

"Why don't you answer me?" asked Carteret.

"I'm afraid to open my mouth," said Chapman; "you'll be jumping down my throat."

Carteret made a movement of impatience as he stood behind his friend. "You are always saying something that's disagreeable," he said. "I don't know half the time what you are driving at."

"O, yes, you do," replied Chapman; "that's what makes it disagreeable. But I don't intend it to be. I'm always forgetting my hypocrisy with you. That's the infernal nuisance of being confidential with a fellow. You can have two of the finest girls in town, but if I let on I see it, you'll cut me dead. It's a bad box to put a friend in, who's got as good an eye for beauty as I have."

"Yes," said Carteret, a little sharply. "You've got one of those deuced artistic eyes that are always seeing a great deal more than exists. It doesn't work well in friendship."

Chapman lowered his brush; in fact, he stopped painting a moment, pushed his seat back a little, half shut his eyes to discover the effects of his scumbling and said:

"Carter, if you'll give me lessons in spontaneous lying, I'll become a pupil of yours myself. The trouble with me is that I'm one of those consummately ingenuous asses that take a man at his word one day and get kicked for it the next."

"I'd like," replied Carteret, "to give you lessons in plain speaking. If I know what you are talking about I hope to die."

"Didn't you tell me," said Chapman, "that that girl over at Hannige's had promised to be your wife?"

"Did I?" asked Carteret with a dreamy kind of wonder at his own assurance, now that it was repeated to him.

"Yes, you did. Didn't I tell you Stonybrook would walk off with her? And didn't you try to jump down my throat then and there? Haven't you made up with the other one, and isn't that radiant goddess over at Hannige's engaged to Stony—perhaps I'm dreaming?"

"You must be," said Carteret weakly.

"With my eyes and ears wide open," added Chapman. "If Hannige didn't tell me that Stonybrook had proposed and hadn't been rejected, and if I didn't notice that you had stopped going to the house, I hope I may never wake up."

Then Chapman resumed his scumbling rather spasmodically and Carteret, who was standing behind him, began to exhibit various emotions which, as Chapman would have said, were "badly mixed."

"Engaged to Stonybrook," he said involuntarily, as if trying to get the full significance out of the sound, and then instantly aware that the tone of astonishment was slightly pathetic, and wishing to hide his feelings from Chapman, he blurted out:

"Well, old fellow, perhaps there isn't much of a dream about it after all. A girl's got a right to marry whom she pleases. I'm booked for Mrs. Sanger's. If anybody calls for me, I'll be in to-morrow." He put his hand on Chapman's shoulder—"You've got that corner a shade too heavy, take out some of that umber. Bye, bye."

When he had slammed the door of his studio, he tried to think it out in his impatient way. There was at first a great deal of indignation felt but hardly understood. But, after a little while, this somewhat irrational anger, by an inexplicable process, changed its object. He ceased to feel aggrieved at Manuella and began to abuse himself. "After all, it would serve me right," he said inaudibly, "if she did marry Stonybrook. He's the braver, steadier, and more reasonable man, and she's found it out. I abandoned the field to him without a cause, expected like an idiot girl would run after me, and stayed away like a baby because she didn't. When I come back, I'll have a talk with Chapman and find out about it. That old woman Hannige is a mischief maker."

All this was very energetic and penitent. It sounded to his conscience like a remedial determination. But he walked over to Doctor Sanger's rather blue and wretched, for there was a grain of possibility that it might all be true and was past remedy. And that, like all final and irremediable possibilities, startled him.

Once or twice the impulse seized him, before he reached Broadway, to go straight to the house in Fifteenth street and learn the truth. Something told him that if he did, he would fail to keep his appointment at Dr. Sanger's and that would be ruinous. So he compromised by walking past Mrs. Hannige's and going up Irving place to the doctor's, only to observe with an acute sense, how dreary and forsaken Fifteenth street looked in its dirty, half-melted snow.

Mrs. Follen Sanger had met him but once before, and then in the dimly-lit reception room where he had been introduced and the arrangement made for the sittings. He now encountered her in a large upper room that had been set apart at her desire for the work of the portrait. It was flooded with light and the mistress of the house had attired herself at her husband's request in the white corded silk. Carteret therefore saw a very handsome woman and his admiration was instantaneous. She had purposely avoided the fashion of the time in her garment, which fashion, it is needless to say, was not the most beautiful ever devised, although hooped skirts had been reduced. Her splendid dress, worn without any of those absurd adjuncts, clung to her long figure almost with the simplicity of the old Directoire gown and fell in chaste folds of drapery at her feet.

"I am glad you approve of it," she said. "for Follen would listen to no other, and it's a little old-fashioned."

"It's superb," replied Carteret. "I hope I may do the subject justice."

He sat down at the canvas with a crayon in his hand and began to scrutinize her with an artist's privilege, and he saw that she was looking at him intently.

"I think," said he, "that you had better sit until I get the head and countenance. It will be awkward and tiresome to stand all the time."

He then got up and placed a chair for her in the right position and she sat down about six feet away from the easel.

"I'm afraid," he said, as he reseated himself, "that Dr. Sanger and Miss Enniston have formed an exaggerated notion of my abilities from that Academy picture. You see I took all sorts of liberties with that, and made it a kind of pastoral poem."

"Miss Enniston, did you say?"

"Yes; I suppose that you know that I am indebted to Miss Enniston for this commission. It was her enthusiasm that attracted the doctor's attention to me. I think that if you turned your head a trifle—that will do—the outline is clearer, thanks. Miss Enniston quite insisted on his meeting me."

"She is an old acquaintance of yours?"

"Yes," replied Carteret, "I have known her some time. I knew the family very well. Her father was one of the best friends I had."

Mrs. Sanger was at this moment the victim of the most contradictory emotions. Once more she was placed in a position where it was necessary that her visitor should watch her closely, and once more the visitor unexpectedly raised emotions which she did not wish to betray. As she thought of this a purely feminine feeling of recklessness and defiance supervened. There was such an obvious malignity and purpose in these recurring events, and fate so clearly meant to torture her, that she drew herself together with the sudden resolve of weakness and with the impulse to defy it. Then, too, there was another incentive. Now was her opportunity to learn safely of the Enniston affair, and what was the version of the story accepted by the public. Carteret did not inspire her with the dread that Dr. Ferris had occasioned. There was nothing occult or suspicious about this poor artist. On the contrary, there was something suggestive in his voice and face that won her strangely.

"*Was* one of your best friends, Mr. Carteret? Is he not still?"

"O, dear, no. I thought you knew. You have dropped your eyes, please keep the same position and expression that you had. When you are tired I'll stop and let you rest, thanks. Mr. Enniston met with an accident last summer. It was a sad affair."

"An accident?"

Carteret laughed. "You've changed your whole attitude and expression, Mrs. Sanger," he said.

"You surprised me," she replied. "I never heard of the accident. Am I in the right position now?"

"Yes. It made a great deal of talk at the time, and was in all the papers. You see it was a most unusual occurrence. Do I agitate you?"

"No," she said, "don't mind me. Tell me about it."

He was looking at her as she said this. Something in the expression of her face caught his quick eye.

"You have weak nerves, Mrs. Sanger?"

"Yes," she said; "they make foolish show of weakness. What was the accident? May I get up a moment? I'll put a little cologne on my temples. I've had a touch of headache for a day or two. You can go on with your narrative."

She got up with a show of apologetic good humor, and Carteret leaned back with his crayon in his hand. When she got to the little table where there was a mirror and several bottles, she said with her back to him:

"Was it a railroad accident?"

"No," replied Carteret, carelessly. "It was a most remarkable affair. Mr. Enniston went down one evening into his garden to cut some flowers with a little stiletto that one of the ladies had given him, and he stumbled and fell upon it and killed himself."

"How singular," said Mrs. Sanger, as she bathed her temples, and she said it with a tone that was not unlike a sigh of relief. "I never heard of such a thing. Cutting flowers with a stiletto."

" O, you see there was a little party in the house and one of the ladies came upon the veranda, and seeing the moon shining on the white flowers in the copse, wanted one, and Enniston took the poniard rashly out of her hair and went down to get the flowers for her. He must have stumbled in the copse and fallen upon the poniard."

Mrs. Sanger came back to her seat a moment later. She was measurably composed, but her woman's curiosity was aroused.

"What a dreadful shock to Mrs. Enniston," she said. "How did she bear up under it?"

"O, Mrs. Enniston is a woman of pretty strong nerves. She was the only cool one in the party that night. I remember that she never lost her head."

"Were you there?

"I was indeed," said Carteret, unconcernedly; "and it was a terrible night I assure you. But as I was saying, Mrs. Enniston surprised everybody by the way she controlled herself. You must know we were all beside ourselves with consternation and grief. I don't know what we should have done without her. You are interested in the circumstances, Mrs. Sanger?"

"Who could help being?" she replied. "It's the most dreadful thing I ever heard of. Mrs. Enniston interests me. I should have thought people would doubt the truth of such an extraordinary story, and in these days of sensations and scandals, I should suppose such an occurrence would give rise to all sorts of stories, suspicions even."

"O, I suppose Mrs. Enniston's good sense and discretion prevented all that. Reporters and detectives came up there, but she froze them all out."

"Detectives?" said Mrs. Sanger. "It sounds like a romance. Tell me all about it, Mr. Carteret. I'm just like a child in my foolish curiosity. What did the detectives want?"

"I was wrong when I said detectives, I believe there was only one and he turned out to be a very decent fellow. I got quite intimate with him afterwards; he is an inspector. I believe Dr. Sanger knows him. His name is John Wilder. That's all there is to it. Have you always worn your hair in that style?"

"No," said Mrs. Sanger, "I was quite ill last fall and it was cut off. Don't you like it this way?"

"I fancy," replied Carteret, "that it would become you better if it were long. At all events, it would become your costume better. I hope you will let me paint it put up in a knot behind?"

"O, no," she said, "Follen would never consent. I must have it short. He's very whimsical about these things and we must let him have his own way. But tell me; is Miss Enniston like her mother? I have met her and she seemed to be a very charming young lady."

"O dear, no. They are as unlike as mortals can well be. Rosamond takes after her father, impulsive, generous, quick-tempered; her mother is as austere as a Puritan. One tells you all she feels and thinks in a breath, and the other always makes you feel that she sees and knows a great deal more than she ever tells. I confess that I was always a little dismayed by Mrs. Enniston."

"She was just the kind of woman, I should say, to protect herself from detectives and other busy-bodies, and your friend, John Wilder—was that the name—would probably have worried her for a long time if he had lived—didn't you say he died?"

"No," answered Carteret, leaning back and regarding the lady with polite surprise, "no, I didn't say he was dead. I saw him the other day."

"True—you said the doctor was acquainted with him—and now I think of it, I dare say I'm acquainted with him myself. We had a case of robbery in the house. One of the maids was suspected and an officer came here who worried me half to death. He was a stout, big-eyed, black-whiskered fellow."

"It wasn't Wilder," said Carteret, "that's not his style. He's gray-eyed, clean shaven, tall and gentlemanly. I'm going to try and get another drawing of your mouth, please keep it in repose a moment."

Here the conversation lapsed for a few moments, Mrs. Sanger looking thoughtfully at vacancy, and Carteret too intent upon catching the curve of her mouth, to watch the expression of her eyes.

She was wondering who John Wilder could be, and as she repeated involuntarily in her mind the words: "Gray-eyed, clean shaven and tall," the ghost of a face seen once before, rose up and a strange feeling, as of iron pressed against her body, overcame her.

The sitting was given up shortly after this, but she preserved a most affable and encouraging manner with the young artist, and he went away unsuspicious, occupied in fact, with another problem, and once more taking the route through Fifteenth street. When he arrived at the Hannige establishment, an overpowering impulse seized him and he went up the steps and rang the bell. Florry looked at him with smiling and significant interest, and when he said he had called to see Miss Castleton, the girl let him into the little reception room with a nod of intelligence that was meant to say she knew all about it. Once in that little room, he grew nervous. It seemed a very long time since he had been there; so long that a great many things could have happened. How odd it was that this sense of a great gap of time with all its dire possibilities, had not struck him so drearily until he got into that familiar room and looked at the little ormolu clock whose hands indicated that it was five o'clock, and at the lounge where her head had been so close to his that her hair brushed his cheek. Would she come blithely down the stairs as she had often done before? He listened while his heart beat audibly with expectation. Would she send word that she was engaged and could not see him, was it after all, too late? Had he thrown away love and hope? He heard voices somewhere and a door was shut. Then the sound of slowly approaching footsteps. A moment later, Mrs. Hannige stood in the light that came from the hallway.

"How d'y do, Mr. Carteret?" she said, with dignity. "Miss Castleton is not at home."

There was something in her manner that nettled him, and he did not feel very friendly towards her at the best.

"Sorry to have troubled you," he said. "If there is any particular time that the young lady is likely to be at home and will receive me, perhaps you would not object to telling me. It would save us both some steps."

This was Mrs. Hannige's opportunity. "Law, Mr. Carteret," she said, "when a young woman is as busy as she is, it's pretty hard to tell when she'll see company. I s'pose her time's all taken up now. You could leave your card, you know."

"Thanks," replied Carteret, very formally. "Mr. Wilder, I suppose, is not at home."

"John's in Chicago," she said.

Carteret then made another informal bow, said something meant to be polite, and came away with a heart that was momentarily growing more leaden. It was a miserably dark and bleak afternoon and the slush was lying heavy on the pavements and roadway. Something of a boy's desperation seized him as he reflected that he would have to carry this weight of uncertainty through the desolate night. There was an early light in the Century Club. He would go in there and wait till Chapman came along; besides he would see if it were true that Manuella was out. Once in a chair by the window, he gave no heed to the two or three sleepy old gentlemen who were dozing over the evening papers, or sipping their toddy by the grate fire. With his eyes fixed on the bleak street he began to give way to despair. He had learned nothing of Mrs. Hannige, and yet the vague assurance of tone disheartened him. Manuella was too busy to see company now. Then it must be true. She was preparing for her marriage. Had she concluded to take this step for her grandfather's sake? Had she been planning it craftily during all those hours of romance? No, he wouldn't believe it. She must have been forced into it by a doting and selfish old man, a scheming woman and a cunning old reprobate who used them both for his purpose.

He sat there till the street lamps were lit, watching Mrs. Hannige's house. But no one entered. The radiance streamed through Mr. Stonybrook's curtains. If Manuella had gone out she had not returned. Even then it did not occur to him that Mrs. Hannige might have deceived him.

It was six o'clock when he saw Chapman coming down the street wrapped in a heavy coat and muffled to his hair.

He intercepted him before he got to Mrs. Hannige's steps. "I say, old fellow," he unceremoniously began, "come and spend the evening with me somewhere, I'm as blue as a wild plum. Come to Pizanni's and eat some dinner; I want to talk to you."

But Chapman was now in what he called his dry season. One might as well try to make a hibernating animal fight when he is laid by for the winter.

"Can't do it, old fellow. I've just come from Pizanni's. Had to put up with soup and potato salad 'cause exchequer's low; must get some sleep and put in my work. Can't really think of it; got five pictures to finish and I'm cold. It's a beastly night. Come up in my den and I'll make you an egg nog."

"No, I thank you," said Carteret, despondently. "Goodnight."

For a moment he seriously thought of calling upon Miss Enniston if only to escape from himself, but reflection told him that her society in his present condition would only be an additional aggravation, and so, after aimlessly wandering about and trying to eat something in a Broadway restaurant, he drifted into the Winter Garden Theatre. The lights and cheerfulness attracted him without his knowing it. Some kind of a comedy performance was going on, but he found that he could not fix his mind upon it, and so at the end of the first act he strolled out to the vestibule and, putting a cigar into his mouth, stood in the entrance way idly regarding the crowds upon the sidewalk. Notwithstanding the night was a bitter one and the roadway was heavy with dirty snow and ice, the scene was an animated one. The glare of the lights and the pleasant con-fusion of people robbed the weather of its bleakness. While he stood there the regular sound of an approaching drum reached his ear, and presently a battalion of men in heavy blue overcoats went by. Nobody gave much heed to them and they passed as if New York had grown accustomed to the sight of men going to the front. As Carteret was regarding them listlessly, someone came up and in a tone of familiarity addressed him:

"Hello! Beg pardon, let me take a little of your fire. You don't know me, of course not, eh? Thanks." He held the cigars together daintily, puffed a moment and said: "Forgot the cup affair, haven't you?"

Carteret recalled him as the young man who had brought the cup to the house in Fifteenth Street. "O, yes," he said, "Kleinbacker?"

"Right. Pretty slow show," jerking his head in the direction of the audi-torium. "War's killed the theatre. Can't get the women out. How's Miss Castleton? I called there the other day. She's going away. Fine girl that. I like her. She's dead level."

"I have not seen Miss Castleton in some time," replied Carteret rather formally.

"No?" asked Kleinbacker. "Wondered why I hadn't seen you 'round. What's the matter? Say, between you and me, she ain't goin' off with that old freezer, is she? I kinder thought from what the old woman said, it was a dead connubial jig. Hang it, you know, I ain't got no more claims than any other young feller with an eye for the sterling, but it's a scorching shame if she is. How is it, any-way? You ought to know something about it. What'd she do with that cup?" Carteret's first impulse was one of contemptuous indignation. But Kleinbacker had a way of frustrating these natural impulses by mere volubility.

"I know very little of Miss Castleton's intentions," he said, with a good deal of superlative haughtiness that was utterly lost on Kleinbacker.

"Certainly, of course. If you had no intentions yourself you wouldn't be apt to notice anything. But you see I was struck with that girl the first time I saw her. She kinder gave me a confidential wrench like when she came back that day at the shop and gave me her address, so I could call on her. I galloped over there two or three times to see how the land laid. I kinder thought you had the dead open and shut thing, don't you know, and all the other fellows would have to look on and applaud. But when I found it was Stonybrook I just took a gasp. Yes I did. I looked up Stonybrook. That's what I did, just for the ten commandments' sake, and when the old woman of the house let the cat out I says to myself, this here *is* a scorching outrage, and if I hadn't anything else to do I'd make a torch light proces-sion of Stonybrook. What do you say to something hot? It's cold standing here."

"What do you know about Mr. Stonybrook?" asked Carteret, feeling all at once that this garrulous companion was not without some interest.

"Not enough to put in a commercial agency's book," replied Kleinbacker, "but enough to make a brother hustle if she had one."

"See here," said Carteret, "I'm not the young lady's brother, but I've got as much respect for her as if I was. Do you understand that if you have got anything to say against her you will have to make yourself perfectly plain and then stand up to it like a man?"

"O, excuse me," remarked Kleinbacker, "if I don't choose to put on frills in her defense I don't think you need to. I'm interested in her, I am. Anyway, you don't want to waste no ginger on me. I kinder counted on your help."

"That young woman," said Carteret, "was a pupil, I might almost say a protégé, of mine. I promised to look after her like a brother."

"That's all right, and you ought to do it. You never had a better chance to keep your word. That Stonybrook's a gull—a regular sea-gull."

"Is he?" asked Carteret, trying to experience a proper awe, and only feeling an improper pleasure at the ornithology. "Well, what of it?"

"O, nothing, only if you took the interest in the girl that I do you wouldn't want to see her gobbled by that kind of a bird of prey."

"Gobbled?" repeated Carteret. "I fancy, Mr. Kleinbacker, your imagination is running away with you. If Miss Castleton desires to marry Mr. Stonybrook, I don't think it's any business of you—ours."

"All right. I don't say it is any of yours. I thought being a friend of hers, you'd hate to see her fooled and I could count on you. But that's all right. You probably don't understand my feelings towards that girl."

"No," said Carteret. "I haven't interested myself much in the matter, that's a fact."

Then these two young steers lifted their horns and glared at each other with an animal instinct to interlock them and try each other's strength.

There was a moment's silence in which they managed to expend a good deal of foolish defiance and then Kleinbacker said:

"Excuse me. I guess I haven't made myself plain. I'm in love with that young lady and I thought you were a friend of hers and I could give you a pointer. It's all right. I ask your pardon. She don't seem to have many friends, that's a fact." And Mr. Kleinbacker moved away with considerable independence as if the matter were closed out.

There is no doubt that several simultaneous emotions have a paralyzing effect even upon such impulsive natures as was Carteret's. He looked after the young man with indignation, astonishment and contempt, in all of which there was a half conscious desire to know what Kleinbacker had to tell him about Stonybrook. But it was now too late. That personage accosted an acquaintance and they went off to take a drink, leaving Carteret in a chilly brown study.

CHAPTER L.
JUST BEFORE EASTER.

Miss Castleton was neither hysterical, nor sentimental, but she suffered a good deal, as day after day went by and Carteret did not come again. She invented all sorts of excuses for him but they could not, however plausible, dislodge the increasing fear that Carteret must have grown tired of her. Instead of making her indignant, this haunting suspicion filled her with a pensive misery. The one pure and happy promise of her life seemed to have withered without cause. She started every time she heard the bell ring and she could feel her heart beat. But after repeated disappointments, she began to adopt a new course. She did not upbraid her lover. She began with a woman's fine will to adjust herself to the new conditions. Once or twice it had occurred to her to put on her hat and go to the studio, but she banished the idea almost as soon as it was born. She had seen one woman running after him, that was enough. No, the proper thing to do was to cease to think about him. She had thought of Otis Chapman and whenever she heard that noisy artist come in and go up the stairs, she imagined he had come straight from Carteret at the studio, and once she went out into the hall and spoke to him with a vague sense that even this was bridging the blank chasm with some kind of a possibility. But Chapman was respectful and close-mouthed and the girl's natural diffidence prevented her from making any inquiries. So, one by one, as the days went by, she gave up her projects and began to shut off her recollections. As for her dreams, they must have been very childish vagaries, and it became her now to look seriously at matters. When Mr. Stonybrook had first betrayed his desire to make love to her, she had actually pictured Carteret coming to the rescue and saying: "O, no. This cannot be. She is mine," and she had kept back all point blank refusals so as to give Carteret that privilege. Wasn't that childish?

But one day, as the reader knows, Chapman, in an extra mood of garrulity, had betrayed to Mrs. Hannige that he and Carteret and Miss Enniston had been to to see the Sanger picture, and Mrs. Hannige not only drew enough out of him to frame a theory of her own, but went immediately to Manuella with it. "There," she said; "you see what young men are. He's gone and made up with that brazen creature and now I suppose he'll keep his word and marry her."

It would be difficult to explain how subtly cruel this was to Manuella's nature. She could not reconcile the perfidy of it with what she knew and believed of Carteret. She thought she could see him happy with some one and not suffer much, but to find out that he was fickle, dishonest and base, that hurt her.

Meanwhile Mr. Stonybrook was pressing her delicately, but urgently to give him an answer and she saw that her grandfather had already accepted that gentleman as a member of the family.

The girl could not help feeling grateful to him. She had no cause to complain of his conduct toward her, for he had preserved a respectful deference and shown a consideration of her feelings that it was impossible to meet with annoyance. She had, too, seen the condition of affairs steadily improve under his supervision, and it looked now as if his interest in her grandfather would permanently relieve her of one of the chief causes of anxiety and place the old gentleman beyond the reach of poverty and distress. Added to all this, Mrs. Hannige had speciously and craftily sung the praises of Mr. Stonybrook on every opportunity. Miss Castleton was not uninfluenced by these considerations. Her judgment, no longer disturbed by the presence of Carteret, was beginning to weigh all these things against what was every day growing to look more and more like an illusion or a mistake, and she had got so far in what to her appeared to be a sensible and proper reasoning process, that she deliberately treated Mr. Stonybrook as if her conscience were on his side. He was instinctively aware of the change that was taking place in the girl's treatment of him, and he curbed his impatience and tried by every means in his power to strengthen the belief that his claims were on the side of right and wisdom.

One morning he came into her room with his cane under his arm and pulling on his gloves. He was in the habit now of running in quite informally, for the door was left ajar in the mornings as if to show that the chamber work was done and that Mr. Evans was in his chair. On this occasion he was less deliberate than usual. He spoke to Mr. Evans as was his custom in a conciliatory and indulgent manner, but Manuella detected the new air of hasty formality instantly.

"I am called away this morning," he said to her a little later, as she stood by the window; "it is rather unexpected and urgent and I may be gone a week." He stopped a moment as if he expected some expression of annoyance or regret on her part. But she only evinced a faint surprise on her face and said nothing.

"I may be gone a week," he repeated; "perhaps longer."

"We shall miss you, I am sure," she was saying. He cut her short, "Perhaps my absence will depend somewhat on you. I should like to feel that I ought to hurry back."

Then seeing that he had taken her unawares and that there was a shade of perplexity on her face, he added: "A word is nothing when your mind is made up, and I suppose it must be made up now as definitely as it ever will be. All you have to do is to tell me that you have thought favorably of my proposition, and then I shall have some excuse for hurrying back."

"I have not thought unfavorably of it," Manuella said, and she tried her best not to have her words sound calculating and chilly against his easy confidential tones. "But I am sure you will not think me unfeeling, Mr. Stonybrook, because I do not want to decide such a matter with a word, and would rather wait till you come back, when we can talk it over with Grandpa deliberately."

"Very well," he said; "so be it; when I come back then, you shall do the talking and I will listen to my fate. Goodbye."

Hardly had he been gone an hour when Mrs. Sitwhite came up the stairs, leading her boy by the hand. Manuella was surprised and pained at her appearance. She was poorly clad and the incongruity of her various articles of apparel showed that some of them were borrowed. Her face was red and swollen and her eyes inflamed. She coughed almost incessantly. She ran and put her arms round her father's neck and gave way to a fit of hysterics. Manuella looked at her with pity and dismay, and as soon as her spasm had subsided, she placed a chair for her, untied the strings of her rusty black bonnet and said, "Whatever is the matter, Cynthy? You look perfectly wretched. Pull the chair up here to the fire. I do believe your feet are soaking wet."

But it was some minutes before Mrs. Sitwhite could quite detach herself from her father. She made several dashes at him, choked him and bedrabbled him, much to the old gentleman's discomfiture, he squirming in a vain endeavor to preserve his usual dignity and mildly remonstrating with ejaculations of "Bless my soul;" "yes, yes;" "there, there," etc. It finally ended in Mrs. Sitwhite sitting down and giving way to a fit of coughing.

"What a dreadful cold you've got," Manuella said. "What have you been doing?"

"I got it," said Mrs. Sitwhite, "over the tubs on Monday; it was a bitter day and I had no hot water half the time."

"Then why didn't you put it off till you had?"

"O, yes, that's very well for you to say. Why didn't I put it off? Because they had to have the clothes and I had to have the money. That's why."

Manuella, who was standing near her aunt staring at her, gave a little sigh. "Then you haven't heard from John?"

"I was a faithful wife to him, and you know it, Ella. I slaved for him and put up with everything, and Pop knows I could have had my pick. I don't deserve it after all I've suffered."

"But," suggested Manuella, "perhaps you are unjust to John. Consider how difficult it is for him to see you now, or write. You talk as if he had deserted you. I'll not believe it. John's all right; remember he's a soldier. What have you done for your cold?"

"Not much. How can I? The baby's down and I had to use all the money for her. I couldn't stand it any longer, Ella. I had to come and tell you. You won't thank me I know, for everybody has their own troubles."

"Where would you go if not to your own father, I should like to know?" asked Ella, who felt, in spite of her pity, some indignation at her aunt's maudlin helplessness. "You know very well you should have sent to us at once."

"Cynthy, my dear," said Mr. Evans. "You haven't got any head for business."

"And you ought to leave that place," added Manuella, "I'm sure there are healthier and better places in New York for the same money, where your children could get out into the air."

At this Mrs. Sitwhite broke down afresh. Between sobs and tears she managed to say: "O, certainly, there's fine places enough and why don't I get 'em? Why don't I move on the Fifth avenue? Why don't I build a home for myself? It's so easy for me when I haven't got even food half the time and have gone to bed hungry because I wouldn't see the young ones suffer. I'm sure, Ella, I wouldn't have come here if there'd been anything else I could do."

Despite the woman's inclination to snivel, Manuella was touched by her distress. Mr. Evans' helpless annoyance at the situation only added to the girl's pain.

She could not help thinking as she looked at her aunt, of the old days at her grandfather's home, when they were all comfortable and life seemed so promising to Cynthia. She could not shut out from her woman's sympathy the wrecked existence, the hopeless and vulgar suffering of her condition. Nor could she help a feeling of reproach directed against herself as she thought of her own changed prospects, her eager hopes, her plans and her new life of promise and comfort, while the only remaining member of her grandfather's family was destitute of everything that made life tolerable. The great pity that took possession of her, wasted itself in no words of familiar consolation. It was made deep and silent by a sense of duty. She did, indeed, allay with little acts of consideration, her aunt's querrulous nervousness and, finally sitting down in front of her, got her to tell enough of her circumstances to make it reasonably certain that John Sitwhite had neglected if not deserted his family. Some acknowledgment there was in the woman's speech of her own wrong-doing which made it all the more pathetic to Manuella. "There's never been a day's luck for me since you went away," she said; "and the Lord knows I've tried as hard as a woman can to do my duty."

The upshot of it all was, that after an hour or two, Manuella fixed her up a basket of dainties, gave her some ready money and sent her away in much better spirits, with the promise that she would come down at once with her grandfather and try and help her out.

The moment Mrs. Sitwhite was gone, the girl's resolution that had been slowly forming, made itself known to Mr. Evans.

"Grandpa," she said, "there's only one thing for us to do. We must go back to the Terrace and help Cynthia. It will only be a little while. We can get her out of that place in the spring, and it's nearly here: but she needs our help now. She is going from bad to worse. We can't do any better and we mustn't give our money to strangers while Cynthia is suffering."

Mr. Evans was quite unreasonable as usual. He delared that it wasn't businesslike. Cynthia could come to Mrs. Hannige's. He couldn't bury himself in that place and Manuella had forgotten that she was a Castleton.

The girl knew well enough that she could have her own way in the end without argument, and so she went about quietly making her preparations for the change. Something, she could not tell exactly what it was, made her feel a sudden desire to get away from Mrs. Hannige's. She made herself believe that it was only duty to her aunt. But whatever it was, there was a good deal of moral heroism required to carry out the task when she came to the details of it. The sunny room, with its grate fire and its memories of bright mornings And pleasant dreams, had to be exchanged for the noxious atmosphere and the dull, ignoble imprisonment of the Terrace. She tried to think that it would all be temporary, a mere visit, but she could not rid herself of the feeling as she put away her many little tokens of her new life and tied up her brushes with a piece of ribbon, that somehow an illusion had vanished utterly and she was to wake up permanently in her old place.

Once, in taking the trifles from a drawer, she came across the folded paper containing Carteret's verses, and then she sat down by the window and read them over again. While she did so, the preparations were suspended. Heaps of clothing littered the floor; the furniture "stood awry in that disorder known as cleaning the room." The old gentleman was waiting to come out of his little apartment, but everything stood still while she read the verses over again with a peering interest as if there was still something behind them that she had not yet discovered. Finally, she gave a little half audible sigh, poked the paper into the folds of her dress and resumed her occupation.

Mrs. Hannige's astonishment was profound and protesting when she heard that Manuella and her grandfather were going away, and the girl, with allowable tact, tried to take the edge off the announcement by saying they were only going to make a visit. Her aunt was in distress and needed them. They would probably be back before long.

"But what," exclaimed Mrs. Hannige, "will Mr. Stonybrook say?"

"He will probably say," replied Manuella, "that we had as much right to go away and attend to our private affairs as he had."

"Yes, I know, my dear; but Mr. Stonybrook told you all about his. Have you written and let him know?"

This nettled Manuella a little. "I don't think it is necessary to bother Mr. Stonybrook with all our little domestic affairs, Mrs. Hannige," she said. "When I see him I will explain matters if he should demand an explanation."

But Mrs. Hannige persisted in looking at it as a breach of confidence and in some sort a violation of an implied understanding. The fact is she had grown to regard Manuella as in some way the ductile creature of her own projects, and mingled with this match-making propensity was a genuine affection for the girl. She could not bear to think of her going away.

Nevertheless, after a week's lingering preparation, Manuella and her grandfather went to the Terrace and took their old place by the window in Mrs. Sitwhite's dingy room. Once, and once only, did the girl give way to sentiment and regrets. It was on the first day in the place, and she had sat down and gazed through her old outlook between the gas tanks and the chimneys. There, gray and indistinct, like a bit of soiled pearl, was the Long Island hill lying in the winter's sunlight, patched with snow and blurred with intervening gusts of smoke. The few inches of the river were dark with the wintry water. Cakes of ice moving across at intervals made the water all the more inky and a tug, straining against the tide, sent off round puffs of steam that were torn and scattered in dissolving wreaths.

For a moment or two this bleak view of a familiar picture caught and entranced her feelings and her fancy. What a sudden transitory gleam of real life she had obtained since she went away from this room! What possibilities; what hopes; what disappointments, had been crowded into the weeks! What tumultuous and unstable things life and love were. What unknown depths they had discovered in her. What a wretched ending it all was to come back here and sit down heartbroken at the starting point, to look upon that bleak and forlorn picture. How mocking were the strains of the "Blue Danube" now, as she stared at the ice and saw the wraiths of mist vanishing into nothingness. How indescribably far away and unattainable were those moments that "moved on perfumed feet, and the joy of absent words was broken only by the sweet disturbance of the birds." Yes, she was quoting it from memory, but how illusory and chimerical it all sounded with the jar of the adjacent streets and the harsh turmoil of Mrs. Sitwhite's children in her ears.

But this mood of sentimentality lasted but for a few moments. There were humble duties to be performed and they would help her. So she put on an apron and went bravely to work to make life in the Terrace more endurable. It was delightful to see how her resolution helped everybody, including herself, and it was amazing to observe how tact and graciousness and a very little money speedily subdued the confusion of the place and shed their mollifying influence over influenza and juvenile infatuation.

She had promised herself to make some inquiries about John Sitwhite at the military headquarters, and to get her aunt away from the Terrace, and her unpleasant duties would only be temporary.

In leaving Mrs. Hannige, she had let that housewife believe that they were going away merely on a visit. "O, I dare say we shall be back sooner than you think," she had said, and Mrs. Hannige had at the very last moment impressed upon her the importance of coming in every chance she got. "I'll keep your room just as it is," she said. "You can come in as if you had kept it. Don't forget."

But Manuella had been very reticent about her aunt's address. She did not want Mr. Stonybrook to come there, or, as she had vaguely said to herself, "anybody else." Her pride insisted upon it that to stranger eyes it would look very much as if she had sunk back to her natural surroundings. "I'll send or call and get my letters," she said. "We are not going far away, Mrs. Hannige, and I expect to see you often."

The moment she was gone the atmosphere of the house missed her. Chapman had said to Mrs. Hannige, "O, no, the house is just the same, mommy, but the conservatory door's nailed up. The halls have lost the trail of the musk pink. I used to find my way up in the dark by following it, now I knock my nose against the turns in the stairs. Where has the perfume gone?"

Then Mrs. Hannige put on a look of suppressed but beamy intelligence and said, "Young men are too inquisitive. You'll hear all about it in good time, I suppose," and the mysterious manner to together with what Chapman called a "wedding expression," were interpreted to mean that Manuella had gone off to get married, and as Mr. Stonybrook had gone off at the same time sagacity had the warrant of coincidence for settling into a conviction.

The best that Mrs. Hannige could do to favor her own scheme was to sustain this conviction in anybody who was likely to imperil that scheme, and hence when Carteret came to the house she was significantly mysterious and misleading. She merely felt in an uncertain way that if she preserved the *status quo* long enough matters would come out as she desired.

And Cartaret, with his worst forebodings corroborated by Chapman, Mrs. Hannige, and finally by Mr. Kleinbacker, passed through successive stages of desperation and despair with their reactions of indignation and reproach. Only one thing was clear. Manuella and her grandfather had gone away, presumably with Mr. Stonybrook, and it could only be for one purpose. Mrs. Hannige did not know where they had gone. She acted as if she were under a pledge of secrecy. She could not even tell if they would come back. Look at it in any light that he could command it bore the same significance. The thing was over. She was done with him, and there was but one sensible thing left for him to do and that was to "brace up" and adjust himself to the inevitable. His effort to do this was marked by more vagaries than vigor, but he deserved much praise for the attempt. Three, four, five weeks passed by; dreary, uneventful weeks they were to him, owing to his condition. The chain of circumstances that held together the personages of this story appeared to be broken.

He had finished the portrait of Mrs. Sanger, and he felt that it was an execrable example of his incompetency. The woman had interested him more than the work, and he never got tired of telling Chapman what an eccentric, wayward, inquisitive creature she was.

Wilder was away. The rascals who were yet to be "hunted from the face of the earth" had apparently saved him all the trouble by removing themselves. Manuella was gone, and even Miss Enniston kept out of sight. These were dull days at the studio. Lent had come and was nearly gone, and premonitions of Easter were already in the shop windows.

One morning Carteret received a check for the Sanger portrait. He took it into Chapman's studio and showed it to him.

"What are you going to do with it?" asked Oats. "Store it or strew it?"

Carteret laughed rather grimly. "If I could get that other check from Miss Enniston," he said, "I think I'd go abroad, spend a year poking about the byways of Europe and try and mix knowledge with *dolce far niente.* I'd like to see Bouguereau work, and fool away some time with a French sweetheart."

Otis stopped and looked at his friend. Then he let down his mahl stick between his knees and threw one leg over it to keep it from resuming its automatic task.

"Carter," said he, "you're getting reckless. What's the matter with you? You're as blue as the devil. I've noticed it for some time. Now you're trying to be desperate. You know that you'll get Miss Enniston's check. Any way, I know it. You are not worrying about that, are you?"

"You appear to have Miss Enniston's confidence," remarked Carteret. "I've noticed you always speak of her with a calm reliance that I don't possess. When did you see her?"

"I saw her last night," said Chapman, somewhat hesitatingly, "and I'm going to see her to-night. I hope to work some profitable trade in that direction." And then, after a moment's pause, and as if this information was felt to be very wide of the mark, he blurted out in quite another key: "Confound it, Carter, I have a great admiration for that young lady. Hang it, I'm fond of her. There's only one thing in the world that prevented me from telling you before; I was afraid you were, too."

Carteret laughed loudly in a forced manner as if the idea were a humorous one. But there was a bitter flavor to the hilarity.

Chapman may have detected it. "At all events," he said, "I was awfully bothered, don't you know. *She* didn't bother me. O, dear, no. It was you. I somehow got it into my head that you were all fixed in that quarter and had everything tied up and labeled. But when I saw that the deeper you got into it the bluer you got, and you ended up by wanting to scurry out and hide away in a Paris garret, I said, 'I shouldn't wonder if Carter would thank me to humbly intervene in my miserable way.' Don't you understand, old fellow. Anyhow, it's as plain as Prussian blue that you may be in love, but it's as clear as Croton that it ain't that girl."

Carteret listened to this confession with some amazement and a great deal of interest. His impulse took the line of magnanimity. "My dear old boy," he said, "why didn't you mention it before? You didn't think I'd let my selfish plans stand in the way of your deep disinterested affection, did you? By Heavens, you wrong me. Miss Enniston's a noble prize; enthusiastic, fine looking, well fixed, loves art, moves in the best society, and doesn't care a cent for me, only as a brother. She pretends to admire my genius and all that sort of thing. Go in and win her, my boy. It's a worthy prize. She'll learn to appreciate you as I do when she knows you."

Headlong as this speech was, the consciousness that he was extending the brotherly illusion in too many directions came suddenly upon him and gave a rather hollow expression to his eyes.

Chapman merely said: "O, cut that, Carter. I've been studying the young lady in my own way, while she was winding me up. She pretended to like me and to get to see her, I pretended to like you. Then I got sentimental and she sat on me. She don't want me for a cent. She don't want art. There's only one thing on earth that she does want and she means to get it if she can."

"What is it?"

"You."

"Rubbish."

"O, no, solemn fact. What do you suppose she bought your picture for? Ha, ha; encouragement of genius! Pickles. She wants to put the heel of her number two boot through the canvas. Why, I'd never have found out how utterly dead gone you were on the other girl if it hadn't been for Miss Enniston's consumate and devouring jealousy. It's worse than Greek fire. Do you know what she wants me for? Simply to wipe her number two boots on when she has walked over your sylvan goddess. Now you've got it straight. If I were you I'd marry her and then you can both of you go into art together. You needn't work any more then, you know. You can buy your pictures of me."

"Never," said Carteret, rather fiercely.

"O, well," rejoined Chapman, "you'll forgive me for making the suggestion. I never would have dared, only I know you can't marry the other one; at least, I don't quite get it into my head how you can, when she has from all accounts, gone off to marry Mr. Stonybrook."

"I don't believe a word of it," cried Carteret, "and you haven't got an item of fact to build such a ridiculous notion on."

"The best you can do is to come over to the house," replied Chapman, "and imbibe a few of the facts. She's gone, bag and baggage and so has Stony. I don't think it becomes me to say that they have gone off together on any other scheme, for I'm not as disrespectful as you are."

Then Chapman whipped out his mahl stick and swung round at his canvas. But it was only for a second. He almost immediately swung back again.

"Besides," said he, "there's a connubial air in the house that's unmistakable. Mommy Hannige actually beams orange blossoms and serves wedding cake for lunch. I don't believe there's anything but a marriage of her own fixing that could plant such an infernal ecstasy on her ponderous jaws, or impart such a benediction to her feather duster."

Carteret was sauntering up and down the narrow studio, but he said nothing. Chapman looked at him a moment. Then he laid down his tools with the manner of a man who knew that it would be useless to paint now that his mind had been completely diverted. He went to the basin and began to wash his hands.

"We are both in the same kind of a canoe, Carter," he said, "and I've got a scheme that's a rescue. I've been thinking about it for a week."

His companion did not pay much attention to the scheme. He merely said: "What is it?" with polite indifference.

"Let's go into exile and rail against the world." Then he held his head down, dashed the water into his face and began rubbing his countenance with both hands to a white lather, as if to extinguish the absurdity before it burned any deeper.

A moment later he was standing in the middle of the room vigorously rubbing his face with a crash towel, and trying to follow Carteret in his movements at the same time.

"That don't strike you. Well, it isn't what I mean exactly. You're flush. In a few days you'll get your other check and I'll be in funds myself. We're both soured with the sex. Let's pack our traps as soon as the season opens and bury ourselves in the White Mountains. We can work, moralize, sleep on pine boughs, and both fall in love with the only girl who doesn't go back on us and won't be jealous—dear old Mistress Nature herself."

Carteret stopped walking and regarded his friend dreamily, and Chapman, seeing that he had struck a sympathetic chord, began to work his variations on it.

"We can build a lodge with an ingleside, own a canoe, take our guns and tackle, live on trout and venison, commune with heaven, sleep when we are tired, and howl our thanksgivings all day from the mountain-tops without fear of the police. What do you say?"

"It's a seductive prospect," replied Carteret; "you've touched me in a run-away mood."

"Good enough, then; we'll stop this 'Lady of Lyons' melodrama and go away and play 'As You Like It.' You'll never do any more work here, in this condition. You've come to a dead stop. Let's cut the world for a couple of months and forget everything but the beauty of outdoors."

Although Carteret did not immediately evince any enthusiasm over this project, he nevertheless fell in with it unprotestingly, as day after day Chapman talked it over and made his plans. It woke up the youthful desires, and both allayed and diverted his thoughts, and so the remaining days, dark and dreary enough in the studio, were cheered and enlivened with the boyish promises of the coming summer.

CHAPTER LI.

LOVE OPENS A CORRESPONDENCE.

Manuella saw matters slowly improving under her management, and one day she unexpectedly got a letter from John Sitwhite for his wife. It was the darkest and most discouraging moment of her toilsome experience at the Terrace. It looked as if Mrs. Sitwhite and her family were doomed to poverty and helplessness and that her own life was to be given to the care of an imbecile grandfather and the support of her aunt. It was not a pleasant prospect for a young woman who had been allowed to look into the enchanted domain of love and romance. But she did not give way to vain regrets. She had tried every means in her power to find a more comfortable abode for the family. She perused all the advertisements and made long journeys, only to come back discouraged at the high rents or the disagreeable places. And in all this she met with no sort of encouragement from her grandfather or assistance from Mrs. Sitwhite. The latter indeed, had settled into a morose condition of mind that saw only the gloomy side of everything. Her husband, she insisted, had deserted her. To add to all this, Manuella discovered to her sorrow that her aunt was resorting to the worst kind of stimulants to drown her trouble.

It was not possible for the girl to keep her face bright all the time, and now and then, as she sat at the window looking upon the winter scene, unobserved by her grandfather or her aunt, the freshet of memory brought the water to her eyes.

Then one day she went to the headquarters of the U.S. Sanitary Commission to enquire, as she had often done before, about the Fifty-second New York, and to her surprise found that a large mail had come from that Regiment which was now on the Red River, in Texas, serving under General Banks.

The bulky document that she carried home from John Sitwhite, created quite a sensation, and when the little group was all properly arranged round the window, she sat, in the middle and read his letter with many new and varying emotions.

And this is how it ran:

"Brazos Santiago, Camp Dana.

Well, Old Girl, I s'pose you thought I had given you up for good, but here I am like a bad penny you see, on hand again. I wrote you at New Orleans and sent you some money two months ago, and when Our Force got to this place I heard that the whole mail was captured by a privateer on the Gulf and I said: just my luck. I s'pose you've had hard times of it anyway with the kids, but there ought to be a pretty good heap of greenbacks to your account in Uncle Sam's safe. We've had the devil's time here in the swamps, first up the Rio Grande and then down again, looking for Johnnies and fighting musketeers. Sojerin ain't no picnic down here, don't you fancy it, and that's a fact. I hope the young ones are all right. I'd like to have a look at 'em anyway. Tell Patsy if he comes to the house that the war's all right and New York had better keep quiet or some of us boys will be marching home to attend to 'em. Poor Sam Bradley, he'll never sling no more coke; he got it in the neck the first day at Brownsville. He didn't live over an hour. He was a straight one. I felt knocked over myself when I heard it. But I'm all right and what's better, I'm acting captain of our company; that is, what's left of it. But captain don't count much down here. Inside the letter is the papers for you to take to the Government office in Chambers street and get your money. I guess you'll find everything all right. I s'pose you never hear anything of the princess or the old man. They was too good for our place. What's become of Dan Sully? Does he come round? If you ever see him tell him the coke bank is child's play to sojerin. I've had pretty good luck so far, got scratched by a shell, that's all; but I'm all right and you can tell the little chap he'll get a bran new set o' sojer togs when Johnny comes marching home. Now that's all I've got to say. Just you keep your temper down and your courage up and I'll be walking in on you one of these days and you won't know your loving husband. If you send a letter, mark it Headquarters Department Southwest, Brazos Santiago, Texas.

Capt. John Sitwhite,

Co. B, 52d N. Y. Vol.

When Manuella had read this letter with triumph and astonishment, she was prepared to burst forth in mixed congratulations and reproaches. But Mrs. Sitwhite had thrown her apron over her head, and it was quite plain from the motion of it that she was having a small turn of hysterics all to herself.

This letter proved to be the first of a series of events, and everybody knows that events move in flocks and packs, like sheep and wolves.

It was the very next day after this letter was received that Manuella managed to get away for a visit to Mrs. Hannige's, and she stopped on her way to call on her old friend, Mrs. Holbrook. What was her surprise to hear that the place was sold out and that the Holbrook's were going to Harlem. "Yes, my dear," the old lady said, as she brought a glass of soda into the back room for Manuella, and sat down for a comfortable recital. "We've got a good price for the place and good will, and we're going up where there's more business. Bob is a little cramped here and wants to do something a little more showy in the littery way; you know how venturesome some young men are. But then I can't blame him; his father was the same way. Yes, he's picked out a nice store on the Third Avenue, and is up there now, tinkering away. We're going to move next week. So, you're not married yet, are you? Why, I heard you had picked up somebody with a lot o' money and was living in great style. How people will talk."

"No," said Manuella demurely; "I'm not married yet. You don't know of a nice cheap place in Harlem for a family, something plain and nice, with air and sunshine?"

"O, then you *are* househunting."

"Yes, for my aunt."

"Why, bless your soul," said Mrs. Holbrook, we've taken a frame house ourselves on a Hundred and Twenty-seventh street; it's for all the world like a country place, and Bob was saying only yesterday, if we could only get a nice, quiet family to take part of it—how many children has your aunt got?"

"Two," said Manuella, feeling her heart sink as she thought how nice and quiet they were.

"I'm afraid Bob wouldn't like the children, my dear. If it was you and your grandfather now—"

"O, but Grandpa and I want it, there would only be three of us with two children and Grandpa don't count. I don't believe Bob would object at all," she added with a half smile, "and I'm coming in to talk to him about it."

"Yes, do, my dear. Bob often asks me if you've been in."

The prospect of being able easily to win young Mr. Holbrook to her view of the case so encouraged her that she set out for Mrs. Hannige's with a much lighter heart than she had carried for a long time.

She was met by that lady with her usual exuberance and the announcement that Mr. Stonybrook had come back and would be awful glad to see her. "You'd better go right up to your room and take your things off. I'm not going to let you go back till after lunch. It's no use, I won't hear a word, go right along."

Once in her familiar room, Manuella began to grow serious. She felt that there was to be a formal interview with Mr. Stonybrook, and that she had no definite course marked out in her mind. A consciousness that in some way Mr. Stonybrook was stronger in his will than she was in her resolution added to her nervousness. How was she to refuse him? What reason could she give; what reason was there indeed for refusing him?

She did not meet him until lunch, which Mrs. Hannige had prepared with him in view, and then he disarmed her at once by his tact and easy naturalness. They chatted about every unimportant matter, even to the making of a salad, which Mr. Stonybrook kindly volunteered to dress for them in a new way, and for which he was graciously complimented by Manuella. He regretted her temporary absence from Mrs. Hannige's home so incidentally, and said so good humoredly that if she missed it as much as he did when he was away they'd soon have her back, that Manuella fell into his pleasant vein and the luncheon was as informal and easy-going as could have been wished.

But Mrs. Hannige, at the right moment, slipped out, and left them alone, and Manuella felt that it was all preconcerted.

Mr. Stonybrook was too tactful to disconcert her by any uncomfortable eagerness or directness. He carefully avoided any little emotional crisis and in spite of herself kept her at her ease by skirting round the dangerous subject with an easy assumption that it was sure to be settled all right.

They were still sitting at the table. He leaned back in his seat, took a sip of the Burgundy that he had furnished for the occasion, and said:

"Now tell me, Miss Castleton, about Grandpa. You must have been doing ever so many things since I've been away. I got so interested in his improvement and so used to his pleasant old-fashioned evenings that, upon my word, I felt quite lost without them."

"He keeps up his spirits most remarkably," answered Manuella. "He doesn't worry, and I think his health is better than it used to be."

"Yes, he used to worry a good deal over you. I think the old gentleman would be the happiest man alive if he knew you would never be taken away from him. I found out a good deal about him when you were not around, and I noticed he always worried secretly until you came back, but he wouldn't acknowledge it. You're a kind of sunshine to him, but he doesn't know it any more than the flower that would die without it."

"Yes," said Manuella, dropping into this vein immediately. "He is so helpless and so far away from the real difficulties of life that I feel toward him more tenderly than you can imagine."

"Quite true. I know it, I know it," said Mr. Stonybrook. "But the difficulties were all disappearing, so it seemed to me, and really, you know, you both of you let me into some of your confidences. I felt at one time that you had let me do a lot of things that it was impossible for a young lady to do. There aren't any new difficulties are there?"

"N—o," replied Manuella dreamily.

"I'm glad of that, because we were clearing off the old ones without any trouble. The fact is, Ella—you'll let me call you Ella? It's an awful waste of breath to be saying Miss Castleton—the fact is, difficulties that look insurmountable to a young lady who hasn't had to win her fight with the world, don't amount to much to a veteran such as I am, and after all, there isn't but one real difficulty in this world, and that is how to be happy. The only real difficulty with that is that we have to suffer half our lives before we find out the right way."

Then he stopped a moment and broke into a hearty ha, ha. "By Jove," he said, "that sounds terribly preachy, don't it, for me," and then learning forward on the table he said: "The thing that we've got to consider, Ella, is this, and we must consider it like two sensible people who have got something to do and don't want to mix any nonsense up with it. Would you be entirely happy if all the perplexities and problems of life were removed and you could feel that all you wanted to do for yourself, and your grandfather in his declining years, could be assured without any sacrifice; if you could have the home, the comforts, the refinements and the pleasant duties of a lady, feeling only that you had somebody that you respected and trusted to think of you, and guard you, and exact nothing from you but your utmost confidence? That's the question, Ella, for us to consider."

She had dropped her eyes, but she knew that he was looking at her, and when he paused and there was some response expected, she said, without looking up:

"Yes, I have considered it."

But he did not jump at her answer. He accepted it as a matter of course and went on in the same strain.

"Of course we have, but I've got to consider the most, for all the responsibility is on me, don't you know, and all the consequences—and I don't want to imperil the happiness of the woman who trusts me. I'd refuse to consider it another moment, Ella, if it didn't look to me as if we had some kind of common duty to perform, and you hadn't shown that you trusted me and depended on me a little."

"Indeed I have, Mr. Stonybrook, and I think you are sincere and generous, and could do more for me than anybody else that I know. I would be very ungrateful, I'm sure, not to tell you so."

"Don't think I can do too much. I'm quite moderate in my estimate of myself. If I can save you from some of the disappointments, some of the failures of life, and protect you with a great affection and consideration from the fickleness, the fraud, the folly, that my own sex will offer you, I shall be very content. Do you think I can?"

This was specious and effective. If there was anything that Manuella at this moment wanted to be guaranteed against, it was fickleness and fraud. Something of the natural weakness of a young and inexperienced woman came to Mr. Stonybrook's assistance, like a cunning ally. He made her feel that with him all the doubts and dangers of the practical side of life would disappear. She would have a discreet, mature mind to think it all out and do it for her. All she had to do now was to accept the position of a lady and let somebody else assume the hard fight of which she had obtained a glimpse. So she answered him softly:

"Yes, Mr. Stonybrook. It seems to me that you might!"

He did not press the matter farther. "You don't know how happy you make me," he said. "I am going to have a long talk with your grandfather.

Mrs. Hannige said, I think, that you were making a visit to your aunt's. O, by the way, I brought you a little present from Boston. It's in my trunk which isn't unpacked yet. If you don't mind, I'll go up and get it," and Mr. Stonybrook jumped up with something of the elasticity of a boy. "And I've got something for your grandfather too. I can send that, but you might as well take yours with you. You'll pardon me a few moments, will you not? I'll fetch it."

Then as he went out, Mrs. Hannige, flushed and bristling with her own affairs, sailed in.

"Upon my word," she said, "I shall have to let my servants run my house presently. That girl takes more upon herself than all my guests put together and it all comes of my treating her better than she deserves. But I've settled her this time, I hope. Yes, I have, my dear. I've given her notice and out she goes on Saturday. I've stood it as long as human patience could hold out."

"Why, Mrs. Hannige," said Manuella. "What is the matter?"

"Matter, it's always the same matter. The moment you give one of them hussies an inch, they take the whole concern. But there, never mind that. I've fixed it once for all. I thought that room of yours was put in apple-pie order for you, and would you believe it, there's hasn't been a broom in it for two weeks."

Manuella smiled faintly. Mrs. Hannige's domestic troubles did not particularly interest her at this moment "I'm going up to put my things on," she said, "for I must get back. Tell Mr. Stonybrook I shall be down presently."

"Well," replied Mrs. Hannige, "if that girl's in your way, push her out. I made her go up at once and slick the place a bit. I'll tell him. Isn't he a gentleman? I tell you, Ella, he's a man among ten thousand."

When Manuella reached her room, she found Florry there in a high state of excitement, swinging a broom viciously and knocking things down generally. The manner of the girl was so unusual that it arrested her attention.

"Don't you think, Florry, that you had better wait a little while till I get through? You are making a terrible dust," she said mildly.

Florry brought her broom down with her two hands grasping its handle. Its whisps bent under her strenuous double clutch. Her yellow hair was flying and had a feather or two nestling in its frowsy convolutions. Her eyes reflected some of the lurid hue.

"I'd do anything in the world for you, Miss, that I would, for you never asked me to lie, and me Christian brought up, that I was. I'm fired out because I had a young man, as if a girl couldn't see company betimes in better houses than this."

She held the broom like a churn handle, and on one of her bare arms there was an absurd silver-plated bracelet that looked like an enormous napkin ring.

Manuella, who was looking at her, merely said: "Well, well, I don't want to hear of your affairs and I don't think Mrs. Hannige wants you to lie. What have you got on your arm?"

"Me young man gave it me," said Florry with a half simper. "It's him that she's down on and without reason. Sure, I meant no wrong and says I if he's good enough to come and see the young lady, that's you, says I, he's good enough for me, and at that she out and abused me like a dog."

Manuella, who had turned to attend to her toilet without giving much heed to the girl, stopped.

"What do you mean," she said, "by the young man who came to see me? I'm afraid Florry that it isn't Mrs. Hannige who taught you to lie."

"It's Heaven's truth, Miss," said Florry. "He came to see you many's the time and when he couldn't see you, he was real good to me and I knowed all the time you didn't want to see him."

"I didn't want to see him? How did you know that, who told you I didn't want to see him?"

Florry let a sudden look of crafty good humor play about her mouth.

"O, it wasn't the wan you wanted to see," she said, "it was the other wan. But it wasn't my fault that you didn't see either wan of 'em, and that's the Lord's truth."

"Either one of them," Manuella repeated. "Florry are you inventing stories to spite Mrs. Hannige? Are you sure there were two gentlemen called to see me?"

"I hope I may die this minute," said Florry, "and when the old woman undertook to interfere with me in the same way, a girl couldn't help takin' your side. O, you don't know the things that's going on in this house, and I'm glad to be out of it."

And then she began, with a desperate impulse, to swing her besom as if she had more indignation than words could accommodate.

"Stop that and listen to me a moment," said Manuella. "Was it Mr. Carteret who gave you the bracelet?"

"No'm, Mr. Carteret don't care nothin' for me. I guess you know that as well as I do."

"Then it was Mr. Kleinbacker?"

The girl nodded her head with a ready and rapid affirmative.

"And Mr. Kleinbacker come here many times to see me?"

"Well, m'm, he's come a good many more times than t'other wan."

"And Mr. Carteret came several times?"

"He just did and he set in the little room two hours and I say there's a young man waitin' to see Miss Castleton and she says: 'Let him wait and you go down and sweep that diningroom and mind your own business. It'll do him good.'

That's what she said, and her puttin' on airs with me because a young man as is a gentleman comes to see me. O, I ain't goin to keep my mouth shut. Seein' as how I must walk out for not lyin', I might as well walk out with the whole truth on me tongue."

"How many times did Mr. Carteret call?"

"Sure I couldn't count 'em when she opens the door herself and I'm in the kitchen. Wunct you'd jist gone out with Mr. Stonybrook and wunst you was in your room with Mr. Stonybrook, and wunst—"

"What did he say?"

It was quite plain to the girl's instinct that she had interested her listener and the same instinct told her how to sustain that interest.

"Indade, and what could he say? He tried hard enough to see you and he couldn't, so he looked pitiful like and went away. I felt sorry for him."

"Why didn't you tell me?"

"Well, then it was as much as me place is worth. I'm tellin' you now, when it's gone."

"Did Mrs. Hannige prevent you from telling me?"

"Did she? Why, you don't think she'd pay me extra wages if I didn't do what she wants. That's what I'm kickin' about. I did it and then she fires me out."

Manuella was now adjusting her hat and furs with increased rapidity. She was thinking, and one's thoughts sometimes betray themselves in the movements of the fingers. She had about finished when she said suddenly:

"And Mr. Kleinbacker came to see you, you say?"

"Indeed, he did."

"Where did he see you?"

"He came into the basement."

"And he tried to find out from you all he could about my movements, which you told him and he bribed you with bracelets and things. There, don't fly out at me. I haven't got time to discuss it with you. Bring that bundle and come down stairs."

"Indeed I'll not," said Florry. "You can fight your own battles. I've told the truth and I'll stick to it, but I'm not goin' to be bull-ragged between the two of yez."

Manuella said not another word. She went down the stairs very thoughtfully. Mr. Stonybrook was waiting for her. He had a little box not an inch square in his hand.

"What an outrage it is to tear away in this manner," he said. "I've only had a few minutes' talk with you. But you'll be here to-morrow, of course. I shall expect to see you. Take your glove off, my dear, I've got your present and I want to put it on your finger."

"Please don't put it on today, Mr. Stonybrook. I—I've overstayed my time and my gloves are tight. Keep it till I come over again. It will keep, will it not? I've a long walk and it will be dark presently."

"But I insist on accompanying you. I can't permit you to go alone."

"But I request that you will not. Mrs. Hannige, can I write a note at your desk?"

"Why, yes, my dear, of course. Sit right down here."

Mr. Stonybrook gave an almost imperceptible shrug of his shoulders and put the box in his pocket. The girl's actions were of course inexplicable to him. She sat down and wrote something hurriedly.

It was folded, put into an envelope and addressed to "Colin Carteret, Tenth Street Studio." She then asked Mrs. Hannige for a stamp and affixed it. When it was all ready, she resumed her jaunty manner, held out her hand to Mr. Stonybrook and said, "Good bye for a little while. I forbid you coming out."

"Shan't I mail your letter for you?" he asked.

"O, no; I'll drop it on my way. Good bye, Mrs. Hannige."

"Good bye, my dear."

And then she ran out before they could follow her.

She had scarcely got to the bottom of the front steps when Otis Chapman came up. In a flash, a new idea seized her. She would send the note by him. It would go more direct. He promised to deliver it promptly and discreetly, and put it in his breast pocket.

"You'll not forget it, will you?"

"On my honor I will not," said Chapman. "Are you coming back to the Hotel Hannige soon?'

"O, yes, at some time," she said gaily, as she tripped off down the street.

The next day Carteret was lying on his back studying a map of Maine, when Chapman came in.

"O, I say Chap," he cried, "we can't get round your route without a horse, and I've made a new tour. Look here, we can go up the Penobscot and cross over to Millinoket—that's our spot. It's only fifteen miles from there to Katahdin. Say, I saw a canoe yesterday that was made of rubber. You can put it in your trunk—what's that?"

"It's a new style of portable soup. Each powder makes a quart of genuine consomme, bean, pea, chicken or beef soup. There's six packages in a box. Only a dollar. All you need is a pot, cold water and a fire. By the way, did you see Fairchild?"

"No, what do you want of him?"

"I want to get that repeating rifle of his; he never uses it. It wouldn't be a bad idea to get Fairchild to go with us."

"There you are again. I wish you wouldn't talk about inviting anybody else. Confound it, I don't want to take my species with me. I want to get away from them and as soon as possible."

"Can't go till the frost is out of the ground, my boy," said Chapman, "so curb you impatience. Besides, I haven't got my work all done, and you haven't got your check yet. Suppose we go up and call on the young lady to-night and refresh her memory. O, speaking of young ladies, I've got a letter for you. It's in my coat pocket, wait a moment."

It took him but a minute or two to go and get the missive, which he put into Carteret's hands as that young man languidly stretched himself out on the lounge.

He tore it open eagerly after he had seen the handwriting on the envelope, Chapman meanwhile filling his pipe and examining his packages of soup.

It ran as follows:

COLIN CARTERET:

I have just this moment learned that you made several efforts to see me and were told that I was out. I write this to remove any impression you may have received that I did not wish to see you. I cannot make explanations without some further information. If you care to send me any word about it, you can address me immediately, care of Mrs. Holbrook, 1149 First avenue, for I am now at my old home in 19th street.

MANUELLA CASTLETON."

"Do you know," said Chapman, "that half the fun of living in the woods is destroyed now by the facility with which we can take the luxuries with us. Fancy the Pathfinder lighting a fire at night and making himself a plate of turtle soup before wrapping the umbrageous mantle of his couch about him."

"Have you got any paper and ink in your room?" asked Carteret.

Chapman laid down the packages he was examining. Carteret was sitting bolt upright, holding the letter out in front of his eyes and staring quite dramatically at it, as if he had suddenly become long-sighted.

"Important?" asked Chapman.

"Yes, very. See if you have any ink."

"I've got paper, but ink I wouldn't swear to."

They both went into Chapman's studio to rummage for stationery. Letter paper they found with various hotel heads on it, and numerous stains of sienna. But the ink was reduced to some dry scales in the bottom of a funnel-shaped stone bottle, and when Carteret turned it over some of last summer's dead flies and a rusty' steel pen fell out.

"Don't answer it till tomorrow," said Chapman, "and I'll buy some."

By dint of inquiries in all the studios on the floor he at last got a bottle of jelly-like ink, which he thinned under the hydrant and then locking his door sat down to answer Manuella's letter.

For half an hour he worked under the spell, and with the inspiration of a hundred emotions. He addressed it to "My lost darling," and heaped reproaches upon himself and upon the young lady, declared that his life was wrecked and his heart was broken; that he would never believe in woman again, and was packing up his traps to leave the country.

Presently, when he had expended all his superfluous feelings on paper, he got up, took a turn about the room and sat down and penned this letter:

"MY DEAR MISS CASTLETON:

It is indeed true that I tried often to see you, and only gave it up when I was given to understand that you had little time to waste on me and even then I relinquished the effort, but not the desire, with a faith in you that had nothing to stand on but my poor heart. Mrs. Hannige did not desire that I should see you and I was told on all sides that you were going to marry Mr. Stonybrook. If I did not rush in and claim. you, it was because it looked more like selfishness than bravery. But I beg of you to believe now and forever that though I may not possess you, you possess all that is best and noblest in me. It does not become me, perhaps, to tell you that I have suffered. I suppose that a man has no right to that luxury. It is his duty to be brave even when his world is a wreck. That is what I am trying to be.

Yours unchanged,
COLIN CARTERET."

After considering this some time and seeing that it offered not the slightest excuse to Miss Castleton for an answer, he wrote this postscript:

" If there is any information that I can give you, would it not be better for me to call and lay it at your feet, where I have laid everything else, than to attempt to write letters about it? Of course I do not know that it would be even proper, until I hear from you."

Then this message was delivered to the mail and Carteret sat down with Manuella's note in his hand to see how much could be got out of it by renewed readings.

CHAPTER LII.

THE CONSPIRATORS DISAGREE.

The Astor House during the war was a much livelier centre than it has been since. Its great granite walls, not unlike the walls of Fort Sumter itself, which were being pounded to dust by the costliest of armaments, looked down on the Park Barracks whose site has since been covered by the peaceful architecture of the restored Republic in the United States post office, and upon the whole nest of newspapers on Park Row and Ann and Nassau streets.

The old-fashioned portal of this famous hostlery was choked all day with officers, marshals and recruiting agents. Its great rotunda was crowded by merchants and politicians and its rooms were always full of guests from the West.

On the topmost floor in the northeast angle, on the morning of the 5th of April, Mr. Chanfleur and Miramon occupied one of the rooms with a low ceiling, which room looked out upon the City Hall Park through two round embrasures. Miramon stood at one of these circular windows with his head and shoulders partly thrust into the recess and he was looking down musingly upon the park, some of whose willows wore the yellow greenish hue of spring. The clatter of the barracks, the regular marching-tap of the drum, the occasional calls of the drill sergeant, and even the tramp of the squads, came up to him mingled with the sharper rattle of omnibuses, the tinkle of the car bells and the shouts of the newsboys.

Chanfleur, who was seated at an absurdly small table in the center of the room, had placed his silk hat in front of him and was rapidly writing with a gold pencil on a sheet of hotel paper.

"I don't suppose we can get a messenger up here," he said, "and I might as well wait and send it when I go down. Now suppose you give me a clear idea of the situation. The man McCune, you say, has been here a week."

Miramon left the window and seated himself opposite his companion. "He escaped, as I told you, on the 20th," he said. "The fellow is a desperate sort of rascal and being detailed with a gang of labourers to work at some improvised fortifications somewhere on the edge of the enemy's line, he escaped during a skirmish, swam out to a fishing-smack, stole its yawl and made his way in the night through the lines. At least that is his story. The only important thing is, that he *is* here and has told me how he and Plonski were trapped and enabled me to set in motion the means of Plonski's liberation."

"That of course you did through Judge Sanger."

Miramon did not answer the questions into which Chanfleur's speech invariably ran. He betrayed the fact that he had a much stronger individuality and a finer perspicacity than his companion, by never allowing these questions to divert him from the vital issue of their conversation.

"Plonski is here," said Miramon. "I have seen him, but I did not think it judicious or safe to have him at this interview. I want to determine at once just how far we can trust him."

"But we've been trusting him all along, haven't we?" asked Chanfleur.

"His return," said Miramon, "makes it tolerably certain that the cup has not been found. The question is, in the renewed search for it, can we employ him and his men? He says confidently that the cup used to entrap him into the clutches of an U.S. Marshal, was hired for the occasion and fooled the man McCune. If you wish to know how he made sure of this I can tell you in a few words. It seems that the fellow who was employed to do the job and whose name is Sully, is a friend of a woman who lives in that row of tenements in Nineteenth street and it is through that woman that Plonski got at some of the facts. The cup was lost by the opening of the water-gate in the Croton aqueduct and not by any mysterious intervention of Providence. From every reasonable probability it is in the stream somewhere still. It was the conclusion of Inspector Wilder, as well as my own that the man Samson had recovered and made away with it. That possibility is set at rest by the fact that he was arrested in Detroit two weeks ago for an attempted bank robbery which he would not have mixed himself up in had he possessed the cup."

"It seems to me," exclaimed Chanfleur impatiently, as he pushed back his chair, "that the bottom defect in our whole scheme is the importance that you attach to the cup. Had the money and time that have been wasted in trying to get possession of this old silver, been employed in a systematic search in the West with such guiding facts as you possess, for the wealth itself, we should be nearer the end of our job. But now it looks to me as if we were at the beginning again, not having gained an inch."

"We are in the situation of men on a vast plain in a dense fog and without a compass," said Miramon. "Any search without the cup will be a hunt in a circle and a fruitless and discouraging task. I certainly possess more information on this subject than any man alive. I've traversed half the globe to obtain it, and I have gone over the whole wilderness of Southern Colorado. The sum total of my convictions and experience is that the cup is our compass. It has on one side the algebraic location of this treasure. I have, by indefatigable research and years of study, arrived at the historical assurance of how those Mexicans designated places and measured distances and have the whole set of symbols in my keeping. But they are only the means of interpretation—they are not the information to which we can apply the means. Had I been able to get the cup into my possession long enough to see the markings, it would have been sufficient, or had there been a transcript in Valadares' papers, this hunt would have been useless. But you know that the attempt to find such a copy in Mr. Enniston's safe failed, and the only transcript of the cup's hieroglyphics ever made was mutilated and the half that is preserved contains only a portion of the treasure list. With these facts well in your mind I think you will see the necessity of wasting no more time in idle discussions. A thorough, systematic search must be made for the cup, as soon as the weather will permit. The question is, shall we employ Plonski and his agents?"

Without waiting for Chanfleur who had stretched out his legs and with his hands deep in the pockets of his trousers, was jingling the contents impatiently, to answer, Miramon went on.

"Plonski has mismanaged the affair at this end. Instead of going into conspiracy and inviting the inspector of the police, he should have gone straight to Enniston and Ackerman and obtained their cooperation or bought them off. He has deceived me in several particulars, which leads me to suspect that he has some intention of betraying us. In addition to all this he has made himself inimical to the Government and is liable at any moment to rearrest."

"You are forgetting one thing," said Chanfleur. "His political influence can protect us against Wilder."

"We need no protection against Wilder," resumed Miramon. "We should have Wilder on our side. He at the worst would be content with liberal pay for his services, and he knows Plonski's career and has a personal grudge against him growing out of Plonski's attempt to deceive him. It is necessary to decide upon our measures at once, for the moment Wilder gets here, he will inform Ackerman that the cup is still in the stream and it becomes then a question of who finds it first and can retain possession of it."

"It appears to me," said Chanfleur, "to be the most hopeless of all undertakings. I confess that I'm dead discouraged."

"I have examined the stream," said Miramon. "It is a small brook, flushed only by freshets or the Croton water escape. About a mile below the point at which the cup was lost, is a dam and a button mill, the flume of which is eight feet high. The pond has not been emptied in four years. The man will lift his gate and drain it for a hundred dollars. It was physically impossible for the cup to have passed it and will be found undoubtedly in the stratum of mud at the bottom. Plonski, who is a practical fellow with all his craft, would have accomplished this if Wilder had not arrested him. Before he could get at it again, the winter closed up the stream. It is a very simple task of engineering, I assure you."

"Very well," said Chanfleur. "It can be safely left in your hands. But it does not appear to me to be prudent to antagonize Plonski. He knows too much, and might seriously damage us."

"I should advise," replied Miramon, "that the services of Officer Wilder be obtained to aid us, and that measures be taken to stop all further risk and delay by making direct overtures to Capt. Ackerman, who is sure to put in some kind of claim of ownership, and may employ Wilder to frustrate our plans. While I am perfecting the details of this, the man McCune can be employed to keep an eye on the stream. He's skulking from the marshals, now, and would be safe up there in the woods. Besides, it would be Plonski's proposition, without doubt, and as we do not wish to fall out with him, we can let him serve us up to the point of actual search."

"You said something about having discovered Plonski's connection with a political junta."

"Ah, yes, I meant to have told you that he is badly mixed up with a set of socialists and Red Republicans. His ambitions are political and anarchical, and I half suspect that he has taken some of them into his confidence and led them to believe that they can carry out their plans by securing this wealth. The danger of such a disclosure lies in the unscrupulousness of the men and their advantage of organization. It was to offset that danger that I desired to secure the valuable aid of Inspector Wilder. I had an interview with the officer, and he said at once that there was no possible excuse for the interference of the police with the proper search for the cup, and that nothing but Plonski's illegal methods of procedure had brought the thing to the attention of the detective bureau. As for the ownership of the cup, he acknowledged that it was not the duty of the police to decide. So you see that even Mr. Ackerman cannot use the authorities in his behalf without bringing suit in proper form. The whole thing, therefore, is in a nutshell. We must get the cup into our possession long enough to obtain its secret, and if possible prevent Plonski from obtaining that secret."

"There is one thing that you haven't made quite clear to me," observed Chanfleur, "and it is who brought about the arrest of Plonski if it was not Wilder."

"It's a great pity," said Miramon, "that we could not know that Plonski did not have the cup and was ignorant of its whereabouts without releasing him. He was captured, I believe, through the efforts of the attorneys of the Enniston estate, who were probably employed by Mr. Ackerman."

"But," said Chanfleur, "the mere possession of the cup can do him no good without the means of interpreting its secret."

"It is probably no part of his purpose to recover the treasure. He would be much more likely to go straight to Mexico and sell out to the authorities either clerical or civil. There's a sort of Rosicrucian society in the church there which is possessed of a great deal of secret information concerning the traditions of the country. It was through that organization that the lost mines of Tlamasco were rediscovered, and the treasure of the Chalco palace unearthed."

"Very well," ejaculated Chanfleur, who had paid little attention to this information. "I'm in the habit of taking my own views of things, and I'm bound to tell you that I wouldn't have anything to do with Plonski. At all events, I'd tell him the cup was found and keep him away from the place until we get through."

"But you must remember that Plonski is a man who also has views. He would very likely tell me I was trying to deceive him."

"How soon can we get to work with the search?"

"I shall be able to tell you in a day or two. I've got to make some inquiries and get some reliable workmen. You had better come here in the morning. If I am away I will notify you. The place is out of the reach of observers, and the mob downstairs is the best sort of guaranty that you will not be noticed."

Chanfleur then look his leave. He had not been gone twenty minutes when Plonski, wrapped in an old-fashioned cloak, knocked at the door and Miramon let him in.

He showed the results of his imprisonment in his face. He was gaunt and a trifle grim about the mouth, but his eyes shone brighter than ever and the red stone was gone from his throat. He had tried to bribe a sentinel with it at Fortress Monroe, and his failure had only added one more to his bitter scores against the world.

He came into the middle of the room, unceremoniously took his hat off and began wiping his bald head with a colored handkerchief.

"You bade me come at eleven," he said; "so I came at ten to see why you set that hour. I waited downstairs and saw Chanfleur go away. Why did you not wish me to see him?"

"Sit down," said Miramon unperturbed. "I am not going into explanations. If I wish to see Mr. Chanfleur alone it's none of your business. Neither he nor I object to seeing you at the proper time."

"You are trying to blind me," said Plonski. "You told McCune to stick to it that the cup he saw in Sully's hands was the real cup."

"So McCune sticks to it that it was, does he?" asked Miramon, with real interest.

"McCune knows the cup when he sees it," said Plonski; "consequently as he didn't see it in Sully's hands, he must have been bribed to stick to that lie. You want to keep me from looking for it in that stream."

"But isn't it possible that it may have been found by Sully?"

"No."

"Well, you speak confidently. Will you tell me how you know that Sully did not see it? I can understand the surmises you made when I saw you yesterday, but your positive manner now leads me to expect some new facts."

"Very well, you can have them. Wilder wouldn't be running after Samson to find out if he took the cup when he knew Sully had it, would he? Job Ackerman wouldn't be still planning to get it if his lawyer had recovered it, would he?"

"Ah, you've seen Wilder," said Miramon.

"No," said Plonski, with a quick leer of triumph, "but you have."

"Yes," responded Miramon, somewhat nettled; "I have seen him."

"And he advised you to get rid of me. You can't do it. In such a scheme as this, an employé becomes a partner. You might as well understand that I am not going to plot for a year for prospective benefits and then be dropped when they are within reach."

"I quite agree with you that such a result would be—disappointing to you. But it might be necessary for us," said Miramon; "still as it has not been contemplated, it would be idle to discuss it. It is only fair to remember that when I got back here you had disappeared and so had the cup. I was completely at a loss to know what to do. Matters have been straightened out since and we are now ready to go to work again."

Then the two men sat down and tried to make each other believe that confidence was restored. It was one o'clock when Plonski went away, and he noticed, as he crossed the park, a blue bird sitting on the dead spray of a maple. "The winter is over," he said to himself, as he pulled his coat about him and went uptown.

CHAPTER LIII.

KISS AND MAKE UP.

Colin Carteret's professional experiences were not at all peculiar. He had suddenly attracted attention by his picture in the Academy. He had seen himself paragraphed as a genius and he had read labored disparagements of his work. He was told by his brother artists that he was made, and his studio, for the first-time, began to be invaded by curious visitors and that class of purchasers which is governed entirely by the vogue or the conspicuousness of an artist. Two or three really good commissions came to him from dealers, and he received several letters from actresses asking what he would charge to paint them in costume.

But notwithstanding all this, his temperament was too genuinely artistic in the best sense to be supremely happy over it. He asked himself several times of what value success was when it had lost its living purpose. Nor could all the aesthetic or philosophical arguments of his reason quite influence him, though they might convince him that it was a sufficient and noble end to work for art alone.

It is doubtful if any young man, at his stage of development, is seriously governed by abstract considerations.

After writing the letter to Miss Castleton, art and nature were both suddenly crowded out of his consideration by the new hopes and emotions that struggled in the most contradictory manner in his mind. It was impossible to sit still before his easel and keep his mind on his work, and the Maine woods were not for the moment dwelt upon with the same zest that Chapman had awakened.

One whole day passed and there was no answer to his letter. Then he began to imagine every kind of accident that might have interfered with its delivery. Might he not have directed it wrong? Might not the jealous Bob Holbrook mislay it or withhold it? Might it not be misunderstood or misinterpreted by Manuella, and might it not be, after all, that she only wrote to him as a matter of formal courtesy, to make her conduct with Mr. Stonybrook appear less heinous, and not with any intention of opening a correspondence? As was usual in these subjective perplexities, he ended by formulating his doubts and suspicions into a sort of conviction, and tried to convince himself that his hopes and imaginings were the most illusory counsellors; that he lost his balance at every whim of a woman who knew his weakness. By the next morning he had worked himself into a grim cynicism and was just about to rush into

Chapman's studio and take up the Maine woods with a desperate avidity when there came two letters.

One was by mail and the other by messenger, and when he answered the rap on his door, there stood the postman and behind him a commissionaire, as the messengers were called at that time, when the first organization of a district service sought to employ disabled soldiers.

The vague thought that shot through his mind, as he returned the postman's official smile, was that it never rains but it pours. "If you please," said the commissionaire, "I want a receipt for this one. Are you Mr. Carteret—Colin Carteret?"

The young man took the letters eagerly enough, saw that the superscriptions were not in Manuella's hand, but his rapid conclusion was that she had got Bob Holbrook to address the letter. One of them *must* be from her. It would be impertinent, he felt, for anybody else to write at such an expectant crisis. So he locked the door—why, it would be impossible to say, unless it was that he felt the emotions of the moment were too sacred to permit of interruption from Chapman. Then pulling his stool round to the light, he tore open one of the envelopes, an unfamiliar hand. He looked at the bottom of the last page of close writing and saw the name "Job Ackerman."

Then he dropped the letter on the floor and opened the envelope that had been sent by messenger.

What was his astonishment when he found that it was a letter from Miss Enniston, and doubled and pinned with a black pin across its inner page was a crisp United States greenback note, the denomination conspicuously showing in bold white figures 1000.

Poor as he was, and anxious as he had been all along to get this money, his one feeling for the instant was that of keen, quick disappointment. He dropped the hand that held the note down by his side. In it was a fortune for him and the first proud prize that his talents had fairly won. But there was a girl somewhere without a dollar and all his talents could not win her. She had suddenly become the unattainable in his disappointment, and now the money of the world had suddenly sunk to the mere attainable.

Presently he unpinned the greenback, looked at it with an instant curiosity, then laid it on his paint stand and leaning over with his two elbows on his knees, read the letter.

"*My Dear Friend:* Mr. Chapman reminded me last night about the picture, and I ought to explain to you that the delay in sending the check was caused by the unsettled condition of my father's estate. But as Mr. Chapman intimated that you had expressed some surprise at the delay, I hasten to send you the ready money. Please acknowledge its receipt, and come and see me either to-night or to-morrow, for I want to consult with you about the picture. A Broadway dealer has asked permission to exhibit it in his art rooms. Don't you think that would be to your advantage? What a goose Chapman is. He actually asked me if it spoiled soup to boil it too long. I tried to see Mrs. Sanger's portrait, but when I called there was nobody at home.

"Don't forget. I shall wait for you and shall not have another opportunity to see you for a week, for I am going home to help Dr. Flockton with his Easter Festival.

ROSAMOND ENNISTON."

He sat a few moments contemplating the sheet, after he had read it. Altogether its effect was to deepen the feeling which already had possession of him, and which might be called a dull sense, that Fate and his desires did not agree. He tried for a while to think of what he would do with the thousand dollars. He tried to recall all the things that he intended to do when he had no money and dreamed only of getting it; but, to save his life, he could not remember what they were, save that during the halcyon hours of an autumn fled into the irredeemable, he had had a boy's vision of some day being able to empty all this into one little woman's lap and take his reward in the surprise and delight of her splendid eyes.

He varied the experiment by trying to get up a counter enthusiasm for what Chapman had called the "Dear old mistress Nature." He turned over a book of etchings, but Penobscot's waters wore a desolate and far away atmosphere, and Katahdin's blue outlines seemed incomprehensibly lonely.

She would not be in that world, but in this, and he would be forgotten. So, love stuck as close as remorse itself, and the next morning, when he came back from a breakfast that he had intended to be of extra relish, and that somehow had been very stupid, there lay Manuella's letter at last. He saw it with what might be called a general throb, and seized it with a diffusive thrill. There wasn't much of it, and he tore it open and swept it all in with an omniverous glance, as if the first thing to do was to determine its general meaning and come down to its particulars afterwards.

"Colin Carteret," it said, "I wrote you a letter because I wished to correct what appeared to me to be an injustice. I do not feel like giving you formal permission to call upon me, because whatever permission you once had was never interfered with by me. I am very sorry that other people should have deceived you. I never have.

MANUELLA CASTLETON."

The effect of this letter upon Carteret was remarkable. His first unpremeditated impulse, when he understood it, was to put the sheet with a sudden movement to his mouth and kiss the name at the bottom of it. Then it began to grow upon him with the calm efficacy of its guilelessness, until it seemed like a revelation. Not a tremor of the vagaries, the doubts, the perplexities, the suspicions that had worried him; not an indication of any struggle, but a simple dignity and a quiet ignoring of everything but the conditions which she had not disturbed. And what a strange authority in this utter refusal to sophisticate or argue; what a stinging reproach under it all; what a noble vindication of herself without words, when she had nothing to explain and no violated conditions to restore.

That was the way it looked to Carteret, whose imaginative mind was apt to run rapidly in any new direction. The moment the spark on his old altar was fanned, all the surroundings began to wear a rosier significance. "I'm a fool," he said. "Didn't she say, 'I'm back at my old home in Nineteenth street?' What more could she say? Didn't that imply that she never thought of marrying Stonybrook, and that I was at liberty to call on her there? Would anything but poverty take her back to that den? Did I want her to send me a certified statement, sworn to before a notary, of her conduct and habits and thoughts? Must I have an embossed invitation to call on a girl who had promised to be my wife and never took back the promise? The fact is, I'm an atrophied jackass, there's no doubt of it, without a jackass' ability to kick, or I'd turn my propulsive forces on myself. Dear little heart, it isn't possible for her to be disingenuous or false and if she marries Mr. Stonybrook, I'll take her word for it he's a brick and make her a wedding present. If there is anything in this world that is certain, it is that I'm not worthy to marry her, for I'm a consummate, hair-splitting, mooning ass."

He got so indignant at himself that he wanted somebody else to share it, and went to Chapman naturally, but as he did not explain the situation fully to his friend, his friend did not enter into the denunciations with much spirit.

"I'm perfectly willing to acknowledge on general principles that you are a consummate jackass for the sake of brotherhood," said Chapman, "but may I be fried in my own oil if I can see any particular reason for cutting ourselves with knives and tearing out our hair today."

But in a very little while Carteret's' effervescent reaction died out and he began to act like a serious lover. Some recollection of Manuella coming down the grand staircase clinging to Mr. Stonybrook, flashed upon his mind, but he put it away and said; "Tomorrow's Easter Sunday. I'll send her a bunch of violets and then I'll call. There's something propitious in Easter—it's a holy renaissance."

Then he looked at his $1,000 bill; curiously wondered if it wouldn't be the proper thing to send it back, but doubled it up again, put it in his pocket and saw Mr. Job Ackerman's letter lying unread on his table.

He found it to be a blunt and friendly business letter, saying that the writer had been twice to see him when in the city and had found him to be absent both times from the studio. It earnestly requested that Carteret would make an appointment, as Captain Ackerman wished to see him on private business of importance to both of them. He would call again if an hour was set, or Mr. Carteret might run up to Coe's Grove, as the weather was fine now, and he was so much younger than his friend and did not have the spring rheumatism in his foot.

Carteret answered this letter, briefly informing Capt. Ackerman that he hoped to be able to get away in a day or two and would run up to Coe's Grove and see him. He also wrote a compact business letter to Miss Enniston, acknowledging the receipt of the money and having accomplished this duty, he gave himself unreservedly to anticipations of the morrow. And when the morrow came, he had calmed down and was much more of a reasonable being than he had been for some time. He heard the Easter bells ringing while he was eating his breakfast, and the glad spring sunshine had in it for him a subtle promise. He went to the studio in a new spring suit and noticed on his way, the children carrying flowers to church. He bought an expensive, but modest bunch of dewy violets and sent a messenger to the Terrace with it as a sort of forerunner, and then about nine o'clock he set out himself. The effusive and impatient lover had now cooled into the reflective man who was presented with a delicate problem. He was going to meet once more the woman who had in some way been estranged, or at least separated from him, and now that he was to see her, there was really nothing to warrant him in believing that she had not seen the folly of their little romance, or that she only wished to appear courteous and kind in carrying out her deliberate intention of marrying a man who could provide for her, while preserving amicable relations with the man who couldn't. Something told him that she would not be back in her old and humble quarters if her relations with Mr. Stonybrook had not been disturbed, and there was in his mind a hopeful kind of suspicion that Mrs. Hannige had been carrying on a systematic deception in Mr. Stonybrook's interest. But he did not give his mind with any kind of seriousness to these problems as he walked across Union Square. The glad influence of the morning was not provocative of grave reflection and despite the uncertain condition of his mind, his sensibilities insisted on singing as he went along.

The result of two forces acting upon him from within and without was not a clearer understanding but a more vigorous executive determination.

Nineteenth street was basking in the morning sun. Its inhabitants were out on the pavement in their best clothes. A group of men stood round the entrance to the Terrace and Fanny Grinch was leaning out of her window. He heard the sarcastic remarks in the group as he passed through and began to mount the dirty and gloomy stairs. It only needed one flight to color his mood. "Good heavens," he said to himself. "Why should the diamond go back to its mine after being cut and polished? I suppose she will be there at the window as I first saw her, in dishabille, perhaps doing the housework like a maid. What a misfortune!" Then when the artist had expressed his sensibility, the visitor reflected that he did not remember which floor it was that she was on, and so he had to ask Cokey Tim, who was holding some kind of a mass meeting in one of the upper hallways, surrounded by all the small boys of the establishment.

In reply to his question the whole convention burst into information—that he had to go up another flight, and proceeded to accompany him—some of them shinning up the balusters, so that when Mrs. Sitwhite opened her door in response to his knock, she found a rather elegantly dressed young gentleman standing in a group of eager and impertinent youngsters, which group when she sheltered her visitor behind her closed door, let out a concerted whoop of derision and defiance and then swept down the stairs.

Colin Carteret suddenly found himself facing a most unexpected scene. Seated on two wooden chairs were the junior Sitwhite's, bolt upright in clean pinafores, evidently on exhibition, in a suppressed condition, for just in front of them on a table was a paper of candy, the ends of the sugar sticks temptingly obtruding from the package.

As if interrupted in some kind of class examination, there stood by the window in attractive and dainty street dress, a young lady whose smile of instruction was arrested by a stare of astonishment, and whose spring-like attire was heightened by a bunch of violets on her breast. In the middle of the room stood Bob Holbrook with his hat in his hand as if he had just been going when the new visitor arrived.

"To think," said Mrs. Sitwhite, "that a gentleman can't call without all the young ones of the neighborhood insulting him at my very door."

"How do you do, Mr. Carteret?" said Manuella, pleasantly, from her vantage ground at the window. "I hope the boys in the hallways did not annoy you."

Mrs. Sitwhite dusted a chair with her apron and gave it to him and he sat down, while she went on with her running comments on the neighbors' children.

And Manuella took up her conversation with Mr. Bob Holbrook.

"Now, I'm sure," she said, "that you can say from the bottom of your heart that you never saw better-behaved children. Did you?"

"No, I never did," replied Bob, putting his hand on his heart. His interest in the children was somewhat disturbed by the new comer. "Why, they're just like two white mice—nobody'd ever know they was about and I wouldn't care a rap if they was. Why, I just like children as if I was a father."

"I knew you wouldn't object if you saw how good and quiet they were," said Manuella; "and once they get where there's fresh air, it will make angels of them. I'll bring them over some morning and buy some of those sugar monkeys. Tell Mrs. Holbrook I'll run in in the morning and see her; will you?"

"Yes," said Bob, backing to the door. "Bring the kids over; the old woman'll take to 'em and everything will be all right."

The moment he had bowed himself out, the two youngsters sprang from their seats and made a simultaneous dive for the paper of candy, with a warwhoop. Mrs. Sitwhite sprang between them and there was a struggle.

Manuella regarded it a moment with the sense of the ridiculous making itself manifest on her face. Then she turned to their visitor, who was beginning to feel somewhat foolish, and said:

"I am going to church, Mr. Carteret. Would it be convenient for you to accompany me as far as the building? It is such a beautiful morning I am anxious to get out. Grandpa is indisposed and we thought it best not to disturb him."

"I shall only be too delighted," said Carteret, as he got up and followed her.

As they were going down the stairs she said, with admirable composure, as she pulled on her gloves: "I ought to explain the absurd scene to you. Mrs. Holbrook has part of a cottage-house to let uptown that I am anxious to get for my aunt, and I was trying to win Bob Holbrook over to my views of the children. It was an absurd exhibition to make to you."

"It would have been more interesting I dare say," replied Carteret, "had I known the plot. Did you get my answer to your letter?"

"O, yes, of course," quite unconcernedly.

He was at her side. He could smell the faint odor of the violets. She was self-possessed and even elegant and some kind of invisible barrier had come between them. It was as if the girl that he knew a few weeks ago had been transformed into an independent lady. He would not for the world have dared to call her Manuella.

"Yes," she said, "I got it. I was anxious that you should know what I only discovered by accident myself, that Mrs. Hannige had deceived us both. She never told me that you called."

"It seems to me," remarked Carteret, "that it did not require Mrs. Hannige, to tell you that I *must* call."

"I certainly looked for you," she said, without recognizing the reproach in his speech. "You had got to be such a visitor I mean, we were so accustomed to have you look in, that when your visits suddenly stopped, we hardly knew what to think. My letter was merely to let you know that I could not be so discourteous as you must have thought me."

"Was that all you wrote the letter for?" asked Carteret.

But they had come to the doorway of the Terrace and had to pass through the knot of men and women, so the answer was deferred if not killed outright.

Their passage made a sensation. There was a general paralysis of admiration among the men, one or two of whom lifted their hats in involuntary tribute as she went through. A subdued but audible murmur of wonder followed her as she passed, and one fellow remarked: "Isn't that rather high-priced for the Terrace?" The Grinches leaned so far out of their window to see, that one of the men extended a brawny hand to them, with the implication that he would assist them to step out.

The moment that Carteret was out of hearing of the group he said, with the influence of the situation strong upon him: "Will you tell me, Miss Castleton, why you came back to live in this place?"

"Oh, I couldn't in a moment," she said promptly. "I suppose it appears very dreadful to you, but it has its advantages."

"Really?" asked Carteret.

"Yes, it is homely, vulgar, if you like, but it has few disappointments, no allusions, no nonsense. It's plain and hard and honest. Besides I'm only temporarily here to look after my aunt."

He felt his heart sink in spite of him.

"O," he remarked with a strong effort to give a flavor of satisfaction to the monosyllable. "Yes, temporary, I see."

"Have you seen our old friend Mr. Kleinbacker lately?" she asked, cutting off all further questions about her future intentions.

"Yes, I met him accidentally one night at the theatre. We had a few minutes' conversation, but his insufferable vanity and impudence offended me, so I got away as soon as possible. He informed me that he was in love with you."

Miss Castleton laughed. "I have no reason to doubt it," she said. "He was treated very much as you were by Mrs. Hannige, but he was not so easily driven from the field, for he bribed the girl Florry and got into the basement, making her believe he was in love with her, and began prying into Mrs. Hannige's affairs and mine."

"To some purpose," said Carteret, "evidently, for he told me that you were going to marry Mr. Stonybrook."

"Did he?"

"He certainly did, with an air of authority," replied Carteret, and then, as the newspapers say, Mr. Carteret paused for a reply.

"That's odd. I wonder what *he* knew about it."

"I don't know. I don't know what anybody knows about it. I suppose the only way to get at it will be to take Mr. Stonybrook by the throat and choke it out of him."

"That appears to me to be not only rude but unnecessary," she said.

They were on the Second avenue now. It was thronged with church-goers and Stuyvesant Park was alive with a warm holiday air. He had no knowledge of where she was going. He let her indicate her own course and she went slowly across the park toward St. George's. A fretting consciousness that he was not gaining an inch in his conversation was mingled with a reminiscent tenderness. Could it be that this handsomely dressed and self possessed woman was the girl in the chip hat of yesterday? What would she say if he dared now to ask her to sit down on one of the benches in the park, as he had done once before, and let him pour himself out to her. What would he not give to feel her clinging to him as she clung to him that morning when they met the crowd on Broadway? It was not a weak sentimentalism that prompted this passing idea. It was perhaps only the acknowledgment, now that he had got at her side, that she was farther away than ever.

Presently they were at the church steps and a dismal conviction that he would have to leave her with no reason for seeing her again, and no sort of satisfaction in having seen her, took possession of him. She had not shown the slightest desire to explain anything or to renew their former intimacy. Her manner was guardedly that of an old acquaintance who wished to retain his respect. He must accept this as the result of the interview, lift his hat and let her go on to her devotions.

But why should he?

They stood at the portal. She had one foot upon the step. The crowd was moving past them into the church. To stop was to attract attention. He hesitated and put his hand to his hat.

She turned partly round with a look of faint surprise. But she said nothing.

"I beg your pardon," he said, "you invited me to the church door."

She put her hand gently on his arm. The tips of her gloved fingers just touched his coat sleeve, and at the same time she stepped up into the doorway, and a moment later they were entering the broad aisle. He found himself in a pew by her side. There was no longer any opportunity for conversation, and he gave himself up to his perplexed thoughts, steeped in a happy knowledge that she was close beside him and wafted by the music of the organ and the boys voices into a trance that had nothing devotional in it, and from which be was awakened by her offering to share the prayer book with him.

Something in the service touched him deeply and kindly, and he found himself listening to the words that came mellow and significantly across the great congregation.

The whole purport of the short sermon was Hope, and it was colored by all the sweet promptings of the awakening season. Then the assemblage stood up and sang a hymn, and he found himself holding the book with her and listening to her low rich voice mingling with the strains of praise.

But the service had no such sentimental effect upon her. When they came out, she said: "You don't go often to church?"

"No, I fancy one has to be led. It is possible to make me go often with a mere touch, I find. Must you go straight home?"

"Straight," she replied. "If you have anything to say to me you must say it as we walk back."

"I have so much to say that it would be impossible."

"What about?"

"About ourselves."

"Is it anything that you have ever said before?"

"Yes, I suppose it is, only made more urgent by misunderstandings and doubts."

"Have you doubts?"

"Have I? I am torn with them."

"Doubts of what?"

"Of everything, of you, of myself."

"I am sorry that you doubt me, Mr. Carteret, because if you do, there is nothing you can say that I would care to hear. Had we not better talk about something else? What did you think of Dr. Tyng's sermon?"

"If I did not doubt you, would you care to hear me?"

"Isn't it somewhat ungenerous to ask me that, when I have spent so much time listening to you? Please don't accuse me or excuse yourself."

"But a word of explanation is only fair—if some things can be explained. I thought when I saw you coming out of the Academy of Design, leaning on Mr. Stonybrook and looking so confidingly into his face, that I could never forgive you for going to see the picture for the first time with him."

"Yes, I went with him," said Manuella, "because I wanted to coax him to buy the picture, and a rude woman insulted me while we were looking at it. Do you insist upon going over these things? They are not pleasant."

"I only insist upon showing you that there was some reason for my being hurt. You will not let me explain, and you will not yourself admit anything. Why did you write me that letter?"

"Because I thought you had been wronged by Mrs. Hannige."

"And do you mean to say that you did not know that I was wronged before?"

"No. I should have told you."

"Then it is not true that Mr. Stonybrook wanted to marry you?"

"It *is* true."

"But you do not want to marry Mr. Stonybrook?"

"Mr. Carteret," she said, "my wants are many and it seems very absurd of me to tell you what they are. I don't think you should even ask me about them."

"But there was a time when you did not wait for me to ask. You commenced by wanting a brother."

"And I ended by not getting him. Perhaps if I want Mr. Stonybrook it will end the same way. Why bother about it?"

"Because," said Carteret, "I might have some rights in the case. I want to find out."

"Well, that would be better than wrongs."

"Yes," said Carteret. "Better to defend. What makes you say you didn't get a brother? What was it you did get?"

"I have been asking myself that question for some time. Don't you think you had better let me go home alone from this corner? It's only a step and there's such a rude lot about the door."

"All the more reason why I should see you to your room," replied Carteret. "I positively refuse to leave you here."

She made no reply to this, and they walked along.

"It's astonishing what a change a few months make in character," said Carteret presently. "Last fall 'you were a child and I was a child in our kingdom by the sea.' Now," he hesitated a moment, "well, now you are—we're both independent. I suppose you know that my picture—I ought to say *our* picture, has made me?"

"But Miss Enniston bought it."

"So she did. I couldn't help it."

"But I wouldn't let Mr. Stonybrook buy it because he criticised it," said Manuella.

At this naive, uncommercial acknowledgment the young man, felt as he had often felt before—like catching her in his arms. But this time she kept him safely enough at a respectful distance; besides, they were at the door of the Terrace.

It was very delightful to see Mrs. Sitwhite push her children into the kitchen and get in herself after them, when the young people entered the room. She instinctively felt that the proper thing to do was to protect them in their interview from third parties. Carteret sat down with his cane between his legs, while Manuella took off her hat and various other outdoor garnishments. "There," she said, as she tried to unpin the bunch of violets, "I didn't thank you for the flowers."

"Of course not. I didn't tell you that I sent them."

"You didn't need to," said Manuella, who had turned her back to him and was trying to detach the bouquet from her dress. She apparently had some difficulty with it or with something in its vicinity, for it was at least a minute before she extricated it, and when she did and turned round to lay it on the table, a folded bit of paper fell to the floor and Carteret picked it up. It was such a worn and soiled little jacket that it attracted his attention and he stood holding it in his hand with a smile on his face.

"Don't open it," said the girl, holding out her hand at the same time, impulsively.

He handed it to her and he noticed that the blood had come into her face with a suffusing magnificence.

"Ah," he said, with the stupid thoughtlessness of a boy, "Stonybrook."

She drew herself up a trifle. "Yes," she replied.

"And sacred," added Carteret.

"Yes," she repeated.

He gave a little shrug, got up, went to the window, bit his lip and then turning round suddenly, said, "Manuella, there isn't the slightest reason in the world why you should deceive me. Upon my honor, I believe that you have made me unselfish enough to see you married to Stonybrook without a murmur, if I thought he could make you happy. If you have ever thought that he could, I'll be hanged if I'll not be the brother I promised, and help you, if I die for it. Only tell me."

She looked at him a moment Then she picked up the folded paper and handed it to him.

He spread it out. It was worn at the folds so that it almost dropped apart, and it was full of pinholes where it had been fastened in her bosom. It was his page of verses, written that dreary night in the studio.

He looked up from the frayed sheet that he held in his hand; the woman he loved was leaning against the only other window in the room with her back to him. Her pensive attitude recalled a similar scene long ago a sudden light came into him.

She had carried this bit of paper all these weeks in her bosom, and her confusion was only occasioned by the fear that he would know it.

He got up and went to her. He put his arm about her. She did not shrink. "My darling," he said, "I'll never ask you another word of explanation. I'm not going to ask you any more questions now, but I'm going to tell you something. You are mine. All the Stonybrooks in the world can't have you. You are fated to marry the biggest booby on earth, there's no help for it—the decree is gone forth. I pity you, my brave and long suffering girl, but I shall do my duty."

Her head was averted, but before she knew it, he had pressed her face gently round and kissed her. Then he rushed out carrying the little splash of a tear on his cheek.

CHAPTER LIV.
MR. STONYBROOK IS REJECTED.

To kiss and make up in this always natural and therefore always unexpected manner, was to produce a change in the condition of affairs that would affect several persons in succession.

Manuella was at first inclined to be very severe with herself for what looked like a cowardly and weak relinquishment of a woman's prerogative to make a man penitent and solicitous, and she even went so far as to plan a little scheme by which Carteret should not see her for a week, in order to punish him mildly for jumping so preposterously at the truth. It is needless to say, the scheme did not work, for he was over to see her the next morning before she had got Mrs. Sitwhite's youngsters into subjection. Then began the long explanations, in all of which the young man was the effusive and humble self-accuser and the young woman was the forgiving agency, and the young man, in spite of all that she told him of the Stonybrook experience and she told him everything with straightforward and fearless candor, felt that it was all his own fault.

It took only a few interviews of this kind to bring matters to the inevitable crisis, and one day Carteret said, "There is but one honest and decisive thing to do. You must become my wife. We should never have encountered any of these difficulties if I had married you long ago. The more I think of it, the more I am convinced that all our troubles have sprung from my dilatory and timid nature."

But the young lady was proof against all his appeals for rash action. She let him lavish his endearments upon her. She did not deny that he had won her heart, but she was not going to rush off and do something unbecoming in a Castleton to accommodate his impatience, and although she never uttered a reproach or whispered a doubt, Carteret felt in spite of himself that he was put on probation again.

He came at the subject every time they met, but with all his arguments, it never got any farther than a promise on her part that it should take place in the summer, if everything went right. Whereupon he had declared in a burst of eloquence—"And everything shall go right, my dear. You shall have your own way and I shall take all the long weary months till summer to make myself better fit, and you will struggle along without anything to help you but your own brave little heart, and I'll come to see you in this God-forsaken garret and keep asking myself why, if you are mine, I haven't got you. I'll do it in spite of reason and sense and comfort and expediency, because you command it, for I'll be hanged if you shall have all the martyrdom of duty to yourself."

And then Manuella would beam all over with an absurd glow of happiness at this boyish fervor. But one day she announced with a tone of disappointment that the Holbrook cottage had been given up. Mrs. Holbrook couldn't let them have it before the first of July, as the owner intended to stay in it till that time.

The prospect of remaining in the Terrace all summer was discouraging enough even to the most rigid sense of duty, and Carteret at once proposed that as soon as the daisies were out, they go back to the aqueduct. He would write to Mr. Manser at once, or better still, he would go up and see him—the old woman would be delighted to have them back, and he'd get Chapman to go with them and so make up a little artistic community, "and Chapman, don't you know, wouldn't be in the way a bit."

It was a seductive idea certainly when placed against the depressing prospect furnished by the Terrace, and although Manuella did not say much about it, she allowed it to enter her mind and Carteret's constant pleas and pictures influenced her.

Something of the same persuasive urgency in the young man won Chapman over from the Maine woods. The Penobscot was too far from a market, don't you know. The very acme of smartness was to secure the isolation and beauty of the Maine woods with the advantage of accessibility and he just knew the spot.

But it must not be supposed that Mrs. Hannige and Mr. Stonybrook acquiesced in this arrangement of affairs without a protest. Manuella had written a letter to Mr. Stonybrook, thanking him for all his kindness and informing him that she had thought over his generous proposals seriously and had come to the conclusion that she could not accept them without doing great injustice to herself and greater injustice to him. She had made up her mind, after much painful thought upon the subject and she knew Mr. Stonybrook too well, she said, to fear that he would try to influence her against her convictions or turn her from what was her obvious duty.

When Mr. Stonybrook read all this, it had anything but a soothing effect upon him. He cursed a good deal and went to Mrs. Hannige with it. It did not take long for that lady, when their heads were together, to enlighten him upon some points. She attributed the girl's actions to the influence which that abominable young scapegrace and painter had over her. "As long as she was here under my eye," said the confident lady, "nothing of this kind happened. Why, bless your soul, the fellow is engaged to one young lady already, that I know for certain, and how many more he's promised to marry, the Lord only knows. He'll just fool that girl to his heart's content and then be making up to somebody else. What idiots girls are."

"You don't think, then," said Mr. Stonybrook, "that this is as serious as it looks."

"I think just this," replied Mrs. Hannige, "that she's just soft enough to be turned round anybody's finger and if you talked to her right and she was told what kind of a risk she was running and was kept out of the influence of that reckless young man, she'd be another sort of person."

"You must get me her address at once," said Stonybrook.

"Yes," answered Mrs. Hannige, "I'll get it out of John. He must know it and he's just come back."

Then Mr. Stonybrook wrote a crafty letter to Miss Castleton. He assumed the tone of injured innocence and reminded her that her conduct for months had led him to make serious plans and build precious hopes, and she had no right to dismiss his claims in such a flippant and inexplicable manner. He was at least entitled to see her and have an explanation from her own lips for she had given him some right to urge his claims.

This letter Manuella received and turned over immediately to Carteret, showing him at the same time a copy of her own letter to Mr. Stonybrook.

Carteret was not as indignant as she had expected, but a good deal more decided.

"My dear," he said, "of one thing there can be no sort of doubt now; you are my promised wife and Mr. Stonybrook has not a shadow of excuse for annoying you. Let me take care of this matter. Don't you think of it again and don't write any more letters."

"What will you do?" she asked.

"Nothing," he said, "that you would not have me do. I am going to explain the facts to this gentleman."

She tried to dissuade him, but he was gently firm and marched straight to Mrs. Hannige's.

A strange girl let him in. But Mrs. Hannige, who was at the end of the hall, recognized him immediately, and called out—

"Why, Mr. Carteret, how do you do? You're a perfect stranger."

As Carteret strode past the girl to the rear of the hallway, Mrs. Hannige, with her greatest complacency, said—

"I didn't think you'd ever come near us again. Of course you didn't come to see Miss Castleton this time. I s'pose I'm the favored party."

"Madame," said Carteret, with most metallic dignity, "I wish to have a few words with Mr. Stonybrook. Will you hand the gentleman my card, and say I am waiting?"

She took the proffered card mechanically, and just at that moment a hearty voice from the diningroom called out—

"Hallo, Carteret, come in here."

It was John Wilder, who got up and extended his hand as Carteret entered. A few words of greeting passed and Wilder said: "You were asking for Mr.

Stonybrook; defer your interview with him until you have had a talk with me. I have something of importance to say to you. I want to talk to Mr. Carteret, Molly; shut the door."

Mrs. Hannige reluctantly obeyed her brother, but an obtrusive curiosity and much amazement accompanied the act.

"Did you get a letter from Captain Ackerman?" asked Wilder, the moment they were alone.

"Yes, I did."

"Have you seen him?"

"No, I promised him to run up there, but I haven't had the chance."

"Suppose we walk over to the club, they know me there; I've got something to say to you."

Carteret hesitated and Wilder added: "As what I have to say to you is entirely in your own interest, I think you can safely let the Stonybrook matter wait until you have heard me."

As they crossed the street Wilder remarked: "Molly is over-curious and she intended to listen to what I had to say. As there is not good reason why she should know it, and several good reasons why she should not, I thought it best to be by ourselves."

When they were seated in the club house, he continued: "Captain Ackerman has something of the utmost importance to tell you. I prefer to have him give you the information, but I can say to you that it relates to that cup."

Carteret gave a start. Some flash of premonition told him that the odious cup was to appear again the moment his hopes of Manuella were brightened.

Wilder observed the look of annoyance and impatience.

"Don't be superstitious and foolish," he said. "The matter of the cup is no longer a mystery. It is worth a great deal of money, and as some sort of claim on your part is going to grow out of the affair, you ought to take a serious interest in the matter. Mr. Ackerman will explain to you who the real owners are."

"But," exclaimed Carteret, "my interest in it is a fiction. I don't care a—"

"You're interest may be worth a small fortune to you, if the cup is recovered by Captain Job Ackerman."

"My interest?"

"Yes, that is what Captain Ackerman wishes to see you about. I have only been back here two days, but I have learned sufficient to make me believe that the cup will be recovered."

"You amaze me."

"It is sufficient for me to tell you at this time, that I shall do my best to get the property back into Captain Ackerman's hands, in which case all interests can be adjusted and yours are safe. You can assist me somewhat."

"I?"

"Yes. What are you going to do with that girl?"

Really, Mr. Wilder, that's a most extraordinary question."

"Are you going to marry her?"

"Yes, sir; I am. And as she is my affianced wife, I don't intend to have her annoyed. That's why I wanted to see Mr. Stonybrook."

"O," remarked Wilder, with an imperturbable smile, "that was it, was it? Well, why don't you marry her?"

"Now see here," cried Carteret, jumping up, "there is a nasty imputation in your questions that I don't like. By heavens I'd marry her to-morrow, if she would give way for an hour to my impatience."

"What did she go off down to that tenement house again for?"

"To get rid of Mr. Stonybrook," Carteret promptly answered. "You can put up a good deal of money on the theory that I didn't want her to go there, and would like to get her out of it."

"Why don't you take her up to that place on the aqueduct again? Don't fly off, if you were up there you'd be very apt to keep your eye on that stream of water while at work. That's one reason. Another is, that there's going to be trouble in the city this summer. That's another reason. I don't want you to be kicking up a shindy with Mr. Stonybrook, as you're pretty sure to do. That's another reason. He's a most exemplary lodger whatever else he may be, and Mrs. Hannige deserves a little consideration from me. If you go up there he will not be likely to annoy you any more and I suppose you can get married up there as well as anywhere else."

"I wish to heaven I could get her away at once," Carteret said thoughtfully.

"O, there will not be much trouble about it if you go the right way to work," Wilder answered rather quizzically. "You see, my young friend, I am what they call a civil officer and I want to keep things as civil as I can in my own immediate circle of acquaintances. You're just hotheaded enough to go to punching Mr. Stonybrook's head and Mr. Stonybrook is just discreet enough to call upon me to preserve the peace. I'd rather you would regard my feelings and domestic relations, and at the same time preserve my sincere interest in your welfare."

John Wilder was looking in his cold, implacable way at Carteret and there was no mistaking his meaning. But seeing that Carteret offered no sort of objection, his manner changed and they fell into a more amiable colloquy, Carteret finally going away in a much better mood than when he entered the club.

It is doubtful if all his coaxing would have induced Manuella to leave her sister and go into the country at this time, if Capt. John Sitwhite had not walked in one day, very brown with exposure and very hearty with liquor. He was home on a furlough and the scenes which ensued were not at all to Manuella's taste. John intended to have a good time while his furlough lasted and it was not difficult to get his wife to join him in celebrating his return. Manuella at this time had formed a habit of walking over to the studio building in the afternoons, so that Carteret could walk back with her. One day she told him that she would have to leave the Terrace now for it had become unbearable and Cynthia no longer needed her assistance. Carteret immediately proposed that she get her grandfather ready and go up to the Manser's to board for the summer. She offered a few trivial objections, as was becoming, and then made a delightful show of being convinced by unanswerable logic. Carteret ran up to see Mr. Manser and came back with fervid descriptions of the country and the hospitality of the old folk. Mr. Manser, he reported, had got to be quite a local antiquary. "He told me," said Carteret, "that General Washington when he retreated from White Plains, crossed the Pocantico just below the old man's house and threw into the little river a lot of English plunder, including a number of silver cups." "Why," said the old man, "the crick's full of 'em; there's been two took out jest over yander beyond the gate."

Meanwhile the days were getting warm, for the summer was come. But these lovers, engrossed in their own happiness, thought of little but themselves. Carteret forgot or postponed the visit to Captain Ackerman, he even neglected his chum, Otis Chapman. He worked at his easel in a hilarious way, it is true, and managed to finish up two or three commissions, but his ears were alert for the step of Manuella and his thoughts were as often at the Terrace as on his canvas.

One morning Chapman said to him, "I was up at the Hardynge's last night and what do you think I learned? Miss Enniston told me that Col. Hardynge was going to send his family into the country and shut his house up for the summer."

"Something he does every season," said Carteret carelessly.

"No," continued Chapman, "he doesn't. It is so unexampled for him that the young ladies have been discussing it, and I learned enough from Miss Enniston to make it pretty sure that the Colonel is afraid to have his folks here this summer and has been advised by Judge Sanger to send them away. It seems that the politicians predict a regular French revolution in our streets."

Wilder's warning recurred to Carteret and heightened his anxiety to get Manuella away, but the days went on and trifles light as air interfered with their departure.

CHAPTER LV.
SOWING THE WHIRLWIND.

During the month of June, 1863, the Astor House in New York was a scene of continual and intense political excitement, such as probably will never be witnessed in that historic hostlery again. The bitterness, the magnitude, the awful cost of the tremendous national conflict now passing through the darkest hours that precede the dawn, were all reflected here in the martial, commercial and political elements of an anxious and heterogeneous mob, that filled the corridors day and night and made the rotunda echo with the blasphemy of the army, the braggadocio of local partisans, the fears of merchants and the enthusiasm of patriots. At no time in the progress of the great civil war, were the prospects of success for the Government so gloomy or the predictions of the anti-war party so confidant and so threatening. Disaster after disaster had befallen the Federal forces. To Milroy's almost utter extinction at Winchester had been added the defeat of Fredericksburgh and the crowning fiasco at Chancellorsville. General after general had been displaced in the desperate effort of the Government to find some capable leader of the Union forces. The Thirty-seventh Congress, at almost the last moment of its existence, had passed the conscription act, and the loyal States, already drained of their sons, were to see the draft enforced which enrolled every citizen between the ages of eighteen and forty-five, in the ranks, to carry on what appeared to be a vain struggle against superior military wisdom and an invincible army.

Everywhere were heard the legal and authoritative protests against the conscription. One of the judges of the Supreme Court of the State of New York, had declared it unconstitutional, and another had stigmatized it as an infamy framed to take away the State rights of the citizen. The Governor of the State was an open and able opposer of it. And while these partisan conflicts of opinion were fanning the embers of popular opposition, the news came that the victorious army of General Lee, flushed with its success over Hooker, was marching north. It was in vain that the loyal ears listened for some faint thunders of hope in the west. Gen. Grant had settled down apparently to stubborn inactivity, held like a bull dog at bay before Vicksburg. Banks was silent before Port Hudson and Rosecrans had spent half a year, inactive, in Eastern Tennessee.

At such a time, all that was weak and craven and ignoble lifted its head. Every petty wrong and trivial sacrifice cried out with sharp voice against the folly of abstract principles and the fatuity of patriotic sentiments, and the baser elements of a dense community, ordinarily held in its darkest corners by the suppressive unanimity of public opinion, began to prick its ears. Some of the grannies of a past political expediency, long since forgotten, mounted the rostrum to dwell upon the blood and the wrongs of national defense. Ex-President Franklin Pierce in New Hampshire within sight of the battle field of Concord, gathered about him all the fatuous and imbecile patriots of his kind and preached the logic of submission and the beauty of national disintegration, leaving in his printed address, the imputation that honest men had ceased to be rational beings and that it was the part of Christian meekness for Philadelphia and New York to turn the other cheek also to the chivalrous Gen. Lee and his advancing hordes.

It is necessary also to bear in mind, before one can understand the feverish condition of men in such a representative meeting-place as the Astor House then was, that Wall street partook of the excitement. The fluctuations in the market, the rise of gold and the rapid change in fortunes, imparted a portentous character to the commercial atmosphere. And under all this was a subtone of social apprehension. All the militia was called away from the city. The Park barracks held only a recruiting squad, and no one could tell what was to be the outcome of the violent antagonisms now making themselves felt.

The steps, the vestibules, the corridors and the rotunda of the Astor House were even more than usually crowded with restless and shifting groups, on this morning.

Streams of eager and anxious men were pouring in and out. The babble of voices in the passageway and the still louder confusion in the rotunda, could be heard at the portal. It was very easy to see by a moment's observation of this center, that public excitement ran high. Animated knots of men, in heated discussion, blocked all the entrances, and merchants, politicians, deputy marshals, United States officers and city officials, speculators, recruiting agents, and army contractors, mingled in a strange mob within. Conspicuous in one of the groups, by his portly person and his florid face and authoritative air, was Judge Sanger. He was in animated conversation and he used a newspaper that was rolled up in his hand to emphasize his remarks.

Not very far away was his son, Dr. Follen Sanger, in another group. He was much more grave and reserved, and listened to a violent speaker with a thoughtful face. Over at one of the lunch counters, was John Sitwhite in a blue army dress, eating a piece of pie with a fork and laughing loudly at a story which a brother soldier was telling him. John Sitwhite had been ordered to report at the Park barracks for recruiting duty.

If this part of the house was throbbing with excitement, the other and remoter portions were choked with transient guests and almost equally animated with coming and going people. In a room on the second floor at the corner of the two principal passages, which commanded a view of the great staircase, sat Plonski busily writing at a handsome table, which was covered with letter paper, envelopes, telegraph blanks and newspapers. He had taken off the silk cap which he usually wore when in doors, for the room was warm and his bald head was moist with perspiration. He had grown visibly older in the months that had elapsed since the reader first saw him. There were new lines in his dark face and the eager alertness of his glance was subdued to one of stealthy and wary intensity. He wore heavy, iron-rimmed spectacles which added to the sombre aspect of his face, and his hand, as it held the pen, showed the long, sinewy and snaky fingers that were curiously indicative of the man, in their delicacy and bloodless hue. He was dressed in a loose blouse, negligently thrown back and near him on the floor, was a small trunk partly open, as if the papers on the table had been taken from it. Seated on a stool by the side of the door that opened into the hallway, sat what appeared to be a servant or attendant, and whose appearance indicated that he might have been pulled from one of the barricades in Paris or hunted up in a gypsy community of Bohemia. The creature was not over twenty and his demeanor and attitude of steady watchfulness were those of an animal.

Plonski looked up at him and made a motion almost imperceptible with his hand that held the pen, and the man stepped, with an instant celerity, from the door to the table and received a bit of folded paper and some instructions given in a subdued voice and in what sounded like a Hungarian patois. He appeared to understand for he nodded his head with the animation of a Southern gipsy and immediately left the room without saying a word.

The moment he was gone Plonski threw down the iron spectacles on the table and getting up, turned the key in the door and then walked about the room indeterminately and nervously, occasionally wringing one hand in the other, or pulling spasmodically at his heavy moustache.

"Yes, yes, yes," he repeated in a querulously reflective tone, as if answering himself. "I ought to consider society." A bitter hard smile wrinkled the corners of his mouth. "Hunted like a felon from country to country; hated, persecuted and betrayed by society—I suppose I ought to kick away the firebrand that is lying on its threshold. Mm—m. Let it burn. The old edifice is rotten. The sleek, smiling hypocrites ought to be roasted out. The old rat can at least gnaw the matches when the household is asleep."

He grew more nervous as he moved about, bent over, but too full of unexpressed emotion to keep quiet. But he changed the action of wringing his hands to that of rubbing them together, as the current of his thought grew a trifle more exultant. "Millions—yes, millions, almost within my grasp—what need I care for society when my turn comes? Society will then fawn and flatter like the hound it is. They shall not outwit me—cunning idiots, they shall not. I will match cunning with desperation. I will meet power with violence. Money,

money is all I want—revenge comes with it and reparation. No, no, my lying friends, you do not know whom you are dealing with. I am not going to be flung aside when you are done with me."

He was interrupted at this point by a knock on the door. He opened it and Mr. Chanfleur entered followed by the attendant who had carried the note.

As usual, he was overheated, fussy and impatient.

"What do you want?" he asked, somewhat brusquely, as he took his hat off and began fanning his face with it. "I'm very busy—have you anything to tell me of importance?"

Plonski shut the door and locked it. "Yes," he replied. "You and Miramon are attempting to deceive me. I wanted to tell you that I know it."

"If you have made up your mind to that, you probably know what to do," said Chanfleur, rather contemptuously. "What the devil did you send for me for? Was it to tell me that?"

Plonski exhibited his nervous intensity in his manner rather than in his voice, as he replied:

"You can't afford to throw me overboard, after making me one of the principals. I thought perhaps if I called your attention to your own danger, you might hesitate."

At the word "danger," Chanfleur started perceptibly.

"You have begun to threaten," he said. "It's infernally tiresome to me. I didn't know you were a principal, and I wasn't aware that you were to be thrown overboard."

"You have made arrangements to have the pond in Westchester county drained. It can't be done till the fifteenth of next month, because the mill has a contract to complete and cannot do without water. Miramon did not think it politic to offer a sufficiently large sum to have it done before. The work is to be carried on systematically, and you expect to recover the lost property, but you did not tell me a word of this. I had to find it out for myself. Miramon has taken that man Wilder into the scheme and left me out. You have used me for all the dangerous and dirty work. I have been hunted and imprisoned in your service, and now, when you are about to seize the result of my work, you intend to sacrifice me."

Chanfleur turned impatiently toward the door, but stopped as Plonski added:

"It's a fight between us. I see that. You have treated me in a dastardly manner."

Chanfleur uttered an oath. "How much more money do you want?" he asked.

"Not a cent," replied Plonski sharply. "I've got all the money I want. I've demanded fair treatment."

"You never intended to deal fairly," said Chanfleur.

"Ha; Miramon told you that."

Chanfleur shrugged his shoulders and went to the door.

"You intend to be mischievous; very well. I only ask one thing of you. Don't bother me with your arrangements, and don't send this cur of your's after me again. If you've got any schemes of vengeance, go to Miramon with them. I don't want to be annoyed."

There was no mistaking his meaning or his manner. They were indicative of contempt, impatience and defiance. He had evidently come to the conclusion that Plonski was no longer valuable or dangerous, and his mingled impatience and impertinence were the direct results of pressing and precarious conditions in the money market, from which he had been summoned almost imperatively.

He had to stand at the door a moment, while Plonski unlocked it. In that moment he merely said: "When you get over your suspicions and want to talk sense, I'll hear you—if I have time."

He was gone. Plonski hesitated but a few seconds. There was a slight tremor in his lip, as he looked at the door which had let Chanfleur out. Then his manner suddenly changed. He spoke to his attendant quickly, in a foreign tongue, and they both began bundling the papers on the table and the few other articles that were scattered about the room into the trunk. There was apparently an understanding that their work in this room had come to an end; a careless hurry in their disposition of articles denoted it. There were upon the table several small handbills, printed in German and French. Plonski picked them out, folded them together, and handed them to his servant with a pantomime gesture. The man put the packet into an inside pocket of his coat, and then went on with his task. In a very few minutes their work was accomplished, and Plonski, after a hasty glance into the mirror, picked up a small hand satchel and, followed by the man, went to the office, paid his bill, got a cab, saw the trunk placed on it, and then drove rapidly away from the hotel.

The vehicle went up the Bowery as far as Houston street, and then turning east struggled through that long and choked thoroughfare toward the river.

This street was at that time and to some extent still is, one of the most distinctive boundary lines anywhere to be found in the metropolis. On one side of it for a mile open up all the thoroughfares of the densely populated district extending south to Grand street; so densely populated that the area between Houston and Grand streets includes three Police Precincts, the 10th, 11th and 13th. On the other side, extending north, are the comparatively new and broad avenues, numbered from one to three and alphabetically designated from A to D. Two phases of metropolitan development thus come together and almost overlap each other, topographically, here. On one side, the oldest and most wretched district, with its squat houses jammed together so tightly, as if by the pressure of life about them that they appear squeezed out of shape and awry; its innumerable dirty little shops and encroaching factories and extemporized work rooms; its almost impassable streets, barricaded with unused articles along the curbs, and its dirty, noisy life, presents old New York in its worst aspect. On the other side, the new thoroughfares with their tall tenements and their appearance of space and light, mark the later addition and the attempt to improve on the old.

It need not be said that none of these aspects of the city with their suggestions appealed to Plonski. He sat with his chin deep in his coat, grimly taciturn, but there was a wicked determination in his glittering eyes. The occasional delays, caused by the obstructions in the street, alone drew him out of himself to the immediate surroundings, and then only to exhibit a moment's nervous petulance of manner. Owing to the impediments it was some time before they reached the river section of this precinct, where the dwellings gave way to founderies and stables and coal heaps, and the street presented an almost impassable array of boilers, derricks and heaps of gas pipes, broken machinery and discarded building material. On the north side, between Goerck and Mangin streets, the vehicle drew up in front of a three story brick house which was plainly enough of a former era of architecture, for its peaked roof had once been covered with slate and had been repaired with strips of boiler iron, and its narrow panes of glass on the upper stories were flanked by shutters that had once been green. Across the lower entrance, was a small and faded sign bearing the inscription, "Hotel Villers. Wines and Refreshments."

Adjoining this house on the east was a long two-story and very much dilapidated wooden structure, whose square windows were boarded up and through whose open doors below one might see piled up in endless heaps old barrows, scrap iron and dilapidated vehicles. It was plainly a receptacle for such rubbish as the neighborhood afforded, and was used by some contractor for storing debris.

Plonski entered the Hotel Villers by a hall door, whose worn sill was level with the street, and whose old brass knocker was a veritable relic. It had one other entrance which had been made from a window into a door, and which led to Villers' little wine room. It was filled half way from the top with a green latticed blind, from behind which a middle aged man of lean and inflamed appearance, in his shirt sleeves and smoking a cigar, was watching him.

The moment Plonski opened the hall door this man opened another leading into the hallway from the wine room and met him face to face. The salutations were practical, brief and succinct.

"Have you got your key?" asked Villers, with the slightest possible accent.

"Yes," replied Plonski. "Did you find the girl?"

"All right. She was here herself. McCune will come when the gas is on. Lay low. The rest of 'em will be here first."

Plonski then went up the stairs, and the trunk having been brought to the door by his man, the cab rolled away.

On the second floor there was an old fashioned bedroom with two small windows in it looking down into the street. It was meanly but not uncomfortably furnished, and Plonski's actions showed that he was at home in it.

He untied and took off the heavy shoes from his feet and put on a pair of loose, well worn and flattened out slippers which he pulled from under a table. The change appeared to afford him a great deal of relief, for he moved about with more freedom. When his man came in dragging the trunk, Plonski addressed him imperatively without looking at him and the man, dropping the end of the trunk to the floor, put his hand into his inner pocket, drew forth the packet of papers Plonski had given him and placed them in his master's hand without the slightest manifestation of thought or emotion, although it was obvious that Plonski had made him carry the papers as a measure of precaution to himself, not desiring to have them found on his person had he, in any of the pressing contingencies of his movements, fallen into the hands of a United States marshal again.

There was something strangely like an animal in the obsequious watchfulness and automatic obedience of his companion, who kept his eyes on his master very much as a trick dog will. As Plonski moved about the place there was an apparently unconscious inclination of the man to follow him. Suddenly Plonski stopped, looked at him an instant and said something in a foreign tone, which sounded very much like the training master's permission to his performing brute to rest awhile. The fellow's swarthy face lit up, a gleam of sensual eagerness came into his eyes, and making some kind of a fawning obeisance, he started hurriedly off and disappeared into a smaller adjoining chamber.

The moment he was out of sight, Plonski went to an upright secretary bed that stood against the eastern brick wall of the house, gave it a pull, and it rolled easily and noiselessly away from the wall, disclosing a narrow, jagged-edged opening in the bricks, sufficiently wide to admit a large man who turned sidewise.

It was closed by an iron door on the inner side, upon which hung a long iron hook. Into this door he fitted a key, pushed it noiselessly open and stepped up through the narrow passage upon the second floor of the warehouse adjoining. He then put the iron hook into a staple in the bed, and pulling the door backward, had moved the bed to its former position. It was so dark when he had done this, that he had to stand still a moment to accustom his eyes to the gloom.

The place on which he stood was a great open loft at least seventy-five feet long, with the angles of its roof showing in heavy beams with here and there a tiny speck of light, like a bright point, indicating the condition of the shingled roof. Save for a narrow space of a few feet about the iron door, the floor was heaped with builders' "horses," scaffolding material, and lime barrels, so as to effectually prevent as if by barricade any approach from the eastern entrance, where there had once been a set of steps, but was now only a trap in the floor, and a loose block and tackle hanging over it. Through the passageway that had been left along the wall from the iron door to the rear floor, Plonski groped his way to a wooden partition which enclosed a room about twelve feet square. He opened an extemporized door of rough boards, lit a candle and found himself in an apartment that had been furnished with table and camp stools. There were two or three glasses on the table and a deal of tobacco and ashes. The unplaned walls of the room were smeared with color as if some chair painter or carriage jobber had rubbed his brushes there, and in one corner was a round gong or bell muffled with rags, but showing its unobstructed hammer attached to a wire on the wall.

When, some days afterward, this place was made a harbor for rioters and was captured by the police in what was one of the most romantic, as well as tragical episodes of the draft riots, it was found that this bell communicated with a lever under Viller's counter and that in case of danger he could ring the note of warning with his foot and not intermit his smiling service of drinks.

There is also a police story that at one time the patrolman on this beat got it into his head that there was something wrong going on in Viller's house, and insisted upon the proprietor taking him through the rooms. While he was making an examination of Plonski's apartment, a meeting was in session on the other side of the brick partition. By the merest impulse, he gave the bed a pull and disclosed the iron door.

"What's that?" he cried, striking it with his club and making a ringing reverberation.

"That," said Viller, "was made by a painter who worked in there and boarded in here, and I had the iron door put on when he went away, for I didn't want to be burned out when the bloomin' shed goes up, as it's sure to do some day. There ain't nobody been through that hole in a year, I'll swear; look at the dust." And he stooped down and drew his finger across the sill, leaving little furrows in an accumulated powder that was quite a sixteenth of an inch thick.

"No," says the officer, "that don't show any travel, does it?" Then he went away and four days afterward he was transferred to the 28th precinct and was killed in that fight with the river thieves at the foot of Spring street, known as the O'Marra Row. But Viller himself told this story afterwards to the chaplain at Sing Sing, to which place he was sent as one of the first fruits of the Whyo gang laid on the altar of law, and he added with a keen sense of pride in his own methods: "You see, I'd just salted that step with road dust, that I kept in a cushion. All I had to do was to knock the bag on either side o' the door, and it made everything sweeter'n wax."

Plonski had not been in this gloomy meeting place a great while before he was joined by four men, who came singly up Viller's stairs and passed through the opening in the wall. The first comer was a foreigner and looked like a Pole; his name was Lavinski. He was a crafty faced, cruel jawed, vulpine man in workman's attire and could not have been over thirty. He shook hands with Plonski and spoke to him in a subdued voice as they sat down at the table.

While thus engaged in conversation, they were joined by a third person; a stalwart, heavily bearded Frenchman, who spoke English and French alternately. He was addressed as Citizen Cremaillon and was known in Viller's wine room as the director of the first section of the American Socialists' Protective Union, an organization having its habitat somewhere in the dense quarter south of Houston Street and made up entirely of disgruntled and effervescent red Republicans from Paris. He was known to the police as the Butcher of Carlton Street, given to enormous drafts of red wine and to a lurid oratory that usually ended in a verse of the Marseillaise.

The three men had evidently been in the room before. They were familiar with it and fell at once into a consultation that needed no preliminaries. In this conference Plonski was the most reticent member. Cremaillon was one of those ignorant proletariats who are most explosive. Lavinski was cool, inquisitive and careful. He spread out the printed circulars upon the table and they discussed their probable effects with little variance of opinion, except that Cremaillon thought that there was not flame and thrill enough in them. They were appeals in German and Polish to brothers in chains and workingmen in poverty, to stand together now against the tyranny of conscription. Cremaillon appeared to think that if there was no conscription, there would be no trouble. Lavinski believed that the crisis had arrived and that the conscription was only an incident. Broadway needed the baptism of the barricades. It was the opportunity of the century. He took a copy of the morning *Tribune* from his pocket and pointed to an editorial which said: "There will be no organized opposition to the draft. Law will be enforced and those alarmists who are trembling at the departure of the State militia, are trying to make a sensation out of whole cloth."

These were men who bore in their natures the wrongs of centuries, but who were ignorant of the advance of the race. They betrayed the weakness of ignorance in the constant reliance upon a movement of the mass to improve the individual. Society under Cremaillon would be a melodramatic bureaucracy, plus force. Under Lavinski it would be revolution, minus wisdom. All of them were men with grudges rather than of wrongs. Their cries for equality were protests against advantages won and held by obedience, patience, conformity. They represented three dangerous factors in every community—greed, revenge, the cowardice of wrong-doing which seeks for strength in solidarity. But it was evident enough that there was no common plan, or even common purpose, in their consultation, only a common apprehension and a possible chance to effect their several schemes. They compared their resources, so to speak, but had no organizing skill to unite them. They represented three battalions of disgruntled and ignorant *sans culotte* whose instincts told them that some kind of a crisis had arrived and that the vigilance and the grip of civil authority were relaxing. They did not even know that an organized opposition to the draft was possible. They only knew that the elements of opposition burned all about them and that if they coalesced, revolution would break out and that revolution, in some way, was the grand opportunity.

Cremaillon counted twenty-two divisions of the French *solidarité* that met weekly in New York, but the organization was social first, political afterwards. It spent moments in dreams of barricades and hours in dancing the can-can. It would fight if it could vindicate the right of revolution and could wear *bonnets rouge*. Cremaillon said afterwards with a shrug, when he heard that an Irish mob had burned an orphan asylum: "*Mon Dieu*, what a waste of *éclat*. They might have blown up the spire of Trinity Church. It would have been the supreme sacrilege. These canaille are only capable of the violent, they cannot understand the beautiful."

It was doubtful to Plonski if the solidarity would be dangerous unless it had a good brass band to play the Marseillaise and a handsome cocotte to lead the procession. But it was equally apparent to Plonski that these excitable Frenchmen would fall in and swell the torrent when the freshet began.

Lavinski, who was the secretary of a council of the Knights of the Golden Circle, was governed by an intense hatred of all kinds of civil authority. It had been the enemy of his class for generations. His mother had died in Siberia and his father had been shot in Cracow. He had himself escaped from the mines. He showed the vindictiveness, the craft and the cowardice of one who has long been hunted, and unlike many of his countrymen, he saw in the American system, a social tyranny which needed only time to become a political tyranny as cruel as that of Russia. But it did not appear that the Knights of the Golden Circle had any well conceived plan of opposition to the Government. They were ripe material for a crisis, but their organization was made up of sore heads, various hued traitors, men who had been ruined by the war, disappointed small fry politicians and inbred ruffians or criminals who made common cause against law and order. Pessimists, anarchists, fatalists, fanatics, they were ready to struggle violently against society because it represented Fate.

In this common purpose both Plonski and Cremaillon shared, but neither of them betrayed by a thought that they sought to control or guide events. They merely wished to avail themselves of them.

The council, therefore, was indeterminate, vague and inquisitorial, until it suddenly received two more members. They were brought up to the door by Villers and shown in. They had evidently not been there before for they looked round inquiringly and unfamiliarly at the place. One was a heavily-built, muscular, and bull dog fellow, with brawny shoulders and brutal Celtic face, upon which he wore a heavy oiled moustache and out of which leered two blue, meaningless eyes. His clothes were of a showy, negligé sort, and his shining silk hat was set at a jaunty and defiant angle on his head. In his mouth, between his white teeth, he held the chewed remains of a segar whose end pointed upward toward his sprawling nose and made little gyrations as he masticated it. There was a heavy plated chain on his waistcoat and a monster seal ring on his hand. His face, dress, and easy swinging athletic gait proclaimed him at once the type of man seen nowhere but in New York; that order of political ruffian whose inherited pugnacity and incorrigibility, held down for generations in one country had sprung into unlicensed activity in another, and whose aptitudes bred of the fighting clanishness of a subjected peasantry have asserted themselves with all the viciousness of brute force in the partisanship and fellowship of our local politics. The one distinguishing trait of this order of man is an over-weening belief in muscular force and an organic inability to weigh any other. He is consequently forever a terror and a nuisance and forever a victim. He was accompanied by a much smaller man of entirely different build and manner, thin, white-faced, narrow-chested, and slightly bent, he had nevertheless, the air of a man of relentless purpose and intolerable bigotry. His mouth seemed frozen in a bitter expression of intolerance, and his flattened cheeks, destitute of color, conveyed the notion that his head had been subjected to some kind of pressure—say, of religious prejudice, that had operated like the compress put upon the skulls of the flathead Indians in infancy. His manner was obsequious but persistent, deliberate but sharp, subdued but intense, and there was in his action a constriction that betokened the clerical rather than the executive habit.

They came in together, the larger of the two announcing his approach by unrestrained and coarse remarks, the loudness of which caused an apparent protest of manner from those who were waiting. The moment the door was shut, he said:

"Well, byes, yez have a good rat hole.What the divil are yez afraid of?"

His companion paid no sort of heed to him. "Gentlemen," he said, "have you brought the papers?"

There was a general assent. The first speaker sat down with his legs under the table and his two elbows upon it, and took in the company with an impertinent glare as he chewed at his cigar stump. His companion, still standing, continued in a sharp and curiously raspish voice: "I brought Mr. Casey with me for personal protection. I have many enemies, he knows the fourth ward thoroughly."

"You bet I do," said Mr. Casey. "Better'n any man in it not barrin' yourself, Mr. Sweeney."

"The general meeting of the delegates from the constitutional leagues," continued Mr. Sweeney, "have decided to oppose the draft, as you know. I was appointed on the committee to ascertain what force we could depend on from the friendly societies outside of the league."

"Has the league determined to oppose the draft by force?" asked Plonski.

"There is no other way to oppose it," replied Sweeney.

"Then it means to fight the United States Government?"

"O, say," interrupted Casey, "you make me tired. Who's running the Government? Any way what's New York got to do with the Government? What we want, is to run ourselves. This nigger Government is got enough to do without tryin' to run New York—hey, Shorty?" and he laid a brawny hand on Lavinski's shoulder, and that rather fragile personage somewhat over assented to the proposition.

Mr. Sweeney paid no attention to the interruption, and Plonski turned himself slightly about with the mute determination not to recognize Mr. Casey in the conversation.

"The Government cannot enforce the draft," said Sweeney; "it has no means at its command to subdue a city like New York, and all we need is to make a show of resistance. If the Government accepts the issue, we put the consequences on the Government"

"And the consequences," said Plonski, "are?"

"Revolution and the overthrow of Government rule in New York," replied Sweeney. "We are anxious to know how far we can depend on your people in that case."

"There are," said Plonski, "from eight to ten thousand Poles, Bohemians, and Germans, who would be glad of the opportunity to oppose the existing social condition of affairs. They are ignorant of such a movement and are without arms. I don't think, of themselves, they could offer any sort of resistance to the authorities."

"Probably'd run quickern'll hell," said Casey.

"Of course," continued Sweeney, "it means war here in New York, and war on our side means using every element of the population for our purpose, that we can get. We count on fifty thousand able bodied men. The militia will be away. The police are half of them with us at heart. The city Government, with the single exception of the Mayor, cannot be depended upon by the Government at Washington. The signal of revolution will let loose a hundred thousand of the lower class, whose main incentive will be pillage. These are considerations that we have not thought it best to overlook, but to avail ourselves of. Two at least of the armories have been under close watch, and we think it will not be difficult to get possession of them by a sudden movement. You are to explain these facts to your countrymen, the time has come for the people of New York to take possession of New York for themselves. I don't feel like going into any further particulars till I hear from your sections. But we mean business and we want to know what you mean."

"Vive la liberte," cried Cremaillon.

"Bully for you, Frenchy," said Casey.

"You see," continued Sweeney, "that there is no child's play about this."

"No," remarked Plonski, "if what you call the lower classes, bent only on pillage, are to come into the game."

"O, well, if you object to that, you will probably not object to be shot down by nigger regiments that the Government will send here."

"Say, old man," broke in Casey, "we can't have no niggers no how. If I had my way, I'd hang all the niggers, war or no war."

"I'm afraid," remarked Sweeney, with a curiously bitter smile, "that liberty can't get along without the gang contingents. Mr. Casey has a list of them."

"You're roight, I have," said Casey. "I've the byes in black and white. Ther's de stable gang is good for forty men, and the Grinnige street gang for forty more. Slim Jim's gang ain't much good, but the Holly Bergens is terriers, and Dutch Harmon swears the forty thieves in Fortieth street is red hot. Then we got the Red Stars and Katydids to hear from, and they know they're biz. You start de picnic and de byes are all right. They'll git a show then, and it's a long time since they was in luck. Some of 'em ain't had a silk hat on since Buchanan was run. What's der matter wid de Never Sweats of Nineteenth street? There's no coppers round dem lads, is ther?"

"If these gentlemen know what's going on," said Lavinski, timidly, "I'm afraid the police will be on to it before we can get together,"

"O, see here," exclaimed Casey, dropping his big fist upon the table; "Don't gimme any o' that. Nobody ain't givin' nothin' to no police. Mebbe these byes ain't as sweet scented as some o' you're daddies, but they stand by the party; hey, Sweeney? and they roll up when the horn sounds. You don't know 'em? All dey wants is a livin' show in de racket Give de byes a chance. Dey ain't puttin' out no fires and savin' no property; not by a d———— sight, but if it comes to sluggin' a copper or cuttin' the legs of a sojer's horse, I'm bettin' on 'em—see Sonny?"

This speech led to a dialogue between Lavinski and Casey, and left Plonski and Sweeney to converse apart. The final result was that another meeting was planned without Casey, and then the party broke up, the men going out through the iron door and down into Villers' saloon, where Casey, still loud and defiant, stood Plonski up for the drinks.

CHAPTER LVI.

THE LAST DESPERATE ATTEMPT.

Scarcely had Mr. Plonski's strange companions separated and left him, when he returned to his room over Villers' wine shop. His first act was to open the door of the connecting room and look in. It was scarcely larger than a closet and the air in it was heavy and filled with smoke. On a rough pallet lay his attendant in a heavy sleep, and the hand that had dropped by the side of the bed had the stem of an opium pipe still between the fingers.

Plonski gave an involuntary aspiration as if to eject the fumes from his lungs and shut the door. As the afternoon wore away he tried to get a nap himself but could not. He then got Villers to send him up a sandwich and a pint of claret, which he disposed of more as a matter of duty than a matter of desire. The man was evidently in too anxious a condition to either sleep or eat.

It was eight o'clock in the evening before the man he was expecting arrived. It was McCune, who stole in guardedly and was clumsily disguised. The moment he was in the room Plonski caught him by the hand eagerly, with something like a greeting.

"I'm glad you came," he said; "I depended on it."

The Mink looked at him as if surprised at his unusual cordiality. "Curley's back," he said.

"What?"

"Curley Samson. I got the word at Mother Masson's fence. He broke a week ago and came straight. What's this that's goin' on? There's a lot of blokes on from Baltimore and Cincinnati."

"There's going to be trouble with the police," said Plonski. "Let's go in here. I want to tell you about it."

He then lit a candle and pulled the bed away, muttering at the same time, "I'm glad you came. I knew you would, but you'll have to be careful. Here, come in here. It's safer."

The moment they were in the retreat, Plonski said:

"You can't stay in the city. They'll take you sure. Now, listen to me carefully and I'll save you and make your fortune, if you do what I want. We've got to get that cup out o' that stream."

"O, say, boss, you're a friend o'mine, I know," said McCune, "but I hate to see you fooled by a bloomin' copper like that; the cup was took out."

"If you'll listen to me and do what I tell you, we'll not be fooled again," replied Plonski, impatiently; "and this time there will be some work for you.

They are going to drain that river and pond to recover the cup. They wouldn't do that if it was taken out. You've got to go up there and get it."

"You doan't expect me to drain the bloomin' river, do yer?"

"No; let them drain it, but you get the cup. No matter how, only get it."

The Mink let out a long-drawn oath. "This is business this time an' no mistake."

"McCune," said Plonski, drawing one of the camp stools close beside him and seating himself, "it's worth more money to you to get that cup for me than you'll ever make in this world. It will set you up for life in a new place. I've got the money, mind, and I'll pay you the solid gold when you put that cup in my hand. There's going to be a civil row here in a week or two that will paralyze the police. They will not have time then to look after us. You needn't be afraid of knocking a man on the head in those woods; I'll have you out of this safely the next day. They'll not have a big party at work there, because it ain't safe. You can find a way to get the thing if you make up your mind and you've done worse jobs for less pay."

The slight tone of appeal in this was entirely new to McCune. He instinctively felt that Plonski was bent upon a desperate venture, and with the feeling that he was more valuable than ever to him, he began to make objections and express doubts.

"O, I d'know about taking that kind of a job," he said; "I'm hunted now and I'd like to be let off from any more chokin' risks. Besides the thing's cursed."

"Don't be a fool," said Plonski. "We've got a plain sailing trick. They'll never suspect that you are around. They'll be hunting singly all along that brook, and not one of em's as stealthy or as quick as you are. You know the country, every path in it, and you've got the Italian settlement to jump into. Take that girl of yours and go up at once; you can send her down to me if you want money or have anything to tell me and nobody will suspect her. I'll give you enough to keep you both in good shape, and you'll be out of scent of the marshals."

He stopped a moment and waited for some response.

"Say, boss," The Mink replied, "I don't go heavy on it, no how. It means swingin' or a lifer, if I slip, and I've had 'nuff mush for the season."

Plonski got up. "Then you refuse. You are fool enough to throw away the one chance for your life. All right. You said you got the word about Samson at Mother Masson's fence, didn't you?"

McCune knew only too well that Samson would offer no scruples about the job, and he did not intend to let that ruffian into it.

"Well, then, I didn't say as how I refused, did I?" he said. "I was only thinkin' as how you'd mebbe sooner hav' Curley do it."

"I'd rather have you do it. You're straighter, but I'll get him if you don't. I'd rather give you the money."

"What'll I git if I don't snatch the bloomin' thing?"

"You must get it," said Plonski. "Don't you understand, I've got to have it?"

He appeared for the instant to forget that he was betraying his desperate determination and necessitous condition to McCune. He moved about the room pulling at his moustache and repeating the idea. "I shall get it. There is no one to deal with but Miramon and two or three unsuspicious laborers. It can be done. It must be done. I must have it now, cost what it may. It must not reach Miramon's hands, and if it does—well, Miramon must go."

Then, as if remembering McCune, he said, addressing himself to his companion: "We'll get it, my man, don't fear. We'll outwit the whole of them and take ourselves out of this before these political idiots begin to kill each other. Then we'll get some rest. We can enjoy ourselves; we'll go to Mexico. Think of that. You'll be a gentleman. We've got to look out for ourselves. Don't you see, for ourselves? But everything depends on my getting the cup. Fair means or foul, my man, get it for me and I'll fix you for the rest of your life. Do you understand me? I must have it. Money is no object. You don't think I'd lie, do you? Why, I'll fix it so you'll be sure to get your money. But you must make sure of it. There must be no slip this time. Why don't you say something?"

He paused again. For a moment there was dead silence. Then a sharp sound was heard as if some one had trodden on a loose board outside.

"What was that?" Plonski exclaimed in a suppressed but startled tone. They both listened. Plonski looked at the bell and lifted the hammer. It was in good working order. His hand shook a little as he did so, and McCune, who was watching him, saw that he was pale.

"Must have been a rat, eh?"

Plonski made no reply but went to the partition and held his ear against it. The thought had forced itself upon him that some one might be listening and had made himself heard in the attempt to get away. If so, it was the same person again who had dogged him so long.

He picked up the candle and, motioning to McCune, went out into the loft and held the light up so that its feeble rays fell upon the heaps of lumber that blocked up the spaces. It was apparently impossible for anyone to have approached in that direction without moving some of the rubbish. If there had been any one in the loft he must have come through the iron door. He went back to it, McCune following him. It was standing ajar. He was sure he had closed it. But the bed was pushed close to the wall. Could the door have sprung open of itself? So agitated was he when he had got into his own room that McCune roughly undertook to reassure him. But it was not until Villers himself had sworn several round oaths and declared that no man alive could get up the stairs without his knowing it that Plonski returned to the subject of the cup.

"Now, then," he said, nervously, "you'll get away to-night. Don't risk it in the daytime. How much money will you want?"

He fussed about, counted out what he said was all he had, and, after many urgent instructions and a few grunted promises from McCune in return, the man went away, and Plonski sending for a bottle of wine drank nearly the whole of it and went to bed.

CHAPTER LVII.

THE RECOVERY OF THE CUP.

New York on the first of July, 1863, was sleeping over a crater. One is astonished now with all the records of the outburst before him, to contemplate the apathetic sense of security which pervaded the community. It is amazing to think that destructive forces stored up in the city could be suddenly left unguarded and unchecked and could be animated by a common restlessness and lawlessness, without creating extra vigilance on the part of the authorities and something like a panic on the part of the law-abiding citizens.

But that such was the case, there can be no doubt. Outside of the detective bureau and the councils of a few hot-headed partisans, nothing was known of the disposition and threatened danger of an insurrectionary class, and the public went about its customary affairs with an unconcern that cost dearly.

One or two considerations will, in a measure, explain this. Public attention was centered on the stupendous drama of the war, and the possibility of local disturbance found no place of lodgment, or if it did, it seemed trivial by the side of the tragedy that had States for its dramatic personae and a continent for its theatre. The mere contemplation of war deadens some of the sensibilities. The constant accounts of slaughter set in the phraseology of patriotism and gallantry and the unending lists of killed and wounded, had taken the edge off squeamishness and a reckless, or at least a careless attention to anything less than a decisive battle, was the natural consequence. In addition to this, there was a general feeling that the Government would not enforce the conscription in New York City. The enrollment was going on, but in view of the unpopularity of the act and the possible furnishing of the needed men by stimulated volunteering, the intelligent public mind had settled into the belief that the draft was little more than a Government threat and that its enforcement would be postponed at the last moment.

On the other hand, the unintelligent, made up for the most part of foreigners, whose experience of conscription, under despotic military governments, was bitter indeed, and whose knowledge of the influence of public opinion upon government acts was gained in lands where such influence was nil, became sullen, apprehensive and vindictive.

On the morning of the second, Colin Carteret was surprised in his studio by the reception of a note from Mrs. Kate Sanger asking him to call at the house as she wished to consult him about a matter of artistic judgment. He had seen the lady several times since the first sitting, and she was an inscrutable puzzle to him. He had observed, he thought, an endeavor on her part, to be dangerously friendly and confidential, and it gave rise to unpleasant reflections. He started out late in the morning to call upon her and ascertain what it was she wanted, and on the way he encountered John Wilder accidentally. The officer scarcely saw him. He wore an anxious look and was stalking along with his eyes reflectively on the pavement when Carteret accosted him and held out his hand.

"I thought you had gone into the country," said Wilder.

"Hav'n't got off yet," replied Carteret, jauntily. "Expect to get away in a few days."

"Where is Miss Castleton?"

"O, she's there in Nineteenth street yet, but she's packing up slowly."

"Is she?" asked Wilder, somewhat absently.

"Certainly. You don't want to hurry us, do you?"

"Yes. I'd like to, not so much on your account as on account of the young lady. It's difficult not to take an interest in her."

As Wilder showed an inclination to go on, Carteret made a movement to accompany him and then they both walked along together.

"What's up now?" asked the young man. "Some new deviltry?"

"Let me give you a piece of advice," said Wilder. "You don't appear to understand that I am in a position to know a great deal more of what is going on than you do, and you are not apt to take good advice, but if you can be made to comprehend that I have a purely disinterested regard for you and the young lady, you will act upon my advice instantly and ask no questions."

"My dear sir," began Carteret protestingly.

Wilder cut him short. "See to it that Miss Castleton is removed from that place immediately. If you can get her to go out of the city for a few weeks, so much the better. Don't ask me to go into any explanations. I've got something else to do just now. I'll explain some other time and don't come any farther. Good day."

With that he quickened his pace and left Carteret standing and staring after him.

This brief and ominous conversation changed Carteret's mind and his direction, and instead of going to Mrs. Sanger's, he went to the Terrace. Before he arrived there, he had made up his mind to a decisive course of action. Wilder had alarmed him with a vague apprehension. He tried for some time to settle in his mind from what source the threatened danger was to come, and lover-like he believed it to be Stonybrook. But he succeeded partly by his intimation of danger and partly by his new determination which Manuella covertly admired, in making her promise to get her grandfather ready and take her departure the next day.

But the next day Mrs. Holbrook came to the Terrace to say that they could have part of the cottage uptown and they must take it at once because there was a very nice party standing ready to jump into it. So instead of going into the country, Manuella stayed two days longer to see Mrs. Sitwhite comfortably moved and to partly fit up, in the cottage, a couple of rooms which she and her grandfather were to occupy when they returned.

She did not know that on the Fourth of July when she was bustling about in the best of spirits putting pots of geranium in the window and helping Bob Holbrook tack down matting in the new and pleasant bedroom, that Curly Samson, who had told the story of her abduction to "Big Casey," as he was called, in the conspirators room at Villers' and had excited that ruffian's wildest passions, had got a female pal to watch the moving Sitwhites and find out where they were going.

Nor did Carteret, who came down from the cottage in the afternoon of the Fourth and heard the newsboys shouting the news of the fall of Vicksburg, have the faintest suspicion of the kind of danger that was hovering over the woman he loved. He only knew that as the days went by he was getting terribly impatient and nervous.

He had tried, on several occasions, to find Wilder and obtain an explanation and had only succeeded on the evening of the Fourth by calling at Mrs. Hannige's where he caught the officer in consultation with Mr. Miramon. The brief conversation that ensued was not satisfactory. Wilder introduced him as the young gentleman of whom he had spoken and Miramon, with considerable cordiality, said, as he looked at him intently, that he was very glad to meet him and expected to see more of him, as he was himself going to the same place up the river in two weeks, to be there several days. All of which struck Carteret as rather strange. But Wilder did not gratify him with any explanations, merely asking him if Miss Castleton had left town yet, to which Carteret had to reply, "Not yet."

It was not till the morning of the sixth, that the little party got off. Chapman went with them and very blithe and exultant they all were. The only person who preserved even the semblance of severity was Mr. Evans. They made all manner of jokes about running away from the draft and about Mr. Stonybrook, and they arrived at Mr. Manser's in the afternoon of a beautiful July day, just after a shower had passed and just as the sun was glinting irridescently from every wet leaf and spray.

It can well be imagined that to Carteret it all seemed like a romantic rescue and that he was carrying off his lady love from some demoniac and unseen enemy. The isolation, the peace and the kindly welcome of the place, reassured him. It was like a new chance in life to come back to this place prepared to rectify the mistakes and guard against the follies of inexperience. One of the haunting illusions of life is, that if we could only go back and re-enact our conduct with a new experience in an old place, we might redeem ourselves.

But our new experience makes a new problem whenever we get this chance.

In a very few days, the guests were at home and the new idyll had opened. They were thrown upon their own resources and upon each other. Chapman, who was an esthetic tramp, traversed the whole country for miles around, sometimes not reappearing till the next day and then coming back with a sketchbook full of smeary memoranda and a head full of trivial, but very delightful experiences. Sometimes they made a little group and went off together under an artistic plea and then spent the time very much as truants from school might. A young artist who felt as rich as did Carteret, would be very apt to give way, more or less, to the seductions of such an experience, but to his credit it should be said, that he made a very determined effort to woo back what he called his former woodland inspiration, and the only way that he could conceive of accomplishing it was to put his easel back in the very same place on the bank and put the same nymph in the foreground. And the nymph herself was not averse to the reproduction. She lent herself to the artist's plans with a winning and cunning subserviency and when he got his easel planted, she came every morning with a book and an extra camp stool and hung round him with a delicate intimacy. They were seldom intruded upon in this delightful employment. Chapman, once or twice, came and looked at the work and then made an apology and went away. There is an unwritten code of etiquette that relates to lovers.

And during these hours, there in the whispering shade, the young people grew very confidential and serious. Love began to be deliberate and somewhat methodical. It had plans and provisions and details to contemplate, as well as past misunderstandings to explain and forgive each other for, and very charming it was to see how everything like reproach had the sting taken out of it by the happiness of the hour and the kindliness of the occasion.

"To think," Manuella said, "that you should leave me to write the first letter and almost coax you to come and see me."

"You didn't, my dear," cried Carteret; "I sat up half the night to write those wretched verses, with the one mad hope that you would respond in some way, and when you didn't, I went about like a suicide."

"How could I respond?" asked Innocence. "You said I was a recollection and was part of a vision or something that had faded. What did you want me to do? Say thank you?"

"I never said anything of the kind."

"O, yes, you did."

"Now really, Manuella, I ought to know what I said."

"You don't really know anything about it, for the verses made no sort of impression on you and you have forgotten them, listen."

Then she recited them, and Carteret said, "Why you've got them by heart, haven't you?"

"Yes" she replied; "by heart. I didn't think they were wretched. I read them over and over. It seemed so delightful to have a poet write them to me, and I was so proud of you. I used to sit with them in my hand and wonder if you ever wrote any verses to Miss Enniston."

Then she nestled very close and he stopped painting and let her lean against him, and if Chapman had been looking at them from the top of the hill, he must have thought they were both painting the same picture. But Chapman was too discreet to do such a thing as that.

"To think," said Carteret, "that here we are back in the same place and doing exactly the same things over again. Isn't it jolly?"

"Not exactly the same things," replied Manuella softly. "I don't think we could do the same things precisely. Don't you feel that you are a great deal older? I do."

Carteret considered a moment. "Yes," he said, thoughtfully, "I suppose we are, and wiser. You wouldn't go off to dinner now with Mr. Stonybrook."

"And if I did," answered Manuella, "you wouldn't run away to New York and leave me here alone, would you?"

"And if I did," said Carteret, "you'd write a letter and bring me back."

"Would I, really?" asked Manuella.

"Pshaw, of course you would, that is, if I were such a ninny as to do such a thing again, which is impossible, you know. It looked very easy and spiteful and forgetful to you, I suppose, but that's because you couldn't see now completely broken up I was. Why, dear, it was actually midnight to me for weeks. You were my sun and I didn't know it, and it grew worse and worse till you wrote that letter. Do you know, it's an awful helplessness for a man to be in love with a woman as I am in love with you? Even my talents refuse to work unless you shine on them. You've got an awful responsibility, my dear. I shouldn't like to have another person's existence and happiness depend wholly on my conduct."

Then the girl laughed a bubbling kind of acknowledgment as if it were, at all events, pleasant to assent to that illusion and she accepted the responsibility without any other tremor than was caused by happiness.

These morning experiences on the shadowy hillside were thus moments of sentiment broken only by moments of what Carteret called work, though nobody but Carteret could have found out what separated one from the other. When Manuella was not reading to him or listening to him, she was posing for him, and when she stood on the tender grass before him with the patches of sunlight dancing an instantaneous bacchantic recognition and all the invisible fingers of the air plucking at the golden gossamer of her hair, he was very apt to drift away into a wondering dream and ask himself if it could be true that this Greek legend from the Vale of Thessaly were a real experience or only a vision.

And Manuella would call him back by saying, "What's the matter? You look discouraged."

In such a vale of enchantment it was not possible to conceive of any threatening dangers. The brook crooned its drowsy music all day. Protecting and kindly barriers swept round them and were peopled only by the phoebe bird and the exultant bobolink, whose "sweet disturbance" as Carteret had called it, was only the beauty of the place reaching an audible gamut. Everything was seductively and harmoniously abeyant, as if the "young dream" of these lovers was the very object and purpose of Nature herself. Carteret was in some danger of falling into the illusion that the struggle of life was after all sweetened with nepenthe.

Nobody save Hi Tucker ever dared to step foot into their charmed circle. Mr. Manser, even in moments of voluble rest, stayed on the outskirts. They could see him sitting on his front porch in his shirt sleeves and they knew that he was explaining to Mr. Evans how General Washington unloaded his silver goblets and other plunder into the "crik" when he took the cross roads from White Plains.

Then came the mutterings of the storm in New York. Chapman brought the papers up from the train on the morning of Tuesday, July 15th, and sat there on a camp stool reading the accounts of the outbreak on Monday, the little group circling round him in breathless interest. Meagre as the details were, they were freighted with something of the panic and foreboding with which they were written. Carteret's first thought was very like an unuttered prayer of thankfulness.

Some of the particulars were too astounding and revolting to dwell upon and Chapman and Carteret sagely softened them to Manuella's ears. The sacking of an orphan asylum and the burning of O'Brien in the streets, she knew nothing about. She only knew that some kind of terrible outbreak had taken place and that somehow the authorities would suppress it. But as Chapman continued to bring his news from the depot, it was impossible for them to ignore the portentous nature of the situation. He reported on Wednesday that the depot square was full of the business men who ordinarily went to the city in the mornings and were now unable to get there. The wires were down. The trains were delayed and irregular. They went down empty and came back crowded with escaping citizens from the city who brought exaggerated and blood-curdling accounts of what was going on. The city was burning in a hundred places; the fire department had joined the mob; the police were helpless; Wall street was at the mercy of the thieves; the streets were barricaded. Superintendent Kennedy had been killed. There was not a regiment of militia in the city. At night Manuella could see the red glow of conflagration low down in the southern sky.

On Wednesday afternoon Mr. Manser received a message from the Croton water department, "Put a guard at every culvert on your section at once and see that the men patrol the stretch night and day. There are threats to blow up the aqueduct."

Here was the first wave from the distant storm breaking with an ominous ripple at their very feet.

And the lovers did not know that the eyes of the grey wolf, again skulking in the copse and grove, had looked into their enchanted domain with curious gleams for several days.

Excited, worried and anxious, Carteret neglected his work and listened to the sounds from New York city, all aflame. Then Manuella on Thursday morning, got him back to his easel with much coaxing and many blandishments, and he made a very heroic effort to resume the idyllic mood and go on with his work. Manuella came down the bank about ten o'clock and found him carrying on a jocose conversation with Hi Tucker, who was dangling his legs over the adjacent abutment and holding a hickory fishing rod over the grass as if fishing for grass hoppers.

Carteret was standing at his easel with his back toward her and she heard him say:

"I guess you'd hunt a long time, my boy, before you got anything but suckers or a few silver shiners out of that river."

And Hi Tucker, with a precocious laugh, replied, "O, I got a silver cup out of it."

Carteret turned round and asked with a new interest, "What kind of a cup was it?"

"Silver—solid, I guess. Anyway it looked like it. It was that big," and he held his hands apart to show the dimensions.

"Where did you find it?"

"In a muskrat's hole."

"Where is it now?"

"Mommy's got it on her dresser."

"When did you find it?"

"Last Saturday."

Carteret laid down his easel and saw Manuella, who was standing on the bank with her big sun parasol, making a ruddy background for her golden hair.

"Did you hear what he said?" he asked.

"Yes, I heard it," replied Manuella. "What is it you are thinking about?"

"It must be *the* cup," replied Carteret, nervously.

They approached and looked into each other's faces.

"Don't bother with it," said Manuella, with a good deal of quiet earnestness.

"I'm afraid I must," replied Carteret. "At all events, I'll take Mr. Manser and go down to the widow's and identify it. I once made you a sacred promise to get it. This looks like the first square chance I ever had. Besides, my dear, I want to get it for myself now. Help me carry these traps back to the house."

Hi Tucker jumped down, threw his fishing rod into the grass, and began to help Carteret. While they were gathering the traps, the boy was answering questions that Carteret put to him. And the upshot of it all was that he had found what appeared to be the stolen cup while hunting for a muskrat hole, and had quietly taken the property home and given it to his mother. But the nervous manner and the sudden impatience of Carteret did not escape Manuella, and as they walked up the bank toward the house, she had a strange foreboding.

"My dear," Carteret said, "if this is Captain Ackerman's cup, I must get it to him at once. It may be of great value to both you and me. Wilder told me so, in fact."

"But," said Manuella, "you must not take Mr. Manser to the widow's to identify it."

"Why not?"

"Because he believes the river is full of cups, and instead of saying it is your's or mine, he will instantly declare that it is another of General Washington's mugs, to which the widow will have a better right as finder than either you or I. If you must recover it, we will go together. I shall know if it is the one we lost."

Her instincts were right. The moment Mr. Manser was told what had occurred, he said: "Of course, that makes the third mug that's been taken out. What did I fell you? The crik's full of 'em. General Washington captured 'em at the Battle of Long Island."

Carteret then concluded to make his visit without this archaeologist, and shortly afterwards he and Manuella started on with Hi Tucker down the long shadowy road that followed the windings of the little river.

McCune saw them. He had come over that morning from the Italian settlement, with Clianthe, and had left her under a tree in the neighborhood, while he made a reconnaissance. The first thing that attracted his attention was a man on the aqueduct armed with a shotgun, and walking up and down as a sentinel. By stealthily skulking through the denser part of the grove, he got round so as to see the great culvert, and there were two other armed men there. This puzzled him, and he started down the stream to investigate. He had not gone far before he saw the light dress of a woman moving along the dark road on the other side of the stream. He kept along parallel with the little party, but with no definite purpose and no suspicion. He saw them disappear in Mrs. Tucker's cottage, and he kept on down to the mill pond.

It was not till an hour later when on his way back that he felt an awakening interest in the lovers who were on their way home, walking very closely together and one of them carrying a bundle under his arm that instantly attracted the man's attention. Had there been the faintest suspicion in his mind that this was the cup, he would not have hesitated at any desperate act to obtain it. The objects of his scrutiny were sauntering along the mossy path with their heads together, utterly unconscious of any danger. To jump suddenly from behind a tree or rock and fell the man with a club before he could defend himself was an easy task.

But The Mink could not so easily get it into his head that the cup which he had seen in Sully's hands had got back into the stream, and that these same innocents were quietly walking off with it. So he let them pass along till they entered the grounds of the gate house and were safe.

Then, as he thought it over, he concluded to go back and find out from the boy, Hi Tucker, what it was they had been up to.

To his unbounded amazement, he learned the simple facts from the lad in a very few words, and with an oath that startled Hi Tucker, he bounded into the thicket and made his way with what speed he could to the spot where he had left Clianthe.

"Say, gal," he cried, breaking in on her unexpectedly: "If the bloomin' mug ain't found agin, break me in two this minnit. Pulled out by a kid and up in that didenticle ranch again. Yes it is. Put your togs on—you've got to whoop it."

"What are you goin' to do?" the girl asked as she got up from the grass and stood looking at him somewhat frightened and with her shoes in her hand.

"I'm goin' to hev it now, if I hev to wade in red to git it—see? Git on yer leather. You're to streak it straight for Beaky. Tell him to wait for me at Setchell's on Seventh avenue tomorrow and next day. Go on. It's the makin' o' yer, sis. We'll cut the biz, if I git this and we'll have the rhino in our poc's. Don't make no bloomin' mistake. I'll snatch it if I hev to knife the gal herself."

"Then I don't go," said the girl, dropping her shoes and assuming a stubborn look and attitude. "If yer that loony, I'll go back on yer, dead. I wouldn't stay in the same celler with you, if you put a hand on her, now—curse me if I would."

"Don't be a d— fool," said McCune. "I ain't goin' into no butcher business if I kin keep out. You go to Beaky and tell him to lay for me at Setchell's. He'll know. I'll bring it or stiffen on the try. Go on now. This ere's our pie—see? We stand in alone."

After a few minute's parley, which ended by a promise on McCune's part not to lay a hand on the girl, Clianthe bade him a rough good bye and started across the hills.

The Mink looked after her a moment and then slowly and cautiously retraced his steps towards the stream.

CHAPTER LVIII.

MURDER MOST FOUL.

The certainty that men had been placed on the aqueduct to prevent any search for the cup, led McCune to believe that, now that the cup was recovered, they would guard the house only until its removal. He proceeded as stealthily as he could in his observations. There was the fellow on the high embankment, strolling up and down with his shotgun. To keep out of his quick sight, he made a long detour and worked slowly round through the woods to a secure place where he could watch the house until dark. He was satisfied now that the cup was in it, and he meant to make the burglarious attempt to get it as soon as the family should be in bed.

Meanwhile there was a consultation, and Manuella and Carteret had their heads together over the mysterious article, admiring it once more with an increased curiosity and wonder. By dint of extraordinary determination, rather than unusual logic, Carteret convinced Manuella that it was his duty to place it at once in Captain Job Ackerman's hands. "We shall neither of us be comfortable while it is here," he said, "and I decline to subject you to any further risk on account of it. Besides there is a mystery connected with it that Captain Job Ackerman must unravel, and there is a reward offered for it which he must pay. I am going to get Mr. Manser to take me down to that six o'clock train, and I am going straight to Coe's Grove with it. I'll be back early in the morning, before anything can happen, and this place is now guarded night and day by armed men."

Reluctant as the girl was to have him go, she had to give in to his will in the matter, and she saw the preparations for his departure with a strange misgiving.

McCune also saw, with a keen interest, the wagon brought up to Mr. Manser's door, and, after some delay, Cateret, with a satchel that undoubtedly contained the cup, got in. Then Mr. Manser followed, and finally one of the men, with a gun in his hands, also entered the wagon and they drove away.

Lithe and wiry as he was he could not keep the vehicle in sight, for he had to avoid being seen. But, by making short cuts through the woods, he managed to keep within a stone's throw of it, as it moved along the devious road, appearing at intervals until it reached the highway. Once there, the driver whipped up his horses and it presently disappeared.

McCune knew enough to conjecture rightly that if Carteret had the cup he was going to Coe's Grove with it. He told himself that the young man would not be likely to go to the city in its present disturbed condition. He also knew that the wagon had started as if timed to catch a northern train, and he concluded that if the cup went to Coe's Grove it would also go back to the house out of which it was originally taken. His course was therefore clear. It was to take the first train he could catch and go himself to Coe's Grove.

It was six-thirty when Colin Carteret, once more in front of Jared Sprinkler's, hailed a vehicle, and twenty minutes later he was driving up the blue gravel road to the Enniston house with the cup in his keeping.

It was half-past nine when The Mink dropped from the rear of a train in the dark at the same town and disappeared in the shadows of the little depot.

Mrs. Enniston and Dr. Flockton were sitting on the front veranda when Colin Carteret mounted the steps. The lady rose and welcomed him in her stateliest manner, and Dr. Flockton added a few formal and flowing phrases of salutation. But the visitor briefly informed them that he had come upon a matter of urgent private business with Captain Ackerman and intended to return as soon as possible. Barney was then sent over to Dr. Wollendorf's and in a little while the captain came across the field.

The moment he and Carteret were in the back room upstairs, Carteret said:

"Well, you are astounded, of course, at seeing me, but I am going to astonish you still more. I have got the cup."

The captain looked at him incredulously.

"You—have got it?" he asked slowly, as if he did not quite comprehend.

"Yes," said Carteret promptly. "I've got it. It's here in this satchel. It was lost in a little stream; a lad who lived on the stream fished it out. I made him a present, captured the property and here it is. You'll know it, I presume, when you see it."

"Know it? Certainly. Show it to me."

And the captain went to the mantel and took down a wax candle that shed a faint light over the large room. "Where is it?" he said, eagerly; "let me see it."

Carteret took the cup from the bag and held it up. The captain placed the light on a table. "That's it, sure enough," he said. "My, God, how you surprise me! Does Wilder know?"

"Not yet. I came direct to you. I shall send him word in the morning. There can be no mistake. The history of its adventures are closely connected up to this discovery. I wanted to see it safe in your hands."

And Carteret handed it over. "Put it away," he said. "I've got a good deal that I want to say to you, for I must be off early."

Captain Ackerman received the cup with eager wonderment. The light in the room was very poor, and he began feeling in his waistcoat pocket for his spectacles. Not finding them, he held the cup off at arm's length and looked at it with a child's eagerness and an old man's dimness of vision.

"Put it away," said Carteret. "There can be no doubt of its identity."

Captain Ackerman carried it in his hand as he proceeded to shut the door. He then went to the iron safe with it.

"H'm," he said, "Jane has got my keys." He then placed the cup on the top of the safe and the two men sat down at the table. "I'll examine it in the morning," he said; "I suppose it is all right."

"Certainly it is all right," rejoined Carteret. "It is the cup that was taken from this room, and after an unparalleled series of adventures, is back here once more. I have done my share in recovering it. I want to know now what its value is and what possible interest I can have in it."

"Did you tell Jane that you had brought it?"

"No. I did not think it worth while to explain to her until I had talked with you."

"I'm very glad you didn't. It would only worry her. I'm all struck abaft, Mr. Carteret; I didn't expect this, you see;" and the captain got up, took a turn, looked at the cup once more and went on: "I scarcely know how to act. You've caught me like a white squall. Sit down, sit down. I'll get my reckoning in a minute. I wish Dr. Wollendorf was here."

The old man seated himself again and Carteret said:

"From something Mr. Wilder said to me I fancied you desired to give me some information concerning this cup that is of personal interest to me."

"I have, I have," replied the captain. "It is of the utmost importance. The cup may be, in fact it is, of the greatest value and you have a proprietary interest in it as part owner."

"I have?"

"Yes, you have. Your father and I were joint owners. When he died he left your interests in my hands."

"My father?"

"Your father was the late Oliver Enniston."

"Captain Ackerman, you amaze me. Good God, man, what are you saying? Then I am—"

"Don't put your helm down that way; you're all right. I knew your mother well. She was Ol Enniston's first wife and died in childbirth. It was purely a politic weakness that made Enniston keep the facts to himself when he married my sister. There was nothing to conceal except a foolish love match and a harum scarum marriage, and Ol was a little afraid of Jane. He always meant to straighten the matter out, which indeed was a matter of record, but as time went on it grew more difficult. When he died, he said to me, 'Job, if there's anything comes of that cup I want my boy to get my share of it.' By the Lord, it fills every inch of canvas I've got to think his boy has walked in here with the cup in his hands. It's a dead strange piece of business, Mr. Carteret, from beginning to end. I could spin a yarn about it that would take the poetry out of these landsmen who write novels."

"My name, then," mused Carteret, "is Enniston. But why was I overlooked by the executors of the estate? Why," he exclaimed, jumping up, "Rose Enniston is my half sister, and at one time I was engaged to be married to her. Captain Ackerman, there's been a good deal of duplicity and considerable wrong in this business. I think I'm entitled to feel outraged."

"My dear sir," replied the captain, nervously, "I don't think anybody wanted to run you ashore. It was a nasty channel, I'll agree, and there was considerable fog, but now we've got charge of the deck, my boy, and we'll 'bout ship. Don't you see?"

"Then Mrs. Enniston knows nothing of all this?"

"It isn't safe to reckon on what Jane don't know," replied the captain. "She can see more fathoms deep and not throw a lead than any woman I ever got acquainted with. One thing is certain. If the Enniston estate was settled up and divided it wouldn't amount to a biscuit bite by the side of your interest in this cup."

"One moment, Captain. I suppose you know that Miss Enniston bought my picture."

"No, I didn't know it."

"Well, she did and she sent me a thousand dollars for it. Where did the money come from?"

"She borrowed it. I happen to know, for she tried to borrow it of me."

"Then she borrowed it on her prospective interest in the estate?"

"I dare say. Rose is a headstrong girl—she's awfully like Ol, her father, in some things. I tried to advise her, but it was like advising a water spout. She didn't tell me what she wanted the money for."

Carteret began to fidget. "I wish you'd tell me," he said, "as briefly as possible, what my immediate prospects are. Do you expect to realize at once on this cup? Suppose you give me a clear statement of the whole matter. I've left my affairs in a bad state and have got to get back in the morning."

"In the morning?" repeated the captain with surprise. "You can't do it. There's too much to attend to. I want you to go over the papers and understand matters. There is no affair so important to you as this. We've got to decide if we will sell out for $20,000 at least cash, or hold on for more, and I don't mind telling you that $20,000 isn't a pin scratch on the amount the cup represents."

Carteret listened to this with a confused sense. The whole revelation was so sudden that he could not instantly adjust his comprehension to it. But in spite of it all, there was one dominant and very urgent feeling that nothing Captain Ackerman had said could deaden or displace, and it was that he had left Manuella with a solemn promise to come immediately back; that some kind of double peril, indefinable but irremediable, lurked round the aqueduct; that he had never left Miss Castleton without subjecting her to danger and now, more than ever, he had cause to guard her. No, he must get back.

"Captain," he said, "I shall have to go back early in the morning and straighten up some things. That done, we can attend to our matters here deliberately—you know the condition of affairs in the city. I'm worried about some friends of mine. See here, there used to be an early milk train went through about half-past five. I'll get up and catch that. It stops at Tarrytown—I can then make my arrangements and come back."

"My dear sir," replied the captain, "every minute of delay after to-night is dangerous. Wherever that cup has been the sleuthhounds of crime have been on its track. I have learned enough to know that in a day or two, if we do not inform Mr. Wilder, we shall have the old miscreants hanging about. I was going to ask you to go to New York the first thing tomorrow and find Wilder."

"Very well, then," said Carteret, "I'll get up early, stop at Tarrytown, and then see if I can get Wilder. You must not forget that he probably has his hands full in New York at this moment."

"Yes, yes, but he can advise us. He must know what has happened and at once. We'd better go downstairs now and see Jane. It's only proper, besides I want to get my keys."

They had talked much longer than they knew. It was nearly eleven o'clock. Mrs. Enniston had retired and the house was locked up. Captain Ackerman opened the hall door and looked out. A great patch of moonlight lay across the veranda, unbroken save by the shadows of the two chairs where Dr. Flockton and Mrs. Enniston had sat. It was a very warm night and the cool air from the shrubbery was fragrant and grateful.

"It's a strange place, Captain," said Carteret. "One never knows how to conduct himself in this house. Here am I, a guest of Mrs. Enniston's and I haven't even asked permission to stay."

"O, that's of no consequence. There's your old room at the end of the hall. There's nobody in the house. When you feel like it, go to bed and don't bother about the etiquette. I generally take a smoke and a turn on the grass before I take my berth. If you feel like loading in some of this night air, I'll get you a pipe."

"No, I thank you," replied Carteret; "I'm pretty tired and I don't want to over-sleep myself. If you'll give me a candle, I think I'll turn in."

When at the door of the little room at the east end of the upper hall, the captain said: "Mind you, if you want a cup of coffee in the morning, you'll only have to get Barney up."

"Thanks," said Carteret, with a half yawn. "I'll snatch it at the Tarrytown depot. Good night."

Captain Ackerman went back to his room, wiped the perspiration from his face, filled a heavy pipe with tobacco, took his coat off and went down the stairs to the back door, which he unlocked noiselessly, and leaving it ajar, proceeded down the steps of the narrow back porch to the strip of lawn on the other side of the roadway. Here, under the maples that stood in a row and threw their shadows over the blue gravel, he had worn a little path by his regular nocturnal watch. He had been driven into this habit partly by Mrs. Enniston's ineradical antipathy to tobacco and partly by his sea-going life.

The night was a beautiful one, and save the sound of the crickets in the grass and the soft rustle of the trees as the air swept through them, not a sound was heard. Even the footsteps of the walker were muffled in the grass. So still was it, that he could, at intervals, hear the rustling and cooing of Dr. Wollendorf's pigeons as he turned in his path and faced the old farm house, lying there in the moonlight, with one or two dancing patches of silver beyond where the effulgence touched the distant river. But the captain was not affected by the external beauty. He was thinking of the cup, without the slightest apprehension of immediate danger. He would see Dr. Wollendorf the first thing in the morning. Carteret would be back at night. They would communicate with Wilder. Means would be taken at once to protect the property. Everything would be straightened out at last and Ol Enniston's wishes carried out to the letter. The kind hearted old sailor was thinking less of himself than of others. "If I can get enough out of it to straighten Jane's mortgage," he said, "I'll have a snug harbor for the rest o' my days and what more do I want?"

But there was one observer of this scene. Not thirty feet away, close behind the trunk of a great overgrown willow, where he had often hidden before, stood McCune, taking in the whole situation. He watched the white shirt of the captain as the sailor paced steadily up and down under the trees. He saw that the stretch that he covered was at least fifty feet, and that a minute or more was consumed as he went up the walk with his back to the door. He felt sure that the cup was in the house, and that everybody but the captain was asleep. He saw that the captain was not thinking of danger, for he had left the door ajar. It then occurred to McCune that if he could get into the house without being seen, he might conceal himself until the captain retired, and then he would have the run of the place. He saw that there was a dim light in the upper room. He felt sure that the cup, if in the house, was in that room. He calculated every chance with the minute craft of a skilled thief. If he undertook to cross the gravel, it would make a sound easily heard in the still night. But he could slip round, come down the south side of the house, take his shoes off, hide himself under the edge of the porch, and when the captain turned and walked up the stretch, he could slip quickly up the steps like a cat and get inside the door, before the old sailor turned again. Scarcely had this idea shaped itself in his mind, before he set about putting it into execution. It did not take him more than three minutes to glide snakelike through the outlying copse round to the edge of the porch, where crouching in the shadow, he looked across the top of the steps and saw Captain Ackerman coming toward him with his head down and leaving little wreaths of smoke behind him. When within twenty feet of McCune, he turned about methodically and began slowly walking back. With marvelous dexterity, strength and nicety, The Mink drew himself over the rail of the porch, crept swiftly up the steps like an animal, and was inside the hallway before the captain had again turned. He pushed the door to its former position and waited to see if the walk was ended. But the captain kept on. Then The Mink slipped noiselessly and quickly up the stairs. The door of the captain's room was ajar. There was a light inside. The moment the thief looked in he saw the cup standing on the safe. Then a new idea struck him. If the captain continued his walk five minutes more, why was it not possible to get back as he came and carry the cup with him? Quick as this thought was, it was scarcely quicker than his action, and in another minute he was descending the stairs with it in his hand. He had got to the door and had pulled it open to look out, when he came face to face with the captain who had returned and had stopped at the entrance to knock the ashes from his pipe. With a sudden ejaculation of dismay and indignation, the sturdy old sailor instantly sprang at him and grasped him by the throat. But he might as well have grasped an anaconda. The Mink was a trained wrestler, a wiry, alert desperado, with steel muscles. He slipped down in a writhing contortion, extricated himself and stepped back, and then drawing a sand club from his pocket, he struck the old man over the head with it. Not once, but twice, with all the force and lightning celerity he could command. His victim gave forth a sound something between a gulp and a moan, and fell back against the door frame. Such was the miscreant's presence of mind, that he caught him as he fell, so that there would be no further sound. He gave one quick, close look into the face of the man and then went down the steps.

Scarcely had he reached the spot where he had left his shoes than a new idea occurred to him. If he left the body there, the discovery and the hunt would be quicker than if he should pull it down into the trees back in the grass and close the door. He put his shoes and the cup down. Then, with a second thought that showed how much more crafty he was than Capt. Ackerman, he picked the cup up again. He was not going to let it out of his sight, even for a moment. He brought it back to the gravel road, where he could keep his eyes on it, and then dragged and lifted the body of the dead captain down the steps, and left it lying about ten feet inside the grove and not two feet away from the path where a few minutes before the hopeful and kindly old man had been walking.

He then went back once again and closed the door, taking a quick scrutiny of the porch and hallway to see if he had dropped anything. This done, he went off through the trees and down the slope toward the railroad track and the river.

It was about five o'clock in the morning, when Carteret opened his eyes, and the first thought that came into his mind, as he got hastily up and began to dress, was: "I wonder if it was the unconscious instinct of a sister that made Rosamond so dead set on me."

He looked out of the window. There was a gray light in the east. The birds were twittering in all directions. Nobody was astir in the house. "By Jove," he said, "I mustn't miss that milk train;" and with that he dashed some water in his face, completed his toilet, seized his satchel and hurried down.

"Well, I'm blessed," he said, as he went out, "if the captain didn't forget to lock the door. The old man will lose that cup again, if I don't hurry back and look after him."

The next moment he was himself hurrying across the lawn and through the woods, almost in the footsteps of The Mink.

CHAPTER LIX.

HOURS OF TERROR AND DISMAY.

A fifteen minutes walk through the trees down the declivity, brought Carteret to the railroad. He stood a moment on the bank looking at the river dancing in the pearly gray light of the morning and at the opposite shore, flushed with the rosy hue of the rising sun. He heard the dull rumble of a heavy train, slow moving, and he scrambled down to the tracks. In the still sharp air of the morning, his sense of hearing was unusually acute and he perceived almost immediately that the noise of the train was growing less. He turned and faced the river so that the sounds would reach his ears from the up and down stretch of tracks. He heard the toot of a whistle and it came from below. The rumble ceased. The milk train must have gone down.

Without a moment's hesitation he started in the direction of the Coe's Grove depot. The way was a straight one over the sleepers. The morning was invigorating and he was too impatient to stand still.

When he reached the depot, he found that his surmise was correct. He had missed the milk train by about ten minutes.

"But great smoke," said the station master, "you must be in a fine state of mind to be getting up to catch a milk train. Why didn't you take it easy and go down like a gentleman in the seven ten?"

"I'm only going to Tarrytown," replied Carteret, "and I could have gained an hour and a half if I'd caught that train, that's all."

"Well," said the official, "you can't count on trains just now. There ain't one on the schedule that's within an hour of its figgers. Why, that milk train'll have to wait at Dobb's for the 9:20 Saratoga Express. There's a block at Spuyten, and a dead tangle at Innwood. If yer was going to the city you'd be liable to be side-tracked for three hours. Why, the rioters rolled about forty tons of stone on the roadway at Fort Washington night afore last and there ain't been a south wire that worked till yesterday."

"Then I've got to wait for that Peekskill train."

"Wait's the word. Everything's runin' wild. You'll hev time to get your breakfast, I guess. She'll be along about nine."

Carteret then went over to Sprinkler's and Nancy Ann got him a plate of ham and eggs, and a cup of coffee. He listened to her gossip and wandered about the depot square impatiently, until he heard the toot of a locomotive and the noise of an approaching train. It was nine o'clock; and as the cars came in sight and slowed up, he ran across the roadway and sprang upon a rear step and entered the train. He noticed that it went slowly through the village but did not stop, and as he looked out of the window he saw the depot men making signals. Throwing himself into a seat with a sense of satisfaction that he was moving, he gave himself up to his thoughts only to be called out of his reverie by the conductor.

"I'm only going to Tarrytown," Carteret said; "how much do you want?"

"I don't stop at Tarrytown," replied the conductor.

"Don't stop," exclaimed Carteret, jumping up. "Isn't this the Peekskill train?"

"No," replied the conductor. "This is the Saratoga Express, and I've got to be at Dobb's Ferry in fifteen minutes. The Peekskill train held over for me. I saw you jump on from the road. You'll have to pay your fare to New York, and next time you'd better come through the depot."

"Don't you stop this side of New York?" asked Carteret, as he got his money out.

"Not if I can help it, and ain't signaled," replied the conductor.

Here was an annoying state of affairs. Carteret settled into his seat and began to calculate how long it would take him to catch a train back from New York, and get to Tarrytown. What would Manuella think, how could he telegraph? Very soon he began to notice that something unusual was taking place. The ordinary humdrum of local travel and the routine system at the stations were interfered with. Great crowds were at all the depots. Trains stood on the side tracks, and there was an enormous amount of shouting and tooting and delay. At Spuyten Duyvil they came to a standstill. Carteret got out and found the tracks, as far as he could see in both directions, were covered with freight trains. It was an inextricable tangle to him, and the only answer he could get was, "all right, road'll be clear in fifteen minutes." So he went back to his seat and waited while the cars backed down and were switched and interminable loads of stock and lumber slowly moved past him, and he did what everybody else does in such cases, he did not get out and walk because he felt that if he did the train would immediately move and get to its destination long before he did. It was twelve o'clock when they slowly crossed the Spuyten Duyvil draw, and moved as far as Manhattanville; and here, seeing that the confusion and delay were more discouraging than ever, he got out determined to find his way to the city by some other conveyance. The factories at Manhattanville were all closed and the operatives were on the streets, but there were no signs of disturbance. A gunboat lay just outside the draw with the United States flag flying and her guns covering the bridge.

To send a dispatch was impossible. The police authorities had control of the wires and the railroad business at the station precluded any chance of getting a private message through to Tarrytown.

Carteret's determination now was to see Wilder if possible and return immediately to Tarrytown, and with this intention he set out eastward along the river to walk over to Harlem, hoping to find some means of conveyance to the city proper and to learn what the condition of affairs was. The great avenues that he crossed were deserted. An air of idleness and quiet hung over the upper part of the town as if the day were an enforced Sabbath. It was insufferably warm and his impatience made him feel it acutely. He had not gone far before he heard the call of a newsboy and presently met the lad on the full run with his bulletins under his arm. Carteret bought one and it proved to be the first edition of one of the evening papers. He looked at the black headlines as he walked along. They indicated plainly enough that the worst was over and making every allowance for the effort of a paper to exaggerate the situation, it was obvious that the arrival of troops and the organization of the citizens themselves had determined the result of the riots. The news columns of the sheet were given up to the reports of local sedition and the National war. All other matters were crowded into the narrowest space. It was therefore by the merest accident as he opened the paper and cast his eye over its scanty news items, that he saw a dispatch not an inch long and in small type, away down in the corner and bearing the caption, "Murder at Coe's Grove. Before he could comprehend the full significance of the brief announcement, he had read it through with his breath suspended.

"COE'S GROVE", July 17th.

"Captain Job Ackerman, a well known and respected citizen of this place, was murdered last night at his residence. His body was found this morning in his yardway. The assassin escaped on an early milk train, but the sheriff has a description of him and has started in pursuit. He is known to have gone to the city carrying a satchel in which is the property for the possession of which the deed was committed."

For several seconds Carteret stood in the street staring at this piece of news with a strangely transfixed eye. It was some time before the full significance of it all was mentally grasped, for the statements were incredible. "How could the captain have been murdered the night before in his own yardway, when I passed out of the doorway this morning?" he said to himself. Then he remembered that he had found the door unlocked and that the last thing the captain had said to him was that he was going to smoke his pipe on the lawn. "Could he have been murdered on the grass while I was sleeping and his body dragged round to the front entrance? If he was killed, it was to get possession of the cup. My God, then it is gone again."

So unconscious was he of his actions that he had turned and was hurriedly retracing his steps, when the final and inevitable thought in this nexus brought him up again. "Who is suspected of this? Known to have gone to the city with a satchel on an early milk train," he repeated; "no one knew that but Captain Ackerman; yes, Barney was up and may have heard me. My hurried arrival; my inexplicable departure; yes, yes, my anxiety at the depot; the remark of the station master, what was it? 'You must be in a great state of mind to be getting up to catch a milk train'; my getting aboard before it stopped; my going to New York when I told everybody I was going to Tarrytown; my wholly inexplicable visit to Captain Ackerman, it must be me they are looking for."

Honest indignation and pride told him that the thing to do was to challenge instant and public scrutiny. The thought that his actions during the morning might look suspicious brought the blood to his cheek.

Agitated and anxious, he turned and set out again with renewed speed toward Harlem. He must find Wilder immediately. As he hurried he thought over all the possibilities of the situation. Might there not be circumstantial evidence enough to make it almost impossible for him to clear himself? Might he not be arrested and held for months under a cruel accusation, while the con-spirators who committed the deed were removing their assassin from the reach of the authorities? What would Manuella say? He pictured to himself Chapman getting the paper, his horror and amazement. Would he take it at once to her? It would be only natural. "I am liable to arrest at any moment," he said. "That sheriff may have got off at Manhattanville." He turned and looked quickly back as if he expected to see a pursuer.

On none of the avenues that he crossed were the horse cars running, and it was not till he reached the Third avenue that he obtained a conveyance. By dint of argument and a round sum of money he finally got a man to drive him to Forty-second street, but no inducement could make him go farther. Carteret then set out on foot and taking to the roadway at times he finally reached Mrs. Hannige's, in Fifteenth street.

At the house he found that the regular order of the establishment had been disturbed.

"Lord, Mr. Carteret," said Mrs. Hannige, "John hasn't been here for a week. Such goings on you never heard of. Why, his life wouldn't be worth a straw if he was seen alone. I guess you'll have to go to the Central Office if you want to catch him. How's Miss Castleton? I s'pose I can call her that yet, can't I?"

Carteret was undetermined what to do. It looked like running his head into the very police net that he wished to avoid if he went to the Central Office. And still it was above all things necessary to see Wilder if he was to be vindicated or to be even assisted in his terrible plight.

While he was debating this matter in his mind, he was hurrying toward Mulberry street as if his feet were stronger than his fears. But he found the street upon which the Central Office was situated guarded by militia and battalions of police. It was only with the greatest difficulty and the exercise of considerable ingenuity that he got through, and then only to learn to his dismay that John Wilder was not at the Central Office. To his urgent inquiries but one answer was returned from the detective bureau: "Officer Wilder is not on duty." Disappointed and despairing, the young man was hustled round and about among eager citizens, officials and officers, and was given plainly to understand by the subordinates that he ought to know better than to come there on private business at such a time. Just, however, as he was leaving the building a detective in the garb of a working man, spoke to him. "I heard you asking for Inspector Wilder," he said. "If you want to see him you'll probably catch him at the headquarters of the Citizens' League, Fifth Avenue Hotel, or at the office of Burton & Dunn."

"Thank you," said Carteret, impulsively, as he hurried away. When he arrived at the rooms of Burton & Dunn, he was compelled to wait a dreary while, after he had sent his name in to Mr. Burton, with the forlorn hope that the lawyer could tell him where to find Wilder. When he was finally ushered into the private office of the lawyer, that imperturbable gentleman had wheeled himself round in his revolving chair to look at him, and Carteret saw a rather handsome and scrupulously dressed old gentleman, with a dewy pink in his broadcloth lapel. The only other person in the office was a somewhat coarsely dressed laboring man, with his cap in his hand, who was evidently waiting for some orders.

"I come to you, Mr. Burton," said Carteret, somewhat impetuously, "to ascertain if possible where I can find Mr. John Wilder. I have very important and urgent news for him; a murder has been committed and a dreadful mistake has been made—"

The workingman interrupted him. "Who is murdered?" he asked, quietly but quickly.

Carteret looked at him with astonishment, but he had recognized the voice.

"Captain Ackerman has been killed," he replied, as he stared. "It is in the papers."

"Sit down," said John Wilder. "You are excited. What do you know about it?"

Carteret dropped into a chair and briefly told all that had occurred from the moment that Hi Tucker had innocently betrayed his recovery of the cup. Both listeners heard him through without interruption, and he concluded by saying: "The circumstances are pretty bad for me, and I naturally looked for you at once."

Wilder merely remarked to Mr. Burton as Carteret concluded:

"Plonski's got the cup. McCune is ahead of us."

"It looks like it," said Mr. Burton reflectively.

"Carteret," remarked Wilder, "you're in a disagreeable box. There's no doubt of it, with this turn. But you've come to the wrong man, I'm afraid. I'm in a box myself."

"You. What do you mean?"

"I am as good as removed from the force. My power to help you is gone, because the only way to help you is to take McCune at once."

"McCune," Carteret repeated with some amazement "But you are not sure that he—"

"O, yes I am," said Wilder; "but to make anybody else sure I've got to get my grip on him, and before I can straighten my own affairs and vindicate myself, which will take time, it will be too late to arrest him or to help you."

Poor Carteret listened to this with a sinking heart and a dull sense of virtuous indignation at the same time.

"Do you mean to tell me, gentlemen," he asked, "that you have no means of arresting a murderer or of protecting an innocent man? If you haven't it is my plain duty to go to the authorities."

Neither Mr. Burton nor John Wilder replied to him. They did not appear to be thinking about him at all.

"John," said Mr. Burton, "I anticipated this from the first. You will remember that I warned you the plot would widen out into politics. I think Dr. Sanger is playing a shortsighted game in allowing himself to be mixed up in this matter."

"Are you quite sure that he is mixed up?"

"Quite. His influence is sufficient to secure that order sending you to Montreal on a wild goose chase. If you disregard it, you will be suspended or asked to resign. There is only one thing to do, get it withdrawn. I wish I had Acton's ear for ten minutes. But even a case as urgent as this would be impertinent to him at such a time. I understand he hasn't had his clothes off for five days. Humph, you were to leave at four o'clock. It's now nearly two. I think I'll go down and try and see the commissioner."

"And I," said John Wilder, "will go and see this Doctor Sanger."

Mr. Burton, who had risen, hesitated a moment. "Do you think that will be politic?"

"It will be some satisfaction," replied Wilder, "to hear what he has to say."

"Send me word here," said Mr. Burton, who was already putting on his gloves. Then turning to Carteret, he added, "if you get time, John, I'd take this young man to the Central Office and have him make his statement to the superintendent."

"Very good," replied Wilder, "but I shall see Dr. Sanger before I see the superintendent—by the way, the superintendent is in the hospital—I suppose you know."

"True, true," said Mr. Burton, as he put his hat on, "but there will be some-body to take the deposition."

"I must go to Fifteenth street to change my clothes," remarked Wilder to Carteret, "Suppose you wait there for me."

In obedience to this request, the men met half an hour later at Mrs. Hannige's. Wilder had resumed with marvelous rapidity his usual attire of blue flannel and he said to Carteret who was impatiently waiting for him: "Perhaps you had better walk up to Doctor Sanger's with me. It will save time. I can tell you in one word, after I have seen him, what I can do."

As they walked along he asked Carteret a thousand questions but furnished no sign of the effect the answers produced. He merely said as they approached the house in Gramercy Park: "This turn in the affairs of the cup is a most unfortunate one for you and for Miramon, to say nothing of Captain Ackerman. Plonski has undoubtedly recovered the property before this and has made all his plans so as to take advantage of the disorder in the city. It robs you of a fortune, seeing that Captain Ackerman's death leaves you the only claimant that Miramon has to deal with."

"Yes," exclaimed Carteret, "and the only one with a sufficient motive to kill the captain."

Wilder smiled, "It is going to cause you a deal of trouble," he said, "unless the real culprit is caught. I can see that. I wish I had my hands clear. What time was it when Captain Ackerman went upon his night watch on the lawn?"

"It was about eleven o'clock," replied Carteret, "Do you think he was killed on his lawn?"

"Yes, I do. It is quite reasonable. McCune must have followed you from the aqueduct. The captain wouldn't walk over an hour. You didn't hear him come in?"

"No. I went immediately to sleep."

"H'm—he never came in."

"O," said Carteret, "I forgot to say that when I went out in the morning, I found the back door unlocked."

"H'm—but you didn't notice anything else."

"No, it was too early and I was in a hurry."

"The murder was probably committed some time during that walk. It gives them a good start. We are fifteen hours behind now. I'm afraid it's a hopeless case. The cup is gone this time and no mistake. Here is the doctor's house. If he is at home, you will wait in the parlor for me."

They mounted the steps and were ushered into the same parlor in which Carteret had looked at the new picture. When the servant came back and said the doctor would see Mr. Wilder in his office, the officer as he was about to leave the parlor, bent down and said in a whisper to Carteret: "Wait here. It may turn out to your advantage." Then he followed the servant to the room at the end of the hall and was shown in.

Doctor Sanger, in a velvet jacket, was seated at his table facing the door. His secretary occupied the one additional chair in the room and it was behind the doctor at the window, where also was a telegraph instrument.

As Wilder entered, the doctor made some kind of remark to his assistant who got up and left the room. Wilder and Dr. Sanger were then face to face alone for the first time.

The doctor, handsome, florid and slightly imperious, ceased writing a letter and looked up at Wilder, holding his pen on the paper as if the interruption was not of sufficient consequence to warrant him in laying it down.

"Officer John Wilder?"

"Yes, sir," said John Wilder.

"Want to see me?"

"Yes, sir."

"Well, Mr. Wilder, make your interview to the point and brief, please, for my time is valuable. What can I do for you?"

"I came to see you," said Wilder, "about my position in the special force. There is a political move to retire me."

"Ah, about that. Sit down, Mr. Wilder. You'll find a chair there," and the doctor jerked his head over his shoulder toward the chair at the window. Wilder went round the table and sat down in it expecting the gentleman to wheel round his heavy chair and confront him, but he did not He began writing again. After a moment of rapid penmanship, he said without lifting his eyes or his hand from the paper: "You'll excuse me while I finish this letter. You can talk; I can hear you. There is a political move to retire you, yes."

"I should like to know," said Wilder, "if you intend to prefer any charges against me and what they are, in case I refuse to leave New York. It might be possible for me to disarm your antipathy, if you have any."

Dr. Sanger blotted the writing, folded the letter, reached over for an envelope, applied the gummed edges to his lips and sealed the letter. Wilder could follow every minute action behind him.

"I think, Mr. Wilder," said the doctor, as he addressed the envelope with a magnificent gold pen, "that you are a very energetic officer, but that you would be a great deal more comfortable out of New York than in it. You appear to have outgrown your sphere here."

"I don't understand you," said Wilder. The doctor had spread another sheet of note paper and was writing the date on it. "I don't think—it will—be difficult if you want to," he said. "It is the opinion of a large number of influential people that your talents could be employed in a fresh field to better advantage than in New York."

Here he stopped writing and turned his head a little so that the man behind him could see his profile. "This is good advice on my part merely. As there isn't much chance of your following your profession here under the present regime and you probably couldn't very well follow any other at your time of life, I should think that a change of locality to Australia, for example, would be a capital thing for you. Think it over, Mr. Wilder. Think it over."

"Do I understand you to invite me to leave the country to accommodate the rascals who are in it?" asked Wilder.

"No," said the doctor, who began writing again. "I invite you to give way to a power that you can neither oppose nor argue with. A man who has been in the habit of arresting innocent people, taking them out of their homes without warrant or suspicion and spiriting them away, to answer some purpose of his own, is not apt to argue with the department or appeal to the public. I should advise you to go to Montreal, Mr. Wilder, and stay there till you are recalled. You'll pardon me if I finish this letter;" and the doctor went on writing.

Wilder was in a cold stage of indignation. This, then, was the end of his career. He had come up against a bloodless political combination that intended to wipe him out of existence. To stand up and fight it might result in slow vindication, but in the meantime every interest in his keeping must suffer. After a long struggle with an unscrupulous outcast whose hand was against society, and just as he was about to reap the reward of his unremitting toil and innumerable dangers, all the means that society had furnished him fell to pieces, and he was helpless, outwitted and disgraced.

His pride and his indignation were not at the moment as great as his sense of discouragement. A deep numb conviction that there was something radically wrong in society when it lent to its enemies all the facilities to baffle justice, oppressed him. Probably a minute elapsed and nothing was heard but the scratch of the doctor's gold pen. But in that minute Wilder understood perfectly well that the doctor had given him his ultimatum and was serenely confident of the power to enforce his desires. Wilder was just about to end the interview abruptly with an expression of his opinion, when the door in front of him opened suddenly but softly and a woman stepped half way into the room with the hurried intention of speaking to the doctor, but seeing Wilder, she stared at him with a strange startled look, the color left her cheeks and she seemed to sink backwards through the door again, which closed upon her. The doctor called after her—"Kate, Kate," as if to bring her back, and then went on with his epistolary work.

The woman had recognized Wilder in the quick glance and Wilder, with an equally good memory and a special training, had recognized her. But he had a preconceived impression to dislodge. Kate Haviland he supposed had died in the hospital. Evidently she had not and Dr. Sanger had married her. It connected itself in his mind in a moment and the doctor was doubtless innocent of her history.

He got up and went round to the other side of the table so as to confront the doctor who looked up and said:

"Have you made up your mind, Mr. Wilder?"

"Yes," said the officer. "I *have*. I do not leave New York. If either of us leaves, it will be you."

The doctor dropped his pen and threw himself back in his chair with the air of a man who did not wish to be annoyed by threats and didn't intend to be. He utterly failed to comprehend opposition to his will. He believed that the policeman would make some kind of threat and go, but it would not interfere with the results as planned.

"If your interview is over," said the doctor, "please retire, quietly."

Wilder looked at the man placidly enough. The self important air and dictatorial manner had not disappeared, but they no longer offended the officer.

"The interview is *not* over," he said. "The entrance of your wife recalls to me that it is you who have outgrown your sphere of usefulness."

The doctor grasped both arms of his chair as if he were about to leap out of his seat. His face flushed, his eyes flashed. He reached over and struck the bell that was on the table.

"By Heavens," he said, "I'll have you flung into the street."

Wilder grew cold and very calm. "Let me warn you," he observed, "that you are making a mistake and a fatal one. Something has occurred since I have been in this room which disarms me of any feeling of anger which I may have had, and I declare to you that at this moment I feel nothing but the deepest pity for you."

At that moment the door opened and a servant appeared in answer to the bell.

"See if your mistress is in the house," said Wilder with an authoritative air.

The man looked from Wilder to the doctor. His master wore a look of growing anxiety. "She went out this minute," the man said.

Wilder opened the door. There was a moment's pause, during which the three men looked at each other. Dr. Sanger suddenly got up. Some kind of apprehension was growing upon him. He could not have interpreted or formulated his feeling. Mainly, it was a fear that the officer would disclose something; he was not perhaps as fearful of the actual or possible consequences as he was intolerant of any dealing with them. To such an essentially selfish nature it was enough that he had set out to ignore and defy the possibilities of his wife's career and the world ought to regard his determination.

"You had better send your servant out," said Wilder, as he held the door open. "You are not prepared for publicity."

There was in his look as he spoke, a sufficiently calm assurance to convince the doctor that a mere show of authority or of anger would be unavailing. "Leave the room," said the master to the servant, and the tones of his voice, always mandatory, had lost something of their imperiousness.

When the two men were left alone they were facing each other. Both were aware that some kind of a crisis had arrived, but they were not sure of its full significance. The doctor was painfully conscious that the mystery of his wife was about to be divulged and he did not want that. He would do anything to preserve his own careless illusion and ignorance. But mingled with this feeling was a suspicion that Wilder might be using this means to revenge himself. On Wilder's part was the sudden conviction that he had come face to face with the murderess of Ol Enniston and that there was one inevitable duty staring at him. This grim thought gave to his manner an unconscious deliberation and something of the placid relentlessness of facts themselves. The mere expressions of the two men's faces as they looked at each other would have told that one represented fate; the other fatuity.

Wilder was the first to speak. "At such a time," he said, "it is hardly probable that a lady would leave her home and go unattended on the streets without an extraordinary motive. The first thing to do is to secure your wife's safety, in case she has fled."

Dr. Sanger, without a moment's hesitation, sprang to the door. He passed rapidly into the hall and mounted the stairs, taking two steps at a leap. He went directly to his wife's room. It was in disorder. One glance told even the man's unobservant eye that something unusual had occurred. One of the drawers of her dressing-case had been pulled out upon the floor, and some of the contents were scattered on the carpet. A slender flagon of cologne had been knocked over on the marble slab and its neck was fractured. The contents had run down the face of the ebony and left a large wet spot on the white cover. The air was loaded with the perfume. On the velvet couch a satchel gaped as if its contents had been hurriedly pulled out in search of something.

The doctor opened the other drawers of the dressing-case, for the tiny keys hung in a bunch to one of the compartments, and the drawers were unlocked. He turned the contents over roughly with his hand. Mrs. Sanger had a quantity of valuable jewels—he found the jewel case. It was empty. The diamond pins that always flashed from the satin cushion under the mirror were gone. As the husband made this strange examination he grew more and more excited in his manner. Some kind of fear accompanied the growing assurance, and it ended by his turning suddenly to rush from the room, and then he came face to face with Wilder who had followed him up and had been watching the tell-tale operations.

Dr. Sanger was now too visibly alarmed to try to conceal his fears. Every other consideration except the recovery of his wife disappeared. He must have her back. He forgot the possibilities entailed—he strode to the door. Wilder stopped him.

"One moment," he said. "You are satisfied now that she has fled. She is on the streets with her valuables. Her personal safety and recovery are what you are thinking of. I can assist you. If your wife leaves the city, I alone know where she would be likely to go. If she remains here, I can find her. What else comes afterward we can talk of later. Do you want my assistance?"

"By heavens," said the doctor, "I'll have the whole force out"

"It is already out," replied Wilder, "and has its hands full. And the whole force is without my personal knowledge and means."

"Then why don't you do your duty? What do you want? Don't stand there."

"I want the authority," said Wilder. "It is necessary to withdraw your charges. One word from you to the commissioner will do it. Your first step is to send a message to the Central Office. Come down stairs."

"Now, then," said the doctor when they had reached the office, "what do you want? Be quick."

"Write," said Wilder.

The doctor seized his gold pen. Wilder dictated:

"I withdraw all charges pending against John Wilder of the special force. Do not send him out of New York. His services are too valuable here at this time."

The doctor signed it, called a messenger and Wilder saw it go.

"Now, then, a conveyance," he said. "I may catch her at the Hudson River depot."

"Do you intend to restore my wife to me?" asked the doctor, with a pale face and a hard voice.

"I do," replied Wilder.

A moment later he laid his hand upon Carteret's shoulder in the parlor and said: "Quick, my boy. I can save you yet. Come with me."

CHAPTER LX.

MR. PLONSKI'S FINAL TRIUMPH.

When McCune stopped in Mr. Enniston's woods, to roll the cup up in an old newspaper, he heard the sound of the waves in the little bay beneath him.

He listened a moment. "If there is a boat down there, I'll swipe it," he said. "By—that old man had a good grip, he's hurt my windpipe." Then he started down the declivity again and when he came to the water, he threw his sand club as far into the tide as he could and he lingered a moment to see it disappear. Mr. Enniston's boat house stood there in the cove, unused since Carteret and Rosamond did their wooing in the summer afternoons. He kicked the door in, pulled out the skiff and sculls, and leaky as the little vessel was, he pushed himself out into the tide and began rowing down the river as fast as he could. It was at once apparent that the tide was against him. He was tired and sleepy but it would not do to stay in the vicinity. So he pulled at the oars laboriously, stopping now and then to listen for a train. He saw the day break but he could not tell the time. Then his quick ear caught the rumble of the approaching milk train. He slipped into a little bay and seizing the cup gave the boat a shove into the stream with his foot, and mounted the track to wait.

Fertile as he was in devices for getting a ride and being well supplied with money, he had little difficulty in accomplishing his purpose. He had made his calculations roughly but shrewdly, but it never occurred to him that Carteret could be suspected of the murder. He knew that the pursuit would begin immediately and that he would be tracked to New York. But he counted on the public disorder in the city and on Plonski's craft and influence. Once in town, he felt sure that he could baffle the police and with Plonski's aid, escape. His chief anxiety therefore was to get there and the confusion and delay on the road were so great that this anxiety increased momentarily. He was too old a thief not to know that the police would be waiting for him at the depot when the belated train pulled up. He meant to drop off somewhere in a secluded spot in the suburbs. But as the reader already knows, the trains were all blocked for hours and only the passenger freight was pushed through, while the stock and milk cars stood waiting on a siding. It was one o'clock when this train had crept across the bridge at Spuyten Duyvil and pulled up again just north of Innwood in a rocky glen.

It was here that McCune, unobserved, slipped off, made his way up through the rocks and set out nimbly in a southeasterly direction, avoiding as much as possible the public thoroughfares. His one object was to get to the rendezvous and get rid of his booty, and he believed that he could safely pass through the upper portions of the city without much danger, as the police were nowhere on patrol duty and the detective force was occupied entirely with the rioters.

It rather encouraged him to find when he had got down to Fifty-ninth street, that there were signs of disturbance on the west side. He thought that he would have a much better chance of passing unobserved when the attention of every-body was given to a street fight. But when he reached the Seventh avenue, he found that it was in possession of the rioters.

The outlying shops were shut. The roadway was full of people, aimlessly walking about, and the outlook southward down the broad street showed that the black masses increased with the distance. McCune had picked up a stave from a bundle of hay, and he trudged on, carrying his bundle under his arm. To all appearance, he was himself one of the many discontented and vicious mischief makers, who had no other immediate purpose than forcible resistance to the efforts of the authorities to enforce the law.

He thought that it would not be difficult to reach his rendezvous at Thirtieth street by keeping with the groups who seemed to regard him as one of the many who, like themselves, had some kind of a personal grievance against the police. But when he reached Forty-second street, the crowds became denser and more uproarious. It was difficult to get through. While he was trying to work his way among the men and women, there was a sudden roar and yell of voices, and there came into the avenue, from East Forty-second street, a wild procession, headed by a hatless man on a drayman's rawboned horse. He was waving a cutlass, and standing in the stirrups, shouted to his followers to come on. The mob that responded could not in its entirety have consisted of more than two hundred persons, many of whom were women, more ferocious and forbidding than the men. But as the body swept into the avenue and began its march southward, it seemed to suck into its wake all the thousands from the pavements and the avenue above Forty-Second Street, and McCune found him-self following a vast billowing and frenzied sea of human beings. Far in front of him he could see indistinctly, at intervals, the figure of the horseman, waving his arms and riding in advance. Behind him, as far as he could see, the avenue seemed pouring its thousands up in the rear. The din was unearthly, and it was impossible even for this thief, bent only upon his own personal deliverance, to escape the effects of the terrible excitement. But he hugged his bundle under his arm, grasped his stick, and went safely enough along with the monstrous human current, hoping that if it continued on the avenue as far as Thirtieth street, he could there extricate himself and find his employer.

The windows on either side of the avenue were filled with excited spectators of the scene. Some of them gazed with silent horror and apprehension, and others cheered and encouraged the mob. He saw, lifted above the heads of the rabble in front of him, rude banners, which were inscribed: "Down with the police," and "No Nigger Government in New York." The street trembled with the tramp of the multitude, and the air was rent with the noise of thousands of throats. But with that deceptive sense of strength which mere numbers, however unorganized, creates in a certain order of mind, he never thought of the possible danger this mad sortie was running. Indeed, he chuckled secretly at the apparently invincible strength of such a multitude, and believed that nothing could stay it. It was in some way directed at law and civil justice, and it was those things which at this moment he had the most cause to fear.

He was marching with the crowd, and could not have been ten feet from the sidewalk, when he thought he heard his name called in a shrill voice. He looked up and saw Clianthe on one of the crowded steps of a residence. She had seen him, and was fighting and pushing her way down to come to him. In such a tumult a reckless woman has more immunity than a man. The girl, with desperate agility, worked her way through the masses of men, and McCune, by dint of hard struggling, got hold of a telegraph pole and clung, waiting for her. The moment she came near enough to speak, she said in a coarse whisper:

"Give it to me. You'll be took."

"O, no, Gal," he replied; "we don't take no risks with a woman in this kind of a circus. Where's Beaky?"

"He's waitin'."

"All right. Come on? This is pie for us. Nobody ain't goin' to take us in this procesh."

McCune was awakened from his sense of security rather suddenly.

It should be stated that the Government had begun the day before to pour troops into New York, and among those that were sent on and were landing in various portions of the city were several batteries of artillery direct from the front. One of these United States batteries was landed at Thirty-fourth street and North River, and at one o'clock it received orders to march to the Seventh avenue with caissons and quell a riot. The commanding officer started with his guns on the double quick, supported by a detachment of the Seventh Regiment. It is now a matter of history that he swept into the avenue at Twenty-ninth street, unlimbered and opened with grape and cannister at short range. These men were veterans, and they made short work of the mob. The result was ghastly enough. McCune was too far in the rear of the advance to anticipate anything, and the crash of the artillery that shook the surrounding buildings, the splintering of glass, the sudden upraising of terror and pain in shrieks and yells, and the frantic leaping of the mob upon itself in the effort to escape, were the first and only intimations that The Mink had of danger. Along with hundreds of others about him, he realized in an instant what was taking place, as the dense smoke swept over his head, and he forgot everything in the desperate struggle to get from the avenue into one of the side streets. Borne along by the maniacal creatures about him, it required all his agility and strength to keep his feet and not be trodden to death in the stampede, and for five minutes his course was over men, women and children. Clianthe, with an equal desperation and a keener terror, hung to him until the pressure gave way and he was flying down Thirty-second street with the panic stricken torrent. He had not got more than one hundred feet before a new wail of despair went up about him — they were rushing upon the clubs of a battalion of police that was coming up the same street in pursuance of some general flanking plan. It was impossible to turn back. Those behind pressed irresistibly on. McCune, who was close to the sidewalk, was seen by Clianthe to run down a cellarway and try to force the door. While in the act a policeman's club fell upon him with a crushing weight and he knew nothing more until an hour later, when he became conscious in a cell of the Twentieth Precinct Station in Thirty-fifth street, and his bundle was gone.

The surgeon who stood near, saw that he had revived, and beckoned to the sergeant. "Where's me bundle?" asked McCune.

"Your bundle?" replied the officer, with a derisive smile. "Where did you steal it?"

The Mink looked about him craftily. He knew where he was. Involuntarily he put his hand to his head and touched the bandage, but his faculties were alert. It instantly occurred to him that as he was in the hands of the police, it was far better to be taken for a rioter than for the murderer of Captain Ackerman, and if they did not recognize him, he could say that he took the cup from Plonski's house and that person's influence would still be in his favor.

He knew that the moment he was able to speak, the routine of the station would require him to answer certain questions, and he tried to fix in his mind what to say and how to communicate with Plonski.

Something, however, of the ordinary procedure was omitted or delayed at this time, owing entirely to the extraordinary state of affairs at the Station House. Men and women, many of them wounded, were huddled into all the rooms and cells, and the place was besieged by citizens and guarded by a detachment of soldiers, who made it in some sort a barracks and headquarters. On the main floor were a number of unsightly forms with rough rubber coverings thrown over them, but unmistakably denoting by their conformation, that they were corpses.

Twenty minutes after the artillery had opened on the mob, the military had possession of the street. The guard was walking regularly from Thirteenth to Fortieth street, and a row of twelve pound field pieces looked up and down the avenue. But the event had been carried over the city by swift tongues, and people were coming from all directions to look upon the scene, and to enquire at the station after friends. Among the politicians and officials whose interest brought them to the station, was Judge Sanger, who drove up in a cab, and went at once into the captain's room. He had not been there a minute when Plonski elbowed his way through the crowd and came in behind him. He was noticeably livid in hue and anxious in expression. His quick eyes ran over the crowds and took in the scenes with sly rapidity, as he made his way through the groups to the sergeant's desk.

He was not graciously received by the officer, who was doing his best to preserve an official equanimity, in spite of the aggravations of an importuning and not very reasonable crowd of citizens.

"Stand back, will you? What do you want to climb over me for? If you don't take it easy, I'll run some of you into the street."

At this admonition there was a moment's hush, and the women who were looking for their wounded friends, subdued their lamentations and objurgations.

Plonski, who had got through the crowd finally, caught the officer's eye.

"I merely wish to identify and recover a piece of stolen property," he said. "It was taken under my eyes, and the thief was arrested with it in his hands."

"O, well, you'd better go in and see the captain," replied the sergeant. "I can't 'tend to you now."

The stick of a roundsman, who stood near trying to keep order, pointed towards the inner office, and after a moment's parley with another roundsman, Plonski got into the private room. There he found Judge Sanger in close consultation with the captain.

The judge knew him. It was a most fortunate occurrence for Plonski. The politician in his easy heartiness, said at once:

"Hello, Plon. What's the matter with you? Looking for some of the boys?"

"No," said Plonski. "I had a piece of silver plate taken from my room in Thirty-ninth street by the crowd. The man that took it was arrested in the melee with it in his hands. I want to recover it and appear against him."

"O, is that all? Well, you're lucky. The captain will fix you up. Captain, this is a friend of mine, Mr. Plon. Anything he wants I'll be responsible for."

The captain nodded his head. "Was the plate brought here?"

"Yes," said Plonski, "I hope so. It was captured with the fellow. He was not in the fighting crowd but was trying to escape when the police arrived. I can describe the property."

"O, it isn't necessary. You will appear against the man?"

"Yes. When will he be arraigned?"

"We'll take a batch of 'em to Jefferson Market in the morning. You see we haven't room for 'em here. You'd better come there."

The captain called an officer in. "Just give this gentleman his property. Take his address. See that the sergeant puts it on the blotter."

"This way, sir," said the officer.

Plonski bowed and thanked the judge politely.

"O, that's all right," said that hearty individual, drawing his chair up to the captain's again. "That's all right. You may be able to do me a turn some time. Good day."

In less than ten minutes Plonski had the cup in his hands. He stood at the desk while the sergeant was entering his name and address. It required all his strength of mind to keep his anxiety from becoming visible. An acute fear possessed him, now that he had the long-sought-for article in his possession, that Wilder would turn up before he could get out of the place. The officer appeared to be maliciously slow in making the entry. He stopped once or twice and leaning over the book, looked inquiringly at Plonski as if some kind of suspicion was awakened or he had seen his face before.

When he had deliberately written the name and Plonski was about to go he stopped him. "You say that you live at 160 West Thirty-ninth. How long have you lived there?"

"Not a great while," remarked Plonski.

"Do you usually reside in a livery stable?"

"No, sir. I do not."

The sergeant called out, "Watson, see if Officer Dennin is there."

"Pardon me," said Plonski, with an admirable show of composure, "why not ask the captain? His orders were to make a minute of my address. He probably knows his duty, as he knows me."

The sergeant hesitated a moment. Then he said:

"All right. If the captain says so, it goes; but it's dead irregular and he'll have to shoulder it."

"Are you through with me?" asked Plonski.

"Pass on."

CHAPTER LXI.

PLONSKI MAKES OFF WITH THE CUP.

It was John Wilder's intention, as it was plainly his duty, now to find Mrs. Sanger and McCune if possible. If not interfered with, he felt sure that he could catch the woman. Some kind of instinct told him she would make her way to her mother in Deposit. But in any attempt to leave the city, her chances of easy exit were at this moment small, indeed, in view of the conditions of travel. The apprehension of The Mink was another matter. To catch that wily thief and murderer, and Wilder had no doubt that he was the murderer of Captain Ackerman, required the machinery of the department and the aid of the special men usually detailed for such work, which he could not at this moment command. There was but one probability to lay hold of—the man was in the service of Plonski and Plonski was in the city. The agent would try to communicate with the principal and turn over the property. For him to come at once to the city would be the safest course in the city's present condition and the only direct means of reaching the city was the Hudson River Railroad.

By some rapid process of induction, the officer arrived at the best means of action. Professional pride was keenly alive to the situation. He was the depository of two extraordinary mysteries. Innocence depended on him—justice expected him to do his duty. His course was not very clear. He was not certain of his own plans and a hundred obstacles intervened.

But with his usual rapidity of mind, he arrived at the only safe course of conduct before he left the doctor's house.

"I will find Mrs. Sanger," he said, "if it be possible. You had better remain here where I can communicate with you. If I want you I will send."

In spite of the doctor's imperious will, Wilder had his own way. Both men were grimly guarded in their manner and conversation and the short colloquy in the hall before they separated was characteristic.

"I will accompany you," said the doctor.

"It will be useless," replied Wilder. "I will find Mrs. Sanger. It is my duty, but I must take my own course. If you will go to the Central Office and wait I can put myself in communication with you."

"What do you intend to do?" asked the doctor with a hard voice.

"Find your wife for you," replied Wilder.

"What else?"

Wilder drew himself up. "Doctor Sanger," he said, "my first duty is to find her. There will be time for explanations afterward. I refuse to say more until I am sure it is necessary, and in that present silence I best serve you."

It was four o'clock when he stopped at Mrs. Hannige's and made Carteret get out. "You will run too much risk in going with me," he said. "Remain here where you are my prisoner. Do you understand? I'll give Molly a word. It's better for them to find you here."

It was three o'clock when McCune was arrested and it was a few minutes past four when Plonski left the Station House with the cup in his possession.

At half past four, Wilder was compelled to abandon his vehicle at the Sixth avenue and make his way on foot through the crowds on the streets to the Thirtieth street depot. Long before he reached the offices of the road, he knew what had taken place in the Seventh avenue. It was discouraging, but he kept on with the pertinacity that had so often brought him out of similar difficulties. Some kind of instinct made him feel sure that the woman he was in search of would come here. There was a mere chance of catching her. But he was satisfied in a very few minutes that he must give up that idea. Only one train had gone out and that had left before she could possibly have reached the station and she was not among the crowd of anxious people that was waiting. He therefore left such directions as would make it impossible for her to take a train without being noticed and went to the road master. Here he got an accurate account of the trains that had come in and after a hunt through the neighborhood, found one of the brakemen who had come down on the milk train. A very few questions sufficed to convince him that McCune had boarded that train somewhere between Coe's Grove and New York with the cup, and once satisfied of this, there was nothing more to do but to get the assistance of the Central Office and capture him if he was in the city.

It was with a vague purpose of this kind that Mr. Wilder set out from the railroad yards to the Twentieth Precinct Station, distant but four squares, though he may have been induced, now that he was in the neighborhood to see and hear for himself what the result of the fight on the Seventh avenue had been.

When he arrived on the Seventh avenue, he found a battery of artillery planted in the roadway and our old friend Mr. John Sitwhite, sitting on a caisson, while a platoon of his men kept the crowd back with bayonets.

A little further on, he met Dan Sully with the badge of a United States marshal on his coat. "Come over to the station," he said; "I want to show you a sight. It gives me a starter."

"They've had bloody work here," Wilder said as they walked along.

"Yes," replied Sully. "There won't be any more of it. This has settled it. If they'd had the artillery here last Tuesday, it would have saved lives."

When they got to the station, Sully went to one of the rubber covers and pulled it down. Wilder started.

"That's not the one," he said. "Wait a minute—"

"Hold on," said Wilder; "I know that woman."

"She's a beauty," said Sully, "but that isn't what I want you to see."

Wilder stopped him as he was about to cover the form and bent down to look at it.

It was Mrs. Doctor Sanger. She was attired in her rich walking dress, but her hand still clasped the folds of the garment on her bosom and it was torn away in a death spasm, exhibiting the clotted blood that had flowed from a bullet wound.

The officer looked at her with a strange sense of pity. Sully saw that he was shocked. "Know her?" he asked.

"Yes," replied Wilder.

"She tried to cross toward the station at Thirtieth street when the mob was firing down the avenue, a stray bullet struck her and she fell on the curb. They carried her into a hallway first and went through her pockets. She had nothin' when she got here."

Wilder drew the covering over the beautiful face as gently as possible. "What," he was saying, "will the doctor say to this?"

"Here," said Sully; "come here. I thought mebbe you'd like to see what happened to Big Casey," and he turned down another of the rude palls.

Even the steel nerves of Wilder shrank a little at the sight He saw the form of a man that had been struck by a discharge of grape shot at short range and it had torn away the whole breast, exposing the viscera. His face was untouched and Wilder, with a quick recognition, turned away.

"That feller hit me with a shoe once," said Sully. "I'm carryin' the marks of it on me yet."

Wilder then went into the captain's office and communicated with Dr. Sanger. He must have had a long consultation with the captain, for when Dr. Sanger drove up, he had not come out.

When the doctor was shown his beautiful wife, he stooped and kissed her. There were no tears in his eyes and not a tremor in his voice.

While they were preparing to remove the body, Wilder and he looked into each others eyes. One man was pallid and stony. The other was patient and unflinching.

"There was a duty," said Wilder. "It has been cancelled. Do you want to know?"

"No," replied the doctor. "Death is silence."

"I will respect it," said the officer, and unconsciously he lifted his hat.

The doctor extended his hand. The men looked in each others faces. There was a quick grasp. Not another word was spoken.

While these events were taking place, Plonski was traveling as fast as he possibly could without attracting attention, down the Eleventh avenue toward West street. He trudged along with his bundle protruding from his surtout coat, very much as if it were a package of cold victuals some one had given him. He appearance was not indicative of prosperity, and his carriage was that of a slightly infirm man. He bent over a little, and might have been taken for an elderly artisan hurrying home. Fortunately for him he encountered no patrolmen, and the usual idlers of this thoroughfare were drawn away by the excitement elsewhere.

When he reached West street, he went into a sailor's store where a number of men were congregated, and bought a hand satchel and a number of other articles which he put into it, including his bundle. Then he went on down West street until he reached that neighborhood below Twenty-third street which is given up to canal boats and barges. Here he stood a moment trying to survey and comprehend the vast snarl of produce boats that stretched out as far as he could see north and south.

He appeared to be undetermined, for he went upon one of the docks between long lines of bleating calves and heaps of hay and lumber, and then came back as if he had made a mistake, and tried the dock one street higher up. He picked his way through the chaos of produce, and came at last to a flotilla of canal boats lying in the ooze and sewage, for the tide was out, and then shading his eyes from the hot afternoon sun, he stood on the string piece looking down on the dirty fleet, and wondering how he could get down the sides of the dock. Some one below came to his assistance and put up a rough stepladder for him. He looked up and down the dock. Nobody was observing him. The next moment he was climbing down the steps guardedly, while the boatman held them at the bottom. "I want the 'Mary Isabel,'" he said.

"There she is alongside," replied the man. "You look as if you could escape the draft without running away. Look out and don't fall down that hole. Here, gim'me your bag; I'll toss it over to you."

Plonski thanked him and climbed over the shingles and potatoes to the next boat which, with several others, was unloaded. The moment he was on the deck of the "Mary Isabel," a man who was smoking his pipe under a small awning on the stern, came up and spoke to him. "Well, old man, you goin' with us?"

"Yes. When do you go?"

"'Spect to pull out in half an hour; that's our tug tootin' out there now."

"Good," said Plonski. "Do you want your money now?"

"Might as well take it fust as last."

"Very well. Come under the awning out of the sun. When will you be in the Valley?"

"'Bout a week"

The two men then went under the canvas and sat down, and Plonski counted out a number of bills, saying as he did so, "You see I always did prefer the quiet way of traveling, and as I haven't got anything to hurry me, it looks as if this kind of a trip would build me up."

While this was going on, Carteret was once more walking the floor of the room which Mr. Evans and his grand daughter had previously occupied. The young man was in a pitiable state of mind; impatience, anxiety and indignation moved him by turns. He at one moment gave way to despair and said that he was cursed, but the next moment he was measuring with a more healthful reason the means of vindication. What would Manuella think? That was the oppressive question after all. Suppose the man McCune was never heard of again; what then was to be the fate reserved for him? Was Manuella to grow, with all the circumstantial evidence and all the dreadful delay of the law, into the slow belief that he was guilty? To an impatient young man this was about as poignant a reflection as he could experience. He hunted up pen and paper. He would write to her at once and explain matters. The accursed ill luck that had separated them again should not have his aid and silence.

He was scratching away hurridly at this epistle, when Mrs. Hannige burst into the room looking very panic-stricken and panting heavily. "Mr. Carteret," she said, "My God, I'm all shook to pieces there's three men down stairs—they want you. Do you know what they say? You've committed a murder."

Carteret jumped up and Mrs. Hannige shrunk at once instinctively from him, as if he were already contaminating.

"I am not a murderer, Mrs. Hannige," he said. "Who are these men?"

She leaned against the wall as if overcome.

"They're officers," she replied. "O, I can't talk to them. You'll have to see 'em."

"Can't I see them here? Ask them to come up."

It was unneccessary. They had come up and one of them had pushed the door open while Carteret was speaking. It was Cob Dutcher.

"There's your man," he said, pointing to Carteret.

His two companions stepped into the room. One was the grizzled and sinewy country official, with much iron gray hair curling out from under his chin and a crook-neck stick hanging over his arm. The other was a policeman in uniform.

"I arrest you," said the sheriff, "for the murder of Captain Job Ackerman. I am deputy sheriff of Putnam county. Put your hat on. You will have to come with me."

"Gentlemen," said Carteret, "I am already in the hands of Inspector Wilder, pending the arrest of the real murderer. You will save yourselves a great deal of unnecessary trouble, and me a great deal of useless annoyance by seeing him first."

"Yes," said the sheriff of Putnam county. "Jess so, but Mr. Wilder can come to Putnam if he don't like my way of doin' business. I jest want you to come with me and don't make no talk."

But Mr. Cob Dutcher demurred at once.

"We'd better see the inspector," he said; "he knows more about this than we do."

"I don't want to see no inspector," said the other. "I never knowed nobody could teach me how to do my duty. We'll talk about this when my man's under lock and key."

The hard, unreasoning face of the man convinced Carteret that it would be useless to appeal further to him. So he put on his hat and was about to pick up the unfinished letter, when the deputy snatched it from the table. "What's this?" he said, as he put on his glasses. "Let's see."

The group stood round in expectancy the door was wide open and Carteret was aware that the household were in the hallway. Nothing could have made the dread fact of his situation so acute as this act of the officer, from which there was no appeal, and the sudden conciousness that all the inmates of the house were regarding him with pity, curiosity and something of horror.

The sheriff having deliberately adjusted his glasses behind his ears with an additional remark that "We'll see about this," began to read:

"MY DEAR MANUELLA:

That accursed cup that appears to be the blight of my life has now plunged me into another and awful misfortune. When I left you to set out for Coe's Grove, I gave you my promise. You see how I have kept it. I believe the cup has ruined me."

"Humph," remarked the sheriff, holding up the paper; "that's your handwritin' you'll allow."

"It is," said Carteret; "and it's a private letter."

"Jes' so," ejaculated the sheriff, folding the paper up and putting it into a big wallet. "We'll see what your peers of Putnan county have to say about the cussed cup. It's ruined many a promisin' young man, but I don't know as it will stand in your favor with a jury of Coe's Grove, seein' as how that's a purty tight temperance village. Why, when a man put it in black and white that the cup is the ruin of him it's agin' a sheriff's principles not to let him hev the benefit of his confessions."

At the conclusion of this speech, to which Carteret did not make any reply, the officer touched him on the arm and the young man went down stairs by his side, a prisoner, and Cob Dutcher and the policeman closed up the rear. The servants were looking over the hand rail and Mrs. Hannige and Mr. Stonybrook had their heads together. The deputy sheriff from Putnam county had succeeded in impressing the household with the importance of his errand, but when they got into the lower hall another consultation took place. Carteret told Cob Dutcher that they were making a mistake. "If you arrest me, I warn you that I will hold you responsible. Inspector Wilder knows as well as I do who the real criminal is and if you insist upon arresting an innocent man, who is already in the hands of the best officer in the city, without consulting him, I want you to understand plainly that I'll make Putnam county sweat for it."

But Putnam county observed that he had "heered young men swagger like that afore. It never skeered him and he wanted to get to Coe's Grove afore midnight."

Cob Dutcher took the sheriff into the little reception room with his prisoner and there they held a long parley, the policeman waiting outside on the steps.

It was six o'clock when Dutcher gave it up and the rural officer, tapping Carteret on his arm, indicated that he was of the same opinion still. Wilder arrived before they got out of the house and he landed, so to speak, in the center of the group.

A quick explanation was made. Carteret was eagerly bending forward to hear his friend interpose in his behalf. What was his amazement when that friend merely said, "Have you got the papers?" and getting an affimative answer, he only remarked "There's your man."

"But you don't mean," cried Carteret, "to leave me under this cruel accusation?"

Wilder shrugged his shoulders. "There's your prisoner," he said. Then he opened the door and called the policeman in. "See that this arrest of Colin Carteret for the murder of Captain Job Ackerman is sent to the Central Office, so that it will go in the morning papers," he said. "Say that the arrest was made by Inspector Wilder and the prisoner turned over to the sheriff of Putnam county."

"In the name of heaven, John Wilder," exclaimed Carteret, "What does this mean? You know as well as I do, that I am not a murderer."

Wilder turned away. The sheriff said, "Now then, we've had enough nonsense. Right face, march."

Cob Dutcher followed Wilder into Mrs. Hannige's back room as the men departed and when the inspector had dropped into a chair with a very fagged air, Cob remarked: "What's your game, Captain? You don't believe that young man killed Captain Ackerman do you?"

"Cob." said Wilder, "you must have seen McCune take that train from Tarrytown to Coe's Grove."

"So help me, I didn't," replied Cob. "I ought to, but I didn't. All I saw was Mr. Carteret take it and he carried the bundle."

"Well," said Wilder, "I wish you'd come over to the court in the morning. You may help me. Will you?"

"Sure," said Cob. "You won't be so tired there and I want to chin you."

Half an hour later when Mrs. Hannige came softly in, she found her brother fast asleep in his chair with his head on the table.

When she woke him with sisterly consideration and begged him to go to bed and get some rest, he got up, took a drink of water and saying "good night" with a gruffness that was not habitual with him and that surprised his sister, he went off to bed.

He overslept himself the next morning and was in a worse humor when he got his coffee.

Meanwhile the mill at the Jefferson market had begun to grind. The court-room was crowded. A double row of policemen was at the doors and the crowd of prisoners in the pen was large. Among them was the rodent face with the peering gray eyes and flattened nose of The Mink and his restless glance wandered over the mass of spectators in search of Plonski. Lawyers, shysters and reporters were gathered about the rail and a malodorous air, dense and moist, pervaded the place. The jargon of the mob subsided at the sharp rap of a policeman, as the judge entered and took his seat and, leaning over the desk, shook hands with an acquaintance below him who evidently made a humorous remark, for they both laughed loudly.

The process of listening to the petty cases that came up was a tedious one. The charges were, for the most part, of disorderly conduct and were dismissed in a perfunctory manner and with a fine. One poor woman was accused of petty larceny and was defended by a young lawyer, which delayed matters. While it was on, the sheriff arrived with Carteret. They were brought down and seated inside the rail by an officer, and a moment after John Smith was called and a policeman shoved McCune to the front. He stepped forward with his head down, but he gave an anxious look around the house. Wilder was not present. He had time to see everybody that was in the courtroom, for the judge was laughing and talking with a politician who had come up and seated himself beside him. He was a fine, portly gentleman with flossy white hair and red cheeks and his broadcloth coat was jauntily thrown back and displayed a wealth of shirt front. In an interval of jocular conversation, the judge turned and said:

"Well, my man, what have you been doing?"

A policeman responded. "He was taken in the crowd yesterday with a piece of stolen property."

"Was he rioting?"

"Well, not exactly, your honor. He was running away and got a rap on the nob."

"Where's the property?"

"It was given up to the party as claimed it."

"Well, well, well," cried the judge; "What is the charge against the man? I can't sit here all day. Where is the owner of the property?"

The policeman looked helplessly around upon the spectators. Nobody responded. The portly gentleman whispered something to the judge.

"You're discharged young man," he said. "Step down. Next."

At that moment two persons in the assemblage rose up. One was a young woman in a rear seat. She got upon the bench to overlook the crowd and see the discharged prisoner.

The other was a tall, sinewy man who had been hidden by the prisoners. He pushed them aside as he entered the pen and placing his hand on McCune, who was just about to leave the dock, he said: "I want you for your job at Coe's Grove," and before the man had recovered from his astonishment he had snapped the irons on his wrists.

At the same moment, Mr. Dan Sully tapped Clianthe on the back and said:

"Sis, it's no use. That's the inspector and he wants you. He told me to stay by you. Don't be foolish or I'll have to rivet you up, too."

CHAPTER LXII.

LOVE LIES BLEEDING.

The morning after Carteret left the aqueduct with the cup Manuella brought her sewing out on the little porch and sat down beside her grandfather. It was one of those dewy summer mornings when the heart of nature sings voluptuously. Very beautiful was the girl as she sat there in her crisp muslin dress, with her little slipper on the rung of Carteret's sketching stool. Chapman was standing in the shadows of the road nearby with an absurd artist's umbrella over his head. He was admiring her with an artist's eye and a man's zest. The keen particularity of his vision made him take in all the details. "What a superb combination of Diana and Gretchen," he was saying to himself. "What a divine unconsciousness of her multitudinous spell. I don't believe she has the faintest notion how bewilderingly and aggravatingly intoxicating she is from her chignon to her foot. Why, the curve of her neck is like a poem of Rossetti's. She seems to grow upward from grace to color and end in a halo."

She was bending over her needle. She was always sewing now. The white material on her lap was flecked with dancing shadows of the vines. Old Towse was lying at full length on the gravel with his tongue hanging out. A couple of humming birds were whirring above her head in the flowers. It was a serene picture. Chapman could hear the Pocantico singing softly in the woods. "Carteret was right," he said; "this is the place for him to paint a picture, but not for me. The inspiration has a despairing envy in it for me." Just then Mrs. Manser came to the door in her spotless white apron and looked out over her spectacles, first at Chapman and then at Manuella.

"I s'pose Mr. Carteret will be back this mornin'," she said, "and be here to dinner."

"I wouldn't count on him," Chapman said; "travel isn't very easy just now."

Manuella looked up. "O, he'll be here," she said confidently.

"I'd like to know," said Mrs. Manser; "'cause if he was I'd put that other chicken in the oven."

"Don't waste it," said Chapman. "Trains are mighty uncertain nowadays."

"He will surely return this morning," said Manuella. "He told me so."

"I hav'n't the slightest doubt of his intention," said Chapman. "I was only fearing his connections. But I'm going down to the depot and watch for him. I want to hear the news." Then he sauntered off and Manuella sat for some time with her needle suspended. She was thinking. Presently she said, "Grandpa, you didn't tell me about the letters you got yesterday. Who were they from? Were they love letters, that you kept them so sly?"

"They were from Mr. Stonybrook, my dear, and were only business letters. A girl like you wouldn't be interested in them."

"Yes, I would. Will you let me see them?"

"Yes, yes. In good time; in good time."

"Have you been corresponding with Mr. Stonybrook, Grandpa?"

"My dear, I always made it a rule when I was in business to answer letters promptly, and I haven't outgrown the habit."

"Did you answer Mr. Stonybrook's letters?"

"Certainly."

"How strange."

"Strange, my dear?"

"Yes, that I should not have known it."

She was thinking how much her time and attention had been absorbed of late to have overlooked her grandfather's occupation, and how slyly he had done this.

"Did you send the answers?"

"Yes, my dear. Mr. Chapman took them with him."

"What—just now?

"Yes, my dear. Mr. Stonybrook's intimacy and kindness would not permit me to neglect him."

"Will you let me see his letters?"

She noticed that her grandfather fidgetted a little.

"My child," he said, "you shouldn't bother yourself with matters you do not understand."

"You don't want me to see Mr. Stonybrook's letters?"

"Yes, yes. You shall see them. I think I'll go and take a short walk in the sun, my dear," and he got up and began to fuss about. She buttoned his coat across his breast and tied a kerchief round his neck, and he strode away striking his stick in the gravel quite vigorously, with a plain intimation that he needed no attendance.

It annoyed her very much to find that her grandfather was in correspondence with Mr. Stonybrook, and it annoyed her still more to find that it had an air of surreptitiousness.

But her thought presently drifted into another channel as she resumed her sewing. She was thinking of Carteret all the more tenderly now that the reappearance of the cup and his departure cast a vague apprehension over her thoughts. How good and kind and gentle he had been of late. Nobody knew him so well as she did. How exquisite was his sense of beauty and how delightful was his companionship. All their old fears had vanished. She was his now.

They had lived the past few days in the full confidence of the fact. What could possibly come between them now?

She stopped, as she asked herself this question, and began to wonder why she asked it. The humming birds were poised over the jasmine flowers. She looked at them without seeing them. A bit of deep blue sky threw them out in strong relief like silhouettes. Somehow they were like little cherubs such as we see on old tombstones, and they were away off in that blue ether.

Why was she growing nervous again? Was it the discovering that Mr. Stonybrook was writing to her grandfather? Absurd. The girl had not the slightest fear of Mr. Stonybrook, and yet she felt that some kind of a growing anxiety indefinable and causeless was there in her mind like a restless shadow.

Was this the premonition of evil that sometimes projects itself upon the delicate texture of such exquisite organizations?

She put her sewing by and tried to amuse herself with Towse. She went out on the aqueduct to enjoy the walk with her grandfather. They watched Mr. Manser in the gatehouse and heard him tell how General Washington threw up redoubts "jess down the road" and how one of his men fired his old Queen Anne musket at the ball on the church spire and how the bullet was "astickin' in it yit." But she was conscious that her gayety was a little forced, and by and by she went to her room and shut her door with the one purpose of enjoying a woman's luxury of being alone with herself.

They waited dinner for Carteret till half past one, an unprecedented thing for a farmer, but neither he nor Chapman appeared. The little group at the table was absurdly gloomy without reason, and Manuella's anxiety was rising with every hour. At three o'clock she resorted to the last device of expectancy and helplessness. She threw herself on her bed and tried to stop her thinking and worrying with sleep. While she lay there, a picture indeed, with a south wind fluttering her curtain and an occasional yellowjacket looking in at her with priviledged wonder, Chapman was waiting at the depot to get the news from the city. It was two o'clock when the first papers came up on an extra train and were thrown off in a bundle as it went through. Chapman secured one, and it was not long before his eye fell upon the dispatch from Coe's Grove. His astonishment and horror were great. The instant conclusion was that the paragraph referred to Carteret as the murderer. His instant thought was that some infamous practical joke was being perpetrated on his friend. He turned it in every possible way to get some kind of reasonable meaning out of it, but failed. He would stake his life on Carteret but why did he not return? It was three o'clock and he dared not go back till he learned something. Eaten up with anxiety and impatience, he tried to telegraph to Wilder, and when at last he succeeded in getting a dispatch through, he was told by the operator that there was no chance of its being delivered in the city.

Finally, a train came south, and on it was the sheriff of Putnam county who got off at Tarrytown to get the assistance of Cob Dutcher who could identify Carteret.

Then Chapman learned that his friend had gone to New York and that the officer was in search of him. Still he wouldn't believe that it was true. There was some dreadful mistake somewhere and he made up his mind not to tell Manuella. There would be a late mail from the city he would come down and get that. It would bring some word from Carteret.

When he returned to the aqueduct, Manuella saw by his face that something had happened. Her own grew a shade paler as she looked at him. He tried to assume a jocular air, but he was a bad actor and it had a ghastly strain in it.

"Something has happened, Mr. Chapman, and you have not the courage to tell it like a man," she said. "Where are the papers?"

"There were none this morning, so if there's anything happened" he said, "we hav'n't heard of it yet," and he turned his head as if her eyes affected him like a blaze of light.

"Mr. Carteret," he said, "has probably been detained by the business he had in hand. We shall hear from him with the afternoon mail."

There was nothing that could be done now, but wait and keep silent. A blight had fallen on the little party. Late in the afternoon Chapman went again to the village to get the mail. There were two newspapers addressed to Mr. Evans, care of Mr. Manser, but no letters, and he handed these papers over to the old gentleman without letting Manuella see him and said: "Put them away. They'll do to read on a rainy day."

Nothing occurred until ten o'clock at night. He had avoided Manuella and gone to his bedroom about nine. He was just ready to turn in when there came a light rap at his door. "Who is it?" he asked.

"It is I," said the voice of Manuella. "Can you come into the hall a moment? I wish to speak to you."

He threw on his dressing gown and came out. She looked like Lady Macbeth as she stood there in the passage, pale and clad in white, holding a candle in her hand.

"I go to the city in the morning," she said, with strange deliberation. "Will you accompany me?"

"I will do anything you require," replied Chapman. "Have you heard?"

"Yes. It is an awful conspiracy. I must see Mr. Carteret."

"And your father?"

"He will go too."

"Very well, Miss Castleton. Get yourself in readiness. I will tell Mr. Manser. You can rely on me."

He wanted to ask her many questions; to offer sympathy and advice; but something in her resolute white face deterred him. She thanked him and he instinctively and formally bowed.

"Good night," she said.

"Good night, Miss Castleton."

The next morning at ten o'clock, the little party landed at the Hudson River depot in the city. Mrs. Enniston, Dr. Flockton, and Dr. Wollendorf had come down on the train with them, and they did not know it until Chapman, leaving Manuella and her grandfather in the waiting room, went out to get a conveyance and encountered Miss Enniston who had left her mother, and come out for the same purpose.

"Isn't this dreadful?" she said with a suppressed voice. "I'm so sick I ought to be in bed. It seems so horrible and incomprehensible that I can't make it out."

"It's all a lie so far as Carteret is concerned," said Chapman. "You must know that. He's got a friend in Detective Wilder who will vindicate him, I trust."

"Haven't you seen the morning papers?"

"No," said Chapman. "I couldn't get them on the train."

Miss Enniston took one from her reticule and pointed to a paragraph.

"The Coe's Grove murderer arrested. Inspector Wilder last night arrested a young man named Colin Carteret, charged with the murder of Captain Job Ackerman at Coe's Grove. He was turned over to the custody of Sheriff Frost, of Putnam County. There can be no doubt, the inspector says, of the young man's guilt."

"I think," said Miss Enniston, "that Carteret must be insane. Why did he fly to New York?"

Chapman looked at her with something like dismay. There was a scintillant light in her eyes that was new to him, and her manner was spasmodic and eager.

"I cannot tell you," he answered; "the whole thing is a mystery to me. But I cannot believe that Colin Carteret has done this deed."

"Yes, you always defended him in everything. I remember. But it almost drives me to desperation. You don't think he could be driven to a rash act by temptation—by an extravagant woman or something—do you?"

"Miss Enniston, I have not thought of it that way. I never saw anything desperate in Carteret's character."

"Did you come down on this train?"

"Yes."

"Who came with you?"

"Mr. Evans and his granddaughter."

She threw her head back a little, and Chapman thought he heard the click of her teeth.

"Are you going to find Carteret?"

"Yes, as soon as I send Mr. Evans home."

"Then Miss Castleton is not going with you?"

"No. You do not understand—"

"Take me with you," she broke in. "I *must* see him."

"Consider," said Chapman, shrinking at once from the task, "it would be a rash undertaking at the best for a woman, and at this time perilous. I do not know where he is, or that I can see him myself. He may be on his way back to Coe's Grove."

"Back to Coe's Grove?" she repeated, with an inquiring tone. "Must they take him back there?"

Then she made a jump at Chapman, catching him by the coat, entirely unconscious that she was attracting attention by her actions. "Where are you going to look for him?"

"I am going to the house in Fifteenth street," Chapman replied. "If I can find the officer, Mr. Wilder, who was always his friend, I may learn something."

"But that is the man who arrested him."

"Yes, so it appears. I don't understand it, but arresting a man doesn't make a man guilty, Miss Enniston."

"Where is the prison or the institution for arrested people?" she asked.

Chapman could not help a twitching smile. "I really couldn't tell you," he said; "I suppose the Police Headquarters in Mulberry street is the best place to get information."

"Is it?"

"Probably."

"If you get any will you come and tell me, on your honor?"

"Yes," replied Chapman, glad of the relief that the promise afforded him.

She put her hand in his and caught hold of him with a strenuous grasp, as she said: "Don't forget, you have promised to let me know immediately if you hear anything."

She turned away and then came suddenly back, saying: "You will not think strangely of my impatience, will you? This dreadful affair has upset my mind completely."

"Don't make any apologies, Miss Enniston," Chapman replied, "I think we are all upset."

He stood watching her a moment as she went rapidly into the passenger room. Something in her manner had struck him painfully and he could not tell what it was.

Shortly after this, he put Manuella and her grandfather into a coach and set out with them for Mrs. Sitwhite's. The vehicle was driven at a rapid rate and they found no opportunity for saying those things which the occasion seemed to call for. Manuella preserved a cautious reticence, either because she did not wish to discuss matters before her grandfather or because Chapman was not exactly the one to discuss them with, so they uttered scarcely anything but monosyllables during the whole ride, which occupied three quarters of an hour.

Chapman saw his charges safely to the little piazza of Mrs. Holbrook's cottage and promising to come back as soon as possible with all the good news he could get, he left them. He was awfully blue. To use his own words: "An ideal loaf with a goddess in it had been blown sky high over night. Hang it, what would his artistic sensibilities do now without this dew and sunshine to feed on? Suppose Carteret should be guilty? Good Heavens. It wasn't beyond the range of human possibilities. Weren't men crazed in all ages by these sirens? What did Miss Enniston mean by saying he was insane? Perhaps she knew that he inherited a taint of insanity."

"Well, Mommy," he said, when he got to Mrs. Hannige's, "here I am, upside down. What in the name of humanity have you been doing since I went away? Where's Wilder?"

"Oats, my boy, I'm awful glad to see you. I never missed anybody so much in all my life. Did you ever hear of such goings on? If a saint had told me such a thing of Carteret I would not have believed it. I can hardly believe it now. I was so taken when they came for him, that I liked to have dropped upon the floor dead. And that poor girl too. Where is she? My, my, what a terrible thing temptation is."

"Mommy, I don't think you know what you are talking about. You don't think Carteret is a man to kill anybody."

"That's what I would have said against the world. But when John makes up his mind about a man, I don't think my judgment amounts to much, and you can't tell what a young man can be led into when he loses his head."

"Where is he?"

"My. I s'pose he's in a condemned cell. You didn't expect to find him here, did you? Mr. Chapman, I always was particular about my guests, no matter what else I may have been, you ought to know that, and I guess I put up with that young man as long as anybody could. If that girl had listened to me—"

"Say, Mommy, if you want me to listen to you, come down to facts. Where's Mr. Wilder?"

"As if I could tell where he is at these times. Why man, I haven't seen him for a week at a stretch and then expected every time the door bell rang to see him brought in cold. If he isn't in court, he's at three hundred, and if he isn't at three hundred, he's on the street. Tell me about Miss Castleton. I s'pose she knows."

"Yes, she knows."

"Does she take on badly?"

"No. She bears up like a brick. She's one of those stubborn kind that thinks she knows Carteret better than a judge and jury. Do you think I'd catch Mr. Wilder at three hundred?"

"Lands, Oats, I can't tell you where you'd catch him. What do you want of him?"

"I want to find out all about my friend, before they hang him. I'm like Miss Castleton, I believe in him."

"Well, I'll tell you, John is in an awful humor. He went over to the Jefferson Market about nine o'clock, where they were going to try your friend. He was that put out that he scarcely spoke to me. Where is Miss Castleton?"

"She's up at her sister's in Harlem."

"O, she's come to town."

"Yes. I think I'll go over to three hundred and try and catch Mr. Wilder. I'll be home to-night. You can shake my bed up and dust off my camp stool."

The inspector's room at three hundred Mulberry street was besieged by a number of people when Chapman got there and he had to wait.

Wilder was closeted with Miramon, who sat at a table in the centre of the room. Wilder was standing in his shirt sleeves. It was a small, plainly furnished apartment with three or four leather chairs in it, a desk upon which were papers and a couple of regulation revolvers. The click of several telegraph instruments could be heard in an adjoining room, when the conversation lapsed.

"It looks to me now," said Wilder, "as if Plonski had got out of the city with the property and I might as well tell you that if such is the case, the chances of finding him are small indeed, and the hunt a tedious one. I know that he obtained the cup direct from his man McCune. He has not been seen since and I have made the most thorough search that is possible. The girl Clianthe saw him go down West street with the property and then lost him. There were no patrolmen or detectives on the whole stretch, every officer in the city being on duty elsewhere, but between Twenty-third street and Pier No. 1, there were fifty boats of all kinds went out that afternoon. Nothing could have been easier than for him to nave slipped aboard and got out of the city unobserved. No sort of police prevision could have prevented this, and your further hunt for the man will have to be determined by what you know of the probable direction he would take with the property."

"Then," said Miramon, getting up, "I am to understand that you believe the man has left the city."

"Yes. The attempt to find him now will be a more expensive one than you will probably care to undertake."

"The expense is no consideration, sir. I represent a syndicate of capitalists who will give fifty thousand dollars cash for the cup. I feel myself authorized to offer you that for its recovery."

Wilder shook his head and smiled. "My success so far," he said, "in trying to recover it, makes your offer anything but tempting. But there is one thing, let me say before you make any move, the claim of Captain Ackerman now held by Mr. Carteret, can probably be bought up for a trifle. It would be a good idea to purchase it outright and get rid of it, that is if you intend to continue the search."

"Continue it? Why, sir, I've been half my life in it and now that all the proofs of value are in my possession, I am not likely to relinquish it."

"Very well, sir," said Wilder. "I will be very frank with you. I don't think you will find Plonski. He is a remarkably shrewd man and you may depend has laid his scheme so as to baffle pursuit. You will be in town for a few days?"

"Yes, until I have made up my mind what to do. I may count on your advice."

"Yes, but at present you can see that I am pressed for time."

While this was taking place, our friend Carteret was moodily pacing up and down in another room of the same building, a prisoner. What was his friend Chapman's astonishment as he cooled his heels in the waiting room, to see Miss Enniston arrive at the entrance, accompanied by a fine looking gentleman with white, flossy hair, and wearing a musk pink in the lapel of his coat. His astonishment did not abate as he saw this gentleman enter the inspector's room and presently return with a piece of paper which he gave to a policeman, who carried off Miss Enniston. It was plain to be seen that she had got a permit to see Carteret.

Great as Chapman's surprise was, it was feeble indeed beside the astonishment of Carteret when Miss Enniston entered the room where he was confined. She came in hurriedly and pantingly and rushed at him with impetuosity.

"Rose," he gasped.

She stared in his face. Her eyes were strangely bright. "What have you done?" she said, with a dramatic intensity of manner that surprised Carteret.

He drew himself slightly up: "I have done nothing to be ashamed of," he said. "Pray calm yourself."

She stared at him a moment and then dropped into the chair that he proffered her and gave way to a meaningless burst of hysterical tears.

Carteret was not in the frame of mind to be comforted by this superfluous sympathy. He walked away. Miss Enniston drew her handkerchief over her eyes once or twice and got up and followed him.

"Carteret," she said, "this is not the time to repulse me."

"I don't wish to repulse you, Rose, but I should like to restrain you. Don't treat me as if I were guilty."

"You mustn't talk in that way to me," she replied quickly. "We should be perfectly frank now, if never before. You know you have treated me very badly. Don't turn away from me. You loved me once. The best proof that I have never ceased to love you is that I am here now to help you. I have brought Mr. Burton. Try and be candid with me."

Carteret held up his hand in dismay. "You do not know what you are saying," he said. "I beg of you to be sensible and not begin that strain again."

"I am quite sensible," she replied. "It is my heart that is speaking."

"Impossible," he cried, interrupting her.

"What is impossible?" she retorted. "Is my past impossible? Is it impossible that you are human?"

"Miss Enniston, in the name of heaven, stop. It is impossible that I should love you, and I do not want to hear you speak of it. You are beside yourself; why did you come here?"

He stopped speaking and stared at her. The expression of her face was new to him.

"No," she cried, answering his stare with a fiery look. "No, you cannot, you will not, because I am a fool; because I have abased myself and crawled to you. Do you know what it will all come to? I cannot have you. I know it, but nobody else shall, for I will destroy you first. I warned you of this long ago, but you would not heed me."

"You are insane," said Carteret. "When I tell you why I cannot listen to your wild talk of love, you will know—"

"It is enough for me to know that you have made me desperate, and they will hang you. It is enough for me to know that I might have saved you, and you would not have it; that baseness and treachery and scorn will bear their fruit in you."

"What will you do, Rose? Listen to me. I am innocent."

"Ah, ha, of what? Of perfidy? Of heartlessness? Of falsehood? Of treachery? Are you innocent of murder?"

"Yes, by heaven, you know I am innocent."

"So, you think no one saw you. You do not know that I looked from the window of Captain Ackerman's room when you stole down the stairs to the lawn at night. Is it incredible to you that heaven sent me to that window, so that your destiny might rest in my hands?"

"You there?" he cried incredulously.

"Yes, I was there. We were there together that night."

"My God," he exclaimed with a wild, despairing tone. "You *are* insane." Then a horrible thought came into his mind suddenly. Was it possible that he had actually committed this deed? Could it be that he had got up in his sleep, impelled by some demon of the night and done this foul murder? He had read of such things. Unconsciously he put his hand to his forehead as a man will when distracted with his own thoughts. It was easier to believe this than it was to believe that a woman could invent such a horrible story for her own selfish purposes.

"Rose," he said, and his voice was somewhat ghastly in his efforts to be calm, "I should have told you; you are my sister."

She threw up her head, and her eyes hashed as she replied:

"You would return to that fiction, would you? Brother and sister; yes, we tried it. Our blood was too hot."

"You do not understand," he cried; "let me explain. Mr. Enniston was my father and your's—it is true."

She stepped back a little, as if the audacity of the speech had impelled her. "Liar and coward," she hissed. "In your extremity you would say and do anything. You would sacrifice truth itself for the woman who has driven you to crime. Yes, a lie; it has been a lie from the beginning, and it has grown steadily to this final enormity; and it will end, like all lies, in disaster."

"Miss Enniston," said Carteret, with an intense calmness that was in strange contrast to her capricious violence; "I do not know what is in your heart; I hesitate even to suspect. It is incredible to me that you can mean what you say, and that even a mistaken love can make such perjury. You will come to your senses and regret your vindictive passion; I am sure of it. As for me, I am innocent of hatred for you or of crime against heaven, and to die innocently is better, by far, than to live guiltily."

Something of the honesty and bravery of this conviction gave a sudden dignity to his appearance, and she looked at him as if her soul comprehended the superiority of his position.

"Yes," she replied in a dreamy monotone; "always above me. You cannot know what passion is. You cannot feel. You would put your condemned foot on me now as if you were superior to me, and I must grovel under it and look up to you. You, who inflame all the devilish impulses of my nature, dare to pity me? They will hang you, and you will look down upon me from the heights of ignominy with the same pity, and I alone could have saved you."

Then, as if the intensity of her emotion could no longer accommodate itself to words, she broke into hysterical tears, and with her hands over her face, she began to sway her body to and fro, emitting the while convulsive sobs and moans.

Something like pity came over Carteret. He began to perceive that in this wreck of sensibility, truth and discretion itself had been swept away. It was one of those exhibitions of feminine frenzy which have no relation to the reason. But its effects upon him would be none the less disastrous, if persisted in.

It was at this crisis of the scene that Carteret was summoned by the door-keeper. "Inspector Wilder wishes to see you in room six," he said; "step this way."

Carteret moved along the corridor with a numb sense. This last blow deprived him of the little resisting power he had left. He felt now that he was to be made a victim, and that it was useless for innocence to fight against destiny. The best it could do was to grimly and silently submit. He passed along, vaguely aware that Miss Enniston was following him, and that her silence and her stealthy, implacable presence were ominous.

When he reached the inspector's room, he found there Mr. Burton, sheriff Frost and John Wilder. They were seated at a table in the middle of the room, and he felt that he was being summoned to a death council. Miss Enniston was brought in a moment later. Mr. Burton gave her a chair, and she sat down a little apart from the group, with a cold and white sullenness on her face. Carteret gave her one glance of wonder and pity, and John Wilder said:

"Well, young man, you have had a close shave for your life. Do you know how much trouble you have made?"

"I apologize," said Carteret, "to you and the community for the trouble I have caused, seeing that I have not been put to any myself."

"Why they'd have hanged you, my boy, if I hadn't arrested you."

"I assure you, sir," replied Carteret, "the result will be the same to me whether they or you do it. You have reserved the privilege for yourself. The only difference is that they are honest. They believe me guilty. You know I am not."

"Mr. Carteret," said Wilder, and there was a curious smile lurking about his usually serious mouth, "it takes more hammering sometimes to unrivet a false suspicion of guilt than it does to weld a just conviction. I have been trying to use the same hammer for both. The facts were dead against you. Nobody had such a motive for the crime as you had, for when Captain Ackerman was out of the way, you were the sole owner of the cup and a fortune came with it. You were on the eve of marriage with a poor girl. You set out mysteriously and suddenly to go to Captain Ackerman. You were the last one to converse with him. He was never seen alive after you left him. You escaped from the house at an unusual hour in the morning. You crossed the lawn near the dead body, with a satchel in your hand. You were seen, agitated and impatient, to avoid the depot at Coe's Grove and jump upon a train before it stopped. You came to New York instead of returning to Tarrytown, as you had promised. There was fifty thousand dollars waiting for the cup here. This chain of circumstantial evidence needed but one link to become fatal, and that link was an eye witness."

Wilder stopped. Carteret looked instinctively, as he held his breath, toward Miss Enniston. Their eyes met. In her's was all the significance of concentrated inquiry, of reckless purpose, of base power, trembling with scintillant light upon the edge of decision. In his were the cold wonder and numb reproach of pity and horror, and he was farther away from her at that moment than he had ever been before.

She rose to her feet slowly, as if about to speak. He knew that back of the icy exterior was an impetuous nature, liable to be driven in any direction by the emotion of the moment. He was acutely aware of what she would say and how, in her dementia, she would exult at the dire result of saying it.

They were all looking at her when the door suddenly opened and a card was handed in.

The inspector read it. "Dr. Wollendorf," he said, with some surprise; "Bring him in," and leaning over to Mr. Burton, he whispered to that gentleman, who nodded his head in reply. "Sit down, young man," he said to Carteret. I shall only detain you a few moments."

Poor Carteret sat down, His face was pale and the lines about his mouth were distinct but there was an air of honest defiance in his expression. Miss Enniston remained standing, and the entrance of Dr. Wollendorf withdrew attention from her.

The benign old gentleman entered the room, hat in hand. His long iron gray hair streamed over his shoulders and his big brown eyes took in the little assemblage with something like a protest. John Wilder jumped up and met him cordially.

"Doctor, I am glad to see you;" he said. "How are your pigeons?"

"I have an important communication to make," said the doctor; "I have come all the way from Coe's Grove to make it."

"Take a chair, Doctor. This is an informal consultation. Mr. Burton, Dr. Wollendorf of Coe's Grove. You have lost a staunch friend. How does Mrs. Enniston bear up under it?"

"She is here in town," replied the doctor. "The coroner has possession of the house and the village is in an uproar. She came down with Miss Enniston this morning."

"Was Miss Enniston in the house when this occurred?" asked Mr. Burton with surprise.

"Yes, sir; I believe she was," replied the doctor.

Both Mr. Burton and John Wilder turned and looked at Miss Enniston as if for explanation. She did not take her eyes from Carteret.

Dr. Wollendorf paid not the slightest attention to the interruption. "I felt it my duty;" he said, "to communicate with you at once in person."

"Proceed Doctor," said Mr. Burton; "these are all interested listeners."

"I went to the coroner, sir, as soon as I heard what had happened, but he wouldn't listen to me. He said he had the man."

"Yes, yes. What was your statement?"

"Well sir, it may not amount to much, but you see, Captain Ackerman was at my house when Carteret arrived at Enniston's and they had to send over for him. I had an idea that he would come back later, but he didn't, and I was sitting on my back porch between eleven and twelve, as I do every night. There was a full moon shining very much as it shone on the night Ol Enniston was killed and I could see accross the fields to Enniston's timber. I was looking that way and I saw a man cross the open space where the properties join; you see the east end of the Enniston estate runs south right up to my fence. My night glass hung on the porch and I took it down to see who was going in that direction at that time of night."

"Did you see the man distinctly enough to know him again?" interrupted Wilder.

"Certainly, he was not a hundred yards distant, and my eyes and my glass are good and the light was unusual. He was moving in a kind of loping way and he had a bundle. My mastiff under the porch barked once or twice, and the man stopped and listened with his face toward me.

"One moment," said Wilder. He rang the bell. "Bring up the prisoner in twenty-six," he said to the officer who came in.

A moment later, McCune, heavily ironed, entered with the policeman and threw a quick, defensive look around the room.

"Is that the man, Doctor?"

The doctor took him in carefully. "Yes, sir," he said, "that's the man."

"Take him back," said Wilder, and McCune was led out.

"Doctor," he continued, turning to the old gentleman, "that is very important testimony, but I shall leave Mr. Carteret to thank you. How long shall you be in town?"

"I think," replied the doctor, "that I shall stop here a week or until the village has quieted down."

"O, go back." said Wilder laughingly. "It will all be quiet in twentyfour hours. Perhaps I ought to explain to you some of the circumstances in return for your assistance. You see, there was a curious network of appearances against our friend Carteret, and it was absolutely necessary to take a very decided step in his behalf, in fact to trap one of the confederates in the crime. That confederate was a young woman." Here there was a slight interruption in the conversation. Miss Enniston sat down and Doctor Wollendorf, whose attention had been attracted to her, said: "I think the young lady is ill."

"No," replied Miss Enniston, in a steely voice. "Proceed. I am not ill."

"I gave it out in the papers." resumed Wilder; "that I had arrested Carteret for the murder and believed him guilty. This resulted just as I had calculated it would. The young woman believing that no suspicion rested upon her confederate, came to the Jefferson Market police court unsuspectingly, where her man was arraigned as a rioter, and I picked her up instantly. She has acknowledged enough to convict the right man, and I got a writ of habeas corpus for Carteret, which is returnable to-morrow. He will not therefore have to go to Coe's Grove. I tell you this so that you can remove the Coe's Grove suspicion against Carteret. He had nothing whatever to do with the murder and I knew it from the first. But I had to complete my evidence against the right man at any cost."

Here there was a muffled cry and the sound of a falling body. Carteret cried out: "The lady." Miss Enniston had fallen from her chair prone upon the floor, and Doctor Wollendorf had sprung to her assistance. "She has fainted," he said and as Wilder turned away, Carteret approached him and made a futile attempt to express in words the new set of emotions that had overtaken him. Wilder cut him short. "Your friend Chapman is outside," he said; "I hav'n't time to see him. Suppose you go to him. Don't forget the court to-morrow morning at ten o'clock, I will be responsible for you till then. Go along, you must see how much I have to do."

CHAPTER LXIII.

MR. KLEINBACKER TURNS OUT
TO BE A GOOD ANGEL.

Mrs. Sitwhite, very rheumy and inflamed, welcomed her neice to the cottage with voluble demonstrations. "If you had only come back three days ago," she said, "you'd have seen it all. Why, we could sit out there and hear the guns; yes, we could, and see the houses burning at night. You ought to hear John tell about it. You know the butcher that was on the first floor at the Terrace? Well, he was killed with a pavin' stone; yes, he was aridin' at the head of his men; and then the Sixteenth street gang set fire to Levers' across the way and throwed all his groceries in the street and Cokey Tim you remember Cokey Tim—he had his back broke; and Mary Grinch, she was run over in Second avenue, and Patsey McGloin was clubbed to death, and my heavens, Ella, I couldn't tell you in a week all the news that John brought home, and there's been a young man to see you twice. Once he came on foot and once he came in a carriage of his own, saying as how it was all right and he'd catch you when you came back and I was to give his love to you; yes, he did as sure as I'm standing here and a scrumptuous young man too, and I never seen him before and there's the name on the card he give me."

It wasn't necessary for Manuella to look at the name on the card to ascertain that her visitor was Mr. Kleinbacker. A passive wonder at his pertinacity and he was forgotten.

"Do you suppose the trouble in the city is all over, Cynthy?"

"Every smitch," said Cynthy. "The troops have been comin' in for three days. John says the city is as quiet as a lamb since the boys came back. You know they flanked 'em."

"They what?"

"They just flanked 'em. I don't know how they done it, but John knows. He says they were flanked and I guess he was there. It's something awful, I could tell by his underclothes. But why don't you take your things off? My, Ella, how you do dress. I don't see how you do it. That hat must have cost a shovelful of money. Pop, will you sit down and behave yourself? You jigger round as if you couldn't stop. Mebbe you ain't goin' to live here. That's your room. Why don't you go and put your slippers on and act human."

"Cynthy," said the old gentleman, who was fussing around in an abstracted manner, "have you got a broom brush. I'm all dust and I've got to go downtown on business."

"Downtown?" both the women repeated in astonishment.

"You're just going to take that coat off and mind me, that's what you're going to do," said Mrs. Sitwhite.

Mr. Evans got his stick from the corner. "I must attend to my affairs, ladies," he said. "That is what I came to town for, and if you must know all these little business details, I've got to draw some money. Cynthy doesn't know that Mr. Stonybrook is my banker, Ella."

"Grandpa," said Manuella, who, as was her custom, approached him coaxingly, "let the business wait till to-morrow and then perhaps I can do it for you."

He shook his head, turned away and began buttoning his coat over his breast with an air of mysterious authority. "No one can attend to my business but myself, my dear. How often have I told you that? You should not annoy me in this manner, for you do not understand these things."

Manuella knew well enough that in these moods of imbecile determination, nothing that she could say would deter him, so she made up her mind to go with him, much to Mrs. Sitwhite's disgust.

Thus it was that they arrived at Mrs. Hannige's early in the afternoon and that lady met them in the hall with her usual effusive want of candor and ushered them into the familiar little reception room.

"Now," said Manuella to her grandfather, "you may transact your business with Mr. Stonybrook and I will wait for you here. I do not wish to see him. He will come down in the dining room for you where you can have him all to yourself."

She heard the maid say a few minutes later to the old gentleman in the hall, that if Mr. Evans wanted to see Mr. Stonybrook, he would have to come up stairs, and it gave her cheek a little unconscious flush, but she saw her grandfather go slowly up the stairs with the maid's assistance.

Mr. Stonybrook was lying on a couch in a handsome dressing gown reading a French novel. He did not get up when Mr. Evans was shown in. He languidly said, "Ah, how do you do, Mr. Evans, take a chair. You'll excuse me for not coming down. I'm deucedly lazy and didn't want to dress. Have you got some business to see me about?"

The old man came across the room beamingly and quite oblivious of the change in Mr. Stonybrook's manner. He held out his hand cordially.

"Yes, yes," he said; "It does one good to get back into this comfortable place once more. I'm very glad to see you, very glad indeed, sir. I hope you have been quite well. I have enjoyed very good health myself, sir. I think I can say, very good. You are looking quite smart yourself. I should have come down to see you before and ought to apologize. As I said to Ella, it was about time that we had a game of backgammon."

"Well, Mr. Evans, now that you are here, what can I do for you?"

"Yes, we'd better come at once to the business. We can chat about other things afterwards. I left Ella down stairs and I—"

"Did Miss Castleton come with you?"

"O, yes, Ella insisted on coming. But I don't think she understands our business. Ella is a mere child in some things. I don't think she'll ever have much of a business head, Mr. Stonybrook, do you?"

Mr. Stonybrook did not think it worth while to answer this question. He laid his French novel on his stomach, print down, locked his hands behind his head and gave signs of being slightly bored as he eyed the frescoed paper on the ceiling.

Mr. Evans had taken a piece of paper from his vest pocket which he laid on his knee while he polished his spectacle glasses with a red silk handkerchief. "You shall hear of our enjoyment in the country," he said, "and O, bless me, yes, and Mr. Carteret—"

"Mr. Evans," said Mr. Stonybrook, pressing his fingers across his mouth to hide a slight yawn, "I wish you would come to the business of this interview. I am as sleepy as the devil. What did you want to see me for to-day?"

"Ah, yes, yes. The last payment you made was a hundred dollars, Mr. Stonybrook. You see I have kept careful memoranda. I always do. It's the result of early business training. There was five hundred dollars on the twenty-first of February, and two hundred on the first of March. That makes eight hundred. It was nearly all used in clothing. A girl is a very expensive thing when she has to be outfitted, sir, very indeed. The balance in my favor is about eight thousand four hundred dollars, according to my books. Does that agree with your books?"

Mr. Stonybrook sat up on his couch, gave the French novel a toss across the room and let out a whistle of astonishment.

"I suppose you stopped in to get eight thousand four hundred dollars, didn't you?"

"O, dear no," said Mr. Evans. "I should much prefer that you retain the bulk of it until I make arrangements to open a bank account. That is, sir, if you do not object to being my private banker. If it is any annoyance, my dear sir—"

Mr. Stonybrook walked to the front window. He bit his lip. "Blast the old idiot," he said to himself. "I've got to dispose of him once and forever."

"Mr. Evans," he said, as he came back, "you are laboring under a slight mistake. I undertook to straighten out your affairs with your former partner on the showing of your books and your representations, believing in them both, and having a personal interest in your granddaughter I advanced certain sums to you. I have to tell you now that I don't believe there is a dollar to be squeezed out of your partner, and that I am not going to advance any more money. Your granddaughter as good as promised to marry me. She accepted all my money and then threw me overboard. If you are as scrupulous a business man as you pretend to be, you will give me your notes for the money I have already advanced, and when the next man puts up for the young lady you can pay me back."

It was impossible for Mr. Evans to grasp the full meaning of this astonishing and cruel outburst all at once. His apprehension was only capable of struggling with some of its details, and when he began a mental struggle he usually floundered into helplessness.

"I assure you, sir," he said, "that the accounts are right. Mr. Rankin must pay every dollar because it is just that he should."

"I dare say he will, when you give him that reason for so doing. But it don't apply to me," rejoined Mr. Stonybrook. "I've already been more generous than just, and neither virtue pays."

"I can assure you, sir, that my accounts are correct."

"I don't want to see your accounts. I have seen enough of them. I found them pretty expensive accounts while I was examining them. Just give Miss Castleton my respects and say that I have got through."

"But my dear sir, it will never do to treat the child that way. We must all try and keep our word, Mr. Stonybrook. I shall see that my child keeps hers."

"When she does, it will be time to talk about business, Mr. Evans."

It now occurred to Mr. Stonybrook that perhaps the young lady seeing that a public misfortune had come to Mr. Carteret, might have planned this interview. It was characteristic of the man to conceive of the possibility of such a thing.

"If your granddaughter wishes to see me, Mr. Evans, I will come down. You had better go to her. You are agitated. We can talk the business better perhaps than you can."

"Yes, yes," said Mr. Evans, and there was a slight tremor in his voice. "But, sir, you forget that she is incapable of business, and I am afraid that she will not understand your way of putting it. I will see her and instruct her. She always obeys me, I assure you—always—always."

Mr. Stonybrook held the door open while Mr. Evans passed out. He rang the bell and saw the maid assist the old gentleman downstairs. But before Mr. Evans had reached the first floor, his sensibilities had overpowered him. Some general sense of calamity and dire disappointment took possession of him. He was wringing his hands in a feeble way and it was plain to be seen that his judgment and his fortitude had forsaken him. He reached the lower hallway in a condition of pitiable helplessness. He was bent over as if with an added infirmity and his breathing sounded like deep-down feeble moans. His eyes were full of water. He went straight to the hallway entrance, and was trying to open the street door, still mumbling to himself inarticulately, when Manuella saw him from the reception room and came to him.

"Yes, yes," he said in response to her inquiry: "I must attend to this matter at once. It cannot be delayed. My grandchild is entitled to the money. It must not be made to appear that you loaned it to her, sir. It is not a correct business way of stating things and I am grieved, sir, to hear a business man take such views, I am indeed, sir."

"Grandpa," said Manuella, "What has Mr. Stonybrook said to you? Tell me, can't you?"

He looked at her dreamily but it was difficult for him to recover from the mental confusion into which Mr. Stonybrook had thrown him.

"I am worried my child, because my affairs are strangely unsettled. I do not quite understand how the accounts should vary. Let me see, what did you say was gone? Ah—yes, it was the cup and the money, I remember. We have no money. Mr. Stonybrook is mistaken in you and you must not permit him to think that you took his money, for he is a business man, my child, and we shall have to pay him back."

She led him into the little room where, left alone with him, he speedily grew more incoherent and unintelligible. It was nevertheless plain to her that he had undergone some unexpected shock and was suffering from something that Mr. Stonybrook had said.

She tried to cajole his reason with her usual blandishments, but with very little success.

"Did Mr. Stonybrook say, Grandpa, that we owed him money?"

"It is very absurd my dear. How can it be when we have received only eight hundred dollars and there is eight thousand four hundred dollars coming to me. I have my memoranda in my pocket. I always carry the figures with me. I have kept them carefully."

A feeling of humiliation and indignation took possession of Manuella but she tried to calm him.

"Never mind these accounts," she said; "We will go back to our little home and fix them up after we have rested. You have me, Grandpa. We can be content and happy and forget all the worry of business. It will be much better for us. Come, let us go. You shall tell me all about it when you are rested. We have no friends now but each other. Do you feel strong enough to walk? I think the air will make you feel better."

She got him on his feet, put his stick in his hand, and with her arm tenderly about him, led him out. They were going out the door when Mrs. Hannige came and said her parting words, "Must you go, my dear? I'm so sorry. My heart just bleeds for you, but I'm sure everything will be brighter and better in the end. Poor Carteret. He's lost everything in the world, even his reputation. Good bye. Be sure to run in again the first chance you get."

Manuella was leading her grandfather down the steps guardedly when a handsome clarence dashed up to the house and Mr. Kleinbacker sprang out in all the splendor of fashionable attire, looking indeed quite indescribably swell, so to speak. He sprang up the steps instantly.

"Permit me," he said, catching the old gentleman by the disengaged arm. "Take it easy, governor. Plenty of time. I caught you at the right second, Miss Castleton. Glad to be of service, you know, and always on deck when beauty calls."

She thanked him when they reached the pavement and was about to move away.

"You look smashed up," he said. "How far have you got to go? The old gent isn't in training for a walking match. What's the matter with taking my trap? Here Gus," he shouted to the driver, "lend a hand."

Manuella began to shrink. "We can find our way in the horse cars," she said. "We came by them and can return the same way. You are very good."

"Horse cars," he exclaimed with a somewhat exaggerated attitude and gesture of horror. "Miss Castleton, you must be without your usual filial affection. Horse cars at this time of day—why, I wouldn't insure the old gent's life for two blocks. Here, I'll whip you to your train in a jiffy, you are going to a train, ain't you? And I'll throw you a benediction when the bell rings."

It was a great temptation; the long distance and the condition of her grandfather made her hesitate, and Mr. Kleinbacker broke out again.

"O, perhaps you object on account of yours truly," said he. "All right, I'll stay behind. You can go it alone. You can let the old gent drive, but you can't shake his bones up in a horse car if the undersigned can prevent it. Step right this way, Mr. Evans."

And Mr. Evans was not so oblivious of the luxury of a handsome conveyance as to hang back with any degree of modesty.

"It is very kind of you, sir," said Manuella, when she saw her grandfather being lifted into the vehicle by two men. "It is a long ride. If you will leave him at my aunt's, I will come up myself immediately on the cars, but it is really asking too much of you."

"I should say it was. It is asking a good deal more than your obedient servant is going to grant. I couldn't think of separating you. If you take to the horse cars, I'll have to go them too, if I hang on to the strap with my upper lip, for I couldn't let a lady risk her life in that way just now, without disgracing my own father and being false to my own mother."

There was a breezy chivalrous determination in the man, and Manuella gave way protestingly to it. She presently found herself being handed into the vehicle, and before she knew it was being tucked up next to her grandfather, Mr. Kleinbacker considerately taking a seat to himself.

"It will blow some wind into him," he said, "and he needs it. You don't look very festive yourself, Miss Castleton. Hav'n't been on the sick list, have you?"

"No," she replied.

"Worried then. By George you look it. I'll bet a tea service, solid, that Stony's been worrying you. Do you know that man worried me for three months, just because he gave it out that he'd gobbled you. I had my tombstone all cut, yes I did. What was life worth to a young man when a cucumber like that could walk off with the finest girl in town? You don't mind my expressing myself, do you? You see I can't keep my feelings—never could."

"Mr. Stonybrook has not caused me any worry, Mr. Kleinbacker," said Manuella mildly, but with a vague sense that an awful lie was being registered against her somewheres. "You are making a mistake."

She was dreading to hear him break out about Carteret, for it was impossible, she thought, that he had not heard.

But he did not. Evidently the news had not reached him of the Coe's Grove affair, and to her surprise his interrogative volubility took another direction entirely.

"Glad of it," he exclaimed; "awfully glad, but you must have had trouble about something. Girls always do, don't they? Nothin' happened to your cup, I hope."

She seized upon this as a happy relief.

"Yes," she said; "I lost it. You can't imagine how distressed I was about it"

"Is that all?" he asked with a laugh. "Couldn't you rake up anything worse than that to worry over? O, come now, there must be something that weighs on you heavier than that does. How did you lose it?"

"Stolen," she replied, "and it has caused me a great deal of pain."

"What, you don't mean the loss of it?"

"Yes, I do. Its possession is of great importance to me. You can't understand how great."

"O, I don't want to understand. All I want to know is that you want it. Set your heart on it, hadn't you? Would you like to have it back?"

"Have it back, Mr. Kleinbacker; what do you mean? Of course I should like to have it back," and she felt an uncanny sensation creeping over her.

"I mean," said he, "that if you want it, I'll get it for you. I don't pretend to know a great deal, Miss Castleton, but on a straight average, I know what I'm talking about."

"Get the cup for me?" she said, wonderingly. "No, indeed, Mr. Kleinbacker, it is gone forever."

"Gone? Pickles! Say the word and it's yours. Happy thought. We'll take it up with us. By ginger, souvenir from yours till death. That's the kind of quicksilver I'm made of. Gus," he suddenly shouted, "drive round to the factory; I want to get a bundle."

Manuela was now in a maze of perplexities, and as her grandfather was inclined to doze off, she listened to Kleinbacker's explanation with the keenest interest.

"I told you," he said, "if anything ever turned up about that cup to come to me. Of course you never remembered anything I said; why should you? But all the same I meant it. You don't suppose I'd give the Martin Shay Home Guard such a cup as that to shoot at, do you? Why, they didn't want it. 'Look here, boys,' says I, 'that's an old fashioned mug. They don't shoot for that sort of prize nowadays. I'll take and make a replica of it and put the shamrock on one side and the American eagle on the other, and I'll do it so fine that you won't tell the difference unless you look sharp and close and I won't charge you nothin' extra, neither. You just give me the old mug for keeps. I've got a museum and it will just fit into it. What you want is a mug that is up to date—a regular target mug.' Did they do it? Well, I guess so. I just got up a new one for them with less hieroglyphics and more gimp, but I'll take my affidavit, Miss Castleton, that you can't tell the hieroglyphics from the gimp unless you look down pretty close and find Martin Shay twisted round the star spangled banner on the new mug and just carefully kept off the old one by your devoted servant."

The amazement of Manuella grew as she listened to this story, told in a rattling manner, and with no comprehension of the effect it was producing.

"Why did you not bring me the genuine cup in the first place?" she asked.

Mr. Kleinbacker's sharp face wore a look of extra smartness as he replied: "You can't blame me for wanting to make the cup biz go as far as possible, can you now? When a fellow gets a chance to serve a girl like you, everything tells. I think you've got more satisfaction out of two cups than you would out of one. Hang me, if I ain't sorry that I didn't make a regular set of 'em. I could turn up then every six months as your preserver with a new deal and you could keep on losing 'em, don't you see?"

He jumped out at Dittmar and Kleinbacker's, ran up the steps and presently came back with the treasure carefully rolled up. He put it snugly in between Manuella and her grandfather, saying:

"There's the simon pure, original Jacobs—it's yours. All you've got to do whenever you look at it, is to remember the undersigned."

He rattled on as they passed rapidly up the avenue, and Manuella continued to listen to him in a maze of wonderment. When they reached the Holbrook cottage in Harlem, the old gentleman was awakened and Mr. Kleinbacker tenderly helped him out. He then bade Manuella *au revoir* as she stood on the steps with the cup under her arm. Mrs. Sitwhite watching his gyrations from the kitchen window with unalloyed admiration. "Don't mind me," he said, "I'm harmless and don't lay that thing around carelessly." A moment later he was flying down the street waving his handkerchief gallantly from the vehicle and telling Gus to put on steam for he had to be at the club to dinner.

Poor little distressed heart. She put the cup once more on her mantel, looked at it a moment with pensive wonder, and then began to think of other and what were to her, at this time, more important matters.

Mrs. Hannige had told her quite enough to make her very miserable, for it was Mrs. Hannige's belief that John Wilder thought Carteret was guilty. The girl's impulse was to go to Carteret and comfort him in some way. She did not for one minute contemplate the possibility of his guilt. She thought only of his misfortune. But she was ignorant of the world and did not know exactly how to reach him. It seemed to her that some terrible and insurmountable barrier of law or injustice intervened. If she could have met the officer, he would have helped her and enlightened her. But she was penniless. Their little stock of money had run out, and it now looked to her as if Mr. Stonybrook had deceived them cruelly. There were three men in the world to whom she had looked with genuine feminine candor, for strength, and all three appeared at this moment to be taken from her. Her grandfather was hopelessly helpless. Mr. Stonybrook was unworthy, and Mr. Carteret was unfortunate. Never before had her condition been so dreary. Never before had she been so keenly anxious and so pitilessly perplexed. Her beautiful face betrayed, even to Mrs. Sitwhite, the condition of her mind, and her aunt's clumsy efforts to reassure and comfort her, though kindly meant, were wide of the mark.

It was not till the next morning that anybody arrived at the cottage. Carteret was, of course, the first to come. "My darling," he said, "look me in the eyes. You never had a moment's doubt, did you? Tell me that and all the rest is forgotten. I have just come from court and I'm a free man once more. I would have been here yesterday afternoon, but I could not see you until this weight was off my mind. Tell me," he repeated, "you never had any doubt."

"No," she said, "I never did. It never entered my head."

He had his arms around her. "With you," he said, "it is possible to defy even misfortune, for faith is greater than facts. But it's all blown over now. Good fortune and bad all gone together. I feel as if I had to begin life over again, but I don't care. I've lost everything but you, and thank God, you are everything."

Having emitted this paradox, he began to regard her white face tenderly. "You have suffered too," he said, "I can see it. That's the accursed part of this tangle, that you should have to take some of the pain, but it's all over now. I've got so much to tell you that is astonishing, that you must prepare yourself. I am not Colin Carteret, I'm somebody else. I've lost a fortune that I never had, but through no fault of mine. I didn't even sell my picture that I sold, for I've got to send the money back; and to cap the climax, Miss Enniston is going to be your sister as well as mine."

Manuella looked at him with open-eyed wonder. "Don't talk that way," she said pleadingly, "I can't laugh at your cynicism, it is too flippant and careless. It seems to me that you are just out of the clutches of death itself. I am trying to realize that you are here and safe. Don't trifle with me."

"Trifle," he cried. "Never was I so serious, every word is true that I tell you. I wouldn't trifle with you, my Gretchen, at this time for you are also my guardian angel. But," he said, "angel as you are, you can't restore the cup or the fortune and so you shall remain my Gretchen."

Never were the conditions of angelhood so easy of accomplishment. She hesitated a moment. Then she got up.

"Should you love me any better if I were an angel—would it make you any happier if I restored the cup?"

"Yes," he said, as he caught her and pulled her back. "If you were to be the regular angel I should be happier with the cup, because it means a fortune to me and I could pour it into your lap. That's all, but why ask such a question?"

"Because," she said, as she released herself, "if the proof of my being an angel depends on the cup, I'll go and get it for you."

It was his turn to look astonished now. "You are trying to be frivolous because you think I am," he cried. "It doesn't become you and I never was so seriously happy in my life. The cup is gone. Let us forget it."

"On the contrary," she replied, "I have it in the other room. Wait a moment. I'll get it for you.'

At this Carteret became speechless. A paralysis of incredulity seized him and converted him into a staring effigy. He saw her open the door of her little bedroom. He caught a quick indefinite vision of her grandfather asleep on the bed, as if he were back in the old studio at Mrs. Hannige's and the mockingbird were singing somewhere. The morning sun streamed in through the bedroom window and made a golden background as she stood there in the doorway holding up the cup with triumph for him to look at.

All at once metaphor was turned into miracle. The angel calmly defied fate.

He sprang toward her, took the cup in his hands, turned it over eagerly and then stared at her with a great inquiry.

There is not that woman alive who at such a moment could resist the temptation and the luxury of prolonging the mystery, and Manuella was too much of a woman to relinquish the delicious advantage too suddenly.

"Are you sure it is the right one?"

"Yes, yes," he said, as he rolled it over. "Yes. What does it mean?"

"You said it meant a fortune."

"So it does; so it does. But, my God, Manuella, there ought to be blood upon it. How came it into your hands? Why don't you explain? It is linked with crime; it's whole history is infamous."

"No," she said, "it is innocent and uneventful. It is the true cup. All others are false."

His perplexity and wonder amused her a moment. Then she sat down and told him all, and it ended with the naive remark:

"So you see, my dear, it is Mr. Kleinbacker who is the good angel after all. I have no right to the wings."

"But," he said, suddenly, "Mr. Wilder must know."

"But you must not go with it," she added just as quickly.

"No. We'll send John Sitwhite, and not take our eyes off it till the inspector gets here."

That is what they did. They shut the doors. They talked in whispers. They wrote a note of startling import and admirable brevity to John Wilder, and then they despatched John Sitwhite under many injunctions to be discreet, to communicate with no one and to come straight back, and while he was gone, they guarded the mysterious treasure with a pagan ceremony of contemplation and adoration, keeping it in front of their eyes, and going through a prolonged mystery holding each other's hands and otherwise acting in a manner very appropriate to such a mystic occasion.

CONCLUSION.

Captain Job Ackerman's funeral took place the next Monday. Colin Carteret Enniston and his wife were going to Coe's Grove to be present at the funeral, and John Wilder had sent a note, saying that he would accompany them. He was going up to spend a couple of days with Dr. Wollendorf and his pigeons. So Carteret had gone down early on the morning of Monday to see John Wilder at Mrs. Hannige's before they started and he there met Mr. Stonybrook accidentally. That gentleman hardly knew him. It was not dress that had changed him, so much as manner.

"By the way, Mr. Stonybrook," he said, "my wife gave me a little commission to execute. There is a small indebtedness of her grandfather's. Let me have the amount, please, and I'll give you a check for it."

Mr. Stonybrook said, with his usual superciliousness, that he really did not at the moment remember what the amount was. It was a bagatelle, a matter of some eight hundred dollars, a personal loan.

"Very good," replied Carteret. "Please write me a receipt in full. I am instructed by Mr. Evans to pay it."

It was with the air of a millionaire that the young man wrote the check. Mr. Stonybrook would have looked amazed if he had not long ago given up the habit of looking as he felt. "Art must be looking up," he said.

"Yes," replied Carteret; "when it looks in the other direction, it isn't art, it is connoisseurship."

"I really never expected to get the money, don't you know," said Mr. Stonybrook, as he put the check in his pocket.

"I dare say not," rejoined Carteret. "What you expected to get was something else, but it is just as well. Each has probably got his own."

The two men then turned on their heels and they never met again.

Rosamond Enniston was not at the funeral. She was in a private hospital in the city, but Mrs. Enniston was present with Mr. Burton. The remains of Captain Ackerman were tenderly deposited in the Hillside Home, close to the one grave in the little twelve foot enclosure, and the grim old superintendent of the place remarked to Mr. Wilder when the last shovelful of dirt was laid upon the mound: "You wanted to be sure that that one was put in, didn't you?"

Mrs. Enniston and Mr. Burton returned immediately to the city. Nothing could induce Mrs. Enniston to live on the Enniston place again.

But Mr. Burton had asked Carteret to go there and remain awhile to look after the property and the interests of the estate. And so it was that John Wilder, instead of spending his short vacation altogether at Dr. Wollendorf's, spent a great portion of it at the house where he had once been so coldly received. It can well be imagined that he and Carteret, as they smoked their cigars on the veranda in the very spot where Mr. Ol Enniston and Anson Seymour had sat and looked into the shrubbery, had a great many curious notes to compare. But the officer kept his pledge made to Dr. Sanger and never broke the silence of the dead. Once or twice he stopped in at Jared Sprinkler's and Nancy Ann showed him a new scrap book that she had commenced, and Hi Tucker asked him one morning, when he was coming to get that dog.

About a week after the funeral, Wilder came up in the forenoon from the Coe's Grove station with quite a large package of mail matter. He found Carteret and his wife sitting on a rustic seat looking down through the chestnuts to the Cove.

"I've got quite an assortment of letters for you," he said "and some papers," and he dealt them out to the eager young people who fell to tearing open the envelopes while he unfolded the morning *Herald* and looked over the news.

"By George," cried Carteret; "listen to this. It is from Dr. Wollendorf," and he read from the epistle in his hand.

"I am glad to be able to inform you that Miss Enniston is in a fair way to recover. She has passed through a remarkable temperamental change for the better. It is a very interesting case. I suppose you have heard the news. She is to be married this winter to Dr. Flockton and they are going abroad for a year. She is so changed that I doubt if you would know her. Flockton says she has been born again. I wish that we could transfer that process from his profession to ours. What a lot of trouble it would save us. However I think Miss Enniston will make a very rabid devotee. I shall be home in a few days, for I suppose my birds must be suffering."

After a few exclamations of surprise which this unexpected news called forth, Manuella said, "Pray listen to my letter," and she read as follows:

"My Dear Mrs. Enniston: I hope you will accept the little wedding present I have sent you by express, it is a solid wine service, and every cup is a reproduction in miniature of the Toltec goblet which I hope you have preserved carefully. Of course I don't mean to say that I have re-produced the hieroglyphics, for I didn't have the original to imitate, but in form and general appearance they will remind you of the antique cup, which I had the honor to pass over. Give my respects to your husband, and say I always appreciate a man who makes a ten strike, and remember that if you should be in need of goods in my line, our house will endeavor to serve you and yours with the promptitude and neatness which I am proud to say have always distinguished the firm of Dittmar and Kleinbacker. I enclose circular. Yours truly,

ADOLPH KLEINBACKER."

Both Carteret and Manuella burst into merry laughter. But Wilder was too busy perusing the *Herald* to give any heed to them.

A moment later he handed the paper to Carteret, and pointed with his finger to a paragraph in the marine news.

"KEY WEST, July 26th.

"The French propeller Eugenie, from New York to Vera Cruz, with passengers and freight, was lost in a hurricane on the morning of the twenty-fifth, about thirty miles west of the Dry Tortugas. Three of her crew reached Fort Jefferson in an open boat, and report all hands lost."

"Why," exclaimed Carteret, "that's the vessel that Miramon sailed in with the cup."

"Yes," replied Wilder thoughtfully, "that eventful cup is now on the bottom of the Gulf of Mexico. It appears to have cursed everybody that had anything to do with it."

"True," said Carteret, "except—" and he looked at the beautiful woman by his side, "except—"

Then he got up and kissed her and the salute was the happy sound that ended the history of the cup.